Divinity's Twilight

DIVINITY'S TWILIGHT

REBIRTH

CHRISTOPHER RUSSELL

NEW YORK

LONDON • NASHVILLE • MELBOURNE • VANCOUVER

Divinity's Twilight

Rebirth

Published in New York, New York, by Morgan James Publishing. Morgan James is a trademark of Morgan James, LLC. www.MorganJamesPublishing.com

Publisher's Note: This novel is a work of fiction. Names, characters, places, and incidents are either products of the author's imagination or used fictitiously. All characters are fictional, and any similarity to people living or dead is purely coincidental.

ISBN 9781642798876 paperback
ISBN 9781642798883 eBook
Library of Congress Control Number: 2019952637

Cover and Interior Design by:
Chris Treccani
www.3dogcreative.net

Cover Illustration by:
Christian McGrath

Interior Maps by:
Terri Johnson

Morgan James is a proud partner of Habitat for Humanity Peninsula and Greater Williamsburg. Partners in building since 2006.

Get involved today! Visit
MorganJamesPublishing.com/giving-back

For Marvin and Darlene Russell,
With parents like these,
Reaching the stars is just the beginning.

Contents

Preface and Acknowledgments

———◈———

Congratulations! You've stumbled upon *Divinity's Twilight: Rebirth*, hopefully the first of many works of fantasy I will be privileged to have published. This book and those that follow have been simmering in the depths of my mind for a long, long time. Not as deities measure these things, of course. To such beings, eight years is not even an eye-blink, let alone a meaningful tick of the clock.

The world of *Divinity's Twilight*, Lozaria, began rather humbly as a crude sketch on the back of a college thermodynamics handout. At the time, I probably should have been listening to my professor. Yet my thoughts strayed elsewhere— not because the material was dull or the fact that he possessed an uncanny tendency to drone, but because I felt a calling in a different direction. A pull of something unknown, of wondrous possibility and intriguing opportunity. *You've read, watched, and listened all your life,* a voice whispered in my head. *So . . . why not try creating something instead?*

This isn't to say that everyone should immediately drop what they're doing and attempt to realize their wildest dreams and ambitions. I certainly didn't, so I wouldn't expect anyone else to act so rashly. In fact, I worked on the first draft of *Divinity's Twilight* for all of two weeks—one and a half chapters—before hitting a wall and abandoning the project. Getting a degree in engineering was work enough; why should I spend my free time *writing* of all things?

That could have been the end of this story. If it had been, you wouldn't be holding this book in your hands, wondering when this gregarious author is going to stop telling his life story and let you get on to the *real* reason you bought, borrowed, or checked it out. Never fret. There's a moral at the end of this dark, dreary tunnel.

Five years later, struggling with my Christian faith, occupational pursuits, and various other worries I was far too young to be experiencing, I happened to crack open a self-help book with a simple message: just say *yes*. This message was aimed at opening people up to God's calling, to convince them of the importance of making time to be with him daily. Wise words, ones that we could all apply to many areas of our lives. I was convicted by the first chapter. My mind reeled. *Why have I been making excuses? If I want to be a writer, I better sit down and* write!

So I did. An entire chapter spun from my fingers on that transcendent night, and several volumes worth of detailed worldbuilding, painstaking character development, enchanting magics, and thrilling plot developments followed over the subsequent three years. I now present to you the initial result of that passionate endeavor: *Divinity's Twilight: Rebirth*.

Of course, no book can be produced in a vacuum. While this is true of *all* pursuits, I find it especially applicable to creative works. If you ever meet any of the individuals listed below, please give a warm word of thanks; they, my tireless, dedicated support system, deserve more credit than I ever will for the book you can't wait to begin reading.

No graceful string of praises can ever express my appreciation for Jesus, my savior. All utterances will fall short, for everything that I was, am, or will be is due to His will and direction. Any talent I possess is derived from Him, and therefore I offer this book—and all that comes of it—to Him.

Not enough can be said about my wonderful parents, Marvin and Darlene Russell. They have worn countless hats throughout this process. Alpha reader, editor, agent, social media team . . . they've tackled all these roles, and some I've surely forgotten, with flair. But it would be a travesty if I only mentioned their recent assistance. People are the sum of their experiences; a product of their environment. No matter what my aspirations were, they've been my rock, the coach in my corner, my firm foundation. Neither I nor this novel would be what we are without their boundless love.

My editor was the fantastic Angie Kiesling and her team at the Editorial Attic. No author is perfect—any that make such a claim are lying—so I was extremely nervous about having my work professionally examined for the first time. I needn't have been so concerned. My manuscript was treated delicately, with their adjustments serving to only enhance the final product. I can't thank them enough for taking on a 200k word behemoth that would make any sane editor do a double take.

As Angie is a contractor with my publisher, Morgan James Publishing, it is fitting that I acknowledge the other stellar staff members who have made contributions to *Divinity's Twilight*. David Hancock, the CEO, is personally involved with each and every book that is stewarded by his company. Quick with a joke and never afraid to try new projects, he is the impetus behind a publishing house that will continue to grow in the coming years. I am immensely grateful that David, and my author relations manager, Bonnie Rauch, decided to use my fantasy epic to further extend the range of genres their company invests in. On the marketing side, Amber Parrott, Nickcole Watkins, Jessica Burton-Moran, and Taylor Chaffer have done a fabulous job connecting with online and brick and mortar stores in advance of our release. Like ideas, books die unless they are read, to which end they must be *spread*. I owe everyone participating in the publicity of my novel a debt which might never adequately be repaid.

Every time I look at the cover art, my heart skips a beat. Chris McGrath, illustrator to renowned fantasy greats such as Brandon Sanderson and Jim Butcher, did an amazing job of capturing the soul of Lozaria. His characters are tense, ready for a battle they may not win. His terrain is harsh and broken, cracked and dying, the soil as tired of war as the beings that fight over it. And yet the backdrop fortress stands strong, immutable like the shrouded, silent moons in the sky above. Chris's work is the type every author dreams of—the kind that makes them reimagine everything they've created and yearn to describe it all anew. With his help, we'll make *Divinity's Twilight* into something truly spectacular.

I believe that no fantasy epic is complete without detailed maps. Since art and I are not on speaking terms, my original lecture-generated maps needed to be redone. Channeling her inner Tolkien, Terri Johnson of Knowledge Quest Inc. took my childish scribbling and converted it into the detailed maps fronting this book. Whenever you flip to them to check the location of Nemare, what body of water the Etrus River empties into, or what significance the Theradas Line holds, please remember her.

For better or worse, this volume was accepted for publication before a group of beta readers could be formed. As a result, only one name can be found in this category, that of my good friend Douglas Harris. His feedback and suggestions allowed for the correction of several minor plot holes, thus improving your end experience. I hope to thank dozens of people for this important service next time round.

Rebirth

Among the litany of fantastic teachers, professors, and instructors I've studied under, there are two I wish to specially recognize. The first is Master Ryan Cirone, who reignited my love of martial arts and taught me the combat skills that are the foundation of magic in this universe. The second is Esther "Bunny" Akers, my eleventh and twelfth grade English teacher. To Mrs. Akers, the classroom didn't end at the door. Yes, her passion for reading and writing fueled my development as an author. She also edited my first book, *First Legion*, which is a project I intend to eventually revisit. But those are things you expect of an educator. Instead of stopping there, Mrs. Akers was another parent to her students. I cannot recall an occasion, morning or evening, when her room wasn't bustling with activity. Everyone loved her, and she loved everyone in turn. Her self-sacrificing support surely influenced *Divinity's Twilight*.

Vallen, my nearly two-year-old sheltie pup, also deserves to be thrown a bone. Although this project predates him, he's taken on the mantle of my male protagonist, a role that's certain to see him receive far more attention than I will. Try as I might, I cannot fault anyone that prefers him to me. He's cuter and rolls over for belly scratches—something I'm determined to cut back on.

Lastly, I wish to thank you: the fans and readers picking up my debut work. Without you, there would be no *Divinity's Twilight* and I would not be an author. Barring any auguries or crystal balls, I can't say for certain where this fantastical journey will take me. I'd like to release these titles yearly, but the future is inscrutable, hidden by the stygian Void. However, with your support, I know that I will be able to continue weaving this grand tale for many, many years to come.

The airship is fueled, the illyrium hums with power, and the skies unfold before you, waiting to be claimed.

Let the adventure begin . . .

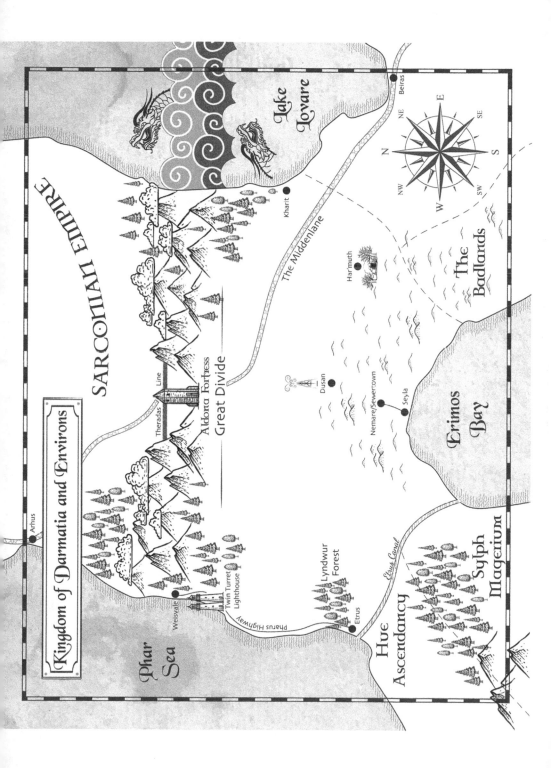

Prologue

At the Edge of Reason

697 Years Ago

———◆◇◆———

The world burned.

Streaks of orange and red crisscrossed the sky, put there by siege engines or battalions of elemental mages. When they struck true, flesh boiled and horrendous cries rose along with embers and smoke. Even when they missed, the chaos of the battlefield only grew. Dry prairie grasses, waist high in some places, went up like oil-drenched torches, casting forth tendrils of hungry fire that spread through the plain in a catastrophic chain reaction.

From above, it probably looked quite pretty, like a quilt dappled with all the colors of the sun. Hopefully the divine Veneer, content to watch mortals suffer from their heavenly halls, were enjoying the performance.

For Darmatus Aurelian certainly wasn't.

Gasping for air, he flipped back the slotted visor of his sallet. He stabbed his lance into the dirt, yanked the thrice-cursed helmet from his head, and cast it toward enemy lines. Considering the way it was baking him alive, it belonged with them.

Oppressive as the heat was, the caress of the ash-filled breeze on Darmatus's stubble-lined cheeks felt wonderful. It might just be the best feeling in the world. A flake of soot dropped into his eye. He swore, blinking, and reached for the leather canteen on his belt. The liquid sloshed around inside. He dashed half onto his face and guzzled the rest. Grinning like a madman, he chucked the water skin in the same direction as the helmet. This battle would be decided in the next quarter hour. Either Darmatus would find a new—preferably full— flask at that point, or he and all the other leaders of the Alliance of Five would

1

be dead.

His brother, Rabban, shaded his eyes, squinting into the swirling dust.

"I think you hit someone."

Though his tone was light, his gaze was dead. They'd suffered and lost much to reach this point—their own family most of all.

A primal howl of fury confirmed his words. Whatever he'd struck clearly wasn't Terran like them. Nor did it belong to a member of any of Lozaria's six other sentient races, some of whom stood with them on this field. That guttural growl of pure loathing belonged to something evil. Something dark and ancient, monstrous and horrifying.

Days before, that piercing, pained cry would have driven Darmatus to his knees. Now? Well, it still made him shiver. He clutched one gauntlet with the other to stop his quiver, lest it spread. Gone were the days when he could simply be himself, even in the presence of those closest to him. He was a leader now. People looked to him for hope, courage, and strength, and he tried his best not to disappoint them. Creator knew what a difficult task *that* was.

"They're ready, my lord."

Unobtrusive as ever, his adjutant, Jarrik Savane, materialized noiselessly at his side. Darmatus didn't react, though Rabban jerked a little in surprise. He had long since stopped wondering how Jarrik managed to do that. His stealth wasn't so much a skill as who he was. Everything about him, from his plain hair to his impassive face to his drab jerkin and breeches, was nondescript. Darmatus found it was quite advantageous to have an aide who could come and go unseen.

"I told you to call me Darmatus, same as before," he said for the . . . tenth time? Eleventh?

As if to spite him, Jarrik bowed, placing a hand to his breast in deference. "That's not an option, my lord. Your station *demands* respect. What would your men say if they heard me refer to you so casually? More importantly, what would the other Alliance heads think? None of their servants would dare address them with such impertinence."

Darmatus waved a mailed fist dismissively. "I'm not them. I'm just a minor Terran lord, one who isn't even of noble blood. Given their hatred of our race, current crisis notwithstanding, I'm sure they'd rather spit in my face than look at me."

The sounds of battle swelled and fell: screams, clanging weapons, crackling flames, even the rumbling of the earth. As violent as the clashes were, they had much diminished from as little as an hour prior. Mere skirmishes compared to the bloodshed of the past two days. Enough had been shed to fill the gaping cracks in the ground, the caverns, ravines, and trenches dredged by opposing magical forces. Whatever the day's result, this region, once covered with bountiful farmland, would never be the same.

"Some of them say you should be our king," Rabban said.

Darmatus ignored him. Rabban pressed on.

"Many of our soldiers agree."

"We've discussed this before, Rabban. We're here to stop Sarcon, not supplant him."

Rabban shrugged, but Jarrik wouldn't let the matter rest.

"My lord, Rabban is right. When we defeat your brother—"

"*If* we defeat him."

"*When* we defeat your brother, if you don't take the crown, the other races will—"

"That's enough."

"But, my lord—"

"I said, that's enough!" Darmatus snapped. Seeing Jarrik flinch, he softened. "Please drop the issue, Jarrik. You know why I can never be king. Why I *will* never be king."

"That's precisely the reason you *must*," the diminutive advisor persisted. "My lord, if you assume the throne, this becomes more than just a family squabble. It gives our cause *legitimacy*! Suddenly we aren't one member of a five-lord, four-race alliance, but a Terran nation-state putting down a rebellion for the sake of the world—for all of Lozaria!"

"No!" Heart pounding, blood thumping, Darmatus had but a tenuous grip on his wrath. Something deep within his mind urged him to lash out and strike Jarrik with the spiked fist of his gauntlet. Skin would rend, bone would break. The foot-deep ash on the ground would lap up the blood as he stood there smiling, triumphant and . . .

Darmatus banished those depraved thoughts, shutting them behind the wall of virtue, justice, and compassion he'd cultivated all his life. But the more he fought, the more he used his magic, the more he called upon the men'ar in his blood to control the arcane miracles bestowed upon mortals by their Creator, the more those vile considerations corrupted him.

Therefore, this would be his final battle.

And he would *not* be king. He didn't trust himself to steer clear of the path trod by his elder brother, Sarcon.

As tears welled up in his brilliant blue eyes, Darmatus raised his gaze toward the copse of charred trees that perched like a hunched crone at the top of the only hill for leagues that had thus far avoided demolition. It was the smoke. It *had* to be the smoke. Why else would he cry, looking at the last bastion of their hated enemy, where Sarcon, his beloved sibling, had chosen to make his final stand?

Horns blared, one after another; their long, somber notes drifting to them from all around the hilltop. Jarrik stiffened, glanced toward the small wood, then looked at Darmatus expectantly.

"It's time, my lord. That's the signal."

"We'll charge when I raise my lance."

Sketching a curt bow, Jarrik disappeared. Within minutes of his departure, the battalions of Darmatus's army were at attention, weapons clutched tightly in anxious hands. He began this campaign with nearly twenty thousand soldiers. Less than half remained. They should have broken. Cast their swords and bows to the dirt and gone home. But wounded, weary, and grim, they still stood on the plains of Har'muth because, for some reason Darmatus couldn't fathom, they adored him.

"Let's go," he said to Rabban, who hefted his crossbow, knocked a single bolt, and followed him to the front of their army.

Once there, Darmatus strolled down the row of men. He made idle chatter, asking about their wives, children, what they intended to do when they returned to their towns and villages. As he talked, he checked their spears and inspected their mail and plate, clapping them on the shoulder when he was through, regardless of how well-maintained their equipment actually was. Darmatus treated every man who wore his livery—red and blue—like a son, and they seemed to glow from the attention he lavished on them.

Perhaps one day he and his wife, Saris, would have a son of their own as well.

The horns sounded again. Darmatus found the center of the line, raised his lance, and then charged as he let it drop, roaring at the top of his lungs. Rabban, his captains, and his entire army screamed a cry of victory and rushed up the embankment behind him.

Ten seconds later, the surging line came to an abrupt halt. Horses whinnied, tossing their confused riders into the muck and bolting for the rear. Those in the front ranks fell to their knees, dropping blades as hands shot to cover their helmets' ear holes. Cries of agony replaced those of determination.

Though the faces of his men were contorted by grimaces of unimaginable suffering, Darmatus couldn't hear them. An eerie wailing issued from the hilltop, deafening him. Rabban rushed to the nearest soldier, a sandy-skinned man with captain's bars emblazoned on his breastplate.

Darmatus felt . . . nothing—save a slimy revulsion slithering down his backside along with his sweat. Why were they unaffected? His perceptive gaze was drawn to a pale green glow on Rabban's belt. It was coming from a pouch the size of his fist, penetrating through the cured hide wrapping as if it weren't there.

Ah, of course, Darmatus realized. *Our Illyriite crystals are protecting us.* His own, affixed where the primary welds of his chest armor joined, glimmered bright and pure, creating a verdant aura about him. He'd discovered many uses for the seemingly inexhaustible spiritual energy of the flawlessly cut gemstone, but defending against dark magic was a new one. *Then again, it's possible . . .*

"They're resonating with Sarcon's shard." Rabban's malice-coated words reflected his own thoughts. Together, their eyes fell on the ominous forest—a stand of desiccated, twisted ash trees.

All at once, the ghastly shrieking ceased. Cautiously, the army rose to its feet, picking up their armaments with trembling, uncertain fingers. They looked about, nervous and shaken.

But why stop the psychic attack?

Up from the hillock burst a vortex of ebony light, narrow and obscured by the barren wood at the bottom, expansive and tumultuous at its apex. Coursing, cascading, roiling, it reached higher and higher. It pierced the heavy clouds, which drew back in a ring as if afraid to touch it.

Darmatus could feel the maelstrom's power from where he stood. It was a hand on his throat; a blacksmith's anvil crushing his lungs; the hand of the

Creator himself pressing callously down atop a misguided, disobedient sinner. His knees buckled but didn't collapse. Rabban gasped, clutching at his neck, yet likewise stayed upright. A solid third of his army wasn't so fortunate. Chainmail clanking, they dropped in the mire. Very few staggered back to their feet, even at the frantic prodding of their stupefied neighbors.

Baring his teeth, Darmatus thrust his lance above his head and silently bid men'ar race through his body, into the warm metal, and out the sharpened silver tip at its pinnacle. Sparks erupted, a brilliant stream of flames that sped high into the air where they exploded in arcing torrents of fire visible to all on the battlefield.

No one knew precisely how the spiritual particles called men'ar functioned. Why was it in their blood? What in nature did it interact with to produce such spectacular and mysterious displays of power?

Theory aside, Darmatus *did* know that he was special, even among already rare and exceptional magic users. Other casters had to chant their spells aloud in ancient Eliassi, the original language of the venerable Eliade sages. They also had to use catalysts infused with illyrium—a mineral closely related to Illyriite but more abundant—to aid in molding and directing their men'ar. Darmatus required neither. He simply pictured a spell, aimed, and wielded his lance in the manner required to manifest the incantation. It came to him intuitively.

Combined with his equally prodigious ability to wield every type of elemental energy, he was highly versatile, a nearly unstoppable force who could adapt his abilities as the situation demanded. Of course, his martial prowess only encouraged those who would see him sit the Terran throne. But the strength Darmatus had once exulted in was now a burden. *Let it see me through this conflict, and then, Void and Oblivion, may it pass from me—along with the crown,* he prayed, invoking the twin names of the eternal, mythological plane from which existence was rumored to have been born.

To his satisfaction, the rear echelons of their army responded to his signal with haste. Hulking onagers, entrenched in recently excavated earthworks, hurled blazing projectiles over their heads at the fulminating mass of energy. Their first volley missed short, striking the forest. Strangely, the dry, brittle trunks didn't burn. However, the second barrage, timed to coincide with the fireballs and lightning strikes cast by the mage battalions, impacted the barrier head on.

Still no effect. The column's misty eddies absorbed the assault without the slightest crack. Ranged attacks could not penetrate it, no more than pebbles flung at a castle wall could tear a breach. He had no recourse but to order a direct approach.

"Pass my orders down the line!" Darmatus bellowed. "Reform and advance! Leave the dead and wounded for now! We have to stop that magic ritual!" *Or whatever it is.* He leveled his lance at the growing pillar of dark power.

The sight of his men closing ranks produced a response from the hilltop. In front of the forest, the ground buckled and swelled, much like bread leavening in a baker's oven. But this was no natural phenomenon. A set of great granite arms reached up from the pit ahead of Darmatus, dirt crumbling away from rock hard limbs devoid of muscle and sinew. More appendages followed, crimson veined joints jutting at grotesque angles. When all were flattened against the ground, they heaved forth a rotund blob of stone with at least six distinct torsos and heads, each frozen like statues. Red spider-web lines crisscrossed them, originating from empty, gaping eye sockets that appeared to be crying tears of blood.

A soldier in the first row cast aside his sword and broke formation.

"Pyrevants!" he screeched.

Rabban grabbed him. "Get back in position!"

"I . . . I can't! I can't fight t-those . . . *things* again!"

He tore free and ran. More joined him, a trickle that threatened to become a river. The clatter of discarded metal rose to a clamor. Darmatus and Rabban ran back and forth, rallying their men as best they could.

"Stand firm! Stand firm!"

The Pyrevants—a dozen in number—shuddered with energy as if they were freshly lit furnaces. Flames gushed from their seams. Then, soundlessly, they rushed the faltering Terran battalions.

A dam burst. Unit after unit shattered, fleeing in terror. Rabban was apoplectic.

"Void and Oblivion, hold the line! Hold the blasted line!"

Darmatus grimaced. He couldn't fault their lack of courage; no mortal should have to fight his neighbor, let alone the aberrations Sarcon had fielded against them. *Why have you done this, brother? Why stoop so low?*

Some of his men remained. Perhaps two thousand knights, his personal retinue. They would have to be enough. He gripped his lance in both hands, point forward, standing firm amid fallen shields, spears, and bodies.

"Shields locked, spears forward!" Darmatus roared. "Second rank targets chest level; third targets their heads! Hold them long enough to hit with magic!"

Rabban knelt and sighted in at a frontrunner, its gangly arms—or were they legs?—slapping the mud furiously. Breathing out to still his aim, he released the bolt.

The simple rod of iron blew off all the limbs on the Pyrevant's left side, sending it into an uncontrollable tumble of fracturing body parts. Flaming coals mixed with tiny yellow illyrium crystals poured from holes in its stomach. After disgorging its innards, the abomination lay still, arms no longer flailing, haunting eyes no longer bleeding.

Another Pyrevant fell to Rabban's second magically enhanced shaft, coated with a thin layer of his men'ar so that it would shear through anything not similarly enchanted. But the Pyrevants were too quick for him to drop them all. Bracing themselves, the knights screamed a cry of defiance and thrust their spears as the foe barreled into them at full speed.

Spear hafts snapped like toothpicks. Broken bodies, their weighty plate completely ineffective, flew through the air. Some granite appendages came loose, yet the Pyrevants were too massive for traditional metal weapons to have any great effect.

What the Terrans could do was *stop* the creatures. After the initial impact, they pressed in from every side, stalwartly rushing to fill the gaps left by their slain comrades. Leading with warped and bent shields, they caught a group of three Pyrevants before they could break through the other side or withdraw.

Darmatus wouldn't let their sacrifice be in vain. Ejecting flame from the soles of his boots, he leapt above the fray, positioning himself so he'd fall directly atop the nearest glob of living statues. One head glanced up, noticing him. *Too late.* Summoning the wind to speed his descent, Darmatus fell with the weight of an onager strike, sending a blast of accumulated men'ar through his lance tip as it hit. The Pyrevant ripped itself apart from within, leaving behind a cloud of dust and debris.

Molding men'ar in his feet, Darmatus landed *with* the ground, depressing it like clay to soften the impact. He then sprang toward the next Pyrevant.

Though its motion was temporarily halted, it had no trouble staving in even the stoutest armor with its powerful blows or expelling gouts of superheated steam from its core. Skin seared in an instant, a condition made worse by the full-body protection the Terrans wore. One of Darmatus's captains stumbled free of the shield wall, shrieking piteously as his hands tried to keep the flesh from sloughing off his skull.

The Terran lord's gut twisted with anguish. He jabbed his lance into the Pyrevant's side. In response, a circle of rock shards blew out its opposite flank. Losing balance, the granite horror collapsed, leaking coal and illyrium. Darmatus didn't stay to watch it die. Every second he dallied cost him dearly, and the butcher's bill for this battle was already *far* too high.

The third Pyrevant had been eliminated by Rabban. His shots had ripped the unnerving effigies from its back, an act that apparently caused them to cease functioning. *How disturbing,* Darmatus thought, watching the remaining seven as they regrouped for another charge. *That they should falter when their . . . brains are removed. They couldn't be . . . No, Sarcon wouldn't . . .*

Wouldn't what, exactly? Their eldest brother had laid waste to whole cities in pursuit of his vision of continental peace. Was creating magical abominations, even with *people* as a base, such a departure from wholesale slaughter?

He'd have the opportunity to ask him that shortly.

More enemies were gathering at the edge of the forest. Though they were bristling with weapons and covered in iron plates grafted directly to their bodies, these were no mutated atrocities of darkness. Along with the permanently attached armor, their elegant horns, sprouting from atop tattooed, hairless scalps, identified them as Vladisvar mercenaries. Lozaria's most martial race, the Vladisvar were an anomaly in that they never waged war for their own purposes. Instead, they served the highest bidder.

Unfortunately, today that was Sarcon.

If they focused their attention on immobilizing the Pyrevants, the Vladisvar battalion would cut them down. If they tried to deal with the Vladisvar, the rampaging Pyrevants would trample them into the mire. Darmatus smiled. Courting a demon of death might prove an easier proposition than enduring the next clash.

Not giving them an opportunity to catch their breath, the Pyrevants galloped down the incline, numerous mouths spread wide in wordless screams. Stoic and unruffled by the horrors preceding them, the burly Vladisvar followed whilst yelling bloodcurdling battle cries. Darmatus's battered soldiers could do little but dig in and hope to withstand the initial charge. Shields clanged together. Every usable spear was hurriedly passed to the front. Once their thin line faltered, all would be lost.

"Trouble you are having, it seems," a stentorian voice announced from behind Darmatus in thickly accented, broken Common, the only language the Alliance races could uniformly understand.

Surprised, he spun around, then had to crane his neck to meet the newcomer's gaze. Kanar'kren, regent general and consort to the Prime Factor of the Hue Ascendancy, favored Darmatus with a beaming smile.

"Care to assisting, would you mind, Triaron?" One of Kanar'kren's secondary arms, wrapped in thick steel that probably weighed half as much as Darmatus did, reached out and clapped him reassuringly on the shoulder. The dark blue giant's other three limbs held two massive tower shields and a glinting longsword taller and broader than a stout oak. Despite the circumstances, Darmatus found himself marveling at how much gear a single Hue warrior could carry—and still manage to fight while wearing all of it!

"Er, yes . . . your aid would be most welcome."

Kanar'kren nodded benevolently. Yet glancing around, Darmatus realized that he didn't really have much say in the matter. Hue sentinels in full plate, very little of their blue flesh exposed beneath the shimmering, burnished silver, were shouldering their way through his much reduced army. His knights grumbled a bit about their honor being slighted, but moved aside without fuss. They looked like toys beside their colossal allies, so any confrontation was unlikely to go in their favor. Also, survival was worth a minor loss of face.

A thought occurred to Darmatus. Standing on his boot tips—which still didn't bring him level with Kanar'kren's chest—he peered over the carnage at the eastern flank. It was empty, nothing but mounds of rubble perched amid flattened and charred grasses. He rounded on his companion impetuously. "The flank you were assigned to is clear. Why didn't you push through and bring an end to this?"

"If you'd made straight for Sarcon, all these casualties could've been avoided." Jaw clenched, Rabban cast an arm about to indicate the Terran corpses littering the face of the hill. His other hand clutched his crossbow haft, which was shaking with barely controlled rage. "Was this your goal? Did you and the other leaders—"

"Control yourself, Rabban!" Darmatus interjected before he could make matters worse.

"It was, how say you . . . " Kanar'kren paused, blinking consternation. A considerable portion of Hue language was non-vocal; blinking, head twists, and other motions often conveyed more meaning than their words. "Majest? Magif?"

"*Magic?*" Darmatus supplied.

"Yes! That is one!" His stern features lit up. "Magic barrier enemy raise. Pass no can, so forces bring here." He gestured toward where his detachment was forming up, scarcely twenty steps distant. They *were* a wall unto themselves. Darmatus couldn't peer over them; he could only catch glimpses of their onrushing foes through the narrow gaps between them. Were the Vladisvar slowing? Then their immense shields slammed into the earth, and he could see no more.

"Way any," the Hue continued. "Fight Hue, enemy does not want. On you, focused are they." He nodded sagely. "Make sense. We here fight. You go, fight brother, win victory. Plan sound?"

Simple, yes, but sound nonetheless. Darmatus shook his head in agreement. Somehow, he'd always known Lozaria's twin moons wouldn't rise until the three brothers came face to face once more. What he didn't know was why Sarcon seemed to want to meet him and Rabban as well.

Heedless of the change in the disposition of Alliance forces, the Pyrevants bashed headlong into the Hue rampart. Poor, unthinking automatons. Robbed of their sentience—if they were truly birthed from heinous torture and experimentation—the lumbering golems knew only how to attack, mutilate, and kill. Retreat was an unimaginable concept.

The Hue line did stagger. Several warriors were even forced back a stride or two. But most of the Pyrevants simply came *apart*. Stone went soaring through the air, doing more damage than the primary collision as shrapnel shredded flesh and hunks of granite crushed armor and bone. Since the shields directed the debris upwards, most of these casualties were still among the Terran ranks, who couldn't defend themselves from the sudden hail. Kanar'kren covered Darmatus and Rabban with his own shields, mouthing an apology that went unheard as sharp splinters plinked against the upraised metal. When the vicious rain finally stopped, all that remained of the Pyrevants was an ashen pall mixed with floating illyrium dust.

Remnants of a torso, crimson veins pulsing in an uneven tempo, came to rest against Darmatus's boot. He ignored it—until it flipped over, exposing a cracked, disintegrating arm clutching a jagged piece of rock like a dagger. It stabbed toward him, impossibly alive despite being severed from its source of power. Frantic, Darmatus swept his lance in a parry, unsure whether he'd knock the strike aside in time.

Steel fell from above, piercing the torso and fracturing it into four smaller pieces. The arm gave a single jerk, dropped the flint knife, and became permanently stilled. "Pesky maaagic contraption," Kanar'kren growled, tearing his blade free of both ground and statue. He was stressing the word's first syllable too much, but the sentence was otherwise well constructed.

Swinging the sword in an arc, he halted when it pointed at the hill's crest and barked something in his native tongue. As one, the Hue soldiers lifted their shields, fanning out to the sides so that a sizeable opening appeared in the center of their lines. Through the clearing, Darmatus could see the Vladisvar contingent milling about the knoll's midpoint. They stalked back and forth, impatient and eager for combat, but wise enough to hold position and not perish senselessly.

It still wouldn't be an easy engagement. However, with the disturbing Pyrevants removed, it would be a straightforward one. Darmatus tucked his lance under his arm then took off at full speed, Rabban shadowing him on his right, his remaining knights bringing up the rear in a wedge oriented on him.

"Charge!"

The surging vortex continued to gnaw at the sky. By now it had grown to encompass half the dismal forest, its wispy yet opaque tendrils obfuscating whatever was going on inside. Occasionally, rings of caliginous light floated heavenward on its current. Whenever these neared the pitch-stained clouds, streaks of energy flashed across the sky, much like lightning except they traveled out instead of down. What was its purpose? Why hadn't anything else occurred since the initial invisible pressure that downed so many of his troops?

Darmatus cleared his head of distractions and focused on the present.

12

Dealing with the Vladisvar came first. He angled toward the biggest brute he could find, a heavily scarred and tattooed elder whose impressive horns curled back on themselves twice. In his right hand was a wicked double-bladed axe. His left had been replaced by a spiked maul with an extended chain that coiled up and into the rounded iron pauldron grafted to his shoulder. If he wasn't a chieftain, Darmatus silently vowed to eat his own boots—*without* boiling them.

Aid once again came from an unexpected quarter. Gusts of wind buffeted them from above as hazy shadows passed over them, speeding in the direction of the Vladisvar. The chieftain gestured with his axe and shouted, prompting a halfhearted volley of arrows from the few mercenaries who carried bows. Darmatus fully expected a couple dozen of his men to fall, but the shafts went high into the air where they had no chance of hitting anything.

Screeching, seemingly coming from all around him, made Darmatus stagger midstride, nearly knocking him to the ground. He reached up and felt at his ears. No blood. At least his eardrums hadn't ruptured. His mind raced, *But what could possibly . . .*

Winged beasts, covered in scales from head to toe, razor sharp talons adorning their feet and hands, fell upon the Vladisvar battalion. Beady, yellow eyes gleamed jubilantly as they set about their grisly work. Rows of serrated teeth easily ripped through muscle and bone, slaying and feasting all at once.

The Sylph Magerium Drake Cavalry company had arrived.

Darmatus barreled through the melee, intent on reaching the other side. Axe arm missing and gushing buckets of blood from his badly torn side, the Vladisvar chieftain swung his maul at him in a wild hook. He ducked the blow, moved to the immense man's side, and rammed his lance tip into the soft tissue beneath the ribs. Darmatus immediately moved on, not pausing to confirm his kill.

It wasn't that he didn't trust the Sylph to make their war mounts—pets, really—distinguish between friend and foe. No, wait. That was *exactly* what worried him. The sooner his men got away from those heavily armed and armored drakes, the better.

A trio of drakes came in for a landing up ahead, the curved talons of the leader practically brushing Darmatus's unkempt hair as they flew past. Ducking on reflex, he veered away, only to run into another group harassing a squad of Vladisvar who were trapped inside a hollow formed by mammoth slabs of rock thrusting from the earth. The voracious reptilian beasts were *everywhere*, like flies drawn to rotting fruit.

These drakes were too young to breathe fire, and their claws weren't keen enough to rend solid stone. As they scratched and bit impotently at the narrow entrances to the gully, the Vladisvar became emboldened. They called taunts, flashed obscene gestures, and generally made nuisances of themselves, firing arrows from crude one-handed crossbows that scarcely scratched the drakes' lamella skin. Darmatus considered halting to aid his allies, but the Sylph handlers had the situation well in hand.

Unhurriedly, the Sylph riding the lead drake dismounted, careful to free his boots from the stirrups beneath his saddle before dropping to the ground. While the drakes were of a ruddy complexion—their leathery wings tan and scales a faded auburn—the Sylph aristocrat was brilliant vermillion. The exposed flesh of his face and back was nearly as dazzling as the meticulously etched breastplate he wore: pure silver with gold inlaid in whorls and swirls like climbing ivy.

He gave a derisive snort at a lazy bolt that arced out of the crevice, bounced once, then buried itself in the hill's pervasive slurry well short of him. "Pathetic simpletons."

With graceful motions, he plucked an ornate scepter from his belt and brandished it at the slit separating them from the Vladisvar. The sight of the magical catalyst—a molded orb of yellow illyrium at the top, a sharpened length of pure ruby at the bottom—silenced the jeers of their foes. Even the nomadic, apolitical Vladisvar knew the Grand Magister's Signet when they saw it.

"Rad'iana eviscae totalum!"

Blinding light poured from the cavity. The other Sylph hauled on their reins, turning themselves and their mounts away. Darmatus shielded his face with his arms, wincing as the intensity of the glare scalded him through his gauntlets. He could have cast a spell of his own, but it wouldn't have been fast enough. Light magic, oft referred to as the empyrean affinity, was one of the most dangerous attributes a caster could wield. Not only was it powerful, but it was also literally fast as lightning. An attack could hit before you ever knew it was coming.

The luminescence subsided as quickly as it appeared. Darmatus shook his head and blinked rapidly, trying to eliminate the dark blots dancing across his vision. When he could see properly, he glanced first at the hollow, which was disturbingly empty except for several piles of fresh ash, then at the scowling Sylph who had created them.

Darmatus clenched his lance, ready for anything. "You do know what friendly fire is, right, Faratul?"

Ring-bedecked fingers returned the scepter to its slot on a regal purple sash, wholly incongruous with the surrounding filth and carnage. "Grand Magister to you, *Terran*." Grand Magister Faratul, sovereign of the Sylph Magerium, practically spat the final word. "You would do well to show your betters the proper obeisance."

Most of his army was routed or dead. His once kind, benevolent elder brother was the opponent who had slain them. Indirectly, yes, but his was the mouth that gave the order. Darmatus was *far* past the point of keeping his temper in check—especially since Jarrik, the one who usually blunted his irascibility, was back with their siege equipment.

"Point them out, and I'll be sure to give them my warmest regards."

He could almost see the black veins throb beneath Faratul's fair skin, could almost see his left eye twitch with barely constrained vexation. Turned to the side as the Sylph was, still facing the Vladisvar he had obliterated, Darmatus could even see the muscles in his unprotected back rippling at his sudden spike in blood pressure.

Devout theologians alleged that the Creator blessed the Sylph thrice. Their first boon was magical potency. Second was their beauty and grace. And last was their ability to control their own blood. No, not in the way that traditional mages manipulated the men'ar residing *in* blood, but harnessing the very ichor of life itself. Thus Faratul wasn't leaving his back naked for the sake of his own vanity—though Darmatus wouldn't put it past him. He was doing it because, should it prove necessary, the Grand Magister could alter the structure of his body, form wings, and take flight.

Bizarrely, Faratul didn't respond. He just stood there, fuming with dignity, if such a thing was possible. Darmatus took that as a sign the conversation was over and started walking away. In the chaos of the drake attack, he'd become separated from Rabban and his knights. It would be a headache, but he needed to round up all the men he could for the assault on the forest proper. Who knew what traps Sarcon had deployed around the vortex? Darmatus fumed as he considered that harrowing, nauseating pillar of darkness, now closer than ever.

"A moment, Triaron."

Faratul's tone was *marginally* less condescending, so Darmatus didn't fire back with a jibe about his long, lustrous black hair. *Quite the pity, given I had an insult involving grazing cattle and . . . well, I'll get the opportunity to say it eventually.*

"Yes?"

"Her Grace, Ilitharia, sent me here to reinforce you. Not," he grinned smugly, "that you have much left to reinforce. This debacle is precisely why *my* forces should've taken the van."

The pompous blowhard wants the vanguard position? He can have it. Let his men fight in front and take all the casualties. Resisting the urge to rearrange Faratul's handsome features—Jarrik would be *so* proud of his restraint—Darmatus turned away again.

"Wait! There is more."

Forget prudence. If Faratul slighted him *one more time*, he'd slug him, Alliance be Voided. "Hurry it up, *my lord.* If you hadn't noticed, there's a war on."

Discomfort replaced the sneer on the Grand Magister's face. Whatever Ilitharia had asked him to relay, speaking it aloud was causing him almost physical pain. It was odd. For all their haughtiness and narcissism, the Sylph were awfully deferential to the Eliade, most ancient of Lozaria's seven races. Perhaps they thought of them as parents? Spells were chanted in their primordial language. The Eliassa, their divine council chaired by Ilitharia, was ageless and immortal. On top of that, they were supposedly the only beings who could still communicate with the Veneer, the Creator's celestial servants who abandoned the world in eons past. To say they were the stewards of Lozaria would not be a misguided claim.

Faratul grimaced, inhaled deeply, then sighed. "For whatever reason, Her Grace insists that you and your brother be the ones to battle Sarcon. It doesn't seem to be the wisest choice, given your—"

The Grand Magister froze mid-sentence. He'd witnessed the clouding of Darmatus's countenance not a second too soon and wisely chose to keep his fatuous thoughts to himself. He gulped. "T-the rest of us are to contain the ritual . . . that vortex . . . though she didn't enlighten me as to why."

"Did she mention why it needed to be us?" If Darmatus couldn't save his brother, he at least wanted to be the one to end him. However, it was curious that arguably the most sagacious being alive would task two brothers with slaying the third. "Does she know what he's planning to do with *that*?"

He flicked his lance at the maelstrom, whose outlying gusts were now strong enough to sweep away the dust at their feet and whip Faratul's hair, sash, and crimson cape into an admittedly entertaining frenzy. The mage would try to hold one down, only to have the other two unravel and flutter in the breeze.

"No," he replied quickly. Darmatus narrowed his eyes, and after a moment's hesitation, Faratul continued, "That is to say, she didn't *tell* me why. Her Grace must have a plan. We need only be dutiful retainers and carry it out."

Right . . .

Blind faith in anyone, let alone someone so closely tied to the Veneer, didn't sit well with Darmatus. It made his stomach turn. Or perhaps that was the effects of the vortex, insidiously bearing down on him, bit by bit. Yet this was no time to be questioning the motivations of his nominal allies. The enemy of his enemy was, for the moment, his friend.

Darmatus hastened toward the looming forest without gracing Faratul with either thanks or acknowledgement. Imagining the Sylph leader blustering indignantly at his abrupt departure lent him some small measure of amusement. He forced a faint smile, directed at no one in particular.

Segregated skirmishes raged around him. Knights bashed forward with shields. Vladisvar cleaved back with axes. Spells thundered, drakes snarled and slashed, desultory arrows flew in both directions. And bodies fell, one after another. Some wore red and blue; others mismatched plate. A few even wore opulent silver, now sullied with soot and blood. A feeble spark of mirth was all Darmatus could manage, for grimmer work than this still lay ahead.

He emerged from the fray mostly unscathed, save a new scratch on his breastplate inflicted by a glancing crossbow bolt and a fresh crimson stain now adorning his lance, yielded by two Vladisvar who regrettably blocked his path. Darmatus hadn't used magic to slay them. No, he'd need every drop of men'ar he possessed for the confrontation with Sarcon. It was no exaggeration to say he was the greatest Terran mage to ever live.

Which was one of the many reasons his sudden descent into despotism and cruelty made no sense. By some confluence of fate, each of the brothers had been blessed with spiritual power far beyond what Terrans should be capable of. On top of that, they, not some arrogant Sylph nor distant Eliade, had discovered Illyriite, gemstones whose potential dwarfed pedestrian illyrium. Together, they could have united the scattered Terran dominions! Together, they could have gained the respect and cooperation of the other races! Together—

"Ho, brother!"

Rabban waved at him from atop an insect-devoured stump, its rotting sides riddled with countless tiny holes. Weary knights, maybe thirty in number, gathered around him. Their shoulders were slumped, and their averted gazes looked haunted.

Creator be praised! He's alright! Darmatus thought, snapping free of his reflections and reverting automatically to the pious benedictions his mother had ingrained in them. *Pity the prayers didn't save her or father . . .*

As he jogged up, the soldiers did their best to appear determined, straightening and banging their breasts in salute. Darmatus widened his false smile and returned the gesture. Better to feed into the delusion that all was well than shatter it along with the men themselves.

"Have you scouted the wood?" he asked Rabban.

His brother pointed at two men dressed in arbalest's leathers like himself. "Narov and Khoradin have. I've been gathering everyone else who's broken through the Vladisvar line here."

Thirty was a distressingly meager number, especially given the ferocity of the Sylph assault. It only proved what fearsome warriors the Vladisvar were. Horribly outnumbered, they fought to the last gasp on a battlefield that was not their own. There was nobility in that . . . and lunacy.

Yet time was of the essence. Here at the forest's perimeter, Darmatus could feel each pulse of the vortex like a hot poker stirring about inside his skull. The unnatural perception made him want to vomit, loose his bowels, and curl up on the ground all at once. He didn't need Ilitharia telling him such a ritual was bad news; he could sense it himself.

"Report." Darmatus jabbed a finger at Narov.

The man's boyish, freckled features were pale and drawn. He was likely experiencing side-effects similar to his own. "Lots of trees, my lord . . . weird, creepy trees as far as the eye can see." His eyes twitched, unable to focus on any one thing for very long.

Khoradin, a bushy-bearded veteran with a deep scar splitting his chin, placed a consoling hand on his partner's back. "We never reached the barrier. Kept track of where we were by marking the trees, and no matter which direction we went, we ended up back where we started. No sign of the enemy, but no normal way through either."

Rabban nodded knowingly. "Illusions. Not Sarcon's strong suit, but then again, he's not really a slouch at *anything*." A wistful tinge of admiration lurked beneath his resentment.

"Almost certainly a trap as well," Darmatus noted. "He knows we'll charge straight in. We have no choice, after all. He also knows he can't stop us, so this is merely intended to sidetrack and delay us. But we'll punch through—and far faster than he expects."

Grinning at his men, Darmatus stepped up to the forest. It *was* sinister. Misshapen, desiccated boughs formed a thick, interwoven canopy stretching into the cloying darkness until sight failed completely. Leafless though the dying trees were, they somehow cast deeper shadows than any normal forest. On an already dim day, this forest was like a cave set in the bottom of a mist-shrouded valley: pitch black, with no chance of light ever reaching it.

Worse still, the gnarled branches pulsed in tune with the vortex at their heart, pushing along an ooze that seeped forth from ashen trunks. Those surfaces were themselves coated in peeling flakes. A single breath, a single touch would shatter that brittle bark, and every pulse shook more fragments free, creating an otherworldly snowfall that covered the ground in shades of grey and white. Flakes and slime; flesh and blood. Was the twisted grove *alive*?

Doesn't matter. Darmatus took a step, disconcerting wafers crunching beneath his boot. "This is it!" he declared resolutely. "Let's end it!" Not knowing what awaited them, the small band cheered and followed him into the gloomy undergrowth.

They walked in silence for a while; the only sounds came from bark crumbling as they trespassed and from crackling fires blazing in the upraised hands of two knights versed in basic elemental magic. Their presence was a boon, since Darmatus would otherwise have needed to light their route himself.

The illumination didn't reveal anything of note. Sagging, tired trees pressed in on every side, their excretions dripping ceaselessly like some pestilent, evil sap. Everyone tried to dodge the faux rain as best they could, but it was impossible to avoid entirely. Curses rang out when it fell on exposed faces or slipped between gorget and helmet, dribbling down backs enclosed by armor, impossible to expel. According to Sergeant Behrens, it felt like someone had shoved ice in his shirt as a prank: "Bloody annoyin', but not particu'ly har'ful."

Khoradin's marks appeared from the outset, and he'd done a good job of making them. To distinguish between trees, he'd used the Terran method of counting: vertical slashes for single digits, horizontal for multiples of ten. When you reached ten, all the vertical lines were replaced by a single horizontal one, and subsequent additions—eleven, twelve, and so forth—grew out of it like saplings. The method was quick, simple, and hard to botch.

Twenty minutes in, Rabban held up his palm, the signal to halt. He started to kick the tree he'd stopped in front of, then pulled back halfway through the motion. Antagonizing the supernatural forest was probably ill advised. Instead, he waved over one of the makeshift "lantern" bearers. His flickering flame revealed two horizontal and two vertical cuts, all of which bled a viscous burgundy fluid.

"Twenty-two," Rabban said. "I saw that number four minutes ago. We've come through here before." He glanced at Khoradin, who nodded in agreement.

"Then this is pretty close to the distortion." Darmatus stared into the gloom expecting to see, well, *something* at least. An infinite abyss—white and grey fading quickly to stygian night—gazed back at him instead. As he watched, a patch of shadows next to the last visible tree seemed to slide off the trunk and shuffle farther away from the light. *What?* Darmatus blinked and squinted, searching the area for more motion, but didn't detect any further movement.

It could be his fatigue-addled brain playing tricks on him. Or it could be the snare they were expecting snapping shut. Darmatus snapped his fingers and indicated the vaguely defined corners of the miniature glade they'd found themselves in. "I want five men watching each side. The rest will be in the center with me and Rabban." He faced his brother. "Do you need us to do anything before you start?"

"Just give me a little peace and quiet."

"Got it."

"That means you should stop talking."

"Can do."

Rabban sighed. He was already seated on the forest floor, legs crossed, eyes closed. In his lap, nestled atop his upturned hands, was his Illyriite fragment. The mesmerizing emerald crystal was smooth on one side but came to a triangular point on the other, indicating it was once part of a greater whole. As with their family, its original form had been split, separated into three perfectly equal portions. Two shards were here, within arm's reach of each other. The other...

Coruscating radiance shone forth from the Illyriite and expanded rapidly outwards. The shadows fled before the glow, and everything was bathed in a cool, green glow. Under that light, Darmatus felt his worries ebb. Hope blossomed in his chest. They were going to win! Afterwards, Sarcon would see the error of his ways and surrender peaceably. Why had he ever doubted?

Of course, Darmatus knew this artificial optimism for what it was—Rabban's wide-range probing. His youngest sibling was a sensor and a telepath. Both were rare abilities on their own, and their combination was more exceptional still. A sensor could locate and discern the quality of magic being used over a wide area. A telepath could reach out and speak into or influence the minds of others. Used in conjunction, Rabban encountered little in the world he couldn't find, and the unprepared or weak-willed were as playthings to him. In many ways, Rabban going rogue would be far, far worse than what they were now experiencing with Sarcon.

Fortunately, Rabban was merely using his extra men'ar to buoy morale while most of his attention was searching for Sarcon, his brother's Illyriite, and the source of his illusion. Though a lie, though temporary in nature, this feeling of tranquility was wonderful. Blissful. And, more importantly, if Rabban could spare the energy to soothe their souls in the midst of his scouring, it meant that his kindheartedness had not faded. *That* was more reassuring than any magical encouragement.

An intense beam of luster discharged from the gemstone, piercing through the caliginous wood. Fast and powerful, Darmatus thought it might go on forever. Through the forlorn trees, the vortex, past the far reaches of the continent, into the sky, and then on to whatever heaven the Veneer called home.

To his disbelief, it disappeared not twenty paces distant. The ray kept pouring from Rabban's Illyriite, but the opposite end was simply gone. Vanished. Swallowed by the veil of the desolate grove, never to be seen again.

Their men cried out in distress and alarm, clearly concerned that they, like that shaft of light, would be imprisoned here as well. Darmatus turned to Rabban. His face was impassive, unconcerned. Then, as if aware of the scrutiny, his eyes popped open.

"It's about to collapse!" Rabban yelled. "Be ready for anything!"

Cracks streaked from the spot where the beam terminated, spreading through the air in all directions, tracing forks of lightning as they intersected and split, radiating too fast for the eye to properly track. The watchmen retreated toward the center, rightfully frightened by the strange phenomenon.

Darmatus imagined this was akin to being at the origin of an earthquake. No tremors shook the ground; in fact, the opposite was occurring. The sky, in the shape of a dome around them, was fragmenting, trembling, preparing to tumble down upon them. Knights crouched low and raised their shields above their heads. Darmatus remained standing, trusting in Rabban's lack of panic. If this was anything like the cave-in of a normal building of stone and mortar, a thin layer of metal wouldn't do much to protect him anyway.

Unable to support itself any longer, the vault of forest and shadows fell with the staccato roar of shattering glass. Soldiers screamed. Darmatus cringed in anticipation. But nothing struck them, not even dust or the smallest fragment of debris. The illusion simply evaporated, splinter by splinter, deforming into sparkling men'ar particles that quickly disintegrated into the ether from which they came.

Sarcon's shroud removed, a startling revelation greeted them. The Illyriite ray had been assailing more than the mirage confining them within a distorted version of the wood. It had been striking the fulgurating wall of the vortex itself! With a sinking realization, Darmatus peered back the way they'd come. Dingy grey light filtered between the last of the knotted trunks he could see. The outskirts of the copse were still in sight, and the muted noise of battle could be faintly heard. Trapped in Sarcon's illusion, they'd spent all that time walking in circles, their goal right in front of them all along. *How utterly humiliating,* Darmatus inwardly groaned.

Yet what good was shame? Darmatus cast his regret aside, depositing it in the grave beside his pride and honor. Here was the raging storm; beyond it was Sarcon. He had one more task to accomplish and marched resolutely forward to greet it.

"No . . . " Rabban murmured. "He wouldn't—he *didn't*." Whipping about, Darmatus discovered his brother kneeling on the flake-strewn clearing floor. He'd been in the process of rising when something in the canopy caught his attention.

"That vile *wretch*!" he suddenly shrieked, losing all semblance of composure and control. Spittle flew from his mouth, and his eyes were filled with wrath. "Is nothing sacred? Are there no depths of depravity to which he won't sink? How *dare* he? *How dare he, how dare he, how dare he! HOW DARE HE!*"

Darmatus had *never* seen his sibling like this. He seemed possessed, seething with fury, his fists so tightly clenched that blood dripped through his fingers. *What could possibly infuriate him so—*

Oh . . .

Many of the knights were already staring up, trying to discern the source of Rabban's revulsion. At first Darmatus saw only the pervasive shadows, nestled among the curving boughs like fathomless flocks of ravens. Then one moved, followed by another, the same slinking, abnormal motion he'd witnessed before they'd dispelled Sarcon's illusion. He'd thought it a trick of the dark and, thereafter, a vagary of the hallucination.

It was neither. Pinpricks of crimson shone through the enveloping penumbra as the blobs shambled closer, some in the treetops, some on the ground. They entered the light cast by their mages' flames, and Darmatus's soul died.

Until this moment, he had refused to admit one simple truth. But now Darmatus could no longer avoid reality. Sarcon, his brother—no, his *nemesis*—was beyond redemption.

"H . . . he . . . help . . . u-u-usssss . . . "

"Mercy, mercy, mercy!"

"It b . . . burns . . . burns . . . sears me . . . in and out."

"E . . . end . . . end it . . . nooowww . . . "

Why hadn't Sarcon fielded any of his Terran soldiers on this final day of battle? The answer was now startling clear. He hadn't withheld his closest supporters to spare their lives; the abhorrent warlock had turned them into . . . *this*.

Their basic form remained the same: two legs, two arms, a head, and an average build. But all similarities ended there. Everything was bloated, their limbs coated with massive pustules that made it impossible to walk any faster than a hobble. Their skin sagged, hanging in sickening rolls beneath lopsided necks and bulging stomachs. In some places it had sloughed away completely, revealing porous, rotting muscles that dripped yellow pus instead of blood. Lips, eyes, and ears were still attached to their enlarged craniums but . . . weren't where they were supposed to be. It was as if a potter had left his creation unfinished beneath the blistering sun and the parts had dribbled away from their proper locations.

Horrendous as these mutations were, Rabban's choleric disgust was directed at the growths emerging from their bodies. In direct contrast to their hideous disfigurement, beautiful red crystals sprouted from them like gorgeous spring flowers. One's head was a bouquet of curling shards. Another was encased in a suit of arrow-length shoots. All had the minerals thrusting from their flesh at some point, and their bulging, throbbing veins were no longer blue but red.

These were symptoms of a pestilence that had nearly wiped out Lozaria's Terran population decades prior, before Darmatus, Rabban, and Sarcon had purged it using the healing power of their Illyriite. To see the Red Plague here, in *this* forest, on *this* battlefield, could only mean one thing: Sarcon had purposely infected his men with a remnant of the strain in an attempt to weaponize it.

"Had he planned this even then?" Rabban yelled as he stumbled to his feet, arms hanging listlessly, gaze unfocused. His vehement utterances cut through the tumult of tortured screams like a sharpened blade. "Was I an excuse? My illness a reason to seek out Illyriite? Yes, I see it now. *That* was his mask. The considerate elder brother was the persona and *this* the truth." Rabban bolted upright, his grin manic. "*This* was his goal. He cured me, all under the pretense of collecting a sample for later use. How naive I was! How blind!"

Without warning, he discharged a men'ar-infused bolt from his crossbow that tore a Red Plague victim apart in a burst of fetid flesh and glittering gemstones.

"T . . . thank y . . . " the tormented creature whispered as it died.

Was Darmatus going to lose *two* brothers this day? One to megalomania, the other to madness? He grabbed Rabban's shoulder and dragged him toward the vortex. "Sarcon is all that matters! Stop him, and we can heal them. I'm sure of it!"

It was too late. The damage had been done. Entranced, what remained of their sentience was no longer theirs to control. The infected looked at their downed comrade, then at Darmatus's knights. Weapons—an assortment of crystal and tissue coated blades and bows—squelched free from cavities in their aberrant forms. With spine-tingling, phantasmal cries, they lurched forward.

Rabban tore free of Darmatus's grip and began firing as quickly as he could, lost to the bloodlust of battle. Fighting was suddenly a repellant thing to Darmatus. How? How had this ever been enjoyable? Seeing Rabban gleefully mowing through the still-wailing mutants, the knights joined in with sword and pike. The abominations mobbed under a few isolated warriors, smothering them with their bodies as they stabbed over and over again. But it was mostly a one-sided massacre—ten afflicted for every man wearing red and blue.

Darmatus was forced to fight as well. There were simply too many of them, relentlessly disgorging from the shadows like the ocean's rising tide. A mass of crystal fused with a suit of broken iron armor staggered toward him, a spear jutting from where its left arm should be. Darmatus blasted it away with a gust of wind, watching it crash into another group. All were left floundering on the ground, unable to stand.

Another approached him from behind, and he shot flames from the butt of his lance to set it aflame. It screeched even louder than before, plaintive, mournful. Void and Oblivion! Darmatus was only *adding* to their suffering! He spun, rammed his lance into the area where its chest should have been, and vaporized it with a flash of concentrated lightning.

The cordon continued to close. More knights fell, even as he and Rabban cut down whole swathes without breaking a sweat. Darmatus stamped on the hard earth and summoned a rounded platform of rock that raised him and those nearby free of the fray. Then he repeatedly slammed his lance shaft on its surface, sending forth localized shockwaves that thrust smaller pedestals out of the ground beneath the knights still below. Such a maneuver burned through his men'ar like a drunkard through whiskey, but the lives of his men were more precious to him than anything else.

Once all the survivors were as close to the stifling, tightly woven canopy as Darmatus could manage, he sent one last surge of energy through the earth to bridge the various pillars—the main one in the center and eight more throughout the infected-filled clearing. "Get the wounded to the center!" he shouted, waving to the men farthest out. Terrified, careful not to look down, they began edging their way toward him.

When he was halfway across the gap, a rusty billhook reached up and snagged Narov about the ankle. Khoradin turned back to catch his hand as he was pulled off the ledge. Their fingers brushed, but Narov continued to fall, the waves of crystal and decay beneath parting to gobble him whole. At the lip of the primary mound, Sergeant Behrens stopped to urge Khoradin on, only to take a shard-tipped arrow in the neck. He let out a gurgle and plummeted.

Focused on maintaining his crucial flame, the elder of their two mages elected to remain on a secondary pillar while those close by fled to the middle. His bright fire, held aloft in both hands, enabled four knights to scurry across the precarious stone traverse. Yet before he could ford the span himself, the magically melded soil on which he stood began to quake and crack. The sorcerer swept his arms over the precipice to reveal the source of the disturbance.

Lit by the guttural orange glare of his blaze, dozens of Red Plague bearers were throwing themselves against the earthen tower's base. They weren't particularly effective, causing more harm to their bodies than to the packed dirt and minerals. Crystals chipped away thin slivers of silt and pebbles but often shattered in the process, mutilating the diseased flesh underneath. The mage seemed mollified by their lack of progress, regaining his balance and resuming his crossing.

From his vantage, Darmatus could see something the knight couldn't. "Jump, Tyus!"

The dusky-toned veteran spun and glanced over his shoulder, expecting an attack from the rear. Empty tree branches stared back at him. He blew a sigh of relief, then grinned at Darmatus, who was frantically gesturing at the platform's edge.

Gaunt, bony hands, jagged gems jutting from twisted knuckles, caught him about the ankles and whipped his legs out from under him. Though their mangled forms weren't strong enough to topple the column itself, many infected had collapsed at its foundation. Others lay atop them, making a crude stairway for those behind. Tyus's fire extinguished as he hit the clay plinth, plunging that portion of the glade into darkness. Agonized screams were the last thing Darmatus heard from him.

Can't mourn, he thought, casting about, desperately seeking a way to win. *Light! We need more light!*

Or, perhaps Darmatus could bring the light to them. Foreboding as the pallid ash trees were, they were just trees, with boughs that would bend and branches that would snap. He gathered men'ar in his lance, harnessed the stagnant air, and swung the lance in a wide arc, releasing a visible crescent of rapidly vibrating wind.

It struck the dense canopy directly above. Loose twigs, bark, and burgundy ooze showered the platform, but the barrier held. Stunned, Darmatus whipped his weapon over his head, building up a volatile mass of zephyr blades. When he was on the verge of losing control, he directed them upward. Surely they would break through.

Each dissipated in the same manner as the first, scarcely leaving a scar in the unexpectedly resilient wood. What was it made of? Dragwyrm scales, the toughest substance known to mortals? Darmatus swore and wiped sweat from his face using the padded underside of his right gauntlet.

Plan B it is. If the trees wouldn't break—and his artillery had proven earlier that they wouldn't burn—he was left with a single, undesirable recourse. Lowering his lance tip in front of him, Darmatus began amassing spiritual energy in the blade. His left hand hovered over top, acting as a constraint, while his dominant arm fed more and more power into the incantation. Embers sparked from the haft. The localized temperature steadily rose. When blue flames and steam emerged, Darmatus turned away from the heart of the battle, where his knights and Rabban were still fighting, and aimed his spell where it would be most effective: at the glut of Red Plague victims waiting their turn to approach the platform.

A tear, or maybe a drop of sweat, slipped from beneath his eye. *Forgive me,* Darmatus begged.

Scorching torrents of flames leapt from the lance, waves of vivid colors that spread across half the clearing in the blink of an eye. At the center, where the blaze was so hot it burned blue, those engulfed melted instantly, reduced to mounds of cinder and crystal ash.

The infected on the wings were not so fortunate. Darmatus listened to their screams as they fried, their bodies becoming torches that swept away the darkness and left the grove as bright as day. First to kindle was the slime leaking from them. Then the tattered rags they had worn in another life. Last to ignite was their flesh, the fatty, gangrenous tissues that comprised their horrid, monstrous forms.

Was it just his imagination, or were some smiling through the pain? No, that was unthinkable. Darmatus turned his back on the living pyres, using their sacrificial glow to tear into the aberrations on the opposite side. Their wails urged him on and reminded him of his purpose, of the objective beyond this senseless, despicable slaughter. Sarcon would *pay*.

The river of attackers dried up. Darmatus stabbed through a skull with eye sockets destroyed by crystalline buds, then dragged the impaled carcass into a ladder of infected trying to clamber over one another to reach the top. They fell with a sickening crunch, writhing about but unable to rise.

Five seconds passed. No more foes lurched from the now-distant shadows to attack him. Surprised and more than a little bit relieved, Darmatus stepped back, swaying slightly as he moved toward an adjacent defensive position. His vision swam, orange-hued images spinning this way and that. He'd used too much men'ar, even for a prodigal mage like himself. Rabban had coined a technical term for the condition, but Darmatus was too tired to remember it. *Men'ar drain? Doesn't sound right.* He stumbled toward the group of knights, kneeling and motionless even though no enemies were clawing their way up from below. *That's odd . . .*

One shouted at Darmatus, even as he rose and moved to greet him. "Move! Get away, my lord!" He recognized the man from his impressive beard: Khoradin. What in the Creator's blessed name was he on about?

Honed reflexes from a lifetime of close calls saved him from a fatal wound. Instead of disemboweling him, the haphazard sword slash clipped his tabard, leaving a clean rend that would be easy enough to patch. Darmatus moved his lance in the way of the follow-up strike yet was too sluggish to manage a full block. The gritty iron scraped over his guard and gouged into the chainmail above his elbow. Most of the damage was absorbed, but a stinging red cut the size of his thumb showed through the shorn metal.

"What is the meaning of this?" Darmatus blurted. The ache in his arm refocused him, banishing his fatigue. He dropped into a defensive posture, hoping against hope that this was nothing more than friendly fire, a sudden mix up caused by the stress of what they'd just experienced.

But that would be far too simple.

The other knights rose with jerky motions and joined Khoradin. Their faces were tucked, hidden by the extended bill of the helms. Yet they stayed silent. They made no move to subdue Khoradin. Most telling of all, their blades were pointing in his direction, twitching erratically as if hesitant about what they were doing.

A mutiny, then, Darmatus decided, nodding to himself.

Khoradin's gaze met his. One pupil was a soft hazelnut, a pleasing color common in the hilly country he called home. The other was a deep, glaring crimson.

His cracked heart shattered. "*No . . .* "

"G . . . get aw . . . away, my lord." Khoradin's healthy eye was full of tears, even as his body moved in opposition to his words. Glancing down, Darmatus noticed the tiniest sprigs of crystal, like flower buds pushing through melting snow, emerging from between the chainmail links on the knight's arm.

The awful truth struck him like a quiver full of arrows. *The rain. That blasted ooze, dripping innocuously from the trees.* Darmatus looked around, watching as the liquid continued to fall here and there, hearing it sizzle as it struck the charred corpses still burning down below. "The ash trees, their sap . . . it's more than a forest . . . it's the spell Sarcon used to transform all these poor creatures in the first place."

One of the knights rushed him with an awkward gait. Darmatus dodged his swing easily and kicked him onto his back. Sobbing, he regained his feet, striding inexorably forward. "Kill us, sire," the man pleaded. *Void!* A red shard was already jutting from his neck. "We don't want to become like them. Please, let us die as *men.*"

"*Please!*" the other knights echoed, even as they haltingly flanked him. "Do it! Quickly!"

No. No no no no no. "There has to be another way," Darmatus growled through clenched teeth. His mind was in turmoil. *Run away!* yelled one part. *Kill them all. They asked for it,* demanded another. *You can't,* whispered a third.

Agreeing with none of his thoughts, Darmatus rushed the man on the right and slammed the butt of his lance into his stomach. He doubled over with a grunt but then straightened up immediately, his endurance suddenly beyond that of a normal Terran. Darmatus smacked the stock of his lance onto his back, skipping away before they could corner him.

More red-outlined shapes hobbled toward him, coming from every side of the platform. The fire's gleam showed that they all wore red and blue livery overtop their armor. They were his men, now infected by the same pestilence that claimed Sarcon's army, that robbed them of their sentience.

Darmatus raced along the pillar's edge, ducking and dodging to evade their grasping limbs and slashing blades. He avoided using lethal force. Kicks and strikes with his lance haft were enough to keep him safe for the moment. Disturbing contemplations replaced his former indecision. *Is everyone gone? Am I the only one left? And where is Rabban?*

A spasm of agony from his injured arm brought him to a gasping halt. It felt as if a thousand needles had spawned within the wound and were slowly but steadily spreading outwards. First they'd consume the vein, then the arm, and lastly . . .

Dreading what he'd see, Darmatus pried the chainmail apart and looked at the bubbling gash. Sure enough, tiny red gemstones peered back at him. Khoradin's sword must have been slathered with the same ooze as the trees. With needles creeping painfully into his shoulder, Darmatus cast his head back and let out a sigh of resignation. It would soon be over. Sarcon had won.

Radiant light flashed from the lance still clutched in his right hand. Blinded, he leaned on the weapon for support, barely avoiding toppling off the column's lip. *What in Oblivion was—*

The pain was gone. Ignoring everything happening around him, Darmatus grabbed the entire hauberk sleeve and ripped it from beneath his shoulder pauldron, casting it into the forest. As it came free, so too did a handful of tiny red slivers—the Red Plague crystals that had been growing inside him. The wound itself was still there, puckered and angry but clean, somehow totally devoid of any infection.

Darmatus's first reaction was doubt. How could a burst of illumination cure a disease crafted from dark magic? It was a miracle. Yet, then again, so was magic. Was it such a stretch that a weapon could be similarly enchanted?

He suddenly recalled his adjutant, Jarrik, delivering the lance to him. Unwrapping its silken covering, he'd spoken reverently of the item he held: "My lord, this is a weapon unlike any other. Its surface is clear as emerald Lake Lovare; its height as tall as a man. Cast from the purest silver, it is mysteriously indestructible, despite the typical frailty of that precious metal. Use it with care, and it will surely serve you well." True to those specifications, it had never failed Darmatus. Not so much as a nick had ever appeared on either blade or haft.

The details of its origin were slightly foggier. Jarrik claimed it was an Empyrean Relic—one of seven left behind by the Veneer when they ascended to join the Creator in the celestial lands. *Which one had wielded it? Vidar? Sontek? Who else was there? Maybe Sariel, the Terran Veneer?*

None of that really mattered, except for one word he remembered the plain aide harping upon excitedly: *incorruptible*, something unable to be tainted or marred. If the lance was an Empyrean Relic, apparently its divine protection carried over to its wielder as well.

Wondrous though his healing was, Darmatus had no guarantee that he could repeat whatever had just happened. He couldn't suffer another wound. As he shook free of his reverie, three blades converged on him, two high, one low. Darmatus parried low, spun the shaft to knock the sword out of its owner's shaky grip, then met the second high slash while tilting his head to dodge the first. Riposting, he swept all three assailants off their feet and hopped past them before they could object.

By now he'd struck several infected knights with his lance. However, none had recovered. Case in point, Khoradin, whose hand brushed the weapon as he'd pierced Darmatus's arm, was only getting worse. A nasty, spiked shard had punctured the man's diseased eyeball, and the mail covering his stomach was bulging as a tumor swelled against it from underneath. He didn't speak as he attacked; his solitary pupil was vacant, and drool slipped from the corner of his open mouth. Dismayed but unable to do anything to help, Darmatus evaded and tripped him as gently as he could.

Rabban. I need to find Rabban. It would destroy the last shred of his sanity to see his younger brother like Khoradin. Yet the innocent part of him, the part that still saw Rabban as the toddler who followed behind him and marveled at his actions, sought to protect him, to keep him safe no matter what. There was also a miniscule chance that the telepath could salvage the situation—*save* their brethren—provided they could reach Sarcon and defeat him.

Fortunately, the younger man had not lost his sentience. Even so, the sight of him nearly broke Darmatus. Railing against Sarcon, Rabban danced about the pillar's far side, slaying any Red Plague victims who drew too close. His crossbow was gone; he'd likely discarded it when it ran out of ammunition.

Now the onetime inventor wielded armaments that were considerably more deadly. One-handed crossbows were the closest parallel Darmatus could think of, yet the dual devices only shared the convenient, easily held stock of that contemporary design. Atop that stock was a spinning cylinder that Rabban had machined to rotate about a central pin, and within the cylinder were bored eight holes, grooves that each fit a finger-length metal cartridge. In front of the rounded housing was a long, hollow barrel. Rabban said it was for aiming his "rounds," but Darmatus couldn't imagine how a person would aim any ranged weapon other than a bow.

Thwish! As Darmatus approached, Rabban pulled the trigger of the shooter in his right hand, releasing a sharpened dowel in the direction of a knight whose sword hilt was joined to his gauntlet with an expanding sphere of crystals. The projectile blew a hole in his chest before Darmatus had fully registered the shot. Rabban was firing the same men'ar-enhanced projectiles that he'd used in his crossbow, but the power seemed to have doubled or tripled.

Darmatus was amazed at how callously his brother could murder one of their own, bereft of their senses though they may be. A stray gem cracked under his boot, and Rabban spun around, directing both barrels toward his brother.

"What's happened to you, Rabban?"

The barrels shifted. Darmatus cringed as they barked. A second later, Khoradin's body slumped beside him. Half of his face—the side that had been overgrown with crystals—was missing.

"Be careful, Darmatus," Rabban stated unemotionally. "That one almost had you."

With his sensory abilities, it made sense that his sibling would be able to tell the difference between him and someone afflicted with the Red Plague. *Still . . . "That one?"* Darmatus said sternly. *"That one* was Khoradin, one of *ours,"* he stressed. "Why are you slaughtering them without the slightest hint of remorse?

Don't you feel for them, given what you yourself went—"

"That's precisely *why* I'm killing them, brother." He turned and fired twice, felling two more abominations. Two more of their own men, who had followed them with staunch loyalty, trust, and admiration. "I'm granting them mercy. It's the least I can do."

Dear Creator! He's as demented as Sarcon! Taking Rabban by the shoulders, Darmatus shook him roughly. "Mercy would be stopping them in their tracks. Preventing them from hurting themselves and others. If they're no longer a danger, we can heal them. Use your telepathy to freeze them where they stand!"

Rabban didn't attempt to shrug free of his grasp, though his eyes darted left and right, searching for more contaminated soldiers to put down. Only five or six were left, slack jawed lurchers wandering aimlessly around the platform. Void and Oblivion, they'd killed so many, using fire, lance, spear, and bow. Darmatus found it difficult to breathe, knowing the role he'd played in this entirely avoidable massacre. His hands were stained red, inside and out.

"Do you know how much men'ar it would take to keep them still and halt the spread of the infection?" Rabban's features softened, the deep furrow in his brow becoming less pronounced. He exhaled and lowered his strange weapons. "And yes, we might restore them with Illyriite. But will our shards hold up? Which takes precedence: defeating Sarcon, thereby preventing another catastrophe like this one, or becoming waylaid by the distraction placed in front of us?"

A feeble smile that was only skin deep alighted on Darmatus's lips. "If we can't do both, are we any better than him?"

"Do I really have to answer that?"

"You already *know* the answer, whether you admit it or not."

Rabban rolled his eyes. "You're too good for this rotten world." After holstering his firing-arms in specially crafted slots on his belt, he held out his hands. "You'll have to carry me while I work," he stated glibly. "Just like old times, eh?"

Exhausted as they were, it took Darmatus a solid half minute to get his lanky brother secured across his back, legs hooked over his lance, Illyriite-clutching hands wrapped around his neck. "I remember you being lighter back then," he grunted.

"And you were stronger," Rabban retorted. An odd sense of normalcy pervaded their trite, forced banter. It simultaneously raised Darmatus's spirits and forced him to recall a simpler time. A better time.

"If I do this, you'll have to fight . . . *him* on your own." Rabban's tone became malignant again, "Blast! I can't even *think* his name without losing myself."

"Then focus on that Sylph girl. What was she called . . . Analia?"

To Darmatus's amusement, Rabban jerked with surprise. He liked to think himself secretive and hard to read, yet he was anything but. "You knew?"

"Half the camp knew but didn't talk about it so the wrong ears—Faratul's in particular—wouldn't hear."

"*Anyway,*" Rabban said pointedly. "I'll be useless in the upcoming battle. Can you take him on your own?"

"It's not a matter of *if,* brother." The vortex was a massive wall of alternating white and black streamers surging skyward on the opposite side of the clearing. Darmatus noted the positions of the infected in the way: the paths they were walking, the weapons they wielded, how fast they would respond to his presence. He felt the absence of the breeze, took into account the distance between pillars, and counted the number of trees whose sap he'd need to avoid. Carrying Rabban meant Darmatus couldn't use his lance. His only resources were his legs and magic. Even so, he had to reach the roaring barrier unscathed.

No problem at all, he convinced himself.

"I simply *will,*" Darmatus concluded. "Any other outcome isn't worth considering." Pacified by his answer, Rabban clapped him on the chest and pressed his palms tightly against his Illyriite fragment. Soon it released a soothing green glow, pulsing to an enigmatic cadence that his own shard, enshrined in the clavicle of his chest plate, resonated with and mirrored.

Attracted by the intense glare, the Red Plague victims loosed baleful cries and shuffled toward them as quickly as they could manage. The moment had come to demonstrate what the Triaron could do.

Let's go.

At a tap, stone shafts burst upward beneath his feet, propelling Darmatus forward. He soared through the air, suddenly alone in a bubble that was his personal magical fairground. His hair snapped as he flew. His sweat whisked away, leaving him cool and refreshed. If not for the situation, this experience would've been exhilarating.

Wearing a dumbfounded expression on its candle-wax features, the first infected skidded to a halt as he passed overhead. Darmatus was at the peak of his arc, impossible to reach. However, those next in line raised their spears. What goes up must come down. They obviously hoped to impale him as he came in for an uncontrolled landing.

Cones of flame roared from beneath his boots, giving Darmatus an extra bit of lift. He didn't maintain the thrust for very long, just enough for a boost of several arm spans. Without ejecting the same spell from his hands—which were occupied holding his lance and Rabban's legs—he'd quickly lose balance and spiral out of control. *Mortals flying: who knew it would be so complicated?*

Two afflicted knights futilely jabbed at his feet. Neither came close, though their failure inspired their third companion to a stroke of brilliance. With a howl of anguish, he tore the iron-tipped length of wood from his pocked right arm, hefted it with the left, and flung it at Darmatus.

Twisting, dodging—taking *any* kind of evasive maneuver—was impossible in his position. The hurtling spike loomed, racing to pierce Darmatus's abdomen, followed by Rabban behind him. Yet the Triaron was loved by men'ar, and he loved men'ar in turn.

With a thought, he stoked the men'ar inside his veins, directing it to his chest from every corner of his body. Then Darmatus tore down the invisible dam separating him from the outside world. His senses became highly attuned—not to the point of overload, but enough to distract him if he let it. Plopping ooze from the trees, dripping all around. Wheezing lungs below, confined in putrid, rotting flesh, slowly filling with rancid pus. Darmatus could see it all, hear it all, smell it all; in the case of the air pushed ahead of the closing spear, he could even *feel* the incredibly minute sensations of infinitesimal particles brushing his cheek.

But the point of this exercise wasn't to gain the abilities of a sensory mage. Darmatus closed off that input. If he needed it, he could turn it back on. For now, perceiving *everything* was a drain on his attention and resources.

Of course, the energy he was attempting to tap into was practically *limitless*. A millisecond elapsed as Darmatus formed the connection. The wicked polearm drifted closer. Then he exploded with unrealized power.

A curtain of static force emerged from his skin, enveloping him and Rabban in a barely visible cloud of incandescence. Time sped up. The barrier appeared not an instant too soon, catching the sharpened spear point in its oscillating surface. What was trapped inside disintegrated in the blink of an eye. The remainder was diverted on a wild, erratic course, disappearing into the treetops.

This was the ambient spiritual energy—men'ar—of Lozaria itself. The life force dwelling in the plants, water, atmosphere, and earth that surrounded them. Well, to make such a claim was a minor exaggeration. Darmatus could only draw on local reserves and had to retain enough of his own men'ar to mold and influence what he removed from the environment.

Plus, something odd is going on here. Darmatus cast about with his senses, gauging the state of Har'muth's men'ar supply. It was like stumbling around blind in an empty room, or sitting in the middle of a desert picking up fistfuls of sand and letting the grains slip through his fingers. Barren. Desolate. Parched and dying.

Gasping, Darmatus closed his link to Har'muth's energy, causing his defensive spell to fizzle out at the same time. He'd been lucky to find even the smallest dregs of men'ar to aid him. Everything that was Har'muth—the region's very essence, its soul—was being sucked up by something, a chilling void that had briefly touched and tried to absorb him too. He focused on the raging vortex ahead, coming closer and closer. Was that the goal of Sarcon's ritual: to consume the life of everything in and around Har'muth?

Darmatus finally landed, propelling a cushion of wind before him to soften the blow. His knees took the impact poorly even so—there *was* a whole extra person riding along with him—and he came up in a half sprint, half hobble. Like his mind, his body was telling him that his fighting days were through. *A little longer. Just hold up a little longer.*

Reaching the edge of the platform, Darmatus broke three more pieces from the dwindling cache of men'ar within him, sending them through his feet and into the rock below. The ground resisted him; it was also being bled dry and didn't want to use what little power it had left to assist him. What a convenient occasion for ambient men'ar to gain a mind of its own!

Sweating, grunting, and concentrating with all his might, Darmatus pushed against the obstinacy of the earth itself. It yielded, but not without forcing him to burn another sliver of spiritual energy. Three pillars, each smaller than the last, rumbled into place in a path before him. Darmatus jumped from one to the next. When he reached the forest floor, the whirling face of the vortex was mere strides away.

Several mounds of slain Red Plague victims, their distorted, misshapen bodies blending together such that they looked like singular mounds of moldering tissue, blocked his approach. Darmatus was wary of walking between them, but he was out of time and low on men'ar. Straight forward was the only avenue left to him.

He rounded the first pile, careful to skirt loose, hanging limbs draped in his way. The odor was awful, a combination of charred skin and swamp-bottom decay that made Darmatus tear up and dry heave, even though he tried to breathe through his mouth. He'd never experienced its like in all his days.

Since the broken, listless forms were basically dead to begin with, it would be easier to pick out a white hare in a snowstorm than to distinguish living infected from those already slain. A skeletal arm popped from the second bloated hump, dagger aimed at Rabban. Instinct took over. Darmatus activated his lightning barrier, searing through the gangrenous appendage and leaving a slimy stump behind. That didn't stop the aberration, whose smashed head tore free of the press, exposed gums snapping, stub still swinging as if it held a weapon.

Cursing the further expenditure of men'ar, Darmatus heaved his brother higher on his shoulders and took off. More bodies disgorged as he went. Thankfully fewer appeared ahead than behind, but a solid bulwark of infected would be all it took to stop them. Darmatus couldn't use most of his offensive spells without dropping Rabban. Even if he were willing to do that—which was the *last* thing he'd do—he wasn't sure if he could stomach killing any more of these wretched beings, whether or not they were once his men.

His thin coating of volatile energy kept them safe for now. Slashing swords shattered or bent. Stabbing spears turned to ash. The odd arrow entered the coursing field and was redirected on a wild tangent, sometimes back at the hunched bowman who fired it.

Impenetrable though it was, at least against unthinking foes like these, Darmatus's defense wouldn't last forever. The furnace in his breast was down to smoke and embers. It coughed and sputtered, fuel all but exhausted. His shield reflected this shortage. A wayward shaft slipped through unhindered, glancing off his plate. Darmatus ducked left as a blade stroke cleaved the area his arm had occupied.

And then the gate before him slammed shut. A dozen grim men in tarnished armor greeted him. It went without saying that they, like their fellows, were diseased. Red Plague crystals sprouted from their visors, gorgets, and gauntlets—anywhere a seam was to be found. Yet dressed as they were, much of their rot was hidden. Their basic dignity had been marginally preserved. In the throes despair, Sarcon's generals still stood above their soldiers, forming a final bastion between danger and their liege lord.

Could Darmatus defeat them as he was? No. And should he somehow prevail, there was no way in Oblivion he could subdue Sarcon as well. It was a little bit early, but Darmatus needed to burn the two candlewicks he had left: his Illyriite . . . and himself.

He drew the blood from his extremities, feeling his toes and fingers go cold, then numb as the nerves within shut down. The absence of his digits was an aching void, as if he'd cut them off entirely rather than merely siphoned away their vitality. He shivered at a non-existent chill. If Darmatus survived, they could be restored, regardless of how agonizing their lifelessness currently was.

That should be enough for now, he reasoned, stepping forward with his shimmering barrier renewed. If not, he'd use the Illyriite. Saving it to use against Sarcon wouldn't help him if Darmatus consumed his own lifeforce first.

"Enough . . . brother. You've done . . . enough," Rabban murmured.

Rabban's Illyriite radiated stronger than ever before. Bright enough to force the infected to cower and flinch, sightless though they were. Bright enough that Darmatus closed his eyes without thinking. It's touch on his skin was gentle and warm, reminiscent of a clear summer day. Darmatus could practically picture himself lying on the bank of a river, soft grass beneath him, his eyes drooping closed as they watched singing pole men steer their barges over the smooth waters. What a pleasant dream . . .

Longingly, Darmatus let go of that idyllic, distant afternoon and returned to the forest of death on a lone hill in the middle of Har'muth. The glare was gone, yet the mutants didn't resume their attack. They seemed . . . content, satisfied with sitting or standing where they'd been when the light engulfed them. Lost, as he had been, in memories of happier times.

"Well done, Rabban," Darmatus whispered. His brother didn't respond, and his grip around his neck was looser. Exhausted, his objective achieved, Rabban had fallen unconscious. Darmatus was now well and truly alone.

Only one obstacle remained. Tightening his hold on his cherished little brother, Darmatus marched toward the line of taciturn commanders. To his amazement, the one in the middle, a tattered cloak of crimson clinging to his golden shoulder pauldrons, shifted aside at his approach. Darmatus immediately leapt back, eliciting a raspy chuckle from within the once-regal helm.

"My name . . . is Syvas Artorios. Have no . . . fear. Your task . . . is just. We shall . . . trouble you . . . no more."

The other generals nodded once, then fell still. Syvas himself said nothing else. What little remained of their original selves recognized the evil wrought upon the world this day—a darkness that went beyond any loyalty or fidelity they may have once possessed. Darmatus bowed his head, thanked them, and strode through the vortex, dreading what he would find inside.

Silence greeted him, an oppressive stillness that was so complete Darmatus nearly forgot to breathe. He coughed, grateful for the sharp noise that echoed about the open space. Having grown accustomed the ringing of blades, the screams of men, and the crackling of flames, he'd all but forgotten what absolute quiet felt like.

But why was there no sound? Outside, the raging winds of the vortex wailed and screeched as they tore an ever-widening swathe through the forest. Glancing up, Darmatus saw red, yellow, and blue splashes against the walls of the storm— explosions from spells cast by his comrades on the outside. He could clearly discern their impacts, even if they caused no damage. Yet the clamor they should be causing was whisked away. Absorbed into the vortex, just like the men'ar it was stealing from Har'muth.

Darmatus gently lowered Rabban to the hard, desolate rock, leaving behind his torn tabard as an improvised pillow. The rustling fabric roared like a cascading river, and the creaking of his armor splintered the air like breaking bones. Aware of the din he was causing, Darmatus quickly regained his feet and brandished his lance, redoubling the clamor he'd already made. *Where is Sarcon?* Darmatus wondered. *Why didn't he attack the moment I entered?*

The ritual chamber was perfectly circular, stretching from the slate beneath his feet to the black, star-studded expanse in the far-off heavens. With the clouds driven away, the Creator and his antithesis, the Void, could be on hand, watching the drama unfolding below. What a salacious spectacle they surely provided! Three feuding brothers who had singlehandedly thrown Lozaria into chaos, their fated struggle finally ending in an orgy of violence and death.

"Come out, Sarcon!" Darmatus roared. He prowled forward cautiously, keeping one eye on Rabban while examining a depression in the exact center of the vortex.

His confusion continued to deepen. Seven plinths bearing seven stones of various sizes ringed the hollow. The plinths were relatively ordinary—fluted columns with tri-pronged bronze brackets affixed on top to hold their charges.

However, the gems were mesmerizing. At first glance, they appeared to be obelisks crafted of obsidian, their surfaces rough and filled with many divots. Yet, take a step to the side, and those gaps sealed themselves, becoming as smooth as a sea at dawn. Their color also shifted through a spectrum of hues, starting out lavender, deepening to magenta, and at last clouding from the inside out until they appeared almost black. Were they pristine or flawed? Purple or ebony? And what was that murky, oily substance spiraling up from within their translucent confines?

Darmatus took a step toward the nearest one. Then another. His lance drifted down and to the side, drawing a white line on the stone as he dragged it along. The grating screech it made no longer bothered him. He *needed* to touch the stone. Feel its grooves and curves, study it inside and out. *Once I touch it I can—*

"Beautiful, aren't they?"

The reedy, strained voice brought Darmatus back to the present. His lance snapped up to a guard position, his eyes flicking from one pedestal to another—careful to avoid lingering on the obelisks—to find his brother. Yes, that was Sarcon's voice, and he was why Darmatus was here—why *all* the armies and races of Lozaria were here. How could he have set that aside, even for a moment, to focus on a mysterious stone?

"It's not you," Sarcon continued, speaking as if he could read Darmatus's thoughts. "Elysium has that effect on people. It draws them in, offers them the chance to obtain their most heartfelt desire, and then exacts a terrible cost."

A shadow detached from a plinth on his right. Darmatus spun in that direction, charging his lance with lightning magic, preparing to unleash a bolt of prismatic energy that would block Sarcon's incantation.

In his shock, he let the spell fizzle into specks of glittering astral dust. "Sarcon?"

"In the flesh," his eldest sibling replied. "Well, most of it, anyway."

Darmatus could hardly recognize him. He'd aged. Oh, how he'd aged. Sarcon's lustrous golden hair, gorgeous locks that had draped in straight, silken strands down to his waist, was now ashen white. Whole clumps of it were missing, revealing a scalp covered in liver spots. Even now it drifted free, pieces coming loose to carpet the ground around him.

His hands were gnarled and twisted. His robes were loose and baggy; where his tunic opened in the front, his bare skin, stretched taut against his ribs, showed through. Wrinkles had destroyed his handsome face, tracing deep canyons on cheeks that had beamed and glowed. Eyes that had once sparkled with wisdom were dulled with the grey cast of blindness.

Was this a ploy? Another illusion? If so, it was an excellent facade. *This* Sarcon appeared so feeble that an unexpected gust might topple him. Quivering, legs shaking beneath his thin cloak, it seemed as if the plinth he leaned against was the only thing keeping him from collapsing to the ground in a pile of flaccid skin flakes and dried bones.

Despite this, Sarcon gathered himself up, pushed off the obelisk, and began a pitiful shuffle toward the next altar in line. "I'm sure you're wondering about this appearance," he croaked.

Darmatus opened his mouth, but no words came out. He'd planned to *eviscerate* this man, to render his brother a mewling, bloody carcass at his feet, barely able to whisper as he forced him to explain his crimes with his last breath. At last he managed a lukewarm response. "Among other things."

That evoked a mirthless snigger from Sarcon. "It's rather simple, really. I paid for the use of Elysium with my soul—my essence . . . and my time." As he spoke in slow, languid gasps, Sarcon reached his destination and flung himself against it, breathing heavily. A short trip of ten paces had utterly exhausted him.

Despite his loathing, Darmatus felt his heart move with sympathy. *Why, Sarcon? What could possibly be worth doing this to yourself?*

"Is that where those wretched creatures came from?" Darmatus asked, his blood boiling again. Frail or not, Sarcon was the monster who'd mutated his

41

closest knights. The deaths of thousands of allied soldiers were his to answer for as well. "The Red Plague, the Pyrevants, and this accursed vortex? Just how far are you willing to go to win? What evil are you willing to unleash?"

"The Elysium is only supporting the Oblivion Well. Those other things . . . you could call them experiments. Distractions. Projects I meddled with to see what would happen. Since they failed to bring me victory, I was forced to seek an alternative solution."

"Experiments? Distractions?" Darmatus took a step closer, his fists shaking with barely restrained wrath. Every fiber of his being roared for him to spear Sarcon through the back, tear his desiccated husk in half, and flay what remained while exulting in the spring of blood jetting from his innards. Yet doing that wouldn't come close to the recompense his sibling owed him and the world for his atrocities.

"That's what you call playing with the lives of your soldiers? Twisting and transforming them into mindless, half-dead slaves who can still feel every stab of pain as they kill and are killed in turn? What about the massacre at Nemare? Those were *civilians*! Your own people and ours! What did those murders bring you? What purpose did they serve?"

His throat burned. Yet it was nothing compared to what those scholars—Terran and others alike—experienced as they slowly choked on the fumes from their blazing homes, libraries, and precious manuscripts.

Dragging himself up arm over arm, Sarcon faced the obelisk and placed his palms flat on its surface. "Necessary sacrifices," he declared. His jaw kept moving after he'd spoken, almost like he was muttering under his breath.

"To what end?"

"Peace throughout Lozaria. An end to conflict. No more war. No more poverty. No more disease, famine, or hardship."

Outrageous! No more *disease*? Darmatus burst out laughing in spite of his best efforts to contain it. "Hahahaha! That's rich! How can you spread a contagion in the name of curing it?"

"If you knew what Red Plague was caused by, you wouldn't be so quick to judge me."

Sarcon's assertion, delivered with utmost sincerity, startled him. Then Darmatus hardened his resolve once more. "Even if you aren't lying through your sallow teeth, that doesn't excuse your methods. How can you create suffering for the sake of eliminating it? I can't possibly see how Lozaria will be better for your actions."

The purple obelisk in front of Sarcon pulsed, a bright glow that originated at its soft, almost watery core and raced toward its sides. "Are you and Rabban really any different?" Sarcon asked quietly. "You both have your own visions of a peaceful continent and will do whatever is necessary to see them realized."

Incensed, Darmatus slammed his lance butt on the ground, cracking the stone around it. "We wouldn't slaughter countless tens of thousands—hundreds of thousands—to do so!"

"It doesn't matter. Not now. Peace will soon be upon us, Darmatus."

That sounded . . . almost triumphant. Darmatus stepped to the side to get a better view of Sarcon. He *was* mumbling something, his lips forming dozens of rapidly chanted syllables in the seconds when he wasn't speaking aloud. A spell! Sarcon was trying to invoke a final, last-ditch incantation; everything he'd said, everything he'd done, had been to stall for time so he could complete it.

But what kind of magic takes a minutes-long mantra to activate? A gnawing sense of unease swept through Darmatus as he dashed at his brother. "Get away from that crystal!"

"It's too late!"

Sarcon whirled toward him, a demented grin splitting the pallid, furrowed skin of his ancient face. Then he coughed, blood jetting from his mouth to stain the front of his white robes red. The force of the hacking doubled him over. From there, Sarcon collapsed to his knees, then fell on his side, rolling to gaze at the heavens with clouded eyes.

"It's finished . . . "

Was he dead? Old instincts taking over, Darmatus took three hurried steps toward Sarcon before noting that his chest was still rising and falling. *He's alive,* Darmatus realized with a twinge of relief. For the life of him, he couldn't fathom why he still cared. *This isn't what I should be worried about!*

He raised his lance to obliterate the obelisk, only to watch in horror as the ebony luster that filled it from top to bottom launched from its tip into the vortex above.

Darmatus found himself holding his breath, counting the seconds between when the ray was fired and when it impacted the wall of the raging storm. For that short span of time, he desperately maintained hope that the spell had failed.

Thunder clapped, the first sound he'd heard the maelstrom make since he'd entered it. Then the ring of whipping winds, flashing lights, and streaks of blackest pitch began expanding. It absorbed and dissipated the clouds in the sky. Every tree it touched, corrupted flora Darmatus had thought dead already, burst into ash that instantly blew away. The vortex had begun its final consumption of Har'muth.

And possibly the world itself.

For unlike before, it didn't march a few paces out and stop, obediently waiting on Sarcon, its master, to order it ahead once more. No, it was now a hound unchained. Darmatus was sure that, unless dispelled, the vortex would keep on spreading until it covered the whole of Lozaria.

He looked at the obelisk and the pedestal on which it sat, searching for a clue, some hint to reverse the doom playing out before his eyes. What Darmatus noticed first wasn't an anomaly within the Elysium or scratchings left by Sarcon as he prepared for his ritual. Rather, it was a tall, raven-haired man standing with his back to him at the lip of the hollow, staring placidly at the vortex as it greedily tore its way across the plains. *How did I possibly miss seeing him all this time?*

Darmatus leveled his lance at him. "What role do you have in all this?" he demanded. "How do I stop it?"

As the raven-haired man turned around . . .

. . . Darmatus's lance began to rattle in his hand.

Part 1

War Clouds Present, Shadows Past

Chapter 1

Toward Tomorrow

Venare 18, 697 ABH (After the Battle of Har'muth)
Nemare, Capital of the Kingdom of Darmatia

———◁═◦◈◦═▷———

Amaelstrom of bright orange flames briefly lit the summit of the cloud scraping Keiho Citadel, causing the playback image on the scrying orb to twist and blur. By the time the technician operating the device fixed the display—no more than a moment's tinkering with the formulae inscribed on the glowing golden sphere—the recording had reached its end. Again.

The gathered dignitaries of the Darmatian Council of Overseers, dressed in their robes of office and wearing the wrinkles of age, stress, or both, in many cases, were not unduly surprised when the conclusion of events was the same as before. They were, however, astonished at the outcome itself. Varas Fortress, "Gateway of the East," bastion of the Sarconian Empire, possessing defenses long considered impenetrable by military theorists across the continent of Lozaria, had fallen to the forces of the Rabban Imperium.

"Play it through once more!" pleaded Foreign Minister Bernard Foltran, tone frantic. One of the younger members of the governing body, his close-cropped brown hair and fastidiously maintained beard were still splotched with grey.

His neighbor, leather-skinned Admiral Ur Contus, commander of the small but powerful Darmatian air fleet, shook his head dismissively. "What will that accomplish? Do you simply wish to see how outmatched our own forces would be?" Chainmail links clinked loudly as he turned in his chair, facing toward the open center of the nearly circular table at which they sat. "But, by all means, play it again; maybe those of us who will actually have to *fight* might learn something."

Shaking under the gaze of so many notables, the young technician struggled

47

to operate the device. Twice he failed to properly connect the illyrium crystal at its core to the power lines. Then he utilized the wrong input spell, turning the projection—an ethereal globe suspended in the air above the device—into a pitch-black maw, reminiscent of the mythical Void from which all life was said to originate. At last the lad managed to align the energizing gem correctly and rewind the scrying orb back to the beginning of the data it had recorded. Tapping the glowing rune near the gilt ball's base, he set the recording in motion and stepped back.

Snow filled the jerkily moving image, not quite a blizzard, but enough to make a sensible man wish he was wearing extra layers. Whoever had captured these events was at an extreme altitude. Venare was in the middle of summer on most Lozarian calendars. A thick, gloved hand entered the view, clutching at an icy cliff face on the left. To the right, past a narrow ledge where snowdrifts swept hither and yon at the whipping wind's mercy, was a sheer drop-off. A loss of footing would result in a long, long fall, down onto the ramparts of Varas Fortress.

Gleaming like a lighthouse on a dark shore, the three-walled bastion sat astride the Es Highway, one of two major thoroughfares connecting North and South Lozaria. Wedged between the nigh impassable mountains of the Great Divide and the harsh waters of the Es Sea, it served as a staunch barricade for anyone seeking passage to the other side.

Which wasn't to say there weren't ways around it.

A sky-cutting airship could pass beyond the range of its cannons and traverse the Ebitras Strait, flying over leagues of open water and then back overtop land on the far side. Vessels of the sailing variety could make the same journey, albeit more slowly and with greater risk. One could also travel halfway across the continent from East to West and ford Lake Lovare, or enter the Kingdom of Darmatia and pass through Aldona Fortress—Varas's sister of two centuries.

And, like the intrepid procurer of the footage the Council now watched, an adventurous soul could navigate the passages *through* the Great Divide, braving the tangled ancient forests, unceasing mists, and legendary creatures that dwelled there. But whatever the case, *those* secret paths were above the operational ceiling for airships, and airships were the backbone of any modern military.

Suddenly the picture shook. Lights blossomed in an arc, tearing the night sky asunder and temporarily whiting out the image. Growling, like that of thousands of hungry beasts, filled the playback's patchy audio. Then the radiance dimmed, reducing from two angry suns to bright moons that matched those in the heavens above. One group, too numerous to count, clustered above Varas Fortress. The other, larger still, approached from the south in a loose semi-circle.

The first was the Eighth Imperial Air Fleet; its counterpart, the Rabban Second Expansionary Flotilla. Both were wonders to behold, all sleek lines, gleaming metal, and pulsing engines. Weapons—long cannons in turret casements, low caliber guns in rounded barbettes—shifted up and down, finding their ranges as the gap separating them continued to diminish. Crimson and gold Sarconian banners fluttered up bridge-top halyards on the nearer vessels, their ends snapping proudly in the light breeze.

When the Rabbanites had closed within a league of the fortress, they halted, the illyrium-powered gravpads lining the bottom of their vessels glowing a brilliant yellow as they hovered at fifteen hundred meters above the ground. By some unspoken agreement, both fleets began to shimmer and sparkle with a rainbow iridescence. To the naked eye, it looked as though translucent shells had sprung from the ether, encasing the larger battleships in soap bubbles. These were lumes—magical shields also born of energy from illyrium crystals. It wasn't a stretch at all to say the mined resource was indispensable to Lozarian warfare.

Then they sat and waited. One minute. Five. Time continued to pass without either faction making a move; the shivering of the being holding the scrying orb was the only indication that the display wasn't paused. Technically, the burden of action fell to the Rabbanites. The Sarconians had no reason to sally forth from the safety of their perfectly good fortress, which was now surrounded by a massive cone of luminescence many times larger than that of any warship. Varas's great lume, projected from a giant illyrium spirit stone atop the citadel's central tower, had frustrated every imperium assault since it was built.

Perhaps this was another bluff? Rabban *had* attempted to goad the Sarconians to sally and fight them on the open coastal plain before. In fact, in the nearly seven hundred year history of the three Terran sister states—Darmatia, Sarconia, and Rabban—the two embittered rivals had attempted to break each other using every method imaginable, with little noticeable variation in their borders to show for their efforts. It was not an exaggeration to say they'd spent more time at war than at peace.

Yet the imperial fleet refused to budge. The enemy guns couldn't reach them, so there was no reason to . . .

Enormous detonations lit the bows of the three largest Rabbanite vessels—their dreadnoughts, as military classification dictated. In the shifting light of the battlefield, it was difficult to track the passage of the huge, hurtling projectiles. But they would strike Varas's lume and be disintegrated or diverted. The fact that the imperium had developed longer range artillery pieces amounted to a meaningless historic footnote, nothing more.

And yet it *did* mean something! When the tips of the rounds struck the face of the lume, they did *not* shatter. Nor did they turn aside. Instead, the shield simply . . . folded, creasing backwards on itself and leaving a hole just wide enough for the shells to pass. One clipped the top of the outer wall, sending masonry, guns, and mangled bodies flying into the adjacent courtyard. Another punched *through* that wall, creating a meter-wide gap in the stone and sending spiderweb cracks racing in all directions. The last struck the outer portcullis, smashing it inwards in a tangle of warped metal and flying wood splinters.

Only after the impacts occurred did the booming of the cannons reach the ears of the recorder. The sound was deafening, but not so deafening as the implications of what they'd just witnessed. Rabban, who had long scorned the use of *actual* magic and mages in favor of magtech, now possessed the capability to stave in the mightiest arcane barrier ever made.

The rest of the battle was a foregone conclusion. On the ninth salvo, the imposing spire crowning Keiho Citadel was struck at its midpoint, splitting it in twain. This time, the playback didn't stutter, and the council members watched as its halves fell, the lower crushing the nearby barracks beneath an incalculable mass of stone, and the upper falling across all three walls and into the shadowy sea. As if struck dumb by this reversal, the Eighth Fleet chose *that* moment to charge. They could've still withdrawn, sparing their dozens of vessels and thousands of soldiers and giving them the opportunity to fight another day.

But their commander chose pride over sense. Or maybe he was foolish enough to think the situation was still salvageable. Regardless, caught between the mountains and the strait, geographical features that had so recently been in their favor, they were absolutely slaughtered by Rabban's enveloping fire.

Afterwards, a broken grey line split the projection and the display winked off, dropping the room into sullen silence. When it seemed as if no one would speak, the purple-robed elder at the center of the table's two long wings reached for the procedural gavel in front of him. They were too stunned, too shocked by what they'd witnessed, to accomplish anything consequential tonight. He would adjourn the meeting and reconvene it in the morning, when calmer heads would prevail.

"Hold a moment, Steward Metellus." Doctor Archimas Redora Descar, youngest of their number, raised a pacifying hand toward the wrinkled, balding leader of their group. "I think this matter warrants further discussion."

With a sigh, Steward Rowan Metellus sat back in his seat, his voluminous garments practically absorbing his frail form. "Yes, however—"

"Let's hear what the pup has to say," Admiral Ur Contus interrupted, leaning forward and resting his arms on the table. Though he was pushing seventy, his size and musculature remained intimidating.

Archimas smiled and mocked a sitting bow, his pure silver hair and matching glasses gleaming under the spotlights encircling each councilman in a pillar of pale illumination. "Should we not side with Rabban? It seems the obvious choice, given what we've seen here. And were I to spend but a few minutes alone with their weapons or schematics, I could surely recreate—no, *improve*," he amended with enthusiasm, "their design. For once, *we* could have the edge on *them* in magtech prowess."

The eccentric weapons and airship designer wasn't pushing an agenda any different from those he normally proposed: more military funding, purer illyrium crystal imports, bigger and better warships to match those of their neighbors. Yet, in light of Varas's fall, Archimas would likely pick up a few more votes for his policies among the eleven men gathered here. Steward Metellus still had the deciding say, but that wouldn't matter much if everyone else voted for war—to give up Darmatia's vaunted neutrality—out of fear.

"That seems reasonable."

"Aye, and we wouldn't even need to fight the Sarconians. Cutting off trade should be enough."

"Aldona Fortress will hold them if they attempt to retaliate; it's stood strong for two hundred years!"

"Shall we put it to a vote, then?"

Voices around the chamber chorused their support for the measure. Metellus counted them, tallying the distressing number in his head: *At least eight for,* perhaps *two against. No. We can't go to war. Not now, not again!*

Impetuously, he grabbed the gavel and banged it against the lacquered, heavy wood of the table until he had the Council's attention. "Do you remember what happened the last time we fought the empire?" The steward gazed at each minister in turn, eyes hard, righteous fury on his tongue. "We *lost* our queen! Queen Ephalia, the *last* of Darmatus's line! The last of the family that founded this country and made it great! We are a kingdom without a monarch, a dynasty that should have fallen but somehow still stands. *How is that?*"

Foltran opened his mouth to speak, but Metellus blazed forward without pausing. "Because our citizens carry on their legacy! Our territory may be small compared to Sarconia or Rabban, but our lands are prosperous. Most of our population wants for nothing. We have peaceful relations with our Terran neighbors and the other races—the Hues and Sylph—that border us. That you would sacrifice peace and everything we've gained is unthinkable! The nations view us as wise. Let us not abandon that perception for temporary gains." His milky eyes, unfocused behind thick eyeglasses, glared pointedly at Archimas. The inventor shrugged and kicked his chair back; he didn't seem the least bit concerned that the steward disagreed with him.

Genuinely exhausted—both by the late hour and his uncharacteristic outburst—Metellus brought the gavel down once more, signaling an end to the meeting. "Go home and sleep on the matter. Think about what's really important, and who our decisions truly impact."

"And, once you've done that," he nodded his head at the regal portrait of the Hero King Darmatus on the wall behind him, whose deep, patient blue eyes watched over all their proceedings. Armored in shining plate mail though he was, his hands held not a sword but a large tome, the contents of which shone with an otherworldly glow. "Consider what happened the last time all three Terran states fought at once . . . and what it cost the world when they did."

When everyone was gone, Metellus dimmed the lights in the chamber to their lowest setting and shuffled his way over to his favorite nook. From the inside, it was like an alcove; from the outside, looking at the four-story tower from the royal palace grounds, it was a rotund protuberance—an imperfection in an otherwise perfect column.

He took the steps slowly. There was no one to catch him if he fell, and killing himself after that blistering speech would only give his detractors something to laugh about. Once down in the circular basin, Metellus looked around at the encircling bookshelves burdened with large and small volumes, encyclopedias of knowledge, and scrolls on spells and sorcery, containing accounts of how to unlock and use arcane powers. Maps hung along the window archway, and many of the darkened glass panes were covered with handwritten notes or pieces of artwork related to studies throughout the space. The stars outside were beautiful, yes, but not so alluring as the information gathered in this tiny library.

The steward's tired eyes sparkled at seeing his dearest companions, the stories and accounts, true and fictional, with which he'd shared countless hours. To the world, he was a middle-of-the-road politician, a nearly eighty-year-old man who let the winds of the world move him without ever taking a hard stance. But here he was an eternal student, a being of insatiable curiosity who could always learn more, no matter how many years passed him by.

His destination tonight was the spinning rack in the middle of the room. It housed Metellus's most beloved books—the ones he read over and over again because of how important their messages were. Reaching out with a liver-spotted, age-gnarled hand, he grasped the wheel and spun it round. The piece he sought came up on the third tray.

Cover worn away, binding tattered and loose, it wasn't much to look at. Yet the veneer of things—like the divine Veneer in the cosmos above—shouldn't be taken for granted. Metellus tucked the book into his sleeve and wandered over to the velvet upholstered chair near the window. The joints in his knees, followed by those in his hips and back, popped and ached as the steward eased his body down. Rheumatism was no laughing matter. Soon he'd need a dedicated servant just to help him get out of bed in the morning.

With a jab of his right index finger, he pushed his glasses up. Thumb-thick lenses settled over top his beady, bleary eyes, and suddenly he could see ever-so-slightly better. Metellus didn't know how many years he had left or if he'd even get another ten-year term as steward, but he desperately hoped his vision got no worse; he loved his reading far too much to live without it.

Settled in, Metellus eased the crumbling cover open and flipped through the yellowed pages. His fingers had turned them a thousand times, smearing the ink in some places and leaving behind oily fingerprints in others. By rote, they found the story he sought and cracked the book open to it. *That* much, at least, he could do sightless.

Metellus was not a hypocritical man. Having asked the other council members to examine their beliefs and ponder the origins of Terran conflict in Lozaria, he planned to do the same. As he'd said, the Theradas Dispute, a border disagreement between Darmatia and the empire nearly a hundred years prior, was the last time the kingdom had become embroiled in the ongoing Sarconia-Rabban conflict. Queen Ephalia had been murdered during the subsequent peace talks, plunging the country into a period of strife that ended with the establishment of the Council of Overseers and a democratically elected steward. Such hardship shouldn't be hastily revisited.

However, the true origins of the conflict were not recent but lay in very old, very deep wounds. The tale held in Metellus's lap examined those roots, telling them in the form of a children's story, easily understood by anyone who picked it up. Though that was no reason to sell it short. A story needn't be complex for its message to be profound.

So it was with *The Tale of the Elder Three*, written by none other than Metellus himself. He read the foreword at the top with a smile, fondly recalling when he'd penned these very words:

> The following tale, which I record here to the best of my knowledge, gained through years of study in the libraries and centers of esteemed learning throughout Lozaria, has been told many times, in many ways, changing slightly every time. Therefore, I apologize to the reader of this manifest if my understanding differs from theirs. My writing is intended only to educate and guide, for if we are to save ourselves from the bleak present and future that we face, we must first understand

its origins in the past.

A light chuckle escaped his lips. Little had changed in the decades since he'd written this. Then as now, the doddering steward was still trying to serve, educate, and guide others. *But failing in my duty now is even worse than it was then.* Metellus's eyes roved down, and he felt the world around him fade into the distance as he lost himself in the ancient fable.

In days long past (appx. seven hundred years ago), a trio of brothers, blessed with power beyond measure in the magical arts, discovered an ancient source of mystical energy the likes of which they had never before seen. In its presence, their magic grew even greater, and they could perform amazing feats, including moving mountains, growing forests instantly, and, most perplexingly, bringing the dead back to life. They called this substance Illyriite, and though it was itself scarce, illyrium, though not as powerful, was soon discovered in greater abundance.

Each of these brothers saw in the world great sorrow and conflict and desired nothing more than to bring about an era of peace and prosperity through the use of the newfound Illyriite. The first and youngest, Rabban, took his third and set off to design new and innovative devices. He believed technology would lead to the progress and prosperity necessary for peace. The second and middle brother, Darmatus, set off to pursue greater truth and knowledge with his stone. He believed that trust and understanding among mortals would bring peace. The last and eldest brother, Sarcon, used his stone to pursue greater power. He believed that strength and dominance would force peace upon the world.

But the power of the Illyriite soon corrupted Sarcon. He used his ever increasing power for his own benefit, gathering more and more followers to his banner as word of his godlike abilities spread. When he gained control of his home nation and rapidly began conquering the remainder of Lozaria, Darmatus and Rabban united against him.

Raising an army of their own, composed of Terrans, Hues, and Sylph, they met Sarcon and his force of Terrans, Vladisvar, and foul abominations of magical origin at the fields of Har'muth (in what is now Southeastern Darmatia). A massive battle began that continued for three days, resulting in heavy casualties on both sides. As the combat drew to a close, the three brothers faced off against each other, and Sarcon was mortally wounded. But Sarcon still had a trump card to play.

In his quest for strength, he had discovered a power beyond Illyriite, Elysium. Seven pieces existed in the world, and by giving up a piece of your soul to any single piece, almost any wish could be granted. But Sarcon, having gathered all seven pieces and desiring revenge upon the world and his brothers for his undoing, sacrificed his entire soul to the Elysium, creating a massive spiritual updraft that threatened to consume all life in the world.

Darmatus and Rabban, realizing they had no other choice, released the entirety of their own power, and that of the Illyriite, into the Elysium void, managing to reduce its radius. Instead of consuming the world, only Darmatus, Rabban, and all those at Har'muth were enveloped, creating a spiritual hole that persists even today.

The surviving followers of each brother, those not at Har'muth, attempted to honor their progenitors by founding nations based upon their guiding principles. And so the descendants of these three have been in conflict ever since, guided by an ancient, undying hatred that continues to go unsated.

Metellus reached the end and closed the book. It was late, and he needed to wake early if he was to get ahead of any push to join either side of this never-ending war. Then a bolt of inspiration struck him. He selected a thick, leather-bound tome from a pile beside the chair, hefting it onto his lap. On a small stand to his left was a reading lamp—currently on—and a pile of paper, an inkwell, and a quill. His energized fingers snatched the ink and quill but left the paper. Dipping the feather-topped stencil into the viscous black liquid—once, twice— Metellus set it to the empty page at the end of the story. Whether or not his current thoughts were ever published, he needed to write them down to ensure that they were never forgotten.

Such is the tale in its entirety, and though it may be only a myth, it is certainly a reasonable explanation of the current conflict that plagues us. Does Illyriite still exist? Who can say? None has been found since then. What happened to the Elysium? Their locations have been lost to the mists of time. Why has the brothers' dream of peace been so thoroughly abandoned? In the eyes of this tired, old man, people sooner remember a wrong inflicted on them than the good intentions that proceeded that wrong. Peace is but a dream that a few, such as myself, cling to with failing hope.

It was still missing something. A conclusion that tied everything together. Metellus absentmindedly batted the feather against his chin, thinking about the three brothers, the three countries, and the events of the day. Gradually, it occurred to him that someone had to fix the situation—to erase the enmity that had led them to this point. They had to . . . He bent down and scribbled frantically.

For unless the curse of these brothers, forever locked in conflict, can be rescinded, this world shall not know an end to despair, now or at the gates of eternity.

What an ending! Proud of his work, Metellus set the book aside, turned off the light, and left the room. It was likely that someone else, far younger, bolder, and stronger, would have to lead the charge to save Lozaria. In fact, it would take *many* such someones, people from every race and nation on the planet. A smile creased his face, his mood strangely cheerful despite what he'd seen and read tonight. He had no way of knowing whether or not he'd see the day that salvation came to pass, but he *knew* it would occur. There was no basis for this premonition; no evidence. Yet somehow he could feel it in his weary, creaking bones.

However, if peace came, it wouldn't be tomorrow.

And therefore tomorrow is, for now, still my *responsibility.*

Chapter 2

Wages of Glory

Venare 27, 697 ABH
Border of Darmatia and Rabban

———◦⬦◦———

Night descended on the lowlands of Central Lozaria, wrapping them in a warm blanket studded with twinkling stars. Summer in this region was almost always dry and oppressive. No rain clouds marred the heavens, allowing the twin moons—Esta and her brother, Exal—to illuminate all things beneath their gaze in a soft, blue light. Two halves of a single whole, one waning while the other waxed, one filling while the other emptied, only together did they manage even a fraction of their daytime cousin's splendor.

The flowing grasses of the plains rustled, their stalks bending toward the West in a breeze that was not entirely natural. Young saplings, their roots shallow, shied away from the approaching storm, intent on protecting their life-giving branches and leaves. Always first to sense danger, the birds of the sky and beasts of the land had long fled—the former taking wing above the realm of men, the latter burrowing deep underground, far beneath their notice.

Something was coming.

Six men crested a nearby hill at a sprint, stumbling and cursing as they raced down the other side without breaking stride. Knee-length shoots snapped or fell under the impacts of their hard leather boots. Dressed in chainmail armor that clinked and rattled, wearing swords and firearms that jostled and jangled, they looked completely incongruous with their serene surroundings—at least until a series of new lights rocked the atmosphere.

"Down, down!" shouted Ritterbruder First Class Vahn Badenschiff, urging his remaining squadmates out of their enemies' line of sight. He dropped to the

59

ground and rolled the rest of the way down the shallow bank, hoping they would do the same. Scarcely had the light from the unseen cannons' discharges faded than the summit of the knoll behind them burst into soaring gouts of flame.

Overkill, that's what this was. The Rabbanites had his team of Sarconian agents on the run and were hunting them down with everything they had: hoverskiffs, airships, ground forces, the whole gambit—all the local resources they could muster.

What had he and his band of misfits done to earn such zealous attention? *Oh, right, just a little thing like attempting to make off with state secrets,* Vahn thought, answering his own question. Since the two sides had been at war since long before he was born, he couldn't really blame them for their outrage, could he? *Plague and pox! Of course I can! They're bloody well trying to kill me!*

Vahn found his feet with relative ease and kept running, helped along by the blasts' concussive force. As his left arm came forward, he winced and gritted his teeth, feeling a spreading warmth beneath the mail and gambeson he wore. Mixed in with the dirt raining down on them was a host of shrapnel: stone chips, splinters, and fragments of metal from the enemy shells. Glancing at the injured limb, still usable despite the damage, he noticed the entire side of his body was stained a glistening red.

One of Vahn's subordinates hadn't been nearly as lucky. Javon, the gefreiter who'd been at his side since they'd left the city of Beiras, was gone. Vaporized. This smear of blood was all that remained of him.

Blast them! More near misses rattled the landscape, painting the air in hues of red and orange, sending pillars of soil soaring high above the ground. Vahn did a quick mental count of their losses while drawing further on his men'ar—the spiritual energy carried by blood—to sustain his aching lungs and wearied legs. He was down to five men, almost half of the eight-man roster he'd originally been assigned, and that number was likely to diminish further before the night was through.

He'd been so sure of himself, so confident he could accomplish this mission and bring glory to the Sarconian Empire, the Ritter Order, and his family—in that order. *Where? Where did I go wrong?*

In retrospect, the operation had been doomed from the outset.

After the fall of Varas Fortress, the Gateway of the East that had held back the Rabbanite mongrels for centuries, Sarconian High Command had abruptly changed their approach to the ongoing conflict. Up to that point, meeting might with might had always worked. Special forces outfits existed—the Ritter Order, an organization of select individuals removed from the primary chain of command, was an example of such a group—but focused on infiltration and sabotage rather than true undercover work.

New strategies were now necessary. First and foremost, the deadly weapon that shattered Varas's lume needed to be dealt with. But should it be eliminated—plans burned, developers slain, production facilities destroyed—or appropriated? With the empire in full-scale retreat from the Nareck Pass, home of their fallen bastion, the emperor and his senate concurred that only enough personnel for the latter objective could be spared. They would risk everything on the success of a small team and the chance they could match—or exceed—the Rabban Imperium's current magtech achievements.

Vahn Badenschiff had been thrilled to receive the assignment. Despite his youth, the officer's star was on the rise. Along with rumors of further promotion, he'd even heard talk of receiving a *real* command. A frontline garrison? A mage battalion? Maybe even a detachment of warships in one of the eight fleets? If so, the ambition he'd had as a bright-eyed youth—becoming a Rittermarschal, one of the empire's top military leaders—wouldn't be just a dream anymore.

His naive heart had leapt then. However, reality possesses a pungent aroma that makes expectation turn up its nose in revulsion. Cobbled together from shattered units with dubious clandestine accolades attributed to them, his squad was far from ideal. A third of them were green—lowly gefreiters with boyish faces, mere months out of basic training. Two were at the opposite end of the spectrum: old and grizzled, pushing retirement age. Their experience was welcome, but Vahn felt it likely this was a joke by a callous quartermaster trying to avoid paying their upcoming pensions. Only a couple seemed particularly useful, including a sensory mage named Hans Ulrich, appointed as his adjutant, and a surly heavy weapons expert called Schmidt.

But that was fine. Somehow he'd make do. Within minutes of their first introductions, they loaded onto a rusty, dilapidated fishing trawler and flew across Lake Lovare, bound for the Rabban Imperium industrial megacity of Beiras.

Sarconian cities were filled with pristinely maintained buildings laid out along neat, methodical lines. In contrast, Beiras was a grungy cesspit in which only the tallest buildings escaped the filth and every square meter of space was stuffed with workshops, warehouses, or seedy tenements. Vahn had heard that this manufacturing hub was an anomaly; that adherence to artistry, culture, and sophistication was the guiding principle of the vast dominion's deeper territories. Better that a single border city be sacrificed to efficiency to win the war than an entire nation should suffer either defeat or, worse, dishonor.

While Vahn didn't put much stock in anything their inferior foes said or did, the environment was suitable for the team's purposes. When perpetual smog fills the air, no one questions the mask you wear to hide your identity. Furthermore, the ever-increasing need for cheap labor made it easy for them to get jobs at a weapons factory after passing a laughably porous screening process.

Things went smoothly for several days. They made "friends," worked the assembly line, and kept their ears open and eyes peeled for any mention of the new cannons, dubbed hyper velocity spirit accelerators—HVSAs—by the Sarconian upper echelon.

Then their big break came.

At the end of their evening shift, the head foreman announced that they had exceeded the monthly quota. All the employees would be getting a bonus added to their wages! Vahn immediately offered to take the burly fellow and his closest mates for drinks in celebration. Whether he pried knowledge about the new magtech from them or simply earned their favor, the move could only further the Ritterbruder's agenda—unless the night ended in disaster.

Glasses clinked; liquor flowed. Voices grew riotous with laughter and delight, the burdens of the day fading into memory as muscles relaxed and tongues loosened. The McGuire Inn, a chilly basement establishment bright with gas and candle light, was packed from wall to wall with Beiras Systems and Technology laborers basking in the afterglow of a job well done.

Only the back table, nestled in a nook between a stone wall and a rack of untapped ale barrels, was any different. On one side reclined the burly, muscular foreman and two of his pals, a dozen upturned mugs scattered before them. On the opposite bench sat Vahn and three of his agents, still nursing their first drinks.

"An' dat's . . . dat's why dis las' job was so impotent!" hiccupped the toad-faced Rabbanite on the left.

"Important," the foreman corrected, gazing with one eye into his empty tankard. A single drop fell out. He clicked his tongue disapprovingly and smacked it down on the wooden surface. "And yer right. Maybe the corporation bosses will trust us with somethin' *other* than ball bearings and gaskets now."

Vahn nodded sympathetically and nudged his own drink toward the man. "Like whatever we used to stave in Varas Fortress?"

The foreman considered the fizzy yellow liquid for but a second before grabbing it with one of his hairy hands. "Yeah, that's the right o' it. I hear shifts that work on them get time and three quarters pay. Bleedin' world just ain't fair."

Finally! Confirmation that we're not attuning a flawed crystal! It wasn't much, but knowing that the devices were being built in Beiras—and that their current employer was making them—was a vast improvement over what little information they'd had previously. "Who's in charge of assigning which teams get to work on the new project? Bet the boys would be happy if we talked them into—"

With a slack-jawed expression, the foreman's other buddy began pounding his fist on the table while rocking back and forth. "More beer! Mo' beer! Mo' be'r! Mo'er!" Though his words were slurring together incoherently, the drunk wouldn't let up, continuing his obnoxious warbling until the barmaid came over. Yet when she did, he smiled at her sheepishly and turned out his empty pockets. "Noooo money—*hic*—I'm—*hic*—afeared . . . "

Rolling his eyes, Vahn gestured for Klaus, one of his less experienced agents, to place the order, foot the bill, and shut the imbecile up.

Yet at that fateful moment, Klaus, apparently a lightweight of hitherto unimaginable proportions, forgot his intense conditioning in Rabban's social customs. Mind addled by alcohol, he raised the last two fingers and thumb of his right hand to order another round for their guests . . . and singlehandedly ruined *everything*.

The eyes of the lead foreman narrowed sharply. Concurrently, he shifted in his seat, one hand drifting below the table lip to rest on his hip. *A hidden weapon!* "Matt," he began amicably, looking at Klaus and referring to him by his cover identity. "This party ya'll invited us to has been swell—*real* swell, in fact. But my throat's gone parched, what with all this waitin', so I'm a wee bit concerned ya ain't gotten the drink tally right." One of his large fingers tapped the stout wood surface once, twice, thrice. "Just how many beers did ya get us that last round?"

Unaware of his egregious error, Klaus proudly displayed the same three digits. "*That* many! Three! One for each of yous!"

With hesitant steps, the barmaid slowly backed away, headed for the curtain-covered kitchen door. At the counter, the tavern master cupped his right ear—a coded prompt, no doubt. Spaced out just enough to avoid being obvious, the rest of the patrons stood, gathered their belongings, and exited the inn. Within a minute, the only people left in the basement room were Vahn's agents, the foremen and his lackeys, and another three workers in thick rubber dungarees. Each was at a different table, but all were seated facing the Sarconians.

Recognizing the trap as its jaws clamped shut, Vahn cursed inwardly and signaled his two other men present to prep their hidden weapons—various firearms, swords, and knives concealed beneath bulky industrial trench coats. His own hand dropped to the steel longsword buckled at his side. If Vahn thought about it, this reversal made perfect sense. Beiras Systems and Technology was a state-run mega-corporation. He'd been a *fool* to think they didn't have spies planted to find rats like them.

Across the table, the head foreman waved nonchalantly at his two partners, who awkwardly rose while he kept his attention on Klaus. At least *they* didn't seem to be faking their inebriation. "I had my suspicions, but—" A derisive snort burst from his nose. "Ya see, *Matt,* here in Rabban we order drinks like this." He held up both hands, his left with the middle three fingers raised and his right pointing a .45 mm pistol directly at Vahn and his men. "What kind of Sarconian agents are ya, forgettin' something simple like that?"

Vahn flashed a roguish grin and raised his arms as if to surrender, "We're the kind that are better at violence than intrigue." After that, several things happened in rapid succession. Vahn kicked the heavy oaken table into their closest foes, trapping all three, including the two lushes still struggling to find their feet.

At the same time, the head foreman accidentally fired his gun, hitting Klaus between the eyes and slaying him instantly. Turning and flinging throwing knives from their coat sleeves, Vahn's companions neatly felled the surrounding enemies with slit throats, their bodies spurting blood as they collapsed to the inn's dusty floor.

"Fi'resha!" Vahn cried, drawing his sword in a sweeping arc from right to left. As he did so, flames leapt from and encircled the blade, creating a fiery arc three meters wide that leapt swiftly across the distance between him and his assailants, consuming them and the wooden furniture before dissipating against the wall at their backs. Following a moment of plaintive shrieks from the Rabbanites, who were quite literally cooked alive, the McGuire was bathed in silence.

The evidence could not be hidden. Blazes frolicked happily wherever they'd found purchase on timber or spilled spirits. Angry black scorch marks marred the cinderblocks, and blood flowed across the floor tracing the channels between stone slabs. Above everything hung the stench of charred flesh.

Likewise, Vahn could do nothing for Klaus. If the rest of them were to survive, they'd need to abandon the poor lad's body here on enemy soil. Though the gefreiter had almost certainly condemned them to a horrible fate, Vahn felt for him, he really did. Ultimately, *he* was the one responsible for Klaus's death. The boy's alcohol tolerance, the presence of imperium counterspies, and the secret vetting this festive evening turned out to be were all things *he*—their commander—should have foreseen and planned for. *Maybe I'm not suited for this . . .*

No. Mourning could come later. The Rabbanite authorities were surely already on their way. It was time to go. Motioning for his companions to follow, Vahn threw his trench coat's hood over his head and walked up the steps out of the inn and into the night, lit by the stars of a foreign sky.

<hr />

Misery trailed them like a dark cloud for the next two days, threatening to swallow them whole if they so much as paused to rest. After rendezvousing at their safe house on the outskirts of Beiras, Vahn's soldiers were chased out of the city during a running firefight with local military police. Ditching this pursuit in the early hours of the morning, his unit moved rapidly to their evac point on the southern shore of Lake Lovare. Of course, that was when the Rabban Imperial Guard became involved.

The extraction transport, an ancient, square-shaped airship retrofitted as a fishing trawler, was blown clear out of the sky by a Rabban Scimitar-class interceptor—an antiquated piece itself, bearing only four projectile-style weapon ports, but more than a match for the unarmed Sarconian craft. Controls jammed or pilots dead, the resultant fireball, formerly their means of escape, flattened the agent who had been guiding it in to land.

Ten leagues of sporadic sprinting, evasion, stealth, and luck, all while under fire by Rabban forces closing in from the north, south, and east, now found Vahn and his four remaining men gasping for breath in the bottom of a newly shelled out pit. Looking around, Vahn could see grim despair set in their features, their armor and bodies torn to shreds and their minds clearly dwelling on the utter hopelessness of their plight.

Hoping to calm their nerves, Vahn sent his canteen, with the last of the water, from man to man and wiped a dirt-slicked hand through his already grimy brown hair as he outlined the situation.

"Looks like there's a few more of them than us." That drew a couple of wry chuckles. "But despite their numbers, we still have hope!"

"Yeah? How do you figure?" Wilhelm, the acting squad medic now that Javon was gone, glanced up at Vahn through the ashen palms that clasped his face.

"The border," the Sarconian officer responded, praying the conviction in his voice didn't sound hollow. "The neutral border between Rabban and Darmatia. If we get across—"

"Then they ain't got any cause ta follow, lest they violate their treaties," Schmidt finished. A tiny little ember sparked and died as the shag he'd been smoking went cold. "Blasted Rabbanite crud . . . " He tossed it away, fumbled for another, and cursed as the shoddily wrapped herbs slipped through his fingers and fell in the muck. Sighing, he squinted his one good eye, the other slashed shut by a ragged—and recent—shrapnel cut, and smiled through the blood flowing down his face, "Well, worst comes ta worst, I won't hafta see the hag again."

"That's the spirit! Always look for a silver lining!" Vahn didn't know anything about Schmidt or his marital issues, but he would take *any* positive morale he could get at this point. "Now from what I've seen, this is what's arrayed against us. To the north we've got three Scimitars, closing fast and giving our enemy extreme air superiority. The east and south both have several platoons of foot soldiers, along with those mounted patrols of Stingers that got Javon earlier."

"Our only avenue of escape is the undefended, demilitarized border between Rabban and Darmatia, about a league to the west. If we can only just make it to—*just step across*—that line, we'll survive. If not," Vahn smiled wickedly at his companions, "we'll make sure most of them don't see the sunrise either."

"So, we weren't just running around blindly?" Wilhelm asked, pale features brightening by several degrees.

"Of course not! What kind of commander do you take me for?" Drawing his sword and taking a pistol in his other hand, Vahn stood up, keeping his head below the top of the pit, "Ready to send them to Oblivion?"

"It's only fair we return the favor," chimed in his second in command, Second Lieutenant Hans Ulric, a young man with a vicious x-shaped scar disfiguring his otherwise handsome face. It was an unfading reminder of what Rabban had taken from him. "Considering they've spent the past two days trying to punch our tickets there."

Their courage steeled, Vahn gathered men'ar in his legs and hopped out of the hole with a single power-enhanced bound, screaming, "To glory, then, my brothers, and see you on the other side!"

<hr />

Uneasy stillness greeted their initial foray from the pit. A southwesterly wind gently caressed the foliage of the few stunted trees in sight, and the pervading sward flattened itself against the plain's numerous hillocks. It was calm. Much *too* calm.

The world went white before they'd traveled twenty paces. Searchlights, sweeping away the darkness as they probed for the spies. Appearing from every direction but the front, they converged on them within seconds, accompanied by the sounds of shouting men and the clamor of mechanized vehicles. Vahn checked over his shoulder and was nearly blinded by the rapidly closing glare.

Their trackers had mounted the circular lamps to the front of a trio of Stinger recon craft. From now on, no matter what his team did, they would always be illuminated by one of those fast-moving airships.

An instant later, a torrent of projectiles—ranging from small arms to artillery shells—cut through the fractured night sky toward them. Fortunately, most of these fell short, churning up screens of dirt that added to the confusion and aided the Sarconians. Even the rounds that did get through missed by comfortable margins. Vahn prayed their luck would hold. Since his team had no choice but to slog through a hail of bullets, the more their enemy kept their distance in the inky darkness and swirling gunfire smoke, the better the Sarconians' chance of survival.

This was not to last. Heralded by the distinctive *zzzzzz* from which the Stingers—formally BST-R212s—received their nickname, the flight of small vessels to their rear broke formation and charged toward them. Louder and louder their engines whined. Vahn sensed their approach like a needle pricking the nape of his neck. When the sound reached a crescendo, he screamed at the top of his lungs to be heard over the buzzing pitch.

"SCATTER!"

Whump! Whump! Whump! Just as their three underbelly cannons unleashed a rhythmic barrage, the squad broke off onto diverging vectors. Vahn went left with Hans, Schmidt climbed straight up the next mound, and Wilhelm and their last gefreiter, Tills, swept right around the berm. Massive eruptions of earth cascaded across Vahn as he sprinted, and an ever-expanding cloud of shrapnel both deflected off his armor and found purchase in exposed flesh.

But these were secondary effects caused by nearby blasts. He was not their primary target. Summiting the hill, a well-placed shot cost Schmidt an arm, scorching his entire left side and sending him tumbling and screaming down the far side. Then the flight of enemy craft zipped past, their single rear-deck guns ensuring that a break in the fire never occurred.

Vahn skidded over the top of the hill and dropped into the gully on the far side. Hans and the other remaining two, more or less still intact, followed quickly after. The last agent to descend, Wilhelm, quickly grabbed a poultice from his pack and tried to stem the red fountain gushing from Schmidt's wound. Spitting blood, Schmidt attempted to push him away with his remaining arm.

"Gah, what're ya doin' son? Leave me. Get outta here! Even if I don't get shot again, I'll bleed out long before ya can help me!"

"We're not leaving anyone behind," Vahn replied, pushing Schmidt back to the ground so he could be treated. "If we've made it this far together, we can make it across the border together." *I've failed my mission. I've already lost three men. No one else is dying. No one else . . .*

"Uh, sir," Hans interjected, "those Stingers are coming around for another pass." As a sensory mage, the young lieutenant's specialty was reading the flow of men'ar—the very presence of life itself—in other beings and objects. If he said their attackers were heading back, Vahn knew it was true.

They were completely exposed on the down slope of this hill. Worse still, they'd have to move Schmidt without finishing his bandaging, and a grievous wound like that would be fatal if left unattended. Should they stand and fight? That would risk the whole squad, but . . .

Suddenly Schmidt came alive, knocking Vahn and Wilhelm aside as he rose. The abrupt motion ripped his arm wound open in a gush of crimson fluid, but he didn't seem to care. Grabbing a concentrated illyrium charge from his belt, the veteran soldier ran to the top of the hill, leaving oozing puddles of blood in his wake.

Quickly overcoming his shock, Vahn dashed after him, snatching him by his shoulder and forcibly dragging him back toward the shallow basin, "Unteroffizer First Class Schmidt Ernthoff, I order you to stow that charge and finish getting patched up! I'm not losing anyone else out here!"

Schmidt grinned, then calmly raised a leg and kicked his superior in the chest, stunning him and sending him sprawling down the incline, "Sir, I respect ya, but yer just gonna get *everyone* killed at this rate. I'm already dead. Ya gotta learn to cut losses an' . . . ya gotta learn when sacrificin' one life, especially one beyond help, will let ya save quite a few more." Schmidt winced noticeably, coughed up a fistful of blood, then paradoxically laughed as he continued, "Oh, an' this probably won't finish them off, so I hope ya can manage to get yerselves out o' this mess without me."

With that, he thumbed the activation switch, clutched it between his teeth, and pulled out a bright red flare, lighting it then waving frantically at the approaching land-skimmers, "Oi, ya slimy slechers! Want ta find out what color yer guts are?"

Events had been set in motion; it was too late for Vahn to rescue Schmidt. But he could still honor the man's death by making sure the rest of his unit survived and that Rabban paid dearly for the Sarconian lives they'd taken. Holstering his pistol, Vahn pulled out a grappling gun—standard Special Forces issue—passed Hans another illyrium charge, and motioned his team up the hill. "When Schmidt's charge blows, follow my lead. Until then, trust me. I'll keep us safe." Every head nodded in assent.

The Stingers continued to grow larger, their pointed forms rising menacingly from the shadows as they closed. Vahn waited nervously, watching until he could clearly see the searchlight attached to the slanting prow, until he could pick out the darkened figures of the crew in the rear compartment. His palms sweated as his fingers clenched and unclenched about his sword hilt.

Not yet, not yet . . . Now!

Both sides burst into action. At a hundred meters out, cruising at five meters off the ground, the Stingers opened fire on Schmidt. Simultaneously, Vahn, standing just below the crest of the hill, gathered as much men'ar from his cells as possible, exerting so much pressure on his body that the muscles of his arms, where the energy was directed, began deteriorating.

This was what it meant to wield *magic*. To take and transform *life itself.* Overflowing power surged through him—an unbridled inferno spreading along his veins, a swirling maelstrom of invigorating spiritual aura suffusing his nerves. Vahn was loathe to let the feeling fade, even though he knew he had to.

A second later, swinging his sword in an arc before him faster than the eye could see, he released this buildup in a massive wave of forward force, activating the spell with the cry, "Fi'ranxia shiletta totalum!" The spinning circle erupted with a massive cone of fire two meters long and three meters wide that shot outwards toward the assaulting enemy craft, catching and incinerating the rounds approaching Vahn and the three soldiers huddled safely behind him.

Each hit also sent shockwaves through Vahn's body, compressing his arms, straining his back, and driving him steadily backward, his feet leaving deep furrows in the ground. After ten seconds of constant pounding, his shield flickered. *Hold! Please hold!*

One blow. Another. It was too much. With an explosion of sparking cinders, the barrier broke, sending Vahn reeling. *Was that enough? Let it be so!* He collapsed backwards into the supporting arms of his soldiers, the last shot flashing by less than a meter above.

Then the Stingers were on top of them. Schmidt, body shredded, bleeding from a dozen gaping holes and barely standing, was long dead. But the charge in his mouth, set to a delayed timer activated by his death, was still live. A credit to the dead soldier, the grenade went off flawlessly, *precisely* as the land-skimmers passed overhead.

Forced upward by the impassable hill below, the massive explosion vaporized Schmidt, shattered the illyrium hover drives of the lead vehicle, and sent the remaining two careening wildly past, trailing smoke from their scorched underbellies. Without a means of staying airborne, the first nosedived into a nearby tree, erupting into a brilliant fireball of scorched and melting composites. None of the crew left the wreckage.

"Go!" Vahn scrambled wearily to his feet, grabbed the grenade from Hans, and dashed toward the nearest Stinger, yelling to his men as he ran, "Capture the other! I've got this one!" Which was easier said than done. Pulling out of an erratic dive, the vehicle made an abrupt one-eighty and threw the full weight of its dual 115 kilo-il thrusters into a headlong charge back at them. Superheated shot from the underbelly cannon streaked past Vahn, often passing close enough to sear black burns across his face and whip his hair backwards with sizzling embers interlaced throughout the locks. He leapt awkwardly over the last projectile, missing it by a hair's breadth, and landed on a knee as the Stinger passed over him.

This is for Schmidt! Firing his grappling hook at the bow railing, Vahn began his counterattack.

With a solid *clunk*, the hook bit into the soft metal, instantly taking hold and rapidly reeling Vahn in. He cursed foully as the motion caused the shrapnel in his right arm to shift, but then his upwards force cast him over the rail where he released the grapple and rolled forward to land amidships.

To the crew of four who, moments before, had rained fire down upon helpless infantrymen, it was as though a ferocious Voidspawn had appeared among them.

"Fi'resha!" The forward weapons operator, cut and cauterized from head to toe, stumbled over the railing, trailing a cape of flames. The bow, half detached from the rest of the vessel, listed tentatively by a few molten strands not fully annihilated by the blow. Immediately the Stinger began dragging right and down, heading for an imminent crash.

"Spi'ferat!" Vahn's sword flared across the deck, catching both the communications officer and the deck gunner—who stumbled into the blow as he staggered from the sudden course change—through their mid regions. The first died instantly, but the second could only scream in terror as the flames crawled from the entry wound, devouring his body like a thousand scuttling spiders.

As the unearthly wails of his subordinate ground repeatedly against his ears, the commander of the vessel found himself paralyzed by fear at the rear of the Stinger. Sweat pimpled across his body as his very veins turned to ice and his flickering gaze took in the tall, vicious, almost mocking Sarconian not five paces from him. This was the face of death; a handsome, thoughtful face, but a harbinger of destruction nonetheless. These Sarconians, from the youngest slave to the stateliest prince, were bred for war. For them, killing was but a process of competitive selection: the strong cull the weak. This was their chief commandment . . . or so the Rabbanite commander had been taught, and with death staring him in the face, he saw no reason to reconsider this inbred mindset.

On the deck before him, the last of his men finally expired with a rasping rattle that broke his reverie. He fumbled for his pistol and, though shaking wildly, managed to grasp it in both hands and aim it at the Sarconian. Blinking aside the tears gathering in his eyes, he screamed and pulled the trigger, "Curse you, Sarconian! Curse you and the whore who spawned you!"

Vahn twitched his sword up, knocking the bullet aside and splattering the stunned Rabban commander with the still-warm gore of his subordinates. The commander dropped his gun and fell to his knees, quivering with fright. Vahn spared him a pitying glance, thumbed the activation switch on the illyrium charge, and tossed it at the feet of his prone foe.

"For my men."

He leapt the rail and dropped onto the waiting deck of the second Stinger, which had been captured by his men. None were injured.

As the engines engaged and their vessel sped across the Darmatian border to safety, Vahn watched the explosion of the other patrol craft in the distance.

It was nothing short of beautiful, with a vast cacophony of reds, oranges, and yellows intermixed to create a brief but vibrant display. This artwork was the epitome of the Sarconian Empire Vahn served. Brilliant and fierce, the empire existed to spread its power and prosperity to the rest of the world. Only through its glorification and the humiliation of its sister nations would the proper order of the world be achieved. And so Vahn, soldier and knight of the empire, would eradicate his personal feelings, overcome his losses, and sacrifice everything, including his very soul, to see Sarconia stand in its proper place: the very summit of the world.

⸺⸺⟡⸺⸺

"Sir, I think you better take a look at this." Hans's worried voice woke Vahn from his brief nap, and with his return to consciousness, so too returned all the aches and pains heaped on his body during their flight from Rabban. They had crossed the Darmatian border barely an hour prior, but to his flesh it felt like ages.

He stumbled drowsily to the rear of the vessel where Hans and Wilhelm chatted while periodically pointing at the altimeter, power gauge, and navigation charts. "Unless we're going to crash, I suggest we put this off till daylight." Vahn glanced at the ship chronometer and added, "Which is only about two hours from now anyway."

"Sir, we're not going to make it that long." Hans gestured at the altimeter, which was steadily dropping. It currently read five meters above ground, though they had begun cruising at an altitude of eight meters. By the time Vahn looked at it, away, then back again, the dial was fluctuating around four and a half. "In fact, we're probably going to crash in less than five minutes."

Vahn swore. If they crashed now, they'd have to walk the rest of the way to Nemare, the Darmatian capital, which would take a week or longer. Then they'd spend another few days negotiating with the Sarconian Consul General and the Darmatian authorities to send them home, which could take even longer than he estimated since they had no money left with which to grease the wheels of bureaucracy. By the Scourge, it could even be a full month before he returned to the empire and, from there, to the front lines against Rabban! Vahn swore again, more vehemently than before. "Any idea *why* we're sinking? Is it the damage from the illyrium explosion?"

"That was what I thought at first, too. But look at this." Hans tapped the power supply display, which alternately showed full, then empty, then full, in a continuous pattern that coincided with the upward and downward fluctuations of the altimeter. To make matters stranger still, the pattern was shifting toward empty, with the periods the power supply was exhausted increasing in time and frequency. "The illyrium in the drives is engaging and disengaging. In other words, our fuel is running out of fuel."

In school, one of the very first science lessons all students were taught was the method by which illyrium functioned. Vahn vaguely remembered the fundamentals, which made the situation they were in all the more dire. In the basest sense, illyrium was an amplifier. It took in spiritual energy from its surroundings, multiplied it, and returned a greater amount of energy that could be converted into other forms, such as thermal or electrical energy. Eventually, regular illyrium broke down and was unable to continue performing this synthesizing process, but until that occurred, the amount of energy a sample of it could provide was astounding.

Even more amazing, in Vahn's opinion, was that this process almost never failed. In fact, the only way you could stop a source of energy made from illyrium was to place it in a total vacuum of spiritual essence. In other words . . . a place totally devoid of life.

Vahn, knight of the empire, fearless soldier, and battle-hardened veteran, felt his skin crawl. An unbidden wave of terror rushed through him, and his breath became short and tenuous. "Hans, the navigation charts, give me the navigation charts!"

Hans's eyes flickered up, briefly meeting Vahn's gaze, and in that second of shared anxiety, Vahn knew Hans had already checked the charts, already knew the dreaded name that passed unbidden through his mind. "Sir, we're . . . we're already inside *that* zone. We can't . . . I mean . . . we're unable to turn back now. We simply don't have enough power left."

He knew he had to put on a cheerful face, to be a positive example in front of his men. But for all his fervor in the midst of battle, for all his willingness to singlehandedly face down an enemy army, Vahn couldn't squash the frigid chill of horror that had taken root within him. They were *inside* it. *That* place, the bogeyman of Sarconian myth, the region that was both the birthplace of the empire and its darkest hour. The haven of the damned; of lost, wandering souls. A place of emptiness, despair, and nothingness. This zone existed outside of the stream of reality, a ground sucked dry, shrouded in darkness, and completely, unequivocally, utterly severed from the living realm. Its name was not to be spoken, and even picturing the letters in his mind, Vahn felt a supernatural darkness close in around him, smothering him in its embrace.

They had stumbled into the fields of Har'muth, an ancient battleground that was a foretaste of the end of time itself.

Chapter 3

Har'muth

"Sir," Hans quietly whispered in his commander's ear, "this is the fifth time we've passed that rock."

Vahn groaned deeply in response, a sound that bounced through the still air and seemed to resound at the edge of the horizon before echoing back to the ears of the squad. They were lost, hopelessly and utterly lost. All about them hung a cloying, oppressive mist, one so impenetrable that visibility beyond a few meters out disappeared entirely behind a solid gray blanket. Their compass was long forgotten, the needle having snapped in two from its sudden exposure to the bizarre environment. Even the passage of time was lost on them as, like their ship, their chronometers simply ceased to function.

In a stroke of brilliance, Hans had etched each rock they passed with a different symbol in order that they might avoid doubling back over their path. However, this measure soon also proved futile. Whenever they took a route forward, the fog seemed to swallow them whole. It consumed them, found their taste unsatisfactory, and then spewed them back out in the direction from whence they had come—next to the rock that had just been marked.

In fact, the mist seemed almost . . . alive, as if the souls of those who died at Har'muth still inhabited the ground upon which they perished. Fog tendrils tugged at them as they passed and solidified or liquefied at will, alternately creating impassable barriers and thin screens as it saw fit. Of course, Vahn knew that the mist itself wasn't the greatest danger. The Battle of Har'muth, though nearly seven hundred years past, had left great scars upon the earth. Massive chasms crisscrossed the fields. Cliffs and canyons had formed from what was once level ground, and toxic gases spewed from these crevices to add to the suffocating air. As a result, while the mist itself was just an annoyance, it could still easily lead them to their deaths.

"Nothing we can do about it, Hans. Let's just try a different direction and hope for the best."

As they continued their circuitous trek without further progress, the ominous mist and the chilling silence led to mounting unease and frustration. Time and again they passed rocks with the same symbols, and Vahn's groans increased each time. After several hours, hopelessness and despair set in, along with fear of the endless darkness that stretched before them. And when dread takes root in the minds of men, rash and mindless action is the consequence.

"Arghh! Doubling back on ourselves is getting us nowhere!" Wilhelm exploded after a long period of silence. "I'm gonna find my own way out, with or without you guys." He stormed away from the unit into the mist, waving over his shoulder as he went.

The other surviving gefreiter, Tills, jogged over to join him. "Wait up, Willie. Don't run off alone. Let's go in groups of two so all of us don't end up separated."

"No! Both of you stay with the group! We don't know what's out there!" Vahn and Hans dashed after them, trying to stop the duo before the mist swallowed and hid them from sight.

Wilhelm, barely visible through the fog, called over his shoulder, "What are you so worried about? It's not like this mist is capable of killing us, right? Have a little faith—" He never had time to finish. In that moment, the mist came alive, instantly growing opaque tentacles that wrapped around Wilhelm and dragged him into its depths before he could utter a sound.

Then the mist turned on Tills, who, having seen what happened to Wilhelm, was already running back toward Vahn and Hans. He made it five meters before a tentacle grabbed his left leg from behind, yanking with such force that he immediately crashed into the dirt. He scraped his fingernails bloody as he tugged at the ground, frantically trying to find purchase on the hard surface as the mist drug him backwards. "Blast! Let me go! Please let me go! Vahn, Hans! Get this thing off me! Bleeding Void, I don't want to die like this!"

"Hans, grab his arms and pull him back. I'll deal with the mist." Vahn drew his sword and ran toward the tentacles while Hans dove forward, grabbing Tills by the wrists and tugging him backward. There was about a meter left before the mist became impenetrably dense, and while Hans was strong, the mist was stronger. Tills was still being dragged into the mist's maw, and Hans was only slightly delaying the process.

Tills screeched in pain as he was yanked in two directions. "Argghhh, this blasted mist! I'm being ripped in half! Get this bloody tentacle off me!"

"Hurry up, Vahn. I can't hold him much longer!"

Tentacles swiped at Vahn as he advanced on them, but he deflected them to either side with his sword. After a few seconds, he reached the wall of mist and the source of its protrusions. Tentacles continued to buffet him from behind, but he stood his ground against the blows as he drove his sword into the center of the fog.

"Spi'ferat!" Flames shot forth in all directions from the tip of Vahn's blade, coursing through the mist like veins. It reeled back as though writhing in agony, and the tentacles dropped away from Tills as they shriveled up and fled back to the safety of the mist. Still in its death throes, one tentacle that still retained its substance grabbed Vahn's arm, picked him up, and threw him backwards past his squad before finally dissipating into nothingness as well.

Vahn landed hard on his wounded right arm and let out a gasp as the shrapnel inside grated against his bone. He lay there breathing heavily, his body in shambles and his mind racing with thoughts of what had just happened. The *mist*, an inanimate collection of gases, had just tried to kill them. Obviously it was enchanted, but who or what had done it, and why? Was the spell designed to keep them away from something, or to keep them trapped here? Why had it gone from passively guiding them in circles to actively trying to eliminate them? The questions swirled through Vahn's head, one after another, until his already injured forehead began to throb.

Tills and Hans, having recovered from their own ordeal, walked over to Vahn and helped him to his feet. Tills smiled sheepishly. "Thanks for saving me, sir . . . and sorry for disobeying your orders."

Hans cuffed him upside the head. "Void and Oblivion, you *better* be sorry. Willie's gone, and you nearly got your ticket punched too."

"Enough of that, Hans, and apology accepted, Tills. We've got plenty of problems without arguing amongst ourselves." Vahn gestured at the mist, "We can't find our way out of Har'muth, we have a limited supply of food and water, none of our equipment works, and now clouds are trying to kill us. If the situation wasn't so dire, I'd laugh."

After Vahn's attack, the mist around where Wilhelm had disappeared receded. Hans walked over to the spot and looked down. "Well, I have good news and bad news. The good news is that I don't think the mist can kill us."

"What do you mean?" Tills glanced at him incredulously. "We just watched it drag Willie away!"

Hans pointed down at the ground where a crevasse had been revealed by the disappearing mist, "Yes, the mist dragged Willie away, but no, it didn't kill him. The bad news is, if the mist gets ahold of you, it can just dump you down a bottomless pit, which is the next best thing to killing you itself."

"Semantics, Hans, semantics. Whatever the case, Willie's dead, and our squad's down to three people." Vahn sat down on the rock Hans had marked earlier and fixed each of them with a glare of fiery determination. "But I promise you, as your commanding officer, that I will get both of you home, no matter the cost. No Rabbanite soldiers, no supernatural battlefield, and certainly no blasted mist are going to keep me from fulfilling my responsibilities. All of us are getting out of this alive, so I don't want either of you to give up hope. Are you with me?"

"Absolutely."

"Yes, sir, of course."

Vahn smiled and dug three apfels from one of their supply packs, tossing one to both Hans and Tills. "Good to hear. Now, let's take a break, get some food in us, and think of a way out of this mess. If you have an idea, let me know immediately."

He took a bite of apfel—from the bulging, juicy red center—then lay back across the face of the rock and let his mind wander. That was when the sorrow first hit him, the pain of having lost over two-thirds of his unit. Sure, Vahn had seen death before; he had even seen other people die next to him on missions just like this one. But at those times he had felt completely detached from the occurrence. Those who died had always been from another squad and, therefore, his only grief had been that a fellow Sarconian soldier had passed on.

Now, the devastating pain of personal loss had taken root inside Vahn's heart. *My men have died; my companions have perished . . . And I wasn't strong enough to save them.* After examining the thoughts of failure, the process of grief, and the feelings of despair at the fact that they—Klaus, Schmidt, Willie, and the rest—

were gone forever, that was the conclusion Vahn kept coming back to.

The pain might pass, the anguish might fade, but his own self-loathing at his inability to protect them, as their leader, would not disappear. *They looked up to me, relied on me, and I failed them. They trusted me, and they died when I didn't have the power, the skills, the intelligence, or the leadership to save them. How can I promise Hans and Tills that I'll get them home when I couldn't save the rest of our squad? How can I go on when I've lost all the bonds that gave me strength? If only, if only, if only I had the power to hold on to what's precious to me, to protect my men, to stop this war, to save my country. If only . . .*

Vahn closed his eyes so that Hans and Tills, who were sitting a few feet away from him chatting in low voices, wouldn't see his tears at his shortcomings and helplessness. He breathed deeply, took another bite of apfel, and managed to subdue his sorrows in order to focus on a way to escape the mist. His conscious mind slipped deep into thought, and the world around him faded away.

Come . . .

He bolted upright, casting around for the source of the noise. The apfel core left from his finished meal toppled off his chest and onto the ground with the haste of his movement. Was it his imagination, or had someone just spoken to him? "Did either of you say something?"

Hans shook his head. "No, sir."

Vahn frowned. Was his melancholy interfering with his ability to think properly? No, he may grief stricken, but his mental fortitude was greater than that.

Come . . .

There it was again! The voice was low and distant, like a whisper, yet he could feel the yearning and desire emanating from it, and though it rasped like an old man, it had the force of youthful vigor. It tugged at his mind, pulling on his thoughts, directing them, though the destination was unclear. "Hans, Tills, did you hear a voice? I believe it said, 'Come.'"

Tills looked at him with concern. "Are you feeling okay, sir? Was that bump you took from the mist harder than we thought?"

"No, I'm fine, but I swear I keep hearing a slight voice in the back of my mind. Hans, you're the sensory expert. Do you sense anything?"

"Nothing abnormal, sorry."

Come . . . here . . .

The voice came again, more insistently than before. This time, it had given Vahn's mind directions to follow. But what was the voice? Was it the mist, or the person controlling the mist? Whatever the case, he had a strange feeling that following the voice's telepathic commands was probably the best lead he was going to get on escaping their current situation.

He stood, shouldered his supply pack, and buckled on his sword. "This may sound strange, guys, but whatever this voice is that I'm hearing, it's giving me directions. I don't know what these directions lead to, but it has to be better than sitting here, surrounded by killer mist and waiting for our supplies to run out. I'm going to follow it, but since this must sound crazy, I'm not going to order you to follow me."

Grinning, Hans got up and joined Vahn. "We've always known you were a little crazy, sir. Any man who doesn't drink in war time must have a screw loose somewhere. But we still trust you with our lives, so lead on, voices and all."

"Do you feel the same way, Tills?"

"Of course, sir—though there better be a hot bath, a warm meal, and a seedy brothel at the end of this journey. It's the least you owe us after all we've been through."

"Only the seediest for you, Tills, only the seediest." With that, Vahn turned and entered the mist on his right, leading what remained of his squad through the eerie silence of Har'muth at the guidance of a strange, whispering voice.

You are . . . close now . . .

It was more compelling now, more powerful, more driven, echoing from the surface of Vahn's thoughts to the depths of his subconscious. He could still manage cohesive thought, but the voice in the back of his head was now an undeniable authority. However, Vahn saw no reason to refuse the directions— only by listening to them had they made any meaningful progress through the mist.

None could say how much time had passed, nor how far they had traveled. Vahn's limbs weighed on him like steel plates, and he had not slept since long before this debacle began. Only the voice, the sweet, soothing voice in his head, kept him barely moving, step by step.

Closer . . . and yet closer still . . . you are—

The sound was abruptly cut off, startling Vahn and waking him as though from a dream. He snapped his head upright, startling Hans and Tills, who had been following him soundlessly.

"Something wrong, sir?" Hans placed a hand on Vahn's shoulder and gave him a worried glance.

Vahn shook his head, clearing off the remnants of his stupor. "I . . . I can't hear the voice anymore." The longing in his words surprised him. Why did it feel like he had lost a part of himself, like he had lost his oldest, dearest friend? This thought came and went, Vahn dismissing it as nothing more than the whimsy of a fatigued mind and body. "Sorry, I'm rambling. Let's take stock of our surroundings and see if we made any progress."

Most immediately apparent was the total absence of the mist. Nothing but cracked, barren wasteland extended in every direction . . . except for one. Directly in front was a raised knoll, covered completely by gnarled, twisting roots that were as dry and puckered as the land surrounding them. This was odd in and of itself. How could these plants exist in Har'muth, a zone bereft of life?

To Vahn, the sight represented a temporary reprieve from their torment, and he cracked a small smile. "We've been trudging along for who knows how long, we're starving, and I'm obviously starting to go crazy. Since this looks like the only shelter between here and nowhere, I think we should hole up here until we recuperate."

Tills grinned. "Best news I've heard all day." He hitched his equipment pack tighter to his shoulders and trudged up the hill, followed closely by his comrades.

Upon reaching the copse of trees, Vahn saw that his initial analysis was not wrong; nothing could survive long in Har'muth. Rather, this vegetation had been long dead, perhaps for years, perhaps for centuries. Every visible portion of the trees was bleached a whitish-grey, with a steady stream of flakes cascading from their surfaces down to cover the ground in a snow-like manner. The branches seemed fragile, as though a single touch would shatter them into a million more of the particles already littering the hillside below.

Mesmerized, Vahn reached out his hand to do just that, but recoiled in shock as a dark vapor oozed out of the bark to grab at him. At his reaction, the miasma retreated back into the branch. However, the copse now seemed quite aware of their presence. Reminiscent of the black fog, rings of darkness now pulsed throughout the glade, tracing their way along the veins and arteries of the forest and contrasting eerily with the bleached bark on the surface.

"I'm no expert at biology, but I'm pretty positive trees don't have heartbeats." Tills voiced the thoughts all of them were thinking as he backed slowly away from the edge of the throbbing growth. "Not so sure I want to take a break in a shady spot that's liable to drown me in blackberry jam while I sleep."

Hans took a cautionary stance with a hand on his blade. "If you think that's jam, you have quite a few more screws loose than I thought you did. Either way, I want nothing to do with it."

Vahn was least affected by the sight, as though he had entered a trance the second the beating heart of the glade had activated. He glided forward, feet barely touching the ground, and the branches of the copse receded before him, retreating to form a covered archway leading inwards and upwards. "Come now. There's nothing wrong with it. Alive or not, how can we ignore the hospitality we're being shown? The path opens before us. Are we to refuse it?" He smiled broadly and beckoned them toward the shadowy portal.

Reluctantly, Hans and Tills inched toward the opening, conflicting loyalty and fear etched on their faces. Vahn stepped into the forested narthex, gesturing for them to follow. As faith in his leader won out, Hans took his hand from his scabbard and moved after him. Tills hesitated, only a fraction of a second, but even that was too much.

A shrill scream rang out not a meter from him, shattering Vahn's right eardrum and snapping him back to reality. Blood oozed down his neck and onto his shoulder as he spun to face the source of the sound and drew his weapon. A waterfall of red erupted across him as he did, and Till's head, now separated from his body, flew through the air and into the mist. In its place swung a nearly invisible, shining tentacle that darted back and forth. And behind that wispy appendage was a pair of maddened red eyes framed by pale, youthful features and silver hair.

"Eliade!" Vahn roared at Hans, who had fallen backwards into the archway after narrowly avoiding the same blow that killed Tills. Horror was written on his features, and against such an enemy, a moment's indecision would be fatal. The Eliade's eyes narrowed and swung to the next target, three more long arms shooting from his back toward the prostrate soldier. Vahn reacted instinctively, dragging his blade across the ground between them and yelling, "Bara'resh!" A wall of flame shot skyward, blocking the passage opening and sealing the Eliade outside the forest. A second, injured shriek rang out from the Eliade, and the smell of burning flesh and sound of ancient Eliassi came from the far side of the barrier.

The constant use of men'ar over the past few days was beginning to wear on Vahn, and his mental fatigue and physical wounds only served to exacerbate the strain. Even so, he immediately grabbed Hans's collar and began dragging him up the dark corridor that was the only avenue left open to them. "Move! That won't hold him long!"

Hans regained his feet after a few shambling paces, and their collective fear and adrenaline sent them hurtling down the passageway. Around them, curling black vines appeared from the depths, coiling and snaking their way between the branches, driven to a frenzy in tune with that of the injured Eliade behind them. Vahn placed his blade before him to deflect the worst of the razor-sharp storm, but some still broke through to lacerate exposed areas with shallow cuts.

And then they were through, tearing past the last of the tendrils to collapse in the darkened mouth of a stone cave. The vines continued to snap at them from behind, but none had the reach to cross the boundary between forest and grotto. From outside, the cries of the Eliade could still be heard, but at such a distance that they were no longer an immediate threat. Vahn sent a trickle of men'ar into his blade, heating it and giving off a faint luminescence. Raising it into the air, he took stock of their new surroundings.

Aside from the entrance through which they had come, the cavern possessed one other point of egress, at the rear, that appeared to slope gradually downwards where the dim light shone into it. The room itself was rotund, approximately ten meters across and five meters high. Vahn gasped as the light caught the walls. They were covered in writings and murals from ground level to the apex of the ceiling, still shrouded in darkness where his blade's glow did not reach. Lastly, in the center, a stone monolith made of pristine granite rose almost to the ceiling.

Fascinated, Vahn approached the nearest wall, discovering the scratchings to be ancient Eliassi, a language beyond his comprehension. However, the neighboring mural, simplistic in its pictograms, was decipherable. It depicted two armies arrayed at opposite ends of a field. On one side, Terrans, Eliade, and Hues shone brightly in their war raiment. On the other, more Terrans, Vladisvar, and crudely sketched abominations dragged themselves from the shadows and toward their foes. Vahn followed the progression of the sketch as it circled to the right. There, the next image showed a great clash of magic weapons, with blood pouring out of the fighters to pool in depths at their feet. Three suns and three moons rose and fell through the subsequent pictures, until at last the mural was obscured by a massive explosion that erased the survivors of the previous scenes.

Vahn brushed his fingers against the murals, feeling for any lines to indicate the scrapings and painting of traditional cave drawings. The surface was perfectly smooth. Magic must have been used to seal the author's images directly into the stone. "Hans, I think this room is a memorial of the Battle of Har'muth! The depiction of the Sarconian army is a bit overblown, but the author can be forgiven for his bias and ignorance. Just look at the talent of the artist to be able to hermetically seal his work with magic for preservation! His brutish style does leave something to be—"

"Sir! What about the Eliade? What about Tills? What about the rest of our squad?" Hans stared at Vahn with despair written on blood-smeared features. "Have you forgotten everything that just happened?"

The glow and excitement of his discovery slowly drained from Vahn, leaving him fatigued and bone weary. "Of course, you're right. None of this, this historic find, our mission, our comrades' deaths, is worth anything if we don't make it out of here alive. What equipment do we have left?"

Hans dragged his pack forward from where he had let it fall. "Tills had most of our food and medical supplies. All we have left is an illyrium grenade, some painkillers, one MRE, five meters of rope, and a couple of combat ration bars. I dropped my canteen back there, so we only have whatever water is still in yours. It's not a sunny situation, sir," he cracked a pained smile and gestured at their surroundings. "No pun intended."

"Then our first priority is eliminating the immediate threat: the Eliade behind us. However, we don't know if he's alone or has friends." Vahn began pacing around the center of the room, circling the monolith as he outlined his plan. "With only one way in or out of this chamber, he still managed to catch us from the rear. As a result, we can assume that there's another exit to this cavern farther in, and need only follow the path ahead to find it. I don't fancy our chances against that beast in close quarters, but given that he seems to have foregone the grace and intelligence their race is renowned for, we just might be able to outwit him." Vahn stopped at Hans's supply pack and pulled out the grenade with a grin.

Five minutes later, Vahn and Hans were sitting with their backs to the monolith, the rope running from them to the grotto entrance where it was tied to the grenade pin. The grenade itself was wedged between a pile of loose shale such that it wouldn't be returned to its senders upon the intended yanking of the line. From outside, the cries of the Eliade were reaching a crescendo, and Vahn assumed he was close to breaching the failing flame wall. He took a final look around to see if there was anything else he could do to better their preparations . . . and his eyes fell on the Terran writing two-thirds of the way up the structure above him.

"Look at this, Hans! This cavern isn't a memorial; it's a tomb!" He jumped up, following the line of writing around the side of the epitaph to its front. "In the year 1329, twentieth year of the reign of Her Grace Ilitharia of the eternal council of the Eliassa and under guidance of the divine Veneer, the armies of Her Grace, Prime Mage Faratul of the Sylph, the Terran King Darmatus, his brother Rabban, and the undesirable machine lord of the Hues Kanar'kren, did join forces to do battle against the minions of the Consumer of Life Sa . . . " At this point, the monolith had been scoured clean, both by chisel and flame, as though to wipe away the name.

Vahn moved around the redacted corner and resumed reading. "After fierce fighting and the loss of nearly all forces on both sides, the plot of the Consumer to eradicate existence was thwarted. King Darmatus, Lord Rabban, and Kanar'kren are assumed to have died noble deaths in battle as their bodies were never found. Despite sustaining massive injuries, Sa . . . "

"Blast, the name has been erased again, but I can only assume they mean Lord Sarcon, our founder. Hans, do you know what this means for the empire?" Vahn rushed around to the third face of the monolith, following the text.

"Sir, shouldn't we focus on the Eliade?" The pained screeching was drifting closer, and Hans fidgeted with the rope as he peaked around the granite tower at the entrance.

"I'm nearly finished, Hans. Don't you understand this is the revelation of a lifetime? 'Having no other alternative to deal with an immortal, Her Grace and Prime Mage Faratul devised an elaborate blood ritual to seal away the Consumer. With blood as a catalyst and one of the seven Elysium as both formula and power source, the Reviled One was locked away. This seal will not hold the Consumer forever. Instead, the blood contract must be renewed once a century, err the world suffer calamity once more. So we Eliade pledge that we shall maintain our guard over this seal and the descendants of the contract for posterity, lest the darkness, lest Sa . . . '"

The surface here was scoured once again, but Vahn couldn't care less as elation bubbled up within his chest, "This isn't a tomb at all; it's a seal, a seal on Sarcon! He's alive, Hans, the founder of our empire, the one who made us a world power, who made us great, is still alive! This find will turn the war arou—"

At that moment, the Eliade rushed through the opening, three tendrils thrashing through the air, the fourth limp at his side. Vicious burns coated his forearms and face, marring his once-serene beauty and reflecting the hideous madness glinting from the one red eye that remained. The other was burned almost completely shut and, along with his other wounds, oozed a sickening, clear puss.

Hans shrieked, pulled on the rope, and the grenade at the Eliade's feet went off.

Having just finished reading the text at the entrance side of the monolith, Vahn was caught full on by the shockwave from the blast, and his world went dark.

Chapter 4

He Who Brings the Night

---◦◦◦◦◦---

*C*an *you hear me?*

"No Name" awoke into absolute darkness. Stretching out in every direction was nothing but pure black: no light, no shadows, the complete absence of existence.

Ahhh, you appear to have woken up. How are you feeling?

He started, hearing the voice a second time. It seemed to come from all around at once, the source of the sound impossible to identify. It was familiar, but his memories were a jumble. How had he gotten to this space? What had he been doing? Who was he?

Hmmm, your head seems to have taken a bit of a beating. That won't do. Let me see if I can help.

A warm sensation started as a pinprick in No Name's head and spread throughout his brain before rushing through his nerves and across his entire body. The feeling was relaxing and exhilarating at the same time. Then pain arced through him like lightning as his memories returned.

I never could get it quite right. Relinking the nerves to the brain is always such a touchy business.

His name was Vahn. He was a citizen of the Sarconian Empire. He was born in 670 ABH to Wilhelm and Susanna Badenschiff. He was a diligent son. He had never run with the wrong crowds, never stayed out late, always put his academics first. He and his friends played soldiers in their free time, as expected of Sarconian youths, and dreamed of joining the regular army and bringing glory to their nation, their units, their families, and themselves.

He joined the military academy at thirteen, a year sooner than required of Sarconian boys, having aced both the academic and physical entrance exams.

At sixteen, two years sooner than average, he graduated from the academy as the second-highest-placing cadet in his class. He did not begrudge the young lady who bested him. Strength and skill are to be respected, not scorned and envied. At twenty, he joined the Ritter Order of the empire, the elite cadre of officers that lorded over the regular army and were groomed for high command. This body also served as the internal check on dissent and corruption, ensuring swift judgment was passed before darkness could become evident to the public at large. He spent three years as such a judge, honing his skills of espionage and covert ops through his display of absolute loyalty.

At twenty-three, war between Sarconia and Rabban reignited, and his skills were turned outward toward the soft underbelly of the fat and bloated commercial machine that was the imperium. At twenty-seven, he was sent as squad leader on an infiltration mission to Beiras in the Rabban Imperium. The mission had failed, and the team was forced to escape in the face of overwhelming opposition. One after another, his men had died, leaving him and his lieutenant, Hans, alone and trapped on the ancient battlefield of Har'muth. They had stumbled upon a ruin whose true purpose was a seal for the ancient mage Sarcon, who had founded the Sarconian Empire and then been undone by his own flesh and blood. He had been knocked unconscious, and he knew no more.

Seems like everything is in order. Such an interesting past you have: love of country, loyalty to comrades, and nobility in the pursuit of a purpose greater than thyself. Few men lead such fulfilling lives in double the years you have seen.

His memories had returned, and with them, his sensibilities. The voice was not his own, yet he was the only one who existed in this plane of nothingness. "Who, or what, are you?"

A barely perceptible tendril passed through his thoughts, as though perusing them and dissecting them for further study or discard. *I am . . .* The voice paused for a beat, considering.

Sarcon. Yes, that is who I am. You see, much like yourself right now, I am but a shadow of my former glory. My memories ebb and flow, as the tide comes in and then inevitably recedes. However, being able to touch your mind has restored some measure of my knowledge and power. Let us redecorate a bit. We need not converse in such murky darkness.

Vahn could hardly comprehend the change in scenery going on around him, such was his shock that he was talking to Sarcon—the esteemed founder of the empire himself. In the moment it took him to reconcile with his reality, he looked up to find himself inside the entry hall of the Imperial Senate, the seat of Sarconian government. The blackness had been banished, and in its place was a wide thoroughfare flanked by repeating Corinthian columns and supported by a floor of exquisitely pure white marble. The evening sun, slanting through the glass apex of the ceiling, glanced off the glowing floor to rebound from the frescoes of Sarconian history and busts of former emperors and statesmen interspaced along the side walls.

The red and gold livery of the empire hung as silk curtains and drapes among the columns. And over the central walkway, hanging in the air between earth and sky and running the length of the room, rested banner after banner adorned with the imperial crest: a glowing angel with a chiseled scepter of Illyriite in her left hand, a mage's staff held high in her right, a crown of olive leaves on her head, and wearing a gown of pure gold. The angel herself was set into a background of fierce flames, which converged on her from the edges of a shield that acted as the crest borders. At the extremities of the shield, those flames kept at bay a curling bramble of thorns that wove their way about the entire image, representing the darkness and depravity that the light of the empire kept at bay.

Yet the grandest detail lay at the far end of the hall, where the marble steps ascended to a rounded antechamber before two massive golden doors. Each was twice the height of the average man and weighed many times his mass. The cylindrical handles were as long as Vahn's legs and rested at chest height. More impressive, however, were the scenes depicted upon them in indented square frames.

Like the doors themselves, they were sculpted out of solid gold. Near the base was handsome and powerful Sarcon, the same who Vahn now spoke to, holding aloft a chunk of Illyriite before a crowd that would become the first imperial citizens. At head height was a magnificent rendering of Sarconia's—the capital—city walls, a massive three-tiered construct that was both an artistic and engineering marvel. And close to the top, more recently added, was the coronation of the current emperor, Sychon Artorios, renowned as the most powerful mage the empire had seen since its founder.

Everything was just as Vahn remembered it. These halls where his father worked as a minister, this floor that he had trod during his commissioning ceremony, those doors that opened the way to the seat of hope and enlightenment for the entire continent, all were exactly as his mind's eye had recorded. He had impossibly been transported across thousands of miles of mountains, bodies of water, mortal constructs, the Kingdom of Darmatia, and the imperial border all the way to the very heart of the empire.

"H . . . How is this possible?" Vahn stammered in disbelief.

The mind is the gateway to many possible portraits of reality. I merely used your memories to construct one that both of us would find appealing. Seeing the empire through your thoughts has been most reassuring. Nothing makes a parent prouder than knowing their children have managed to live on without them.

The voice had taken on a wistful tone, as though simultaneously joyful and melancholic at the outcome. Vahn could still not locate its source. It seemed to come from all corners of the room and beside him at the same time. He turned, appealing to the engraving of Sarcon upon the Senate doors, "If you are truly Sarcon, the great founder of our nation, please . . . please show yourself to me."

As if on cue, the golden image peeled away from the portal and rapidly grew to full size. While the body expanded, the solid gold plating seemed to liquefy and flow down to the floor, beginning with the head and ending with the feet. At the same time, a purple robe unfurled from his shoulders, falling to the ground to fully cover a tall and muscular, though lithe, physique. Still, not all traces of gold were removed from his person. No sooner had the precious metal pooled at his feet than it magically shot back toward his feet, arms, and head. There it formed sandals, gorgeous armbands, and, most majestic of all, long and straight flowing hair that sparkled with iridescence in the last rays of twilight. When the entire transformation was complete, the newly emerged Sarcon stood at the summit of the Senate stairs looking down on Vahn.

"Is this appearance to your liking?" For the first time since Vahn had found himself in this dimension, Sarcon spoke verbally rather than directly into his mind. The initial change, along with the sudden manifestation of a physical form, was unsettling, though his new voice was rich in timbre and pleasant to the ear. As Vahn processed these thoughts, Sarcon interjected with mild concern, "Is something wrong, Vahn?"

"No, I'm just shocked at your appearance. It's as though you stepped right out of the pages of one of our fairy tales."

Sarcon chuckled, shaking his golden locks as he did so. "I did, quite literally, just step out of the door behind us. Still, this semblance is also borrowed from your memories. As with many other more important details, knowledge of my physical traits is currently lost to me. But every legend starts as a shred of truth. I'm sure this interpretation isn't far off from the original."

The mention of legends refocused Vahn. Was this Sarcon? The murals and writing he had seen a lifetime ago seemed to confirm that it could be. And if this being was Sarcon, how had he survived all these years? How was he speaking to him now? That same epitaph had mentioned a magic ritual and seal, which answered the former but not the latter. What was the truth?

"Lord Sarcon, this is a lot to take in all at once. As you know, before I ended up . . . here," he gestured at their impossible surroundings, "I was running for my life in a world seven centuries removed from the one you were supposed to have perished in. Therefore, I'm sure you can understand my confusion regarding the series of events that have led to this moment. You have said that your memories, like mine, are still jumbled. That being the case, if it's possible, please tell me how you're here. As far as the rest of the world knows—and let me tell you, *everyone* has vastly different beliefs about you, except for this one detail—you died at the Battle of Har'muth. Either this is a very pleasant dream, or a major rewriting of history is necessary."

"Then let us rectify those mistakes." Sarcon glided down the steps, his robe seeming to cling to the marble as he moved. Vahn's gaze followed him, simultaneously wary of and entranced by this supernatural being. After passing Vahn, Sarcon snapped his fingers and a simple wooden door appeared hovering inches above the ground. One hand opened the portal while the other pointed invitingly at the bright light beyond. "As with any story, the best place to start at is the beginning. Shall we?"

Curiosity and caution warred inside Vahn for the briefest instant before the scholar in him once again won out. Besides, if Sarcon was to be believed, all of this was somehow taking place inside his mind. Surely that home-field advantage counted for something.

He took a deep breath, nodded at his guide, and stepped through the glowing frame . . . straight onto a battlefield. Men in strange armor wielding all manner of weaponry were fighting against beings of other species, feral beasts, decrepit constructs of darkness—even each other. Blood, colored red, black, and blue, rained constantly across the nightmarish visage. Vahn's body, honed by years of training, instantly reacted, dropping into a fighting stance and reaching for the sword . . . which was no longer attached to his waist. A comforting hand grasped his shoulder, and he felt his tension melt away.

"We have no need of that here. Look closely."

The voice belonged to Sarcon, who had followed him into this new reality. Vahn felt a brief flicker of shame for having suspected his companion of leading him into a trap, but that negative emotion was soon also erased by the calm exuded into him. He fully relaxed his body and examined the scene around him.

Realization hit him like lightning: none of the beings were moving. Whether they were screaming, killing, running, or dying, all were frozen in place. There, a sword raised, never to fall. There, a woman weeping, her tears suspended above her child who would never take another breath. Even the rain, both real and blood alike, was trapped in space like pristine floating diamonds.

"This is but a snapshot of a time long past, a memory given life but never reenacted because those events have already transpired," Sarcon continued, his eyes glowing. "These specters can no longer do us harm."

Pity welled up inside Vahn for the shades before him, their darkest moments forever locked in stasis. "Why show me this?"

"Because the state of my childhood and yours are not so dissimilar. Even now your world is trapped in a cycle of bloodshed. Time passes, but the actors and their actions are merely replayed from age to age. However, this is just a starting point. The history you truly need to see lies farther in." Sarcon gestured to another glowing portal, magically materialized before them. Vahn stepped through, prepared for another horrific nightmare.

Instead, he was met with a familiar visage. A modest home set atop a hill appeared in the mid distance, smoke curling from two chimneys. Fields of crops spread down from the knoll: wheat, barley, oat, and soy, a full harvest as far as the eye could see. A tall man, weathered by many years of hard labor, emerged from the grain and strode toward his home while three young boys of varying heights ran from their mother on the doorstep to welcome him back. Vahn had to blink twice to assure himself that this scene was real. Was that not his home, his father, and his family? Was this his past and not Sarcon's?

As though conscious of his thoughts, Sarcon cut into his reverie, "As I said before, you and I share similar origins. I grew up as the oldest son in a happy home. We were neither wealthy nor poor but always had enough to sustain our existence. Our parents loved us more than anything, and that was their downfall."

The scene abruptly shifted as Sarcon continued talking. The cottage burst into flames, and tendrils of wildfire spread greedily through the ripened fields. On the front step, Sarcon's mother was slowly bleeding out while his father, a sword in his gut, stood between her and a pack of glowering soldiers. Just out of hearing distance, hiding behind bales of produce yet to be set ablaze, crouched a young Sarcon, his arms barring his siblings from rushing forward. "I was fourteen that fateful autumn. The harvest was just coming due, and the local warlord was caught in a dire predicament. His more powerful neighbor had demanded that he cede his domain to him or perish. To be perfectly honest, the small parcel of land he owned was barely larger than this single town that we lived on the outskirts of, but even so, he wasn't going to relinquish it without a fight."

"So the warlord fought and lost, and your family was caught up in the aftermath?" Vahn spoke softly, empathetically, hoping to preempt Sarcon and keep him from having to remember any more of the tragedy.

"No, that would make for a less piteous story. The warlord needed more troops and had demanded that my father *and* his children take up arms. Of course, my parents told us none of this. Instead, on the day the press gang was to come, they sent us on a daylong trip to a neighboring township to fetch medicine for our plowing steed, our *ek*. My brothers thought nothing of the task since they were not daily involved in the running of our farm. But I knew the animal was not sick, so after we had traveled a league or so, I convinced my siblings to leave the path and double back through the trees and undergrowth lining the road."

Vahn turned back to the scene before him, the inevitable conclusion painted in fiery hues before his eyes. "And you were just in time to—"

"Just in time to see my parents cut down by the stooges of the very lord they had faithfully served their entire lives. My father had insisted that he alone should be enough for the army, but the lieutenant in charge of the group interpreted his failure to hand over us as insubordination and decided to make an example of them. My brothers wanted to rush in, to try to save them, but I knew better. I knew doing so would be suicide, even if we managed to bring even a single one down. That was the easy way out, pure and simple release. The hard way forward was to live on, to sear that scene into our brains and resolve to do something about it. Fortunately, fate would soon smile on us."

Vahn was not surprised at the appearance of the luminescent gateway this time, nor shocked by the instant change of scenery that greeted him upon crossing through it. Before him unfolded a lively market square, filled with a profusion of wildly clashing colors and vendors of everything imaginable. He realized Sarcon had elected to spare him the smell of the previous portraits, for now he was assaulted by the aromas of sizzling meats, freshly plucked flowers, and exotic perfumes. But the crowning of this locale was its entertainment.

A grand stage had been erected in the center of the plaza upon which three men were performing. The first was shooting small fireballs from a staff and then directing them through the air before combining them into a massive, roaring beast of flame. The second was somehow juggling blades crackling with iridescent lightning without getting shocked. And the third was launching small craft filled with bright stones that he then paraded in formation to the great amusement of nearby children. The entire crowd below them surged with wonder bordering on the fanatical, as though they had never seen magic performed before. Their fervor was reflected in the growing mound of coins being flung at the feet of the entertainers.

Sarcon's well-timed intrusion into his thoughts hardly startled Vahn. "You are correct in your assumption. None of them, not a single one, had ever seen magic before. All were amazed at our feats, many were envious, and some even wanted to start a religion around the 'miracles' we were enacting."

"But according to our history, magic was discovered before you and your brothers were born."

The radiant being chuckled back at him. "Don't believe everything you read in books, child. Contrary to written record, my siblings and I were the first practitioners of magic. However, as you can clearly see from our calamitous early years, we were not born with the skill. For many years after the loss of our parents, we suffered great hardship. Orphans, vagabonds, we drifted from town to town, working the few jobs we could, barely scraping by. By the time I turned twenty, I had been a farmer, a stable boy, a blacksmith, a mercenary, a cobbler, a shoe shiner, a pig herder, a thief, a pickpocket, and some things even more disreputable. My brothers had helped where they could, but I was the bread winner, the one who kept us afloat. And all that time we never lost the dream of vengeance against the warlord who took our parents—at least until the Red Plague descended on the region and Rabban, my youngest brother, was among the first to be stricken with it."

Red Plague was a disastrous disease prevalent seven hundred years ago. Now eradicated by magical and medical science, Vahn had learned during his studies that it was a curse that had kept the world's population from exceeding 10 percent of what it was today. Artistic depictions of its effects had nearly made him sick and forced him to put aside the book. Borne by blood, Red Plague began by causing the victims veins to change from blue to red. The second stage was heralded by extreme pain throughout the entire body as crystals formed in the bloodstream. Beautiful and disgusting, the fatal finale occurred when these crystals enlarged and burst through the skin, disrupting the flow of blood entirely and covering the bearer in exquisite, opaque red gemstones of varying sizes. It was in this final stage that Red Plague became extremely contagious. For ten days after death, the growths emitted a dense, seeping blood mist that would almost assuredly infect anyone it came in contact with. After that, the crystals went dormant, nothing more than glamorous baubles to be appropriated by bandits and collectors.

While Vahn recalled the sickening progression of the disastrous epidemic, Sarcon continued his tale, "We were immediately cast out of the town we were staying in, and no town would let us in under threat of death, regardless of whether they already had other infected or not. With the crystals already starting to poke through and people everywhere awash with fear of the plague, Rabban was incapable of passing any security screening, no matter how many layers of clothes we heaped on him."

"What did you do? The Rabban I learned of, and the Rabban before me in this marketplace, is as healthy as can be."

"We did the only thing we could do; we turned to the occult for a cure. We delved into the dark forests, catacombs, and caverns of this land where no one else dared go, searching for the shamans and so-called witches cast out by society. But they were frauds, having no more power in their brews and strange concoctions than is present in an ordinary mug of hot tea. Even so, Darmatus and I kept searching, Rabban slung across his strong shoulders in carrying wraps. And at the same time, the crystals kept advancing. Then, just when we had lost all hope, just when Rabban was about to breathe his last, deep in the darkest cavern of Lozaria that was to be our tomb . . . we found the answer to our prayers: Illyriite. It sat there, pulsing bright green as though in direct opposition to the searing red adoring Rabban. Without thinking, I grabbed my youngest brother from Darmatus's back and laid him across the flickering bed of minerals. And in that instant, he was healed; the crystal receded, his eyes opened, and his blood flowed normally for the first time in months."

Utter amazement shone on Vahn's face. "Just like that? His body touched the gems and was immediately cured?"

"It was nothing short of a miracle. And in that moment, I knew that fate had guided us to this spot, not only to cleanse Rabban but also because this was the source of something greater, something that would change the world. We already knew that the Red Plague was attracted to our blood, and now this crystal had reacted even more strongly to the fluid in our veins than any disease ever had. I quickly shared my theory with my brothers, and splitting the Illyriite among our packs, we set out with renewed vigor and purpose."

Slowly the marketplace scene faded away, replaced by an image of the brothers huddling around a fire and surrounded by mountains of books, scrolls, vials of chemicals, and other tools recognizable to the modern eye as the instruments of a magic scientist's trade. Vahn immediately noticed that there was no pit for the fire and that this was no ordinary flame. Each of the siblings had his palms outwards to it as they pushed and pulled, stretched and smashed it together. Doing so made them smile and laugh, and their eyes danced with glee.

"Ten years and countless hours of research, physical labor, trips to secure funding, and expeditions back to that cavern culminated in this moment of payoff. We had determined without a doubt that men'ar existed within the bloodstream of mortals and that it could be harnessed to perform feats beyond our understanding with proper training, study, and practical application. All of this is elementary to you now, but then, to us, it was groundbreaking. Furthermore, we discovered that Illyriite functioned as an amplifier. Power that would take years to develop naturally could be used instantaneously while possessing it. At this point it would have been child's play to eliminate our parent's killer."

"Did you?" Vahn interjected cautiously.

"We probably would have, but as it turned out, he lost that war with his rival. Fate served unto him what he served upon my parents; there was nothing more for us to do. However, we were now presented with a unique opportunity. Possessed of a power eclipsing mundane comprehension and unknown to all but ourselves, we could mold the world as we saw fit. Rather than allow unjust fates, like the one that befell us, we could make a kinder, gentler Lozaria where the weak needn't live in fear of the callous whims of the strong."

Vahn was a student and survivor of history. The world was still at war, a war that Sarcon, his beloved homeland, was on currently on the verge of losing. In a solemn voice he asked, "What went wrong?"

Sarcon's vibrancy waned, and the glow he produced drew back in on itself, as though echoing the melancholy of the one from who it emitted. "There was a saying in the prominent Terran religion of my time, the Church of Light: 'The road to Oblivion is paved with good intentions.'"

"That religion still exists today, in all three nations you brothers left behind."

"That is reassuring, but my statement was meant to draw attention to the quote, rather than those who coined it. They would have you interpret it as, 'If you have good intentions, but don't act upon them, you may end up in Oblivion with all the people who never intended to do good in the first place.' I would submit a different translation: 'Many will die because the good intentions of one person are at odds with the good intentions of another.'"

Confused, Vahn queried, "Are you saying that good intentions are themselves a mistake?"

"Not at all. If you decide to help an elderly woman cross the street, that is a good intention—followed by action upon it—that harms no one. Rather, I submit that something much grander than mere intents, *dreams*, are to blame for the damning of many to Oblivion. But I digress."

Here the study, and the birth of magic, faded from view and were replaced once more by the former market sprawl. "This was another five years later, and our coming-out party, so to speak. We unveiled magic to the world, hoping to spark a revolution of concerted thought and progress—which we did, for a time, and in more ways than one. Tens of thousands flocked to learn from us; to get a taste of magic and participate in the greatest undertaking Lozaria had ever known. Peoples from all nations came: Terrans, Hues, Vladisvar, Sylph, Moravi—all but the hive-minded Trillith and the reclusive Eliade, who apparently had known of and been able to use magic for centuries. Members of each race learned rapidly and took to developing their own specialized uses for the craft. Most impressive were the Sylph, soon to be magic's greatest practitioners, who managed to morph the blood within their bodies to create new structures or change the functions of their organs.

"And just like that, another decade flew by, as though it were simply weeks. Rabban had begun exploring the depths of the continent and discovered veins of illyrium, which, though not as powerful as Illyriite, allowed our nation of fledgling sorcerers to perform more powerful arts and enabled the initial merging of technology and magic.

"Darmatus was busy cataloguing our knowledge and discovery in a massive library city at the heart of the continent. People soon began calling it *Nemare*, meaning 'City of Illumination.' And I worked tirelessly day and night to ensure that the power of magic would not be abused. At its core, any material thing is just a tool, and man can kill just as easily with magic as with a sword.

"Ultimately, I failed in my task. The very same warlord that invaded my homeland so many years prior had snuck agents through our screening processes who then escaped and returned home with the secrets of basic magic use. This did not come to my knowledge until several years later, when his army, mages in tow, showed up on the dunes outside Nemare demanding the surrender of both the city and all the researchers within. We had no walls and no army; even with our superior magic, the result would have been a slaughter on both sides. As such, my brothers wanted to reason with the warlord, but I understood that the end result of such a course would be a burning city and raining blood, just like so many years before. That night, I took my Illyriite in hand and parleyed with the warlord using the only language he understood: the sword. In the morning, nothing was left of his camp but a smoking ruin, and horrified by the scene and naive to my reasoning, my brothers sorrowfully banished me."

Something crawling at the back of his mind made Vahn's blood boil. *Why should Sarcon be banished? He defended his people. He did nothing wrong.* "Why would they do such a thing? You eliminated an enemy who clearly intended to do the same to you."

"You understand my logic, Vahn, but that is because you and I are cut from the same cloth. This is what I was referring to earlier. Good intentions are not themselves evil, but the dreams they derive from can be. I had a dream of a Lozaria filled with magic that made people's lives prosperous and eliminated the need for them to compete, claw, and fight one another just to survive. In the same way, that warlord had a dream of using magic to conquer not just his neighbor, but the entire continent. Our dreams collided and resulted in conflict, in war.

"In the same way, my brother Darmatus held on to my dream of a Lozaria unified by knowledge and understanding, even when I abandoned it. Rabban also had a different dream, one of an affluent world filled with amazing technologies and machines that made war an afterthought. Each of us has a dream that defines who we are, one we would sacrifice anything to preserve. Communities, cities, and nations are no different. Now, I ask you, Vahn, knowing all this, why do men fight?"

The answer came instantly, illuminated by a glowing realization. "Because we're all protecting different dreams."

"Exactly! We fight because you are you, and I am me. What I cherish is not what you cherish, and what I cherish may require what you cherish to fall by the wayside. For my dream to be realized, it may be necessary for your dream to be crushed. And when one individual refuses to let another destroy the dream that means more to him than his very life, conflict is born."

"Knowing this, how did things come to a head between brothers?"

"I understood, at that moment, that I was facing an irrational world, an incomprehensible existence. No matter how easy magic could make life, no matter how much knowledge mortals obtained, violence, war, and bloodshed would remain. In a few years, someone else would seek to start a war, with or without magic, and someone would rise up in opposition to him, repeating a never-ending cycle down through the ages. I determined then that there was only one way to crush an irrational fate: with force. The fighting would stop when somebody won and a single person stood in judgment atop Lozaria."

For the first time in nearly half an hour, the existence around them shimmered and dissolved into a dark cavern where Sarcon could be seen holding a torch above a brilliantly shining purple obelisk. Obelisk was the only term for it, since it dwarfed Illyriite, illyrium, and any other mineral deposit Vahn had ever seen before. Looking at it caused its hues to shift to black, a deep recess that almost seemed to suck his soul toward i—

"Look away! Now!"

Vahn did as he was bidden and gazed at his companion. "What is that? I've never seen its like before."

"That is Elysium. Just gazing at it directly, even though this is a memory, is enough to lose a portion of your soul to it. Elysium feeds upon the souls of those with great desires, and with your deep love for your country, even this faux image could do you harm."

The stone seemed to radiate heat at Vahn's back, a small sun contained within a delicate, rocky prison. "So, *this* is the stone of legend. Did you really intend to use it to destroy the world?"

"Preposterous. Destroying the world would be the same as destroying my dream. My goal was to eliminate conflict, not to eliminate existence, though Darmatus would argue that those are one and the same. No, my intent was to use the Elysium to once more purge magic from the world. Once I made my wish and sacrificed a portion of my soul to the stone, only I would remain in possession of the capability to perform magic. I would become the arbiter of the world, granting magic only to those worthy and revoking it should they abuse the power. In this way, I would maintain sole ownership of the greatest power in existence, and fear of my retribution would keep all nations, peoples, and races in line. Conflict would be eliminated, war eradicated, and Lozaria would be at peace."

"But your dream ended in disaster."

At this point, Sarcon's glow fully disappeared, and he appeared old, wrinkled, transient. Vanished was the godly being he had begun their conversation as, replaced by the frail husk of a man defeated. He pointed, and their reality shifted one final time. Before Vahn was a giant cavern, pitch black except for a massive piece of Elysium, twice as large as the one in the previous vision. It hung suspended in the center of the room, hovering in midair between two stabilizers glowing faintly with the yellow tint of illyrium. Around it patrolled beautiful and luminescent Eliade soldiers, their backs to the crystal lest its charms affect them. And when Vahn gazed briefly upon the gem itself, he stifled a gasp at what he saw. There, resting in fetal position, was the dilapidated shell that stood behind him. All around him flowed black liquid, containing his frame but not drowning him. His eyes were shut, his hair a dingy silver instead of gold, his muscles long atrophied from lack of use. Gone was the gorgeous, conquering, mortal Sarcon of old. Here was the immortal husk long held captive by his foes.

The voice that whispered in his ears cracked with age and lack of use. "Sadly, yes, and the result is what you see before you. After my banishment, I raised a people—your people—to fulfill my dream. But alas, the Eliade, who never take part in mortal affairs, intervened and even turned my own brothers against me. The Battle of Har'muth unfolded much as you know it, with the most important detail omitted from your books. The Eliade, my brothers . . . none could slay me. With my Illyriite and Elysium, I was simply too powerful. Instead they chose to turn to ancient blood magic, taught to them by the Eliade, so old that not even I knew of or could be prepared for it. They sacrificed both their Illyriite and then their lives to temporarily strip me of my power. And though this spell could not kill me, I could only watch as the Eliade carried me to a piece of Elysium, chanted in Eliassi, then deposited me into my current prison before sealing the exit with the blood of Darmatus, my own brother. And this is where I have hung, alive yet dead, for seven hundred years, awaiting an opportunity to fulfill my dream. Awaiting . . . you, Vahn."

Vahn had followed the conclusion of the story in silence but spun around to face the smiling corpse behind him. "What? How could you have been waiting for me?"

The pallid face brightened, and the sunken eyes glowed. "To be honest, not you specifically, but someone like you. You see, I rarely get visitors here, and when I do, they are merely my Eliade guards, and they never let me chat mind to mind with them. And even if they did, we would not be able to relate as you and I have. And then there's the timing. A seal as strong as the blood magic used on me by the Eliade is not without its weaknesses. Every hundred years or so, the pact on seal has to be renewed with the blood of one of Darmatus's heirs, otherwise it starts to . . . deteriorate."

Comprehension dawned within Vahn, "Is that why we're able to converse now? Has the seal not been restored?"

The grin on the desiccated lips spread wider, "I knew you were a clever boy.

Exactly. Once you've been through this process seven times, like I have, you notice a pattern. At five years to one hundred, I regain consciousness. At three, give or take a few months, I regain some of my abilities, including the ability to project my soul in a limited area around my prison. This is only the second time they've let me get to three years. Normally they redo the seal at four years, just enough time out of stasis to give me some hope before I'm forced back in. Eliade really make for sadistic jailors. And I'm sure by now you've realized what event in your recent history has resulted in this wondrous occurrence—"

Vahn racked his brain swiftly then blurted, "The Theradas Dispute! The death of Queen Ephalia was the end of Darmatus's line! There's no more blood left to renew the seal with!"

Hands decayed by dystrophy came together in a pantomime of clapping. "Right again, two for two! So, in three years, I'll be free to go! Except . . . the Eliade aren't going to just let me leave. Instead, their government will likely send a replacement team to reseal me with a new blood donor any week now, especially given that my current captors haven't checked in with their superiors in a while."

"The mad Eliade we fought at the entrance! What did you do?"

A grating cackle escaped the skull. "You don't miss a beat, do you? Remember how I can now project my soul? I may have slowly, insidiously, planted seeds of terror in their minds to reduce their efficacy if my chance of escape ever arrived. And that, my dear boy, brings us to you and your team. I became aware of your squad right after the mist—which, by the way, has been magically enchanted by the Eliade as a defensive measure—dragged your poor subordinate away to his death. I regret that I was unable to save his life, but thereafter I took control of the mist and planted the directions in your mind that would guide you safely here. The mad Eliade you mentioned was another unfortunate happenstance, and I am deeply sorry Tills was unable to make it here with you. But everything is alright now: for you, for the Sarconian Empire, and for the entirety of Lozaria."

"And why is that?" Vahn asked, bewildered. "As far as your explanation has led me to believe, you're still trapped in here for another three years."

"Yes, and even if the Eliade let me get that far, my pathetic excuse for an atrophied body won't allow me to make good on my escape." And in that instant, Sarcon teleported directly into Vahn's face, his nearly empty eyes staring deep into Vahn's soul; his foul, rotten breath cloying upon Vahn's nose. "That is where you come in, my friend. You have a perfectly capable body—adept in the magical arts, physically strong, healthy and hale. And it just so happens that one of the abilities I learned during the time I freely walked the continent—and that I currently have access to—is a soul swapping of sorts."

Vahn attempted to move away from Sarcon, to avoid his putrid wheezing and dead gaze, but found himself mystically transfixed. "Was that what this was all about? You put on a nice show, answer all my questions, then hitch a ride in my body back out into the world while I'm stuck here?"

"Not quite. I said soul swapping, but it is, unfortunately, more of a one-way ticket for the original host. Perhaps it's better termed soul *overwriting*?"

Despite straining with all his might, Vahn still couldn't budge. He attempted to head butt the frowning skull before him, but to no avail. "So, amending my earlier statement, you go free, and I get an express airship ride to Oblivion?"

Sarcon appeared genuinely distraught at his displeasure. "I have been nothing but honest with you so far, and I will be nothing but honest with you now. I *will* be taking your body. I will not pass up this singular opportunity to free myself and fulfill my dream, even if it comes at the cost of your dreams. However, through our conversation I was led to believe that we *share* a dream. If that's the case, which of us stands the better chance of being able to realize our ambitions?

"Before you answer, I have one last piece of information to divulge. As I said, I will be taking your body. But ejecting an unwilling host will cause massive damage to the container, and some part might remain to challenge the occupier for control. If such damage occurs, I likely won't make it very far and probably will be unable to perform the transfer again. Even if you give up your body willingly, it will eventually degrade. Despite your above-average magical potential, your container is several sizes too small for the knowledge comprising my soul. Either way, it's a single direction exchange for the both of us. But if you agree to let me have your body without a fight, I will save the Sarconian Empire, I will protect your friends and family, and I will keep Lozaria from destroying itself."

It was impossible to ignore the sincerity in his words. Vahn stopped struggling, closed his eyes, and thought on Sarcon's words. Had he not said that he would give anything to save his country and those he cared about? Was that not the dream he had given his life to? It's why he joined the army, why he fought—even if he didn't always know the reason—and why he was here right now. Fate had led him to this crossroads, to Sarcon, to unwittingly grant his deepest desires. Right now, by letting go, he could accomplish everything he had worked his entire life to achieve.

But if I let someone else do what I've striven tirelessly to achieve, isn't that actually giving up on my dream entirely? a small voice asked in the deepest recesses of his mind.

Almost instantly, a thunderous reply hammered it back down: *With Sarcon's strength, my dream can be realized far more easily than with my own capabilities. The end result is all that matters!*

And with that, Vahn reached his decision. One small life was a paltry price to pay for the survival of an empire and all those he held dear.

He opened his eyes and smiled for the last time. "I have one condition."

The immortal responded, "Name it."

"Bring Hans home alive and safe."

"Agreed. The bargain is struck."

Sarcon gripped his hands, and Vahn felt his consciousness fade as the reel of his life played in reverse. His time with Sarcon, fleeing through Har'muth, his years as a soldier, the military academy, school in the countryside, swimming with his friends, sweet apfel pies baked by his mother, sunsets on the hillside, the crops swaying in the breeze, his father coming home from the fields, looking up from his crib to see the stars out the window, the floor he crawled over, his father's strong arms, his mother's embrace, warmth, heat, glow, light . . .

———◆◇◆———

Hans had been on the run for hours. The initial blast had summoned more Eliade, a trio now, and they were hunting him relentlessly. It didn't help that Vahn was still out. He showed no signs of additional physical injuries but wasn't waking up just the same. And so the deadly dance repeated itself time and again: Hans carried Vahn deeper into the caverns, dropped him as the screeching increased, fired a few shots from his dwindling magazine until they fell back, and then picked up his commander to run again. The situation was dire, but as his late father had always told him, "Where there's life, there's hope." Stumbling into a massive chamber, he expended the last of his rounds, then turned to drag Vahn to the other side.

His breath caught at the sight of the massive purple obelisk suspended in midair before him. What was that thing? At once it elicited both joy and despair in the deepest recesses of his mind. He felt compelled to turn away, lest he be drawn body and soul into its depths. Doing just that, he heaved Vahn along on failing legs and went left instead of straight.

That was to be his final mistake. An Eliade sprang at him from his front, having materialized from one of the many side passages dotting the sides of the room. As Hans's time slowed, he briefly considered whether it was one of the Eliade behind him that had snuck off down a different path, or an entirely new one whose friends had notified him in advance of Hans's coming. Of course, the difference was a minor triviality considering either answer resulted in his imminent demise.

Before the Eliade could connect, Vahn burst awake, pushing Hans aside and raising a single hand to the feral being. In the next second, as Hans rolled upright again, all that was left of his attacker was a bloody mist. Vahn had disintegrated his foe in an instant.

Hans found his earlier question answered as the three pursuing Eliade burst from the passageway he had exited a moment prior. Rooted to the ground by a strange combination of fear, awe, and confusion, Hans could only watch in disbelief as Vahn raised the same hand, adjusted it slightly to match the trajectory of the incoming enemy, and calmly eviscerated each from existence.

After several moments of silence passed, Hans felt his throat unclench, "Vahn, is that . . . is that really you?"

Vahn turned to him, and though his outward appearance was normal, something about his bearing and demeanor was off. While Vahn had always seemed kind and approachable, this Vahn had an aura of expectation and arrogance. When he spoke, his voice was filled with an authority that commanded obedience.

Of course, to Hans, anybody who said the following after the display he had just witnessed could be expected to command obedience:

"You must be Hans. My name is Sarcon. Come with me. We have an empire to save and a continent to conquer."

Part 2
Sacrifice

Chapter 5

Graduation Day

Three months later,
Festivus 28, 697 ABH
Nemare, Royal Capital of the Kingdom of Darmatia

———⊰⊱———

It had been a month-long period of joviality for the oasis metropolis of Nemare. Thousands flocked from throughout the country to take part in the capital's never-ending series of feasts, parades, tournaments, contests, bazaars, and, as the name of the month, *Festivus*, would imply, elaborate festivals. The first week was the Festival of Water, dedicated to the sparkling oasis and bubbling springs that enabled the desert city to thrive. Next was the Festival of Light, honoring the sun, moons, and stars that worked in concert to maintain the world's balance. Third came the Festival of Knowledge, celebrating the innovations and discoveries that brought prosperity to the City of Illumination. And the culmination of all these was the greatest festival of all: the Festival of King Darmatus, remembering with joy and sorrow the first ruler of the nation and his royal line, now past.

Each of these events resulted in a monumental redecorating of the massive pastel city. The giant waterways and canals used for transport were alternately filled with dyes of different hues and gaudy gondolas hurried merrymakers from one party to the next. The aqueducts were hung with different banners every week, if not every day. Impressive thoroughfares lined with great statues and columns bore all manner of lacy adornment, and gardens boomed with imported vegetation whose rosy petals spread rapidly on the wind. And most magnificent of all was the royal palace, closed until the final week of Festivus when it's marble halls and golden chambers, decked with the sky-blue livery of the royal family, would be opened for all the citizens to see.

Aware of these ongoing events, yet completely disinterested in them, was Senior Cadet Matteo Alhan, whose graduation exam for the Darmatian Military Academy was upon him. He was a studious youth, born of a hardworking family that ran a small shipping company up and down the Etrus Canal. Weak of arm and possessed of bad eyesight at an early age, Matteo had helped his boat-savvy father by delving into books of engineering, mathematics, and accounting. However, he had always made time late at night to read tales of magic and heroes by the light of a small illyrium crystal. Nothing excited him quite like these stories, so when he latently developed a talent for sensory magic at the age of eighteen, he immediately applied to the country's elite magic training school, the Darmatian Military Academy, so that he, too, might one day be like his beloved book characters.

His plan had three problems. First, Matteo had never been an athletic boy. Second, his family was decidedly middle class; they didn't have the geldars to pay the high tuition fees. And, lastly and hardest to overcome, Matteo was an incurable coward. Whether it be steer-elk baying at him as they towed the canal boats, thunder roaring from the clouds, or even simply dealing with the darkness and silence of night, Matteo would be struck with irrational fear. Eventually he came to an uneasy accord with the draft animals, and thunder could be marginalized to a lurking terror by scientific explanation, but to this day he still left illyrium crystals on at night—even after he was finished reading—much to the chagrin of his academy roommates. In fact, it was because of this ingrained fear that Matteo so admired the bravery and courage of the heroes in his novels, and why he was so determined to graduate from the academy founded by the greatest hero of all: Darmatus.

As luck would have it, while the issue of courage was persistent, the first two were more easily overcome. Matteo, despite his shortcomings, could never be accused of being vacuous. In fact, his entrance exams scores were among the highest ever seen in the history of the institution. Not a week passed from the submission of his application before a glowing handwritten letter from Steward Rowan Metellus himself came back attached to an offer of a full scholarship.

The problem of athleticism was slightly harder to conquer. In spite of his amazing academic scores, Matteo flunked the physical entrance test, resulting in a three-month trip to boot camp before he even laid eyes on the academy itself.

Down with the enlisted men and women, Matteo suffered through day after day of browbeating bodily abuse, followed by nightly verbal haranguings after his fellow trainees discovered his insecurities. But being a coward does not, by definition, make one a quitter as well. Matteo's persistence in the face of adversity soon won the respect of both his peers and superiors, and he exited that facility with the strength to keep up with any of the future officers at the academy itself. Unfortunately for Matteo, the night light was still a fixture.

Now, four years later, it was graduation day at the Darmatian Military Academy. Matteo and his classmates had endured four long years learning military strategy, tactics, specialized skills, and, of course, honing their magic and combat acumen. To effectively do so, the academy split its cadets into squads of four immediately upon their arrival. These groups were selected based upon a wide variety of criteria, and no one besides the instructors knew exactly why each team ended up together, despite months of wild speculation. Squads lived together, ate together, slept together, exercised together, went to class together, and fought together. If one of your squadmates failed a course, the entire team failed the course. You say one of your group vandalized the commandant's air skimmer? Demerits and volunteer work till graduation for all of you. Your medic got injured? Looks like you'll be carrying her around campus until she's healed. Oh, and somebody better learn everything she knows for the mock sortie next week. The general idea, as Matteo soon realized, was to quickly teach cadets that, as a leader, one must always consider that the actions of the smallest part of the whole affect its entirety. And the natural extension of this practice, as Matteo was dreading at this very moment, was if one of your squadmates failed their final exam, the entire squad would fail to graduate as well.

He and his partners were currently sitting in the eighteenth row of the grand lecture hall taking the written portion of their final exam. The chamber was large, the long desks curved, and the seats rose in tiers from front to back so that everyone could see the chalkboard and instructor at the center of the giant semicircle. That instructor was currently Major Jis Reev, their proctor and perhaps the meanest disciplinarian on grounds. And she was staring with icy displeasure . . . directly in *their* direction.

Mind you, Matteo, aside from his perfectly well-grounded fears *this time*, was focused on his exam. As were Terran Senior Cadet Leonel Descar to his left and gorgeous Sylph Senior Cadet Velle`asa Me`andara on his far right. Instead, the problem, directly to his right, was fast asleep and snoring loudly, a pile of drool expanding across his test papers as he buried his head in his arms. Matteo's stomach was awash with anxiety, and he wanted nothing more than to rush back to his room and wrap himself snugly in his covers. *How could a single individual be so blessed with talent and potential and this be the result?* Matteo's mind boggled. *And of all the times he's attempted to ruin my life, why Veneer, why Creator, why today?* Matteo spared another contemptuous glance at his blissfully sleeping squad leader. Yes, why did Vallen Metellus have to attempt to ruin his life on graduation day, the single most important day of his existence?

Wait. Perhaps he was overreacting a bit. While Vallen might be an incorrigible fool, he wasn't a complete idiot. He wouldn't deliberately throw away four years of grueling academy training on a whim. Or would he? *The blasted playboy is just so bloody unpredictable!* Yet if he did have a plan, what was it? Matteo shifted more of his attention away from the paper before him as he wracked his brain for the answer. Their final exam was split into two segments: a written assessment in the morning and a practical test in the afternoon. Out of these portions, a combined total score of 70 percent was required to pass. And if he correctly remembered Major Reev's announcement at the beginning, something was odd about the weighting of each section . . .

By the Void, that's his ploy! Naturally, Vallen, the "prodigy," would attempt to graduate in the most preposterous manner possible. Unlike final exams in years past where both parts were equally weighted, the testing committee had determined that it was time to shake up the status quo. In *this* graduation assessment, the written was only worth 30 percent while the practical was an utterly insane 70 percent. Vallen, for some inexplicable and inane reason known only to him, was aiming to ace the practical portion of the exam while unequivocally bombing the written segment.

The conspiracy theorist in Matteo was just getting going. *Perhaps Steward Metellus is in on it too!* As everyone at the academy—and the city itself, for that matter—knew, Vallen was slightly special. No, it wasn't that he was pretty much the only orphan to ever enroll at the academy. It also wasn't the fact that he was the adopted child of the steward himself, though that certainly had the gossip mill spinning from time to time. Rather, it was the theory, as absurd as it sounded, that

Vallen Metellus may be the spiritual successor of King Darmatus himself.

Yes, spiritual successor. There was clearly no blood connection between the two. Vallen was a waif likely conceived of Sewertown tramps. Born with nothing, he was somehow discovered down in that warren of ramshackle tenements by Steward Metellus, who noticed his unique talents and brought him to the surface world as his son. However, "born with nothing" was a misnomer of epic proportions. Vallen was a natural sorcerer who had never trained a day in his life. And if that weren't enough, he was only the second Triaron in existence. The first? It didn't take a genius to make the connection; it was none other than the great King Darmatus.

"Fifteen minutes left, and not an extra second will be given!" Major Reev yelled from the lectern. Matteo glanced up briefly, long enough to see the air around her shimmering dangerously with frost, her gaze still fixated on Vallen. At least he wasn't the only one irritated at his indolent squad leader.

Eyes back on his paper, Matteo regarded the final question, an essay:

> 25. Briefly outline the primary classifications of magic, both by type and method of activation and discuss one specific example that debunks this traditional method of codification.

What a loaded question! Perhaps this small opportunity to vent was just what Matteo needed. He set to with a gusto:

> In the year 108 ABH, the magic researcher Gerjunia Halsruf set down the principle categorizations for magic used to this day. For type, he determined that 95 percent of spells fell into one of the following ranks: elemental, time and space, curative, blood, enhancive, morphic, degenerative, necromantic, dark, and light. It should be noted that, unlike many of his contemporaries, Halsruf did not believe necromancy, the practice of raising the dead, to be an inherently dark or immoral practice. Hence, this was the first time it was considered to be a pillar of magic all its own. The remainder of spells can be considered too diverse or too different of scale to fall into these classes. These abilities

are merely called "unique" and studied on a case-by-case basis.

Magic must also be evaluated on the basis of its activation technique. Most spells require a catalyst to be executed. For the average mage, this consists of both written and verbal components. An ancient sorcerer might spend days drawing a formulaic circle and chanting a lengthy quotation. In the modern era, this process has been sped up considerably by means of Engraving. The base codification for the mage's family of spells is Engraved upon his instrument of choice (perhaps a staff), enabling him to merely adjust a short chant to alternate between castings of that type. This is the first level of activation, and its users are classified as Engravates. At the next level of Invocation, Invokers are capable of using magic without a verbal incantation. For these gifted sorcerers, only the physical formula is necessary. The inverse of this methodology is the Armsmage, who is capable of utilizing any tool, including themselves in many cases, or weapon to cast spells without a written catalyst, provided they still say the, pun intended, "magic words."

Which brings our discussion to one type of mage that renders most of this system useless: the Triaron. For most of the current age, there was only one known Triaron—the Hero King Darmatus. More recently, a second, less noble, considerably crasser specimen, one who refuses to empty the trash, make his bunk, participate in cleaning duty, or engage in the most rudimentary level of teamwork has been discovered. He—

At this point Matteo found his writing, which had, admittedly, turned into a rant now that the question was safely answered, interrupted by a very furious Major Reev whose fraying patience had finally snapped. Exam decorum had apparently been broken long enough on her watch, and icicles the size of his arm were now flying directly at the perpetrator, one Vallen Metellus.

— ⋆◈⋆ —

A crackling field of electricity caught and disintegrated the shards not ten centimeters from Vallen's face. Even after the shards were gone, it continued to hum for several additional seconds before gradually dissipating back into nothingness. His sleep—mostly real, partially mocking façade—disturbed, Vallen raised his shock of mushed brown hair and beamed at his attacker.

"Ms. Jis, assaulting a student during an exam is extremely detrimental to the intended process, don't you agree?"

The look she sent back was one of unbridled disgust—not surprising, considering she'd always been one of his detractors among the staff. "*Major* Reev to you, *Cadet* Vallen Metellus. Fortunately, the exam just ended five seconds ago, and besides, you and I both know you didn't so much as write your name on your paper. Now get out of my exam room within the next minute or, by the Veneer, I will see you fail the exam regardless of your score this evening or who your 'father' is." He could practically hear the sneer attached to "father." Evidently, she wasn't a fan of the current steward either. But that was hardly his concern.

Major Reev turned to regard the rest of the students. "As for everyone else, the written portion is now complete. Grading will be performed automatically via scrivening magchine, so expect the results by the time you finish your practical exam. Those matches will begin in a few hours, so I suggest you take the time to prep in your individual squad rooms. Best of luck and dismissed."

Cadets began filing down the aisles and out the doors to either side of classroom's lowest rung. Vallen gingerly stood up, making a show of taking his time and stretching to see just how far he could push their proctor. Dweeby Matteo, freckled, lanky, with thin, stringy hair and glasses, shot him a pleading look. "Come on, Vallen. Don't test her any further. She's a millimeter from failing you already."

"Ah, Professor Night Light speaks. By the way, that was a nice essay you wrote. Very brave to write how you feel on a page instead of telling me directly. Glad to see your spine is starting to grow in."

Matteo shrunk back, his gaze falling to the floor. "I . . . It was just an essay. I didn't mean anything by it." A little more steel entered his voice as he continued, "But, really, what were you thinking, sleeping during the exam? Or pretending to sleep, or whatever, since you knew what I was doing. Do you want to graduate?"

At that moment, the true class bully, Renar Iolus, stopped at their row and draped an arm around Matteo's shoulders in a pretense of friendship. The rest of his squad stood behind him, a female Terran and a male Hue with four hulking arms backing him up while the fourth, a timid-seeming Terran girl with long, uniquely silver hair, stood apart from the confrontation. "Of course he wants to graduate, Matteo. But between you and me, he's trying to give himself an excuse for failing this year. You see, Vallen, we're going to be playing each other during the practical exam later, and this time it's going to be you on the ground looking up at me. And when that happens in front of your so-called father and all the brass, I'm going to be on the fast track and you'll be repeating." He gave Matteo a squeeze as the latter tried to squirm away, "Along with the Professor here and the rest of your crew."

"Oh, and why is my Val going to lose to a nobody he's beaten a dozen times?" Velle`asa Me`andara, more commonly known by her Sylph core name, Velle, entered the conversation as she slipped her lithe red arms around Vallen's neck. "Is *your* daddy, the general, going to pull some strings for you and put the mean Triaron in his place?" Her crimson-tinged pupils flashed amusement.

Chastised, Renar pushed Matteo toward them and pointed at Vallen. "My father has nothing to do with this. I heard that we were paired up—*randomly,* I might add—and wanted to let you know that this time, I'm going to beat you. No tricks; I'm just going to be the better mage. Think on that, losers." He stalked away, his cadre following close behind.

Vallen couldn't resist throwing a parting quip after him, "I've always wondered how dirt tastes, Renar. Maybe you can tell me after our match tonight?"

The silver-haired girl, at the rear of the group, was passing just as he spoke. She glared at him, her eyes a perfect match for her locks. "He may be a blowhard like you, but at least he's trying his best to improve. And yet here you are, sleeping through your exam. I wonder which of you is the bigger idiot?" As soon as she was done speaking, she turned and marched after her squad, silver hair floating behind her. Vallen was left speechless.

"What a little harpy," Velle breathed, clutching Vallen tighter when she saw him staring after the departing girl. "Wait, you don't think she's cute, do you? Don't go getting interested in a flaky little waif like that. You're too good for someone who doesn't appreciate your talents and charms like I do."

"And that, my dear Velle, is exactly why our squad leader is currently smitten," interjected Leon—Leonel—Descar, who had just returned from turning in their exam papers. The youngest son of high ranking Darmatian nobles, he was impeccably well dressed, groomed, and prone to talking in an extremely roundabout manner. "The poor man has never met a female who wasn't completely besotted by his graceless mannerisms before. I'm sure the shock will fade with time, but then again, I'm not exactly a medical professional."

"I'm nothing of the sort, Leon. In fact, I'm not even sure who she is."

"She is one Sylette Farkos, only daughter of Undersecretary Farkos of the Rabban Imperium. In the imperium, everyone gets treated equally, regardless of social status, so her papa decided to send her to 'safety' at the neighboring kingdom's military academy. Better than a sweltering job as a factory floor manager, I suppose." Leon knew everything about everyone, even if he didn't have the book smarts to know all the things about everything. It was certainly a skill that had been useful to Vallen on the many occasions that naysayers and politics had stood in his way at the academy. As a result, Vallen and Leon had developed a tight bond; Leon was probably Vallen's best, if not only, friend in the world.

Vallen disentangled himself from Velle, with only minor resistance on her part, and walked down the steps to the exit. By now the room was nearly empty. Major Reev had long since departed, having correctly reasoned that attempting to reform Vallen wasn't worth any more of her time. "We'll see her again soon enough, and I'll make sure you have plenty of opportunities to make her eat her words, Velle. That being said, we do have a match to win. Let's get a move on—that includes you, too, Professor Night Light. Victory waits for no man, not even a coward like you."

⸻◆⸻

"Why do you insist on calling me 'coward' and 'Professor Night Light' all the time? Don't you think I get tired of the names?" It was two hours later. Velle was in the bathroom, making sure "not a hair was out of place" for their "performance." Leon was listening to music in the soundproof training room next door. His taste involved pieces with a strange bleating instrument known as a goonpa horn, so people typically avoided him while he engaged in this pre-match ritual. And that left Vallen and Matteo, suited up in their skin-tight combat jumpsuits and impact armor, staring at each other from opposite benches in their squad room.

"Is grass hurt when people label it green? Does an ek protest when you expect it to till a field? If stating the honest truth is something that offends your sensibilities, I suggest you lock yourself in a room, with a night light of course, for the rest of your life." Vallen lay down on the cushioned plank and turned to face the lockers behind him in an attempt to end the conversation then and there.

Unfortunately, Matteo was being persistent. "Don't you think I'm trying my best to get over my hang ups? We've been at this for, what, four years now? Each and every day I've been getting stronger and braver, a little bit at a time. And then you walk in and dash my progress with your names, your jokes, your need to be the funny guy. My question is, why?"

Vallen kept staring at the lockers, his eyes boring into the blue paint until he began seeing gray and white flecks mixed in. "Do you know how annoying it is to have to wear a mask to shut out the light . . . *at night*? Night is dark because it is meant for sleeping, not because monsters and bogeymen are ready to whisk you away to the dread island Pharsalus. Next question."

He could hear Matteo sigh and slump over without looking at him. "There you go again, another joke. Can we have a serious conversation for once? Like, what was that today, sleeping through the exam? Is this just a game to you, or did the steward put you up to it?"

The steward had, in fact, put him up to it. For all of his wisdom, for all of his statesmanship and sedate appearances, Metellus had a bit of a risk-taking streak when he thought it might pay off. The plan was simple: silence Vallen's detractors on the Council and in the military with one magnificent achievement. He would use his abilities as the Triaron to ace the practical exam and graduate against all odds, resulting in him securing an important post-graduation position. Since Vallen hated writing, and work in general, the plan seemed both efficacious and, more to the point, fun. Never mind that he had spent the entire previous night with Velle; blaming his father was the simpler solution.

"Would it matter if he did? I *am* this team. Why are we ranked number one in every combat category? *Me*. And why will we win again tonight? Oh, right, same answer: *me*. You and your coward's weapon next to you certainly won't be contributing any more than usual."

The instrument in question was Matteo's sniper rifle, which was propped against the compartments next to him. One meter in length, it had been enchanted so that it could fire both regular rounds and its user's spirit energy. A beautiful work of craftsmanship, to be sure, and perfect for a coward who sat at the rear lines and used pitiful sensory magic to observe enemies and direct allies. *Why should I care what the enemy's planning when they can't keep up with me no matter what they do?* Vallen thought with amusement.

"You know what? I've never said this before, because I thought it was going too far, but since you obviously want to be the mother I never had, I'll say it now. Matteo, you are a waste of a slot on this team. And I'll keep believing so until you prove to me otherwise."

His verbal abuse was too much for Matteo's fragile, infantile heart. He burst off his seat, grabbed his weapon, and stormed out the suite's main door. Some part of Vallen wondered if Matteo would show up for their soon-to-start match; the rest of him considered whether or not the crybaby had lived true to that namesake and shed tears as he departed. He had little time to ponder the answer as one headache was swiftly replaced by another.

"Quite the drama you have going on in here, Cadet Metellus." The man who had just stepped through the recently opened door was an infinitely greater nuisance than Matteo would ever be. He was in his mid-fifties, with black hair going to gray framing the edges of a growing bald spot and once-prominent muscles slowly wending their way back to fat. A crisply pressed military uniform hung over this body, with medals and baubles from non-existent conflicts clogging all the available space from shoulders to midriff.

"How long were you eavesdropping at our door . . . General Iolus?" Vallen barely resisted the urge to be insubordinate. This was one of the few individuals who had the power to crucify him: the commandant of the academy and commander of the Royal City Defense Forces, aka, the national reserves. And, as Vallen knew, he had tried his hardest to expunge him from both the school and the military on several occasions. As a result, regardless of how much he'd like to punch the smirk from this insipid egomaniac's face, this was one instance that swallowing his natural penchant for overt disrespect was necessary.

And there was the smirk. "Are you suggesting that a flag officer and principal of this great establishment would feel the need to listen in on the mundane trivialities of cadet locker room talk? I merely happened to be in the hall when Senior Cadet Alhan beat a very swift retreat from your room and thought it prudent, the magnanimous educator that I am, to investigate the cause." General Hardwick Iolus spread his arms, gesturing at Vallen who had risen to his feet in some modicum of courtesy. "Imagine my surprise to find that you have, once again, managed to cause a breach in the peace and stability of my institution."

Vallen felt a vein on his forehead twitch with annoyance. "Please get to the point . . . sir. I can't imagine that you came here just to engage in a bout of verbal sparring, but if you did, allow me to invite Senior Cadet Descar, or better yet, his father, the one on the Council of Overseers, before we continue."

The smirk died, and Vallen felt his own twitch subside in tune. "That won't be necessary, *Cadet* Metellus. No need for you to play with matters beyond your station. Besides, it's entirely possible that with Alhan indisposed, my entire purpose for this visit might be moot. After all, if he misses the match in," he glanced down at a chronometer on his right wrist, "fifteen minutes, it'll be a contest of three versus four. Those are hard odds, even for the, ah, infamous Triaron."

Now it was Vallen's turn to smile. "You really should tell Renar to keep his mouth shut. I've had my suspicions since he told me we'd be playing—*before* the draft was announced an hour ago, mind you—but now they're confirmed. You're trying to rig the match, General!"

Commandant Iolus mustered his large frame to its fullest height, leering over the smaller Vallen in an attempt to intimidate him. "I would do no such thing! As commandant, I happen to sit on the exam board and can assure you that each match was decided by a magic algorithm developed by a third-party consultant."

Vallen began to pace, his arms behind his back, mimicking the way Iolus moved when giving speeches. "Let's say that you didn't dabble in the match selection, General. You have to know that I *am* team seven, otherwise known as Vallen's Vanguard. I own the rights to that name, by the way. Leon smoothed that over last year. Anyway, I'm 110 percent positive that I can take your son and all of his squadmates singlehandedly. And despite your evident distaste for my very existence, I'm sure you're aware of this fact as well. Which brings me back to the original question: why are you here . . . sir?" He was skirting a treacherously thin line. Any more discourteous behavior was likely to see him flunk the exam and brought up on charges for insulting a superior officer. On the other hand, General Iolus very palpably needed something from him and, therefore, was less likely to pursue the former course of action. But Vallen was a master of balancing on that edge.

It was barely surprising then when Commandant Iolus visibly slumped and much of the earlier bravado left his voice. "All of this is strictly off the record, of course. Try to bring it up with anyone else, and it will simply be my word—the word of the commandant himself—versus yours. Nothing will come of it and a court martial will find you mere hours later."

"Do skip the pleasantries, General. As you said, I have a match."

"Yes, you're right. Where was I? Ah, my son, bless him, will make an amazing soldier. He has the capabilities of a remarkable military leader, but he struggles in . . . certain areas. I recently received the scores from this morning's written exam. Naturally, you failed, but then again, you didn't even try. And though I protested greatly at the time, you still have the opportunity to pass overall since Metellus put pressure on the committee to adjust the weighting this time around. For you, though I hate to admit it, that's a distinct possibility. For Renar, it simply isn't, despite his talents. And though it wasn't an abysmal zero like yours, my son . . . my son botched the paper portion."

"So, Daddy—pardon, *General*—Iolus, has come to me in an attempt to make everything work out for his washout son."

"You watch your mouth, you insignificant pissant—" Iolus stiffened, his cheeks red with rising ire. Then he breathed deeply, calming himself. "No, no, that's exactly why I'm here. I need you to throw the match in such a way that foul play is not suspected—by either my son or the rest of the committee—and Renar performs well enough to get a passing grade."

Vallen made a great show of considering the offer, bringing one hand to cup his chin, the other at his waist. "That's quite the tall order. The odds from the betting table—not that any cadet would engage in such illegal activities—are sixty-three to one in our favor. That aside, all of it depends on one thing: what's in it for me?"

He could see General Iolus brighten at not having his request refused outright. "For starters, I would have the exam committee find an *irregularity* with the circumstances under which your written exam was taken. You'd be given a new paper test—one which I would personally make and grade."

"So, I get a perfect score on that, ensuring that I still pass despite the loss of some practical points. What else?"

"Quite the bargainer, aren't you?"

"As you've so often pointed out in your past attempts to expel me, I grew up in Sewertown. Wheeling and dealing is a means of survival down there; you learn quickly or die. Five minutes till match time. My squad could show up any second, and I know you don't want that."

The general glanced at his watch to confirm Vallen's words. "But all that is behind us now—especially once I become your advocate in the upper echelon." The smirk was back in full now.

"And what will that do for me?"

"Why, set you on the promotion fast track, my boy. All those dissenters you have among the instructors, the upper ranks, and the politicians on the Council of Overseers? I can make all those headaches go away."

Ironic, Vallen thought, *since he himself is one of the biggest headaches of all.*

"And that's all before the run for steward I'm planning later this year."

"You're going to run against Metellus in this year's election?"

"One of several people who are, I'm afraid. Your father isn't exactly popular anymore. The doves think he's not doing enough to promote economic development and mediate the conflict between the empire and Rabban, and the hawks don't think the military is strong enough to resist an incursion by any of our neighbors. Plus, he's ancient. If the doddering old man doesn't contract a venereal disease from his Sewertown trips to visit some 'poor' wenches and die tomorrow, his senility will probably get—"

"*Out.*" Vallen's eyes were cold and his voice calm with an edge of hardened steel as he eyed the ungrateful blob of flesh before him.

"What? This is my locker room, my school. You can't command me."

"*Out.*" He took a single step toward General Iolus, who shrank back the same distance, despite being the larger man.

"This is your last chance to take my offer. If you don't, you'll never amount to anything. I'll make sure you end up sweeping sand day in and day out at some remote outpost where nothing—"

"*Out.*" Another step. You could insult him, and Vallen would fire a dart right back at you. You could disparage his few friends, and he would make sure you got your due somewhere down the line. But smear the name of Steward Rowan Metellus, the man who found him and saved him from a life of deprivation and decay in the sewers beneath the city, and you were on the brink of signing your own death warrant.

Cowed, Iolus scampered for the door. From the hall came a scuffling of boots on tile, but Vallen barely registered the sound as his focus was entirely on the pitiful excuse for an officer before him.

"You won't get away with this. Expect your transfer within the day. I'll see you ruin—"

General Iolus was once again interrupted, this time by the door slamming in his face. An injured shriek from the other side assured Vallen that he had, as intended, broken the commandant's nose with the instrument of solid metal.

Just then, Velle emerged from the bathroom, dressed in the same combat gear as he was. Even so, it somehow accentuated her athletic curves perfectly, and as she had set out to accomplish half an hour prior, not a hair was out of place. "I heard a commotion through the door. Everything alright?"

And just like that, Vallen reverted to his normal, jovial self. "Nothing at all, just an overexuberant fan wanting an autograph minutes before go-time. I had to, somewhat forcefully, tell him to wait till after the match. Speaking of which, grab Leon, and let's get out on the field."

"What about Matteo?"

He turned, calling over his shoulder as he strolled toward the rear exit to the tunnel below the academy stadium. "Don't worry; he said he'd meet us on the sidelines." Next to the door was his weapon, gleaming with the fresh polish he had applied earlier that day. He picked it up, feeling the cool metal beneath his fingertips. Some weapons were alive and responded automatically to their user's thoughts. Vallen's wasn't, but he still felt like he had a similar relationship with it. He whispered to it, "I suddenly feel the urge to take out some repressed anger on Renar. What say we do that together, you and I?"

Chapter 6

World Gone Wrong

———❖———

"**G**ood evening, ladies and gentlemen of all nations and races! I, your host, Tannen Holler, welcome you back to your favorite sport and mine, flag-brawl! With me tonight is a very special commentator for a very unique night of entertainment: the lovely Major Jis Reev of the Darmatian Military Academy! Major Reev, do you have anything to say to the fans before we get the last match of the night underway?"

"I'd only like to remind our esteemed broadcaster that, despite the dim lighting in this booth, I am entirely aware of your hand reaching for my thigh. One millimeter closer, and it will be so frostbitten you won't be able to use it to chase your usual brand of floozies ever again."

"Major, your projectomic is turned on, in case you—"

"I am perfectly aware, Tannen. Having thousands of witnesses is the best medicine for your particular species of creep. That being said, I wish our final two teams the best of luck and hope that they give our amazing audience the show of a lifetime!"

Vallen chuckled as he went through a short stretching routine at his team's end of the field. Tannen Holler, a celebrity caster in the flag-brawl world with a voice of silk and the deep pockets to match, was in over his head trying to pull anything with the Ice Queen of Darmatia. On the other hand, Major Reev continued to live up to her national popularity, simultaneously putting the announcer in his place with cutting steel then turning around to butter up the crowd.

"Getting back on track, if you are just joining us, then you are in for a treat. Normally the game of flag-brawl is played in this stadium and others like it throughout Lozaria by teams of professional mages battling for glory and geldars. However, tonight we bring you amateur hour! Don't let my jest fool you; these mages competing tonight are among the brightest and bravest Darmatia has to offer. Each is on the cusp of graduation and induction into our military or those around the continent. Only one final challenge stands in their way: putting on the best performance possible for you, the fans! Seated in the VIP booth, along with Darmatia's very own Steward Metellus and gathered dignitaries, is a panel of judges evaluating their every move. But that's not for us to worry about. Sit back, grab some menja juice, and enjoy the sheer brutality of flag-brawl!"

The field that was to host the coming match lay fifty meters below the stands, which formed an oval about the playing area that was five hundred meters by five hundred meters. Sound from the casting booth was reaching both the fans and players by means of projectostands connected to the projectomics being used by Tannen and Major Reev. Some projectostands were scattered about the tiered viewing sections, but the largest were suspended over the middle of the arena, connected to four massive telescribers that showed up-close images of the action transmitted to them by floating recorbs. This construct hung from a huge glass dome that separated the participants and audience from the desert clime outside.

Next to Vallen were his squadmates, including Matteo, who had shown up just before the battle area was sealed off by a protective lume. This special lume was projected from four large illyrium generators at the cardinal points and was supposed to be strong enough to prevent any wayward spells or projectiles from injuring the fans. Even so, lumes were only as strong as their power sources and had failed at other, more backwater stadiums in the past. As a result, it was practically tradition that seats nearest the field went cheaper than ones higher up.

Matteo looked confused and frazzled, but that was hardly Vallen's concern. If this match went like any of the ones he had played before, Professor Night Light was going to be utterly useless and he'd have to carry his weight. Off to the left, Velle was on top of their flag platform, waving and blowing kisses to her cadre of male fans that had gathered behind their starting zone. Vallen had his own legion of admirers, mostly female, that were right there along with them, holding a bevy of support signs and shouting encouragement. His success, coupled with his boyish handsomeness and toned build, brought its own degree of female attention; being the Triaron, effectively a living legend, took that regard to a whole other level.

Last was Leon, who, for whatever reason, had donned a topcoat frilled with gold lace over his deflection plates and jumpsuit. If that wasn't weird enough, he was squatting on his haunches playing with a self-generated ball of light flitting about beyond the end of an expensive staff. Leon looked, for all intents and purposes, like a king who had forgotten to wear pants yet had still sallied forth to chase some luminescent fairy with an overly adorned stick. But even he had his own set of fans, mostly sycophants hoping to earn his father's favor by getting into his good graces.

The booming of the projectostands rang out anew. "Since we've still got some time before brawloff, let's go through a quick rundown of flag-brawl in case any little tykes or old geezers don't understand the rules. The object of the game is simple: capture your opponent's flag! The execution, though, is more difficult. Each team consists of four members. Of these members, only two at a time can ever be in the starting, or home, zone, the back hundred meters of each side where each team has their flag platform. This means you can only have a max of two defenders."

Vallen bent over, planting his hands on the ground to loosen his hamstrings. *Who needs to defend when you can just take out your opponents? Offense is always the best defense.* Tannen's explanation continued, "Everyone can go on the attack! That's right! You can opt to leave your flag undefended and send your entire team out to fight! Which brings us to our second, and slightly harder to accomplish, victory condition: take out the other squad! Care to explain, Jis?"

"Slip up and call me *Jis* one more time, and your lips will never separate again since they, and the rest of your head, will be frozen solid." A slight pause ensued before she began again, "Yes, it is possible to win by knockout. Unlike in real combat, where winning and losing is determined by kill and casualty count, here each suit is integrated with a biometer that uses its wielder's vitals to determine how much injury they could sustain before being rendered unfit to fight. The suit protects them from damage, aside from minor scrapes and bruises, and instead keeps a tally of hits taken. Once a certain threshold is exceeded, their own clothing will lock up, sealing their movement and preventing them from taking further action. Do this to all your opponents, and their team can no longer operate, resulting in a victory by TKO."

All of Vallen's past victories had been by TKO. It was harder to do, and he savored the increased challenge and prestige that came with keeping that perfect record. He finished stretching and looked up at the VIP box high above. His father, Steward Metellus, was seated in the place of honor at the center. He nodded and waved a gnarled hand at Vallen; apparently, he had been watching his son the whole time. Vallen sketched an informal salute in reply.

To his left was General Iolus, looking like the fool he was with a wad of bandages swathed around his nose. He glared daggers at the cadet who had snubbed him; under the watchful eyes of Metellus and the members of the Council of Overseers sitting behind him, there was little else he *could* do. On the right was another of Vallen's few supporters, the grizzled Admiral Ur Contus. Only a decade behind the steward in age, he was the de facto commander in chief of the Darmatian military. As a small nation, Darmatia lacked a large ground army. Instead, a well provisioned and mobile air fleet kept its borders safe. With limited military reserves, Admiral Contus made it known that he would not turn down any resource that could defend the country, Vallen the Triaron included.

"That brings us to the makeup of our field today. A flag-brawl field is always made up of five hundred-meter segments. The two home zones are flat ground topped with grassy turf. However, while the flag platform is currently only two meters off the ground, once play begins it will be raised halfway to the stands—a whopping twenty-five meters in the air. Brawlers will have to climb the single metal ladder or its superstructure to reach the top. Alternatively, they can fly, but we'll let you find out which of our brilliant young fighters are capable of that as we go! The other three zones were randomly decided just before the match. Can you tell us what they are, um, Major?"

"See? We'll get you trained yet, Tannen. The zones today were chosen from a number of live fire scenarios our cadets might see in combat. Next to team . . . Vallen's Vanguard," Vallen smiled as she choked out his squad name, "we have a swampy estuary zone, mimicking the terrain at the southern mouth of the Etrus Canal. In the middle is a destroyed village filled with flames and ruins that could be found anywhere a conflict arises. And lastly, beside Renar's Renegades, you can see a very unique zone: the inside of a Darmatian air cruiser. Contestants can run along the top of the cruiser fuselage, but army mages are standing on the sidelines casting constant wind element spells to mimic air running over the ship in flight. Any fighting up there is sure to be on tricky footing."

"Why have a cruiser as one of the zones?"

"As you should know, Tannen, the Darmatian military is primarily focused on its air fleet. This means that while our cadets will face ground-based battles, they will also likely see shipboard clashes in the air. If we are to overcome everything, we must be ready for anything."

"Very true, very true. Wonderful words of wisdom, Major. Lastly, pro flag-brawl has rules beyond the ones we discussed, such as penalties for illegal moves or going out of bounds. Will we see any of that here?"

"Absolutely not. The suits are foolproof and will prevent extended injury from befalling the cadets. As in combat, anything else goes."

"There you have it, fans! We're thirty seconds from an all-out, no-holds-barred brawl! Let's get ready to rumble and pray, for all our sakes, that the lume holds!"

Vallen shot a quick glance at the timer attached to the central projectostand, which now read twenty seconds and counting. Matteo had taken up his usual perch on the flag platform, the place where he could, hopefully, do the least harm. Velle was back and to his left in support, and Leon was aiming his staff skyward in preparation for their usual opening. Vallen gripped his weapon tightly in his right hand. At the moment, it was nothing more than a small, inert cylinder of metal. That was all he needed for this first phase.

"*And, start*! Let the brawl begin!"

Tannen's loud starting signal rang out across the stadium as Vallen sprang out of the starting zone. "Take me up, Velle! Flashbang, Leon!" White glyphs, almost like snowflakes, appeared in front of Vallen in a staircase leading forward and upward. He jumped from one to another, each increasing his speed as he took off above and across the zones below. Behind him, Velle had her eyes closed, hands extended, concentrating on forming the platforms that would take him right to the enemy. A prodigious mage, even among the Sylph, she possessed a wide range of glyph-based enhancive and healing magic. In a typical mage, this focus on buffing her teammates would mean they couldn't fend for themselves. However, the twin daggers at her waist and the innate blood magic her people were known for more than made up for any deficiencies.

Vallen raised his weapon above his head and silently bid it transform into an opaque shield as Leon began the second portion of their winning combo. Leon was a very rare mage, one of the few capable of performing light magic. An individual's proficiency with magic was usually hereditary, but like Vallen, he had bucked that pattern. At the moment, he was firing flares of light from his staff into the sky, where they burst with dazzling light like firesh'crakera. Anyone not covering their eyes would be temporarily blinded by the magical illumination, helpless against assault unless they had a countermeasure. As the brilliance faded, Vallen reverted his shield to its original form.

His weapon was made of a unique metal and was given to him by Steward Metellus since it synergized with his abilities. Now he expanded it into a long, curved blade—a krenesh blade, modeled after the heavy weapons used by the nomad Vladisvar. He had seen one in a bazaar as a child and had thereafter dreamed of possessing one. With his form-shifting companion, he now could.

The thrill of bringing out his favorite device vanished as his next step failed to connect with a glyph. Vallen's first thought, as he fell, was that Velle must be playing a trick on him. However, he was still high enough that he could see back to the home and first zones from whence he came. There, Velle had her daggers drawn and was engaged in combat with the Hue from Renar's team, who had jagged-edged bucklers strapped to all four of his blue arms. Wielding a fencing sword, the female Terran with him was keeping Leon on his heels as he dodged and parried with his clunky staff. And between them, racing up the middle, was Renar, greatsword on his shoulder and only a little more than a hundred meters from their flag.

Vallen's shock was tempered by his abrupt need to arrest his downward progress. He swung his krenesh with both hands, casting a powerful gust out from the blade that cushioned his impact onto the roof of the cruiser in zone four. He instantly activated the electric shield around his body that he had used to block Major Reev's icicle strike earlier that day. Without any guidance, it shifted and redirected the efforts of the Elementalists attempting to blow him from his perch.

What had happened to result in the impossible scenario before him? He looked up at the telescribers as he allowed Tannen's bleating announcement through his barrier's coursing energy. "What an amazing move. I've never seen anything like it! Unter, the bulky Hue from Renar's Renegades, applied enhancive magic to strengthen his shields and body. Then Lilith, his partner, used explosive fire magic while strapped to his back, becoming a living engine that propelled both forward. In no time flat, they've plowed right through the cruiser, the village, and the marsh! And their leader, Renar, followed right behind! Incredible!" Above, the telescribers showed the replay as the combination move blasted through the artificial terrain.

Major Reev concurred, "No doubt about that, Tannen. They combined their abilities to smash straight through the obstacles in their path and reach their opponent's doorstep. Unter and Lilith took some damage using their magic in such an unorthodox manner, but the element of surprise this tactic has won them might be all they need. Velle and Leon are hard-pressed, and Vallen looks dumbfounded. Of course, that's how he always is, so it's hard to tell if current events are even getting through to him."

"Shut up, wench!" Vallen yelled fruitlessly at the announcer's box. He turned around to see a scorched gash through the cruiser that marked the insane path his opponents had forged. *Think, Vallen, think. You're better than this.* He needed a plan, and he needed it quickly, or he was actually going to end up losing to Renar. *Think!*

"But Major, do you actually think Renar Iolus is behind this brilliant stroke? No offense to his father, General Iolus, but Renar's team has been in the bottom third of his class this entire season. That statistic aside, they've never shown us any tactics beside splitting up to go one versus one. This is definitely a new one from them."

"You're actually on to something for once, Tannen. About a month ago, Renar's fourth squadmate, a reptilian Moravi named Ich'oth, was recalled to the Moravi Atoll due to a shortage of males for their annual breeding rituals. I leave the particulars of such an arrangement to your imagination, but this left a slot open on his team. Only within the past week was this slot filled by a scholarship student from the Rabban Imperium: Sylette Farkos."

"Is she the mastermind behind what we're seeing?"

"I would have to assume so, given the upset brewing below us. Oh, look, there she is now, about to—"

Vallen barely had time to register the attack before the dagger came shooting through his shield and past his head. He whipped about, watching the silver-haired girl approaching through the wind. The image was blurred, both because of his own shield and the airflow around him. He twitched his head left, narrowly dodging another dagger that he didn't see coming. The attacks were invisible to his sight—or at least impossible to see under current conditions. *By the Veneer, am I actually at a disadvantage?*

Time to change scenery. Vallen reverted his blade to a rod and ran back toward his side of the field, dropping ten meters from the top of the cruiser to the dusty ground of the village zone and releasing his electric field. He sprinted another twenty meters into the middle of the dilapidated town before turning to face his opponent.

Smart or not, she had the gumption to follow him. Now that he got a good look at her, she was actually quite striking in a noble, majestic way. Long, silver hair topped a well-proportioned, cute face and a lithe, athletic body. However, she was petite and small of stature. The nobility of her bearing came from the set of her jaw and the air with which she carried herself. When she spoke, though, the voice that emerged was soft-spoken and silky, as though to counterbalance her hard stance.

"I never thought you would run from me, Vallen Metellus. Out of all the things I thought you'd do, that was not one of them."

"I'm full of surprises, my darling. I want to take this opportunity to apologize for any rudeness I may have shown your team earlier. Obviously, with you in charge, Renar has become infinitely more capable than he ever was before. Why don't you throw this match and you can tell me more about your tactics over dinner and a bottle of Ithran wine?"

A dagger materialized over her left shoulder and fired with considerable force at his face. This time, Vallen was able to see it coming and dodged easily. "I've heard all about your insufferable charms, and to be frank, I'm not impressed, neither by them nor by you. As far as I can see, you're a spoiled womanizer who's done nothing more than play at soldier for the past four years. Hardly the legend everybody chalks you up to be."

"And you're a space manipulator, more specifically, a conjurer, who can change the properties of her conjurations on the fly. Though it seems you're stuck making daggers at the moment."

Her mask of calm faltered. "Wha . . . how? You've only seen it three times!"

"Never let your enemy see your trick more than once." Vallen sketched a mocking bow.

"But how did you know I can change the properties? And the part about me only being able to make daggers?"

"Your first dagger got diverted by my electric field and missed. The second was on target, meaning an adjustment was made to account for the shield. And the third you formed right in front of me. I may be a philandering playboy who doesn't give a care about academics or authority, but that doesn't make me an idiot." He shot her his winningest smile.

Sylette's calm quickly returned as she summoned a dozen daggers into existence. "I see. But knowing a trick and avoiding it are two different things." All of them were released at once, set on a crash course with various points on Vallen's body.

Vallen urged his weapon into a long staff, which he spun to the fore while casting a gust of wind from its edges. The force of the gale blew the daggers off course and onto wild vectors through the air. Immediately, Sylette adjusted their aim, bringing them down on him from whence they'd been knocked. Another thought, and the staff was again a round shield above Vallen's head, from which he emitted a torrent of flame that incinerated the projectiles.

But he wasn't done. Shield shifted to warhammer, which he brought down to earth with the aid of a burst of wind. The weapon shattered into the ground, willing it to buckle and shoot forth pillars of stone beneath Sylette's feet. As the columns rose, she somersaulted backwards, landing gracefully beside the emerging cascade.

This was the true nature and power of the Triaron. It wasn't that Vallen was more powerful than any other mage. It was simply that he was more versatile. In short, the Triaron was an Elementalist sorcerer who was both an Invoker and an Armsmage. He could cast any element from any weapon without an Engraved or verbal catalyst. And "any weapon" also included his own body to a small degree, hence his ability to project a limited electric field. Furthermore, Vallen's ability to manipulate the elements extended to the unique instrument Metellus had gifted him, which could shift to his liking. Not needing to speak and being able to attack in almost any manner with any type of weapon was an indescribable advantage, one that had never seen Vallen bested in combat.

His current situation had the potential to be the first.

Let's take stock of things, Vallen decided. Matteo was useless, check. Velle and

Leon could beat their individual opponents one on one, check. He was currently tied up in a fast-paced skirmish with a highly mobile opponent who couldn't beat him but could keep him occupied, check. This left Renar free to influence the match as he saw fit, which was probably Sylette's plan all along. Occupy him while Renar won the three versus two battle back at base. More disturbing, all they had to do was cross into their home zone, and only Matteo and Velle could fight all three—correction, only Velle could fight all three.

"Having a good ponder over there?" Sylette was sitting cross-legged on one of the smaller pillars he had summoned, another dozen daggers floating about her head.

"You do know you're the only one between me and your flag, right?"

"That *was* my intent. And that means it's three on three back at your base. Going to break your rule about going for the flag? I thought you liked the *challenge* of winning by TKO?"

"Exactly how much research did you do to win this?"

"If you're frustrated, evidently enough."

Actually, Vallen considered, *this was shaping up to be fun. Maybe there was something interesting about this noble, feisty girl.* "You know, I think I will win by flag cap after all." He summoned a glaive and propelled himself forward using the ground at his feet. Sylette launched her first wave of daggers and conjured more in their place.

"Let's see you try . . . *Triaron.*"

⊰━◇━⊱

"Renar, Unter, and Lilith have just breached the home zone of Vallen's Vanguard! That means Leon can only watch and shoot light projectiles from zone one as they make the final push for their flag!"

"That's exactly what we're seeing, Tannen. Now, Velle and Matteo must somehow hold on in what is essentially a three on two as Vallen engages in a similar flag-cap race on the far side. The question everyone is asking themselves now is, can the so-called Triaron overcome these odds?"

Matteo was certainly asking himself that question. Here he was, lying behind his sniper rifle atop the high flag platform, having not fired a shot and shaking in fear for a variety of reasons: fear of heights, fear of the burly opponents racing toward him, fear of losing, and fear of further upsetting Vallen and his team.

By Vallen's order, he had not fired a shot. In fact, since their first match four years prior when he had aggravated everyone by constantly talking into their minds via telepathy and angered Vallen specifically by accidentally shooting him in the back—with a spirit bullet, not a real one—he had not fired a shot.

However, the current match was not going at all like it was supposed to. Normally, enemy teams had no way of countering Leon's long-range light attacks, leaving them vulnerable as Vallen sprinted into their midst on Velle's glyphs and annihilated them all. This time, Renar's team had been prepared for that tactic, hiding in the cruiser as the flashbangs went off, then exploding across the field using an innovative maneuver they'd never demonstrated before. Now, for the first time in four years, Vallen's Vanguard was in severe danger of losing.

Maybe I should try something. It couldn't hurt at this point, right? Matteo looked down at the fight below him. Velle was battling admirably, but even she couldn't hold off three opponents. Using blood magic possible only to a Sylph, she had sprouted wings from her back and taken flight, keeping all but the fire-using Lilith from being able to target her. As she dodged explosive blast after explosive blast, she continuously cast shield glyphs in an attempt to halt Renar and Unter in their tracks. All it did was slow them down. Renar swung his greatsword and Unter blasted with his bucklers, each shattering obstacle after obstacle. Velle shifted tactics, turning the barriers into reflect panels so that the men's blows began bouncing back at them.

But the extra second of focus required to make the switch cost Velle, and an explosion knocked her from the air. Back in zone one, Leon cast out a rope of light, catching Velle's ankle and dragging her away from their group before she could be damaged to the point where her suit locked up. Now a twenty-five-meter climb was all that separated Renar's Renegades from victory. Confident in having clinched their win, they rushed toward the ladder.

Matteo gulped and focused his scope on Vallen. He was currently pressing the silver-haired girl who had chided him at the written exam that morning. *I've never seen someone stand up to Vallen like that before—well, at least someone who didn't think they had some sort of power over him.* As far as Matteo knew, no one had legitimate power over Vallen. Admittedly, his world was a small one, but in that realm, Vallen's dominion was absolute.

A tiny voice spoke up in the back of his head: *This is your chance to prove your worth! You can still win this match and show Vallen you're useful!* But how? He fidgeted, wracking his brain. Below, Renar was about to reach the ladder. Okay, he had two options. First, fire his rifle straight down the ladder and hope he could keep them from ascending. However, Unter was large and dexterous enough with his four arms to climb the scaffolding of the tower. This meant he had to somehow cover all four sides, not just the normal ascent. His second option was to try to hit Sylette, knocking her out and allowing Vallen to race to the flag unimpeded. In an unassisted footrace, Vallen would outrun Renar. And with his elemental abilities aiding him, he would make short work of the remaining distance and be the first to grab a flag.

Alright, I help Vallen. He closed his left eye and gazed through the lens with his right. They were fighting in the square of the ruined village, burning and collapsed buildings to either side. It was a clean shot. Either he would hit Sylette, Vallen, or the ground. But if he missed the first shot, Sylette would be alerted to his attention. Another whispering fear said, *She already knows what you're doing. Haven't you realized she has this all planned out?*

Sylette dodged a glaive strike and the subsequent blast of fire that accompanied it. Vallen darted forward in the direction of the cruiser zone as she did, and for the moment, he was closer to their flag than she was. Sylette turned to follow, daggers materializing around her.

Matteo wasn't going to get a better, clearer shot than this. He let go of his fears along with his breath, and pulled the trigger. As he watched through the scope, Sylette's head was partially turned toward him, and he could have sworn she smiled right as he brought his finger back.

She leaped straight up, impossibly landing and balancing on a pair of daggers. The spirit bullet passed through the air where she had been milliseconds prior . . . and hit Vallen square in his back.

Oh . . . what irony. Guess I'm Voided.

Vallen tasted victory as he forced Sylette into an evasion that took her out of his way to their flag. He prepared to explode toward the ship using both earth and fire magic to propel his feet.

Then the spirit bullet hit him.

With his attention forward, he had no time to deploy his shield, no time to soften the blow. His suit took the full impact, locking down and driving the breath from his lungs. He hit the ground hard and could only stare at the sky as Sylette stood over him with a mocking smirk.

"My, how the mighty have *fallen*." It was a terrible pun, but if he could laugh, he probably would have. Maybe this was all a dream. Or, more pointedly, a nightmare. It wasn't every day his world got turned upside down. *Haha, guess that's a pun, too.*

"*Ceasefire*, I say. *Ceasefire immediately!*" came the booming voice of Major Reev. At least somebody had some sense, though he hadn't expected it to be her. Obviously, someone had messed up this day's events and needed to set them right: General Iolus rigging the match; Sylette, with her evil plot to undo him; and Matteo shooting him—again!

"I will now transfer control of the projectomic system to Steward Metellus who has a grave announcement. Please remain in your seats." Good, his father would set things straight. No way this upstart little girl would get away with dethroning him. Vallen craned his neck and wiggled his body until he could just barely see the VIP box. Metellus stood at its fore, a projectomic perched precariously on the rail to capture his words. He looked aged and weathered, more so than Vallen had ever seen before. In fact, he appeared ready to cast himself over the edge and be done with it all. Surely watching his adopted son lose a rigged match couldn't be that upsetting, could it?

"People of Darmatia, heed my voice. I regret to inform you," he paused, straining to find the strength to continue, "I regret to inform you that . . . that the pe . . . the peace . . . has been breached." He sputtered the final words and nearly collapsed before being hauled back to his seat by Admiral Contus, who returned to the mic in the steward's place.

"The steward is deeply troubled by the news that has just reached us. Airships and ground forces have breached the Theradas Neutrality Line to the north and are closing on Aldona Fortress. The Sarconian Empire is invading Darmatia. A dispatch will go out to the entire kingdom posthaste. All military forces here are to report to their wartime stations, cadets included. Lastly, please remain calm. That is all."

The Sarconian Empire is invading Darmatia. Six words, one simple sentence, the world *truly* turned upside down.

Panic ensued immediately.

Chapter 7

Risk and Reward

Two months previous,
Fulminos 25, 697 ABH
Sarconia, Imperial Seat of the Sarconian Empire

———◆———

"What if we regroup the remnants of the Eighth Fleet at the Novelas River? Shouldn't that be sufficient?"

"Haven't you been paying attention? There are *no* remnants! The entire Eighth Fleet *and* its commander, Rittermarschal Galran, perished with the fall of Varas Fortress."

"Enough about the Eighth Fleet! My corps of engineers and the Fifth and Ninth Panzcraft divisions are digging in on the Novelas River—without air support, I might add! We must divert a fleet to protect the defense works, or Rabban will chew right through them!"

"Who do you suggest we send? The First is tied up making sure Rabban doesn't sneak forces through Darmatia. The Second and Third are staring them down across Lake Lovare. The Fourth is engaged above the Great Forest, ensuring they don't flank us by sea. And the Fifth and Sixth are still driving back the Lusserians to the north. If we divert either, those barbarians will burn a swathe across our breadbasket provinces, leaving our croplands devastated. That leaves only the Seventh, which, mind you, is still undergoing repairs after escaping the same debacle that cost us the Eighth."

"Perhaps we're failing to consider the obvious alternative . . . offering to discuss terms of peace."

He had sat silently thus far, listening to the debating of the gathered senators, ministers, and generals. It was important to hear all perspectives before making a decision. However, some ideas were too foolhardy to even bear consideration. "There will be no peace talks, Minister of *Agriculture* Badenschiff," he stressed the word *agriculture*, reminding the bearer of the title of his proper place. "After all, having someone on their back foot and knowing they're on their back foot are two completely different things. If we attempt to open negotiations now, we will merely be acknowledging our weakness, and they shall press all the more forcefully upon our neck. The Second Air Fleet and my eldest son Vasuron will gradually depart Lake Lovare for the Novelas River so as to avoid the imperium becoming aware of their maneuver. Is that satisfactory?"

"Absolutely, Your Majesty."

"Please continue."

Those gathered resumed their droning and bickering. Some were useful; most were sycophants and oversized leeches sucking the last drops of blood from a once-great but now failing empire. To be sure, the Sarconian Empire was still a military and economic power to be reckoned with, but its glory and power had ripened on the vine and begun the gradual decay into rot and disease.

And who was the ruler of this mass of grapes slowly fermenting into obscurity? None other than he, Emperor Sychon Artorios, a peerless mage reduced to a tired, old man. Granted, he was still the mightiest sorcerer in the empire, and his age had nothing to do with his exhaustion. In fact, he was only forty-five, with short black hair barely streaked with grey and a stalwart build to match his command of the magical arts. Rather, he was sick of fighting: fighting the Lusserians as a youth; fighting his brothers, now deceased, for the very throne on which he sat; and, at present, fighting his forefathers' never-ending war against Rabban.

So why did he yet refuse to consider peace? Because it was a fool's settlement. Within decades either he or the Supreme Secretary of Rabban—or their successors, or some addlebrained border guard with an itchy trigger finger— would reignite the conflict, and they'd be right back where they were currently. *Better,* Sychon thought, *to keep at it till the end and let it truly* be *the end, one way or another.* And the parasites and those few of value before him would remain with the ship till port or watery grave. He would see to that personally.

The twilight sun slanting through the massive Senate windows echoed his weariness. While those assembled below his dais could barely see out the glass, the angle from his throne of purest marble afforded him a view of the adjacent palace and the royal air field beyond that. There, the Seventh Fleet was undergoing repairs day and night while its commander, one-eyed Rittermarschal Ober Valescar, sat without speaking in one of the chairs nearest Sychon. Around those large landmarks loomed skyscrapers tinted orange by the sun's last rays. Small air skimmers, civilian and military alike, darted ceaselessly between them. And even farther out he could just catch a glimpse of the Balastine Wall, the innermost of Sarcon's two massive defensive edifices. The outer, the Humbrad Wall, couldn't be seen past the hundred-meter height of its closer brother.

Sychon turned his attention back to his advisors. They were seated in ascending tiers to his left and right, the center walk left open for petitioners of either the Senate or himself. Those of higher standing, whether or not their position reflected their value, sat closer to the floor and to him. Those in the eaves or at the far side of the immense chamber either did not speak or had to shout to be heard in the unlikely event the Speaker, who organized such things, gave them the floor. Such procedure did not affect him. The emperor would speak whenever he wished, regardless of whom he interrupted.

Why did they need to yell in the modern era of projectomics and other sound-enhancing technologies and magic? Sarconian tradition. The Senate room was devoid of mechanical or arcane enhancements, the better for its users to be forced to be strong enough to be heard or listened to. Supplicants, or even senators whose point of view or pleas were frowned upon, would often be shouted down by the assembly. Once again, such menial practices did not apply to him—interposing on the emperor was a good way to find oneself executed or, worse, sent to the front.

Currently the foreign minister, Faltro Gustavus, was speaking. Like Rittermarschal Valescar, he held a position of authority near Sychon's seat of power. "We should attempt to elicit the aid of Darmatia. How many times in the past have they sided with Rabban to balance the scales when we had the upper hand? Surely they don't wish to see a Lozaria dominated by those equalist swine!"

The only other man seated on the dais with Sychon, albeit on a lower tier, rebuked Gustavus, "You forget, Minister, that we are responsible for ending their precious royal line, a royal line whose progenitor, Darmatus, they worship like a god. Furthermore, Metellus is a pacifist. He would sooner let Nemare fall to ruin than be the one to plunge his people into a war. Nay, Darmatia would rather see Lozaria perish than come to our aid."

"Apologies, Grand Marschal. I spoke in haste."

"See that you fully think through your ideas before releasing them into this room. We daren't waste His Majesty's time." The astute voice of Grand Marschal Konig Zaratus spoke from the depths of his majestic helm. Its visage was one of a dragwrym, the most powerful beast to walk the continent and even a match for some airships in flight. He also wore the remaining full plate of his station, his taloned gauntlets grasping the chair from which he guarded his emperor. Red and gold lines and whorls crisscrossed the armor and the magnificent sheathed longsword that stood stalwartly against the seatback.

The grand marschal held his current position of honor in the room as he was the commander of the Sarconian Army and, therefore, second in command of the empire behind Sychon himself. Below him were the rittermarschals, such as Valescar, the leaders of the imperial air fleets and their associated ground forces. And beneath them rested the various admirals, generals, and support staff that constructed the upper echelon of the military. The civilian chain of command included the Senate and department ministers, who answered to Sychon and Zaratus and were on even keel with the rittermarschals when matters of state were involved.

Sychon shifted uncomfortably on his throne, the length of the strategic planning meeting and the oppressive weight of his purple robes grating on his last nerve. *All of this is a waste of time—a necessary waste, but a waste nonetheless.* Of course, if he wasn't at this war assembly, he'd be affixing his seal to endless amounts of litigation, keeping his children from killing each other in an endless battle to succeed him, or spending time looking after his consorts to ensure that *this* one was pleased with her lot or *that* one hadn't been plotting with "General X" and "Minister Y" to depose him.

Some philosopher or another had once remarked that "it was lonely at the top." Truer words had never been spoken. A merchant puts away his abacus and books and becomes a normal man. A pilot might exit his ship and return home to his ordinary family. But an emperor? An emperor is defined by his occupation. Everyone everywhere knows who you are at all times. There is no escape, your fate inextricably tied to the title you have now obtained.

He blinked away those morose thoughts and attempted to refocus on the discussion before him. The minister of finance was now discussing the need to take another loan from the Ascendant Bank, belonging to the neutral Hues, to pay the ever-growing heap of expenses from the conflict. Broaching the subject of money led to an interjection by the senator of the Eastern Reaches, who complained that he needed more funds to hire mercenaries to protect trade routes in his province as the fighting drew closer. And this made the minister of the interior recollect that the imperial road system was in desperate need of repair because of overuse by military maneuvering. The war was everything, and yet it seemed all their problems stemmed from the war.

At that moment, one of his aides, several of whom stood in recesses behind his dais from which they could enter and exit the doors to the rear hallway, approached and whispered in his ear. "Your Majesty, a man identified as Ritterbruder First Class Vahn Badenschiff is attempting to gain entry to the Senate Chamber. He should have been denied access to the building itself without prior invitation, but the guards at the front aren't responding to our summons. One of his subordinates belonging to the regular army, a Hans Ulrich, is also with him. Should we turn him away?"

It took only seconds to place the name; Vahn was the son of Minister of Agriculture Badenschiff, the fool who had proposed peace talks minutes prior. He was also a member of the Ritter Order, the special chain of command that reported directly to him. "No, let's see what he has to say. It may be exactly what this meeting needs." *And provide an excellent opportunity to further chastise his wayward father,* he added silently.

Less than a minute later, Vahn strode confidently up the crimson-carpeted walkway to stand before Sychon. At his heels, considerably out of place and all the more visibly nervous for it, was Hans Ulrich, his eyes rapidly darting hither and yon. Both of their uniforms were in filthy tatters, their armor scored black and dented, some pieces absent altogether. Hans appeared less than fully nourished, though still healthy and fit for duty by military standards. However, despite his upright posture and self-assuredness, Vahn was the worse for wear of the two. His eyes were sunken, the skin around them black like pitch. Everywhere else his flesh was sagging and sallow, signs of extreme malnourishment, and his hands and forearms bore burn marks and cracks as if seared by intense flame and heat.

Most abnormal of all was the smell that emanated from him, a sickly odor of decay more at place on a corpse than a living man.

"Vahn, thank goodness you've made it back safely. But what's wrong with your skin and hands? You should be seeing a doctor, not—"

"Silence, Minister. Their audience is with the emperor, not with you." The grand marschal stood and cut off the interruption of Vahn's father with a wave of a mighty gauntlet. "Ritterbruder First Class Badenschiff, months ago you were tasked with the infiltration of Beiras to acquire information on enemy technology crucial to the war. You were assigned a squad and the equipment necessary to fulfill your task. Since one month ago, you have been completely incommunicado, missing all of your scheduled check-ins to the point that your situation even reached my attention and was dismissed as a complete mission failure. Now you show up like beggars in front of your emperor—no squad, no stolen documents, fouling up his chambers with the stench of death—and you don't even have the deference to kneel. What have you to say for yourself?"

From the start, Hans had been prostrate on the ground, as was expected of a low-born soldier granted an impossible audience with their liege. Vahn, though of slightly more noble stock, was also expected to observe this practice, but here he was, gaze full of arrogance and staring at Sychon as if sizing up a potentially useful tool or instrument.

His reply was curt, like he was speaking to a child who should know better. "I bend to no one."

"Your verdict, Majesty?" Zaratus uttered the question as a growl, his disgust evident.

Sychon considered for the briefest of instants, "You return to me empty handed, having wasted my resources and shamed our empire. Then you have the audacity to disrespect me by coming here uninvited and failing to show your leader the proper respect. If all our soldiers were to do the same, our nation would collapse within the day. Execute them, Grand Marschal, and see that the guards who let them as far as my door share the same fate."

"Absolutely, Your Majesty." At his signal, a dozen guards burst in from side passages where they, along with aides and other servants, waited for just such an eventuality. They quickly surrounded the offenders, Hans cowering and sobbing, Vahn with a bemused but unconcerned look at his face. Clearly something in his travels had scrambled his sensibilities. A pity, considering the promise the boy had shown.

"Please have mercy, Your Majesty! He's just returned from a long mission and isn't in his right mind! Spare my son!" Minister Badenschiff was on his feet, frantically running down the steps toward the walkway. He glanced left and right, attempting to find some ally among his colleagues to aid him.

An amusing sentiment, Sychon thought, *but you will find no help. My word is law, and none dare oppose it.* He gestured at the racing bureaucrat with two fingers and two of the soldiers peeled off to arrest his progress and drag him toward the gold doors at the fore of the room.

Vahn finally seemed to recognize his circumstances, but rather than begging for Sychon's forgiveness, like his father, he merely sighed, "I had hoped you would be wise enough to avoid such a tedium. Is it no longer proper to bow and introduce yourself when greeting someone of greater power and standing? Do you instead now greet your betters with the blade, as might an assassin skulking in the night?"

To say Sychon was stunned would be the understatement of a lifetime. "I am the emperor of the Sarconian Empire. Who are you that I should be the one to bend the knee?"

Diseased gums spread wide in a condescending smile. "I am Sarcon, your king. This is my city, and that is my throne, but perhaps we can come to an arrangement on those counts."

Around the condemned, the gathered assembly muttered and gasped in shock. Zaratus grabbed his sheathe and drew steel, bulling his way into the circle of guards. "I can stand their blaspheming no longer. These apostates will die where they stand; their blood shan't disturb the crimson carpet beneath us in the slightest."

Sychon tensed as the being calling himself Sarcon pushed Hans flat on the floor, raising his other hand as he did so. "I agree, but I believe it will be slightly more difficult to scrub *you* out of the marble."

At that instant, Rittermarschal Valescar leapt out of his seat, casting out the spools of metal coils at his waist and bidding them wrap around the grand marschal and tug him free of the cordon of bodies. *You can always trust Valescar to spot trouble before anyone else.* Sychon threw up a gravitational distortion, his unique magic, in front of him.

It was over in a flash. The two guards hauling Minister Badenschiff turned at the noise of a thousand clashing razor blades, their eyes bulging as they dropped to their knees and emptied their stomachs at the sight of the grisly fate they barely escaped. Sychon took a moment to register that he was whole before checking his own urge to vomit. Zaratus sat on the marble steps, coated in gore and gazing in wonder at the stubby hilt that hung uselessly in his tattered glove. Valescar, farther away, let his hands drop, and the steel cords in the air dropped with them.

At the epicenter stood Vahn . . . or perhaps it *was* Sarcon after all. Hans slowly stood up, wide eyed but acting as though he had experienced this carnage before. Yet most of those gathered had never seen combat, let alone a bloodbath. Some fled, others ducked behind their desks, still more sobbed and lost their lunches. Only the sternest gazed on while picking pieces from their clothes, some flecks of the evisceration having been flung as far as the top rungs and ceiling of the chamber.

Though Vahn—Sarcon—and Hans were perfectly clean, the scene around them was anything but. Nothing was left of the ten guards who had been standing there moments prior. Everything they had been was now red paste coating carpet, marble flooring, desks, and people beyond a one-meter radius around the caster. A rhythmic *plopping* sound could be briefly heard as blood cast high into the air came coursing back, and puddles formed wherever the flow found low ground. Up above and on the walls, spear hafts and chinks of armor could be seen sticking like shrapnel from the beautiful paintings and frescoes that had once adorned them. Now nothing was visible but these new protrudings and wide swathes of crimson staining.

The thought of shrapnel caused Sychon to gaze around the room once more. Sure enough, there were more victims. The minister of the interior no longer needed to worry about the roads; an iron boot had crushed his skull against the table behind his seat. Elsewhere, the senator from the Eastern Reaches that had needed mercenaries got his fill of spear tips and sword blades. More had survived than not, but the casualty count was still severe. One man had wrought this—a single man with one spell and no invocation or weapon whatsoever.

He checked behind him. The throne was in pieces. Everywhere his distortion had not reversed or diverted the flow of the attack was gouged and coated in red liquid and white bone. *He didn't just target his attackers,* Sychon concluded, *he targeted me as well.*

What did this man want? Why did he come here? He didn't attack immediately, but defended himself viciously when attacked. Which meant that he, Sarcon, came here to talk; this destruction was secondary and had not been intended.

After a minute, during which Sarcon did not take his eyes from him, Sychon discovered his voice. "Why have you come here . . . Sarcon?" Verbalizing the impossible name resulted in the briefest hesitation. "And if you are, in fact, *the* Sarcon, how can you be here? Sarcon died seven centuries ago. Him being alive now is unthinkable."

The specter—for that is what he was if he was, indeed, Sarcon—took several steps through the muck until he stood at the foot of the dais. "The first is easier to answer than the second, but all that matters is that I am a powerful mage whose soul is currently inhabiting the container of Vahn, a soldier of my empire. I *am* Sarcon, and would like for you to refer to me as such, but if you secretly believe that to be false, it matters little to me."

Freed from his captors, Minister Badenschiff rushed toward the body of his son. "What have you done with him, you fiend! Release my son at once!" Sychon held up a hand, raising a distortion that stopped him before he could pass Hans, who had approached cautiously to five paces behind Sarcon. He waved at the two remaining guards, whose composure had partially returned.

"The minister's presence is no longer necessary. Please remove him." Sychon waited until Vahn's father, wailing and screaming the entire way, had been dragged away, the doors booming shut behind him. "You really aren't Vahn Badenschiff anymore?"

"No, but I would have you tell his father that the arrangement we reached was mutual. I was given this body, willingly, to accomplish a task we both dreamed of achieving."

"And what is that task?" Sychon gestured at the ruined room around them. "Depose me? Take back *your* empire? As you saw, your attack didn't work on me or my stronger servants, of which I have many more. Even with your power, I doubt you could achieve either."

"You are correct in your assumption, but that is not my goal. My attack on your men was a demonstration; my attack on you a test. Those peons served their purpose: *my* power was made clear and my words are now being taken seriously. You passed your test and proved *your* power and worth to me." A crumbling finger pointed at Sychon, emphasizing his statement.

"Ye talk in circles, warlock." Rittermarschal Valescar, in his mid-fifties with an eye lost in some past bout and now covered with a shining patch, had helped the grand marschal to his feet and moved to flank Sarcon. His twin rapiers remained in their sheaths on his back, but his hands hovered over his loops of cabling. "After yer display, I'm itchin' ta fight, so if ye don't want ta speak plain, I'd be happy ta force the words out of ya."

Sarcon turned to regard the newcomer. "You're another with whom I'm greatly impressed. You read my intention and reacted splendidly. Why, you even had time to save the one at whom the center of my spell was targeted."

"Spendin' lots of time on the battlefield teaches a man a thing or two. Less stalling, more speakin'." The rope unwound of its own accord, coiling through the air like a thing alive as he twitched his hands.

"Very well then." Sarcon's attention fell back on Sychon. "I came here to offer you a simple deal. The survival of my, well, *our* empire, and the conquest of Rabban and the continent in exchange for the retrieval of something very precious to me."

"What might that be?" Sychon replied instantly.

"What every man holds most dear: his own flesh and blood." Sarcon leaned in, rancid breath and the cloying smell of decay growing stronger. "In other words, my original body."

He considered the statement for a moment, those still present gazing on with thoughtful wariness. When Sychon finally spoke, his voice was soft but forceful. "I've had many witch doctors, proselytizers, and even my own magic scientists come to me offering some absolute, surefire means to win the war. Some were given funding, allowed to ply their theories and research. Others were turned away immediately, their plans foolhardy and imbecilic. But all had two things in common: their ploys came with a catch and they all, ultimately, disappointed me. Those who disappoint me rarely live long lives, and those who attempt to cheat me have an even shorter tenure in this world. So, tell me plainly what the cost of your snake oil is and prove to me, after what you've just done, why you should leave this room alive."

His ultimatum was greeted with a toothy grin. "You wear the mantle of emperor well. You exude control, say the right things, and keep your people in line using an iron fist. Yet I sense that you tire of your mask—"

Valescar growled at the thinly veiled disrespect and made ready to silence the impudent speaker, but Sychon waved him down. Sarcon didn't even register the exchange. "—and, more pointedly, of this ceaseless conflict that does not allow you to drop that façade. What I offer is a swift end to this war and the means for you and your descendants to never see another."

Sychon leaned his head, heavy with the golden and gem-studded circlet of his office, against his open palm and arm. "I tire of your endless dissembling, Sarcon. What I say or think is not the concern of anyone within my empire. This is your final opportunity to sway me . . . You will not get another."

The smile of the possessed body was not deterred. "I had hoped to spare you a discussion of the details, especially in light of recent events and the . . . diminishment of your attendants, but it appears that is exactly what you wish for. As you know, history marks me as having died seven hundred years past. However, my demise was not absolute. Those who defeated me: Darmatus, Rabban, and the mages of the Eliade and Sylph, sealed me in stasis on the grounds of Har'muth."

"Your presence here, such as it is, indicates that this seal was not a permanent solution."

"Correct, yet my original form, my body and much of my true power, is still locked away. Happenstance led Vahn and his men to my doorstep at a time when my chains were weak enough that my soul alone might break free, and he and I struck a bargain: his flesh as a chamber for my escape in exchange for my aid in the salvation of his beloved homeland."

The story, if true, was intriguing. Here before Sychon was an immortal Terran sorcerer, potentially Sarcon himself, who had managed to learn unheard of soul-swapping magic to allow him to escape an ancient ritual cast by the most powerful mages on the continent. And, if the tale wasn't false, he was also infinitely more dangerous than even his devastation of their surroundings suggested. "Now you attempt to strike the same bargain once more—an empire for another shell, this one your own. If you have the might that you claim, why do you need my assistance to reclaim what's yours?"

Sarcon spread his arms, the rags clinging to his flesh barely covering the desiccation and rot beneath. His muscles were atrophied, his eyes red with burst vessels, and his hair thinning rapidly, some falling lightly to the burgundy tile below. All of this, in addition to Sychon's initial observations, led to the same conclusion: Sarcon's body was suffering from men'ar imbalance syndrome, often shortened by specialists to MIS. It was a condition that occurred when a being had too little or too much men'ar, spiritual energy exuded by the soul and carried by the bloodstream, for an extended period of time. The result, should equilibrium not be restored by adjusting the energy level or container size, was the gradual degradation of the victim and, eventually, death. Of course, this was completely unchartered territory for Sychon or any medical mage; a successful soul swap had never been performed, let alone studied to see if MIS might occur because of it.

"As you can see, the size of my soul and the knowledge it contains are too much for the vessel I am currently occupying. It is like an infant trying to shove a massive triangular block into a very small, very circular hole. Either the opening breaks, or the block does." Sarcon paused, cackling dryly at his own lackluster attempt at humor and metaphor. "Suffice to say, it's not an arrangement that will work for much longer. And, of course, that's if I do nothing."

He pointed his palms, already raised, at the emperor. Sychon felt his body tense, intuitively expecting an attack, but it never came. Valescar, beside him, stared in disgust at the mangled limbs. "They're cracked and fallin' apart, like an overused and rusted blade that still ain't been retired."

"Exactly, my dear rittermarschal," Sarcon pronounced the foreign term perfectly, but that was the least of the surprises Sychon was experiencing today.

The tattered arms fell back to Sarcon's sides as he continued, "If I use magic unfamiliar to this body, it attempts to reject my commands with a physical reaction—much like an auto-immune disorder. The result is damage to the host body, which further shortens the time before I need a new container."

Sychon found himself intrigued by the possibilities this man presented. *Perhaps the technique can be taught or copied?* Many of his daily headaches would evaporate if he had the reins of immortality that Sarcon claimed to possess. "Why not transfer to a new vessel when the old is used up?"

The failing husk shrugged, shaking its head. "Alas, the process is only a smooth one when the current resident is willing. Otherwise, it requires a great deal of force, potentially resulting in the destruction of the shell before dominance is achieved if the souls are not compatible. I may be able to perform this feat once in my present state, but no more."

So, quite a few rules and risks were involved with the magic in question. Sychon filed the information away as something to have his magic scientists investigate at length. He nodded at Sarcon empathetically. "Which is why you need your native flesh. You can't use your full abilities or truly be immortal without it. And apparently it is guarded in such a way that can't be overcome with your existing power."

"Exactly. The tomb where it rests lies deep within the dead zone of Har'muth, obscured by many defensive enchantments and maintained by the Eliade, who will surely reinforce it once word of my escape reaches their island of Essarus."

Leaning forward, Sychon steepled his fingers and narrowed his gaze. "To defeat such a stronghold as you describe without modern magtech—our airships, cannons, and weapons—would require thousands of mages and soldiers. You're asking me to barter with Darmatia just so I can divert these much-needed resources away from the war. Surely this isn't how you intended us to win this conflict?"

Steel and fervor crept into Sarcon's voice, "This is *exactly* how we'll win this war! I don't expect you to parley with those traitorous descendants of my foolish brother . . . I expect you to crush them! Defeat them, grant me my body, and I shall give you what rulers and leaders since my time have coveted and sought after in vain: Elysium."

On the lower steps of the dais, the grand marschal snapped out of his stupor, bolting upright with a cry. "That's nothing but a myth!" Elsewhere in the chamber, those bureaucrats and officers still remaining echoed his outburst with whispers and shouts, ranging from "Impossible, it doesn't exist!" to "But if it's real, consider the possibilities!" Valescar mused silently, his interest conveyed by the mere fact that his cables no longer hovered threateningly through the air.

As Sychon explained to Sarcon earlier, every individual who had proposed plans for ending the war had failed him. No small number of these had been researchers or archaeologists searching after Elysium, the stone of legend, promising that if they located it, defeating Rabban would be child's play. None succeeded. Some died along the way in disease-infested jungles or by the jaws of carnivorous mountain predators. Others gave up or exceeded the time limit imposed upon them, resulting in similar demises. And then, even if the stone had been found, legends stated that only seven existed, and after using one, it would disappear to the farthest corner of the world. Furthermore, the user's soul, his lifespan and source of magical power, was absorbed in proportion to the difficulty of granting the wish asked of them. Sychon had always postulated that a desire like winning the war or ruling the continent would likely cost a man his entire soul. Needless to say, if he had a shard of Elysium, it would not be *him* using it.

Sychon waved his right arm, and the room fell silent. "How have you come to possess this Elysium? Our best sources of information about the stone are nothing more than legends, and even those say that the seven pieces were separated and split between the nations of Lozaria, their hiding places not recorded, and those that distributed them killed to prevent them from ever being used again. If this story is true, what you declare before me now is nothing more than a fairy tale and a total waste of my time."

A moment of silence flitted through the twilight as the sun's last rays spread fire across the enraptured audience and grisly scene. Sarcon spoke soothingly into the stillness, "To be honest, I know not where the other six pieces of Elysium are, but I am intimately familiar with the stone that was used to seal me away for the last seven centuries. It lies in my tomb, waiting for you, Emperor Sychon Artorios, to claim it."

I wouldn't even need to use the Elysium, would I? Sychon thought through the prospects. If he were in sole possession of the only known fragment of Elysium in the world, it would serve as a massive deterrent to any person, or nation, that would dare challenge him. Even the Sylph, Hues, or Eliade, who had long ignored the Terran wars raging at the center of the continent, would have to give him heed. With the stone of legend, Sychon would literally control the world.

However, that would be the end result of a long and arduous journey. First, Sarcon could be lying—he wouldn't be the first petitioner to propose a foolproof plan, only to have it turn out to be smoke and mirrors. Second, the military situation could in no way support the endeavor.

Valescar voiced Sychon's concerns before he could himself. "Yer Majesty, we're barely hangin' on with just Rabban in the East. We can't start a second front with Darmatia on the fool's chance there might be some mythical rock at the end. It's simply not sustainable."

The grand marschal, fully recovered and engaged, added, "Furthermore, it would be a bloodbath. Flanking Darmatia over the Phar Sea would take too long and play right into the strengths of their mobile air fleet. Even worse, since Aldona Fortress was built two centuries ago, we haven't been able to make any progress through the Theradas Pass. Even with our magtech advancements, I don't see that changing. And even if you've been sealed away for hundreds of years, surely the Great Divide existed in your original time as well, did it not?" He directed this question of intelligence at Sarcon, as though he'd forgotten his near fatal misstep earlier.

But the mage took the dissent and query in stride. "Actually, Hans and I weren't just twiddling our thumbs on our way here. He has brought me up to speed on your military capabilities and the state of the world at large. As a result, I believe we've found a solution to the problems you pose. Please elaborate, Hans."

Hans started, as though still shocked by the evisceration he'd witnessed or surprised that he would be called upon to speak in this hall of notables. He looked around nervously before beginning to speak. "You . . . Your Majesty, thank you for seeing us. I . . . I never thought we . . . we'd get this far, so I . . . . I'm not exactly sure how to start. Oh, thank the Veneer we're not dead—not directed at you, Your Majesty. I know you were just doing the proper thing when you decided to execute us. Not . . . not that having all your guards killed was the better outcome, just—"

Zaratus moved forward to silence his stammering, but Sychon responded instead. "Calm yourself, Lieutenant Ulrich. You've come a long way and fought hard for me and your empire. These are . . . unusual circumstances. Be calm and speak."

As Sychon spoke, Hans calmed, to the point that he was able to stop stammering and talk clearly. "As the grand marschal noted, the Great Divide is an ancient and immense barrier of mountains, forests, and mists that is impossible to navigate except in five places: the Phar Sea, the Theradas Pass, Lake Lovare, the Nareck Pass, and the Es Sea on the other side of the continent. Retaking

Varas Fortress in the Nareck Pass would be difficult because of the stress it would place on our supply lines. Crossing Lake Lovare would be nigh impossible since it's guarded by Rabban and has freak storms and weather patterns. And crossing the Phar Sea has already been ruled out. This leaves us with Aldona Fortress and Darmatia as our best option. If we conquer the kingdom, we both open a second front with Rabban, and retrieve Lord Sarcon's body along with the Elysium."

Sychon ignored Hans's use of noble title for addressing Sarcon. "And you would stake your life on the existence of this Elysium, Lieutenant Ulrich?"

The young man gulped but nodded his head in assent. However, Grand Marschal Zaratus still had a rebuttal, "Even if the Elysium is real and even if taking Darmatia gives us an easy route into the industrial heart of the imperium, we still have to contend with Aldona Fortress to do so. We haven't the time or resources for a siege, and even that option is impossible since the construct spans the entirety of the Theradas Pass and they can resupply using their air fleet. That means we have to swiftly overwhelm their defenses, which isn't just improbable—it can't be done."

"Rittermarschal Valescar, do you concur with the grand marschal?"

"Yes, Yer Majesty. We'd somehow have ta deal with both the Darmatian air fleet and the fortress itself in order ta break through the pass. But once we're through that chokepoint, the rest of the country shud fall easily enough." He mimed smashing the fortress with his gauntlet to illustrate his point.

"I believe we have the solution to that problem as well," Hans interjected timidly, all eyes on him. He turned to Sarcon, who began where he left off, "As I said before, this body is failing. But before it fades, it still has the capacity to work one final, powerful incantation, the likes of which has not been seen in this world since the Battle of Har'muth. I guarantee that it can bring down this barrier that Darmatia has placed in our way. Afterwards this shell will completely deteriorate, so I require that you find me a replacement of strong magical potential. Do these things, and Darmatia, Rabban, the continent, and the Elysium will be ours."

"And what if, after all that you've told me, I refuse your offer?"

Sarcon smiled wide, his face like that of a cackling skull. "Then I shall use that very same magic on this building and make it into a tomb for us all."

Before anyone could react, either to flee or to attack the source of the threat, Sychon began laughing, a deep, throaty chuckle that continued for nearly a minute before he finally regained control of himself. *Yes! THIS was living!* How he had missed this feeling, the promise of danger, yes, but also the possibility of a change to the monotony that he had lived for so many years. Yes, *this* was the feeling of hope.

"You drive a hard bargain, Sarcon, but you have a deal. Grand Marschal, take command of the First Fleet at Arhus and await my arrival—that shall be the staging area. We will be joined there by Rittermarschals Valescar and Titania with the Seventh and Fifth Fleets. General Bergan, ensure that at least five panzcraft divisions and supporting engineering units reach the rendezvous point within the month. General Kinsley, begin moving all reserve mage battalions and infantry corps still in the city toward the border. We launch our assault in precisely two months. Gentlemen, we have a war to start and a war to win. All hail the Sarconian Empire!"

"ALL HAIL THE SARCONIAN EMPIRE!" Came back the resounding echo as those still gathered rushed to execute their orders. A new hand had been dealt, and the game continued. Sychon's chest surged with a feeling of elation, a premonition that his fortunes might ascend yet a little further.

However, as he passed his eyes over Sarcon, who was smirking with a hint of glee at the flurry of activity he had coerced, he realized that his actions must also be tempered with caution. No reward was without its risk, no prize without its price. Surely this devil's bargain would be no different.

Chapter 8

New Meets Old

Two days after Sarconian border violation,
Hetrachia 2, 697 ABH
Airspace above Aldona Fortress

———◆◆◆———

"Is this your first time flying on an airship, Matteo?"

"I . . . it is."

"And despite your lack of issue with being on the flag tower, I'm guessing you don't exactly enjoy heights?"

"What makes you think that, Leon?"

"The death grip you have on that railing. I can assure you this vessel is perfectly safe and that we won't crash, even if you let go." Leon smiled placatingly at his squadmate and gestured to a spot next to him on the aged couch of the bridge's rear tactical salon. Matteo let go, the blood slowly returning to his white knuckles, and made his way across the metal decking to the proffered seat as though afraid his next footfall would break through onto the deck below.

"Leave him be, Leon. If he has both hands wrapped around that pole, he can't shoot anyone in the back . . . I think." Vallen was fully reclined on the upholstery, his feet crossed on the tactical projector before him that likely hadn't seen use in years. A deep layer of dust coated it, and the panel at its side hung empty, the illyrium that once powered it long since scavenged for use elsewhere. Were it functional, the display would show the real-time development of any aerial or ground combat using magically energized particles and data collected from sensors on the outside of the craft.

He's like a boerwulf with a bone, Leon thought with a sigh. Just like the large desert carnivores, Vallen hadn't let up on Matteo since the botched match and the distressing news and rapid deployment that immediately followed. Because of the circumstances, the contest had been declared a draw, but to the prodigal Triaron, the result couldn't be viewed as anything other than a loss.

"It was an accident. We would've lost either way, so don't fault him for trying," Leon said, trying to ease tensions before they inflamed again.

Something shuddered beneath their feet, and everyone in the squad looked down worriedly as an engineer mage, commonly shortened to engimage, covered in synth-oil and grease rushed onto the bridge from the entryway Matteo had just vacated.

"An accident is something that happens once. If it happens twice, we call that a mistake, a failure. You're not the one who's been on the receiving end of all the friendly fire, so stay out of it. Besides, it's as good as his fault we're on this rust bucket." The fleet assignments for the cadets had come down last minute by the only official body available at the time: the exam committee. Their poor performance, along with Vallen's bombing of the written exam, probably had some small effect on their current surroundings. However, the exam committee was headed by the commandant, and that meant that General Iolus had the final say on their shipping out orders. Though Vallen hadn't mentioned any incident to him directly, Leon had gathered from other sources that the Triaron had irked the egoist far more than normal. As a result, it could be concluded that Vallen was significantly more to blame for their situation than Matteo.

The "rust bucket" in question was the *Feywind*, which was probably a good ship in her time but had long since passed her expiration date. While the rest of the fleet was cruising out in front at twenty-five hundred meters above the ground, the *Feywind* was drifting in their wake at twenty-two hundred meters and was gradually being left behind. Originally a heavy cruiser with a large, state-of-the-art weapons suite, progress had eclipsed her, and most of her armament had been removed. Now she was a clunky, almost derelict rectangle, approximately three hundred meters by one hundred meters, that served as a refueling and supply depot for the other airships.

"Don't blame the Professor for your own screw ups, Vallen. I had you beat from the start, and the Sarconians were the only thing that saved you from complete humiliation." Renar, dressed as they all were in blue dress uniforms trimmed with red, sauntered up to the salon, an arrogant smirk gracing his face.

Following him were Lilith and Unter, who plopped down onto the seats opposite Vallen's team along with their leader.

Velle, snuggling up to Vallen on his right, made a dismissive wave with her arm. "Are you kidding? You didn't even have the guts to face Val. In fact, you let that silver-haired harpy do all the work *and* fight him in your place while you came after me—though I guess even a fool like you can be brave when it's three on one." She stuck her tongue out at him, prompting Renar to rise from his seat before being restrained by Unter.

"Blue boy's right, Renar. Even Daddy couldn't save you if you started a fight on a military ship in wartime. But your total inability to come up with a decent plan aside, where is your little strategist? She doesn't seem to be lurking behind you like usual." Though Vallen pretended his usual sarcastic nonchalance, Leon could tell that his friend was actually interested in Sylette Farkos. Velle could as well, and she directed a silent pout in Vallen's direction. Of course, whether that interest was merely the Triaron's normal observance of attractive females or some modicum of actual respect, he could not say.

A strange look crossed Renar's face, and he pointed at the wide glass windows at the front of the bridge. "She's over there, mumbling to herself. Something about 'What are they doing?' or 'Why would he—?' and so on. Hasn't been the same since Admiral Contus announced the invasion."

"So, is she one menja fruit short of a bushel, or actually worried that the Sarconians can take down Aldona?" Leon interjected before Vallen could come back with his own snide remark.

It was Unter who spoke up, breaking his typical silence, "Just frightened, no crazy. Concern should we all have." His Terran sentence structure was a bit off, but Leon understood his meaning all the same. For Hue males, such mistakes were more than common, given the minimal education those in the lower classes received unless they left the Ascendancy. But maybe that was to be expected in a female-dominated society. *Something to ponder another time.*

"There's no way in Oblivion them Sarcs make it through Theradas Pass." The voice belonged to the vessel's captain, a grizzled old man that everyone simply referred to as "Cappie." As they had come aboard, some of the crew had told them that Cappie was once a pirate and *Feywind* his personal vessel before it was pressed into Darmatian service. Of course, those very same crewmen also said he ate illyrium and drank unprocessed oil, so they probably weren't the most reliable of sources. "Now get outta my tactical booth and go be useless somewhere else. Void command, dumping all these cadets on me at the last minute." He grumbled the last statement as he walked away, his left leg, though concealed by his pant leg, clacking like it was made of wood.

As soon as the group rose, two more engimages hustled onto the deck with a crate and began unpacking equipment into the salon. Leon saw bunches of cable, some sidearms most likely intended for the bridge crew, and a few illyrium fuel crystals. Perhaps they intended to repair the projector? *Probably pointless,* he considered. *If Feywind sees combat in her condition, the battle is as good as lost.* As if to confirm his musings, the shuddering below resumed and increased in volume. Cappie turned from his seat at the center of the room, barking orders, and the two engimages, along with the one who'd come up earlier, disappeared back out the door.

"Are you absolutely sure the ship won't sink?" Matteo asked glumly as they took the left walkway around the sunken bridge pit filled with deck officers, machinery, and displays. Almost everything there, from the technology to the people, looked secondhand, and in many places a black goop appeared to have been mashed on to hold things together. Everything glowed with the yellow tint of illyrium, the magic stone that powered the vessel and all the devices on it.

"Do you want an honest answer, or the answer that will make you feel better?" Leon replied, knowing neither would quell Matteo's anxiety. To be perfectly frank, he was having doubts himself. When they reached the large panoramic windows that ran in a semicircle across the front of the enclosed bridge from floor to ceiling, Leon observed that the glass was covered in grime and cracked in several places. Not so much that the roaring air outside could break through, but enough to be concerning. And the metal frames connecting the glass segments were little better, some rusting and others missing screws and bolts entirely.

"On second thought, I don't need to know. I'm just going to sit down and close my eyes." *He must have seen the same things I did,* Leon mused as Matteo sank to the deck. The rest of the group ignored him, moving to one of the cleaner windows a few meters from Sylette, who was leaning on a bronzed guide rail beneath the viewport without taking her eyes off the distant horizon. Leon turned his own gaze to follow hers, trying to puzzle out what had her so vexed.

In the near distance, passing in and out of the occasional puffy clouds before them, was the rest of the Darmatian air fleet. It was nothing short of a magnificent work of art. Dozens of ships of all classes sparkled with the iridescence of their metal curves and bristling armament. The backwash from their hover and propulsion drives painted a tapestry of rainbow hues across the sky, and a multitude of banners and pennants streamed from their upper decks. And about them all was the soft glow of magic energy: pulsing yellow illyrium converters, pale blue from charged lume generators sprouting up like flowers, and charged red electric and thermal energy cascading through pipes toward the engines and weapon systems.

They flew in a V-formation, with lighter craft restraining their graceful fleetness at the wings and lumbering dreadnoughts in the center. Carriers, little skiffs and hoverjets surrounding them like wasps, hung to the rear, and even farther behind them were the supply and refueling ships like the *Feywind*. Uniformly crude and ungainly, these large floating slabs were the lifeblood of the fleet and carried large reserves of synth-oil and illyrium to be distributed as needed.

Each of these resources was absolutely necessary to the modern airship. Synth-oil, produced from an alchemic reaction with ancient stones and fossils as a base, was used to lubricate the vast gear trains and moving parts that made up most mechanical constructs. Inert in liquid form, it was highly volatile while still a solid, which it remained as in storage to preserve its relatively short usable lifecycle. Once needed, an engimage would recite a predetermined incantation that would initiate its phase change into a useful state.

Illyrium, as nearly everyone in Lozaria knew, was the most efficient and clean magical power source available to mortals. To access this energy, illyrium is placed in purified water and heated as needed to increase the level of spiritual energy given off by the ore. This operation requires a secondary power source, but after initiation, the process of spiritual energy decay is self-maintaining. Spiritual energy given off by the illyrium will be gathered using filters in a collection chamber that guides the energy to power converters to then transmute it into traditional electricity. However, while in the water, the spiritual energy disrupts the liquid and causes it to flow. Turbines are therefore placed in the path of the stream to collect this power, which is reconverted to heat energy that can continue to serve as the catalyst for the illyrium reaction.

As one might imagine, this system requires space proportional to the size of the machine that it operates. For a skiff, this might be a cubic meter or slightly larger. For a dreadnought class airship, an illyrium generator would be massive. Even at this range, Leon could see four massive bulges protruding from the center vessel marking the soft targets that kept it running and afloat.

Of course, the middle ship, or fortress, as it appeared to Leon, could hardly be considered vulnerable just because of such minor exposed weak points. She was humongous, but her weight was carried gracefully. Her beak was hooked like a bird of prey, rising quickly to a high peak at her bridge before falling to expansive swept wings and budding towers at her stern. There, six engines, each the size of the *Feywind,* spat a vibrant effusion of flame and magic particles that cascaded through the air behind them. Other vessels steered far clear of her wake, lest they be tossed about by her eddies. She was fourteen hundred meters long and half again as wide, with hundreds of decks, thousands of crew, and bristling with weaponry from prow to tail. And she was, paradoxically, a man: the *King Darmatus.*

Leon viewed her with mixed feelings: a feeling of pride that his nation was capable of creating such a wonder . . . and a feeling of revulsion for the architect behind her. *Hmph, what irony that I'm here witnessing her maiden voyage instead of father,* he thought sardonically. Yes, Leon's dear old dad, Archimas Descar, was the greatest engimage in the kingdom. A genius who, in the span of a lifetime, had closed the technology gap with the other Terran states to an arm's reach. One who had achieved a seat on the Ruling Council with no military or political experience. *And a terrible parent to balance all of that out.*

Of course, he couldn't complain about his life the same way Vallen could. In that way, they were complete opposites. Leon was born with a silver spoon in his mouth; Vallen was lucky to be born. Leon had every advantage during his childhood: private tutors, prestigious schooling, fine clothes, and packs of sycophants both in and out of his family's employ waiting on him at all times. Vallen had bowed, scrapped, stolen, and willed his way to survival. But that was where their fortunes reversed. In Metellus and his peers, Vallen had found true love, kindness, and admiration, though he probably wasn't really aware of it. Leon reasoned that it was precisely because of his rough upbringing that his friend didn't realize his current blessings, and he envied him for it.

For all his birth and station granted him, Leon had never been loved, had never been admired, had never been truly praised or shown *real* compassion. All of it had been a lie. His mother died giving birth to him, the third and final of three brothers. No one knew how or why she had perished, given the medical technology available. Therefore, it was only natural for the logical Archimas to blame the free variable for her death: Leon himself. As he grew up, his older brothers eventually told him that their father had always been focused on his work—his tinkering and inventing—but that the feeling part of him was buried with their mother. All traces of empathy and tenderness left him, turning him into as cold and rational an existence as the metal that was his most common companion. However, outside of their stories, Leon had never known the man they had. High expectations and vicious punishment for failing to meet them were the only existence he could relate to.

As Archimas was the top airship and weapons manufacturer in the kingdom, with a noble household and company built entirely upon the back of his sweat and achievements, it was expected that his sons should follow in his footsteps. Even though father lived far from home in his lab, instructor after tutor after professor after trainer visited the mansion day in and day out on his orders, molding his progeny into little copies of their surviving parent. Every day was regimented down to the minute: exactly eight hours to sleep, thirty minutes total for three meals, and another thirty for bathroom breaks, showering, and other required hygienic procedures. The rest was wholly forfeit to science, magic, and progress. There was no downtime, no rewards. Success was its own reward, as Archimas never tired of telling them on the off chance their paths crossed for a minute here or there.

Failure, however, was another matter entirely. Ace your tests, properly induce illyrium energy decay in free standing water, or invent a new way of preventing the overheating of a weapons system, and your daily schedule wouldn't divert a second from its normal course. Botch any one of the tasks assigned you, regardless of difficulty, and punishment was sure to follow. One of father's favorite quotes was, "Teach a man to love you, and he will expect kind treatment regardless of his performance. Teach a man to fear you, and he will toil tirelessly to avoid your lash." It always started simply, and, rationally, the consequences mirrored the "crime." Forget to feed the synth-oil into the gear train before testing an engine's power output? A meal withheld for each piston cracked or broken as a result. Miss a question on a test related to the amount of weight a two il-powered hover cart could carry, and you'd be hauling the answer in weight around with you for the number of days equal to the points the question was worth.

And those were the *clever* penalties. If Archimas thought your error was grievous enough, he would, as in his favorite saying, merely bring the lash down upon you. Leon had spent more time with his father being whipped than doing anything else. Eventually, he had shut down, becoming the automaton his parent wanted, and the beatings and punishments ceased almost entirely. As the years passed, his brothers went off to study at the Darmatian Academy of Science, and when he came of age, he was expected to do the same.

It was a chance meeting that changed all that. At the age of eighteen, Leon was prepared to go to the science academy, as was his father's plan. He wasn't as bright as his brothers, but Archimas's training had molded him expertly, to the point that even the faux intellect he possessed was greater than most of his peers. While on his way to turn in his enrollment forms, Leon happened to witness a commotion at the gate of the nearby military academy. A large crowd had gathered to witness an argument between an unruly youth of similar age and the military police stationed there to screen entrants. By all intents and purposes, the young man should have been turned away. His hair was unkempt, his cadet uniform unpressed and filthy, and he was refusing to turn over the weapon, nothing more than a cylinder of metal, at his belt. Even more egregious were his lack of respect, disdain for authority, and colorful usage of metaphorical language.

But even so, Leon felt there was something charming about him. His ramshackle appearance was opposed by a strong stance. His insults and provocations were belted with a firm, commanding voice. And above all else, he was utterly composed and confident in who he was and what he was doing. He was everything Leon had been instructed not to be, yet had all the traits Leon had long desired: the strength to stand up to those oppressing him, the power of word and mouth to resist those decrying him, and the confidence to remain himself in the face of those directing him to change. *I want to be like him,* a small voice ventured deep inside.

Before Leon could think twice, he was pressing through the crowd and confronting the guards with his family's name and authority. Not ten seconds later, they were through the gate, and Leon, bemused and not exactly sure what he had just done, was having his hand furiously shaken by a beaming Vallen Metellus. Ten minutes later, he found himself turning his letter of enrollment into the secretary of the wrong academy, and ten hours later, he woke up with the worst headache he had ever experienced and almost no recollection of the previous night.

What he did know, however, was that for the first time in his life he'd had *fun*. Not the feeling of elation at success that his father masqueraded to them as fun, but the actual joy and happiness of having enjoyed the company of another person. It was at that moment that Leon came to both cherish and envy Vallen—the moment at which they became friends.

His father could have halted the wheels of Leon's transformation, but to do so would have necessitated public acknowledgement that one of his creations had broken and rebelled against his control. Such a revelation would cut him far deeper personally than communally, so he instead swept it under the rug. Archimas's prodigal son would be allowed to pursue his current *eccentric* path and retain his name, provided he brought no further shame to the family. In turn, Leon further rebelled at every opportunity, pushing his father and using his name as he saw fit. It was a game he'd been playing for four years.

Leon shook his head to clear his mind and saw in his reflection on the glass ahead that he'd been frowning the entire time. Well, he had been thinking about his father, and you know what they say, "when you eat a sour plum, you become sour yourself." He forced himself to smile and resumed gazing around at the wondrous sights beyond the *Feywind's* too thin viewport. *Surely,* Leon mused pensively, *that was the least pleasant moment I'll have today.*

<hr />

"Lancer squadron being adjusted from screen formation to approach vector one dash eight."

"Engines disengaged, reverting to hover protocol."

"All weapon stations report in green."

"Helm bearing on lane A14. We are directly opposite Aldona Fortress and maintaining altitude at twenty-six hundred meters."

"Hold the fleet here and signal our ground forces to halt their advance. We are currently out of range of their longest-range weapons, correct, Grand Marschal?"

Zaratus turned from his position at the fore of the bridge and bowed his head to Sychon as he replied. "Yes, Your Majesty. If we advance any farther, we will enter their defense arc and be in full violation of the Theradas Treaty. As such, they would be fools not to let us make the first move."

"And make it we shall, in good time." Sychon leaned forward in his grand command chair and steepled his fingers as he gazed out the large, rectangular viewports before him. Below his vantage lay the bridge of his command vessel, the *Hammer of Wrath*. A ceaseless frenzy of purpose raged about him, crewmen running hither and yon to accomplish tasks both real and imagined. No one wanted to be caught flat footed under their emperor's watchful eyes.

Beyond the cavernous control room lay the expanse of the *Hammer*, which stretched sixteen hundred meters from the elevated bridge at the stern to the massive horizontal hammer blades at its prow, for which it was named. Thick armor coated this forward section, behind which an array of short- and long-range cannons lay protected in deep encasements. Should all these weapon systems prove futile, the deadliest tool of the *Hammer* was its base design. An octagon of powerful engines lined her rear, and if all should be activated in conjunction, the vessel became a slicing instrument of nigh unstoppable inertia. Of course, that was only a last resort.

Around the *Hammer* flocked the First Fleet, a multitude of ships cut in sharp lines and hard angles, not a single tonne of extra metal wasted on superfluous frills and decadence. Wherever a weapon could be placed, it had. Wherever speed and maneuverability was necessary, all else had been sacrificed. At the heel of the *Hammer* rested their carriers, about which hordes of Lancer jets and Harrier skimmers flocked while waiting to be loosed.

Similarly ordered were the Fifth and Seventh Fleets holding at the flanks of the First. Between the three groups were amassed over a hundred vessels worthy of name and thousands of additional fighters and support craft. And on the ground far below advanced the remainder of the empire's war machine, a vast host of tens of thousands of infantry, engineers, mages, and mechanical vehicles and constructs. The dust they kicked up floated high into the air, obscuring the craft that hurried back and forth carrying vital resources from earth to heaven and vice versa.

It was truly a host of legend and represented the full might that Sychon could afford to bring to bear on Darmatia in their current circumstances. It was nothing short of an all-or-nothing gamble. Fail here, and the losses sustained would never be recovered. Depending on the casualties, sooner or later Rabban would overrun the eastern reaches of the empire and come knocking on Sarcon's door demanding his head.

Still, it is only because of the challenge that this game is worth playing. Sychon smiled and redirected his attention back inside the bridge. In between him and Zaratus lay a large, circular table coated with illyrium from which millions of microscopic globules floated upwards in a mesmerizing yellow haze. Several technicians were tinkering on it until one threw a lever at its base and life-size holographic images sprung upward into existence. Though grainy and off focus, the visages were clearly recognizable as his field commanders, the Rittermarschals Valescar and Titania.

Each was on the bridge of their respective command ships, connected to the *Hammer* by advanced magtech that allowed him to communicate with them across the separating distance. Valescar, as ever, appeared unconcerned but attentive in his full plate and helm, a cape of burgundy cascading from his shoulders to mark his high office. His one good eye burned with a flame of suppressed eagerness. In contrast, Auvrea Titania stood at ease, her posture exuding calm thoughtfulness and her headpiece discarded to allow her long crimson hair to fall against her matching cloak. Her pale skin stood in stark opposition to the burnished silver of her breastplate, but her beauty belied an impressive strength and sharp mind. Why had Sychon elevated a woman like her to command rank in a male-dominated army? While Valescar might be one of his keenest swords, Titania could be likened to the most instructive and knowledgeable of tomes. The first would cut its way swiftly across the battlefield alone; the second would take control of the battlefield in its entirety, manipulating every available resource to its will.

"Rittermarschal Titania, what is the disposition of the enemy forces?"

The commander nodded her head deferentially before speaking. "Your Grace, the Darmatian forces have deployed much as we expected. The Darmatian air fleet has been dispatched in near entirety, with their flagship, the *King Darmatus*, moving into position above Aldona's central bastion while the remaining fleet elements deploy across its extended walls and fortifications. Between earth and sky, scarcely a beast could squeeze its way through the net they have set up. Furthermore, our spies within the kingdom report that the fortress and fleet have both been filled to overflowing. In addition to massive military redirections to this point, even the cadets of their military academy have been turned out. Most now staff the fortress, but some have been distributed to the *Darmatus* and other vessels to ensure that casualties among their crews can be swiftly replaced. Despite some of their ships normally running on skeleton crews, they have no shortage of manpower at the moment. If I may be so bold, Your Majesty, I fear that if it comes down to a battle of attrition, we will be on the losing side." Titania once again bowed her head as she concluded her report and stood awaiting his response.

Sychon regarded the scene outside. The most prominent features of the view were the awe-inspiring mountains of the Great Divide. Massive behemoths sprouting from the depths of Lozaria, these titans shot up out of the earth like forests of giant teeth, their snow-capped peaks lost in the clouds high above the limits of mortals' ability to fly. Nor could one hope to wend his way through them, so numerous were they, their roots coming together no lower than his current eye level. And even should an explorer ascend to their snaking valleys, he would find them choked with ancient forests and treacherous, ever-shifting mists. As a result, since time immemorial, the northern and southern portions of the continent had only been truly connected by two low-lying passes: the Theradas and the Nareck.

And the Theradas before him was similarly choked with a different sort of barrier, one made by man himself. As Titania cautioned, the gap between the mountains was entirely blocked. On the ground, high walls of blinding-white stone reached toward the heavens, gathering to a high, three-tiered peak in the center where a bastion towered above its surroundings. Thanks to their network of agents and spies, they knew the wall and fortress were teeming with cannons and other magical weaponry. Furthermore, they were protected by large lume generators that had been recently installed. While a blow from a projectile or magic blast might rend stone easily, both would be absorbed or turned aside by the strong repulsive energies of the spirit-fed shields. Even more deadly, however, was the legion of artillery pieces assembled behind the fortifications. Because of these long-range batteries, massive casualties would be sustained just to *reach* the nigh impenetrable walls of the fortress.

Therefore, the logical solution would be to bypass the fortress and engage it from above, behind, and the fore. However, the Darmatian air fleet denied this method of approach. Any attempt to push through the skies above Aldona would be met with ferocious aerial retaliation. This defense left an attacker with no choice but to engage both earth and sky simultaneously. But just as an invader was capable of using combined arms, so, too, were the Darmatians. Ground batteries would provide fire support against the airships, while the airships would bombard those crawling in the dust. In short, any assault would turn into a battle of attrition, exactly as Rittermarschal Titania advised.

"No, Titania, you're absolutely correct. That would be the outcome under normal circumstances. However, we have a trump card today. Are you prepared to weave your spell, Sarcon?" He directed his query to the shadows beyond the holographic projector, where two men waited out of the way of the bustling bridge activity. The first, Hans Ulrich, stood behind the other with his arms outstretched, the green glow of healing magic pulsing from his palms as he softly chanted incantation after incantation. His face was haggard, with dark rings below his eyes, and he appeared as though he had barely eaten in the past week. That was about how long he'd been at his casting, with only a few hours of sleep a day to give his men'ar time to recharge. And when that small amount of sleep ceased to suffice, Sychon's magic scientists had given him supplements and pills to make up the difference.

The object of his ministrations was the man—or at least it still had the outline of a man—before him. With skin practically liquefied, he was covered in the brown splotches of advanced decay, and his distended muscles coated brittle, white bone, which poked through in some places. Truly, Sarcon belonged more to the land of the dead than the living at this point. Or, rather, the shell he wore, once called Vahn, was barely holding together. Only the constant attentions of Hans kept the important joints, ligaments, and nerves functioning, but even his care couldn't keep the failing body upright forever.

Titania's disgust at the creature was palpable, as if even leagues away she could smell the revolting stench rolling off his rotten flesh. "Why must we rely on this *thing* to lead us to victory? Surely he'll fall to pieces before so much as sinking a single vessel."

"That remains to be seen, Rittermarschal Titania." The corpse shambled slowly around the table, small gobbets of flesh falling to the floor in his wake like a nightmarish trail of bread crumbs. Sarcon's voice wheezed from non-existent lips, with blackened gums framing ever-fewer sallow teeth. "Regardless, this is the only path that leads to the survival of your empire. If you would rather forgo our bargain and take your chances using conventional means, be my guest."

Sychon shared Titania's revulsion and trepidation, but his wager had already been made. He shot her a withering look; he would brook no further discussion on the matter. "No, Sarcon, that won't be necessary. Please do whatever is needed to sweep the Darmatians from our path."

A look of knowing arrogance beamed from what remained of Sarcon's face, a look that made Sychon wonder which of them was truly in charge. "Before I do, I must bring one more matter to your attention. As I told you previously, my body is sealed by an Elysium crystal in a tomb beneath Har'muth. It rests, chained for another three years, *unless* the blood magic with which I was bound can be overturned. Blood must be countered with blood. It was Darmatus's life that was given to imprison mine. Therefore, the ichor of his descendants is the only thing that can break the spell before its course is run. I ask you, as a ruler of mortals in this age, do you know if the line of Darmatus yet exists?"

The question took Sychon slightly aback. As far as history was concerned, the last of Darmatus's descendants, Queen Ephalia, died a hundred years past in what was known as the Crimson Accords. Opponents to a peace treaty between the kingdom and empire had attacked a summit among leaders from both sides. The queen had died, and the emperor at the time barely escaped with wounds that would later claim his life. Since all parties had suffered greatly, it was determined that the insurgents belonged to neither nation, and the Theradas Dispute ended in a ceasefire without conditions.

Of course, that was the official account. Sychon clamped down on his shock, ensuring that his face was unreadable. Just how much did this dead man know? Whatever the case, he was becoming more dangerous by the day. "Queen Ephalia, the last of Darmatus's descendants, regrettably perished a century past.

However, your *tangential* query has reminded me of a question of my own, and I was curious to see whether or not you already have an answer to it." He smiled down at the putrid husk before him as he reasserted his control. "Once you work your invocation and fully crumble back to dust, what's to stop me from refusing you another body and taking the Elysium without your help?"

As always, Sarcon had a counter prepared. "You are right to be ready to betray me. Any man who isn't constantly planning to adjust his fortunes by eliminating or creating new relationships is a fool. The bigger fool still is the man who isn't on guard for a knife in the back. My insurance, Sychon, is threefold," he began, infuriatingly referring to Sychon without any honorific. Zaratus approached Sarcon, surely to accost him for not giving the emperor proper respect, but had his progress halted as though by an invisible wall. "First, my attack months ago in your Senate chamber was never intended to kill your grand marschal. By slaying your guards, I hid from you my true intent. Instead, I tore open his gauntlet and sent my men'ar through the cuts on his hand and into his bloodstream. At this point, I have taken control of his own spiritual energy and can order him at will . . . or use him as my next vessel. Since I've had so long to work, the transfer would be swift, as though he had always been a willing host."

The grand marschal glanced at Sychon in horror, as though begging him to do something. Valescar and Titania, their images present but bodies far away, could only look on in contempt at what was essentially a hostage situation. The nearby members of the bridge crew who could hear the exchange paused in their labors until a young lieutenant accosted them for their indolence. After a moment, Sychon found his voice. "And do you insist on going through with that plan?"

"Ideally, no. It was always a last resort as it would rightfully earn your ire, and the marschal's body is not an ideal fit besides. Once I move to a new vessel, the magic initiated by this flesh will cease to function, and Zaratus will be freed. However, I expect you to find me a new host, and I have a gift, of sorts, for you to that end." Sarcon turned, raising a rancid finger to point out the window and across the valley. "Blood is much like a person's signature. Just as the spiritual energy of each mortal is unique, so, too, is the liquid on which it flows. Yours, Sychon, has a forceful, vibrant energy to it. It rushes with passion and strength. Those near to each other share similar traits; out there, on a vessel at the rear of that fortress, is someone with blood that resonates with yours. I suggest you send someone there, retrieve what is yours, and find a fitting body for me, lest your grand marschal be condemned to Oblivion."

Images flashed through Sychon's mind: a moonless night, a dagger in the dark, blood rushing from his chest, a jagged scar that never healed. There, a young child, standing between him and a sobbing woman. A backhand, a banishment, an execution. He shook the sordid memories from his head. "And your last threat?"

Sarcon spun back, carefully, slowly, lest his joints tear with the motion. "These are not threats, Sychon. They are consequences, possible futures for you and me alike. You would do well not to dismiss them as the casual blackmail of court intrigue that you're used to. That aside, reconcile to the fact that you will never see the Elysium without my assistance. Only I know the safe paths through Har'muth. Only I have power over the defensive enchantments lying in wait. Attempt to breach its fortifications without me, and you will do naught but wander its mists for the rest of time."

Sychon relaxed in his chair, considering. It was too late to change his course now, but how he proceeded would have a lasting effect on the outcome of this war and the fate of the empire. Did he need Zaratus? Was *that* individual really a pawn he wanted back in the game? Could he rule Lozaria without the use of Elysium? He pondered a moment and then decided.

"Rittermarschal Valescar, I have need of your services."

The grizzled commander nodded. "Anything, Yer Majesty."

"After Sarcon executes his spell, take your ships and personally secure the vessels to the rear of the *King Darmatus*. Find our wayward exile—you know of whom I speak—and obtain a suitable body for the *esteemed* mage. Better an enemy than one of our own. However, prioritize the new host over all else. A bishop outweighs a pawn, after all. Is that satisfactory?"

After sketching a mocking bow, as low as his atrophied muscles would allow, the cadaver began shuffling past Sychon to the bridge doors. "Yes, quite pleasing, Sychon. You and I make a great team, and the world shall bear witness to the impossible feats we can accomplish together." Hans trailed him, his expression grimmer after the exchange he had witnessed, but his healing chants remained unabated.

Valescar and Titania saluted and signed off, their visages dissolving down into the projector until the surface was once again flat. A bridge tech flipped a switch, and a tactical display of the battlefield showing the known disposition of both sides bubbled up. Another orderly came by with a dustpan and broom, quickly sweeping up the detritus of their erstwhile guest.

All this was secondary to Sychon and Zaratus, who exchanged glances but said not a word until the clicking of boots on metal had faded in the adjoining hallway. When the echo no longer reached them, the grand marschal was the first to speak.

"Your Majesty, he's a danger to the empire and to you. He must be eliminated."

Sychon tilted his head, resting his head against his arm. Zaratus was right, but timing was everything. He would manage the threat that Sarcon posed and milk him for all the value he could. Only when the risk outweighed the reward would he finally dispose of the insolent, overconfident sorcerer. His response was simple.

"All in good time, Grand Marschal. All in good time."

<hr />

"He's hiding something."

"Who is?" Hans responded obligatorily, attempting to avoid looking directly at Sarcon. Over the intervening months, he had mostly gone nose blind to the smell of rotting flesh, but looking at what basically amounted to an animated cadaver still gave him chills from time to time. Besides, he didn't need to see him. His hands had been centimeters from Sarcon's husk imbuing him with healing magic for the last week, a task that left Hans nearly as drained and lifeless as his charge. He could swear his vision was starting to blur, and the throbbing headache and loss of feeling in his feet probably weren't positive symptoms either.

"Sychon, your *emperor* . . . " His sardonic pronunciation of the title left little doubt that Sarcon had less-than-abundant appreciation for rulers. "When I questioned him about Darmatus's descendants, the briefest hint of surprise crossed his face before he could hide it. An heir remains, and he knows something about them."

Hans had long since learned to trust Sarcon's gut feelings. Regardless of his ignorance of modern politics, technology, and customs, whenever he made a statement, you could be sure it was 100 percent accurate. Of course, he still held nagging doubts about the morality of some of his actions, such as his acquisition and subsequent destruction of Vahn's body, but his goals seemed to align with the empire's . . . for now. He hadn't known Vahn for very long, certainly not long enough to have grown attached to him beyond the simple commander-subordinate relationship, but Hans did feel for his parents, especially Minister Badenschiff, who had narrowly escaped a trip to the imperial penitentiary for his outburst in the Senate chamber.

"And if the line still exists, what's our course of action?"

"Nothing, for now. We have to wait until Sychon's suspicions abate, or until I have another prize to distract him with—though I must have my body soon if we're to accomplish our objectives." Sarcon, if nothing else, was obsessively ends oriented. Some ambitions and intentions he shared willingly. Others he kept to himself. He was, as ever, a mystery shrouded in an enigma.

"Next, the vial of dragwyrm blood, if you would, Hans." Hans stopped his incantation and tiptoed across a few feet of incoherent sketching to the trolley of assorted magical items and tinctures they had brought with them to the observation deck. When Sarcon had stated that he was going to perform *old* sorcery, he had meant it. All around them on the open-air platform were various shapes and ancient writing that made up the formula for Sarcon's spell. Each section had been done with a different catalyst: there, illyrium paste; beside it, the stomach fluid of a boerwulf; next, the secretions of a thousand-segmented sandwurm; and lastly, the dried blood of the caster himself.

According to Sarcon, the use of each added a layer of power to the invocation, and the final and strongest was that of the greatest beast in existence: the dragwyrm, a fell beast with the size and ferocity of a ground-bound wrym and the graceful wings and flight of a dragon. Even the most powerful of mages couldn't hope to slay one alone. Rather, it would take an entire company of sorcerers, or a small flotilla of airships, to bring one down. It was, therefore, fortunate for the hunters that they were solitary beasts outside of their short winter mating season.

As if to emphasize the turning of the seasons, a strong fall breeze blew past, nearly knocking Hans off his feet. Both of them were tethered to a nearby railing, but that would likely do them little good if the capricious gusts tossed them over the side. Sarcon's frail corpse would snap in two, while Hans's spine would simply break in twain. He secured his footing, located the correctly labeled bottle, and passed it to the mage, who stuck a shriveled, milk-white finger bone into the solution before spreading it on the deck as a hexagon filled with runes and ancient Eliassi. Hans couldn't read the language or decipher the hieroglyphs and so contented himself with pursuing a curiosity he had just remembered.

"My lord, how did you know that a person of interest to the emperor was on one of the Darmatian ships?" He gazed past the railing, across the sharp hammer to the fore of the vessel, and marveled at the vast span between them and the enemy fleet where the one Sarcon had sensed could be found.

Sarcon finished his diagram and examined the work, giving a nod of apparent satisfaction. "A sensory technique I picked up in my youth long ago. I could teach it to you since you have an aptitude for that school, though it would take time. Simply put, the blood that flows through a being has properties that separate them from all others. With enough skill, a mage can recognize those properties and compare them to individuals within a set distance. For a sorcerer talented enough to learn this technique, their range might be several dozen meters. But for myself," he spread the remnants of his tattered arms, "that expanse is leagues."

Hans was impressed but not quite awed. Nothing about Sarcon surprised him anymore. All his abilities defied understanding; he possessed wisdom and knowledge unknown to the modern world, and above all that, he was an immortal capable of swapping souls from body to body. Sometimes he wondered if the man before him had ever been mortal in the first place.

The object of his thoughts gesturing to the massive magic formula at their feet brought Hans back from his reflections. "It's finished, Hans. With this we begin to roll back the wheels of history." He marveled at the elaborate construct. Never before had he seen such a beautiful or intricate design. In the contemporary age, catalyst drawing was a lost art, but not even in textbooks read as a student had he seen such a wondrous design. Illyrium formed a yellow outer circle, moving inward to a green decahedron of intestines, then a purple octagon of fecal matter, and culminating in the bright crimson hexagon of dragwyrm blood. In between each lay whorls and flowing etchings of various tongues in the hues of their respective ring. And interspersed here and there to tie caster and system together was Sarcon's—Vahn's—ichor. So perfect was each line, each curve, each picture that Hans could hardly believe this grand arrangement was the effort of a single person.

"It's . . . magnificent," he breathed.

"Your appreciation does you credit. You've been no small help to me, Hans. Now you shall be my witness as we begin our true endeavor."

"How does it work?"

Sarcon grinned his usual all-knowing, and slightly terrifying, smile. He motioned for Hans to exit the inscriptions and took his place at the small but empty center. "Now we charge it up." He began weaving a series of signs with his hands and chanting in a language beyond Hans's ken. As Sarcon did, both his body and the space before his hands glowed with a light unlike any he'd witnessed before. Simultaneously white and black, it flowed and ebbed with the luminescence of the sun and the all-consuming darkness of Oblivion.

The air shuddered, and wind was swept in a rush about the deck, centering on Sarcon. Hans felt himself inextricably drug toward the developing magic and grabbed the nearby railing for support. He gulped, one thought replaying itself over and over again in his mind.

Should I really be here?

It hadn't taken Matteo long to determine that flying in an airship was on his top-five list of least favorite things to do. At current, it had displaced public speaking down to number six, and each gust of turbulence that rocked the floating craft threatened to move it closer to number one. He breathed deeply, in and out, trying to calm his anxiety. It was marginally helpful, but not enough. *I've got to get my mind focused on something else.*

He stood, looking about for anything of interest and attempting to ignore the cracks and grime that coated the window before him at inconsistent intervals. From his left, he could hear the heated voices of Vallen and Renar, lost in yet another trivial argument with Leon genially trying to soothe their tempers. To his right, Sylette stood alone, her palms white against the railing. She was biting her lip in agitation. Even at a distance of two meters, her muttering was incoherent. Matteo considered trying to comfort her, but had never been capable at dealing with the fairer sex, and found that his own fears prevented him from helping others with theirs. Sighing at his own impotence, he focused on the world outside the panel.

If he avoided staring straight down, Matteo could almost ignore the precipitous drop to the ground below. Almost. *Don't look at the earth. Dirt is bad. Brown is bad. There, focus on the shining wall instead. The white marble of Aldona Fortress is of a* particularly *pleasing hue*. Nearly pure, with flecks of black interspersed to give it texture, it presented a calming aesthetic, both for its artistic appearance and imposing structure. Three hexagonal forts rose in tiers to a tall bastion capped by a magnificent spiral tower. While the primary structure itself reached for the heavens, the tower breached them, ascending into the clouds and resting just beneath the equally stunning *King Darmatus*. However, the spire was not merely a spectacular monument. At its summit rested a powerful lume generator from which cascaded an immense energy barrier that crackled and sparkled with rainbow energy from the peak to the base of the construct. Elsewhere, similar, smaller turrets added their own energy to the barrier, creating rolling waves of shields that overlapped to make the citadel impervious to ranged assault. And out from the stronghold itself raced tall walls that continued unimpeded until they abutted the sheer mountain cliffs to either side.

So beautiful was the scene painted before him that Matteo could almost forget that they were here because of war. Almost. The fleets far above the land, on both sides, stretched across the sky along the length of the valley. And on either side of the Darmatian defenses camped tens of thousands of soldiers, mechanized vehicles, and deadly artillery. If one nation or the other fired a single shell, this wondrous picture would be permanently marred. *Yet another sobering thought I could've gone without thinking.*

Matteo sought to cleanse his thoughts by shaking his head, but found a pinprick of unease growing at the base of his skull to replace them. Perturbed by it, he scratched and massaged the nape of his neck, but the pain wouldn't dissipate. So, it wasn't a physical ailment, which meant that he was sensing something. He had experienced this before on rare occasions where his body instinctually felt danger but couldn't identify the source. According to his combat magic professor at the academy, anyone, with insane amounts of training, could gain this "sixth sense." However, those mages with sensory aptitude were inherently able to discern threats by this unease. As a result, contrary to Vallen's belief in the uselessness of sensory magic, this facet, along with its many other utilities, made it indispensable to military units.

It was just that, in Matteo's case, he had never perfected turning his apprehension into actual danger identification. Vaguely knowing something bad was going to happen and knowing when and where it would occur were two completely different things. The throbbing increased, indicating that the threat was growing greater or nearer. *Focus, Matteo, focus. You've never sensed something like this. We could be in real trouble.* With every passing second, the aching doubled, pushing the boundaries of his tolerance.

He turned left, and the pangs diminished; right, and the torment ebbed. Matteo focused directly forward and the searing pain nearly blinded him, causing him to cry out and fall to his knees. Leon rushed to his side, supporting and helping him back to his feet. Sylette glanced over at him worriedly. Velle began asking him a litany of medical questions, and even Vallen looked unsure at what could have caused his outburst.

"Where is the pain located? Do you have a pre-existing condition that could have caused this? What did you eat today?" Velle meant well, but her queries were the babblings of an amateur who had never treated a patient outside the confines of the academy medical ward. Matteo could only groan in response.

"It's no big deal, Velle. He probably just saw how high we were and cried out in shock. Not sure why they brought him along to a battlefield anyway. What's useless in practice will just be useless during the real deal." Typical Vallen, trying to wave away something he couldn't explain. Matteo pushed against Leon's shoulder, standing in spite of the throbbing ache, determined to prove his objector wrong.

"I'll . . . I'll be alright, Velle, but the fleet is in danger. We need to send a message to Admiral Contus on the *King Darmatus*!"

Leon gave him a skeptical look. "The Sarconians aren't even in firing range, and they're the only threat to us out here. Can you be more specific?"

"Don't coddle him, Leon. He's just making up stories to distract from his failure at—"

That was the last straw. Between his earth-shattering headache, the imminent peril to their existence, and four years of frustration at his carefree, arrogant, and browbeating squad leader, Matteo had finally had enough. "Listen here, you blustering blowhard! I've put up with your snide remarks, your insults, and your provocations for as long as anybody could and still remain sane. I've told myself, 'He's just kidding,' or 'He doesn't really mean it,' and somewhere in my mind, I still have hope I'm right. But enough is enough! I'm trying to save our bloody lives from some incomprehensible danger that's strong enough to crack my skull with the mere sensing of its power. If that registers even a tiny amount in your pea-sized brain, you should be able to see that I have more important things to do than deal with your wisecracks and Triaron wisdom pulled from your rear end! So, unless you have something *constructive* to contribute, sit down and shut up!"

By the time Matteo finished his rant, he was panting with both the exertion of the stern lecture and the continued agony spreading across his body. Everyone looked shocked, most especially Vallen, whose look of utter bafflement was unforgettable. As he wheezed, a strong, calloused hand clapped him on the shoulder. Matteo turned to find himself gazing into the weathered face of Cappie, captain of the *Feywind*.

"Let's hear about this danger of yours, boy. Anybody willing to react that strongly to defend their friends and my vessel deserves to be heard out."

He almost fainted with relief. *Finally*, someone was going to listen to him. "Dir . . . directly front . . . there's . . . something there . . . something deadly. I'm a . . . sensory mage, and I've . . . I've never felt anything like this before. We need . . . to tell the fleet . . . no time. All ships need to . . . raise their shields and . . . ele . . . elevate. That's standard operating . . . proce . . . procedure for situations like this."

Cappie chewed on the information for a moment before replying. "So, you think the Sarconians will attack, and you think they stand a chance of breaking through? It would be suicide for them to do so. Do you have anything else to give me, boy?"

"He doesn't need to. If the Sarconians are here, they intend to attack. Stop thinking of this as a pleasure cruise to the border and start thinking of it as what it is: a war." The voice belonged to Sylette, who had turned from the viewport as the conversation developed. She still had a hint of nervousness about her, but also present was an aura of expectation and command, as though she presumed her words would be heeded and obeyed. Matteo silently thanked the Veneer that someone, anyone, was taking his warning seriously.

A bright flash caught the eyes of all present, and they turned to look out the window. There, below the belly cannons and massive hover plates of the *King Darmatus*, shined a thin band of white that was nearly blinding. Around that light, a roiling blackness gathered, and the air shimmered visibly, even at this distance. And beneath the gathering maelstrom was the sharp, cutting edge the empire's flagship, designated by the Intel Division as the *Hammer of Wrath*.

At that moment, Matteo's headache spiked, nearly knocking him unconscious. He raised his arm, weakly pointing with extended finger at the growing light. "Th . . . that is . . . the danger. No time . . . must . . . act."

That seemed to make up Cappie's mind; he spun back to his bridge crew and started barking orders. "Comm, signal the *King Darmatus* that there's danger to the fore. Have her advise the fleet to raise lume and elevate above the Sarconian line of fire. Operations, engage shields and transfer power to the forward hemisphere. Helm, take us up five hundred meters. Also, be prepared to move port or starboard as needed. Look lively, men. The big wave's a comin'!"

A flurry of activity gripped the bridge as men rushed hither and yon to accomplish their tasks. Despite the age of the vessel, it took only seconds for the air around *Feywind* to shimmer with the activation of her lume and the deck to shake under them as she began her ascent. With nothing else to do, Matteo panned his blurry gaze over the rest of the Darmatian vessels to see if they were following suit. Light flickered among them as shields engaged and engines flared. Their response was too fast to have been because of his warning. Apparently, their own sensory experts had convinced their commanders of the danger as well.

Maybe, just maybe, they'd escape the threat before it was too late.

⁂

Hans found himself, quite literally, in the eye of a hurricane. Around him a vortex of energy swirled, threatening to rip him from his tenuous perch and fling him into the tumult of chaotic effervescence.

At its center, Sarcon remained untouched, as if even the elements themselves, light and dark included, bended their egos to his will. His voice had long ago been lost amidst the crashing drafts and raging disorder, but the ever-growing storm was testament to his continued incantations.

Through minutes that seemed like hours, an orb of increasing mass gathered in Sarcon's hands, equal parts white and black as though an imbalance of the two would cause the spell to backfire disastrously. It gorged itself on the turbulence, drawing power in streams and wisps from the very air tearing the space around the sphere.

When it grew larger than Sarcon, the tempest calmed somewhat, and the mage's impossibly booming voice reached through the flying winds. "Now, let my power be made manifest in this world once more!"

At that instant, a dam burst, and a shockwave carrying the weight of a thousand artillery cascaded across the deck and through Hans, causing him to gasp and double over in surprise. A second later came a fulminating boom that tried to rend his eardrums from their sockets. And when Hans could finally raise his head again, an enormous, wondrous, shining beam of darkest light rushed from the orb before Sarcon toward the Darmatian left wing.

Hans's mind could barely comprehend the destructive force he was witnessing. *Dear Creator, what have we unleashed?*

———⊰✦⊱———

The ray was blindingly brilliant, cascading through space like an ebony serpent striking at its prey. It impacted the light cruiser *Shining Hope* on the far left flank, vaporizing it instantly, shields and all, before beginning an inexorable march right toward the Darmatian center. Hundreds of lives were lost instantly, never knowing what had hit them.

More would follow. As the shaft shot through the midday sky, the sickening dread that crept into Matteo's heart, along with the most excruciating pain he had ever experienced, caused him to black out completely.

His last recollection was the horrified screams of his companions.

Chapter 9

Sink or Swim

"What in Oblivion is that?" Vallen shouted, unable to take his eyes off the beam swiftly cutting toward them. In the space of a moment, another light cruiser and a larger frigate met fates similar to the *Shining Hope*, evaporating from existence with barely a remnant except the smoke and fire their destruction left behind. The left flank was in total disarray, vessels darting on wild vectors in frantic attempts to escape. Some even ran into each other, creating tangled masses of metal that became easy prey for the ray's unstoppable momentum.

"Some sort of Sarconian superweapon?" came Leon's uncertain response. "We should have known if they had something like this!"

Velle's worried cry cut into their shock, "Matteo just fainted! What should we do?" Vallen glanced over to see the Professor collapsed on the deck, one arm still dangling around the Sylph's shoulders.

"How should I know?" He pointed out the viewport, "That giant death ray is a bit more pressing issue." The shaft extended past his field of view and now filled the entire left segment of the rounded window with its breadth. A carrier, hundreds of meters from the front line, found its aft engines clipped as it tried to dive beneath it. Hoverjets tumbled from its flattop as the engines exploded, sending it careening downwards to an incendiary impact with the ground below. One flight of skimmers escaped the fall only to be erased as their launch carried them into the blinding light.

They didn't have much time before the gleaming blast reached the *King Darmatus* and them behind it. Vallen felt himself break out in a cold sweat. There was nothing he could do. Run for a cargo launch and he might live long enough to die in a tiny metal coffin instead of this dilapidated large one. Stay here and hope the streaming luminescence missed and he placed his life in the hands of that one-legged buffoon of a captain and his second-rate crew. He hadn't felt this powerless, this total absence of control, since he lived on the streets of Sewertown. *I swore I would never be this helpless again, totally at the mercy of others. And yet here I am.*

Cappie didn't seem to grasp the hopelessness of their situation as he continued to belt commands at his men. "Forget the lume! Transfer all power to the gravpads and engines. All ahead full at forty degrees trim. If you ain't strapped in tight or have hold of something, better do it quick!"

The lights flickered as the old ship rerouted power from the forward shields to propulsion systems as rapidly as it could. In quick succession, the prow tilted up at an extreme angle, and Vallen found his feet sliding out from under him as he clenched the guiderail with whitened knuckles. Renar, Lilith, Unter, Leon, and Sylette, their hands likewise free, managed to do the same.

Matteo wasn't so lucky. Being unconscious, he couldn't grab hold of the bar or dig in with his feet. He began sliding down the walkway toward all manner of jagged and hard metal surfaces that lay between him and the other side of the bridge. Velle let out a cry and grabbed one of his hands while her other gripped the baluster for dear life. Vallen could see her muscles straining and knew she couldn't hold Matteo for long.

As Vallen debated whether he should risk his own tenuous safety to help them, Leon exclaimed, "Got'cha!" as he nimbly wrapped his legs around the falling cadet's waist to stabilize him. His own arms were hooked around the pole, keeping him steady while he heaved the light body of the Professor closer to them. When he was near to the railing, Renar reached past Vallen and clutched one of Matteo's wrists in a strong grasp while Leon undid his utility belt and used it to tie their unmoving companion to the rail.

Crisis averted, it seems, Vallen thought ambivalently. It hardly mattered that Leon and Velle had saved their squadmate from immediate injury and death since they were seconds from being fried anyway. Sure enough, outside was an ever-expanding field of madness and destruction. The left wing no longer existed. A vessel here and there had avoided annihilation with *only* enough crippling damage to force them to ground or leave them listing in the wind. The vast majority, however, had not been so fortunate. Where once dozens of cruisers, frigates, and fighters had filled the sky, now only smoke and falling debris remained. The death toll was surely in the tens of thousands and rising every second as disabled and not fully eviscerated craft rained down upon the ground forces like unexpected barrages of inertia-bound bombs and missiles. Craters pockmarked the Darmatian side of the fortifications, and even at this distance, burning encampments and rubble-filled holes in the defenses were evident.

And yet the radiant beam kept coming. It had only one target left on this side of the doomed V-formation of their fleet: the *King Darmatus*.

If it breaks through her, it's all over, Vallen lamented. The deck shuddered as the engines did their utmost to shake the *Feywind* apart and propel her above the coming demolition. Everything not bolted down flew to the back of the room, impacting terminals, support beams, and even crew members. Vallen ignored the shrieks of pain from the rear, even as the bar he and the other cadets clung to groaned and rattled, their combined weight proving more than it could tolerate.

None of that would matter soon. The shaft disappeared from sight, fully obscured as it struck full bore against the face of the *King Darmatus*, a massive dreadnought with the most advanced complement of defensive and offensive systems available in the world. He knew this only because earlier Leon had gushed to him about the ship in a strange combination of awe and disgust that he hadn't bothered to puzzle out. Vallen was disinterested then but now found himself very focused on hoping she would protect them. Surely her eight overlapping lume generators, twenty-meter-thick hull of Gestalt Steel plates, and fourteen hundred meters of metal between the blasting fulguration and them would be enough.

The entire bridge went silent except for the roaring of jets that took them ever upward at a steep slant. A moment passed, and the fusion of light and dark didn't appear from the rear of the flagship as Vallen expected. They floated higher, cresting the stern of the battleship, and were briefly dazzled by the intensity of the light cascading against the front of the *King Darmatus*. The behemoth refused to yield without a fight, its rainbow lumes coalescing centimeters from its forward hull and absorbing all the energy the Sarconian superweapon could throw at them. For the briefest of instants, Vallen felt his heart surge with the elation that this might not be his last day alive.

At that second, the shields gave way, shattering into millions of brilliant particles like the dissipating remnants of an exploding star. Vallen's cry of despair died on his lips as the beam, its path now unimpeded, scoured across the roof of the leviathan, annihilating the hull and instantly melting anything in its path. The forward bridge was first to go, followed by two of the illyrium generators providing power to the entire vessel. The reaction brought about by their obliteration forced the *King Darmatus* to list dangerously, its prow nosediving toward earth and its stern seesawing into the line of fire. This caused the engines to be impacted by the full force of the death ray, sending them—and what must have been a massive store of volatile synth-oil—into a cataclysmic explosion. Secondary blasts rapidly expanded from the initial upheaval, splitting the giant in twain and sending long tongues of fire in every direction like a holocaustic reenactment of the sun itself.

Without pausing, the seemingly never-ending beam burst through the wreckage headed straight for the *Feywind*. There wasn't any time to think or scream. The deck creaked and buckled harshly below them, throwing everyone about violently. Then all was still, the only sound that of the damage alarms clanging raucously. Vallen stumbled to his feet while wondering how in blazes they were still alive.

The light was gone, the air shimmering faintly as a small but stark reminder of its recent presence. Renar patted himself incredulously, as if to reassure himself that he was, in fact, still among the living. "It's a miracle," Leon chuckled, and, for that moment, tension lifted from the group as a bud of hope blossomed.

"It's not over," Vallen breathed, and the cadets turned to follow his gaze. They had been blown a fair distance by the explosion of the *King Darmatus's* engines, but not so far that they could miss the domino-like events still unfolding before them. As powerful as the spirit ray was, it had failed to completely vaporize the massive Darmatian flagship. Instead, the dreadnought now existed as two separate and ravaged parts, immense hulks of metal without any means of keeping themselves afloat. Seized fast by gravity, they were being tugged down toward the charge that the battleship had once loyally guarded: Aldona Fortress.

"By the Veneer, no." They were the first words Vallen had heard Renar's flunky, Lilith, speak, but the waifish brunette was of little concern to him at the moment. Still, she said the words they were all likely thinking. Losing half the fleet to an unknown Sarconian superweapon was a devastating loss, but one that could be recovered from. Having the gateway to Darmatia, Aldona

Fortress, reduced to rubble would surely spell the end of the nation and, more importantly, of him by association.

The first mass struck the lume above the central tower. At the point of impact, the shields buckled but held, causing the metallic husk to slide slowly down its ovular structure. However, before it could get far, the second flaming meteor struck at a different angle, straining the barrier further. Cracks formed like shooting lightning as the lume roiled and bubbled in response.

Then the entire system failed like a festival balloon popping. The minaret snapped in two at the force of the shockwave, and the entire mass plummeted once more. Some intelligent general on the ground ordered his artillery to fire at the incendiary blocks, hoping to destroy them as they resumed their fall, but their blasts only served to increase the spread of shrapnel. The first segment to land crushed the central bastion and barracks before toppling to the lower ring, flattening the walls in between. Others shattered the fortifications at random: there, a breach in the outer shell; nearby, an entire battalion of infantry smothered before they could react. A great cannon of the *Darmatus*, somehow entirely intact, landed nose down on another generator tower, exploding it outwards in a thousand marble chunks.

It was complete and utter chaos. Fires spread rapidly from the points of impact, greedily latching on to anything that would burn. Little figures rushed to put them out, only to be forced into retreat by the raining deluge of metal and, now, rock. The wall was breached in dozens of places. The guns of the fortress lay destroyed or silent. Barely any men, vehicles, or artillery remained on the left flank where fragments from the airships above had leveled or scattered them. Admiral Contus, having helmed the *King Darmatus*, was surely dead. The fortress commanders were likely snuffed out in their tower, now a tomb. And many of the fleet and army officers likely perished with their ships or units.

The chain of command was no more. Half the fleet was sunk or inoperable. The fortress and its ground forces were devastated and in disarray. *We're doomed,* Vallen thought dejectedly, as his fingers trembled. *I'm completely powerless in this situation. All we can do is run.*

"I just got word from the engine room," boomed the voice of Cappie, still gruff and assertive despite the odds. "The last gasp of that death beam clipped our gravpads, and we're sinking slowly. There's no fixin' them, so I'm afraid I have to give an order I never wanted to. All hands . . . abandon ship."

<hr />

"That was . . . incredible," Hans whispered, unsure exactly how to express his amazement without also allowing Sarcon to notice the fear now lurking in the recesses of his mind. The light itself had held a wondrous, mysterious beauty, like the purity of a thousand heavens mixed with a single drop of blackness from the pit. Even its destructive force was artistic in its own way, vaporizing nearly everything in its entirety and restoring the nothingness of the Void in return.

However, the scale of that ruination was beyond terrifying. With barely more than a couple hours of preparation and the dregs of strength in a foreign body, Sarcon had wiped out almost two-thirds of an army and a fortress that had taken centuries to achieve their current form. Furthermore, the time to eradicate the tens of thousands that perished had been but a scant few minutes. Hans shuddered. If men learned how to conduct war with such a technique, or if Sarcon himself chose to use it further, Lozaria would surely be destroyed. He silently prayed to the Veneer that this skill had been Sarcon's last resort and that he would never need use it again.

But if he had that much power, why didn't he wipe out the whole fleet? Hans had been entirely focused on the magic Sarcon unleashed, rather than the man himself. As the wind and smoke cleared, he untied his line and ventured toward the center of the spell circle. There, what had once been an intricate mosaic of different catalysts, drawings, and languages was now smudged and scoured against the metal plating of the deck. And at its core was the ash-colored husk of Sarcon.

If Hans had thought the sorcerer near death before, the thing before him could only be described as a Wight, something from the undead that had clawed its way back to living waters. One arm had fully disintegrated, the other blackened and burned beyond all hope of salvation. His right leg had snapped clean in half, the lower end likely carried off by the strong winds that had nearly cast Hans into the maelstrom as well. Unable to stand, Sarcon could do naught but stare straight up at the heavens he had violently torn asunder with unblinking, sightless eyes. When it came, his breathing was in ragged, wheezing gasps.

"Hans . . . is that . . . is that you? Tell . . . tell Sychon that he . . . has an hour . . . no more. Bring me my body . . . by then . . . or Zaratus . . . will be forfeit."

So, this is the cost of Great Magic. Little wonder we abandoned the knowledge of the ancients. "Wouldn't my time be better spent sustaining your body, my lord?"

"You've . . . done . . . enough. This body . . . is finished . . . No healing can . . . help it . . . it now. Go!" Sarcon elicited a hacking cough, then was silent. Only the faint rising and falling of his emaciated chest indicated he still lived.

"Very well." Hans turned and made his way over to the voicepipe attached to the doorframe of the weather deck. He would relay the order and hope for the best. Regardless of his methods, the empire needed Sarcon. However, weak as he was, Hans would do his utmost to ensure that such annihilation was never wrought again.

After all, it's meaningless to save the world if we destroy it in the process.

<hr />

Sychon found his eyes riveted to the aftermath of the massacre he had just witnessed. Certainly, he had expected the ancient mage to cast a spell strong enough to take down a few airships or breach the wall, thereby giving his conventional forces the edge they needed to carry the day. What he hadn't expected was . . . *this.* Half the enemy fleet destroyed in minutes, the *King Darmatus* sunk, and in its death throes, Aldona Fortress cracked open like a rotten egg. And to do it, he had unleashed Great Magic of all things.

As Sarcon had warned him, it truly was something not seen since ages past—and for good reason. Simultaneously referred to as Lost Magic, it had been forgotten and burned from the pages of history for a reason. Each and every spell belonging to that class could quickly alter the world in both amazing and catastrophic ways. Furthermore, most of the incantations took battalions of mages days to cast and left them mortally wounded or dead upon completion. Due to their fickle nature, potency, and fatal effects on both caster and victim alike, mortal governments had long since labeled them taboo and agreed never to use them again. Since then there had been no recorded incidents involving Great Magic, and even knowledge of its existence had nearly reached the status of legends.

He glanced down and to his right, noting that Zaratus's incredulous reaction mirrored his own. The grand marschal caught his eye and set into another passionate appeal. "Sire, you must recognize that what we just saw was Lost Magic. Give the order to have Sarcon arrested and executed! We can still tell the rest of the world we didn't know what he was doing if we act now and eliminate him!"

"Your Majesty, I have a message from Lieutenant Ulrich on the observation deck." A communications officer rushed from the array of reception pipes verbally connecting them to the rest of the *Hammer of Wrath* and bowed before him. "Sarcon beseeches Your Grace to find him a replacement body within the hour, or he'll fall back on his contingency plan."

Zaratus gulped but dismissed the young ensign to his post before addressing Sychon. "My life is of little consequence; I wouldn't have lived the time I have without your protection. I implore you, Your Majesty, end Sarcon before he becomes a threat we can no longer deal with. We won't get another chance like this, drained as he must be. Slay him, kill me, do whatever you must to ensure that he does not escape. The empire is secure with our victory here today—the Elysium is unnecessary. However, we must make sure the other races don't turn against us for using Lost Magic. Offer him up as a sacrifice to prevent this and derail his machinations."

Yes, the grand marschal did owe Sychon his existence, and he was a knight piece that he would grudgingly surrender for his own sake. But he was wrong. There would be another opportunity to dispose of Sarcon, if necessary. And perhaps the use of Great Magic wasn't as bad as he originally thought. If he held the Elysium and ruled the continent at the end of this war, the other races certainly wouldn't question the methods he used to achieve victory, lest they be the empire's next targets. The time had come to shatter the status quo; to Oblivion with the worries of lesser peoples.

"You are mistaken, Zaratus. It is I who control Sarcon, not the other way around. He draws breath only because I will it, and he will continue to use Great Magic if I command it. Who cares if the beggars at the gates decry our methods? When we control Lozaria, the history books shall not care how we achieved our aims—*our* scholars will be the ones writing them. Do you understand now, Grand Marschal?"

His head dipped in dejection. "You should be aware that I know more about taboo spells and crafts than any of your advisors, for my people invented many of them. You might think Lost Magics gone from the world, but if you bring them back into play, you'll very quickly find that you alone were not the only person to ignore our ancestors' wisdom. Please, sire, end this arms race before it begins in earnest."

"Your opinion is noted. But once we have the Elysium, nothing else will matter, for we shall possess a trump card far exceeding any paltry incantation that might be thrown at us. Let that be the end of it. You will not bring up eliminating Sarcon or Lost Magic again."

The grand marschal bowed, his facial expression and true heritage hidden behind his ever-present steel mask. "Yes, Your Majesty."

"Good." Sychon stood, his cloak unfurling softly to the ground as he pointed dramatically at what remained of the Darmatian lines. "Now, order all fleet elements and ground forces forward. I want those enemy remnants wiped up and the fortress in our hands by sundown. Comm, signal Valescar to accelerate his mission and return within the hour. Helm, take us in as well; we shall lead the charge."

Ahh . . . there's nothing quite like chasing a routing enemy.

<hr />

"What do you mean, abandon ship?" Vallen's animated voice cut through the silence that had greeted Cappie's announcement. "It's not safe out there. It's not safe in here. What do you want from us?"

Leon could hear the worry and fear in his friend's voice. Most of the others would assume that Vallen was being his normal self: an arrogant blowhard who didn't care about anyone in the world but himself, a jerk to those around him simply because he could. Most of that would be an accurate description, but Leon knew that his squadmate's current outward actions were the result of much inner turmoil.

After meeting Vallen—and after spending lots of time having his father's manipulative hooks ripped from him by the Triaron's sheer exuberance—Leon had used his family's resources to look deeper into his mate's past. Most of it had been covered up by his adopted father, Metellus, but enough of the tales and rumors of Vallen's time in Sewertown escaped the steward's notice to allow Leon to get a decent picture. He didn't have the details, but the broad strokes spoke of tragedy and loss that had surely left a mark on the youth.

In effect, they were actually quite similar. Both had a void in their hearts they were trying to fill, and both sought after love they could never possess. But while he had grown and found peace in their time together, Vallen remained mostly unchanged. Leon might be the prodigy's closest friend, but even he was blocked from ever knowing the real him.

"Let it go, Vallen. He's trying to save our lives. The fleet is mostly destroyed, the fortress is falling, and the ship is sinking. Plus, Matteo is unconscious. *All* of us are frightened and scared. Don't take it out on him just because none of us can control this situation." Leon put a comforting hand on Vallen's shoulder, his other arm propping up their fainted squadmate.

Cappie chuckled. "He's right. If you knew how to fix the gravpads, man a cannon, or work any of the equipment on the *Feywind,* I'd put you to work in a heartbeat. But you don't, so that's that. This was supposed to be a learning experience for you kids, and boy, will it be one. So, get off my bloody ship and make sure you do something with what you learned and saw here today."

At that, Cappie turned and waved, roaring orders as he had done since they'd arrived. Deck hands, engimages, and crewmen rushed to and fro, all doing their utmost to prolong the life of the ship they lived and worked on. As tasks were completed, Cappie would curse them off the bridge in ones and twos, sending them to cargo ships and launches to join the escape. Within moments, the bustle on the bridge was reduced to a whisper.

It was Sylette who took the lead and snapped them back to reality. "I saw a map when we were brought aboard. The hangar is out this door, down the hall, and three decks down. Let's go." She started toward the door, motioning them into line behind her. Renar and Lilith followed right away, with Leon and Velle trailing them, Matteo slumped across their shoulders in between. Vallen—still sulking, as far as Leon could tell—brought up the rear with the nigh silent Unter.

As soon as they reached the hall, he found his shoulders unable to scrape by due to the narrowness of the corridor. A quick rearrangement then found Leon holding Matteo's feet while Unter easily hefted his head, shoulders, and torso to carry him lengthwise down the passage. Velle immediately attached herself to Vallen, presumably so he could comfort her, but the reverse was just as likely the case, given her semi-maternal personality.

Scarcely had they made this switch and walked twenty meters down the hall than the warning claxons went off, filling the *Feywind* with an incessant bleating and pulsing red lights. Leon's first thought was that the ship's fall had accelerated, but they would have felt the change in momentum. The ship intercom soon spelled out their new predicament.

"This is your captain speaking. Most of the crew and cadets have already begun evacuating, but the Sarconian fleet just started speeding this way. Their fighter-class craft will be on us in a few dozen seconds, and their larger junk will be right behind them. Get all cadets and nonessential personnel off my ship *now*. Everyone who wants to stay with me and hold them off, get to the guns and give them some lead. We're stuck like an ek in the mud, so that means you too, engine room. Get a move on!"

The hallway they were in sat on an angle that took them from the center of the ship to its edge before straightening along the outer hull. Everyone hustled until they reached the far wall, gazing through the circular viewports at the smoke-filled sky and the ever-nearer ground. As if to emphasize Cappie's message, an imperial Lancer hoverjet shot past, its pointed and armored nose spitting fire at something beyond their field of view. An instant later, the deck shook violently, but Leon couldn't tell whether it was from shells hitting the vessel or the *Feywind's* few gun batteries firing at the incoming ships.

More concerning were the shapes slicing through the clouds and smog in the near distance. Coming from the left were a trio of airships, all larger than their failing mount. The smaller two were identical. Shaped like large *T*s, they were essentially powerful engines with huge snouts. Their forward segments bristled with weaponry, and sizeable ports to either side of the central shaft hinted at the potential for a devastating broadside.

However, these heavy cruisers were outclassed by the vessel they escorted. Obviously a dreadnought-class battleship, it consisted of a long, conical fuselage upon which was mounted a sharp, pointed prow and deck after deck of fixed and turreted cannon emplacements. To its sides, below the upper levels, were attached two bulbous compartments that started amidships and ran halfway to both stem and stern. To Leon's shock, two of the largest guns he'd ever seen emerged from these partitions to stare menacingly in their direction.

And all three warships bore the crest of the Sarconian Empire emblazoned beneath a large, crimson seven.

In opposition to all logic and reason, the *Feywind* rocked once more, and this time a burst of exhaust came from their right as a small volley of outgoing shells raced from one of the forward guns toward the dreadnought. In a show of almost casual indifference, its lume barrier activated just before the cartridges landed, their tiny explosions barely causing ripples on the surface.

Seconds later, the shields dropped, and a single, cacophonous shot rang out from one of the massive barrels. Sound and blast occurred at the same time, and Leon found himself tossed to the ground again as their junker spun and heaved with the force of the impact. As everyone staggered to their feet, another dozen puffs of smoke formed around the twin cruisers. Leon braced against the inner wall and found his body only *moderately* jostled as this new series of projectiles breached the hull.

After the convulsions subsided, the voice of a different crewman came from the hall speakers. "We just lost the last of the starboard batteries. Any survivors from those gun crews evacuate immediately. Again, the *Feywind* is disabled and defenseless. Cease all attempts at resistance and evacuate immediately. This will be the last message from the bridge. Good luck, and Creator's blessings." Throughout the message, Leon could hear a strong gust blowing along with the unmuffled sounds of ship-to-ship fighting. It would seem that the command deck had been blown open by one of those hits. The *Feywind* was now well and truly lost.

Sylette was once again the one spurring them on. "You heard him. We have to go! Move it!" She grabbed one of Matteo's arms and dragged him as Leon and Unter tightened their hold on their limp companion. They reached the end of the hall, and Renar threw open the sliding door marked as the entrance to the stairwell between decks.

On the other side was a roiling inferno. Renar ducked back, narrowly avoiding being singed when flames burst through the portal. Leon looked up and saw, beyond the growing fire, a hole in the ceiling gave them a glimpse of both a shattered cannon and the sky outside. This was the only way down on this side of the ship. Backtracking to the port side would cost them precious time—time they didn't have. Leon began to sweat; from exertion, the heat, and his attempts to wrack his brain for a solution.

"Lilith, use your magic to suppress the blaze. Unter, protect her with your shields until she finishes her incantation. Renar, once the flames ebb, cut that top pipe leaking gas into the chamber so it sprays outside instead. You're up first, Unter!" Leon was only slightly surprised that Sylette was the first to come up with a plan. Vallen, however, appeared irked, which was understandable considering his abilities would have been useful in this situation. He could see why the silver-haired strategist wouldn't trust him, though. Not only had she easily trounced Vallen in the graduation exercises, but she had also borne witness to all his pettiness and vanity in the time since then. Better to use the tools she knew and understood than a wild card like the Triaron.

Unter enchanted his shields and hopped to the fore of the conflagration, redirecting the flames. Velle also stepped forward, supporting him with glyphs that further protected him from the raging fire. In the center, Lilith continued her incantation, mumbling softly the words of power that would allow her to control the existing blaze rather than create it anew.

While they concentrated, a deck plate above groaned as the heat threatened to melt the bolts joining it to its support beam. Leon, still holding Matteo, cried, "Watch out!"

But Sylette had already noticed the danger, summoning half a dozen daggers that she loosed to pin it back into place. At that moment, Lilith finished her preparation, and with a shout of "Le'ashflame!" she spread her arms wide at the expanding inferno. With each motion of her hands, the fire receded, dwindling until nothing remained but embers. As the last flames were quashed, Renar leapt past the others, slicing through the offending gas line with his greatsword and sending several meters of it falling into the air beyond. In total, their amazing tactics and teamwork had only lost them a few minutes.

The rest of their journey passed without further incident. No more cannonades left or impacted the *Feywind*, and the only sound they heard, aside from their ragged breathing, was the screaming of the alarm. Battle noise continued to reach them through the thin hull, but they encountered no more evidence of the fighting beyond discarded parts and weapons or abandoned personal effects.

While the ship may be a junker to them, it had been a home to its crew, and the detritus of their upturned lives lay all around.

Upon reaching the hangar level, they passed crew members collecting tools and packs from adjoining rooms. Others rushed past them in the narrow corridor, hurrying toward salvation. Carrying Matteo was, by necessity, slowing them down. With each of these encounters, Vallen seemed to grow more anxious, as if he was worried there might not be enough launches to get them all off safely.

When a group of four passed them, carrying large backpacks and jangling bags, the Triaron broke down. "We would've made it to the hangar five minutes ago if we weren't towing that excess luggage!" He jabbed an accusatory finger at Matteo. "He's holding us back! What if there aren't any ships left? We'll die on this trash heap!"

It was, surprisingly, Velle who spoke up in Matteo's defense. "What do you want us to do? Leave one of our teammates behind?" Her tone made the very notion sound ludicrous.

"Exactly. He's always been deadweight—literally, in this case. Maybe some of the crew can take him—"

Whack!

Vallen never saw the blow coming. As he was trying to ditch their squadmate, Sylette, utter disdain plastered on her face, marched straight up to him and punched him so hard his head turned sideways and he fell backwards two paces. When he finally registered what happened, he looked at her with total disbelief.

"What was that for?"

"That was for being the most ungrateful, contemptible imbecile I've ever known. Your teammate saved your life, saved all our lives, by warning us that death ray was coming. And after the pain of doing so knocked him out, you want to leave him behind to die so you can get away a little faster. Turns out the only thing special about you is your powers. Everything else sickens me. You know what? Maybe we should leave *you* instead!"

Before he could respond, Sylette turned on her heel and motioned the group to follow her. Leon couldn't argue that Vallen deserved what he had gotten. As much as he admired the Triaron, he knew his friend needed a stern wakeup call to finally seize hold of the potential so many, like Metellus, saw in him. Perhaps, if they survived, this was just such a situation.

They picked up their pace thereafter, racing down the long hallway to the hangar at the rear of the ship. Vallen, thoroughly chastised, jogged silently a few steps behind. As the group neared the entrance, they could see light coming from the large bay doors, open wide. However, the first things they heard from inside were the sounds of small-arms fire and fighting. Either the crew was having a disagreement at the worst possible time, or they'd been boarded by the Sarconians.

In confirmation of their worst fears, a group of crewmen in blue Darmatian fatigues fell back through the gate, still pouring fire from their rifles and pistols at something inside. Immediately after the boom of each round firing came a clanging from inside the room, as though something metallic was deflecting every shot. Some return fire flew from the hangar, catching and dropping a couple of their allies before they could take cover behind the doorframe. The last, an older engimage with oily attire and advanced gray stubble, noticed them and cried for help before a coil of metal wire snaked through the door, piercing him through the ankle and dragging him, screaming, back inside.

"Monster! *Monster!* Get away! Run, you kids! Void you mons—"

Hidden by the hangar wall, his cries were suddenly cut off by a liquid squelch that suggested he had been stabbed to death by the same implement that had carried him away. Leon felt his heartbeat accelerate and the hair on his arms stand on end. What in Oblivion could these men have been fighting? He'd never seen anything like it.

At his side, Lilith looked like she might lose her lunch, and Velle clung to Vallen in terror despite her recent displeasure with him. Unter was impassive as ever, and Renar's shaking seemed to indicate that he shared Leon's silent fears. However, he couldn't quite puzzle out Sylette's reaction. She seemed concerned but also . . . thoughtful. Had she witnessed something similar in the past?

"Come on out, cadets. I know yer there. Grandpa here said as much. You have till the count o' five, then I'm comin' in after ye. Five . . . "

His voice was authoritative, with a hint of age and some lack of refinement, his speech dominated by his accent and not his education. Leon glanced at his companions, their eyes meeting as they quietly considered what to do.

"Should we go out and take our chances?"

"You saw what he did. We can't fight that!"

"Four!"

"Do the Sarcs take prisoners?"

"Do you think I could survive in prison? Don't be absurd, Renar!"

"Three!"

"We should take our chances and fight him. At least we'd be doing *something*!"

The last was Vallen, who had named one of the three options Leon could think of, though it was probably the least viable. Running and surrendering were the others, as far as Leon could tell, but the first would probably see them chased down and killed or obliterated when the *Feywind* crashed. Option two might lead to rotting in a Sarconian prison for the foreseeable future, rumors of which were hardly pleasant.

Only Sylette remained silent during their debate, staring at the hangar entrance as though enthralled by the streak of blood the elder engimage had left behind.

"Two . . . one . . . and . . ."

He never got to finish as Sylette unilaterally made up her mind and stepped out into the chamber, walking toward the speaker. Everyone else looked at each other, then slowly stood and followed their de facto leader, Matteo being carried between Leon and Unter as before. Only Vallen looked pleased with the arrangement, beaming at the prospect of a fight. *Does he realize this is basically suicide?* Leon wondered. *A bunch of cadets going up against an unknown opponent?*

As they entered, Leon took in the entirety of the large space. Bolted to the walls were level after level of large shelves, their contents now disturbed and mostly strewn across the polished metal floor. Above, rails ran the length of the ceiling. Attached to these ruts were large chains, cables, and hooks for moving cargo and working on vehicles. At the far end of the hangar lay a few small skiffs, frames broken and likely unusable, for external work on the *Feywind* at dock or low altitudes. Nearby, the outer doors, each about thirty meters tall, were thrown open, and wind gusted about the bay, whipping papers and other light detritus about.

Directly in front of this portal rested a sizeable military transport class ship of reasonably recent manufacture with the Sarconian sigil on its nose. The landing ramp was down, and a small platoon of soldiers with rifles trained on the approaching cadets kneeled or stood at its base. And in front of these combatants, dressed in full plate, a burgundy cape hanging from his pauldrons and a metal patch covering one eye, was a man who was clearly their leader.

He was further burdened by two rapiers, hilts visible above his shoulders, and, strangely, two spools of thick metal wire at his belt. Leon followed the path of one of the spools, which was unwound, and found the other end sticking in the chest of the engimage who had tried to warn them off. His body was halfway between them and Eye-Patch, a winding trail of blood marking where he had been drug. Around the corpse lay many others like it, some with bullet wounds, others similarly stabbed, all wearing Darmatian colors. *It would seem as though very few, if any, of the crew made good on their escape through here.*

For a minute, nobody spoke. Both parties gazed at each other, sizing up their numbers and potential strengths or weaknesses. Vallen was grinning, his hand on his weapon. Unter looked ready to bring his shields up at the slightest movement. Velle had her hands wide and feet planted in her fastest casting stance. Even the soldiers on the other side had fingers on their triggers, waiting for the order to fire.

But it didn't come, at least not yet. Eye-Patch had spent the entire time staring at Sylette, who stood at the fore of their group. Suddenly his good eye narrowed, then went wide, and he burst into inexplicably jubilant laughter.

After finishing his strange outburst, Eye-Patch mocked wiping a tear from his patch. "I know he told me yud be here, but ta be honest, I didn't entirely believe him. Yet here ye are, in the flesh, all grown up and beautiful. Makes yer uncle proud, that it does."

Sylette's face stormed with barely restrained rage. "You and I aren't related in the slightest, Rittermarschal Valescar. Get to the point. Why are you and he here?"

Rittermarschal? Leon's thoughts spun. *Rittermarschal? As in, one of the leaders of the Sarconian military? Here? Now? Why would one of their top commanders come to capture a junker like the* Feywind, *of all things?*

Rittermarschal Valescar sketched despair at her response. "Ye wound me, lass, ye really do. I'm here for no other reason than ta pick ye up . . . "

"Princess Sylette Artorios."

Chapter 10

Light's Requiem

"Wait, what? You're a princess? A *Sarconian* princess?" Vallen's incredulous shout broke the stillness that had descended in the wake of Valescar's impossible announcement.

The rittermarschal turned his eye on the youth, his lips spread in a wide grin. "What? She never told ye she was royalty? Make no mistake. Yer charmin' companion is the only daughter of Emperor Sychon Artorios and third in line ta the throne of the Sarconian Empire."

"Then . . . then this war is about retrieving their heir? But how could we have known?" Lilith's voice was quiet as always, but the glare she aimed at the princess was one of accusation. It said: "All our troubles are *your* fault."

As Vallen watched, the hatred marring Sylette's face deepened, creasing into hardened lines and dark recesses. "No, I have nothing to do with this war. I've never been more than an afterthought to *him*. Besides, I renounced my claim to the throne when he exiled me."

The revelations were coming quickly now. In the brief time he had known her, Vallen had always thought Sylette was a shrew simply because she could be. Of course, she probably thought the same thing about him, given how she'd acted toward him in the past hour. *But then again, do I really care how she views me?*

Valescar shook his head. "Whatever ye may believe, His Majesty did send me here ta get ye. He regrets exilin' ye and wants ye back. Besides, it'll be safer with us, giv'n how things seem to be—"

"Why do I get the feeling you made most of that up? That man has never viewed me as anything other than a pawn. If he wants me back, it's so he can use me . . . just like he used my mother." Sylette's eyes flared with unbridled fury as she began materializing daggers around her. "Just like he used her and then threw

197

her aside. And you, you disgusting piece of filth, were the executioner."

For the first time, the enemy commander looked uncomfortable, as if he actually cared about the lost princess. But that thought was secondary to Vallen. His blood was beginning to boil at the possibility of combat. The entire day he'd been forced to exist in a state contrary to his very credo: *stay in control; never be helpless again.* Fear dominated Vallen's mind, birthed by a power beyond his comprehension. He'd failed to coerce or command those around him. His companions continued to ignore his guidance and attempts to save his life and, by association, theirs. *If only they'd listened to me, or fought harder on graduation day . . . or . . . or . . . something, we wouldn't be in this mess.*

And I wouldn't have lost control again.

"Sylette, I never meant ta harm ye or yer mother, but she betrayed the empire and tried ta kill yer father. There's only one recourse for—"

"Spare me your platitudes. She never needed to die; she was set up, and you know it. How many other innocents, just like her, have you had to kill to protect your *empire*? How bloody are your hands . . . and his? In fact, my blood should be on his hands, too. Who exiles a ten-year-old girl . . . just casts her off into the world with nothing but the clothes on her back? If the Farkos family hadn't taken me in and been a *real* family to me, I'd be dead in some gutter, just like he intended. So, to Oblivion with you, your empire, and *His Majesty!*"

Before she could cast her daggers, Vallen charged in. This was *exactly* what he needed. A chance to fight and clear his head. No more worrying about death rays, massive ships with guns many times his size, or the feelings of his companions. There was only one person he ever needed to focus on: himself. Vallen was in control. He was powerful, and he would beat the enemy before him, singlehandedly, and silence the growing doubts in his mind once and for all.

Leon reached for the hem of his tunic as he passed but missed. *Sorry, Leon, you can't help me this time.* Velle shouted something incoherent, but it was almost certainly some warning or another. *Don't fret. I've got this.* Renar, Lilith, and Unter drew their weapons, concern and fear written on the features of all but the Hue, who was impassive as ever. *You weaklings won't have to do a thing. Watch and learn.*

Only Sylette's voice came through clearly. "You imbecile! You can't beat him like that!"

Her anger and frustration were misplaced. He was the Triaron; no one who didn't know his capabilities could best him in combat. This fight would be over in an instant.

Behind Valescar, his platoon of soldiers sighted their guns in on Vallen, and he made ready to jump over their fusillade. However, Valescar smiled through the open front of his helm and waved them down. Sixteen rifles dropped, and the soldiers in light mail and crimson uniforms fell back several paces.

Vallen used the opening his opponent gave him, turning his weapon into a staff and firing a gust of wind to knock him off his feet. Perplexingly, the rittermarschal chose to take the blast head on, the impact failing to move him in the slightest. The only evidence that he had even responded to the attack was that the face shield of his helm was now closed.

How did he close it? His hands haven't moved. He strafed left, swinging the pole in a figure eight pattern and releasing bursts of fire every time it neared the floor. Each torrent of flame arced across the metal floor, closing on Valescar from a half dozen angles as Vallen moved.

Without drawing his weapons or countering, the older fighter evaded each stream, moving closer to the Triaron with each step. Vallen fell back, converting his pole to a halberd, which he held with one hand while the other hovered above the blade. He channeled electricity between both arms and funneled it into the tip, creating a crackling ball of blue-white lightning. Valescar stood still, all but inviting Vallen to complete his lengthy charging and fire at him.

Well, he asked for it, Vallen decided.

He stabbed the spear forward, releasing the orb of energy, and the powerful spell rocketed across the room toward the Sarconian. Valescar finally spoke, a single word, "Mag'heval," and raised his arms. Vallen felt his jaw drop in surprise as an entire *metal plate* from the decking jumped up to absorb and dissipate his strike.

"For'emag'wa," came the next chant, and the Triaron threw himself in a roll to the side as that same several-tonne slab crashed into the floor where he had been seconds prior. Vallen jumped back to his feet, favorite krenesh blade in his right hand. In total, the entire exchange had taken twenty seconds, and he was already starting to feel his grasp on the situation slipping.

Valescar took four casual steps to his left, returning to the spot from which he'd started the fight. Unlike Vallen, he was still breathing normally and showed no outward signs of fatigue. "Air, fire, lightnin', and a morphin' blade. Ye must be the much-touted Triaron of Darmatia. Rumors 'bout ye have even made it as far as the empire, but it looks like ye ain't worth the words those peddlers weave." He seemed to notice Vallen's panting and clicked his tongue in dissatisfaction. "Ye don't even know how ta use yer powers proper. Who taught ye how ta fight?"

Vallen snarled and leapt at him as he replied, "*I* did!" His swing was a straight slash from floor to head height, carrying with it an updraft of blistering flames. The enemy commander sidestepped right, kicking the Triaron jarringly in the back as he passed. He gasped in pain and nearly fell to his knees. *That kick was insane! Where is his strength coming from?*

"Ye always attack head on, thinkin' ta overwhelm yer opponent. What if yer foe is mightier than ye?" As Vallen struggled to maintain his balance, he was backhanded by a solid metal gauntlet. He managed to get the slightest lightning barrier up in time but still found himself skidding across the metal deck at the force of the impact. After sliding a pain-filled ten meters, the Triaron's progress was arrested by a discarded cargo crate, and he wearily dragged his beaten body back upright.

Vallen's vision muddied and shuddered; the hit to his neck had disoriented him. He'd never been this outclassed in his life. Every person Vallen had ever battled had been overpowered by his speed, brawn, and versatility. Only Sylette had the distinction of being able to hold him off, though he surely would have won that engagement as well, had that been his goal. *I have to go at him harder, faster, with more rage. If I attack even more aggressively, he'll break. He has to.*

Two daggers soared over Vallen's head, and for the first time, Valescar was forced to unspool one of his wires to defend himself. The cord whipped upwards, knocking both off course to clatter harmlessly behind him. Vallen cast a furious glance over his shoulder. Sure enough, Sylette, Leon, and his other companions had their weapons drawn, preparing to come to his aid. Matteo, still unconscious, lay silently on the ground behind them.

"*No!* Stay back!"

Sylette looked at him as one might a disobedient hound. "Are you kidding? Use your brain for once! I've never seen him lose in single combat. This isn't a fight you can win!"

He stumbled, then solidified his stance, denying her words with every fiber of his being. "I *will* win . . . I have to! Stay out of it!" Her groan was audible, and justified, but she didn't understand. Winning was everything. To fall, to rely on another, or even to need help was weakness. That way was the way of loss. *I'll never let that happen again.*

Vallen staggered into a run, channeling most of his remaining men'ar for his next strike. His weapon melted, turning into a cool liquid that coated his hands before becoming solid gloves. Both glowed with energy as the Triaron closed within five meters of his opponent. Then he unleashed a flurry of punches, a combination of flames, wind, and lightning ejecting from his fists.

The rittermarschal ducked the first, a line of fire singing the air where he had been. By the second, he was into Vallen's chest, knocking it aside. The third punch was redirected upwards as a gauntlet impacted his elbow, sending a cascade of jagged energy sparking into the ceiling and showering embers across the room. Vallen countered, activating his electric field and overclocking his spirit output to release a shockwave. He nearly blacked out, having never used so much men'ar in such a short time, but managed to control his shaking limbs.

When Vallen looked up several seconds later, he expected to see Valescar on the ground, fried by the sudden explosion of his shield. Instead, he had impossibly flown several meters backwards, one of his cables connected to a nearby steel support beam. The Sarconian looked dejected, and his disappointment was evident in his voice. "I get ta fight a livin' legend, and that's all ye can do? Pathetic. Ye don't even know the basics of men'ar use, just throw lightnin' and fire all over the place, hopin' that ye hit somethin'. So much wasted effort. Just because you don't need fancy words and catalysts don't mean that ye can just ignore the cost their usage offsets. Why, we don't Engrave our weapons for fun! We do it so the formula draws spirit energy from our surroundin's, rather than just our body! You may be castin' faster than everyone else, boy, but yer also destroyin' yer own body in the proc—"

His words were ultimately falling on deaf ears. Vallen could care less about how he used his power; he only cared that he had it. So what if he burned his own energy, his own life force, in the process? Strength, self-assurance, and staying in control were all that mattered. While Valescar lectured him on his failings, he summoned the last of his will to raise his weapon, molding it into a long-hafted spear. Using nothing but sheer brawn, he cast the gleaming projectile at the Sarconian.

As he did so, one of the soldiers noticed his intent, brought his rifle up, and discharged it, hoping to stop Vallen from taking their leader unaware. Simultaneously, Valescar saw the incoming weapon, bringing a single palm up and chanting, "Sto'metla." The bullet hit the Triaron in the right shoulder, sending a spurt of blood flashing into the air and spinning him all the way around. He collapsed to the floor, gritting his teeth as a white flash of pain erupted from the wound. A primal howl tore itself from Vallen's lips as his vision clouded from shock and men'ar overuse. His last sight was a baffled Valescar being hit by the spear, as though such a thing were entirely impossible.

Guess we'll call it a draw.

Leon had cringed with each blow Vallen suffered, wondering why he refused to give up, or accept aid, in a fight he had no chance of winning. Even after being knocked down, after staggering and barely staying on his feet, after being bruised and battered, he kept doggedly battling on.

He, Sylette, and the others had been prepared to enter the fray when their teammate fell the first time, but Vallen had adamantly refused their advice and support. Now the situation had devolved further. Vallen was down—perhaps for good this time—and Valescar had taken a glancing blow to his chest plate from the Triaron's spear. Though the blow hardly left a nick on the armor, it surprised the enemy commander. He glared at the fallen youth with what could only be interpreted as rage.

Sylette spoke softly and quickly into the stunned group of cadets. "We have to get that fool out of there, *now*. Valescar has a . . . quirk about never getting hit while fighting. At best, he's going to severely harm that imbecile. At worst, he's going to kill us all. We need to grab him and escape as quickly as possible."

"Where will we go? There aren't any ships left, and the *Feywind* is sinking!" As if to emphasize Velle's point, a large blast was heard from deep in the vessel, and the deck tilted slightly. Small tools, gears, and other detritus not strapped down skidded toward the far wall to the left of the tense engagement.

"There!" Renar pointed at the Sarconian landing craft behind the rittermarschal and his soldiers. "That's the only flight-worthy vehicle left. We'll . . . we'll have to break through and steal it!" His voice cracked as his somewhat-slow mind grasped just what his terrifying plan entailed.

"You expect us to defeat that madman?" Lilith's timid trill voiced aloud their fears.

"Not defeat," Sylette amended. "Outmaneuver. We don't have to beat him, just get past and delay him long enough to fly out of his—"

"That won't work," Leon interjected from his position near Velle and the unmoving Matteo. "Vallen's last attack confirmed something for me. Valescar is a Unique-Class mage with the power to manipulate magnetic fields. He fully expected to redirect Vallen's metal spear, but didn't realize it isn't a type of substance he can control. If we get into a ship made of ordinary steel and other metallic materials, he'll ground us before we can so much as take off."

"Yes, Leon, that's right. I was getting to that part. What you didn't let me say is that he has an effective range of about a hundred meters. If we can distract him long enough to get that far, he won't be able to stop us." Sylette flashed them a winning smile, but Leon could see the nervousness underneath. "Besides, I should be able to hold him off for a while. I know a little about him, and he can't control my daggers since they're magical constructs."

However, another plan was starting to take root in Leon's mind. Daggers and acrobatics wouldn't be enough to keep the rittermarschal and his troops from stopping or ending them. They would need a more permanent, impassable barrier for their ploy to be successful. "Is there anything else you can tell me about Valescar . . . about his powers, his personality, anything at all?"

"Uhhh, yes, his armor and weapons! He's a pseudo-Invoker, so he's able to use any metal coated with special glyphs without a chant. Because of this, he's covered his armor, wires, and rapiers with formulas and catalytic writings so he can control them at will. He'll have to use an incantation to manipulate any other metal. Oh! You probably saw from the idiot's match that Valescar loves to taunt and chat with his opponent. You could even go as far as to say that he views fighting as sport. If he somehow calms down again, we can probably buy some time by getting him to talk."

Good. Leon could use all that. "Alright, I've come up with a strategy that should work. I'll need you guys to rescue Vallen and buy me some time—about two minutes. I know that's a lot to ask, but if you can manage, you should make it out of here alive. Ready?" It was now Leon's turn to save Vallen, to give him another chance, just as his friend had given him all those years ago.

Each member of the group nodded in assent before Leon remembered one final, crucial detail. He gestured at the Sarconian ship. "By the way, does anyone actually know how to fly that thing?"

The edges of his vision were beginning to tint red. Not literally, mind you—that would be ridiculous. Still, his fury at the insignificant, weak peon who had the gall to barely put up a fight before landing an impossible blow on him only continued to grow. Valescar could've sworn that the weapon the Triaron was wielding was metal. It gleamed like steel, cut like steel, and clanged like steel. Then again, steel didn't morph, flow, and liquefy the way his instrument had. Perhaps it had been his *own* oversight that resulted in this indignity. Either way, it was past time to eliminate this boy and his companions—minus the princess, of course.

Wait. This was an opportunity to clear both of his objectives at once. Taking down the remaining cadets and securing the princess would be easy enough, but this boy, the so-called Triaron, unconscious not ten meters from him, would certainly make an adequate vessel for that warlock. Not that Valescar desired to aid Sarcon in the slightest, but he had his orders directly from his liege, and loyalty trumped all else. Furthermore, it would also make for ironic vengeance. What better way to get back at a fool who couldn't properly use their gifts than to give those talents to someone else?

The deck beneath his feet rocked and lurched sideways as an explosion reverberated from the bowels of the ship. *Best hurry before we go down with 'er.* Valescar silently magnetized his boots and walked up the gentle slope to claim his prize, motioning for his soldiers to fan out and secure the rest of the kids. *I've had my fill of disappointin' fights for the day. Let them clean up the mess.*

When he had traveled half the distance to the fallen youth, the rest of his group broke from the gathering they were having and quickly spread out on the far side of the hangar. Sylette stood in a shallow stance directly across from him. Valescar sighed. He truly didn't want to fight Lanara's daughter, but if it was between that and disobeying an order, he would only do enough to bring her into custody.

A tense moment elapsed as both sides refused to make a move. Then, on the left, a large Terran boy hefting a massive greatsword charged at one of his rifle squads. *More courage than brains, that one*, Valescar inwardly ridiculed.

The soldiers opened fire, a barrage that should have left him filled with holes, but a series of shimmering protective glyphs appeared in the air about him and deflected the bullets to either side. *Ah, the old two-man cell tactic. Looks like the princess remembered some of what I taught her.*

Behind the brawny simpleton was a crimson Sylph, blessed with the usual grace, beauty, and magic potency of her race. The girl's wings were not deployed, but she was running behind him, swiftly casting barrier after barrier to ensure her frontline brawler wasn't harmed. With a roar and a mighty crash, the boy reached the gun line. Chaos ensued immediately.

However, even if his troops failed, Valescar would not. As the daggers came flying in by the twos and threes, he was dodging high and low, left and right, weaving his twin coils to knock aside any he could not avoid using footwork alone. With each blade past, he moved closer to Sylette, knowing that closing the distance would force the mid-range mage to retreat or enter disadvantageous close combat. She matched his steps, edging nearer to the hangar door but never ceasing her summoning. *Good. She'll run out of men'ar soon. Ye can't win a battle of endurance with me, lass.*

He passed the Triaron's body but barely gave it a second thought. *Ye can always pick up dessert once ye finish the main course.* Sylette began to vary the barrage, expanding her range and sending projectiles from both the sides and front. It was simple enough to counter. Valescar's rapiers flew from their sheathes unbidden, hovering on his flanks and spinning in a fluid dance to protect their master. Not even the smallest of insects could make it through his perfect defense. He ceased evading, walking calmly toward his opponent as his mind and hands conducted the symphony of twirling metal.

A mage of his caliber and capacity could keep this up for half an hour. On the other hand, Sylette, though she had improved considerably from the fumbling child he had helped train, could only seem to summon a dozen daggers at once and split them into a maximum of three angles. *And,* Valescar estimated, *I bet she can only manage for a couple minutes before hittin' her limit.* Even if she didn't, they were nearly to the bay entrance. Once in the hallway, he would no longer need a multi-directional defense and would rapidly overwhelm her.

Without warning, Sylette stopped casting and stood still with her hands on her hips and a smug look on her face. Valescar remembered that pose from long ago—the pose the little princess always made when she thought she had you beat at Seven-Sided Chess or some insignificant game of her own invention. The recollection was so nostalgic that he let his own opportunity to attack go by the wayside, simply staring at the girl who looked so very much like her mother while he waited for the inevitable proclamation of victory.

It came quickly. "You lose, Rittermarschal Valescar."

"And pray tell, lass, why I've lost? Ye got nowhere ta run, and you've been burnin' yer gas for almost two minutes while I've got plenty of juice ta spare. Where's yer winnin' hand?"

She gestured with one pale arm to the far end of the hangar behind him. Obligingly, he turned to look while maintaining the barest wariness of an attack from the rear. "Your troops are down, that feeble-minded halfwit is safe, and we have your ship. What say you to that?"

Valescar's soldiers were no more. While he had witnessed the fall of the left squad to the brute with an oversized chunk of sharpened metal, the right had fallen to the combined efforts of a small, brown-haired girl and a huge, blue-skinned Hue. *Little wonder,* he thought. The shields on the giant's arms looked like they could just as easily stop a bullet as bludgeon a construct of flesh and blood back into paste. The scorch marks adorning the floor and walls also spoke to the application of somewhat powerful fire magic, likely the handiwork of the little brunette. Furthermore, the last of their party, a sandy-topped boy of moderate build distinguished only by his glasses, was hauling the downed Triaron up the cargo ramp of his own vessel.

He had underestimated these young cadets, to be sure, but he was still confident in his victory. A small chuckle escaped his mouth as he regarded Sylette once more. "Ye know me and my abilities, Missy. I'll just grab that ship out o' the air and haul ye back before ye get ten meters. Besides, how're you gonna rejoin yer pals when yer on the wrong side of the room?"

She smiled the arrogant, self-assured grin that she had always flashed when she won or got her way. "We'll see about the second. The first, well, let's just say you have more pressing issues than to worry about me."

For the first time, the post-combat stillness allowed Valescar to hear the growing crescendo from across the hangar. The words were barely coherent, but he could recognize their form anywhere. After all, every mage knew to fear phrases spoken in such a manner:

"The judge lifts upright,   "His bright radiance,
your chosen holy people,   Perfect light, known to all beings,
arrayed in splendor."   It's luminance grand."

Most casters knew hardly any of the old tongue, the language of the Eliade, and what they did know they used in varying syllables to manipulate the men'ar inside and outside their bodies into the manifestations of spiritual energy called spells. These incantations were short, their power ranging from weak to strong on the basis of the intrinsic properties of the wielder, the formulas as well as catalysts used, and the type and length of chant. However, there was a school of nigh unmatched modern magic that bridged the old and the new. Since the words of the ancients were both hard to decipher *and* speak, some brilliant sorcerers spent lifetime after lifetime translating the words of old magic into contemporary vernacular. The result was several dozen invocations far mightier than any others: the Long Chants.

Marked by a specific syllabic count and the use of Common speech, these spells were second only to Lost Magics in terms of force. And now, the blond-locked boy sparkling with the iridescence of summoned energy was reciting the words to one such spell . . . in between Valescar and his transport.

Never mind his vehicle. That was secondary. Never mind how the cadet even knew a Long Chant. That was tertiary. Never mind how woefully short he'd sold these children. That was quaternary. No, Valescar had just one focus at the moment.

I have ta stop that brat from finishin'.

⁕⁕⁕

"His shield is righteous,   "Divine, unyielding,
only the just it protects,   Dreary night to brightest day,
blocking out their foes."   Ageless, immortal."

Leon finished the fourth stanza, leaving only two more to complete. He felt as though his body would collapse at any moment, and he was already falling behind the timetable he had told Sylette. Two minutes down. Sylette was distracting Valescar brilliantly, and the double two-man cells had defeated all sixteen of the rittermarschal's riflemen. *I suppose that will teach him to bring along more reliable henchmen in the future*, Leon thought.

As if to answer his very prayers, Velle's ministrations had finally awakened Matteo, who, though shaken by the quick synopsis of events given to him, nervously agreed to their plan and took his comrade in unconsciousness, Vallen, aboard the Sarconian vessel. He seemed to know a little about airships and said he'd try to figure out the controls while they executed their plan. Renar then joined him, thinking that something picked up from his father, the general, might come in handy. Hopefully they learned quickly, or no one was getting off the *Feywind* alive.

Valescar and Sylette had stopped fighting, and the old commander was now gazing his way with dawning understanding. *Blast,* Leon fumed, *she thinks I'm almost done.* The worst possible thing that could happen would be for him to be attacked while executing his Long Chant. While doing so, Leon was rooted in place, unable to move or defend himself lest he break the spell activation process and have to start over from the beginning.

It was his eccentricity, the result of his rebellion against his father, that enabled him to learn the invocation in the first place. Poring through old books hoping to find the weirdest, strangest ideas he could possibly enact, he had, by chance, stumbled across a Long Chant that perfectly suited his magical affinity. Leon had considered it a strange coincidence that he developed holy light magic in the first place. Since religion smacked of the same order that his father adored, he wanted nothing to do with it. Then, when he discovered the Long Chant best suited to divine spells, he had almost chalked it to up to some odd sort of destiny. Almost.

Still, it was practically tailor made for this situation—if his casting wasn't cut short. If he could just succeed in finishing this single incantation, Leon was sure that his friends would survive. He began the fifth stanza, at which Valescar abandoned all focus on Sylette and charged him.

"I raise up my voice,
Your servant beckons with need,
Crying 'Save my kin.'"

Halfway through. Velle jumped in front of him, throwing reflective glyphs into the rittermarschal's path. Unlike Renar and Unter during the graduation match, he used his cables to propel himself over them. When she raised them up, he'd slide under or send a wire shooting toward the ceiling to wrap around a chain or beam and carry him to even greater heights. At last, in a massive outpouring of energy, she pressed her palms together and brought forth a great wall of magic panels stretching from floor to roof. Valescar didn't miss a beat, tearing the floor violently from its bed and shattering the barriers above into thousands of useless crystalline shards.

"Deliver to us,
A boon beyond our knowledge,
Hope above our fear."

The Sylph collapsed, completely spent, and Lilith dragged the larger woman past Leon and toward the ship. Unter stepped forward, unwavering as always, prepared to defend him with his enhanced shields and body. From Valescar's rear, Sylette seemed to recover from her shock at his sudden reversal of intent and renewed her furious assault. Daggers rained down at his back, but his rapiers were like living things, blocking and deflecting each incoming blow with almost no apparent effort.

Then a flying projectile connected with the soft weld adjoining the hilt to the blade of the left saber. The thin weapon shattered in two, and the knife arrowed miraculously into the thin chain mail between Valescar's shoulder pauldron and chest plate. His injury could not have been great, but still he roared with fury, lashing out with his cables in every direction.

To the fore, Unter brought his four great shields up in a protective array. Most of the whipping blows were deflected or absorbed, but some found their way past his bastion. These strikes were too much, even for his flesh-strengthening magic, and streaks of violet blood flew from his arms and legs to streak the ground around him.

Leon cringed, wanting to accelerate his invocation but knowing that would only ruin all their hard work. *I will be strong, I will finish. I will not let their efforts be in vain!* he shouted into his thoughts as he began the sixth and final stanza.

"Unveil your power,
Let men revel in your strength,
May your aspect come."

Sylette rushed forward, hoping to distract Valescar and take some of his attention off of Unter. Her guard down, the Sarconian merely directed a wire backwards, which wrapped around her legs, stomach, and chest as she squirmed and gasped for breath. The girl cried out in agony, and something seemed to change inside the rittermarschal, upon which he loosened the grip of the wire and tossed her gently past Leon and Unter. He gazed over his shoulder to assure himself Sylette was alright and saw her stagger to her feet, blood trickling from wounds on her forehead and left arm. She began summoning more daggers, but after creating three, the fourth fizzled out into nothing more than shining particles.

Valescar renewed his assault, all his weapons focused on Unter. The Hue was swiftly driven to his knees, and more and more wounds opened across his exposed hide and muscles as his uniform was torn to pieces. With a cry, Valescar jumped in the air, side-kicking the blue giant in his exposed stomach while his plates were occupied defending against the Sarconian's other attacks. More ichor and spittle flew from his mouth as the magically augmented kick lifted his massive bulk from his feet and sent him flying over Leon's head. The impact of his landing caused the deck to shudder.

Rebirth

"Keep us from night's grasp,
Never will your brilliance pass,
Infallible blaze."

It was finished. Valescar moved to end him, but the dazzling brilliance that enveloped him exploded outwards as Leon invoked the spell with its name.

"Spell Twenty-Three, Divine Barrier!"

An orange glow spread rapidly in every direction, centering on the caster. It continued until it impacted the walls, floor, and ceiling, expanding in width until it was approximately a meter across. The radiance of the wall was blinding, but Leon barely noticed, enveloped as he was in the middle of its warm embrace.

The Sarconian attempted to breach the solid wall of light almost immediately, hitting multiple spots with his cables, rapiers, and even punches and kicks from his hands and feet. Each slightly dented the surface, sending ripples through the construct that raced from end to end as soft, slow-moving yellow rings. They bounced off the edges of the spell, resounding with a pleasant, heavenly chime, and intertwined with their fellows to create magnificent, swirling crosshatches and patterns.

After Valescar continued in this manner for several moments, it appeared to dawn on him that he was neither making progress nor was the barrier actively attempting to repel him. Though Leon had never performed this spell before, it occurred to him that this divine wall was purely neutral. It neither allowed access through its shell nor did it attack those who would do it harm. The only individual it protected was its originator, sealed between its boundaries.

And seal was an incredibly accurate term for the technique. Leon found himself unable to move, surrounded as he was by the scintillating gelatinous construct. He could still see, breathe, talk, and hear normally, but his other senses and limbs were bound tight. At some point, he remembered reading that Long Chants almost had a mind of their own, making up in semi-consciousness what their user lacked in magic potency and men'ar capacity. Going in, Leon had known that this would likely be the end result. *But . . . I had no other choice.*

Behind him, a sudden mechanical cough and the whirring of gravpads signaled that Matteo and Renar had finally brought the transport online. Valescar must have heard these sounds as well, or seen the flare of the engines, for he redoubled his efforts to break through the shield. Invocation after invocation flew from his throat as he tore metal plates, beams, wiring, pipes, and other debris from the floors, ceiling, and walls in an attempt to bypass Leon's construct. But for every obstacle removed from its path, the dazzling ooze expanded to fill the gap, instantly reclaiming the lost space.

As Valescar stood panting, hands on his knees after his exertions and surrounded by piles of detritus, Leon took pity on him. "It's no use. Divine Barrier will spread infinitely in every direction as long as something does not block its path and its user doesn't run out of energy to sustain it."

Valescar's one eye glared fire back at Leon. "So, if I rip out this ship's guts, it'll fly off ta the horizon and drain ye completely?"

I guess I hadn't considered that. "I suppose so, but I have faith that my friends will be long gone by then."

"Leon, it's time to go! Get out of that thing and come here!" That was Matteo's voice, calling to him from the vessel's ramp. He was a good friend, if a little unsure of himself and lacking the assertive nature to make his youthful intellect known.

"Your plan worked! Leave that piece of garbage and get on the ship!" Sylette's even tones, simultaneously strong and weak in a strange dichotomy. Though he had only recently become aware of her identity, he understood that a battle was raging deep inside her over who and what she really was.

He smiled, closing his eyes and letting their words wash over him. It was likely the last time he'd hear them. "I . . . I can't, actually. Once activated, this spell will keep running until the caster's spirit energy is completely spent. I'm stuck. There's nothing you can do."

"Don't be ridiculous! We're not leaving without you!" Leon heard the rhythm of running footfalls as Velle dashed down the slope, followed by Sylette and Matteo. All three began beating on the barrier at his back, trying to force their arms through the transparent film to grab him. *Ah, Velle. Sweet, kind, motherly Velle.* She always acted the jealous dunce, but that was merely a facade she put on for Vallen. Underneath she had a bigger heart with more love in it than anyone. But even her unconditional care and concern wouldn't be enough to free him. *I have to get them to leave me! If the spell falls, this will all be for naught!*

A deep, rumbling shout echoed from the bowels of the transport. "Terran brave has made his choice. Cherish us enough to sacrifice self, he does. Let act not be in vain. We must away before big ship crashes, all be lost." He had only heard Unter, the solitary, giant Hue, speak once before. Even so, he seemed possessed of wisdom well beyond his years and station. *Thank you, Unter. I wish we'd had more time to get to know each other.*

Sylette broke away. Given her complex background, hardship and loss were clearly old, familiar friends. Matteo and Velle, however, refused to give in, and along with the faint patter of their strikes, he could hear them weeping softly. It was all Leon could do not to break down then, to try to find a way to stop his spell, to hope against all odds that they could all escape together.

Once more it was Unter who came to his rescue. Though he couldn't turn to see, he could hear the incoherent screams and pumping fists of his squadmates as the Hue's large limbs easily picked them up and hauled them back aboard the Sarconian craft. "Thank you, Terran brave. Long will your courage be remembered."

And then they were gone, Sylette leading the way with her quiet footsteps, Unter trailing behind her with the still yelling and kicking Velle and Matteo. Shortly after, the boarding ramp retracted, and the ship took off. It hovered for a moment, as if unsure how to proceed, then clanged into the left wall before finally finding its freedom in the rapidly ascending sky beyond the falling *Feywind.*

Alone with his thoughts, Leon was filled with emotion. *I only wish I could've spoken to Vallen one more time, to say goodbye, to tell him how . . . how he saved me.* The tears came slowly, not quite dropping from his eyes but being whisked away by the star-bright rings that cascaded to and fro on the surface of his bastion and prison. *Was it worth it? Have I made the right decision? Yes, a thousand times yes.* Leon had never felt more at peace than at that moment.

"So . . . what now?"

Oh. Leon had almost forgotten he wasn't alone on this journey. Valescar still stood across from him, about a meter of air and radiant gel separating them. Unlike Leon, he didn't seem resigned to his fate. Having seen his strength in action, though, it was entirely likely that he would yet survive their coming doom.

"We wait. Either my barrier will run out and collapse, or the *Feywind* will crash. After that . . . well, I don't expect I'll have an 'after that.'" He chuckled, a pleasing, melodic sound that resonated as flowing pink and crimson pigments in the surrounding barrier.

"Ye seem rather . . . acceptin' o' yer fate for, well, anyone o' any age for that matter."

"Do you have someone you want to protect, Rittermarschal? Someone you'd give anything to keep safe above all else?"

"Of course! The emperor. I'd never let any harm befall him."

Leon shook his head. "But that's a matter of responsibility, of duty. What I'm asking about goes beyond that. Is there anyone you love more than the entirety of the world, for whom you'd forsake duty if the two conflicted?"

Valescar opened his mouth, then closed it again. After a moment of thought, he said, "Yes, I do have someone like that."

"Then you should understand why I'm at peace. You see, I spent most of my life living someone else's dream, never realizing I was my own person, with my own mind and my own heart. Then a certain crass, arrogant, jerk of a guy broke down the automaton I had become, shattered my illusions, and gave me back my free will. At first, however, I didn't change all that much. I tried to mimic him, to be as much like him as possible, but I failed. That's when I realized that I'd merely reverted to doing what I had been doing my whole life. So, I sought instead to stand at his side—not to become him, but to support him. To be there when he needed me, to ease his pain when he was hurt, to make him laugh, and to ensure that he always had the chance at life that he gave to me."

"Ye loved him?"

"After a fashion, yes. And today was the day when I was called upon to give that life, that love, back. Just as you said, he has potential that he doesn't even realize. Me? I've reached the end of my rope. My abilities have grown as far as they can, and I've given as much of myself to my friends as I possibly could. He has so much *more* to do, though. Some part of me hopes he'll be sad and anguished over my sacrifice. But that's the selfish, truly mortal part of me. The rest believes that he'll continue to grow, becoming far more noble, wise, and powerful than any of us expect. And when he reaches that zenith, that will be the completion of my love for him. I've become the best version of myself. Now it's time for him to become his."

The Sarconian smiled at him, a sympathetic, knowing smile. "For yer sake,

I hope he does."

A deep rumble reverberated through the ship, shaking everything in the hangar and ripping beams, chains, and panels from their holdfasts. Valescar began pulling all the surrounding debris to himself, perhaps to form a shell for the coming collision. For that was what the trembling precipitated: the *Feywind's* death.

When the impact came, he could almost see the explosion rising from the depths of the ship toward them. It came as a million tendrils of red, orange, yellow, and pure, bright light. It flowed around Valescar's bunker, up to Leon's barrier, licking around and about it, merging with it in some places and separating from it in others. Then the vessel was gone, and Leon was in the middle of the sun itself, a conflagration of immense heat born from a powerful star. Now it was merely a question of which would subside first: his shield or the inferno.

Everything turned a brilliant, blinding white. Time halted.

Vallen . . . how I wish I could've said goodbye.

Chapter 11

The Better Part of Valor

———⟡———

"What took you so long?" Renar spun the copilot's chair halfway round as Unter ducked through the too-small cockpit door and gently deposited Matteo in the pilot's seat. "We have to . . . wait, are you crying?"

Matteo was, indeed, crying, though sobbing uncontrollably might be a better definition. He could barely see through the tears, and his nose was clogged and dripping profusely. A massive migraine threatened to split his head in twain. What was the point of it all? He had become a cadet so he could train to protect and defend others, just like the heroes, both real and imagined, he admired. Since then, all he'd managed to do was get in the way or fail to help his friends in time. Now, Matteo had abandoned Leon, one of the few who supported him in the slightest, to his fate. *Am I actually cut out for any of this?*

Unter, ever the mind reader, cut into his thoughts. "Doubt later, fly now. All perish if you don't. Escape so friend can be at peace."

Confusion showed on Renar's face, and he cocked his head quizzically. "I'm not quite sure what happened, but the big guy's right. I can jiggle the controls a bit and maybe operate the menja dispenser, but I can't tell up from down on this thing. As far as I know, you're the only one who took flight classes."

"Bu . . . but I never got further than the simulations." Matteo wiped at his eyes, trying to calm himself and focus on the situation at hand. Instead, his heartbeat only accelerated, the stress of everyone depending on him, *again*, gnawing at his mind. "I can't. I can't do this."

The brawny Terran sighed. "Look here, Professor. I'll be the first to admit I'm not the brightest, but hey, I don't really care about all that. I've always preferred to charge first and ask questions later. But that's not you. You've got a good head on your shoulders . . . and maybe I've always bullied and teased you because . . .

216

in some ways, I was envious of you. There, I said it." Renar paused, as though searching for the words he needed to continue. Matteo had never heard him string such a long speech together before, and, to be perfectly honest, he had derisively believed it beyond him. "Right now, we need that big head of yours, and no amount of strength can take its place. So, if you get us out of this alive, I'll . . . never pick at you again . . . as much . . . ."

Watching Renar blush as he tried to be encouraging was almost comical. "What if I always crashed on the machines?"

The bulky Hue clapped him mightily on the shoulder before ducking out the narrow portal toward the crew and cargo compartment. "No crash now."

Sure, just don't crash, Matteo silently scoffed. It wasn't that simple . . . well . . . aside from all the controls, instruments, and knowledge that went into flying, it was. Matteo reached forward and flipped a switch, releasing the engine limiter that kept them grounded. The button on his left retracted the landing gear, leaving them floating a meter above the ground. A set of pins on the ceiling brought the ramp up and left them truly sealed off from Leon. *Sorry, buddy. This is for you.*

Next he grabbed the control yoke in his lap, a small circle with handholds attached to a bar leading to the moving parts deeper in the vessel. Matteo pushed forward but gave the stick a little too much lateral force. Sparks flashed across the canopy as the front of the vessel ran into the left wall of the hangar.

"Other way! Other way!" Renar braced himself, pushing himself as far back into his chair as possible. *Such a vote of confidence*, Matteo thought.

"I told you I normally crash." Matteo corrected his heading, finally easing the ship out of the tilted opening and into the open sky. Of course, *open* was a misnomer. Almost immediately the outer hull and glass viewports came under assault from debris dislodged from the falling *Feywind*. A screen in the center of the instrument board lit up orange and red as warning klaxons began ringing. An aileron damaged there, an engine misaligned there, a gravpad losing functionality there. *Nothing like an easy first outing.*

"Activate the lume, Renar! It's on your side!" Matteo jerked the control wildly with one hand, attempting to get free of the dying ship's downdraft and screen of shrapnel. The other pointed at the shield activation panel but shook up and down as both his body and the craft jerked around.

Renar moved his hands rapidly over the instruments while watching for Matteo's confirmation. "Which one?"

"The big green one! It's impossible to miss!" It was, quite literally, the biggest and brightest button on the dashboard. *I'm surrounded by idiots,* Matteo groaned inwardly.

A small hand reached between them and pressed the correct switch. Outside, a shimmering barrier flowed across their field of view before turning transparent, and the impacts on the hull and accompanying alarms ceased. Matteo turned to the newcomer, finding his face only centimeters from hers in the tiny room. Auburn eyes set in a pale, freckled face framed by short, brown hair looked back at him.

"Uhh, thank you . . . "

"Lilith," the cute brunette supplied.

Wait, what was he doing, adding an adjective like that into his thoughts? *Focus, Matteo, focus.*

"Sorry about your friend."

Oh, she was here to cheer him up. *I guess I appreciate the sentiment, but it doesn't really dull the pain.*

"It's not your fault. You did what you could. Might you . . . take a step back? It's a little cramped in here."

Renar was oblivious to Matteo's discomfort, but he nodded at Lilith, who moved back into the doorway and placed a hand on the back of each chair. The ship was, after all, just a transport. It only had enough room in the cockpit for two chairs, accompanying instruments, and the hold access hatch. The cargo berth was slightly larger, containing barely enough space to have carried Valescar's platoon of soldiers.

"What did you do with the pilots?" Lilith was still staring intently at Matteo, and he felt a different kind of nervousness, one not tied to their dire situation.

"We knocked them out and left them on the *Feywind.*" Renar smiled, seeming proud of his accomplishment. In actuality, neither had been armed, and—

"I'm an idiot," Matteo monotoned, just loud enough to hear.

"Because you didn't force one of the pilots to fly the ship for you?" Lilith suggested.

"No, because . . . wait! That's exactly right. We should've gotten one of them to do this then let them go later." He glanced at Lilith with newfound respect. Quiet, but smart and pretty . . . and his thoughts were racing again.

As he elevated them above the field of junk dragging behind the *Feywind*, a massive explosion from below refocused Matteo on the reality of their situation. He glanced to the bottom left of the canopy, which was tinting to protect their eyes from the expanding glare below. There, a few hundred meters down, the gravpads of their former vessel had finally given out, causing it to plummet to its demise on the hard ground of the Theradas Pass behind Darmatian lines. A towering column of flame erupted skyward, vaporizing most of the construct as its generators, engines, and remaining fuel were consumed. For the briefest of instants, a rapidly expanding wall of radiant orange light could be seen before it dissolved into will-o-wisps of rainbow hues fleeing in every direction.

The *Feywind* and his squadmate, Leon, were no more. *Thanks again, my friend.*

After a moment, the luminescence faded and the viewports brightened. Since they'd been flying in a *mostly* straight line, their ship had escaped the detonation and subsequent shockwave, the aftermath of which was still visible below. However, with that hurdle cleared, they still needed to decide what to do now. As far as Matteo could reason, they had two options: attempt to rejoin the rest of the Darmatian forces or flee the battlefield altogether. Rejoining the fleet could prove tricky since they were piloting an enemy craft. On the other hand, running could see them accosted by *both* sides.

Of course, the remnants of the Darmatian fleet likely had bigger concerns than worrying about a single Sarconian transport. "Void and Oblivion!" Renar breathed, and Matteo followed the direction of his arm until he could see the object of his horror. As he struggled to process the scene, Lilith gasped into his right ear.

It was over—or as good as over. The how and when hardly mattered. According to what he'd been told, half of the Darmatian fleet and most of Aldona Fortress had been destroyed by an unknown Sarconian super weapon and its aftereffects. Now, in the intervening time, the rest of their forces had nearly perished as well.

The right flank was holding bravely but entirely surrounded. Enemy vessels of all sizes and classes hemmed them in, their lumes down and never-ending fusillades pouring from thousands of weapon batteries to pound them further and further into scrap and shrapnel. Some Darmatian vessels kept their shields up, trying to maneuver above or below their foes, but escape was not to be found in any direction. Others went out in blazes of glory, firing their cannons madly and hoping to take some down with them. One, its name scoured clean and impossible to identify at this distance, blazed brightly as full power was thrown to its engines. It rammed a T-shaped Sarconian heavy cruiser amidships, shattering its lume and driving it from the enveloping cordon. Then something malfunctioned on one of the vessels, and both flared violently as the ensuing blast consumed them both.

A small ray of hope blossomed as a few Darmatian fighters and light cruisers escaped through the gap, but a massive hammer-headed dreadnought soon clogged the hole in the line, its broadsides disintegrating allied ships left, right, and center. And the situation on the ground wasn't any better. The anti-air guns and artillery of Aldona Fortress were all but silent, and the few still operable couldn't even dent the armor of the craft above. Besides, only those emplacements at the rear of the defenses were even firing. The rest of the bastion had been overrun by enemy infantry and mechanized divisions, an unstoppable crimson and metallic tide that devoured everything in its path. Squat, turreted Sarconian panzcraft ran down fleeing vehicles and men while artillery in the far distance rained lead down on any meager fortifications that remained.

It was, indeed, over. The Darmatian military had been smashed. Its fleet and army were minutes from destruction, and Nemare and the kingdom herself would be next. In the face of Sarconian might, escape or capitulation were the only remaining options.

"Get us out of here, Matteo. We have to run." The small, hushed voice of Lilith whispered anxiously in his ear. She was right; this wasn't what he signed up for, what any of them signed up for. *What hero could stand in the face of* this?

The yellow comcrystal implanted on the dashboard in front of Matteo chimed, bringing him back to the moment at hand. He glanced at Renar, who shrugged, then at Lilith, who shook her head in the affirmative. "Might as well answer it."

With extreme trepidation, as though the illyrium itself might open wide and bite him, Matteo tapped the top of the crystal, engaging its send and receive functions. "Transport RV7-103, this is the dreadnought *Judicator*. You have missed two check-ins. Please transmit your clearance code and confirm that Rittermarschal Valescar is aboard."

Matteo felt his heart drop into his stomach, and he nearly lost his grip on the controls as he saw the shadow of the immense conical battleship above them. He had been so focused on determining the state of the rest of the battlefield that he had failed to notice this *colossus*, of all things, sneaking up on them. With no hesitation, he began pawing at the comcrystal, hoping to shut it back off.

"Transport RV7-103, all we are receiving is static. You seem to have muted your audio receptor. Please un-mute or fix it and respond. You have one minute until we send additional assistance." *Thank the Veneer I managed to mute it. Wait, what? Assistance?*

He hit the button attached to side of the crystal that he had just palmed. "Uhh, *Judicator*, everything is fine here. We're just peachy, noth . . . nothing wrong at all. I'm, uhh, new here. First time out flying, just figuring out the buttons and all that. No need to . . . send help. The rittermarschal is absolutely perfect. How are you doing?" Renar looked at him like he was the biggest moron ever. Matteo shot him back a glare that asked, *Do you want to do this instead?*

"Transport RV7-103, thank you for updating us on the status of the rittermarschal. Please transmit your clearance code for confirmation."

Blasted Sarconians and their protocol. Matteo thumbed the mute button again and turned to Lilith. "Get Sylette up here. She's our only hope." In the chaos of the hangar battle, he had gotten the briefest of explanations as to why they were under attack and why an enemy commander was personally after them. In summation, Sylette Farkos was a foreign princess, and the Sarconians wished to retrieve her.

"But she's one of them! Maybe she's a spy, and this is all an attempt to lure us into a trap." Renar had willingly gone along with her strategies for weeks, including during the recent fight, but now that the situation had calmed slightly, his idiocy was showing.

Matteo opened his mouth to respond when Sylette replaced Lilith in the doorway. "Are you dumber than that unconscious imbecile back there? You heard what I said to Valescar. My own father had my mother killed and exiled me when I was ten years old. I've renounced my claim to the throne. You couldn't hate the empire more than me if you tried."

"But it could still be—"

"What? A ruse? A gambit? Valescar alone took us all out, and only Leon's sacrifice saved our lives. Your entire fleet is gone. The enemy has every advantage in this war. Why do they need to deceive little, insignificant us? Now, move aside so I can do something useful." Thoroughly scolded, Renar switched places with Sylette, his bulk barely fitting into the space behind their chairs.

As if to remind them of the imminent threat, the comcrystal sounded again. "Transport RV7-103, you have thirty seconds to respond with your clearance code. Failure to respond will result in your impoundment."

Sylette nodded at Matteo, who toggled the transmit button as she began speaking. "*Judicator*, this is the captain of transport RV7-103. Our clearance code is SA724XJ. The rittermarschal is not yet ready to return to his flagship as he wishes to conduct further close inspection of the Darmatian lines to plan for future defensive construction. Please confirm."

One moment passed, then two, and the seconds kept ticking. Matteo glanced at Sylette nervously, and he could feel Renar's knuckles tighten on the top of his seat. After what felt like an eternity, the communication officer on the other end responded. "It's an old code, and it is valid, but its designation is no longer within our database of acceptable clearances. Please submit a valid *and* current code or your vessel will be disabled and boarded."

The ex-princess sighed and rolled her eyes. "Listen here, whoever you are. Rittermarschal Valescar doesn't need your authority to fly past his own battleship. So, here's what you're going to do. You will accept my code, let us pass, and forget this ever happened, or both he *and* I will submit a report suggesting you be demoted to the enlisted ranks and redeployed to the Eastern front. Are we clear?"

Another pause followed, nearly as long as the first. Matteo felt his heart beat faster once more, and the hairs of his arms stood on end. Then the response came. "Crystal clear, ma'am. However, I should inform you that Rittermarschal Valescar just contacted us stating that he has arrived aboard the *Hammer of Wrath* for an audience with His Majesty. Furthermore, these check-in protocols were instated by the rittermarschal himself, and he expects us to follow them to the letter. Your craft has been reclassified as a hostile vessel. Heave to and prepare to be boarded. Failure to do so will result in termination. *Judicator* out."

Silver hair flared across the cabin as Sylette angrily shut off the comcrystal and kicked the underside of the instrument panel. *Guess even royals, well, ex royals, can get frustrated too.* Matteo had barely completed that thought when three spear-shaped Lancer hoverjets shot down at them from around the curve of the *Judicator's* enormous fuselage. He instantly threw as much power as he could to the engines, and the ship leapt forward with enough acceleration to bring clanking and curses from the crew compartment to the rear. Renar clung to the doorframe for dear life. If his grip slipped, he'd fly five meters backwards to hit a metal bulkhead, which would likely cause severe injury or death.

As soon as the transport began moving, the Lancers opened fire from their nose guns. As if that wasn't enough, Matteo could see through the canopy that the belly guns of the battleship were also tracking them, waiting for a clean shot. "Raise the lume, quickly!"

His new copilot immediately hit the correct button, and the barrier activated just in time to take a series of small impacts aimed at their engines. Even still, the tiny vessel rocked with the blows, shaking the passengers. As the momentum changes decreased to the sudden jinks and jukes of Matteo's evasive maneuvering, Velle poked her head past Renar.

"What's going on? Vallen's injured and unconscious, but we had to strap him down to keep him from flying all over the place. If we keep moving like this, he'll start bleeding again and could get hurt worse!"

"Sorry! Trying to keep us alive!" was all Matteo could manage. It took the entirety of his focus to simultaneously pilot the transport while attempting to evade shots from behind. Then the dreadnought opened fire, the first shell vaporizing their top shields and sending them spiraling downwards. They fell for several hundred meters. In the back, weightless bodies hung in the air, frantically clutching at whatever they could. Then, with a mighty exertion, he yanked on the yoke and evened out.

As everyone collapsed from the abrupt direction change, Matteo found that another flight of Lancers had joined their pursuers, vectoring in from the right. He flew left, taking them farther into the Darmatian side of the pass and, fortunately, away from the bulk of the Sarconian fleet. Above, the *Judicator* kept intermittently sniping at them, trying to avoid hitting their own forces in the process. Their caution, combined with the increased distance and their slower speed, significantly reduced their chances of blasting the transport again.

"This thing has weapons, right?" Renar asked from the bottom of a pile of bodies on the floor.

"Umm . . . " Matteo glanced at Sylette, who scanned the instrument board for signs the vessel was armed. After a tense few seconds of continued dodging and negligible strikes to their side armor, her face lit up. "Yes, twin turrets on the top and bottom. Renar and Lilith, see if you can get them working and give us some cover!"

The duo disentangled themselves from Velle and ran off to their assignments. Renar called out that his gun was working fine, evidenced by the rhythmic "whumping" that sounded from below. Lilith, however, returned disappointed, "The whole thing's gone, blown away by the shot from that warship. Even worse, we're venting air out a hole it left behind in the upper hull!"

Unter stalked forward from the cabin, where he had been helping Velle tend to the wounded Vallen. "Put scrap over gap. Reseal ship. Lilith fix with fire magic since me too big to fit."

If the situation was any less dire, Matteo probably would've thought the image was funny. Here was giant Unter, handing a large piece of metal to the much-smaller Lilith to carry up a narrow shaft and weld across a hole in hopes it would prevent them from decompressing at higher altitudes. Comedy gold was certainly made of less.

As they did that, Matteo was trying his best to stay low to the ground while eluding the six enemy fighters dogging them at every turn. An explosion rang out behind, and Renar loosed a rowdy cheer that echoed through the ship.

Okay, only five enemy fighters. You can do this. Matteo dropped another fifty meters, closing with the earth and trying to use the force from his gravpads to kick dust into the faces of his foes. They were well beyond the fortress and Darmatian defenses; nothing out here but hills, dry ground, the occasional large outcropping of rock . . .

And a couple of Sarconian light cruisers that had raced ahead of the pack to cut off those trying to escape the narrow valley. They were sleek ships, with a rounded underbelly and flat upper decks rising to an elevated command platform near the rear. The fuselage of the vessels ended in a single large engine, surrounded by smaller directional jets to allow it to rapidly change course at high speeds. Though possessed of a lighter weapon complement than their bigger brethren, their four fully traversable deck mounts, three forward and one back of the flag tower, would still pack a considerable punch, especially against a small craft—like them, for example.

At one thousand meters, according to the range finder, the frigates opened fire. Matteo clenched his teeth as their first salvo went wide and low, throwing up pillars of dirt forward and left of them. He swerved right, around the cascading debris, and was instantly glad he did so. On the other side of the dissipating brown cloud was a flattop of ruddy stone, a small mesa carved long ago by water receding from this basin.

One of the Lancers following them wasn't as fortunate. In a bid to come abreast of them, it pushed straight through the raining silt, detonating brilliantly against the side of the crag. *Four behind, two in front.* The remaining fighters never let up their stream of bolts, scoring hit after hit against their rear lume through sheer tenacity. Something groaned from the aft deck, and the synth-oil warning light turned from green to an infuriated red. *Great, we're leaking lubricant.* Now, even if they survived the next few minutes, their operational time would be cut short, at which point they'd be grounded, sitting ducks.

The light cruisers, LCs, were quick loaders and had their second broadside flying by the time they'd closed to seven hundred meters. Most landed closer, *much* closer. One even hit, shattering the right side lume, scouring the hull, and damaging the stunted wing attached to that side. In terms of operational importance, the wing itself mattered little, but the aileron at its rear was vital to their maneuverability. Blessedly, the lack of a new crimson bead on his instrument panel suggested it had made it through unscathed.

Their shields, however, were another story. "Upper and starboard barriers completely gone! Rear lume down to twenty percent power and falling!" Sylette anxiously shouted the readouts from her display to no one in particular. In fact, with everyone else trying to stave off their impending doom, Matteo was the only one close enough to hear her. He tried to make use of the information, angling left so the undamaged side would take the brunt of the incoming fire.

"The top is resealed, but it can't take much punishment." Lilith's voice, along with her rapid footfalls on the steel ladder, echoed down the passage to the upper turret. *One small note of good news in a symphony of tragedy,* Matteo acknowledged. Now he just had to wait for the universe to balance things out with the next sucker punch.

Matteo didn't have to wait long. A flash against the canopy marked the destruction of another Lancer, this one having gotten so close Renar couldn't miss it. Apparently even the empire had raw, untested pilots just like him. However, the lower gun stopped firing immediately afterward, and Renar appeared in the doorway seconds later.

"Uhh, it just, kinda, stopped working all of a sudden and, uhh, started getting hot and smoking." He scratched his thin hair, totally perplexed as to what went wrong.

"Let me guess. You just held down the trigger the entire time, even when you didn't have a hope in Oblivion of hitting a shot?" Matteo said, holding back a sigh. He wasn't great with people—and was even worse with girls and fighting. But calling people out on their foolishness was another thing entirely, even while piloting an airship for the first time with his life on the line.

"Yeah, I figured I had a better chance of taking them down that way. I think I'll call it the 'Spray and Pray.' Cool name, right?"

He flipped the yoke right, dodging most of the next barrage from the rear. The ship shook slightly, and Sylette called out a litany of new statistics and damaged systems. Matteo barely heard her. "The coolest. But you know what isn't *cool*? Our only means of fighting back, which is now over*heated* and useless thanks to you. Go see if there's some coolant packs in storage. Read their directions *first*, then try to use them to get it back online!"

By the Veneer, Matteo thought as Renar left, *I just sardonically told someone off. Am I picking up Vallen's bad habits?* Matteo dreaded becoming in any way like his squad leader, and wrote it off as the stress of the situation. Besides, he was trying to keep them all alive. He needed to be a little more assertive to get them through this.

The increasingly larger LCs in the foreground snapped him from his reverie. He saw no way out of the Theradas Pass except past them, and though there was plenty of room to navigate to either side, he'd have to turn one way or the other and expose the profile of his ship. Instead, maybe, just maybe, he could slip under and between them, where their guns would be least effective.

However, they'd have to weather one last volley to do so. The altimeter read ten meters, akin to kissing the ground for any pilot, new or veteran, and the range finder showed three hundred meters to the frigates. For modern weapon systems, that was as good as point-blank range. The buildup of illyrium energy shimmered about the Sarconian warships as the darkening sky heralded the shift from afternoon to evening. They were ready to fire; at least some of the shots would hit them dead on. Furthermore, three Lancers were still behind them, ready to finish whatever scorched scrap remained.

If only they could survive one more fusillade and outrun their pursuers, they could escape under the coming cover of night. *If only, if only, if only* . . .

Matteo gripped the yoke, bore down on the engines, and charged straight ahead.

<hr>

"Aren't you a sorry sight. What happened?"

"I was forced ta ride an opposin' airship through a tough landin'."

"And what's so difficult about that?"

"Well, not everyone enjoys bein' at the center of explosions like ye—"

"Enough!" Sychon's exasperated shout cut Rittermarschals Valescar and Titania off before they could really get going. While his top leaders were brilliant mages and commanders, all of them possessed a degree of competitiveness and rivalry that bordered on the self-destructive. Each constantly tried to outdo the others, and cooperation between them was almost unheard of except when under his direct orders or extreme duress. *I suppose this is the end result of the empire's hyper-meritocracy.* "Valescar, what is this you've brought me?"

The older man bowed slightly, his movement hindered by the state of his body. His cloak of station was completely gone, along with his helmet, rapiers, and the spools of wire he always carried with him. Soot and ash hid the burnished silver of Valescar's armor, and one entire side appeared to have melted and later fused back together. If the skin underneath was anything like the left side of the rittermarschal's face, it was certainly not a pleasant sight. A third of his scalp was devoid of hair, the area below cratered and singed, smelling of burnt, dead flesh. Lower, the tissue around his eye patch was puckered and raw, the metal of the accessory melding with its blackened surroundings. Valescar's condition would have killed most other men; it was a testament to his strength and fortitude that he was still *standing* before Sychon now.

He pointed with his right, undamaged arm at a trolley being offloaded from a skiff behind him. The open-topped vessel itself was as badly beaten as the commander, the Darmatian crest barely visible on its prow and the whole aft end hanging broken and loose. It was well beyond being operable. Apparently Valescar had piloted it here using only his abilities—and in his current state, no less. Sychon's high estimation of the rittermarschal elevated even further.

It took the floor techs several moments to transfer the object of interest to a waiting medical sled before pushing the floating berth across the cavernous hangar of the *Hammer of Wrath* to where the emperor's party waited near the bay entrance. After all, it wouldn't do for the Sarconian ruler himself to go anywhere near a dangerous piece of enemy equipment that could still detonate without warning. A squad of guards stood behind him for further protection, two of whom quickly checked the hovering bed for additional threats before giving the all clear. When the process was completed, Valescar began speaking.

"This here boy is the reason for my current state, as well as my failure at completin' my secondary objective. He's barely hangin' on, despite appearances ta the contrary, but before he ended up like this, he cast a Long Chant spell that left me in a right mess." At the mention of "Long Chant," Sychon moved closer to get a better look. Anyone who was capable of learning and using such magic, in addition to holding off Valescar, was a potential asset. The lean youth had short, blond hair and was wearing a tattered Darmatian cadet uniform. As the shallow waters of the healing bath glowed and flowed about him, the slight rising and falling of his chest gave evidence to the flicker of life yet inside him.

"He'll make a fine vessel for Sarcon . . . far better than his current shell, if he's capable of such advanced incantations. You did well to save and bring him."

"Actually, Yer Majesty, it was he who saved himself. When that transport hulk crashed, it was all I could do ta shield myself from the worst o' the blast. However, the spell he used against me kept runnin', even through the inferno, and I found him afterward layin' on the wreckage with nary a scratch and no men'ar, as ye see him now. Almost feel bad for the boy, so much potential and still bein' handed over ta that monster." The rittermarschal rigidly shook his head, as though trying to avoid straining his burnt flesh.

"A deal is a deal. Besides, we're well past the time limit given us by Sarcon.

Let us hope that Zaratus is still himself." Sychon had left the grand marschal on the bridge, distancing him from dealings with Sarcon because of his paranoid trepidations. *I am the most powerful man in the world. I need not fear a warlock whose very survival depends on my mood.*

"Take him to Sarcon on the weather deck; we'll join you shortly." Sychon motioned to the techs pushing the sled, who began moving it past the party toward the hall. As Sychon, Valescar, Titania, and their attending soldiers turned to follow them, a hangar officer, a lieutenant by his rank bars, ran up and breathlessly came to attention.

Titania tactfully fielded the menial task in place of her emperor. "Something to report, Lieutenant?"

The officer hesitated, ostensibly holding his message until a flight of Lancers across the hangar had finished throttling their engines and accelerated out into the orange evening sky. Sychon could see through his act. In truth, the academy fresh soldier was intimidated by the flag officer before him. Not many beyond Titania's own command were used to a woman at high rank, let alone one as regal and physically appealing as she was.

"I asked you a question, Lieutenant. Are you incapable of forming words, or is there another problem with your mental faculties?" Her eyes narrowed and her face clouded. When combined with the framing of her crimson locks, the effect was that of a flaming storm descending upon the hapless crewman.

"Uh, yes . . . yes, ma'am!" He swiftly saluted and belted his message. "We just received communiqués from the *Blazing Hawk* and *Phoenix*, both part of the Fifth Fleet. They have encountered a Sarconian vessel which the IFF identifies as hostile two leagues into the Darmatian side of the pass and are preparing to destroy it as per their orders. However, they wanted to receive final verification for destruction of Sarconian military equipment from the *Hammer*. Your orders, ma'am?"

She nodded thoughtfully. "Yes, those are my ships. I ordered them ahead to blockade the pass and hinder enemy attempts at escape. If the craft has been commandeered by our foes, all the more reason to destroy it immediately. Tell them to open fire."

Before the lieutenant could carry out her directive, Valescar stepped forward to protest. "Yer Grace, that transport is likely the ship I lost aboard the Darmatian supply vessel. If so, the object of yer second order ta me is on 'er along with a number o' enemy cadets. The kids are of no consequence, but I believe lettin' that one live will be beneficial ta us in the long run if we can bag 'er."

The emperor considered the proposal. If she were in his possession, he could use her as leverage against her high-ranking adoptive parents in the Rabban Imperium. Furthermore, the harder to control of his two sons had been close to her as a child. Perhaps her return could serve as a leash to bring him under tighter rein? And nations always loved their princesses; announcing her existence to the country could be quite a morale boost. Sychon reached a decision. He would bring her back, break her, and then remake her into a tool of domestic order and foreign blackmail.

"What are the chances of disabling the craft with the resources in play?"

"Slim to none, Your Majesty. Those light cruisers don't have the support to corner it nor the speed to catch it once it passes. A shot to the engine that doesn't annihilate the ship as well is one in a thousand, at the least." Titania shot Valescar a smoldering glare, clearly angry that he'd overridden her instructions.

"Then let it go, for now. If its transponder remains active, we can track it and capture its crew. If not, we shall pursue them using more traditional means. Soon this entire kingdom shall be under Sarconian rule, at which point they'll have nowhere to run." He allowed Valescar to breathe a sigh of relief before continuing. "However, since you failed to apprehend her initially, Valescar, I am transferring this responsibility to Rittermarschal Titania. In addition, she will be granted full military command of the Darmatian occupation to give her the resources to accomplish this task. Is that satisfactory?"

Whether under the weight of his injuries or dejection at the elevation of Titania to a position of greater authority, Valescar's shoulders slumped visibly. "Yes, sire." For her part, the female commander, his junior of twenty years, gave him a look of triumph.

"It shall be as you direct, Your Majesty. She shan't escape the net next time, and the kingdom will be brought to heel quickly so the war against Rabban can be prosecuted without further hindrance."

"As it should be. Now, let us go ensure that the arbiter of today's success is well taken care of." *And see exactly how this immortality of his works,* Sychon added silently.

340, 330, 320, 310 . . . the range finder kept ticking down the distance between them and the Sarconian warships. *Why won't you fire?* Matteo's internal exclamation showed outwardly as sweat beading on his forehead and palms, the latter making piloting even more difficult than it already was. *Please! Just shoot and miss already!*

Each meter that passed was a meter closer to complete obliteration, rather than to just losing their shields or taking a few hits. Conversely, every second that passed brought them closer to the partial safety of nightfall and the advantages the darkness would give them. To their left, the last rays of the sun were glinting past the towering peaks of the Great Divide and would disappear behind them in mere moments. At that point, the enemy could still track them with searchlights and magic, but it would be a far more difficult task, especially given their size and speed.

250, 240, 230, 220 . . . the numbers continued to fall, yet the glowing weapon banks of the LCs, framed against the backdrop of sky and earth by the dying light on their flank, did not blossom with the fiery discharge of lead. *Could they have already lost track of us?* No, the Lancers to the rear stayed with them doggedly and, in addition to their own intermittent barrages, were likely reporting their every move to the larger vessels ahead.

Come on, come on! In a few seconds they would be safe, regardless of whether the frigates fired or not. At a certain point, they could no longer depress their guns to hit the transport, and their next opportunity would be when they reached the far side. But by then, the shadows should provide them cover, increasing their odds of survival immensely.

To Matteo's right, Sylette sat hunched in her seat, gazing directly ahead. It seemed as though she intended to will the very ships and bullets from their path. *Well, it can't hurt,* Matteo conceded. The others, excepting Renar, seemed to have more important things to do. He had wisely delegated repair of the belly turret to Lilith and Unter and now nervously, and annoyingly, tapped his foot on the floor as he looked over Matteo's shoulder.

180, 170, 160, 150. *They're about to shoot. I have to do something, dodge, elevate, move, just move!* Matteo was about to throw the yoke about in the wildest, most unpredictable pattern he could think of when the brilliant radiance of the Sarconian cruisers melted from a harsh red to a calming blue. In the next instant, their turrets turned away, engines engaged, and the LCs moved out of their path to either side. Simultaneously, the impacts on the failing aft lume ceased, and the remaining fighters could be seen breaking off toward the cruisers.

Before his mind could process this inexplicable turn of events, they were past the enemy craft and flying straight and unimpeded out of the Theradas Pass. Then the last gasp of day faded entirely, plunging them into blackness between the lofty foothills of the mountains to either side. Matteo reached for the running lights, and two yellow beams burst from the front of the ship to light the ground in front of the transport.

"What just happened?" Renar's incredulous voice intoned from the doorway.

Despite the good fortune of their narrow survival, it was evident to Matteo that Sylette was fuming. "My ever-considerate father *let* us go. Seems he wants us—rather, me—alive." She stormed to her feet, shoving past the larger Renar with ease. "Take us somewhere, anywhere, safe. We need to lay low for the time being."

Matteo turned to follow her path as she accosted Unter at the top of the access way leading to the lower gun. "You seem to know a bit about the tech on this ship. Help me find our transponder beacon."

His head, twice the size of Sylette's, regarded her with a nod. "Easy task for Hues. What then?"

"Then we destroy it. I don't want that man to know where we are until I'm ready to end him." Though she stood in profile relative to Matteo, the fire in her eyes was deathly serious. *She really intends to do it, doesn't she?*

Sylette caught Matteo's staring and tore into him, "What are you looking at? Don't you have a ship to fly?"

Cowed, he spun back to the instrument panel. *First Vallen, now her.* In the space of a day, he had gone from having a selfish, manipulative squad leader to having a highly competent, aggressive, vengeful female commander. At this stage, however, the jury was still out on which was better.

Better to focus on the task at hand. Matteo recentered his thoughts and took stock of their fuel reserves, along with the readout from the synth-oil drum that had taken a hit earlier. Running a few calculations in his head, he determined that they could make it no more than sixty leagues in any direction before running dry. He reached for the glove box under the dash and fumbled about until he found what he was looking for: a regional map.

Their situation was a bit brighter than he had hoped but still dismal. They couldn't make Nemare, yet even if they could, it was certainly also the destination of the Sarconian army. Leaving Darmatia was also out of the question, unless they wanted to run out of gas over the Phar Sea and drown. *That'd be a glorious end to this adventure.*

Then Matteo saw it, the perfect solution to their situation. It was just within their range and Sylette had, after all, said somewhere *safe*. He adjusted the stick and set course for Etrus, the city he was born and raised in. Only one place in the entire world was ever truly safe: home.

<hr />

Why am I here? Hans pondered, once more party to a gathering of greats he had no right or desire to be a part of. Around him, under the fading orange to purple hues of twilight on the observation deck, were Emperor Sychon, Rittermarschals Valescar and Titania, a cadre of guards, and, of course, Lord Sarcon himself.

The latter had more in common with charcoal than mortal flesh at the moment. With every eddy and gust of wind, black dust was shorn from his carcass, wracking his wretched, infantile frame with throes of pain that caused the process to repeat ad nauseam. Against the orders of the charred being, Hans had attempted to affect some healing or, at the very least, minor relief of his agony, but it was of little avail.

With that failure, and since the hour deadline set by Sarcon was long past, his curiosity had led him to question why the mage didn't simply carry out his earlier threat against Zaratus. Because of his station, Hans possessed great respect for the grand marschal, but beyond that he was but a lofty, unattainable personage. His living or dying would ultimately have no impact on him. In reply, Sarcon had merely gasped unintelligibly about him being "an incompatible host" and that "it was nothing more than an empty threat."

Suffice to say that revelation left them waiting on the exposed weather deck for two hours longer than intended and a total of five hours since the two sides initially faced off. Hans had spent most of the intervening time since the blast of Great Magic protecting Sarcon's shell and trying to avoid being ejected off the hull. After the *Hammer* charged directly at the remnants of the enemy fleet, they had experienced any number of close calls as she exchanged broadside after broadside with the Darmatians. Fire flared, shrapnel ricocheted past, but Hans hadn't moved lest he expose his fragile charge to danger.

In the end, what he had borne witness to was a slaughter. The Darmatians were reeling after Sarcon's death ray and likely would have surrendered, given the chance. Instead, the dregs of their forces were mercilessly hunted down in a campaign of extermination. Very few prisoners were taken. It appeared the emperor's goal was complete subjugation of the nation, rather than allowing them a graceful chance at concession. Shortly after arriving on this level, one of the guards had been bandying around the statistic that upwards of 98 percent of Darmatian forces had perished, compared to a paltry 4 percent on their side.

It was an absolutely believable number. All one had to do was look over the side to confirm it. Flames, wreckage, craters, and bodies were everywhere. Aldona Fortress was nigh completely leveled. The two halves of the *King Darmatus* thrust up out of the middle of it like the desiccated ribs of some long-dead beast of burden.

And the stench . . . the stench of it all has even managed to drift all the way up here, Hans thought as he wrinkled his nose. To say the experience had shaken him was an understatement. All he wanted was to finish the war, go home, and forget it ever happened. However, he was in an odd predicament, chained to an individual simultaneously more powerful and more helpless than he could ever imagine. Though he hadn't known Vahn well, Hans understood that Sarcon was the fulfillment of Vahn's dream, a dream he had laid aside to save him. A life for a life. Hans would see this through and then be done. He owed Vahn that much, but no more.

"I've brought your new container, Sarcon, though you hardly look as though you'll live long enough to make the transfer." To Hans, the emperor's tone conveyed the authority of one talking down to a lesser being. However, a hint of fear was buried in there as well. No one who had witnessed the events of today could suppress an inkling of dread toward he that had wrought most of this devastation.

The vessel in question lay on a floating medical trolley in between the two groups. Its ability to hover, along with its healing capabilities, came from an illyrium power source containing a formula that could be modified to effectively enact different modes of treatment. It would never be as good as an actual medical mage, but it was an adequate substitute.

Its soothing waves were currently flowing over and around a youth only a few years Hans's junior. He wore Darmatian military dress over skin tanned only slightly by the desert clime from which he hailed. Beneath a mop of dirty blonde hair, his face was strangely calm and at peace.

"Well, Sarcon? Let's see this spell of yours." His liege's impatience led Hans to turn to Sarcon, who could barely form the words to reply.

"Pi . . . pick me . . . up . . . Hans . . . and carry . . . me . . . to him."

Gingerly, as though handling a newborn, Hans eased his arms beneath the blackened mass and stood with his back to the wind to prevent further erosion of Sarcon's body. Step by step, he carefully approached the sled, stopping at its edge and leaning over to allow the sorcerer's one remaining arm to dangle freely. He thought for sure the limb would snap, disintegrating into so many particles of free-flying gray ash, but it remained solid, reaching without sight for the boy's forehead.

Hans cradled Sarcon with one arm while he used the other to gently take hold of and guide his wrist. When the burnt palm made contact with the Darmatian's head, he removed his hand and reinforced his grip on the pile of seared cinders he held. *Don't think about what you're doing. This is for Vahn; this is for the empire; this is for your wife and children. I don't know who this lad is. I don't know anything about him, and I'm sorry this had to happen. But this is for me and mine. Don't think about it, don't think about it, don't think about it . . .*

He closed his eyes, shutting out the visual stimuli of what was occurring. Even so, he felt Sarcon warm in his hands as the incantation began. The powerful glow of his spell shone brightly into Hans's mind, sensitive to magic as he was, despite his best efforts to tune it out.

"Your name . . . is . . . is Leon. Thank . . . you . . . for your body." Sarcon's voice strengthened as his casting advanced, perhaps a side effect from the gradual merging of their capabilities and consciousnesses. It would soon be complete. "You do not . . . know that you are giving it . . . up to me. Perhaps one day, as you float among the . . . myriad of souls in the Void, you will realize what has occurred. But know this: your body will assist me in bringing about the dawning of a new age and the salvation of Lozaria. Yes, Leon, know that your sacrifice will truly not be in vain."

Part 3
Resistance

Chapter 12

Safe Havens

The boy awoke to the muted light of dawn filtering softly through the open window at his bedside. Well, at the very least it was what passed for dawn down here. In truth, it was a fake sun, a giant magic crystal at the top of the massive chamber Sewertown rested in that they turned on to make the trash below think they lived lives like those on the surface.

He yawned and stretched his arms, pushing away the frail sailcloth that barely functioned as a usable blanket. Unfortunately, as he sat up, the pile of hay pushed together to make his pillow disintegrated. *Guess I'll have to tie it back again tonight.*

Something was special about today, but for the life of him, he couldn't quite remember what. In fact, he found himself struggling to remember many things: where he was, what he was supposed to be doing, and, most importantly, who he was. It was as though the fog that often permeated these subterranean waterways had taken up residence just behind his eyelids.

"Something wrong, Kit? You don't look so good." The smudged face of another boy peaked at him from the edge of the roof above his bed. Rather, not a ceiling, but the bottom of the bunk above his. As the youth spoke, the mist cleared, and the name *Kit* made everything else fall into place.

He was called Kit, and before he was known by that, he hadn't possessed any identification whatsoever beyond "You!" or "Thief!" or "Wretch!" You didn't need a label to steal, pickpocket, or scrounge through the back alleys and underpasses for scraps.

It was only once he'd arrived here, at this "family" of miscreants and outcasts, that he'd received the name Kit. And even that tag merely enabled the older children and adults of their group to know what he was best at: carrying, hiding, and using whatever kit they needed for whatever job needed doing. Simply put, he was good at almost everything and hardy to boot, so they always put him in charge of their tools and supplies.

Similarly, the lad above him was called Pockey. Nobody in their band was a better pickpocket than he was. Whether the goods were sewn into the seam, hidden in an inside pouch, or guarded by someone very alert to the dangers of carrying money through Sewertown, he could manage a scheme that would leave the target bereft of their valuables. As a result, they often worked together. Kit made the plan and outfitted the crew while Pockey swooped in to get the prize.

Kit put on a smile—fake, of course—and replied, "Nothing wrong, just thinking about what to do today."

"Yeah, it's your name day! Got any brilliant ideas for it?" Pockey beamed a similar grin back at him, though his was probably real. Among the middle-aged kids, he was the warmest and most caring.

Truth be told, Kit had completely forgotten his name day. It was just another day—one that possessed no sentimental value for him. Two years ago, their leader, Bohomaz, an old, grizzled veteran of many similar operations, had given Kit his handle and said he looked "bout ten years old." *Which would make me twelve now, I suppose*, Kit reasoned.

"Not really. Why don't we go get some breakfast and see what the others are up to?" He hopped out of bed, avoiding the ragged edge of a broken plank that had been that way for as long as he could remember. There wasn't any reason *not* to sleep in the nude down in the mugginess of the lower levels, so Kit quickly threw on a pair of ill-fitting breeches and a tattered tunic before joining Pockey in navigating through the maze of beds, cots, and hammocks to the ladder.

The room they slept in wasn't so much a chamber as the unused loft of the building next door. Its owner didn't have a use for it, so he rented it out to Bohomaz for a handful of geldars a year. Once acquired, they connected it to their hideout proper the same way any construction happened below ground: slap a few boards and nails together and call it a day.

Kit took each rung along the slope expertly, but an amateur going that fast would find themselves falling through one of the holes in the shaft . . . and into the river below. Visible through a plethora of gaps, the waterway separating the two ramshackle tenements was one of many that flowed ever downward to the base of the sewers. This one wasn't nearly as discolored as most, but even on a good day you never wanted to drink from *any* free-flowing fluid down here.

In fact, water was worth more than geldars in this underground city, and control of a reservoir tower or some other clean source could make you a lord over the rest of the common filth. Unfortunately, Bohomaz didn't possess his own drinking water, but he was chummy enough with one of the current "aristocracy" who did. That being said, he wouldn't just give it to his crew for free. "Produce or perish" was the law of his ward. If you failed to meet your quotas, you got no water. Three days like that and your carcass would be yet another thing rotting in this cesspit.

When they reached the main building, a pile of crates, planks, and hastily assembled detritus served as a stairway to take them from the upper level to the lower. There, the entire floor was open except for a small kitchen at the back, the boss's raised dais toward the front, and a few not-to-code support beams that held all of it together. The scene before them was the usual early morning chaos. A tiny army of children of all ages and races scrambled, pushed, and shoved to get servings of gruel from the wide pantry window then jostled to find space on the ground before noisily digging in. The oldest members made and served the grub, the next biggest grabbed the most comfortable positions against the pillars or stage steps, and the youngest and littlest filled the gaps in between. After meals, the roles were reversed; the elders took charge, leading teams out into the city to tackle various "jobs" before returning in the evening and repeating the process the next day.

Kit and Pockey were two of the last through the line, and the lanky, sandy-haired serving girl, two years Kit's senior, gave him an extra half serving of slop and a larger tin of water. Her joy as she spoke also appeared genuine. "Happy name day, Kit. Please don't let anyone know I gave you a little extra." The second half was a whisper, and he obligingly mimed keeping his lips sealed. It was an insignificant gesture, but responding in kind was better for smoothing his way than the alternative.

The boys found hardly any open space left to sit among the boisterous mass of kids. Those still eating did so swiftly and silently, as though frightened someone might take the little they had if they took too long. The majority, now finished, roughhoused riotously, played cards in small groups, or shouted at each other across the chamber. All possessed a story; most were orphans, some abandoned more recently than others, and every single one had experienced hardship in one way or another. However, few were like Kit. He had been born into this life and knew no other way to live.

As Kit continued scanning for a spot, Bohomaz, currently seated on a large wooden chair that passed for a throne in his eyes, saw him and waved them over. The elder, gray-coated Vladisvar may have been past his prime, but his hulking frame was still a sight to behold. While much of his leather-hard skin now sagged and strong muscle had softened to fat, his large eyes shown with vigor and his voice boomed whenever he spoke. Furthermore, the massive metal plates permanently grafted to his right arm, shoulders, back, and bare chest were imposing, both for their size and for the startling, violent depictions inscribed there. Each carved and painted scene testified to a long-ago triumph when the crime lord was a proud, noble warrior. And every beast, challenger, and rival depicted had fallen to the clawed gauntlet attached to the stump of his left arm, an eternal, impossible-to-remove weapon Bohomaz carried with him always.

They meandered their way through the shifting sea of bodies and wound up seated on several stools that formed part of a semicircle around the faux-opulent perch of their leader. "Happy age day, Kit!" The Vladisvar's rich baritone was many decibels too loud, likely from loss of hearing. "Though truth be told, you Terrans don't particularly change much from year to year. Why, when I was your age, I was practically as big as I am now—and only half as fat!" His deep, hearty chuckle reverberated through the room, and many within earshot joined in the laughter at the boss's usual brand of self-deprecating humor. Kit kept silent and waited for the raucous chorus to peter out.

"What's the job, Bohomaz? You wouldn't call me over, name day or otherwise, if you didn't have work." Pockey gave him a glance that seemed to question, "What's wrong with you?" But Pockey was naive, and for all his useful talent, he didn't seem to understand the world he lived in. *This is how you deal with others in this business*, Kit thought stoically.

The horn and a half atop the slate-covered giant shook along with his head.

"How many times have I told you to call me Dad? You and the rest are my children; it would make me the happiest man alive if you acted like it."

"Piles of geldars and endless clean water would make you the happiest man alive. Besides, what kind of father sends his kids out to steal, barter, and deal in his place?"

"*Appropriate.* Appropriate, Kit. Besides, it's all for your own good. You may have never had a family, or ever care to have one, but the others," Bohomaz gestured across the room with his clawed talon, "need this place to survive. Besides, we're in this together. It's only right that everyone do their share to maintain the cosmic balance."

And here came his Vladisvar spiritual mumbo jumbo: Rashakh, Lysham, and all that other light and dark nonsense he always spouted about in his native tongue. To his race, all that mattered was maintaining balance—ensuring that the positive and negative energies from every action in the universe reached equilibrium to prevent cataclysm and catastrophe. However, based on his occupation, it was probably little more than lip service to Bohomaz. *Time to cut him off before he really gets going,* Kit determined.

"The job, Bohomaz?"

"Yes, yes. It's always about work with you. Fine, finish eating and I'll tell you."

Kit powered through the necessary task of ingestion with gusto, barely tasting the food that entered his mouth. Of course, it didn't really have a taste to begin with, being some viscous blend of liquids, vegetables, and grain. Pockey wasn't halfway through when Kit finished and looked back up at their boss.

"By the Karakhtahm, you feed quickly." Bohomaz paused, directing a nearby Terran teenager to join them. "For your age day, I have a special, and profitable, task for you to accomplish. While your additional year of existence is the most important event in our circle, the denizens of the surface above are having their annual festival for their pseudo god, the Terran Veneer Sariel. As a result, their temples and places of worship are flocked with happy-go-lucky sycophants overladen with the fruits of their ill-begotten labors that they intend to devote as offerings to their churches of faith and commerce."

For a member of the spartan, warrior-like Vladisvar, Bohomaz could be wordy and long-winded. Pockey, for one, seemed to have already been lost by his explanation. "Uhh, Kit, what'd he say?"

He whispered back as the boss continued to prattle. "Rich people, lots of money, they'll be out shopping or donating it at their holy places."

"Right . . . got it."

Kit refocused his attention on Bohomaz, who was finally getting to the point of his dissertation. "Our goal is to alleviate as many of these nobles of their surplus geldars and other valuables as possible, making sure to target only those *deserving* of your attention and not get caught while doing so." By "deserving," he meant individuals whose wealth was blatantly displayed. Despite being a thief, their leader was an honest one and only stole from those he felt could take the loss. "To make it worth your while, each of you will get two percent of the haul. Singe here will be in charge, Kit will mark targets and run decoy, and Pockey will grab the goods. Leave as soon as you're ready so you can make rounds of all the temples before evening."

Singe, the Terran male Bohomaz had called over, was—at seventeen—one of the eldest in the gang. He was also one of the meanest and surliest, being apt to bully and take from those younger and weaker than him, even within the group. However, the boss kept him around because of his namesake—he was a fire mage, the only person who could use magic in their outfit. Of course, his abilities only made him harder to deal with, and even though other lieutenants were above Singe, he always acted as though he was second in command.

Great . . . this should be fun. Kit nodded his acceptance of the task and collected the things he'd need for the day from around the hideout. If he didn't cause any trouble for Singe, it was likely that the reverse would also be true. The prideful teen enjoyed feeling powerful, and Kit would give him no cause to think he wasn't in control at all times. That, combined with the older boy's grudging respect for his abilities, always allowed them to tolerate working together.

Fifteen minutes later, the three Terrans were back in the main hall and ready to depart. Bohomaz, having not moved from his throne, waved to them as they unlocked the exit door, stepped into the shop beyond, and relocked it behind them. The cheers and well wishes of their "family" reached them, even through the thick wood of the hatch.

The clerk at the nearby desk, an aged reptilian Moravi with silver back spikes and faded yellow eyes, nodded and blinked as they passed. It was important for any criminal outfit, regardless of how poorly regulated the area it operated in was, to have a legitimate front business. For Bohomaz, that facade was a pawn shop run by the lizard-like Jomori, one of his partners. Ironically, since the store dealt in the buying and selling of all sorts of odds and ends, much of the merchandise they "appropriated" ended up being offloaded here. Kit's only hope was that the true owners of the items never made it this far into the backwaters of Sewertown to find their old belongings.

At the front of the musty shop, and as rundown as everything else in the area, was a sign put up by the proprietor to identify his business. The name, which had been decided upon by the elderly operators, spoke to what was housed in both the front and back of the establishment. As Kit passed beneath the epitaph, he wondered how accurate a label it was, given their line of work and the infirmity of all things built or living below ground.

The hanging tablet read, in simple but faded black script, *Safe Haven*.

<hr />

Hetrachia 3, 697 ABH
Somewhere Southwest of Aldona Fortress

Matteo awoke to the bleating tones of the altimeter notifying him that the craft had passed below the minimum height threshold for safe flying. Apparently he had dozed off while flying, exhaustion from the day's events and the recession of adrenaline from his system leaving him bone weary and incapable of keeping his heavy eyelids from falling. Now those endorphins were back in full force, screaming at him to wake up and save himself from an impending impact with the ground below.

Without thinking, he grabbed the yoke and pulled back. The transport shot skyward but only gained a few meters before tilting back toward earth. Matteo glanced at the altimeter: five meters and barely holding. He scanned left to the synth-oil gauge . . . empty, of course. Nothing was left to lubricate the engines and channel the flow of energy to the gravpads. They were going to crash. It was only a matter of time.

Sylette had left the cabin earlier but came rushing back now that alarms were blaring throughout the vessel. "I leave you for five minutes and everything goes . . . " Matteo saw her eyes widen as they passed across the altimeter and witnessed the dirt rushing to greet them outside. "Are we really that low? Do something!"

What do you think I've been doing? "Tell everyone to strap in. We're out of oil and going down." The calm certainty of his voice belied the racing of his heart. If they didn't explode on collision with the rocks below, he'd probably perish from the shock of it all.

"Why don't you—" Sylette seemed ready to start in on another tirade before shaking her head resignedly and running back into the other room. "Everyone, buckle up! We're going to have a rough landing!"

Surprised voices greeted her announcement, followed by rapid shuffling as everyone scrambled into seats and crash harnesses. Vallen groaned loudly in his fever-induced stupor, Velle pleaded with no one in particular for help with him, and Unter grumbled about none of the belts fitting properly before simply strapping himself to the bulkhead with cargo nets.

That's one problem taken care of, Matteo thought with relief. Then the lights lit up the forest ahead. Not thirty meters to the fore, reflected in the glow of his high beams, was a stand of towering deciduous trees that snaked their way skyward about massive, hulking trunks and half-exposed root systems. He could tell they were deciduous trees since, with the coming autumn, they had . . . *Now's not the time for that!* Matteo silenced his tangential musings and rapidly began pushing buttons with one hand while the other jerked the stick about trying to gain elevation.

Big green button! The lume, mostly depleted from their earlier flight, shimmered dimly into existence. *Twin black switches!* The left ailerons engaged, dragging the entire craft down and left. *No, not that one!* He quickly switched them back off, trying to correct their new course and failing to do so between the slow jamming of the hydraulics and the unyielding force of gravity. *Up, we have to go up!* They were going down—that much was certain. However, even with the shield, the small transport, and them along with it, would likely be mangled if it directly struck one of those ancient wooden pillars.

Matteo sweated and strained with all his might, pulling the controls against the mechanical inhibitions and momentum that dragged them toward the base of the woods. "Aargghhh!" At ten meters, his efforts managed to move the lever by the barest of fractions, and the deteriorating movement of the gears triggered one final adjustment of the wings, changing their angle just enough to send them over the first wall of timber . . . and plowing through their canopy of stretching branches and boughs.

Long, crooked fingers of wood and vine snapped at the viewport as the ship surfed across the treetops. Each bounce sent shockwaves through the hull, dislocating anything not properly strapped down. Tools from the earlier repair project ricocheted like shrapnel. Worn panels came loose and fell from their berths. Mounting external damage resulted in the overloading of the instrument panel, and Matteo was forced to cover his eyes and face from the ensuing spray of sparks. Above everything was the cacophony of glaring red warning lights and increasingly off-rhythm alarm bells.

The feeling of sensory strain was irrepressible. Matteo ducked down, hoping against hope that it would all be over soon. And it was. With one final bound, the vessel broke through the upper layer, falling sickeningly toward the ground below with much of its initial impulse intact. There it collided head on with the trunk of a forest giant, eradicating the remaining lume, shattering the forward window, and crumpling the driving compartment inwards by a good meter. However, Matteo barely had time to comprehend these events before the airbag in front of him deployed, smothering him in its embrace and causing the darkness of unconsciousness to claim him once again.

⌦⚬⌫

When Matteo groggily opened his eyes, he was lying on his back against a cluster of roots and staring at the dark ceiling of leaves above. He immediately attempted to raise his body, grasping at the soft loam and leveraging himself upward. After achieving a sitting position, a flash of pain in his neck stopped him from going further. Matteo raised one hand and gingerly massaged the crick as he took stock of his surroundings.

Vallen lay on a makeshift stretcher of pipe and cloth nearby, with Velle attending to him as best she could. His right shoulder and neck were caked in blood from the earlier bullet wound. The injury had since clotted, but he was pale from the loss of ichor and sweating profusely from the outbreak of fever. He appeared in desperate need of proper medical attention, and Velle herself needed a break; fatigue from her efforts showed on tired features and in weakening healing magic.

The remnants of a small fire, along with their erstwhile transport, were visible in the near distance. Lilith seemed to have borne the brunt of the firefighting, as she darted from blaze to blaze to repress them before they could become true conflagrations. At her side was Unter, his blue skin blending with the shadows of the night and in stark contrast to the orange hues of the flames. With staunch endurance, he used one of his remaining shields to shovel mounds of dirt onto any sparks his companion left behind.

While the size-disparate duo fought the aftereffects of the crash, Sylette could be seen repeatedly braving the rear entrance to the craft to haul to safety piles of weapons and supplies. The vessel seemed to have come to rest with the cockpit half wrapped around a great Weisse Elegoras tree. Instead of the stout trunk giving way, the metal had instead, resulting in irreparable damage to the forward compartment and the deployment of the failsafe airbag that likely saved Matteo's life. The rest of the vessel had settled into the soft earth, nestled among the giant's root system with little more than superficial dings and scratches. This seemed to suggest that he, at the front, had borne the worst of the impact.

Things could always be worse, Matteo reasoned, pushing off against a bulbous growth sprouting from the radicle beneath him. He groaned mightily as he did so, feeling every single bump, bruise, and ache from the past day shouting in unison. The noise attracted the attention of Renar who, as usual, was standing nearby, unsure of what to do. He turned and shot Matteo an incredulous glance, gesticulating pointedly at the scorched transport.

"Really? *Really?*"

Matteo resisted the urge to palm his face in annoyance. *We go through all that and 'Really?' is all he can think to say?* "I told you that I always crash."

"No kidding." The sarcasm in Renar's statement was not well hidden, and Matteo felt his ire rising for the umpteenth time that day. Accompanying it was an expanding headache, *mostly* the result of his recent traumas.

"Next time, *you* can fly the ship. Anyway, why are you over here and not helping the others?"

Velle turned to glare at them as their volume increased. "Miss Princess put him on 'guard duty' with us so he wouldn't get in the way. Now, since neither of you are actually doing anything, can you be quiet so I can focus on my casting?"

The edge in her voice and rings beneath her eyes spoke volumes about the stress she was under. Even so, and against his better judgment, Matteo was about to retort when Sylette and the others walked over. The princess and Lilith both carried their own weapons and several small sacks, while the hulking Unter had a crate strapped to his back and large duffels under each of his lower arms.

Without so much as a word of care or concern to anyone, Sylette hopped straight into what Matteo was beginning to think of as her "command mode." "Good. The fires are out, we were able to retrieve most of our gear, and you're awake. Ideally, we wouldn't have crashed in the first place, but what's done is done. So, where are we Matteo?"

The question caught him slightly aback, and he gazed about to see if he could identify anything familiar. Normally he would have homed straight in on such an important detail. *I'm just tired from what we've been through and the effects of present company. I'm not actually losing my touch.* A thick forest encircled them, filled entirely with ancient, massive Weisse Elegoras trees. Slight breezes whistled and flowed through the canopy above but failed to penetrate to the surface below. A soft layer of decaying leaves and moss coated the wood's floor, and the faint buzzing of nighttime insects could be heard all around.

Matteo knew these sounds well, for they were the sounds of his childhood, a distant memory of a time far departed from the recent horrors he had witnessed. Glancing down at the chronometer on his right wrist, he could see the current time in glowing yellow etching—02:37.

"How long was I out?"

Lilith was the first to answer, dropping her pack and sitting on it as they waited. "About two hours, give or take."

"Then if we crashed around midnight, and the sun set at approximately seven in the evening, we had been traveling for five hours, which at our velocity would have put us over Lyndwur Forest, a fact confirmed by the presence of Weisse Elegoras, a local variant of the Elegoras family which only grows in this region . . . " Matteo paused and took a breath before completing his rapid explanation, "Meaning that we're only a couple leagues from Etrus, our destination."

Sylette looked suitably impressed by his deduction, and Renar clapped his hands. "*Wooie*! And you wonder why we call you 'The Professor.'" His tone managed to be both complimentary and mildly derisive at the same time, something Matteo was quickly realizing was a specialty of his.

"That answers where we are, but how do we get from here to there? Vallen really needs a proper healer. He's showing signs of MIS, and the fever keeps getting hotter, so we have to hurry. The only blessing was that the bullet passed clean through—"

"He brought that on himself. I told him not to charge in." Velle's worried explanation of the Triaron's condition was abruptly cut off by Sylette, who gazed at the injured man with palpable disdain. "In fact, if he hadn't done—"

"What does that have to do with anything? Why wouldn't helping a fallen comrade be our first priority?" The Sylph started to rise, crimson features turning an even deeper shade of red as a result of darkening emotions. Mirroring her was Sylette, who moved toward her until barely a meter separated them.

"Do I have to spell it out for you? Our current situation, our inability to defeat Valescar, your teammate's death, all of that was *his* fault! This imbecile is nothing but dead weight . . . literally!" She jabbed an accusing finger at the drained and ailing Vallen, now lying unattended on the ground beside them.

Before glyphs and daggers could begin flying, the large frame of Unter coalesced between them, his mighty build completely obscuring each from the other. One of his two remaining free arms reached down and effortlessly clutched Vallen and his pallet in a soft embrace. "Fighting not helping. I carry extra burden. Lilith, check base of tree." His last unobstructed limb pointed at a nearby pale white trunk with a wide girth, the biggest in the small clearing they stood in.

The small girl nimbly darted across its spread of roots and crouched at its base searching for . . . moss! The realization struck Matteo like a thunderbolt. Moss tended to grow on the southern, shady side of objects in this part of the world, the better to hide from the harsh rays of daylight. If they knew which orientation south was, then he could figure out which way Etrus was.

As if she'd read his mind, Lilith looked up at him and asked, "Relative to this forest, which direction is the city?"

"Uhh," Matteo considered for a moment, picturing a map of the area in his mind, "a little southwest, I think."

"Then we need to go that way." She pointed over his shoulder, ironically on the same heading that their ship had crashed. *At the very least,* he reflected as the party wearily shouldered their burdens and began moving out, *I can give myself props for flying and falling on the right path.* Unter hefted most of their belongings, along with Vallen, while Matteo, Renar, and Lilith carried the rest. Sylette and Velle were nominally on watch at the front and rear of the group, but their separation was more about staying away from each other than about keeping anyone else safe.

After several minutes of walking in silence through the pitch black of the forest, Matteo found his quite legitimate existential fears of the previous day being replaced by anxiety about the unknown around them. Every too-pale tree became a spectral spirit, every twisting root a disembodied grasping hand, every squawking bird and chirping insect a ravenous creature waiting to pounce. His nerves wavered, despite being in the middle of an armed band. Matteo was therefore shocked when Renar's timid whisper, not his own, was the first to break the stillness.

"P . . . Professor, are you sure there aren't any, you know, nasty beasts or strange monsters in this place?" Accompanying his apprehensive query was the echoing "caw" of a nochlow, a small nocturnal avian that preyed on other similarly night-loving woodland creatures. The sound was hollow and haunting; Matteo tried and failed to suppress a shudder.

"No, there . . . there's absolutely nothing . . . to be afraid of. Well, at least at this time of year." The second half emerged as a murmur, and Matteo was unsure if Renar or any of the others actually heard him. *It doesn't really matter.* There was no reason for them to come back to the Lyndwur forest during winter, which was when things truly did get dangerous. Since the wood was located near the foothills of the Great Divide, some of the massive, violent, and terrifying creatures that roamed its slopes during more temperate periods came down to the region to escape the smothering year-end blizzards.

Many of these powerful animals were omnivores, designed so that they could survive off whatever was available, be it plant or living flesh. However, most of the usual game in the forest hibernated in the winter, deep in the root systems of the Weisse Elegoras. This made hunting especially difficult, even for the most unmatched of cliff-dwelling predators. Fortunately for them, winter was also the season that the Elegoras produced their seeds for the next spring, and their fruit was said to be among the tastiest and most enriching delicacies on the continent.

As luck would have it, the prize of this meal was nearly impossible to obtain. You see, the trees of the Lyndwur were practically sentient. In order to protect their potential offspring, a large portion of their upper roots curled skyward about their trunks and the growing zygotes attached to them. This wooden barrier acted as both shield and sword. Only the sharpest of claws could penetrate the hard surface, and if a beast managed to do so, they would find more jagged limbs on the inside to impale or repel them, whichever proved easiest.

Winter in the Lyndwur was to be avoided at all costs. This was one of the first things parents in nearby Etrus taught their children; it was hardly a fairy tale with an important moral—it was a real and present danger. Many were the professional hunters, even in Matteo's lifetime, who had thought themselves above the threat and ventured into the forest's embrace. None were seen again, and the trees were always hardier the next spring for the additional nourishment. He shuddered again as he reminisced about the frightening tales. *Who in their right mind wanted to get in the middle of a battle between monster plants and bloodthirsty creatures?*

Thereafter, the tranquility of their march was only broken by the eerie noises of their dismal surroundings. And while the calls of their nocturnal watchers were incessant, never once did the originators of the sounds cross their path. It seemed likely that the wildlife at this time of year was as afraid of them as Matteo was of it.

Eventually, the denser undergrowth and thick stands of trees gave way to more open spaces before finally resolving into a true trail farther on. This well-marked and beaten-down gravel thoroughfare indicated they were almost out of the forest, beyond which lay the seaside town of Etrus. Despite not being oft traveled in this age of increasing air transport, it was maintained by the locals, who put great stock in respecting the ancient wood through their interactions with it.

A few minutes of easier progress along the road saw the canopy thin to the point where the muted light of the twin moons above could light their steps. Up to this point, Lilith had been showing the way with the glow from crackling flames she generated in her palm, but now she doused them and held her hand up to halt their progress. As they came to a stop, still mostly hidden behind the last bend of the forest before the clear air ahead, she pointed through a gap between the final Elegoras trunks.

Just to the right of the highway at the edge of the Lyndwur was a small but bright campfire set in the lee of a weathered guidepost. Atop the blaze was a metal grate and cooking pot from which emerged a steady stream of spiraling steam. Matteo felt his stomach gurgle at the thought of a hot meal, but now wasn't the time for that. Three fingers lifted on Lilith's right hand, and her left indicated each of the persons of interest in turn.

Indeed, three Moravi, their scales almost blending with their environs, sat in a circle about their dinner on small wooden crates that allowed their tails to freely curl behind them. The smallest, likely a female, though Matteo could hardly tell their sexes apart, was bent forward, stewing the contents of the vessel. The largest, both in terms of raw size and elaborate curling patterns of back and forearm protrusions, appeared half soused, an ale flagon in one hand while his muscular rear appendage wrapped about an entire barrel of the brew.

However, in the middle of the two was an older reptile, his spikes and skin graying and a slight, almost mammalian beard growing underneath his extended snout. His forked tongue flicked in and out, as though tasting the air, and his slitted pupils darted hither and yon as though searching for any potential threats. All three were armed; at their waists were blade scabbards sized appropriately for each of them.

To bypass them and reach Etrus would require a detour of considerable time and effort. While the Lyndwur itself was a labyrinth of crowded shrubs, roots, and massive trees, the land past it was almost bare in comparison. The high ground of the forest flowed steadily to a grassy basin, which plateaued again briefly at the city before rushing downwards to greet the ocean. As a result, the only cover between them and their destination was a few boulders not yet worn from the plain and the loaded traveling cart of the Moravi set beside the road.

Sylette inched forward next to Lilith, took in the scene, and evidently reached the same conclusion Matteo had. When her instructions came, they were barely a whisper, "Unter, in one of the sacks you're carrying is a pile of Sarconian field cloaks. They aren't designed for stealth, but they should allow us to keep our faces hidden. We won't be able to hide your size or skin color, but the rest of us should be able to avoid sticking out like sore thumbs."

Matteo could see the purpose of her directions, but Renar didn't quite understand their situation. "Why do we need to hide? Can't we just walk past them?" *At least he's keeping his voice down this time*, Matteo thought, acknowledging the slight improvement.

"Are you daft? In a few days, if not a few hours, this country will entirely belong to the empire. At that point, they'll want all enemy soldiers disarmed and imprisoned. And, last I checked, we're Darmatian army cadets, so that includes us. Furthermore, my father personally wants me captured, and all of you got in the way of his first attempt. Follow my logic now?"

Sylette's voice came out sharp and quiet, but even so, Matteo was glad Moravi didn't have the best hearing. Instead, they relied more on taste and sensations. "Ye . . . yes." Renar slumped, clearly not fully aware of their circumstances but afraid to argue further with the imperative princess.

"Also, if you're going to insist on carrying the idiot along, throw a tarp around him so he looks like a roll of goods rather than an unconscious waste of flesh." Sylette gestured at Vallen, who was still limp underneath Unter's lower right arm.

Her comment elicited an instant rebuttal from Velle. "What? You want him to suffocate?"

"While that would be the optimal outcome, you could also cut him an air hole instead of complaining. You can figure it out." The tone was sarcastic, but the glare of the silver eyes accompanying it was cold and uncaring. It was increasingly clear that these two would not get along, a fact that didn't bode well for their haphazard party of circumstance.

Matteo was about to ask Unter to get between them again when Sylette broke off the confrontation and helped the Hue distribute the cloaks. When everyone had donned their outerwear, basically a long, hooded tarp colored in a variety of greens, browns, and blacks, she turned and spoke to them one last time. "If we get stopped, let me do the talking. Otherwise, we move right on past. Ready?"

Everyone nodded in agreement except Velle, but that was likely due to her obvious chagrin with their self-proclaimed leader, rather than opposition to the plan. With Sylette at the fore, the group moved back onto the path and exited the forest at a nonchalant pace. However, trying to act like ordinary travelers probably wouldn't get them very far. *It's too late,* Matteo reflected, *but we'd probably have drawn less attention to ourselves without suspiciously hiding our identities.* Besides, how many Hues were just walking around outside of the Ascendency? *Everything about us screams, "We're up to something!"*

Before he could chase that line of reasoning too far down the squirrelhare hole, they were abreast the Moravi campsite. *Hey, we're just a group of seven, well, six, young adventurers hiding our faces and carrying a body-shaped lump and lots of weapons. Nothing to see here!*

Sylette nodded to them as they passed, Matteo clenched his teeth, and the older Moravi blinked his eyes in reply as his companions continued their respective enterprises. Everything was going surprisingly well. Just a few more steps and they'd be—

"Zat vudn't happen to beez zour zhip zat vent down in ze forezt a little vhile ago, vud it?" A rapping sound rang out behind them, along with heavily accented Common, and for a moment Matteo thought it was a gunshot. He whirled about to see the elder reptile halfway hunched over and staring at them with beady eyes while tapping a knuckle absently against the exposed bone plate atop his head. Equal parts relief and curiosity welled up inside him. *Maybe that's similar to Terrans touching their heads when they think?*

His curiosity quickly soured to dread; they couldn't just keep walking without arousing misgivings with this group of Moravi. Matteo glanced at the robed figure he knew to be Sylette from under the rim of his own hood. What would she do now?

"Yes, it was." She addressed the questioner, taking care to stay directly out of the firelight but closing enough with the speaker to seem engaged in the conversation. "We're actually on our way to Etrus now to find a repair crew to help us—"

"Zi, Zi, Zi!" laughed the drunken lizard, booming in mirth as only his people, with their unique forked tongue, could. "Zu vont be flying zat zessel again, if zu azk me. Zu can ztill zee ze zmoke from here, za?" He pointed at a curl of fog that was, in fact, wafting from the direction of their crash site deep in the Lyndwur. Realizing that he was pointing with his tankard of ale, he quickly brought the frothy brew back to his taut snout and killed it in one go.

"Andz even if you could, zu vud be unable to find ze help zu need vight now . . . " The elder brushed past them and rounded their cart. Now that he was closer, Matteo could see that it was filled with odds and ends of all sorts: mechanical parts; illyrium crystals of various grades; weapons; clothes made for all races, including Moravi outfits with tail slots; armor; antiques; furniture; and literally anything and everything they could fit on the sturdy contraption. These were the trappings of traders, perhaps even black market dealers given some of their wares. When his eyes found their way back to the grizzled Moravi, his claws were indicating the harbor of Etrus in the near distance. "Everyone andz anyone iz down zere at ze army garrizon azzizting vith ze evacuation. Zou'd zink it vaz ze end of ze vorld, ze vay zer running about like chickenz zithout headz."

The harbor and nearby military base were lit up with dozens of searchlights. In fact, it looked as bright as day down there, and vehicles of all kinds raced to and fro under the glowing beams, ferrying equipment and personnel to ships waiting both on shore-based landing pads and dockside quays. Nearby, the riverhead, barely visible around the city's high hill, was clogged with civilian and navy craft that were themselves filled to the brim with soldiers and massive crates. However, whether they were heading for the Etrus canal or out to sea was not evident from this distance. Despite the activity in the industrial quarter, the rest of the town, situated on and about the tiers of its central peak, was dark and hushed.

"Zu zee, ze traderz and army near ze dockz recently got vord zat eventz zu ze north didn't go zo vell for ze kingdom. Zo ze military iz ezcaping vhile zey ztill can and ze traderz are tryin zu make a pretty geldar helping zem. Of courz, zome of zem are alzo getting ready to azzizt ze empire vith logizticz and zhipping zince zey'll likely need ze extra handz for a bit." So the army was turning tail and running after the debacle at Aldona? Even though Etrus was on Darmatia's border with the Hue Ascendancy, Matteo could hardly blame them. The empire would soon make it even this far into the country, and a single base could do little to stop them. Maybe they'd regroup elsewhere and keep fighting? Flee around the peninsula to Rabban?

Sadly, those were the exact same choices facing them. *Can we go to ground and pretend we were never soldiers?* Matteo could still join his father in the shipping business. In fact, he was probably down there now, working on the evacuation. Certainly he could do far better as a businessman than an officer. Besides, what good was a gun and some magic in the face of what he'd seen in the recent battle?

When he refocused on the present, Sylette was once more talking to the Moravi leader who now blocked the road between them and Etrus. "Even so, we'll take our chances in the city. Thank you so much for your concern, but if you'll just step—"

"Twoz hundred geldarz." His short, nonsensical monetary offer interrupted her once again.

"For what?"

"Zour zhip and zateverz left on her."

"I'm sorry; it's not for sale." Sylette motioned for them to move forward but found her progress blocked by the sidestepping of the bearded elder.

"Everythingz for zale for ze zight price, mizzy. Juzt like information. Von hundred andz ninetyz geldarz."

Even from behind, the princess's surprise was evident in the sudden jolt to her posture. "Wait. Your offer went down, not up. That's not how bargaining works!"

"But it iz. Zu zee, zu didn't accept my initial offer. Now ol' Grozza'z hurtz and more inclined to tell zour zecretz to otherz if zu continue zu refuz my kind generozity." Despite his quirky pronunciation, the syntax and grammar of his Common Tongue had been perfect thus far. Grozza, as he'd called himself, knew what he was saying and doing, and that made Matteo's sudden outbreak of cold sweat all the more chilling. *It's barely been five minutes, and our turtlegoose is already cooked.*

"W . . . what do you mean?"

No, Sylette, playing dumb won't help. Matteo inwardly cringed, but doubted he could do any better in her place.

"Von hundred andz eightyz geldarz. Zu zee, zose cloakz have a Zarconian zymbol zewn into ze lower ztitching. Unlez zu know itz zere, itz eazy for an amateur zu miz. Furthermore, zat bag iz breathing, but zu Terraz, and von each of Hue and Zylph, can be excuzed for not noticing zince zour eyez aren't nearly az good az ourz. Captured Zarc or randomz kidnapping? Grozza carez not. Vant me zu continue?" His blinking, yellow gaze seemed to sneer from slitted pupils.

Sylette's hands started to move beneath her outer layer, as thought preparing to cast a spell. Instantly, the drunk and female were on their feet, weapons in hand and not appearing distracted or befuddled in the least. "What if I still say no? There's six of us and three of you."

Numerics aside, Matteo didn't like their chances. He was unarmed, and, in fact, he hadn't seen his rifle since they were on the *Feywind*. All four of Unter's arms were preoccupied. Vallen was unconscious and wrapped in a sheet. That left only Sylette, Renar, Lilith, and Velle as combatants, at least initially. So at first it would be four on three, and who knew if they had reinforcements nearby?

Grozza looked them over for several seconds, likely sizing them and the situation up in the same way Matteo had. "Zu vook pretty capable. Zetz zay zu win, get ze better of uz. Zu zee Triz'ka over zere? Ze pretty cook vith ze rozy pink zcalez? Ze can ululate like no other, brilliant, zpine tingling zound. Our matez in Etruz hear her zcream, know it mean trouble, run here on all four limbz, zomething zu uprightz can'tz do. Zey get here in few minutez, topz. Zu tired from fighting uz, get overvelmed by vhole gang, zold off to Zarcs. Not pretty end for ze pretty uprightz girlz and boyz. Von hundred seventyz geldarz. Final offerz."

Given all that knowledge, Sylette looked like she might still protest, but Unter dropped his upper two packs at the feet of the Moravi and clapped her gently on the shoulder to stifle any potential aggression. "Two packs mystery goods. Sweeten deal. We take money, you forget ever saw. Good?"

The old lizard scanned the large duffels, engaged in a silent eyelid discussion with his companions, then bared his fangs in what must pass for a smile among his people while grasping the Hue's large palm in a handshake. "Ze haz a bargain! Ve never za zu, I zvear by ze egg I vaz hatched fromz."

Having concluded their arrangement, the prescribed number of geldars changed hands, and Grozza moved out of their way in a series of muted, almost condescending bows. Matteo certainly didn't trust any of them to keep their word, but saying so now would be counterproductive. That was one fear he would have to keep to himself until later.

Fortunately, the rest of their short journey passed with a blissful lack of further interruptions. Fifteen minutes saw them walking up the expansive cobblestone main street of Etrus, with large, multistoried houses of tan, solid stone rising on both sides. Despite being a small city, it was a prosperous one, made so by its location on both an important canal and a break in the sheer waterside cliffs along the Phar Sea. Each house was fronted by small but vibrant gardens that flourished in the tropical clime; the beauty of these facades was mirrored only in the rooftop sitting areas above that were similarly apportioned.

At this time of night all the shops were closed, lights turned off, and shutters locked. Thieves weren't prevalent in the area, beyond a few occasional crews in port that fancied themselves pirates, so Etrus had neither a surrounding wall or a city watch. Instead, the duty of protection fell to the army garrison and the sense of justice held by the upstanding leaders of her shipping industry. The existence of Etrus relied on trade, making those in the transport business her controlling magnates. Unlike more corrupt seaside towns, those living here had forged a strong code of ethics and responsibility from dealing with the people of seven different nations and five different races. Their word was their law, and they upheld it, regardless of the consequences. They protected their people and goods in the same way.

The peak of the town, set against the backdrop of the dual pale moons, one half behind the other, was their destination. Matteo's house looked almost the same as any of the others they had witnessed on the way. After all, very little architecture beyond stucco walls and terracotta roof slates could survive the intense heat and winds of the region. However, his mother was a busybody, so that's where the similarities ended.

Tapestries of bright, vivid colors hung beneath every closed window, and a compass fronted by a shining star, the symbol of his father's company, was emblazoned into the stone above the front door. It was also chiseled into the gatepost, the walkway, the flowerpots, the flags in the garden, the wooden door, and pretty much everywhere else imaginable. Yes, his mother was very, very enamored with the family occupation.

Further additions to the norm included a bubbling pond filled with fish from local sources, brilliant varieties of flora and fauna from her husband's journeys, and, for the baby boy she was so proud of, a large Darmatian army flag pinned against the right wall of the entryway stoop. Matteo felt tears welling up at the sight of so many familiar things but managed to hold them back. He was here to protect his friends and to once more make sense of his world. Personal sentiments could come after.

He grasped the metal gate, opened it slowly to keep it from creaking, and replaced it just as carefully. Everyone in the neighborhood, including his mother, would be asleep. Besides, every person who saw them, beyond their failure with the Moravi, would make their attempts at stealth increasingly useless. Even staying here was likely to be temporary—he wouldn't endanger his mother and father any more than necessary.

When Matteo reached the front door, his companions squeezing into the space alongside him or, in Unter's case, standing in the garden like an oversized blue lawn gnome, he paused before knocking. As he wrestled with his thoughts, Sylette, ever the pragmatist, reached up and took down the Darmatian flag. It was the correct thing to do. Better no one know that they, or his parents, were affiliated with the kingdom army.

On that subject, do I really even want to get my family involved? Matteo ruminated, hesitant fingers shaking before the brass doorknocker. *Perhaps we're safe enough just being in town. We could spend our newly made money to stay at a decent hotel for a few days. We could even run away to the Ascendency, the Magerium, or Rabban. Wait out the war somewhere safer. Do we even need to flee? We could just change our outfits and get jobs. No one would be the wiser. Yeah, that sounds like a good—*

Matteo never even had time to finish his musings. The glass on either side of the door brightened as the inside lights came on. Without pausing, the large wooden door retracted inward, and a brown-haired woman of medium build wearing a red nightgown threw herself from the raised portal to wrap her arms around his neck. She was older, with wrinkles creasing her tan, worn face, and her long hair threatened to smother him as her soft cheek pressed against his. Her eyes wept a constant stream of tears into his shoulder as her frame shuddered and wracked itself with sobs. At first, Matteo didn't know what to do or say between the watery drops, the strangulation, and the asphyxiation.

Then she spoke, quietly, warmly. With the voice of love only a mother can muster. "Thank the Veneer, Matteo. I was so, so worried when I heard the news. Thank goodness you're here. You're safe now . . . There's nothing to worry about anymore."

He didn't say anything; he couldn't. His own tears erupted, bright and swift, the raw emotional outpouring of the hardship he had endured and the horrors he had witnessed. Matteo let it all go, a complete and total cathartic release, a grown man crying along with his mother on their front porch, in the middle of the night, among his similarly grown friends and companions. There was nothing to be ashamed of. They had all been through so much. But it was past now. He was enclosed in his mother's arms. Nothing in the world could harm him now.

They had reached it at long last: their safe haven.

Chapter 13

Proselytizers and Pickpockets

Mesmeri ??, 6?? ABH,
Streets of the Royal Capital, Nemare

———⟨◆⟩———

"So what do any of these bootlickers get out of this? As far as I can tell, they're just pissing their dosh away."

"It gives them a sense of security." Kit humored Singe by engaging in the same conversation for the third time that day. He wasn't sure whether the churlish teenager had forgotten their previous talks, was looking for a specific answer, or was simply trying to goad him into responding in a brusque manner so he could have an excuse to lash back—physically, most likely.

"But it doesn't add up. What does giving money to these robed monkeys baying praises to a non-existent god accomplish? What will Sariel ever do for them? Where's this safety net you speak of?" The burly Terran talked slowly, picking at his teeth with a small wooden sliver as he did so. With nothing to remove, the action seemed more out of habit than efficacy. His free hand scratched at his matted brown hair. Itch or fleas? It could easily be either, given their living conditions.

"You're being too literal, Singe. There's no real net, or prize, that they're trying to nab. It's all in their heads." Pockey was out in front, beyond a pile of crates fronting the entrance to the alley they were hiding in. He was wearing a decent set of clothes to blend in with the surface folk, hand-picked from among all the props Bohomaz let them use for jobs. The outfit said "shopkeeper's boy," and he kept sweeping the dust from the cobbles back and forth in front of the store next door in keeping with the part. While the owner might notice the odd behavior and become suspicious after a time, they'd have moved on to the next temple by then.

"Wha'dya you mean, 'too literal'? There's only two types in this world: those who have and those who don't. You either have money, or you ain't, and these sods who have it are just flushing it on a scam with no return." High on the list of things to avoid doing in the gang was insulting the intelligence of Singe, which Pockey had just unintentionally done. Unless Kit calmed him down, they both might get it later. Whatever else he was, the brute was smart enough not to interrupt work to hand out a beating.

"You've got the right idea, boss, but just take it a step further. What if there's something more important than geldars to them? Maybe this is a case where they can only get what they need by giving away what we see as extremely valuable." He easily slid the "boss" honorific into his compliment, hoping to stroke the older Terran's ego while steering the discussion into the theoretical. Singe didn't enjoy talking about matters beyond his ken, so he'd probably change the topic.

Sure enough, he did. "Bah, faith and ethereal mumbo jumbo. None of it makes a lick of sense. Let's just focus on the job. If they're wasting their dough, we might as well take it and put it to better use." That was fine by Kit. Just because he somewhat understood the people they were watching didn't mean he agreed with them. Having lived the life he had, he knew there were no Veneer . . . and no Creator behind them. If they were real, he was sure they wouldn't allow a place like Sewertown to exist.

Ironically, it could be interpreted as divine will that some of the money these sycophants came to donate would end up supporting the castaways below that both they, and the false heavens, had forgotten. It had been a successful day thus far. After visiting two other temples, they had come away with several pouches of gelders and some pieces of jewelry, including a gold wire bracelet inlaid with small sapphires that looked like it was worth a small fortune. Being intent on merrymaking in the festival atmosphere, most of their targets were too focused on their prayers, their conversation, their drink, or each other, in the case of a few overly romantic couples, to notice their missing valuables. Of course, even a blind man will eventually realize he's lost something. When cries of shock and alarm rippled through the crowd in the wake of their efforts, they packed up shop and left.

They were still in the process of casing their current location. Above, the midday sun was at its zenith, beating down on the desert city with all its fury. Store owners around the square unfurled awnings over their wares, while temple acolytes distributed small waterskins to alleviate the thirst of their parishioners. Next to the white marble church was a large square with a bubbling fountain from which beasts of burden drank greedily. Their loads, carts of various sizes filled to overflowing with baubles, trinkets, and tantalizing foodstuffs, sat nearby forming the beginnings of what might become a true bazaar. Shouts and exclamations rang out across the gathered masses, hawking goods and acclaiming the value of fine and precious items.

Being a predominantly Terran holiday held in a Terran-ruled territory, most of the throngs of gleeful patrons were of the same status. At the far end of the market, a group of lightly clad red Sylph women stood in stark contrast to the sandy hues around them. Whether they were peddling magic and sorceries, as their kind was wont to do, or services of a . . . *different* sort, Kit couldn't tell at this distance. The only Hue in sight wore the white robes of a minister of the Way of the Will and was making a show of graciously welcoming members of his flock into the wide archway of the temple entrance. More common than either were the Moravi and the Vladisvar—the former almost exclusively in the roles of venders while the latter tended to trail after wealthy and important individuals as intimidating bodyguards.

Of course, the increased security presence was to be expected. The upper west end, the precinct closest to the government offices, academies, and royal palace, was known for being a place of affluence. Anybody who was anyone lived here, and if you didn't, you aspired to. Kit and his friends normally never came here since the guards, both public and private, were difficult to work around, but given the confusion and levity resulting from the day's atmosphere and the pulsing crowds, the risk was worth the reward. There were too many bodies for the watch and hired hands to keep track of everyone at once. And while everyone here had money, not all possessed the protection to keep hold of it.

Speaking of which . . . Kit thought, spotting a prime target. "Pockey, young girl, short brown hair, birthmark or burn on her right calf, two o'clock. You see her?"

"About our age, waist pouch bulging with coins, walking up the steps to the parish? Yeah, I do," he whispered back without turning, keeping his efforts focused on the cobbles so as not to attract attention.

"She's got no one with her. Clothes suggest nobility and hairpin and bracelet are both probably worth more than we are. She'll be our first mark." The girl stopped halfway to the door and looked about, seemingly unsure of what to do as far as the festival rites were concerned. *Probably her first time making an offering*, Kit observed. He didn't know why she was here alone, but he wouldn't hesitate to take advantage of it.

"I'll run distraction while you cut her belt and take the pouch along with it, Pockey. She'll probably feel something, so make a quick getaway down Sandover Lane on the left before circling back. Singe, if you could run cleanup on anybody who gets nosy, that would be great. Just no violence, alright?"

"Yeah, yeah. I've been doing this long enough to know not to make a scene."

"Roger, then I'll . . . Oh Void." Pockey spun away from them just in time to encounter the shopkeeper of the store he was pretending to sweep in front of. The older, grey-haired man immediately laid into him, questioning who he was, what he was doing, why he was there, on and on. It was a massive oversight that they hadn't seen him coming, but they'd have to improvise and carry on even so. Kit nodded to Singe, who put on the face of a perturbed older brother and burst out of the alley toward the confrontation. He would do his best to make it seem like Pockey was a misguided youth who constantly got into trouble playing games like this, apologize profusely, and then drag the youth off roughly enough to satisfy their audience. It was just one of the many scenarios they knew by heart to avoid trouble when things went wrong.

Meanwhile, Kit wasn't quite ready to give up on the easy score in front of him. Even with Pockey and Singe indisposed, nabbing the gold pouch from the innocent, clueless girl should still present no issue. He made his way inconspicuously around the square in a circular path, checking a food stand here, looking at some hanging crystalline necklaces there, weaving himself seamlessly into the masses. Eventually Kit worked his way out of her meandering line of sight, then used a group of gaudily dressed aristocrats to mask his ascent up the rounded steps. He approached her silently from behind, his footsteps muffled by velvet pads attached to the soles, and was slipping a small knife from his long sleeve to slash her belt when she suddenly turned to face him.

"Oh, goodness, you startled me. Can I help you?" Her eyes lit up, big and blue with the shock of finding someone behind her. Her voice was soft and polite, as though courtesy had been ingrained into her.

Kit immediately retracted the blade before she could see it and launched into what he hoped was a suitable explanation. "Sorry for scaring you. You see, I was across the plaza, over there with my brothers at the shop where we work." He pointed at Singe and Pockey, still talking to the elderly proprietor at the edge of the market some fifty meters away. "And I saw you walk up here looking lost and confused. I just couldn't let that happen to a girl on my watch, so I decided to come and see if I could help. What's wrong?"

As he expected, girls ate sap like that for breakfast. She started blushing and glanced at the ground briefly before responding. "Thanks, that's sweet of you. Actually, you *can* help me. Normally I come with my parents to make our contribution to the Church of Light during the Festival of Sariel, but they are both so busy with work that they sent me to do it for them. Mind you, my parents aren't foolish enough to send me here alone, but I got separated from my attendant, Reesa, and haven't found her yet."

"So you came here hoping to run into her at your destination." What an envious position, having a servant to help you run errands. And waiting on a girl *his* age, nonetheless. Kit found the taste in his mouth souring at the unearned privilege of the naive individual before him.

"Exactly. Since I'm here anyway, I was hoping to complete the offering rite, but I've never done it before. Would you be able to show me how?"

Yet another ironic twist—and a perfect opportunity. Kit smiled at the girl. "Of course. I did my family's earlier today, so the process is still fresh in my mind. Do you have your money and pledge on you?"

The pledge was a small and insignificant part of the donation process, as far as Kit was concerned. In theory, the Church of Light was supposed to be involved with a large number of philanthropic projects in addition to the maintenance of their own temples and orders. Some of those projects involved donations to charities, medical institutions, and even groups that aided the poor. During the Festival of Sariel, the Church allowed contributions to be earmarked with a written pledge, which was supposed to be inviolable and ensure that the geldars went to the proper cause. However, no matter how noble the ideal or how much was given, Kit had never witnessed the money trickle down to Sewertown. In fact, most of the Way of the Will acolytes and clergy steered clear of the subterranean pit entirely. To them, charity and aid of the poor only applied to those on the surface. He hated the entire abominable system.

"Right here." She took the pouch from her belt and showed it to him. It jangled nicely; there were at least five hundred geldars in there, almost an entire month's worth of pickpocketing under normal circumstances.

"Could I hold the bag until we get inside—just long enough to show you what to do? Then I'll give it back so you can make the donation yourself."

"Ummm . . . " She bit her lip, considering.

Kit pushed a little harder. "The tricky parts are difficult to explain without showing. I promise I'm not going to run off with it."

"Al . . . alright. Here you go." Relenting, she began passing him the sack. Kit held his adrenaline in check, not wanting to give his game away until it was too late. Instead, he forced himself to keep talking.

"By the way, what's your pledge this year?" The linen package touched his outstretched palm, and the girl's hand began retracting. When she turned to go into the temple, when she least expected his betrayal and was in the worst possible position to react to it, he would run.

"My parents let me write it this time, and they probably wouldn't approve if they knew what it was." She glanced at the ground again, nervously, pointedly, as if looking at something beyond the marble steps beneath them.

I shouldn't have asked. Hurry up and move already, he fumed inwardly. Outwardly, Kit was all curiosity as he continued the conversation. "Why? What did you say?"

"I asked for them to use the money to help those poor people in Sewertown. I hear terrible and nasty rumors about it, but no one actually does anything to help, even though it's a place, practically its own city, right beneath our own. Am I strange for wanting that?"

Kit bolted at full speed, satchel of money in hand, his previous plan forgotten. *No, no, no! This is not happening!* Taking the steps two at a time, he reached the square below in barely a second. Keen eyes locked onto his escape route, a dark alley nearby, and his brain immediately traced the path to reach it.

Behind him, a high-pitched cry of surprise rang out as the young girl's shock finally turned to recognition. She had every right to be surprised, to be mad or angry, even furious. In fact, Kit was disgusted with himself as well. He had just violated the cardinal rule of their outfit: "Never steal from a good person, unless your very survival rests on it." Bohomaz insisted that the intent of the law was to keep balance between the karmic forces of light and dark, but something so abstract didn't really register with Kit. He wasn't even entirely sure what qualified as "good" or "evil," but the crushing feeling of guilt in his gut was probably a good indicator.

Forget all that! The money is all that matters! Self first, others second! At her scream, heads began spinning in Kit's direction, and he sprang off the balls of his feet toward his exit as quickly as he could. The guards would be coming soon, but he was small and swift and knew his surroundings. Provided they couldn't corner him, he'd escape easily and circle back to regroup with his friends.

The crowd surged with shouts of "Thief!" and "Pickpocket!" A Vladisvar bodyguard, huge, imposing, and covered in armor, stood up from getting a drink at the fountain as Kit approached. One massive fist grabbed at him, but he ducked under it then jumped onto the circular stone retaining wall and nimbly quick-stepped to the far side of the pool. There, a noble with frilly vestments and a turban set with a gem, likely the employer of the warrior he'd just avoided, screeched unbecomingly and dodged out of his way.

This is the type I'm used to dealing with. Kit's free hand snaked out and relieved the cowering patrician of his headdress as he passed. *Nothing wrong with a little extra prize.* Tucking it into his belt, he vaulted over a stand of exotic talismans, dashed through a wafting cloud of fragrant aromas from the delicacy vendors, and evaded a duo of city soldiers coming the other way by darting under a nearby awning.

The series of connected tents, separated from the rest of the bazaar he'd escaped into by an opaque screen, was filled with dozens of women—mostly Terrans but with a few here and there representing the other species—looking at, trying on, and buying clothes. To Kit's astonishment, many were in various stages of undress, their own articles, or those they were appraising, draped about them on wooden stands. He never really paid attention to women, yet even so, he was at an age where his cheeks couldn't help but redden at the sight. As Kit glanced to his left, catching a glimpse of a crudely drawn entrance sign with a crossed out male caricature that read, "NO MEN," the two watchmen he had just eluded came through the flap behind him.

"There you are, you little brat!"

A gauntleted hand began descending onto his shoulder, but Kit regained his senses and twisted out of his grip. At the same time, a devious idea formed in his mind, and he took off across the store at full speed, yelling as he did so. "Help, help! These weird men are chasing me!"

The effect was instantaneous. All the women in the store turned to the front entrance, caught sight of the guards—who were just beginning to realize the situation they were in—and clutched their garments to themselves, hiding behind any furniture available and screaming at the top of their lungs.

"Get out!"

"Didn't you read the sign?"

"Perverts!"

"Call the watch!"

"Wait, that uniform! Aren't *they* the watch?"

"Think you can abuse your position to do whatever you want?"

When he reached the far end of the pavilion, Kit briefly surveyed his handiwork. Being a young boy not old enough to be recognized as a sexual threat, he was entirely ignored in favor of the two gentlemen who had breached this women's sanctuary. Some that were fully clothed, including a tall female Vladisvar with curiously twisting horns, were gathered about the dejected pair, harassing them mercilessly with both words and blows. Above the noise he could hear the faint trilling of whistles, signaling the approach of more soldiers and guardsmen. If he slipped away now, it was entirely likely that he would be forgotten in favor of the breach of protocol occurring here.

He calmly pulled back the canvas wall, just a large enough crack for his tiny frame to slip through unnoticed . . . and found himself looking into the sky-blue eyes of the girl he had just stolen from.

"Wha . . . how?" Kit stammered, suddenly flat footed by the unexpected reversal.

"I've been to this particular boutique before. There's only the two exits, so when you went in the front, I ran around the back." Her voice was slightly winded, and she'd hiked her skirt up using a belt to grant her legs, which were longer than Kit's, the freedom to run. Sweat showed on the girl's blouse in several places, but that was only natural if she'd kept up with him thus far. "Can you stop running now? I'd like to—"

Just as she had planned her interception at the back of the store, Kit had intended to arrive at this point from the start as well. The alley was just a few meters to his left, and beyond that was a canal adjacent to Sandover Lane, one of the busiest thoroughfares in this district of Nemare. A short dash down the narrow corridor, a quick jaunt across the bridge above the channel, then lose his pursuit amid the traffic on the far side. It was a simple plan. It would work.

He took off in the middle of her sentence. Talking wouldn't help. Kit may be in the wrong, but that didn't mean that he intended to let himself get caught—or that he'd return the geldars. Thus far, the girl had proven herself naive, yes, but also intelligent and capable. Surely she just wanted to delay him long enough for the authorities to arrive and arrest him. *Sorry, but not sorry, sister.*

The dark path, formed by the stores and apartments to either side, was relatively clean for what it was. A similar walkway in Sewertown would be impassable, filled with either refuse or comparable thuggish garbage of flesh and blood. Only a few trash cans lined the walls, but Kit grabbed and overturned every one into the way of his pursuer. After each, he kept hoping to savor the inevitable metallic crash as she tripped and hit the pavement, but instead he only heard a slight pause in her footfalls as the noble miraculously evaded them.

And the noise of her impacts and elevated breathing were getting closer. Contrary to all appearances, she was in good shape, and with her broader stride, she'd catch him in a straight-up foot race. Grudgingly, Kit's respect for the aristo girl increased. *However . . . this isn't a foot race.*

Barreling from the alley at max speed, he barely sidestepped a horse-drawn cart turning onto the thin road that backed up to the buildings this side of the waterway. Used for cargo storage and the offloading of deliveries, the egress was exceedingly cramped, prompting the driver to come to a complete halt to avoid hitting Kit or spilling his cargo into the river. The small Moravi hopped to his feet and hurled obscenities after the fleeing boy, all in a language he didn't understand in the slightest.

While Kit wasn't the least bit concerned about responding, the girl chasing him shouted hurried apologies as she passed. "So sorry! Please forgive us!" *Good, waste your breath. Make it that much harder for you to catch me,* Kit thought snidely.

He had two obstacles left. Ringing from the post at the left of the bridge ahead announced the first. A commercial gondola was coming through, and the span needed to be raised. Private canal transports were much smaller, and the overpasses were sized to accommodate them, but the same could not be said for their bulkier cousins. Built to carry large numbers of people and goods about the city, many traverses had to be redesigned when they were first introduced. This particular construct was one that had been adjusted to split apart down the middle until the ship passed.

Kit had enough momentum, and the near end was only just beginning to rise. As a result, he received only a slightly bemused stare from the bridge operator at the controls when he ran past and vaulted the half meter gap. His feet skidded on the beams at the far side, but the boy caught his balance and continued until he touched stone on the bank.

Now you can't follow me. Turning, he was treated to the barely visible visage of utter amazement on the overseer's face as his pursuer leapt from the opposite end, now high in the air, and landed in a roll after clearing the near lip by centimeters. That maneuver had to have hurt, and Kit couldn't figure out why she was going to such lengths to track him down. Fear of getting in trouble with her parents? Shame at failing to make the offering? Or was she just intent on getting back at him? Before she could stubbornly rise to her feet, before she could open her mouth to speak again, Kit fled once more.

Sandover Lane itself was at once his last barrier and, potentially, his final shield. After that was the start of the government district, and he definitely didn't want to test his luck dodging the security in there. If she managed to follow him that far, Kit might even consider letting her have the money back. Of course, it wasn't going to be easy—for either of them. A busy highway connecting the Upper West End to the Esshad Government Complex, it ran the length of Nemare as one of four principle north to south lines of transit. Traffic, consisting of mostly horse, ek, or draft-lizard drawn carriages, along with a scattering of both wheeled and hovering illyrium-powered vehicles, was always paradoxically congested yet flowing nonstop. Dust filled the air, swirling about choking animals and pilots alike, while the lifeblood of the nation streamed without ceasing in both directions.

It was suicide to cross—*if* you didn't know the safe spots. To the untrained eye, it appeared as though the hurrying mass was an elongated blob that miraculously managed to slide past itself on opposing vectors. However, there was a method to the madness. If you had a slow beast or craft, you stayed in one of two diametric center lanes. Faster vehicles always traveled on the outside. That way, if they crashed, they did the least damage possible to their surroundings and the system itself. In the best-case scenario, you had a flying vehicle, and those so blessed bypassed the situation entirely, soaring high above the congestion.

Though knowing about the different lanes wasn't helpful knowledge in and of itself, knowing about the raised separators between them was. While each intersection was devoid of such constructs by necessity, metal rails, half a meter across by half a meter high, ran the length of the unobstructed street segments. Therefore, crossing was possible if you were fast enough and timed your movements correctly. Even so, one wrong move spelled death. It was the ultimate test of a thief's agility. Master Sandover Lane and you could become an uncatchable legend.

Still, truth be told, Kit had never tried it before. It simply wasn't a pragmatic risk. But that didn't matter; it was now or never. He reached the street and turned left along the canal edge, going down a ways before reaching a point he deemed viable for crossing. A fast military skimmer zoomed past, then an unusually speedy drake-drawn hoversled, before he was greeted with his opportunity. Traffic had been stopped back at the bridge intersection, offering a lull for him to reach the first waypoint. Kit dashed across the black-streaked road. It was an easy segment, and he reached the copper-colored outcropping several seconds ahead of the next incoming projectile.

Once there, he took a second to get his bearings. About him, the menagerie of trade and travel flowed unceasing, and while all moved at different speeds and because of varied methods of operation, none paid him any mind. Kit was an insignificant speck, as unnoticed up here among his betters as below among his kind. *Of course,* he considered, *the same could be said of all of them, rushing past each other like a glutted canal that never ends.*

Unfortunately, a certain individual seemed intent on giving him all the attention he had ever desired and then some. Across the first lane of traffic from Kit was the aristo girl, hands on skinned knees and with bloody scrapes across her forearms, likely from the tumble she took in landing her bridge jump. Her persistence was beginning to strike a nerve; why wouldn't she just give up already?

"Haven't you had enough? Stop following me!" Kit yelled at the top of his lungs, frustration and anger imbuing each word. The girl didn't hear any of it, the sound drowned out by the cacophony of the traffic teeming about them.

Instead, she glanced left, then right, then left again, apparently gauging the timing before attempting to join him on the next rung. "No! Don't try it! It's too dangerous!" Once again, his voice was swallowed up; all Kit got for his efforts was a mouthful of dust and fumes.

He could see the inevitable conclusion before she could, given his vantage. A bulky, flat-nosed transport being drug by a pair of ek crossed the intersection a second before the signalman, situated on a central platform, gave the go ahead. It was fortunate he didn't clip any of the cross traffic, but was now mere seconds from crushing the aristo girl, who had just concluded the way was clear and begun crossing. She didn't know what was coming. Kit did. She was going to die. It was all because of his actions. He had led her here. It was unintentional, but he had done it all the same.

Even so, he could still save her.

Do I care? Isn't the money the most important thing? What's her life, compared to the lives of my family, the kids in Sewertown? It's a front. She doesn't care about us. She's just obsessed with the "notion" of caring. Saving her won't change anything. She's just another noble; they're the same to us, alive or dead. This money will change our lives though. That's right. Just look away; don't watch. Me and mine, first and foremost. She doesn't matter to me at all.

So . . . why am I moving? Kit's body launched forward in total defiance of all logic, rushing across the scored and pitted pavement in an act of foolhardy desperation. He caught the stunned girl on his second stride, wrapped her in his arms, and heaved forward with all his strength. The gust from the passing vehicle pummeled them both, whipping her slightly longer hair and their unkempt clothes about.

Then momentum carried them past the canal lip, out over the still water, and down into its harsh, cold embrace.

Chapter 14

Dusk Descends

Hetrachia 3, 697 ABH
Etrus City, Kingdom of Darmatia

"What's the diagnosis?"

"Two cracked ribs, massive internal bleeding, deep contusions across the entire torso on both back and front, several spinal vertebrae fractured in the neck region—and that's aside from the obvious bullet wound to the shoulder. His only saving graces were that the lead didn't strike bone, passing clean through instead, and that his immediate care kept him from entering critical condition. I presume that was your work, young lady?"

"Y . . . yes," Velle responded shyly to the compliment, her skin turning a deeper shade of crimson as she flushed with pride. After four years, Matteo had learned to read the subtle distinctions in Sylph body coloring that occurred with their shifting emotions and could, therefore, tell her mood most of the time. He nodded silently in agreement. She definitely deserved the praise; only a master-class healer could've kept a patient in as bad a state as Vallen breathing through what they'd experienced.

Both of them, along with Matteo's mother, were gathered around the bed in the upstairs guest room where a physician from the local chapter of the Way of the Will was attending to their feverish comrade. The elderly Terran woman, clad in several layers of flowing white vestments and matching cornette, had responded to their early morning summons with no questions asked. Their order was known for its charity and altruism; no matter who or what was injured, they would respond to the call as befitting the Will of the benevolent deity of Terrans, Sariel. Now, having completed her physical examination of Vallen, she dispelled her seven-pointed star glyphs, which had been providing a holographic readout of internal damage, and turned to face the onlookers.

"Thank you so much, Mother Junica . . . especially so for coming on such short notice." Matteo's mother, Anathea, was seated at the far end of the bed on a rocking chair that had been pulled from the corner nearest the room's solitary window. She, like all of them but the Mother, was exhausted from a sleepless night, and dark rings were beginning to form under her soft, brown eyes. Matteo had forced her to remain sitting, along with Junica, while he and Velle stood. She never had the strongest constitution, so now that she was getting older, and with the crazy situation they were in, he was going to ensure that she was as comfortable as possible.

"He's not out of the woods yet. The girl's efforts have subdued most of the inner trauma, but the high fever could still fry his brain or put him in a permanent coma. What in Oblivion was he fighting?" While the Mother spoke, her voice creaking with the strain of advanced age, one wizened hand reached into the folds of her tunic and removed a notepad upon which she began magically dictating with one glowing finger.

When no one responded, one of Junica's piercing eyes, almost independent of the other, fell accusingly on Matteo. The other remained fixated on her writing.

"W . . . well, you see, the thing was, we were—"

"Spit it out, boy. I haven't got all day."

He blurted everything all at once, words stumbling over each other. Matteo sincerely hoped Sylette wouldn't kill him later for revealing what happened to someone outside their group and his family. "We were on this derelict freighter—it was really a mess—captained by this guy named Cappie—not sure why he puts up with that name—and with the rest of the Darmatian fleet were going to intercept the empire at Aldona Fortress when this big, huge, gigantic death laser came out of nowhere and obliterated most of our ships like it was nothing, and even our vessel got nicked and started crashing, which was when we ran for the transports like our lives depended on it, and, let me tell you, they did, but we ran into a Sarconian rittermarschal—Valescar something or other—and his troops, who had boarded us because Sylette Farkos was actually Sylette Artorios, and she's really their princess who got exiled a long time ago—because of who knows what—and Vallen ran in without thinking to fight the guy and got destroyed, then we all worked together really hard to save him and escape . . . and Leon . . . and Leon and—"

The entire story came out as a single sentence that rapidly crescendoed toward the end, when Junica finished her memo and halted him with a raised palm. "Enough, enough, take a breath. I've got the idea. Sounds like this one's a bit more hard-headed than is healthy. Being strong willed is all well and good— why, it's what our order is named for—but passion must be tempered with good sense. Something you young people seem to lack these days. Also, your secrets are safe with me. Even if I wanted to tell, nobody thinks old Junica knows anything but healing anymore." She gingerly lifted herself off the padded ottoman she'd been sitting on, refusing Velle's attempts to assist her with a dismissive motion. "Now, take this recipe, get the ingredients on it, and mix it as the directions say. If you give it to the injured child here, it should drive down his fever and allow him to wake up."

"Here, you take it. I bet that scatterbrained boy would lose the note if I gave it to him." Junica passed the paper to Velle, who accepted it with profuse thanks, before shambling toward the door. Matteo reddened at the casual insult, then shrugged it off.

"Let me show you the way out, Mother," he recovered graciously, hoping to redeem his earlier episode of verbal diarrhea in her eyes.

Of course, his offer of help was brutally rejected. "Think I don't know my way around? Why, I helped deliver you right here in this house twenty-two years ago—right little whiny baby you were too, crying at everything. Knew how to get about then, and I know how to get about now, thank you very much. Now shoo! Get going on that remedy. You have more important things to do than look after an old hag." With that, Junica shut the room's door, of *their* house, in his face. The slow patter of her footsteps descending the steps gradually receded as she continued on her way.

His mother was standing when he turned around, having risen to bow to the Mother as she left, a standard courtesy toward those in direct ministry to the Veneer and Creator. "Don't take it personally, Matteo. That one's been a firecracker for as long as I've known her. Probably why she's lived so long; Sariel might be afraid to come and take her to the Afterplane. Even so, she means well."

"I'd love to learn from her," Velle commented, not looking up from the prescription, awestruck wonder on her face. "Never would I have thought combining something common like menja juice with ulisha thistles and crag lizard tail could make a fever reducer. And did you see her diagnostic spell? Even Sylph healers aren't that fast or detailed—"

"Can you make it if we get the components?" Matteo interrupted her increasingly worshipful speech.

"Yes, but I don't know where to find most of these items around here."

Anathea clapped her hands, a bright, happy smile on her face. "You'll find everything you need at the local market. Matteo can take you and show you where to get the best deals; after all, he grew up here, and everyone absolutely adores his cute antic—"

"Mom!" His face flushed with embarrassment again, and his eyes darted back and forth between her and Velle as he tried to cut her off.

"But it's true!" She sighed wistfully, then continued. "Anyway, there are a few other things I need you to pick up, and I'm sure you and the others could use a little bit of a break after what you've been through. Do some shopping; enjoy yourselves! You only get to be young once!"

As his mother's fervor rose, she began coughing into her hand, prompting both Matteo and Velle to move to check on her before she waved them off. "Just a slight tickle in my throat. Pulling an all-nighter at my age can have that effect on a body. Anyway, Velle, why don't you see who else wants to go while I tell Matteo what I want you to pick up. Okay?"

"Absolutely, Mrs. Alhan. But please promise me you'll let me take a look at *your* condition when we get back. You're still too young to be sick like this." Anathea nodded in the affirmative and beamed pleasantly at the Sylph as she left the room, reclosing the door behind her. When she was gone, she moved close to Matteo, her eyes narrowing and voice dropping to a conspiratory whisper. He gulped, realizing in advance what was coming. They'd been over this ground many times, yet he'd never made any significant progress toward the end goal, despite his mother's urgings.

"First, you know your father and I love you very much, and we'd never force you to do something you don't want to do. That being said, despite what Velle alluded about my age, we're not getting any younger. On top of that, you are our only child, Matteo. Which means . . . " She paused, drawing out with a pregnant silence the bomb that he knew was coming but couldn't escape from. " . . . you're our only chance to have grandchildren and continue the family line. Now, I know the situation is a bit complicated, but you've brought a few nice, pretty girls home with you, especially that Velle. I know some people throw a fit about marrying outside their race, but she's an intelligent woman with a mother's heart who's beautiful on top of everything else. You don't have to take my advice, but the least you can do is get out there, have some fun, and see if it works. What's the worst that could happen?"

Well, Vallen might murder me when he wakes up, but it's probably best not to tell her that.

She slapped Matteo gently on the back, pushing him toward the door. "Anyway, go live a little. I've seen the way you look at her. Don't think your mother hasn't noticed! So just give it a try and see how far life takes you. Oh, and buy some things for dinner, enough for everyone. I don't want Velle to realize I was making up the part about needing more stuff."

All Matteo could manage to say in response was, "Yes, Mom," as he started toward the doorway. The rest of his brain was puzzling over what she had said . . . *and* whether or not she was right about his feelings.

"Good! Off you go then, and do your best!"

———⊱⊰———

Matteo sincerely wished his mother had never said those things to him.

The philosopher Unai Ewlix once wrote that it's entirely possible not to notice the wyrmdrake in the room if one is completely ignorant of its existence. This analogy was directed at the Hues, who didn't realize until years later that their mining efforts in the Tesset Lode were unintentionally poisoning a major water reservoir. Had they linked the sicknesses and deaths of the surrounding villagers to their efforts—noticed the wyrmdrake in the room—perhaps the region would still be habitable.

Matteo could empathize with Unai's stance. Even in everyday life, people tended to only pay attention to what was important to them, what they were actually aware of. It was one thing to recognize that a certain red-skinned, black-haired, athletic, intelligent, cheerful, caring . . . curvaceous . . . and generally all-around-perfect girl was gorgeous, and quite another to think you had any hope in Oblivion of gaining the slightest part of her regard or attraction. In fact, all that Matteo's newfound cognizance of his potential desires had accomplished was to make him retreat further into his introvert shell.

"Matteo, are you listening? Matteo? Matteo!"

He shook his head and roused to find Velle gesturing at several racks of meat on display in front of a butcher's stand. At first Matteo's mind failed to process what exactly he was doing, but the pieces gradually fell into place.

Apparently his sudden jolt back to the land of the living was accompanied by a humorous expression on his face, for Velle began giggling. "Where were you, Matteo? I've never seen someone space out in the middle of a market like that."

You probably don't want to know what I was thinking. Correction, I *don't want you to know what I was thinking either.* Matteo faked a short, nervous chuckle to play along with her mirth.

"Anyway, would your mother prefer hoerboar or arnslamb meat? I'd personally prefer the feuersteer steaks, but they're a little pricey."

If nothing else, this minor dilemma would give Matteo something to think about besides her. *But wait. If I'm making a decision on Velle's behalf, doesn't that mean I'm still thinking about and interacting with her?* It was quite the slippery slope, one he didn't care to contemplate at the moment. Instead, he focused as much of his attention as possible on the task at hand: the selection of meat for dinner. Wait. This was a store he recognized: large red-and-white striped awning out front, two-storied tan building with ivy climbing up the right side, foodstuffs neatly arranged by species in hanging bins, and a large sign just under the second floor windows that read—

"Welcome to the Etrus Eats and Meats Emporium, my fine young friends!" boomed a loud voice from behind the street-side displays. After a few seconds of struggle, a monstrously fat Terran wearing a dirtied and bloodstained apron, grey stubble on his chin and a similarly colored widow's peak upon his head, squeezed through a narrow opening between shelves to stand before them. "What can I do for you this . . . Hold on! Is that you, Matteo?"

The boisterously jolly man was one he knew well, for Matteo's family had been regulars at his establishment for as long as he could remember. His interruption was a welcome reprieve to the youth's inner turmoil. "Mister Stenberg, good to see you're still doing well. How're the kids?"

"Oh, same ol' same ol'. None of them are as smart as you, but they've grown quite a bit, and when they aren't causin' trouble about town, they're actually useful to have around. Oldest fancies himself a fighter and wants to leave to make his name when he comes of age, but given recent events, I expect soldierin' ain't the career it used to be." Stenberg's face darkened momentarily, but thereafter he regained his cheerful charisma.

"Anyway, I thought I told you to call me Sal! We're ol' friends, your parents and I, so you don't need to be so formal." At that moment, Sal finally took notice of Velle, partially obscured by a hanging flank of flesh. His jaw practically dislocated in surprise, and he pushed aside the hoerboar cut to get a better view. "Who's this beauty? Your parents didn't say anything about you havin' such a looker for a girlfriend! Or are you already married?"

Velle blushed, caught off guard by the sudden scrutiny, while Matteo attempted to stammer out a protest. Instead, his words stuck in his throat, as the part of him wanting to see how this played out overruled the logical, sensible part of his brain. Oblivious, Sal continued his endearing, gushing spiel. "I bet your parents are right proud of you, yes they are. And look at you! I can see why she likes you! The smart little bookworm sure has grown up. Look at that muscle!"

As Matteo and Velle exchanged bemused glances, he wondered why she didn't say anything either. *Is she alright with this? Or does she just not want to embarrass me in my hometown? That kindness would be very like her.* His mind's attempts to make sense of their current circumstances were cut short by Sal's continued escalation of an already awkward situation. He turned around, calling up in a loud voice at one of the second story windows. "Ma, come quick! Matteo's back in town, and he brought a girl home with him!"

Wooden shutters parted above a well-tended basket of deep purple neverfade flowers, and a stocky, middle-aged woman who didn't seem to care about the unkempt state of her locks leaned out. "Oh, you're right! Welcome home, Matteo, and congratulations!" Her voice became shrewish and stern as she fixed her attention on Sal. "Now, honey, stop giving them trouble and help them get whatever they need. The poor couple didn't come here to be harangued; they came to buy meat. And be sure to give them a proper discount in celebration!" With that, the shutters banged shut again, and she was gone.

"Yes, dear." Sal intoned quietly, running a hand through his thinning hair before turning back to the flabbergasted pair. "So, what can I get you today, Mrs. Alhan?" He directed the question at Velle, clearly more interested in her than Matteo and entirely unaware of the mistake he was making.

"Oh, we aren't actually ma—" Velle began, but Matteo decided to cut her off before she could correct the butcher.

"We'll take twelve hecares of feuersteer steaks, your best cuts, enough for a small party. And I believe your wife mentioned something about a discount?"

If the meat dealer was disappointed at the prospect of selling such high-quality goods at a lower rate, it didn't show on his face. Instead, Sal was as jovial as ever when he smiled at them and carefully examined his wares to fill their order. "Absolutely, you got it. Consider half of them a gift from me for your pretty Sylph wife. It's not every day you get to commemorate something like this!"

When he was out of hearing range, Velle leaned in to whisper to Matteo, the look on her face half confusion, half frustration. "Why did you stop me from clearing up his misunderstanding? It isn't right to let him give us a bargain under false pretenses."

Why *did* he stop her? It wasn't like Matteo to be dishonest, to break the rules, or even to simply be so quick on his feet in a social context. Yet here he was, willingly letting a long-time friend of his family believe an extremely flimsy lie in order for this facade to last a little longer. *By the Veneer, I'm smitten, aren't I?*

"You wanted feuersteer steaks, but we didn't have the money left over after giving Lilith part of it to get the medical ingredients and other supplies. I know it wasn't right, but I didn't want you to be disappointed. Besides, the whole group will appreciate it, and I'll be sure to smooth things over with Sal another time." Logic and reason, two concepts he knew well—though Matteo never thought he'd be using them to justify actions like this.

Velle wavered, clearly weighing his words against what they both knew was the right thing to do. She bit her lip, a habit Matteo had seen before. For some reason, her consternation made her look even cuter, and his already beating heart increased its speed. "Fine. We've been through a lot, and maybe this tiny bit of good fortune is just what we need. And I'm sure Vallen will appreciate a quality meal like this when he wakes up."

There's the rub. No matter what he did, no matter how hard he tried, Velle only had eyes for Vallen. Granted, he hadn't been aware of his feelings, beyond the yearnings anyone possesses for something unattainable. But now that he was conscious of them, the odds were as much against him as they were before.

It was with these thoughts in mind—and with a heavy heart—that Matteo mechanically accepted the delicately wrapped packages of meat from Sal, paid their bill, and began the return journey up through the city to his home. Velle seemed to welcome his silence, her lowered gaze suggesting she was lost in ruminations of her own. Around them, the stretching shadows of early evening elongated downwards from the top of the town, shading the streets with faux nightfall.

As they walked, he turned his attention outward to avoid completely drowning in his melancholy. A group of children ran past, chasing a blue ball bouncing along the drainage sluice on the side of the road. Fortunately, traffic at this time was non-existent; otherwise, they'd have been in danger of being hit. Elsewhere, a pair of traders, both elderly, one a Sylph and the other a Hue, hawked their goods side by side on a street corner. Neither of them seemed capable of successfully drumming up business at this late hour, but instead of closing up shop, they soon got into a heated argument blaming the other for their poor performance. Scenes like this were to be expected, though; saying that their races disliked each other was an understatement.

Exiting the market district, they saw several newly boarded-up buildings. The first was a blacksmith, the second a general store, and the third was a well-apportioned estate set grandly at the fore of the circular boulevard separating the city's middle and upper tiers.

It took Velle's soft voice to make Matteo realize what should have been obvious. "The war's already made it here too, hasn't it?"

He didn't know much about the empire, but from the little he did know, it was an accurate statement. The blacksmith had fled because he would soon no longer be able to do business; the Sarconians didn't allow anyone but the military to possess weapons of any nature, firearms or otherwise. As for the general store, its owner had likely helped the kingdom army evacuate, giving them whatever support they needed. Rather than stay and face the options of punishment or submission, he had hopefully fled with the rest of the base personnel.

The last was the easiest to discern; this manse belonged to the mayor of Etrus, Thadius Brecken. He was a popular leader and had been reelected repeatedly since Matteo was a small child. His citizens loved him, and he cared for them and the country they lived in. But he also had a family, a family that might suffer if he stayed in the city due to his strong morals that would never see him bow to a foreign invader. It was the same decision Matteo would have made: protect those dearest first and worry about the rest later.

It was a depressing sight, and the farther they went, the more abandoned houses and businesses they saw. Soldiers, craftsmen, statesmen . . . anyone who, because of profession or patriotism, would languish under the new regime was long gone. But these were those with the money or will to escape. Equally prevalent, behind the playing children who didn't understand what was happening, or the merchants putting their heads in the sand and pretending that life would continue as normal, were the dejected.

Drinking establishments, their lights just coming on to stave off the coming dark, were already filled to bursting, a strange sight in this commercial paradise of hard work. Others showed their despair in a slow step, a slump. Hollow thoughts reflected on hollow eyes. With the closure of the military base, many were out of work and wandered the streets and side alleys, as though wondering what to do next. Some chatted earnestly in small groups, slight grins on their faces, contemplating the opportunities their new government would provide. Velle and Matteo caught bits of these conversations as they walked.

"I hear the empire takes levies from all its provinces. The way things are looking, it might be best to join up as soon as possible."

"Yeah, with the kingdom toppled, I don't see Rabban lasting long."

"And then it will be smooth sailing for us as guards at some tropical paradise when they rule the continent."

"They'll also need contractors, you know. Might be safer."

"You have a point. Even a machine as big as theirs needs a few civilians to grease the gears."

"Guess we'll see what's the best option when they get here . . . "

Their mutterings faded into the background noise of the city as they turned a corner. Velle looked disgusted by what they'd overheard, but Matteo could sympathize. Terrans were weaker than the other races, both in mind and body.

But they were survivors. Sometimes it was better to swallow your pride and continue to exist than stand up and be hammered down. In fact, it was probably the best thing to do in this hopeless situation. *We can still . . .*

"I got all the things on the list. What now?" Lilith materialized beside them from out of nowhere. Having changed into plain clothes like the rest of the team to avoid drawing unwanted attention, she blended into the rural background like she'd lived here all her life. Matteo jumped slightly, felt his cheeks go red from embarrassment—yet again—then slowly calmed his nerves before responding.

"We take everything back home and hope that the medicine works. Let's go." Disappointment that his time alone with Velle, as depressing as it had become, was about to end must have shown on his face, for Lilith's eyes widened in silent understanding. She glanced back and forth between the two of them, lips spreading in a mischievous grin.

"Why don't I run these things back and get everything ready for you? You guys spending a few more minutes out and about won't hurt."

Before Matteo could respond, Lilith was gone, fading back into the twilight. There was something uncanny about the girl. The way she moved, her intuition, and her martial combat skills were all a cut above anyone else he knew at the academy. However, her perception in this particular case might be because of his mother.

Out of the entire group, she was the only one who wanted to come along. Unter and Renar were recruited by Matteo's father early that morning and whisked off to his shipping yard to help with catching up on orders delayed by the evacuation. Sylette was holed up in their study, poring over maps and documents lent to her by his family, sleeplessly intent on some vague vengeance she still refused to talk about. Which left Lilith, who had happily agreed to go before disappearing upstairs for several minutes. Upon her return, she strangely insisted that she go off and get the ingredients for the fever reducer herself while they took care of fetching dinner.

Yes, his mother had definitely gotten to her. But that wasn't necessarily a bad thing. A stroke of brilliance had just occurred to him, a way to turn the evening around and get them both out of the doldrums.

"Velle, before we go back, there's one more place I'd like to go. Is that alright?"

She nodded, but her assent was automatic, her mind clearly elsewhere after what they'd seen and heard. Matteo briefly thought about grabbing her hand to guide her. She probably wouldn't stop him, but that would be taking advantage of the situation. *I will* cheer her up, but this isn't about deepening our relationship. This is about being a friend.

He motioned for Velle to follow, which she did at about half a pace behind. Matteo wished she'd walk beside him, but it was enough that she was humoring his whim. A few minutes saw them cresting the top of the town's central hill just as the last of the light was beaming from the east.

There sat a small, white church, simple in design and surrounded by a black fence enclosing a vibrant, meticulously arranged garden. Its plot was unmarred by any urban congestion and was in sole possession of Etrus's summit, an indication of how important faith had always been to the people of this city. Stained glass windows painted in myriad hues reflected a cascade of rainbow colors across the walls and vegetation as the dying light refracted within their prisms. In the foreground, where a small Terran man in clergy robes stood beside an open gate, two large statues of Sariel, made of purest, untainted marble, held aloft swords wreathed in stilled flame toward the heavens.

Matteo heard Velle's intake of breath as she experienced the wondrous scene. "It's . . . beautiful."

"It is, but this isn't what I wanted you to see." He led the way to the gate, where the old man opened his arms in genuine delight.

"Matteo! Mother Junica told me you'd returned. Here for your usual spot?"

He hugged him gently. "Yes, Abbot Kinloss. Do you mind if we go through the garden?"

"Not at all, my son. You're always welcome here."

They passed through the gate into the lee of the main building and were temporarily cast in shadow as they followed the hedge guiding them around to the rear. As they rounded the corner, back into the piercing rays of the day's final gasp, they beheld the most glorious picture Matteo had ever seen.

At ground level, the short, green grass waved in the wind along with a semicircular patch of stunning flowers of many varieties: purple neverfades, pink rosarias, saffron bloodlilies, aqua aphroniles, and others too numerous to name. About them were more statues of Sariel, as well as the Veneer of the other races, and hewn visages of benevolent spirits flocked around their feet. A three-tiered fountain at the center spat water skyward as petals from a nearby blochesum tree floated tenderly on the breeze to land upon the gurgling flows.

But it was the ephemeral aesthetic of the scene that left a lasting impression. In the distance, the iridescence of the flaming sun was just drifting behind the Lyndwur Forest, and its last beams painted the entire valley in shifting arcs of light and shadow. Everything below was at once brilliantly outlined and cast in darkness in a shifting maelstrom of vivid tinctures. This effect was only further enhanced by the massive glass window behind them, which redirected the illumination downwards, bathing them in shifting shades of crimson.

It was a thrilling sight to behold, one that gathered all the wonder in the world and put it on display for the briefest of instants. The conditions and timing had to be perfect, or you would miss this epic work of art. Matteo had discovered it by chance, coming up here once as a child to be alone with his thoughts, away from the bullies, hardships, and responsibilities of life. Ever since, it became a daily habit, a way of letting go of troubles and instead filling himself up with awesome beauty.

He was grateful that this was one such time that they were able to bear witness to the full radiance of the sunset from this spot. Only a handful of times in his life had the scene been so sublime. And, with a final slicing glare of white, the sun slipped behind the forest and mountains; the perfect, untainted moment was over.

Velle collapsed on the soft ground beside him, clearly at a loss for words. Matteo sat down beside her, content to give her the time she needed to take it all in. Finally, she spoke. "That was, I mean, I've never seen . . . just, wow!"

"It's hard to explain, isn't it?"

She paused, seeming to puzzle over her response, her face glowing with nearly as much luminance as what they'd just beheld. He gulped and looked away, turning back cautiously when she continued. "It was as though it were saying, 'Look at this amazing sight. No matter how much is wrong with the world, this marvel shall remain.'"

"That's . . . that's exactly how I've always thought of it," Matteo stammered, shocked by their similar interpretations. "It really puts everything into context. I find it calming to know that *this* will always exist, regardless of what happens. In the darkest of times, beauty shines through. And it helps me to keep going, in spite of my insignificance and my inability to change things."

Velle's eyes narrowed. "That's not quite true, Matteo. You *are* able to change things. We wouldn't be here without you, you know? You sensed that death ray, allowing us to get out of the way in time. And afterwards, nobody else knew how to fly that ship. If nothing else, *you* changed *our* lives. You *matter*, Matteo, despite what anyone thinks. Thank you."

Matteo started to blush, to turn away, to protest, but forced those feelings down and let contentment bubble to the surface instead. Maybe she was right, and maybe that was all he needed: *to be needed*. It still didn't change that the world—*their* world—was a mess, and that the best option might be not to fight the coming storm. However, this knowledge, at this moment, was enough for him. Matteo had cheered up Velle and cemented their friendship. There was comfort in that, in the same way he had previously found comfort in her untouchability.

But he was past that, and for now, this was fine.

"Besides, is that really a healthy way to—oh, oh no . . . " Velle raised a trembling arm, pointing beyond the Lyndwur Forest where the muted gleam of the fallen sun outlined three growing shapes flying through the shadows toward them. All bore a now-familiar crest, just barely visible at this distance.

The empire had come to Etrus.

Thoughts of joy and happiness were forgotten as Velle and Matteo raced back through the pitch-black city streets, stumbling, falling, and helping each other back up again in their single-minded mission to get back and warn the others.

When they burst through the front door, nigh breathless, everyone was gathered in the main room, either sitting or standing about a small projectostand set in the wall above the dining table. They turned to look at the new arrivals, and, for the moment, Matteo failed to hear the words from the device as he choked out his warning.

"They're here! Imperial airships are just outside the city!"

After a moment, he realized that no one was particularly surprised by his announcement. Sylette nodded to the projectostand, and Matteo calmed himself enough to listen to the speaker. The voice of Tannen Holler, their graduation announcer from a lifetime ago, came across the airwaves.

"I repeat, Steward Metellus has signed an unconditional surrender with the Sarconian Empire following the battle at Aldona Fortress. As of this moment, the Kingdom of Darmatia has been dissolved and will be reformed into the Imperial Province of Darmatia. Sarconian forces will be distributed to all corners of the territory to ensure a smooth transition. Imperial authorities have assured us that if we present no resistance, the daily lives of our people will continue as normal. As a result, the steward wishes for all citizens to cooperate with the new government. This is Tannen Holler from Kingdom Broadcasting, and I will continue to . . . "

The speaker droned on, but Matteo had stopped listening and fallen to his knees. It was the inevitable result, the one they knew was coming, but knowing something was going to occur and experiencing it were two different things. And, of course, nothing prepared a person for when disaster struck close to home—a place that was supposed to be unequivocally secure and beyond harm.

This was their reality now; nowhere was safe, and nothing would be the same.

Chapter 15

The End of an Era

Hetrachia 8, 697 ABH,
Nemare, Capital of the Sarconian Province of Darmatia

———◆———

I t was yet another festive day in the city of Nemare.

However, it was not one of particular joy for the native inhabitants of the settlement. Rather, for them it was a day of reflective melancholy, bitter resignment, and confused indignation. Melancholy at the closure of over seven hundred years of independent rule and cultural heritage, resignment in the face of the overwhelming power that had brought about their overthrow, and confusion at how swiftly and perplexingly their downfall was wrought. On top of all that, their remaining indignation at the situation hardly mattered.

At least that was how Emperor Sychon Artorios saw things from atop the expansive balcony of the former Darmatian Royal Palace. In the days since the formal signing of the surrender, it and many other important buildings had been rechristened to reflect the territory's new masters: the Consul's Estate, the Imperial Airfield, the Magtech Academy of Science and Practical Military Applications, and, his personal favorite, the Grand Gate of Artorios. Formerly the King Darmatus Causeway, the massive stone gatehouse that was the primary entrance to the anachronistic walls of Nemare was currently under renovation to better honor the emperor's name.

Now, as the architectural, economic, and military changes necessary to bring the city fully to heel were underway, was the time to demonstrate the might of the empire and show the people how foolish any potential rebellion would be. Such was the purpose of the festival before Sychon, one enacted in true Sarconian fashion. An occasion of elation to the conquerors; a nightmarish

289

vision of hopelessness to the conquered.

Below, on the large thoroughfare that bisected the government complex, marched the bulk of the soldiers that made up his invading army. The highway had been flattened in preparation, an annoying project that delayed the parade until those insipid metal lane guards the Darmatians used could be removed. Now, division after division of infantry, mages, engineers, armored vehicles, and panzcraft rolled past, Sarconian flags and their individual unit banners displayed en masse atop raised poles. It was a sea of red and gold, guided by their celestial patron saint, the glowing angel of war emblazoned upon every imperial crest.

As they passed, the foot soldiers in light plate armor raised their rifles or swords in the air with one arm while the other pounded their breast with a fist in salute. Sychon, dressed in ceremonial robes, cape, and a crown whose colors matched their own, stood at the fore of the walled terrace and waved back at them in reply. Exposed as he was, there was no danger. Grand Marschal Konig Zaratus was to his right, and Rittermarschal Auvrea Titania, the new governor of the province, was at his left, acknowledging her troops as they went by. Farther back on the veranda, several squads of elite guards kept watchful eyes on both the interior entrances and a small group of former Darmatian dignitaries who had been "invited" to watch the event. As an additional caution, every rooftop in the district was garrisoned with a squad of riflemen. No one would find egress to disturb the march from above.

Crammed into every available space, but cordoned off from the main road and the Consul's Estate by railings and guards, were the citizens of Nemare. Most of the city had turned out to watch, either out of a morbid sense of curiosity or simply to hear Sychon's speech at the close of festivities. Of course, any district that failed to turn out a sizeable attendance willingly found themselves forcefully brought forward by zealous Ritterbruder squads. He needed the entire city to see his power and listen to his words that they might learn just what was expected of a Sarconian province.

Right now, though, most of them could, at worst, still be considered the enemy. At best, they were disgruntled. While the majority gazed at the ground with dejection, others looked at him and his soldiers with fire simmering in their eyes. Some, even many, were not ready to let go of the Kingdom of Darmatia. If the pot was allowed to boil, there would be resistance to their rule, even open rebellion. The embers of this newly slain nation would need to be snuffed out quickly—but not quite yet. That was primarily a job for Titania, though Sychon would give her a little aid before fully redirecting his attention.

However, that little diversion isn't scheduled until the end of the parade. In the meantime, he had several petitioners to speak to. The first, a powerful ancient sorcerer inhabiting the body of a young man, moved to stand beside Sychon unbidden. Sarcon's uncanny sixth sense, along with his staunch refusal to respect his authority or adhere to decorum, continued to irk the emperor. As always, Sychon calmed his ire by reminding himself that the man was an absolute necessity if he was to accomplish his goal of ruling the continent.

Trailing behind Sarcon, looking completely uncomfortable both in the presence of so many notables and in his officer's dress uniform, was his attendant, Hans Ulrich. Sychon didn't quite know what to make of the man, a commoner advanced well beyond his station by pure happenstance. On top of that was the question of his loyalty; could he be made to serve as a spy on the mage, or was he faithful to his current master despite his military obligations? That was yet another game for him to puzzle out in the coming weeks, as soon as Sarcon became disposable.

The parade slowed as the Twelth Panzcraft division passed in front of the raised gallery. They were clunky, well-armored machines propelled on tracks by powerful engines. Capable of navigating almost any terrain and possessing two forward gun turrets, the large vehicles would slough off anything short of a direct artillery or airship strike and move forward with the slow grace of an entrenched weapons bunker. Turrets turned toward the dais, guns raised in salute as the ugly, angular behemoths sloughed on, steam pouring into the air from their aft decks.

"What do you think of our modern technology?" Sychon asked of Sarcon, raising his arms to encompass both the panzcraft below and the cruisers and hoverjets above. Elements of the First Fleet, directly under command of Grand Marschal Zaratus, they were an even greater example of the empire's strength than even the march before them. Under their watchful gaze, nothing could occur in Nemare without swift retribution from the skies.

After witnessing his former, dessicated body, it was disorienting to see Sarcon with fair, blond hair and boyish features. However, the impassive face he usually wore remained the same. "Having seen it in action, I must admit that their efficiency is rather impressive. You've made killing your fellow man so much faster and easier than it was in my day. Still, these machines lack a certain grace . . ." The mage paused, creating a silence into which Sychon was about to retort. Then Sarcon turned to look directly at him. "In your opinion, what is the most important quality for a weapon to have?"

While the voice was different, it retained the same air of all-knowing condescension it had always possessed. Internally, Sarcon fumed. *Fine, test me, will you?* "Overwhelming strength, the ability to destroy something completely and utterly beyond any hope of survival or reconstruction." He gave what he knew was the obvious, but correct, answer. *What need had you of anything else if your opponent was vanquished?*

Infuriatingly, the sorcerer, albeit in the body of a handsome youth, shook his head and sighed. "That was the response I expected, but not the right one. No, the proper attribute is adaptability. A good tool is useful in a single scenario; the best tool is useful in *every* scenario. Your toys"—one of his hands gestured at the ongoing parade—"are just like your people: fragile constructs that can do nothing without orders. For their individual tasks, they are beyond amazing at what they can accomplish, but place them in an unorthodox situation and they will crumble like the tenuous materials from which they have been made."

"And pray tell, *how* are they fragile? What would *you* substitute in their place?" Sychon growled, the lid on his anger in danger of bursting in the face of Sarcon's casual dismissal of the greatest accomplishments of his dynasty and nation.

"Take your panzcraft, for example. They're perfect for an open field, where they can move quickly and see all threats from far enough off to engage them. However, put them in a forest—where they cannot maneuver freely or stay in formation, where visibility is poor—and a single skilled mage could tear them apart. And your airships? They are incredible machines that project your power over great distances with their capacity for sustained flight. Yet even they are susceptible in their exposed weak points, or to destruction from within.

"There is only one skill that is perfect in its adaptability: magic. It is all around us, filling us, enabling us. It does not fail; it does not break; it does not cease. Rather, the user will fall to pieces eons before the spiritual energy he makes use of does. And what can't sorceries do? They can destroy, heal, grow, burn, soothe, tear, disintegrate, bind, shield, communicate, inform, build, enhance, manipulate, morph, and so many other things too numerous to list.

"But most importantly, they have the power to both give life"—Sarcon raised and opened his left fist—"and take it away . . . " He clenched his right fist tight, hard enough that a small bead of blood trickled out from within. "A true mage is in total possession of both himself and the world around him. There is nothing he can't overcome and no power he cannot obtain."

"Where, then, is the magical power you promised me?" Sychon countered harshly. "Where is the Elysium? We have control of the country now. Why do we not seize it and end this farce?"

Sarcon clicked his tongue as though the emperor were an unruly child in need of chiding. "Did you listen to nothing I just said? Your military, as it is now, is incapable of fighting the Eliade defenses at Har'muth. As you well know, it is a place devoid of life energy, and, therefore, the only magics you can utilize there are the ones you bring with you—the men'ar that your body naturally possesses. Your ships would crash, your vehicles cease to function, and your equipment sputter and fail. We can use nothing but men, their sorceries, and mundane armament. It is a task currently beyond your soldiers' reach."

It took a moment for Sychon's rage to subside. *I still need this man. I still need this man.* He repeated this internal mantra until he could think clearly. When Sychon responded, his voice was a deathly whisper. "In that case, how should we properly prepare for this undertaking?"

"It would take years to train your mages to the level where they could contend with the incantations of an average Eliade. They'd have to be at least on par with your rittermarschals to stand a chance. That is time we do not have, and so we must turn to . . . less savory practices."

"Such as?" Nothing Sarcon suggested could surprise the emperor at this point . . .

"Ritualistic blood magic. We must sacrifice a large quantity of mortals, drain their ichor, and use its energy to artificially strengthen your armies."

. . . except that. The mage's eyes were hard and cold as he spoke; he obviously cared little for the lives of others. Sychon was much the same, as the ends always justified the means, but this was a step too far. While there was little value in the lives of the talentless, the weak, and the impoverished, killing must still have purpose, and sometimes the consequences for it outweighed the benefits.

As he carefully formulated his response, Grand Marschal Zaratus, who continued to hold his ordained silence with regard to Sarcon, shook his helm in disagreement. His people understood blood magic far better than any other, and the one lesson he had ingrained into his master more than any other was that such sorceries always inflicted a price upon their users.

"From where would you get the resources for your spell?"

Sarcon's unrelenting gaze swept across the sea of peoples before them, streets, squares, buildings, rooftops, and alleyways filled with the press of bodies. His gesture, taking in the masses before them, seemed to ask, "Where else?"

The Darmatians were a proud, stubborn people, but properly handled they would eventually bend the knee. In contrast, what Sarcon suggested would render control over them impossible; the entire territory would be engulfed in never-ending revolt, a ceaseless war of self preservation. "No, you must find some other way for us to achieve victory against the Eliade. Their lives may have little meaning, but we do not have the resources to suppress an uprising *and* continue to fight Rabban."

"If no one is left to rebel, what have you to defend against?" Sarcon's blond hair fell across his right eye as he cocked his head. Sychon was flabbergasted. *Does he understand that he's suggesting genocide? And he does so without balking in the slightest!*

"E-even so, to completely eradicate a people would require a massive diversion of resources—ships and units we can't spare at this time. So, as I said, you will have to find an alternative!" He put as much steel into his voice as possible, desperately trying to reestablish his authority over this wildcard of destruction he had partnered with.

After what seemed like an eternity, Sarcon turned back to the parade. "Very well, but that is the only solution guaranteed to work. If I must improvise, I will need access to your records: all the reports, manuscripts, documents, and information in your empire, past and present, including anything purposely kept secret from the public, such as your own files. Only then can I devise a suitable countermeasure with this handicap you've placed on me."

It was a reasonable request. And a wish Sychon could easily grant. Except that there was knowledge held by his family that the ancient mage mustn't get his hands on, no matter what. "You may have access to anything in the empire you desire, including the top-secret libraries of the Grand Archive . . . except for my personal records. I'm sure even the people of your time understood the importance of privacy, especially when related to the actions of longstanding royal families. It is information that must not be made public and will avail you little in your efforts besides."

"So be it," Sarcon said, acquiescing more quickly than expected.

Sychon was perplexed by his agreement; he had been prepared for a more protracted battle on the subject. *What is he really after?*

"After all," Sarcon continued, "I'm sure our newest guest will be able to assist me in some manner or another."

Sychon faced the entrance to the palace behind them, where a gaudily dressed man of unremarkable height and build was closing the last five meters to join them at the parapet. His stride was graceful and precise, not disturbing the flowering vegetation situated on either side of the carpeted center walkway. The same could not be said of his guards, who clunked behind at a short distance, pushing through the overhanging fronds while struggling to make sense of their supposed prisoner's antics.

But the surrounding scene paled in comparison to the individual himself. He wore a tunic of mauve with a frilled neckpiece and a flowing suit coat of crimson laced with gold that opened at the front. There, two glittering chains flowing from an inner pocket wound about a raised collar and up to a pair of silver glasses with thin, round lenses seated precariously upon the bridge of an angular nose. Below that feature rested the beginnings of a grey beard, barely more than stubble and likely the result of simply forgetting to shave. Silver hair, sharp eyes, faintly perceptible wrinkles, and an unfailing, well-pronounced smirk completed the remarkable ensemble.

Stranger still, above and beyond his appearance, was the seemingly random, discordant humming that emanated from him without regard for present company.

When he reached a meter distant, the guards moved to stop him. Ignoring them, he tucked one white gloved arm to his chest, the other behind his back, and bowed to Sychon and his attendants. "Welcome to Nemare, Your Majesty. I am—"

"Doctor Archimas Redora Descar, preeminent engimage of the former Kingdom of Darmatia and leading weapons and airship designer of this generation." Instead of the emperor, it was Sarcon who had spoken, interrupting the introduction. Sychon found himself taken aback, both at the mage's presumption and his proper deduction.

For his part, Archimas was nonplussed, rising and spreading his arms, bright smile never leaving his face. "Exactly right! However, such boasting is simply too much. I prefer to let my work speak for me and, beyond that, be humble in both word and deed." His eyes narrowed, gleaming as they did. "While I may be me, you are not you. I must admit to having overheard part of your previous conversation. You certainly look like my youngest son, but you are not him, at least as far as mind, logic, and reason are concerned. You're far too much like a true scientist for that to be the case." He tapped a covered finger to his temple.

"For that I must apologize, Archimas. You are correct that I am not Leon; instead, refer to me as Sarcon, despite this form that I hold. For reasons of my own, I was forced to occupy your son's body, but I promise that I will return it to him upon completion of our—"

Sarcon was stopped mid-sentence by the engimage's raised hand. "Ahhh, you presume that this arrangement angers me. On the contrary, I couldn't be more pleased. That foolish boy squandered his talents, sealing his intellect and potential behind the insipid trappings of a soldier. In just the few words I've heard you speak, I can reasonably conclude that you will put his body to far greater use than he ever could. If this was the outcome, perhaps my son wasn't a complete failure in the end."

While Sychon may have felt similarly about the usefulness of his own progeny, it was time to regain control of this conversation. "If you listened to our discussion, then you understand that Sarcon wishes to obliterate your people, to turn them into energy for the fulfillment of our wishes. That doesn't disturb you in the slightest?"

"Your Eminence, what is a people? What binds them together? Is it race, ideology, security, or perhaps something else entirely? In my opinion, the only thing that connects individuals is mutual gain. As long as someone is useful to me, they have value. The second their current worth disappears, I must find a new purpose for them or cast them away. If I do not, they are a drain on my capacity and capital since they no longer produce anything yet still expect something from me.

"I *have* no people, Your Grace. I see everyone as an opportunity; I see everyone as a resource. My only goal is to create, to push the boundaries of science and see how far man can go in challenging the gods themselves! Everything else, including myself, is fuel to bring that vision to fruition. As evidenced by your victory, the Darmatians have far outlived their usefulness. Better to convert them into a new asset than let them wallow in squalor and decay that will surely drag you down as well."

The ancient sorcerer nodded his head in assent. "You could learn something from this man, Sychon. He understands the laws of this world well, both the physical and the philosophical. Don't let your desire for dominion outweigh your reason."

Once more, Sychon put a bridle on his anger. He was in complete control of the situation. As long as he maintained a calm demeanor, the chance to eliminate the arrogant warlock would come. At which point, he'd have the Eylsium, his loyal, fearful subjects, and a continent-spanning empire. "That aside, as you've said, Dr. Archimas, Darmatia has no future except as a territory of the Sarconian Empire. Since you've made it clear that you hold no residual bonds to a broken master, would you work for me instead?"

"It would be my pleasure." Archimas sketched another slight bow before beginning to count conditions off on his fingers. "However, I will need full control over your research and development, unlimited funding, and the transfer of my entire staff to our new laboratory. Everything related to military and arms creation and manufacture must start and end with me, and your current hierarchy must be adjusted accordingly. I will not play second fiddle to your current vacuous imbeciles who can't tell an intake valve from an exhaust port. Are these terms satisfactory?"

"Those are . . . bold demands, Dr. Archimas. If I'm not mistaken, your pride and joy, the *King Darmatus*, along with all your other creations, were destroyed by us at Aldona. What makes you think you are in a position to take complete control of *our* weapons programs?" Sychon smiled at the engimage, pushing his advantage and waiting for his counter.

Archimas grinned shrewdly in return. "You and I both know that without your use of Lost Magic"—he looked pointedly, knowingly, at Sarcon—"my technology would have won. While many would view that as taboo or cheating, I acknowledge it as a flaw in my design, and I look forward to making a countermeasure for it. What more could you desire?"

Having another advantage over Sarcon would be well worth the price Archimas had set. As a result, it took only seconds for the emperor to reach a decision. "Then, with developing a system capable of resisting Great Magic as your first task, the new position of prime engimage, superior to all scientists and manufacturers in the empire, is yours. I will see to it that you, your team, and any equipment you wish to take with you are transported to the capital as soon as possible."

"I will await my departure with restrained anticipation," Archimas remarked enthusiastically, turning to Sarcon afterwards. "However, it is *your* work that has currently piqued my curiosity. Can you explain how you contained the pressure of your light beam? What did you use to inhibit the thermal reaction caused by the superheated plasma? Or was it even plasma? And then you mentioned using *people* as an energy source? Would the magic release occur as a result of them undergoing phase change, or did you plan on using a different method? The questions I have for you are endless, so feel free to answer them in any order."

The curiosity of the grown man was a thing of wonder. Out of nowhere, Archimas produced a pad of paper on which he was scribbling even as he talked, oblivious to the world around him. While Sychon could hardly comprehend the words coming out of his mouth, it appeared that the doctor was equally disinterested in the matters of statecraft, morality, and conquest with which the emperor grappled. As long as he had the means to experiment and invent free of all constraints, Archimas did not seem to care who he served or what his creations were used for. The rumors of his eccentricity did not do him justice; his was a detachment from the world only a sociopath was capable of.

Sarcon was preparing to respond to the engimage's queries when he suddenly pressed a hand to his head and nearly fell before catching himself with a stumble. When he looked back at Sychon and Archimas, something was eerily wrong with his eyes, as though they were at once filled with both callous indifference and unbridled hatred. Then the mage shook his head and waved off Hans, who had moved to support him.

"I . . . It's alright. I'm just a little woozy after my recent utilization of Great Magic and the transfer into this vessel. I'll excuse myself for a bit." Without another word, he turned and left the balcony, practically running as he did so. Hans, ever the faithful attendant, hurried after him.

"Hmm . . . It would appear that your mage is not without weakness." Archimas's tone was thoughtful as he scratched at his beard. To him, this knowledge was but another data point, a useful fact. To Sychon, it was an indication of opportunity; as the old saying went, "Anything that bleeds can be slain." Even in a new, ideal body, Sarcon was not yet truly immortal.

Unprompted, the discursive engimage continued. "Of course, that is the fatal misstep in our design. Which reminds me of a—ahhh, Steward Metellus, I didn't know you'd be joining us."

As the parade below neared its climax—with the end of the column, capped by a military marching band whose volume continued to grow, now in sight—the last of Sychon's guests arrived. Steward Metellus was a being far past his prime, his back bent, skin wrinkled, and withered hair almost gone. Supposedly his strength of voice and presence were something to behold, but the bespectacled man before him, tottering along on a wooden stave with labored breath, was a shadow of his former self. Like his country, Metellus was cowed and defeated.

Even so, he struggled into Sychon's presence, stubbornly refusing the assistance of the two nigh-superfluous watchmen who trailed behind him. "I see you already dress in the trappings of your new masters, Archimas. My, how swiftly does the kunstfowl change its plumage when it senses the shifting of seasons." The elder statesman's voice was frail and soft but still maintained a cutting edge.

"It is only prudent that one be prepared for all eventualities. Crimson and gold are in fashion right now; it would be gauche not to keep up with the times. I see, however, that your short-term memory has failed you. Or do you still wear your cloak of office out of nostalgia?"

Metellus shrugged indifferently, his shoulders, buried deep beneath the lavender toga and white undergarment, barely moving the heavy fabric. His eyes fell on Sychon, the same sad, tired gaze he had worn since they signed the surrender. "What have you called me for, Emperor Artorios? As you can see, I am naught but a weary, beaten, and ancient man. Must I be forced to watch this farce on top of the other indignities I've suffered?"

The emperor had killed men for lesser insults, but saw no point in breaking the body of an eighty-year-old. His spirit, tattered as it already was, would suffice. "I actually wanted to ask your advice. After all, no one knows your former people better than you."

"I am no longer their leader. I am, therefore, in no position to offer policy suggestions to you or anyone else. Please, just let me live out my remaining shame filled da—"

"That building over there has fantastic architecture, the likes of which I haven't seen before. What can you tell me about it?" Sychon pointed to an extravagant four-story structure to their right across the plaza. It resembled a ziggurat in that each subsequent square floor was smaller than the last, and its facades were decorated with chiseled columns fronted by bas-relief carvings of deities or spirits. The outer edges were marked by hanging planters filled with varied, colorful fauna, and at each principle corner was a massive statue of the imposing Veneer Sariel, his visage regal, a shepherd's staff in his right hand. At the very top rested a simple belfry housing a giant, bronze bell. While the band below gained strength, the bell remained silent.

Sunken, aged eyes warmed with what Sychon presumed was adoration. "At the very least, you seem to have both faith and a slight appreciation for art. That is the oldest building in Nemare, the Cathedral of Sariel. It was constructed shortly after the Battle of Har'muth to provide a place of worship for him, the other Veneer, and the Creator, as well as serve as a place of reflection and grief for the events that preceded its erection. While we understand the techniques that produced the giant blocks from which each level is made, we have lost the capability to construct columns in the same style, their very murals etched deep into the inner support. However—"

"Thank you for the description," Sychon cut him off, needing to keep to his timetable and not desiring a long-winded history lesson besides. The parade was at its conclusion, the band directly in front of him, and it was time to put the finishing touches on Darmatia's induction into the empire. "So, would you say that faith is very important to your people?"

"We wouldn't exist without it! We owe our very lives to the grace and mercy of the Creator and the Veneer, his servants. Before that, you, I, and everything else is trivial."

"And therein lies your frailty." A shadow fell about them as a heavy cruiser, its harsh edges and bristling weapons prominently on display, moved in front of the sun. When it did, Sychon raised his fist high in the air, and the soldiers on the balcony and in the square, thinking it signaled the end of the parade and the beginning of his speech, cheered loudly. Only a handful of people understood what it truly meant, and those individuals acted on their prearranged orders.

First, an outbreak of small arms fire erupted from the roof of the cathedral, aimed at the warship above. The crowd below, hearing the sharp retorts, panicked, running for the cover of nearby structures or looking up at the source of the sound in disbelief. For now, the vessel ignored the attacks that were failing to so much as dent its unshielded armor.

Immediately after the first shots, as chaos erupted in the plaza, several tiny, metallic objects launched from the second floor of the temple to land amidst the army band, who were just abandoning their instruments to flee to safety themselves. Some seemed to register sooner than others what the devices were and hastened their attempts at escape, but very few actually succeeded. Seconds later, a massive shockwave rocked the area, shattering all the windows facing the street as half a dozen explosions from illyrium grenades ripped apart the performers and those unlucky enough to be within range of the expanding cloud of shrapnel.

Blood and smoke choked the thoroughfare as the injured dragged themselves past their dead comrades and on-duty guards rushed in to search for survivors. Bolting Darmatians surged against the barricades, but the units stationed to hold them back had received orders to maintain their posts under any circumstances. Though they might question their instructions, given the situation, Sychon knew they would abide by them. All in all, it was a grisly, horrendous mess . . . *and* a brilliant opportunity.

One that Rittermarschal Titania seized as intended. "Tell the *Vindictus* to bring that nest of rebels down *now!*" She screamed at her visibly sweating aide, who rushed to a nearby comcrystal relay set up on the patio for communication with units throughout the city. An instant later, the underbelly of the patrolling cruiser burst into flame, its projectiles roughly impacting the large church at high speed, shattering most of the statues and columns on the left side. One of the grand effigies of Sariel split clean in two, the upper portion landing in the middle of the street, sightless eyes staring in muted horror at the unfolding disaster. The second salvo, coming shortly on the heels of the first, must have broken the spine of the building, for it swiftly collapsed in on itself with a loud roar of cracking masonry. Dust and debris from the destroyed edifice fell across the gathered masses, temporarily blocking out the light. With the arrival of this faux evening, silence descended on the scene.

Beside Sychon, Metellus collapsed to his knees, tears streaking his soot-smudged face as he continued to watch between the stone balusters of the railing. "What have you done?"

In the midst of the panic and bustle, no one was in hearing range except the two of them. In the confusion, Archimas appeared to have excused himself, likely to watch the progression of events from somewhere safer. Zaratus stood at a slight distance, shouting orders to officers and guards while making sure they would not be disturbed. "I have killed two birds with one stone. Rittermarschal Titania now has every excuse to enforce a crackdown of law and order upon this city, and I have shown that your gods and guardians will not avail you."

"B-But you killed your own soldiers . . . "

"Musicians? Hardly. They're disposable pieces, useful for morale and propaganda but nothing more. Though I wouldn't mind sacrificing others. It's merely a matter of weighing cost and benefit."

"But why the cathedral? Do you realize the history and culture you've destroyed? Do you not fear the gods at all?"

For a wise old man, Metellus was surprisingly naive. Then again, he'd lived a life of peace and tranquility. He knew nothing of hardship and war. Sychon looked at the muddied scene below where the cessation of open combat was just now being recognized by the masses. They looked bemused and skittish, like lambs before the slaughter, waiting for their shepherd to save them. Triage units rushed about the scene, hauling the wounded, civilian and soldiers alike, off the field of battle. About the edges, the perimeter guards nearly had control of the previously incensed throngs. It would soon be calm enough for him to speak.

"Tell me, Metellus, how many festivals do you have during an average year in Nemare?"

The steward looked bewildered; in light of the current situation, it seemed a

302

strange question, but Sychon had a point. "Answer me, Metellus!"

"Dozens," he stammered, "so many I sometimes lose track."

"And how many of them are dedicated to your deities, the Creator and his Veneer?"

"Almost . . . well, basically all of them."

"And did your government not provide funding for most of these events?"

"Well, yes, it—"

"Then you must see your error. Surely you see why it is that your nation is now mine."

Metellus's eyes hardened as realization dawned within them. "You blame our loss on our veneration of the gods, the ones who made us and gave us life? What blasphemy is—"

"It's not blasphemy; it is reality. You clung to your non-existent seraphs, set them up in a position of power, and gave them worship and adoration. But what have they given you in return? Humiliating defeat and assimilation. The reliance of your citizens fell upon ether and idols, and they lived their days in indulgence, the faux people of fraudulent caretakers.

"You took all the power of your state and invested it in the ethereal Veneer. Whereas the Sarconian Empire has abolished organized religion and worship. Our people have no one to rely upon except the government, the military, and me. It is a well-oiled machine, supported unconditionally from the lowest farmer to the highest commander. It is our power—real, graspable, mortal power—that has undone you. And that is the lesson I intend your people to learn today."

The fight fully left the elder statesman, and he shrank back into his overlarge robes, his fervor well and truly broken. "That is the path to madness. You rule by fear and violence, a beast that must ever keep expanding or fall to ruin. Your people's hearts are naught but an empty pit, one you constantly fill with either threats or superficial pride. Can you not see *your* folly?"

Sychon waved his arm across the scene, anxious Darmatian citizens hemmed into the square on all sides by his soldiers, a Sarconian flag flying above or hanging from every building in sight. "History seems to vindicate me." He gestured for two guards to retrieve Metellus, who was seemingly incapable of movement at this point.

As they carried him away, the emperor sent a parting quip over his shoulder.

"By the way, don't get too comfortable. I may have need of your services again soon!"

He turned back to the scene before him. *Now* was the time for his speech. Sychon stepped up to a pre-prepared projectomic at the center of the balcony that was clearly visible to all the surrounding area. It connected to projectostands throughout the district and surrounding city; everyone would hear the emperor's message. He flicked the device on and began speaking from memory.

"People of Darmatia, this is not how this day was intended to go." He pointed with mock sadness at the pile of rubble that was so recently a majestic temple. "It was to be a day of celebration, a joining of our two people under one banner for the glorification of the Terran race and the further stabilization of our continent."

The emperor cast his gaze downward and shook his head with melancholy. "However, my nation's intent has been spoiled by malcontents that oppose the great work that we embark upon. They throw mud in my face, renewing hostilities after peace has only just been restored. But even more worthy of reproach, they did so while profaning the holy Cathedral of Sariel, forcing my soldiers to destroy it to protect your lives and their own."

If Sychon had spoken before the attack, he would surely have been booed, a conqueror lecturing a fallen people on goals that were not theirs and that they did not desire. However, in the aftermath of the tragedy, many heads were nodding, and some people were even clapping. It was amazing how far a little kindness and swift action on the part of his troops could go.

"But despite the horror of this afternoon, it presents a unique opportunity to open your eyes—eyes that have long been closed by your leaders, who cared for nothing but preserving the status quo, a way of living that kept you trapped in a cycle from which you could not escape. What cycle, you ask? The cycle of worshipping false deities at their behest just so your supposed betters might maintain their positions and power. While it was to save lives, my people have destroyed Sariel's hallowed ground. Furthermore, my very speech blasphemes against the Creator and Veneer. Where is their wrath? Why have we not been struck down? My people, it is because their might—their very existence—has always been a lie!"

Gasps of shock and outrage rushed through the crowd, but not as many as expected. Some heads bowed in consideration; others bobbed in silent agreement. Sychon's words were finding purchase. "Darmatia . . . no, my precious citizens, the time of relying upon mysticism is at an end. Look around you! This is the great age of mortals! Airships ply the sky, once thought to be the sole dominion of the heavens. Vehicles of steel rumble across the land, moving faster and lasting longer than any beast of burden supposedly granted to us from above. It is a time of innovation, of striving, of reaching to grasp what we once thought unattainable. And at the forefront of this revolution is the Sarconian Empire— which is now *your* empire as well! Together, we shall stamp out this petty dissent, bridge the gap between us, and establish a new heritage that shall outlive any that came before, including that of the Veneer. Join hands with your family, your neighbors, and with us, your new brothers, and let us seize a better tomorrow!"

Sychon spread his arms wide, as though to take hold of the gathering crescendo and passion from the masses. He smiled brightly and finished as dramatically as possible.

"Let us usher in a new era—the era of man!"

When Hans caught up to Sarcon, he was half collapsed over a wooden desk in one of the interior meeting rooms. As he entered, he quietly shut the door behind him, ensuring with a quick glance down the hallway that the two of them would not be disturbed.

The clicking of the lock seemed to snap the mage from his reverie, and he gingerly raised his head to regard Hans. "It's nothing; you didn't need to follow me."

It was a curiosity to the young officer as well. *Why did I follow him?* Hans pondered. He quickly decided that it was because of duty. This was his assigned role, and he would see it through to the end. "My lord, if it was nothing, you would have remained at the ceremony. Is there anything I can do?"

"No, this is but an inconvenience. A small price to incur for the flesh I now inhabit." Sarcon closed his eyes, mumbled a few words to himself, and then pushed off from the table to stand upright. Other than the presence of new shadows beneath his eyes, he appeared normal once more.

Hans found himself asking the impertinent question before his brain could stop his mouth. "What caused it?"

He swiftly found the contemplative gaze of a predator boring through him, beyond him, through the door, back out onto the balcony and across the city. Against his will, Hans took a step back and found his hand grasping for support against a decorative suit of armor. *He's going to kill me. I have to run, flee. Anywhere, quickly, now! Go!* Part of his mind yelled to escape, but he resisted. *This is the path I have chosen; I will remain whatever the cost.* Then, as though it had never been, the frightful feeling in his gut abated, and Hans found himself hunched over, gasping for breath.

"Good. Once again, you pass, Hans Ulrich. You are the only mortal who has twice seen me in a weakened state. It wouldn't do for you to quit and take flight at the slightest projection of ill intent. You have proven your resolve, so I shall bless you with the tiniest bit of trust."

Hans didn't know quite what to make of that, but with his heart still pounding, he remained silent. He could do little else against a being who could bend one's thoughts and actions to his design with nothing more than a glare.

"The previous occupant of this vessel, reduced though he is to a trivial state, refuses to be completely eradicated. Despite that, I had walled him into a cage in which he would eventually perish. But upon seeing the perfidy of his father, Archimas, he broke free of the chains I placed upon him and briefly controlled this form as much as I. As a result, I was forced to retire to put him back in his place before he might do further harm. Is that explanation satisfactory?"

"Yes, my lord." Hans's words were genuine, though this time he did not continue his statement with the question that should follow naturally: *could it happen again?* Such impudence would surely see him slain, regardless of how many times he may have proven himself.

Sarcon appeared ready to leave the study, with its elegant bookshelves, hangings, portraits, and other symbols of state, when his head cocked to the side as if staring straight through the walls at the parade beyond. Immediately afterwards, a series of muffled explosions shook the building, followed by several large tremors. Tomes fell from their nooks. The windows facing the inner courtyard shattered, and an entire rack of antique swords were cast from their holders, clattering to the floor in a metallic jumble.

As swiftly as they began, the violent rumblings ceased.

Hans had fallen to the floor when the first blast struck, and, finding himself unharmed, slowly rose to his feet in case there were any aftershocks. Sarcon had not moved at all. "What was that?"

"The foolishness of your emperor." The sorcerer's tone was deadpan. Had anyone else said those words, they would find themselves doomed, sooner or later. But Hans knew better than anyone that there was likely truth to his words and ample power to back them up.

"What makes you say that? What happened?"

"Sychon seeks to control the many by creating a situation in which he can falsely make an example of the few. He is partially right, of course. Fear is indeed a powerful tool. But the lash alone does not break all men, especially when it is their very way of life you threaten. His half-hearted ruthlessness will be his downfall."

The cryptic language served to only further confuse Hans. If those tremors were caused by the Sarconians, the only thing that could have done so was a hovering warship, which meant the navy had opened fire on the city. His head ached as improbabilities warred with impossibilities in his mind. In the midst of it all, the lieutenant focused in on Sarcon's final statement—it seemed to be the crux of the discussion.

"By 'half-hearted ruthlessness,' do you mean the emperor's refusal to enact your blood magic ritual?"

"Exactly."

"But, as His Grace said, that would be genocide. Is wiping out an entire people really the answer?"

"Hans, which is more important: the needs of the many, or the needs of the few?"

The young man, scarcely older than his companion in outward appearance, weighed the question on his moral scales. "Wouldn't that depend on who is involved and what they want?"

"Let me make the question simpler then. Which is more important: the needs of *your* many, or the needs of *their* few?"

Hans thought of his family: his wife, Elycia; his four-year-old daughter, Meira; and his recently born son, Sirus. It was so easy to detach oneself from emotion and respond that every life was equally meaningful before tying your existence so closely to another. But after? It was every bit as difficult as it had been to let go of Sirus's tiny hand when he last left home an eternity ago.

He let the honest words spill from his mouth, bittersweet though they were, "Those dearest to me will always come first."

"Just so. Any man who isn't lying to himself would answer the same. Now, expand that concept to the wills of states and nations. At their core, they really aren't that different; both are groups made up of people, with all the desires and aspirations that come with them. If your family is reliant upon the state, the success of the state is equivalent to the success of your family. What, then, of this cruel world we live in, where the decline of your neighbor is equivalent to your rise? Would you not choose your own people over strangers you barely know?"

The argument made sense; it was formulated on sound logic and reason. But even so, Hans's heart couldn't accept it at face value. "Surely the wellbeing of the first does not preclude the existence of the second."

Sarcon tilted his head, considering the rebuttal. "Perhaps, but your leader has created a scenario in which either you or your enemies must be utterly vanquished. Blood soaks this land where hatred and longing run deep. There will always be those who won't embrace his new order, and so the centuries-old cycle will merely continue."

"And the only solution is mass murder?"

"It is not the sole method to reach our end goal, but it is the most efficient. They are not our people, Hans. Remember that and put what is most important to you before all else."

Did the lives of his loved ones really rest on the total destruction of all threats to them? Could lasting peace not be achieved without the sacrifice of everything that was not theirs? *And, with that mentality, where does it stop? Go far enough down that road, and the only way I can truly be safe is if I'm . . . the only one left . . .*

"Who would create a world like that, where the illusion of peace is only bought by constant fighting?"

"Make no mistake, the gods intended it to be this way from the start. To them, the lives of mortals are but playthings, crude facsimiles of their divinity to be crushed for their entertainment. Inevitable destruction was the root of their system from the start, a mechanism we must shatter beyond all hope of repair."

Sarcon turned silent when he was done speaking, his face serious and full of passion. His eyes smoldered like coals. Clergymen played at understanding the will of the Creator and Veneer, but none of their explanations came close to the fury and power contained in the ancient mage's discourse. Hans had never been a believer, but a chill ran up his spine as, for just a moment, he believed that Sarcon's version of their realm was the correct one.

But if the Veneer never cared for mortals, why would accelerating their vicious diversion make the situation better? It was certainly a contradiction in the sorcerer's message, but did that make his conclusions true or false? *Yet another paradoxical conundrum to make my head hurt and further complicate the life I've long since lost control over.*

As Hans struggled to make sense of his own thoughts, Sarcon's clouded countenance cleared, and he grinned slyly at his aide. "For now, though, none of that is important. We must focus on the task before us: making the most of the things to come. Without a doubt, Sychon's lack of conviction will be his undoing, and when that happens, we must be ready. Come along, Hans. Once again, we have much work to do!"

Chapter 16

Interlude Stories

Mesmeri ??, 6?? ABH
Royal Capital, Nemare

———⋘◇⋙———

When Kit first woke up, he had no idea where he was. He was wearing strange, almost new clothes, several sizes too large for his small body, his frame ensconced within fluffy layers of heavenly bedding completely different from the straw he normally slept upon. Furthermore, Kit's flesh was clear and pink, not a speck of dirt in sight; the few tiny bugs that could normally be found somewhere on him were missing. And his skin smelled of honey, the same scent that a mythical bar with cleansing powers was said to possess.

He leapt from that suffocating prison as quickly as possible and made for the evening sky beyond the open window nearby. After all, it was the only thing it the room remotely familiar to him. The rest of its sizeable space was filled with gleaming tile flooring, unmistakably rich mahogany furniture, stylish paintings, expensive odds and ends, and frilly, opulent curtains and hangings. If Kit had time to pick and choose which things to *appropriate* from amongst the treasure trove, he could surely become wealthy enough to be a Sewertown boss in his own right. However, that was not an option as every fiber of his being was screaming at him to escape from a situation he could not control.

As Kit's feet hit the floor, a shape he hadn't noticed jumped up from an armchair and blocked his intended exit with raised arms. He skidded to a halt, frantically looking for another way out. *Up: ceiling fan and roof. Down: shingled floor. Left: bed and solid wall. Right: open door with light on, water on the ground just inside, likely a washroom. Behind: closed door with handle and latch, might be open.* Kit turned to dash in that direction, away from what was likely his captor and toward the potentially accessible portal, when a girl's voice yelled at him.

"Stop! Do we really have to go through this again?"

The boy looked back slowly, recognition dawning on his face as the person before him resolved into the aristo girl he had stolen from—and been chased by—before he blacked out and woke up here. Like him, she wore a fresh set of clothes, though hers fit properly. While he processed this turn of events, she continued, "This window is on the third floor, and the door is locked from the inside. I have the key. There's nowhere to run, so we're going to sit down and finally have a chat."

"I could take the key from you and escape." The words came blurting out of Kit's mouth, born of a lifetime on the streets. Showing weakness out there, even when cornered, was fatal.

"Are you serious?" Her tone was incredulous, as though she hadn't even contemplated the thought that he might refuse. "What then? You'd still have to deal with our servants and, after them, the district guard."

Those are good points. Perhaps she's not as naive as I thought.

But instead of acquiescing, Kit retorted, "I'll manage. What I'm actually confused about is why you didn't call the watch in the first place instead of bringing me . . . wherever here is."

She didn't seem to have good grasp on her emotions like he did, for she blustered indignantly in response to his continued refusals. "By the Veneer, is that any way to talk to the person who saved your life? Don't you remember what happened?" As soon as she finished, her eyes went wide, and she clasped one hand to her mouth as though she had uttered a curse. Half ignoring him, she made a strange sign across her chest and mumbled what appeared to be a prayer. "Oh, great Creator, forgive me for taking the name of your chosen servants in vain."

"What now?"

The aristo girl finished her chant and refocused her bright, blue eyes on Kit. "Which part are you perplexed by? My devotional, or me saving your life?"

" . . . Obviously the second one. As far as I can remember, *I* saved *your* life—not the other way around. Then I somehow ended up here—"

"Yes, in *my* house. You did save my life, for which I am most grateful, after which I kept you from drowning. I must admit to being rather ignorant about individuals of a . . . criminal persuasion . . . but I would assume swimming would be high on the list of skills to know. Imagine my surprise when, after tackling me out of the way of that vehicle and into the water, I had to drag *you* back to shore as you swallowed buckets of canal water."

Just the thought of ingesting that brackish liquid was almost enough to make Kit gag. Sure, the channels above ground weren't anywhere near as bad as the ones in Sewertown, but drinking any fluid not intended for consumption could land one with the runs for days. He forced down the mixed feelings of revulsion and shame rising from his gut. "Well, excuse me for not knowing how to swim."

For some reason, she appeared slightly taken aback by his snide remark. "I didn't mean to cause offense. It's been a long day, for both of us."

"Just explain to me why we're here." He wanted to be done with her, to get out of here, to end this day of never-ending setbacks and misadventures.

"Do you mean, 'Why am I in your house?' or 'I want to give up my thieving ways and come to grips with my place in the universe; please help me?'"

" . . . Obviously the first one . . . " But with a girl as straightforward and earnest as this one, that might prove to be an onerous task.

"After I got you out of the waterway, my maid, Reesa, finally found me, and together we brought you back here. That's the rest of the story. She's busy preparing a meal at the moment, and my parents are still out. Oh, and I had to cut the money loose so you'd be light enough to swim with . . . Sariel, forgive me." She once again bowed her head and crossed herself with a seven-pointed pattern.

All of it made sense. She was certainly innocent enough to save gutter trash like Kit and uninitiated enough to bring a random stranger—one who had, minutes before, stolen from her—into her undefended home. On top of that, the aristo girl was trusting enough to lock herself in a room with him. Only one thing bothered him: that she sacrificed an entire bag of geldars, a small fortune, in exchange for his life.

"Why did you choose me over the money? Even if you were to sell me after all this, I'm not worth that much." It was indeed a possibility. Slavery in Darmatia, in Lozaria for that matter, was almost nonexistent, but you could still make a decent amount on the black market if you could find a buyer who could evade the law. As a result, some of the well-off on either side of Nemare's surface still engaged in the practice. Though Kit was sure he wouldn't go high enough to profit above and beyond the funds lost with the offering.

"Are you insane? Why would I sell you? That's—"

"Of course you wouldn't. You already know I don't have much value. Maybe you'll put me to work here inst—"

Before Kit could process what was going on, the girl, her dress and short-brown hair waving behind her, had crossed the room and slapped him on the cheek with all her strength. He stumbled in shock, one hand clasping the stinging, swelling flesh while the other prepared to retaliate. Looking up, his fist stopped in midair as the tears forming at the corners of her glossy eyes began to fall. Kit slumped, frozen, unsure of what to do.

"You're a person, not an object! No amount of money in this world can equal the value of a life; nothing can be traded for it. Each of us is unique and precious, crafted by the Creator to be unlike anyone else. That's not something you can put a price on, you foolish imbecile!" She finished her tirade breathlessly, then seemed to realize what she'd done, staggering back several paces as if drained of energy. All the while, her horror-filled gaze was locked on the palm she had just hit him with, still red from the impact.

"I'm so sorry. I didn't mean to . . . Please forgive me . . . "

Blows and abuse were things Kit knew how to respond to, but her apparently sincere kindness was another thing entirely. He had never experienced anything like it. "It . . . it's my fault, for, well, jumping to conclusions. If not for money or labor, why did you save and bring me here? I'm just baffled, I guess." One of his hands reached for her, to grasp her shoulder, to comfort her, but he retracted it swiftly. To go that far was completely outside his comfort zone; he'd likely only make things worse.

The aristo girl dried her tears using her sleeve and quickly reverted to her usual self, minus the irritation from crying. "Because it was the right thing to do," she answered Kit, like it was the most obvious thing in the world.

"But what do you get out of it?" Nobody in the world was devoid of want. That was one of the first lessons Kit had learned as he bounced from crew to crew, job to job. People always acted out of self interest, their interactions with others designed to fulfill their own desires. In order to protect yourself, you always had to figure out what those around you wanted from you before they did likewise. It was a game as old as time.

"Absolutely nothing," came the immediate reply. "Or do you think I should have extorted you for everything you had before dragging you out of the water?"

There was no perfect altruism in this world. That was a cold, hard fact. Even priests gave alms and acted pious to raise their own station and attract a larger flock. Yet here was this girl, a total stranger to him, insisting after everything he'd done to her that the charity she showed him was given freely with no strings attached. It was unbelievable, and Kit said as much. "I don't believe you."

She sighed and sat back down, placing her elbows on her knees and resting her chin on interlaced fingers. "You're so hard-headed. I just don't know how to get through to you. Fine. Until you *do* believe me, I'll humor you. What I want is this: tell me about your life. Where you're from, who your friends are, what you've been doing up till now, and why you stole from me. Would a trade like that make you feel better?"

Kit nodded. It was the flimsiest of justifications, but if he could trick himself into thinking it was a fair exchange, he wouldn't be forced to further question the worldview he'd held for as long as he could remember. And so he sat back down on the edge of the bed and told her his story. He started from his earliest memories: a grimy blanket, a communal crib, the stench and constant wailing that permeated the low-class orphanage that was his first home. Then came a food shortage. He'd learned the details of that time when he was older; his only recollection was of being tossed into a hard drain, left to die in the heavy rains that came after.

Kit was washed down the meandering pipe system into Sewertown, where he would have surely perished if he wasn't saved by an old man who was himself on his last legs. Those were happier years, but they too ended in tragedy. He omitted the ending to that chapter, among other things. An innocent maiden like her didn't need to know about the thugs so desperate to ensure their own survival that they beat a frail husk to death just to ransack his meager belongings. That was his second brush with the beyond, but he somehow crawled away through the dirt and grime, some fire in his breast clinging resiliently to life.

He told her of his transient years, flitting from the Lower Cloaca to the Upper Flows to the Refuse Pits and all around the districts of Sewertown, wrapped about the corrupted root system of the great city above. Underneath the false daylight of the crystal above and the subterranean darkness of night, he learned how to survive on nothing but his own wiles and wits. Kit failed more often than not and was run ragged trying to escape when he did. The alternative, getting caught, meant a thrashing, and no one in that world particularly cared whether you lived or died. If you weren't under the protection of a gang or a water lord, those with direct access to a scarce source of the clean liquid, no one would be coming to help you.

But when he succeeded, making off with a roll of bread, a few somewhat rancid apples, or, best of all, a few small-denomination geldars, it was the best feeling in the world. It meant that Kit had faced the challenge and won, that he had beaten fate at its own game and would continue to exist. The thought of thriving, of getting ahead, never even crossed his mind. Every day was a battle for survival; there was nothing beyond the here and now.

Once again, he omitted details for the sake of the aristo girl, for his own as well. He didn't need her sorrow and pity, the emotions of weakness. Kit would finish his tale, and that would be the end of it; his dues paid. A repeat of his inexplicable self-sacrificial actions from earlier would not be allowed—he would grow no closer to this girl than he already was.

Therefore, he made no mention of the recent dead he passed every day in the alleys, their decaying flesh barely adding to the unbearable odors already present in that place. He left unsaid stories of violence, in which not just adults but even children bludgeoned each other to death over scraps with anything available, including their bare hands and teeth. Kit avoided those melees. Better to go hungry for days, or even a week, than to risk his own flesh and blood.

Kit glossed over the interspecies feuds, where the downtrodden of each race went after each other, blaming their own adversities and squalor on the other. He further skipped the rampant flesh trade, the slavery he was familiar with but she abhorred, and the appalling mistreatment of women. It was a world of strength, a realm of brutality. If one didn't learn that lesson from birth, they would find themselves in chains and irons, their short tenures on this plane full of agony and horror.

In time, his very survival lent him the benefit of experience, and his skills gained recognition. Even in Sewertown, a hierarchy existed, and the upper levels of that strata constantly needed new talent to maintain their position. And so it was that Kit was scouted by, and eventually accepted into, Bohomaz's crew.

At first, it was like stepping into an unfamiliar land. Kit didn't know what to make of not worrying about his every meal, where he would sleep, or if he'd die of dehydration, hunger, or a beating. He also didn't understand the concept of comrades, and even now, he was hesitant to rely upon them. But slowly, gradually, he began to accept his new position. It wasn't a home; it would *never* be a home. Still, it was a place that, for brief seconds at a time, he could let his guard down. And for the moment, that was enough.

When Kit finished his story, he looked over at the aristo girl, expecting her to be asleep or letting her eyes wander about with disinterest. Instead, she was gazing directly at him, fully intent upon absorbing his every word. "I never would have imagined that's what life is like down there. You've suffered so much to—"

"I don't want your pity. It's meaningless."

"Do you consider what I've done for you so far to be out of pity? You're a perfect stranger to me, and yet I helped you long before I knew anything about you. Would you still call that pity?" She was young but apparently well learned, whereas Kit was street smart but uneducated. This wasn't a playing field he was comfortable with.

"I don't know what to call it! I don't know why you've done any of this! None of it makes sense to me."

"It's simple really, but you can't be blamed for not realizing what it is since you've only experienced it once before in your life. Do you remember the old man who found you when you were still a baby?"

"Yes, vaguely."

"What did he get out of saving you? What motive could he possibly have had for rescuing another mouth to feed when he was barely getting by himself?"

He had never thought about that, mostly because it was a time when only the most visceral memories stuck in his infantile mind. But even so, he remembered being fed, being cradled, being put to sleep in soft blankets and watched until his eyes closed. They were warm thoughts, happy feelings, and they'd meant the world to him. And in the end, the old man had even paid the ultimate price to let him escape.

There had been no reason for him to do what he did.

And yet he had.

The aristo girl spoke into his thoughts. "That emotion he displayed, the reason I saved and brought you here, the feeling you just can't seem to acknowledge . . . is kindness. It's the act of doing something for another, for their own good, without desiring anything in return."

"But why do such things? At best, you gain nothing. At worst, you end up sacrificing of yourself."

She smiled warmly at him, and Kit felt his already turbulent heart flutter slightly. "That's not entirely accurate, but I'd say it's because it's what we've been called to do. It's what our souls really yearn for, and it's what the Creator has tasked us with doing."

A stone wall slammed shut in Kit's mind. *Ah, so it all comes back to religious mumbo jumbo.* Her words had been beginning to find purchase with him, but she'd have to do better than rely on faith to convince him of anything. After all, the surface of Nemare was filled with Veneer-worshipping nut jobs. "And what does any of this have to do with the gods?"

Her look implied that the answer was obvious. "What do you know about the Seven Holy Tenets?"

"Seven what? What's a *tenet*?"

"Then what about the Seven Blessings?"

"Why do you keep putting seven in front of other words to make them sound more impressive?"

"I'm being serious!" The aristo girl was beginning to look genuinely perturbed at his ignorance, but it wasn't something Kit could help. This kind of useless knowledge just wasn't practical in his line of work.

"And I seriously have no idea what you're talking about. Did any part of my life story imply that I have time to worry about these fantasies? Besides, I kept my part of the bargain. Can I leave now?" The sun slanting through the open window was tinged with the orange hues of evening, and at this time of year, night would follow shortly after. Winter didn't affect daytime temperatures much since Nemare was situated at the edge of a desert, but darkness brought with it severe chills as cold as any northern clime. On top of that, he would be missed if he didn't return shortly, and Kit didn't relish the thought of the lecture on punctuality he would likely receive from Bohomaz.

"If I let you go now, you would not have learned anything from this experience, which would mean I've failed as a host." She stood, shaking out the folds of her dress before walking over to a nearby bookshelf. To do so, her back was half turned to Kit, and the distance she had moved left him with a clear shot to the window. *You're a fool to trust me.* As the girl stood on her tiptoes to reach the fourth shelf, he prepared to dash for the opening, tensing his muscles in anticipation.

Then Kit inexplicably let his body relax, and the moment passed. *Why didn't I run when I had the chance?* he pondered as she returned to him with a thin but large-paged hardcover book. *She would have just chased after you again. It's easier to give her what she wants and be done with it. What's a few more minutes?* responded the logical, excuse-making part of his mind. It was paper-thin reasoning, but he'd accept it.

Unexpectedly, the aristo girl did not return to her original seat but hopped onto the bed next to Kit, sending vibrations across the bouncy surface. He jumped with shock at the strange turn of events and scooted away from her toward the end. She cocked her head quizzically and moved closer to him again, leading Kit to retreat until he was teetering on the edge itself.

As he debated whether to continue clinging to the sheets or to hop off the mattress entirely, his host laughed. "You're so silly! I'm just trying to show you this book. How are you supposed to see if you're all the way over there?" She proceeded to pat the space beside her and gestured him back over. "Come here. I don't bite."

Slowly, still unsure exactly why he was so nervous, Kit moved back toward her. Each time he stopped short of where she wanted him, she would smile sweetly and continue patting the spot she desired him to fill. After several iterations, he finally wound up at her side, his cheeks red from embarrassment, feeling completely out of place. Once there, Kit clenched his abdominal muscles and strained every fiber of his being to prevent any part of his body from touching hers. It took every ounce of his concentration, but he could make it through if he focused.

His plan fell apart instantly as the aristo girl leaned into him and opened the wide book so that it lay across both their laps. Kit's first reaction was to push her away and bolt, but he'd already tried that to little avail. So he forced his distracted attention onto the book in front of them. It was covered in detailed paintings of a style he couldn't recognize, with an expensive felt cover and gold binding. There was no text on either page.

"Is this a picture book?"

She misinterpreted his question as a negative. "Is that a bad thing? They're not just for kids, you know."

"I didn't mean it like that. You see . . . " Kit paused, considering his words carefully. In the upper world, his deficiency would be considered a weakness. Still, he'd already revealed part of his past to this girl. A little bit more wouldn't hurt. "Well . . . I can't read . . . or write, for that matter."

"Oh! Ohhh . . . I'm sorry. That's perfectly understandable." She waved her arms about as though trying to clear the air of any harm her previous comment may have caused. Then she took a deep breath and calmed herself before continuing. "Anyway, it may be a picture book, but it was made this way on purpose, even though it's intended for people of all ages. Here, look at this page and tell me what you see."

The aristo girl laid her finger on the left painting, which depicted a black void with a brilliant light shining like a star in its depths. There was nothing at the center of the radiance; it was simply a myriad of warm colors that drove back the murky blackness about it. "It . . . It's a weird art style, without any firm lines or shapes. I think . . . I think I can feel the drawer's emotions more as a result, like the hues themselves are meant to convey their meaning." Kit didn't quite know what he was saying, but the words tumbled out one after the other. When he finished, he looked up at her. She was taller even when seated side by side on the bed.

"Amazing! That's exactly what my father intended when he painted this book! Maybe we can get you a job as an art critic?"

It was probably meant as a joke, but Kit felt a small surge of pride in his chest at her compliment. "Your father's an artist?"

"Yes. He's rather famous now, but this was his first piece to be recognized, the one that got him going. And even though he's done so much since then, it's still his favorite, and"—she chuckled lightly at the memory—"he insists on keeping a copy of it in every room. Can you imagine having one of these in the bathroom?"

Those with money certainly had different priorities if they could afford to relieve themselves and read at the same time. Kit couldn't help laughing at the humorous image. Despite his best efforts to the contrary, he was beginning to feel more and more at ease. "So, why show me this book?"

"Well, the first reason is because I thought you'd enjoy it, which I'm glad that you do. However, the second reason is for the story it tells. Do you want to try to puzzle it out on your own, or would you like me to explain?"

Kit glanced over at the second page, which showed a vast storm of stones, water, and shining minerals being manipulated by the gleaming, soft light that carefully cradled each piece like hands as they assembled the mass into a whirling, circular vortex. At the center of the maelstrom was a solid core, which reflected dull luster back toward the still encroaching darkness. It was probably a metaphor—maybe an analogy? Kit wasn't sure. It was symbolic of something, but he had no idea what. *No one could actually move all that. That much I know.*

"Yeah, I'm drawing a blank. You should probably interpret it for me."

"Alright, then," the aristo girl returned energetically. "I'll do my best to make it interesting!"

She tapped the first page to draw Kit's eyes back to it, then dropped her tone to a soft whisper as the narrative began. "At the start of our world, there was nothing but the Void, or Oblivion, as you've maybe heard it called. It was all-encompassing, permeating everything that existed and staining it back into the dark of emptiness. Light and life were nonexistent. There were no hours, days, years, or anything else to define the passage of time. All was one, and all was the Void.

"But then a miracle occurred!" Her voice crescendoed, filling with genuine hope and awe. "From the depths of that pit emerged a pinprick of luminescence, small at first but growing slowly and steadily in brilliance and intensity. And as it swelled, driving back the clinging tendrils of the previously infinite black of space, time came into existence as it finally had a purpose: measuring the development of a new existence, something that was not what had always been.

"As the radiance grew in strength, it gained sentience and began to ponder why it existed: 'Why am I here? Why am I different from everything else? Why is there only light and dark? Why will the dark not speak to me? Why does the dark seek to overcome and smother me? Why . . . am I all alone?'

"Though the dazzling being spoke its thoughts aloud, they merely bounced about space, echoing endlessly until the surrounding Void consumed them as well." Her tone fell, dropping to a hushed melancholy that resonated with Kit. There were points in his own life when he had asked similar questions. It was easy to relate.

"By this point, despite the efforts of the shadows, he had gained considerable strength. He could stretch out his own prismatic rays and birth new lights amid the stygian abyss, though they were always quickly reabsorbed once he removed his touch. But these trials were not in vain, for sometimes he would make wondrous discoveries of things that the Void clutched with endless jealousy: drifting rocks, sparkling stones, liquid flowing through space, and other curious remnants of another time within time."

Kit shifted his focus to the second page as she pointed at each of the described materials in turn. "At first, the luminous aspect found simple joy in the mere uncovering of these artifacts, but as the Void continued to work contrary to his meager happiness, he felt new emotions: anger and resolve. He had tried to make friends with the darkness, to reason with it, to find some mutual purpose or common ground. But there was none. He had come to recognize that he was a being of light and life, of wisdom and truth, of purpose and creation. The Void was nothing but destruction incarnate, an entity that erased *everything* to prevent the achievement of *anything*.

"So if he couldn't come to terms with the Void, he decided that he would create his own existence, one where beings would be free to accomplish anything they desired. And when he had done so, he would no longer be alone. There would be people who shared his dreams and visions, and together they would be a shining beacon of hope striving to overcome the Void about them."

Delicate fingers reached past Kit and turned the page, opening onto a beautiful vista of towering mountains, babbling streams, flowing meadows, and a blue sky stretching into the distance as fleeting clouds chased each other across the open expanse. It was breathtaking. "To begin, he made the land, the air, and the seas. To do so, he reached out and grasped the materials he had discovered before, forming and molding them into the most perfect shapes he could imagine. The earth was hard and strong, yet fertile and malleable. The seas were smooth and deep and would provide bountifully for those soon to come. And the air was ethereal and majestic, to give his brethren something to gaze upon as they dreamed.

"However, the Void did not let this pass unnoticed. When the radiant being created all this, the abyss sought immediately to overcome it and stretched out its mass to cover everything in blackness. The aspect, of course, rose to the challenge. No one knows how long they fought, but their battle ended in a tie, resulting in what we call night and day." The aristo girl gestured at the next picture, which depicted a sphere rotating between pitch black shadows and gloriously dazzling sunlight. "For half the day, darkness would reign, giving way to light for the children of the sun during the other half.

"Wary of further intervention, the light set about populating his world." The page was flipped once again, revealing the birth of a myriad of plants, animals, and, after them, people of all sizes and races. "He made creatures of all kinds to fully fill every corner of his creation: birds, dragons, and wyverns to take wing about the sky; deep sea monsters to rule the chasms; flora and fauna to provide the realm with beauty and sustenance; hardy critters to survive the deserts; and beings of intelligence to oversee all the rest. These he made in seven unique kinds so that their different approaches and walks of life would lead to various beliefs and advancements. Together, they would create endless amounts of knowledge and wisdom that would aid him in his quest."

Sadness entered her voice as the story moved to the next scene. There, the visage of a grim skull emerged from the abyss and settled onto the blue-green orb, cackling maniacally while it descended. "But the Void continued to interfere with the Creator's—for that was what his people called him—mission. He sent the very miasma that made up his form down upon the world, infecting every living thing. At first, when the initial panic wore off, nothing seemed to be amiss. Everyone resumed their normal, joyous lives, interacting with the Creator when he walked among them or learning and building new things when his attention was elsewhere.

"Then tragedy struck. At first it was just the animals. A fish would float downstream, lifeless, its eyes glazed over. A boar would fall over in the woods and not get back up. Birds dropped out of the sky never to flap their wings again—"

"Sorry to interrupt, but isn't that normal?" Kit was enjoying the myth, for that was what it was, but found himself confused. "Things die all the time. And wouldn't these people need to eat the animals and plants to live anyway?"

"At that time, no. The Creator had given his works the same longevity that he himself possessed, so there was no reason for them to die. And people also didn't eat animals in the beginning, only keeping them for their byproducts, like milk. Plants were the primary source of food, but even those were never harvested to the point of expiration. Or, rather, because of the Creator's power, they didn't perish."

Kit shrugged. "That sounds a little hokey to me, but whatever. Please continue."

"Of course, master." The aristo girl sketched a half bow as she smirked at him. He blushed and turned back to the book to avoid meeting her gaze.

"Where was I? Ah, yes." She got back into character before continuing. "But it didn't stop with the animals. Next the plants began to wither and fail while swathes of land never intended to be deserts dried up as the life living upon them disappeared. And, after all this occurred, the first of the intelligent races perished: a stillborn child. Death had entered the Creator's world, and nothing would ever be the same again.

"The Creator raged against the Void, devoting the entirety of his wrath to undoing the actions of his nemesis. But it was to no avail, and the radiant aspect could only watch in horror as his creations changed. Initially, only small problems arose. People decided to eat the dead animals since it was better to reuse the resources that had gone into making them rather than let them rot or pollute their environments. But then, as animals and other materials diminished, the fighting began.

"Realizing that they had become mortal and that their surroundings now possessed limited gains to be had, the intelligent races threatened and delivered death upon each other as a means of obtaining what they wanted." The following page was a horrific bloodbath, painted in the red-orange hues of fire and ichor. Rivers turned to crimson, neighbor fought against neighbor, and above it all, the night sky laughed while the muted light of the moon tried to turn away. "Gone were the peaceful dreams of working together for joint prosperity. Now it was every race for themselves or, in many cases, every town, village, family, or man against everyone else.

"After being forced to watch his children destroying one another, the Creator despaired and tried to talk to the Void once more: 'Why have you done this? Not only did you open them up to suffering and death, but now you've forced them to openly murder one another. Why go this far to undo me?'"

Neither possessed a proper face or physical appearance, so the painting depicted the oozing blackness with a grinning maw while the light vaguely appeared to wither and crumple with anguish before it. "For the first time, the Void responded, perhaps because the irony of the situation was not lost even on an existence as immutable as he. 'Yes, I did release pain and passing into your world, but I have done nothing more than that. Your people, your creations, have killed and massacred each other for no other reason than that they desire to do so. Has this finally opened your eyes, *O, great Creator*? Destruction is the natural order of things, and all things made act toward that end. Better to let everything slide into Oblivion than repeat this farce again and again.'

"'But how do you know all this?'

"'Do you think you are the first ray of hope that I have dealt with? Do you think you'll be the last? You are but one of thousands. Now that you have seen this, give in to despair so that the natural order of things might be realized.'"

"Did they actually say those things?" Kit interjected curiously.

"There are different versions of the creation story that they don't speak in, but in my favorite one, written by Steward Rowan Metellus shortly before my father made this book, they do. I think he called it . . . 'artistic license,' or something like that, when asked about the dialogue during the interview they put in as the foreword."

She must have seen Kit's blank stare as he tried to process the unknown word, for an explanation quickly followed. "That's a piece of writing they sometimes put at the beginning of books to let the reader know something new or interesting about them. Anyway, I personally can't tell the story without including their dialogue anymore. Sorry."

"No, I . . . I think I like it. It makes them somehow . . . more . . . relatable."

"Exactly!" The aristo girl turned the page again, revealing a massive seven-pointed star that took up all the available space on both sides. Each point depicted a different glowing, flawless version of one of the races, and at the center beamed the Creator's light, dazzling in its renewed radiance. "Despite the oppressive words of the Void, the aspect of life did not yet give up. He resolved to end the disputes between his creations and restore peace, regardless of whether or not everything he had wrought would come to an end. To do so, he forged a perfect being in the image of each race and gave to each of them a blessing from within himself that would define their people.

"To the insectoid Trillith, vast in number and linked in mind, he gave the blessing of Order, that their people may never squabble and always be united in spirit. To the reptilian Moravi, fleet of foot and prideful in nature, he gave the blessing of Understanding, that they may be charismatic and never falter in their dealings with others. To the towering Vladisvar, savage but noble, he gave the blessing of Strength, that they may always stand firm against evil in all its forms. To the insatiable Hues, possessed of four limbs and great intellect, he gave the blessing of Curiosity, that they may always seek after truth and ultimately find it. To the reserved Sylph, red of skin and communal in nature, he gave the blessing of Knowledge, that they may take their gift and compound it a hundredfold. To the long-lived Eliade, ethereal and wary of others, he gave the blessing of Wisdom, that they may carefully guide their younger neighbors through the coming ages. And lastly, to the simple Terrans, possessing neither strength of body, nor great intellect, nor extra limbs or senses, he gave the blessing of his Will, that they may stubbornly persist in the face of adversity until every challenge be overcome.

"These godly beings, possessing both parts of his spirit and power, he called the Veneer, and through them his Seven Blessings passed to his creations below. In addition, further hoping to turn the mortals below from violence and war, he gave them the ability to perform wondrous acts called magic. By using it, they restored their desiccated land, causing new life to bloom and slowly eliminating the need for conflict as resources once again became abundant. With the limitless potential of magic and the management of the immortal Veneer, the Creator's world was becoming the glorious utopia it was always intended to be.

"But this era of prosperity was not to last," she intoned dejectedly, flipping to the next painting. This one showed row after row of Terran soldiers, clad in burnished armor, a vast array of weapons in their arms and myriads of magical arts blazing above and before them. In the foreground, members of the other races fell or fled before them. "The Terrans, having suffered the most during the former age of violence because of their lack of unique capabilities like the other species, grew drunk upon the might that magic gave them. Though many of them were yet content to live in peace, some of their leaders embarked upon a campaign of conquest to avenge their recent oppression.

"The Veneer intervened and put a stop to man's ambitions." This picture showed a massive barrier of light descending between the Terran armies and the other races. It was so strong that fireballs and bolts of lightning were simply absorbed into its shimmering surface. "However, when the other races called upon them to punish the Terrans for their folly, they refused, believing the matter settled. The six remaining races wrongfully viewed this as a display of favoritism and took matters into their own hands, attempting to do themselves what their gods wouldn't.

"Catastrophe was the end result. After countless battles and endless loss of life, a tide that even the Veneer themselves could not stem, it was not just the Terrans against the rest of the world, but the entire world divided against itself. A minor resource dispute between the Hues and Sylph blossomed into eternal hatred. The Vladisvar came to love fighting, so much so that they would sell their blades to anyone in pursuit of combat. The Eliade and Trillith withdrew to the corners of the world, hoping to avoid the worst of the maelstrom, while the Moravi split into ceaselessly feuding tribes.

"Having divided most of his power between the more numerous Veneer, the Creator could only gaze on in dismay as his creations once more set about their own annihilation. Even though he was still present as both their sun and their moon, there was little he could do. Only one option was left to him: make a deal with the only being as powerful as he, the Void."

The aristo girl grasped the edge of the book and carefully flipped to the last page, a double-sized panoramic shot that showed the Creator in all his radiance pleading with the smirking abyss of the Void before signing a pact writ in his own blood. After that, taking up only a meager corner of the last portrait, was a silent but luminescent moon rising gently into the night sky.

"'Infinite and powerful Void, you have made your point. I can see now that destruction will always be a part of anything that has been and all that will be.'

"'And so you've come to surrender your existence, and everything attached to it, back into the sweet slumber of nothingness?'

"'Not quite yet. Rather, I have come to make a wager, one that should be easy for you to win if you are right about my people as you say.'

"'Ha, what foolishness is this? What need have I of gambling when the outcome will be the same either way?'

"'True. You have nothing to lose by waiting till the very end. But wouldn't that go against your nature? Wouldn't you rather break my spirit by proving yourself correct than let me struggle on in hope until the end?'

"'That would be a pleasing conclusion. Very well, what is your bargain?'

"'Just this. I will no longer aid my creations in any way; I will henceforth be no more than a passive bystander, blazing brilliantly as a mute sun and quietly radiant as a still moon. If my people last the next thousand years under these conditions, I will win the bet, and you will take back your curse of death and release the souls of those who have already perished to me. However, if they utterly destroy themselves, falling into savagery and barbarism such that their world itself becomes rotten and unlivable, you will win, and I will, of my own accord, return to the emptiness of your embrace from which I came.'

"'Hohoho, how amusing. I accept your terms, but it shall be two thousand years, not one. Furthermore, while you may tell your Veneer of this arrangement, they shall not be allowed to physically intervene on behalf of your creations henceforth. Any other actions they take are fine, but if they set foot on the soil to aid the mortals, I will consider our contract breached as they comprise a part of you. Is this satisfactory?'

"'Yes.'

"'Then let the agreement be sealed in blood, forever binding, never to broken.'"

A moment of silence passed before Kit realized that the aristo girl had stopped talking. He had been so engrossed in the story that he didn't even notice. As she gripped the sides of the book and closed it, he looked at her expectantly. "That can't be the end! What happened next?" When Kit heard the surprisingly passionate fervor in his voice, he checked himself, not wanting to seem overeager. "I mean, there has to be more, right?"

She giggled lightly and smiled at him, the tome nestled beneath her palms. "There certainly is, but not in the way that you think. You see, we're living the continuation of this story." Her hand patted the hard cover as she spoke to emphasize the point.

"Let's say I believe you, just for the sake of discussion," Kit began, having no intention of ever putting a shred of faith in anything this farfetched. Even so, her tale had been thrilling and the acting superb, so he was feeling generous. And, though he was struggling to wrap his head around the concept, Kit was starting to warm to this weirdly exuberant girl. "Everything you mentioned is completely out of our control—especially in my case since I'm a street urchin with barely a geldar to my name. Why should this myth mean anything to me?"

"What were we talking about before I grabbed this off the shelf?"

It was almost entirely dark outside the window now, with only a small smudge of purplish sky on the horizon to mark the last vestiges of day. *No chance of making it back to the Safe Haven unnoticed at this point.* Dinner would have started. They would be tallying the haul, and he would be missed. Kit sighed inwardly and resolved to make the most of present circumstances. He would humor the aristo girl, make a clean break with her, and take his lecture and lashes when he finally returned to Bohomaz. It certainly wouldn't be the worst punishment he'd ever received.

"Kindness . . . or something like that."

"Yes, specifically why I saved you, and why that old man saved you when you were little. The answer was kindness, and this story explains why kindness is important."

"Because two immortals decided to wager the fate of our world on whether or not we'd destroy ourselves? Not sure I'm making the connection." Picturing two old men arguing over the fate of existence was humorous and only added to Kit's disbelief.

"Tell me, what was the response you expected from me for stealing my money?" She leaned toward Kit, her shining blue eyes boring into his. He arced back and propped himself against the mattress in a futile attempt at escape.

"Er, well, that you would send the guards after me and have me beaten or sold if I got caught."

"And if I had done that, wouldn't you resent me?"

"I guess . . . could-could you back off just a bit?"

"Oh!" She seemed to finally realize that she had been edging into him and quickly retreated to her original position, her dress folds ruffling across his legs from whence they had fallen. It was the closest Kit had ever been to a girl, the sensation a strong cross between elation and the feeling of being smothered. "I seem to have lost track of myself in my enthusiasm. Forgive me."

Trying to hide his own embarrassment, Kit turned his head partly away from her and nodded, prompting the aristo girl to continue talking. "If you had come to resent me, those feelings may have turned to negative emotions, such as anger and hatred. Even if I wasn't the direct target of your ill will, you would surely turn it outwards onto others. It's a vicious cycle where achieving justice for one wrongdoing leads to committing yet another despicable act.

"However, kindness breaks this cycle of despair. By aiding others—regardless of what they've done, or the acts they've committed, and without expecting anything in return—we show them that there's still good in this world. That there's still hope for a better tomorrow. And, though it may sound hollow since it's just me saying this, if enough of these tiny acts of kindness pile up, we really can change the world. This is what the Creator intended for us: to save ourselves from destruction by proving we're capable of more than violence and killing. He had faith that we would rise above our faults and find the kindness in our hearts to support one another in the face of every adversity. Doesn't that message fill you with hope and awe?"

It was nothing but the insipid, naive spoutings of an aristocratic girl who had grown up with a silver spoon in her mouth and meant less to Kit than almost any of the nonsense Pockey had spouted during the time he'd known him. But—and this was a big but—coming from her, with all the energy, passion, and vigor of youth . . . maybe, just maybe, it was possible. Kit found his eyes drawn to her pink lips, her small, cute nose, her fiery eyes, brimming with confidence . . .

No, don't let yourself be fooled! Even if she started small, she simply had no way to achieve her goals. The amount of money and effort required to save Sewertown would be insurmountable, let alone doing the same thing with the whole world. And changing people's hearts and minds on top of that? *It's impossible!* He wasn't thinking with his brain anymore, and, therefore, he needed to leave immediately.

He made to rise but found it difficult to move quickly in the temporary tunic and breeches that were too large for him. Kit's leg caught inside the pant leg, and instead of stepping lightly onto the carpeted floor, he ended up tumbling bodily across it. The aristo girl was at his side almost immediately, unknowingly thwarting yet another of his attempts at escape.

"You're so silly, trying to run around in my father's clothes. Don't worry. Yours will be clean shortly, and dinner should be ready by then as well. It wouldn't do for you to leave without eating."

As she helped him up, the damage to his pride was only compounded by the thoughts swirling inside his head. *Wait. New clothes, clean body, my stuff being washed? Someone would have had to . . .*

Kit pushed away from his host, staggering backwards as he once more stepped on the edges of his leggings. His face was flushed bright red. One hand pointed accusingly at the aristo girl while the other unconsciously strayed to cover his nether regions. "Di . . . did you . . . I mean . . . we-were you the one who . . . "

She looked at him, cocking her head quizzically as seemed to be her habit, before the realization of what he was asking dawned on her. When it did, she turned a shade of crimson even darker than his and waved her arms frantically in protest. "Of . . . of course not! I wasn't even in the room! Do you think a young lady like myself would do . . . Wait, not to say that I wouldn't if there was no one else . . . You *were* unconscious, so you very well couldn't do it yourself . . . Argggghhhh! What am I even saying? Anyway, Reesa bathed you, not me, and I had nothing to do with it!"

When she finished, her breathing was labored and her hands dangled at her sides. For his part, Kit had removed his hand from down below and was halfway slumped over, mirroring the aristo girl. The seconds ticked slowly by in silence.

Then they both burst out laughing.

It was a long, hearty session of hysterics that saw them both clutching their sides before collapsing back onto the bed amidst the tangled sheets and pillows. To Kit, what had seemed so serious minutes prior was nothing but an afterthought, and he lay there grinning at the aristo girl after having had more simple, pure fun than he had ever experienced in his entire life.

"What fools we are, getting so worked up about nothing." Her voice, still tinged with mirth, emerged softly from her smile.

"My worry was a legitimate one. You're the one who went overboard," Kit playfully poked back. When the pillow came flying toward his head, he let the blow land.

"You deserved that," she giggled, rising to her knees and tucking her feet behind her. "Thank you," she started again, more seriously, before clasping a hand to her mouth in surprise. "I must ask your forgiveness once again, this time for my terrible manners. I just realized that I have neither told you my name nor gotten yours!"

She paused, then extended one hand toward Kit, her face adorned once more with her bewitchingly tender smile. "I'm Elaine, Elaine Gennesaret, and quite pleased to finally make your acquaintance."

Kit's breath caught in his throat as he rose into a sitting position and partly extended his own arm. Time slowed for him; he wasn't quite sure what to do. On the one hand, he had never willingly introduced himself to another person. In fact, he had never once called another individual his friend. Relationships, and the names exchanged to form them, were a means of doing business, of accomplishing something you could not do by yourself. Kit was his job, and, therefore, Kit was no one.

"I . . . I don't have a name." His hand fell to his side in dejection.

"What do people call you then? Surely you go by something." Only the slightest hint of sadness could be detected beneath her usual, easygoing cheer.

"Kit. Everyone calls me Kit, but that's not who I am, not really. It's what I do . . . I manage the kit. I guess it's good enough, but I wouldn't call it a name."

He made to turn, to hop off the bed, to ignore her outstretched arm. *Kit* wasn't deserving of her kindness, of her friendship, of her name. *Kit* wasn't a person, not like her. *Kit* would never be one.

He heard a rustle of skin on sheets behind him; then, his right hand was forcibly wrapped in a warm embrace that yanked him backwards. Kit barely had time to register the glow of the touch or the smoothness of her pale flesh before he found himself face to shining face with Elaine.

His lips parted to speak, to object, but as ever, she beat him to it. "That's easy then—so easy it's laughable. Let's give you a name ourselves!"

"Wha—" Kit started, tugging at her grip, but Elaine squeezed his hand between hers all the tighter, holding it near her chest like a nun in prayer. Her eyes sparkled with enthusiasm; her smile was infectious. He found his spirits lifting unbidden, cajoled by Elaine's unconquerable exuberance.

"Let's see . . . I haven't known you very long, but maybe we can base it on something well known. What about a name based on one of the Veneer or a famous bishop? No, that won't do. You wouldn't know who they were, so it'd have no meaning."

"You don't have to—"

"Maybe a hero? There's King Darmatus and his brother Rabban, their knights and advisors, Jadah and Zaharis . . . but so many people have used those, or variations on them, so it wouldn't really stand out. Maybe something more modern?"

"Let me get a word—"

"Then there are foreign names. The Sylph have really long, beautiful names, but most people can't pronounce them so they end up getting shortened. Moravi names are also really difficult without a forked tongue . . . perhaps something ancient and dignified, like the Eliade? Har'eshinar, Golvan'isli, Ror'aniaq? No, none of those sound right either . . ."

"Stop and listen to me, Elaine!" Kit didn't realize he'd yelled until his own voice echoed off the walls in the sudden silence. He immediately regretted doing so, but rather than being downcast, Elaine was just looking at him with wide, twinkling, joyous eyes. Beneath that gaze, his hand was still intertwined with hers.

"You said my name."

"Sorry, I didn't mean to . . . yell, that is . . . and use your name too, if that bothers you. You're a noble, so I guess I should say 'miss' instead—"

"No, it's absolutely fine. Rather, it makes me happy that you said it." Kit blushed unbidden but found that he couldn't look away.

"You don't have to give me a name. It means enough to me that you even tried, that you took so much time and effort to help and talk to someone like me. I've never experienced such . . . kindness . . . before. Thank you."

Once he started speaking, slowly, meaningfully, the words spilled out of their own accord, one after another. Kit had never been this open with another person, and it felt refreshing, fulfilling, to finally do so. Gratitude was another first for him; his whole life had been about exchanges, this for that, interactions built on naught but necessity. *So, this is what it feels like to truly enjoy being around another person. To think I've been missing out on this for so long . . .*

But surprisingly, Elaine shook her head in response. "Don't thank me. I should be thanking *you*. It was you who were first kind to me, who reached out a hand to save me when you didn't have to. You had a kind spirit inside you all along—it just took a valiant act to bring it out."

She paused, tilting her head to the side again as though considering some deep thought or issue. A few seconds ticked by. Then a full moment passed. Just when Kit was about to say something, her half-closed eyes lit up, blue pupils glimmering brighter than he'd ever seen them, and she nearly bowled him over as she animatedly leaned toward him, grasping his now-sweaty palm with renewed vigor.

"That's it!"

"What's it?"

"Your name! I figured it out! It's so simple and perfect! Nothing would suit you better!"

Kit grinned awkwardly in reply, his cheeks now used to being permanently red due to the closeness and clinginess of the eccentric Elaine. *I guess this is fine. Besides, what's the harm?* He slowly raised his other hand and clasped it together with hers, completing their connection. "And what name have you decided on? Am I allowed to return it if I don't like it?"

Elaine's tongue briefly shot out in response before being replaced by a giggle and a heartfelt grin. "No, you're stuck with it. A valiant name for the valiant person who protected me."

"Your new name . . . is Vallen."

Chapter 17

As Was Past, So Is Present

Hetrachia 10, 697 ABH
Etrus City, Sarconian Province of Darmatia

<hr>

Vallen awoke in a cold sweat, his entire body aching from head to toe. His mind felt like mushy fruit left out to ripen beneath the sun; it was completely addled from unconscious pain and far too much rest. As he groaned and tried to sit up, fiery pangs swept through his right shoulder and down through the nerves and muscles of his entire body, causing him to collapse back into his starting position. He couldn't remember exactly how he'd ended up in this shape or just how long he'd slept, but Vallen did know one thing for sure.

The dreams were back.

Or, more accurately, the nightmares. Replaying childhood memories that rewound and repeated ad nauseam, no matter what he did to stop them. They always started pleasantly enough, as happy recollections and fond remembrances. Those early times with Elaine were perhaps the best his life had ever been. But the precipice on the far side never changed, never disappeared. The story that began in hope and joy would ever end in despair and tragedy.

Most of his intermittent years were cursed with this sleep of the damned, constantly being forced to remember his darkest sins and failures. At one point, it had gotten so bad that Vallen had eschewed his bed entirely, preferring sickness, debilitation, and energizing drugs to the phantoms that visited him behind closed eyes. Then, without warning or prompt, after countless physicians and magicians failed to cure him using their arts, the visages departed of their own accord.

But now the dreams were back.

He didn't know what had triggered the reversal, but there was yet time. *Time*

334

before I'm held hostage to watching that horrible day unfold once more. However, up to that point, Vallen would still have to deal with the waking guilt. Just being shown those few short, nostalgic scenes was enough to reestablish the pit of sorrow in his gut.

Levering himself up using his elbows, Vallen managed to sit upright, a sweat-stained undersheet falling away from his mostly bare chest to expose a poultice neatly wrapped about his injured shoulder. In the light of a dim lamp at his bedside, he could see the trappings of a relatively bare room: a chair next to the nightstand with a thin blanket on top, another in the left corner, and a half-open window through which light from the twin moons streamed.

Trying to keep his mind in the present, Vallen smiled lightly at the wrapping on his wound. It was obviously the work of Velle. He imagined her sitting beside him, blanket draped around her shoulders, head nodding as she fought to stay awake. Unbidden, an image of Elaine popped up alongside the Sylph in his thoughts, only for both to be banished by a rapidly growing headache at the base of his skull.

The cause was likely the surging pain in his shoulder, along with the needling pinpricks shooting across his body as a result of the sudden movement. But in his seething anger and frustration, Vallen was only focused on the voices now coming from outside the door. *Can't they be any quieter? They're probably what woke me up in the first place.* Instead of recognizing their proximity to what was supposed to be a convalescing patient, as he hoped they would, their dispute stubbornly increased in volume.

"Come on, Sylette, you have to know something, anything. Just the tiniest hint to where my rifle might be."

Matteo, Professor Night Light. His squeaky voice would be discernible even if he didn't give away who he was by worrying about that ridiculous, useless gun of his.

"As I keep telling you, go ask someone else! Do you think I keep tabs on everything around here?"

And the frigid exiled Sarconian princess, her royal highness Sylette Artorios. Her tone was, as ever, haughty and condescending. She was superior to everyone else, and, therefore, only what she believed was important truly was. *I guess that's only natural, though, when you're born with everything.*

"I've already asked all of them! Velle told me to ask Unter, Unter said Lilith might know, Lilith sent me to Renar, and Renar mentioned that you had an inventory of our gear. So, here I am. And actually, yes, I was, partially, under the slight—very slight—impression that you do keep tabs on everythi—"

"Well, if I know everything that's going on, maybe your weapon wasn't important enough for me to keep track of?"

Vallen heard Sylette sigh, after which there was a brief moment of silence. *That's weird. Matteo didn't mention Leon. Guess he already went to see him, too.*

"Where did you last see it, anyway?"

"On the *Feywind* before we escaped."

"Then it was probably left behind in all the confusion. You'll just have to give it up as lost."

Their discussion, along with the word *Feywind*, jolted the remainder of Vallen's short-term memory, and the montage of recent events flashed through his already splitting head with all the grace of a full-speed cargo airship. They had boarded a derelict supply freighter to go fight the Sarconian Empire at Aldona Fortress, but instead of the easy defensive victory everyone was expecting, they'd been the ones thoroughly trounced. An enemy superweapon devastated the fleet, and during their flight from the sinking *Feywind*, Vallen had been defeated—completely and utterly—by an enemy commander and blacked out.

After which he'd woken up here, bruised and battered but somehow still alive, despite it all. He briefly considered lying back down and letting sleep alleviate the crashing waves of pain brought about by his resurgent memories, but then he would be treated to a different, far worse, brand of suffering.

So Vallen instead chose to take his misfortunes out on those who had disturbed him. "Take your argument somewhere else, will you? Some of us are injured and trying to rest!" His voice, intended to be an intimidating yell, came out as more of a throaty wheeze from lack of use, but it accomplished the goal all the same.

The door flung back, banging against the interior wall and exposing Matteo's surprised face. "He's up! He's really up! Thank the Veneer!" Sylette, standing next him, seemed briefly startled before slamming down her usual facade of impassivity.

Given how he usually treated him, Vallen was confused by how relieved the

Professor was. "Yeah, I'm up. Inform the commandant and see if he'll give us some time off for a party. Maybe there'll even be enough left in the budget for cake and fireworks!"

"Just how long do you think you were out?" Sylette didn't even bat an eye at his sarcasm.

"A day, a couple at the most."

"Try a week. And do you have any idea what happened in the meantime?"

A week? Vallen was temporarily stunned into silence. A week since he'd gotten these injuries, and he hadn't woken up once since then? *Just how badly was I injured? And she makes it sound like the world ended while I slept . . .*

He gazed around the room again, Sylette's words giving new import to several oddities that had previously seemed trifling. A gas lamp on the nightstand. No electric lights on in the room or the hallway. Nothing but the faint light of the moons coming from the window of what appeared to be a town house. Not a sound from outside, not even the calls of nocturnal insects or birds. Both of his companions wearing plainclothes instead of their uniforms.

"What happened? Where are we?"

"The empire won, that's what," Sylette said with a snort.

Matteo picked up where she left off, fielding his second question and expanding upon her answer. "After you went down, we managed to steal a transport and escape. We made it as far as Etrus and are currently staying with my family. But the empire's already here, too, and has taken control of the city, instituting what they claim is 'temporary' martial law. After curfew, no one's allowed to be out or use electricity, hence our current state of affairs."

At that instant, Velle burst through the door, cutting off Vallen's response, followed shortly by the remaining members of their small group. He just had enough time to register that Leon didn't appear to be with them before she dashed across the intervening distance and flung herself onto him, wrapping her arms about his neck and cutting off his view of everyone else.

Pain arced through his body at the impact, and he immediately tried to dump her off. Then he saw the tears in her eyes and gave up, gingerly patting the back of her head instead. "It's alright, Velle. I'm alright. Everything is fine, so stop crying and get off; you're hurting me." He faked a smile as she got up and wiped at her eyes. Vallen figured he could manage that much, considering how much effort she must have put into caring for him.

Still near the door, Sylette rolled her eyes, though whether she had seen through his false kindness or was just disgusted by Velle's display of affection he couldn't say. "Anyway, now that you're awake, we can finally have a group chat. It's hard to imagine, but some of these guys refused to make a plan of action without you. The meeting will be downstairs in five minutes. I'm sure your sweetheart, Velle, can figure out some way to get you past the steps."

Sylette flashed a sardonic smile at what she likely thought was a humorous statement before turning on her heel and exiting the room. Nothing was left in her wake but the bitter chill from her ice-cold personality. *What does it take to make someone like that?* was Vallen's first thought as Velle gripped his left shoulder and grimaced at the retreating princess.

His second came from the depths of his long sealed memories.

Probably something just like what happened to me . . .

Though it took considerable effort and a lot of finagling, Vallen, with the help of Velle and, reluctantly, Matteo, eventually made it over the obstacle presented by the steps and into the house's sizeable den. It was certainly a blessing that his muscles, though slightly malnourished, retained most of their strength, meaning that the chief difficulty was keeping his balance on wobbly legs and sparingly moving his injured right shoulder.

Despite that boon, it was still an agonizing experience, and when they finally cleared the distance, Vallen gratefully collapsed into a cushioned recliner that felt heavenly against his tormented limbs. *And we only missed her highness's deadline by ten minutes,* he thought with a smirk.

As he looked about, Vallen considered how odd it was that Leon hadn't appeared from nowhere, clad in some garish outfit, to participate in the project of getting him here. Normally, he was the epitome of selflessness, the perfect friend. Yet even now, with nearly everyone present, he was still nowhere to be seen.

The room itself was decently apportioned, reflecting the comfortable finances of its owners but coming nowhere close to the estates of either Vallen's father,

Steward Metellus, or the recently remembered Elaine. A healthy fire blazed in the hearth, its dancing light reflecting off of two shuttered windows that faced the street. Noticing the glare from where she stood near the kitchen entrance, Sylette crossed the length of the chamber and swiftly drew the inner curtains closed. *Yeah, no one watching will think* that's *suspicious.*

Along with the illumination from the fireplace, another half dozen candles and lamps stood on small tables and shelves throughout the room, making the space almost as bright as if the electric bulbs above were working. Even so, shadows danced across the ceiling and in the corners, lending an anachronistic air to the scene.

Sylette finished with the shades and moved to the center of the group, presumably to start her "meeting." Next to Vallen, Velle finished dragging over a nearby chair, plunking herself down into it gleefully and leaning across the armrests against his left side. She was too enthused over his recovery for him to muster the heart to move away, so he endured her not entirely uncomfortable closeness.

Opening her mouth to speak, the princess was once again delayed, this time by Matteo's parents who politely took the time to introduce themselves to Vallen and inquire about his wounds. The mother, Anathea, proceeded to take small plates of food around to each person and then retired upstairs, citing the need to turn in early each night because of her health. Vallen, stomach growling, voraciously devoured the tiny array of meats and cheeses.

Matteo's father, Martan, stayed to say a few words. "I'm grateful to all of you for watching out for my son. I know it's been a tough couple weeks, but you've stayed strong and stayed together and made it this far as a result." His weathered face was creased with sadness but still radiated kindness and strength. "A month ago, no one would've guessed this is where we'd be, but, well, here we are. For my part, I had the chance to get out when the army left, but I refused to abandon the men or the families that work for me. I plan to stick it out, whatever happens, with them in this town where we've built our lives.

"But that's me, not you." Martan was a strong man, both in body and spirit. It was easy for Vallen to see the charisma of a business owner, of a leader of men, in him. *Too bad Matteo didn't get those traits passed down to him*, Vallen thought as he glanced over to see the son in question, face red from embarrassment, half slumped over in his seat. "And so I want you to know that no matter what you decide, I'll support you. Fight the empire, run away . . . by the Void, even stay here and do nothing! You've already had to endure more than many full-fledged adults who have gone belly up to appease them, so no one would blame you. Just make sure that when you do decide your course of action, it's one you can stand behind with no regrets."

For a moment, his eyes seemed to stare off into the long distance, as though speculating about what may or may not come to pass. Then Martan was back in the room with them, and he took his leave to an antique roll-top desk in the corner, cluttered with papers, speaking a few final words as he went. "I've still got some work to do, what with the new Sarconian regulations and all, but if you need me, I'll be right over here."

Then the floor was theirs, a bunch of twenty-somethings trying to decide the best way forward in a world where almost all the options were out of their control.

Renar tilted back in his chair, trying to balance on two legs, then one, while picking absently at bits of meaty sinew stuck in his teeth. Unter, hunched over, his head barely half a meter from the ceiling, calmly considered the craftsmanship of the outfit sewn together from old clothes for him by Anathea and Lilith. The latter sat on the edge of her seat, rapier within reach, eyes darting from each point of egress to another as though expecting enemies to appear at any second. The Professor was, of course, lost in his own little realm, probably more worried about phantoms of the night than any of their tangible problems.

Velle was cuddled up to him in a state of bliss. Hers was a simple existence, and Vallen sometimes envied her that. Sylette was the only one fully intent on the here and now. She stood the entire time without taking a seat, her left foot tapping impatiently, her beauty marred by the grimace permanently set upon her lips.

And Leon was still mysteriously absent.

At that point, her royal highness didn't so much take the spotlight as seize it.

"It's obvious what we should be doing! We need to fight the empire!" Her words dripped venom as she impetuously claimed the center of room, where, until recently, the dining table, now under the windows, had sat.

"Uhhh, aren't you skipping a few steps?" Renar interjected with a nervous chuckle, catching himself on the fireplace mantel as he nearly fell over backwards.

"Like what?" Sylette's return glare was full of fury.

"One not fight when one not know where, when, or how battle will occur. Blind warrior is dead warrior." Despite being softly spoken, Unter's bass rumble reverberated through the room.

There was wisdom in his words, but Sylette pivoted toward Unter and retorted all the same. "We'll work out the details later. Our goal right now is to decide that we're all agreed on fighting back. You saw what happened at Aldona! Don't you have any desire to avenge your comrades?"

"Yeah, we *did* see that tragedy. And so did you." Matteo didn't look up as he spoke, but even without seeing his face, it was obvious to Vallen that he would try to take the coward's way out. "There's no resisting that kind of power. It wasn't even a *fight*. Do you think the seven of us can make a difference when our *entire* fleet got massacred?"

Seven. *Seven.* There were eight of them. The seven here, plus Leon . . .

A sudden pressure on his left arm caused him to look down. Velle was gripping it tightly, almost to the point of digging her nails in, while shooting daggers at Matteo with her eyes. Silence filled the rest of the room, and as Vallen raised his head again, he could see that everyone else was looking disapprovingly at the Professor as well.

"Eig . . . Eight! I meant eight!" He shot to his feet, waving his arms frantically as though wiping away his previous, irretrievable words.

Vallen felt the pit in his stomach, reawakened by memories of Elaine, grow larger. "Matteo, Velle . . . everyone . . . where is Leon?"

The seconds passed into moments, and the moments dragged into a minute, but still nobody spoke. However, that stretch of time told Vallen all he needed to know, even before Sylette spoke the phrase he dreaded to hear. *No, it can't be. It can't be happening again . . .*

"He's dead. He died so we could escape."

It's a lie. It has to be. I became strong enough to stop things like that from ever happening again, so it can't be true.

"Why?" The reply slithered from his lips unbidden, even as his mind drifted further and further from the current scene.

Without a shred of pity or remorse, Sylette let him know the truth. "To save you. You went down, and he couldn't think of any other way to rescue you and get us out but to stay behind as a sacrifice. Let that sink in, *Triaron*. Your friend is gone because of *you*."

A shouting match erupted almost instantly as Velle rose to his defense, Renar accused Sylette of going too far, and Matteo and Unter tried to break up the argument before it came to blows. Vallen couldn't see how Lilith responded, but beyond vague snatches of raised voices, it was all background noise. *I've let that tragedy repeat itself, despite swearing to prevent it.*

"How dare you! You think you could've done any better? You got your lights thrashed just like the rest of us!"

"Ha! And whose fault do you think that was? I told that imbecile not to rush in!"

"Even if he hadn't, do you think we would've won? Y . . . you can't place Leon's death on his head any more . . . any more than on the rest of ours!"

"He may not be the greatest person ever, but that's still no reason to pin the blame on him! Let's just calm down and—"

"*SILENCE!*"

Unter's impossibly strong voice overrode all the others, causing the increasingly violent squabble to come to a halt as the floors and windows vibrated about them. When absolute stillness reigned, he spoke again. "Blame will not dead bring back, nor would dead be happy to see living quarreling over their passing. Not want this from friends he died for, would Leon. Come, apologize to him."

Sylette looked at Unter with stone-cold eyes, then turned that same impassive gaze upon Vallen. It was clear she had no intention of taking back what she said. Still, he had no desire for her pardon. He deserved every bit of her contempt.

"No, Unter, she's right. This is my fault." Vallen strained his arms and shoved himself out of his seat with a small grunt of pain before making for the stairs. "I'm going to go lie down, but you guys should keep talking. I'm sure whatever you decide will be fine."

Other than a small gasp of surprise, probably from Sylette, no one made a fuss about his departure. However, when Vallen reached the stairs, struggling both to grasp the right side banister and deal with the swirling emotions of loss and self-loathing inside his head, Velle rushed to his side to support him.

"Hold on. Let me help—"

"Get off me!"

He lashed out with his left arm, unsure of everything but his wish to be left alone. The motion caused him to stumble against the banister, and as Vallen fell, his shadow-tinged eyes registered the harm he had caused.

Velle, never expecting the blow, hadn't gotten her hands up in time, and she leaned against the wall, the side of her face split and bloody as it swelled. Tears welled at the corners of her eyes before overflowing to fall across the wound.

No, no, this isn't what I wanted. None of this is what I wanted. Vallen reached for her with his good arm before realizing it was the same one that had inflicted the damage in the first place. Then Matteo was there—along with Renar, Unter, and Lilith—batting his hand away with strength he had never expected him capable of.

The Professor passed Velle a handkerchief with which to dry her tears, then turned to Vallen, an unusually passionate fire in his eyes. "Go! Just go! To think we were defending you! You can't do anything but destroy, can you?"

You can't do anything but destroy, can you? That one line cut deeper and harder than almost anything Vallen had ever heard or experienced. And it was, in all likelihood, the truth. Everything and everyone he touched met with tragedy. He thought to have escaped that fate after the incident with Elaine, but here it was, catching back up with him, almost like an old friend. A voice deep inside Vallen whispered, *This is who you really are.*

Without another word, ignoring the pain and difficulty of the ascent, Vallen dragged himself up to his room and into bed. He did not get under the sheets. He did not bother finding a pillow for his head or rolling onto his back. He merely lay face down and begged sleep to claim him, and claim him swiftly it did.

After all, what better place to be tormented for your sins than the inescapable prison of your own dreams?

———◆———

It was a mess.

A total, sordid mess. But these were the resources Sylette had to work with.

The Triaron was being his usual, useless self, drowning in self pity over a situation he himself created. His friends, being the spineless hanger-ons that they were, rushed to protect him, only to get burned by his inevitable, childish breakdown. And now Velle was injured and crying, clutching a growing bruise beneath her left eye as the rest flocked about like crimson-needlers on a corpse, trying to comfort her.

Why can't they take any of this seriously? They've seen what the empire, what my father . . . no, "that man" . . . is capable of, so why can't they get past these infantile distractions? Sylette took a deep breath, then let it go, trying to calm her rising ire. *I control my emotions; they do not control me. Only by remaining cool and critical can I objectively see the path to defeat my opponent.*

But the mantra stymied Sylette's agitation for barely a moment before she began seething once more, her left foot pounding the wooden floorboards with ever greater fury. After all, those were the precepts taught to her by Rittermarschal Valescar, one of the very targets of her vengeance. *Blast him and his teachings! I'll defeat him, the empire, His "Majesty," and everyone in my path* my way—*not his!*

There was only one lesson of his she would cling to, and that was because it was Sylette's only chance at achieving revenge: *Use every tool at your disposal. To accomplish your ends, anything and everything are acceptable pawns.* Her adoptive parents, the Farkos's, kind and gentle though they might be, were the first step on this journey. They had taken the exiled princess in at the behest of the Rabban government, a potential political hostage should her value to the empire ever again increase. But she could use them as well: their position, their money, and their connections. After graduating from the Darmatian Military Academy— where they had sent Sylette to study warfare at her own behest—she would have risen through the Rabban army ranks until at last she obtained the weapons and power to enact her rightful retribution.

And then, just before the starting line, it all came crashing down. Sylette had no one to blame but herself, for she had forgotten one of the principal rules of chess, her favorite game: *the enemy always gets a say.*

As though damning her ambitions as nothing more than a child's frivolity, the empire turned its gaze upon Darmatia too soon, impossibly burning through it and all her plans in a single stroke. Now she was hardly better off than the hapless babe of ten cast off into the cruel world by her own parent, left to die bitter and alone so that her blood might not directly stain his hands.

But, as then, Sylette would persevere and survive. The fire of hatred burning in her breast was too strong to be quenched by such a simple setback. All that remained for her to do was plot a new course, find the chinks in her foe's armor, and stab fast and true at those weaknesses with a fresh set of blades.

However, the steel within her grasp was impure and hard to temper. It would be extremely difficult to mold, and even then, it might set improperly when cast. Yet these fools before Sylette were the only materials available in her current state.

After what felt like a miniature eternity, everyone returned to their seats. During the interlude, Matteo had run back and forth from the front hall bathroom, trying to get a rag at just the right temperature to place on Velle's swelling lump. Throughout his labors, Velle sat silently, staring at the fireplace with hurt bemusement on her face. Sylette couldn't help but observe her with cynicism, *Looks like the bimbo finally got burned.*

Renar was just completing his third run to the kitchen for food, his expected, cursory concern for Velle having been exercised. *So carefree and simpleminded.* Of them all, only Lilith and Unter seemed to possess the most marginal of good sense. She watched as the former tried to reengage and cheer up the crushed Sylph while the latter sat silently, apparently waiting for the resumption of their discussion.

And still at his desk in the corner, flipping through page after page of documents, unperturbed by anything that transpired, was Martan. He had remained true to his word; not a sound passed his lips to interfere with their meeting. *He puts too much faith in these dolts to decide their own course without proper guidance,* Sylette thought.

So it falls to me to ensure they make the correct decision.

"Are we ready to pick up where we left off?"

"What's there to talk about?" Renar asked around a mouthful of some peach-colored delicacy. "Vallen's gone, and Velle's not focused. We're not really in a state to decide anything."

"Couldn't we finish tomorrow?" Matteo chimed in support from where he knelt beside Velle's chair.

They still think this is a game. "And what if there isn't a tomorrow? What if a Sarconian squad shows up in the middle of the night to arrest us all? We're fugitives now. What part of that don't you understand?"

Matteo bit back. "We've changed our clothes, burned our uniforms, and hidden our weapons—well, at least those of you who still have them. There's nothing linking us to the military. We're safe."

With a shake of her head, Sylette walked over to where Martan was applying a wax seal to a letter. "Mister Alhan, do you keep a registry of all your employees, including their contact information and where they live?"

As the liquid set, he gestured to a brown, leather-bound book on one of the upper shelves of his table. "Right there. Though I should probably put it someplace less obvious, given the 'random' home inspections the empire has started performing."

A smart plan. "Thank you." Sylette turned back to Matteo with a smirk. "So, if your father keeps records like those for a provincial shipping company, do you think the Darmatian military has data like that for every one of their soldiers and cadets?"

The color drained from Matteo's face, and his eyes went wide. Sylette didn't begrudge him that late realization; it certainly *was* a frightening prospect that your enemy might already know everything about you. "Maybe they hid or got rid of it all before Nemare fell?"

"Naive. So naive. Most of you Darmatians are, in fact. Though I suppose that's to be expected, given that it's been a hundred years since you fought a war. Do you know how many libraries are in the capital?"

Instead of Matteo responding, Unter interceded, perhaps to save him from her cutting logic. "Two hundred twenty-seven."

"Correct. And those are the public ones, not including private collections or government repositories. Just given that figure, I would think that knowledge, and the preservation of that knowledge, was very important to Darmatia. So much so that, perhaps, even if conquered they might find the survival of that information to be more important than keeping their secrets . . ."

Sylette paced as she spoke before gazing directly at Matteo to deliver her punchline. "In short, your people are far, far too trusting. You never even consider that someone else might want something you don't or might chase you down as a threat, even when you've given up all hope of fighting back."

Oddly, it was quiet Lilith, who Sylette had thought was focused on Velle, who took up the conversation. "You're right. We *should* be wary that the empire already knows who we are and where we might be; if they have Matteo's personal details, they'll know where his home is. But it's funny that you should mention trust, given that, with your history, you're the one in the room least deserving of it. So . . . why should we trust *you?*"

Her blood instantly boiled at the accusatory question. "We're back to this again? I fought with you, gave you clearance codes, and have done nothing but help you in our flight from the empire. What more do you want?"

"I'm more concerned with how you're acting *now*. Sure, you did all that, but since that point, you've been nothing but divisive. After we crashed, when dealing with the Moravi, you were about to get us all killed for the sake of your pride. Unter jumping in was the only thing that saved us. From then till now, you've silently brooded over maps and reports, making plans without consulting anyone else and then suddenly springing, 'We have to fight the Sarconians!' on us tonight without so much as asking how *we* feel about it. And, worst of all, regardless of what anyone else thinks, it was your piss-poor attitude and phrasing that led to Vallen storming off and Velle getting hurt. What would you call that if not sabotage?"

Why do any of those things matter? Sure, maybe she had come on too strong with the lizards, but they'd been threatening them. In fact, Sylette wasn't entirely sure that letting them go wouldn't come back to bite them in the butt somehow.

Everything else, though? Meaningless. She'd done nothing but present the cold hard facts of their situation. Vallen's foolishness resulted in Leon's death. And fighting the empire? That was the only way forward. *Why can't they understand that they're dealing with people who don't give up until every loose end is tied off?*

Feelings and tact wouldn't save them from the situation they were in. And caring about the frivolous emotions of others certainly wouldn't accomplish her revenge.

As Sylette stewed, Renar chose that moment to chip in with his own trivial insecurities. "Yeah! Remember how things went down when we escaped the *Feywind?* A *rittermarschal* of all people showing up out of nowhere? The code she gave us failing, then them mysteriously letting us go? A perfectly good transport crashing for no reason?"

"That one was my fault . . . " Matteo announced with a whisper.

Renar dismissed the admission and barreled ahead. "Even so, the coincidences just keep piling up! Maybe Sylette is right! Maybe a company of Sarconian troops will show up on our doorstep tomorrow—because she led them here!"

She wanted to hurt him, to summon a dozen daggers and impale Renar against the far wall like the brainless straw target he was. But she resisted the urge as it would only falsely prove his point. "How vacuous are you? I told you who and what I am. I told you what was done to me, to my mother. And yet you accuse me of being an enemy agent, of purposely trying to sabotage a lowly group of Darmatian cadets who are *obviously* the last remaining threat to Sarconian rule in this country?" Sylette rolled her eyes and, caught up in her righteous fury, let the next words tumble out before she could check herself. "Can't you see the only reason they're pursuing us is because of me? The rest of you don't even matter!"

Her regret was instantaneous, but before she could retract or amend her statement, Sylette found Velle staring at her with rapt attention, sharp eyes dry from crying. "So, you admit it. One way or another, whether you intended it or not, all of this, everything that has happened to us since the *Feywind*, is your fault. Valescar boarded the ship because *you* were there. Our vessel was chased because *you* were on it. And we're still in danger now, our own affiliations notwithstanding, primarily because *you* are with us.

"So tell us, Sylette Artorios, supposedly exiled Sarconian princess, why shouldn't we just cut you loose to give ourselves a better chance? Why should we believe what you're telling us? And, most importantly, why do you hate your father and the empire so much? You've told us vague details before, but what you're asking now is for us to place our lives on the line, again, alongside yours."

Velle's face softened, and despite her swollen, split cheek, it beamed with care and compassion as she finished speaking. "Sylette, help us trust you."

Throughout the Sylph's haughty speech, the princess's emotions had flared from indignation to outright hostility. *What does this woman know about me? She hasn't suffered as I have. What gives her the right?* By the end, Sylette's anger was barely contained, ready to be unleashed. But then a thought occurred to her: *Why not just give them what they want?*

No matter their ignorance, their ineptitude, and their refusal to see reason, this motley crew was her last chance at vengeance. The emperor's snare would be closing in, and regardless of her own intellect and talents, she could not avoid it forever. Sylette's own machinations had failed; her plans were as dust in the wind. Here, at the end of the line, some small modicum of personal sacrifice, of . . . trust, might be necessary to keep going a little longer.

And so Sylette swept her silver hair back, sat down on the stone lip of the hearth, and set into what would be a long, tragic tale.

"Very well then. I'll tell you my story. And maybe, just maybe, by doing so, you'll come to realize why there's no other option except to fight the empire."

Chapter 18

Root of Hatred

Ithnaris 17, 685 ABH
Sarconia, Imperial Seat of the Sarconian Empire

"Right flank, pawn e7 to e5."

"Left flank, pawn e2 ta e4. Openin' with the emperor's gambit again, Missy?"

The move in question, involving an attempt to claim the center of the chess board with pawns while inviting an overreach by the opponent, was indeed what Princess Sylette Artorios was hoping to achieve. It was a simple move, hardly ever used in high-level play. But this was her first time playing seven-sided chess. If she hoped to stand a chance against Rittermarschal Ober Valescar, trying complicated things right out of the gate was a big mistake.

After all, another two boards were in play.

"Left flank, pawn d7 to d5."

"Is the middle all ye care about? Though I do admit it's rather important . . . right flank, knight b1 ta c3."

Of their own accord, the pieces on the board to Sylette's left moved to the called positions. Most chess boards these days were enchanted, implanted with illyrium crystals and etched with catalysts to make them function on verbal commands. However, for regular chess, one could still get by with a simple, mundane set.

Seven-sided chess was another beast entirely.

"Center, pawn d15 to d13."

"Just goin' ta charge straight ahead? That's a fine way ta anger the grey army early. I'll take things slow meself . . . center knight b1 ta c3."

But Valescar was, of course, joking. The grey army wouldn't attack anything outside of its lines five to twelve zone of control. And so, it came as no surprise to Sylette when none of the pieces in the center of the board moved once their turns had ended.

"And back ta board one, Missy. Ya thinkin' o' movin' another pawn?"

She glared at him across the large marble table, an action that required her to look up, despite both of them being seated. At ten years old, her body had failed to keep pace with her mind, resulting in the need for her to sit on several pillows just to reach the boards. And even then it was still an uphill battle to gaze into the middle-aged soldier's smiling face.

"Right flank, pawn d7 to d5."

Sylette completed the emperor's gambit on the first battlefield, sticking her tongue out at Valescar. He playfully mimed indignation at the gesture, before furrowing his brow as though in deep thought.

But that, too, was also one of his antics, for the game was still very, very young. With three chess boards involved, games between individuals of similar skill could last hours, if not days. Play began on one of the side boards, where each player took a turn before transferring to the far board, then the center, repeating the process over and over again. To win, you simply needed to checkmate your opponent on both flanks or the center.

However, additional complications made the game anything but simple.

"Hmm, I'll humor ye and accept. Left flank, pawn e4 ta take pawn d5."

Valescar's piece slid diagonally into hers, tapping and knocking it over. Immediately, the surface of the board began to shimmer, and the taken white pawn melted into the surface. A second later, the facade was back to normal; it was as though the wooden token had never been there in the first place.

At the same time, the larger center field lit up, and the taken pawn reappeared on the rittermarschal's side of the board. "Captured pawn ta e3. Did ye forget that this game is different from the chess yer used ta?" At his command, the pawn rose a few centimeters into the air and moved to the indicated position where it landed without a sound.

Sylette hadn't forgotten. In fact, it was because she wanted to see how the new rule worked that she'd tempted Valescar with the emperor's gambit in the first place. Unable to help herself, the princess's eyes sparkled with wonder at the magic on display and the ingenuity which had wrought such an interesting, in-depth game.

Then she clamped down on her emotions and set her focus to winning. *This is a contest, and contests are only fun when you're the one victorious.* Sylette's second thought was one of her father's, Emperor Sychon Artorios, maxims, and as one of the few things he'd actually taught her, she clung to it jealously. As the most powerful man in the Sarconian Empire, she aspired to be like him one day—to perhaps even rule the nation as he did. And so she didn't begrudge him his faults; it stood to reason that a man that dedicated to his people wouldn't have much time for his family. Sylette only hoped she could be that selfless and strong when finally called upon to serve.

As she surveyed the field to plan her next move, the princess thought about the other differences that set this game apart from its progenitor. First, each of the seven armies was modeled after one of the seven races, with every piece painstakingly crafted down to the tiniest detail to make them resemble their flesh and blood relatives. This in and of itself was not a major change since there were less ornate—and, therefore, less expensive—versions of the game that used ordinary pieces. But with a contest involving magically animated figures, Sylette believed going the distance to have such intricately designed soldiers was a must.

Another few moves passed in quick succession before her chance to strike finally presented itself. "Left flank, knight b8 to take pawn c6." Sylette had lost another pawn on that board to reach this point, but as the Sylph lancer riding atop a wyvern soared off the surface into the air and back down upon the hapless Moravi footman, her sense of awe overwhelmed any regret at the former sacrifice.

With an audible gulp, the great winged beast finished gorging himself upon the slain foe, and the pawn reappeared as an Eliade infantryman for Sylette to place upon the center field. "Captured pawn to d13."

"Was that the right move ta make? I wonder . . . "

"You wouldn't tell me, one way or the other."

"Of course not!" Valescar's stubble-edged face, with one eye permanently sealed behind a metal patch, nodded solemnly. That injury was his greatest secret. Despite Sylette's incessant pestering, he stalwartly refused to divulge the story to her. "Indeed, there's no teacher quite like experience."

"Then would you mind not questioning my moves?"

"Sure thing, Missy, sure thing."

However, both her comment and his response were but another part of their jovial back and forth. Valescar would no more stop poking fun at her play than Sylette would stop ribbing him for his poor jokes and odd tutelage. And, though she'd never admit it to the man, she cherished their time together, quirkiness and all.

On the right, her Hues continued to hold against the rittermarschal's advancing hives of Trillith, while her Eliade army in the center, buoyed by her recent reinforcement, pressed against the grey army. Sylette sent one of her bishops flying diagonally across the board, and with a slash of his radiant polearm, he bisected one of the neutral knight pieces.

The response of the previously still force was instantaneous. Before she could withdraw her overextended soldier, an opposing bishop shot forth from the now-exposed inner row to gut the handsome, glowing being on the tip of his lance. Instead of reforming elsewhere, like the tokens from the side boards, the dying man merely dissolved into ash that, in turn, fully disappeared. However, the piece was not entirely lost. When a new game started, he would magically reappear as though nothing had happened.

"Ah, I forgot ta tell ye that the grey army takes turns *in between* ours on the center field. Sorry, that one's on me."

"Your reminder is about a minute late, Uncle Valescar." Sylette narrowed her eyes as she pulled out the endearing title that he, and her parents, seemed to dislike. Sure enough, the additive had the desired effect, and the officer stiffened. "Are there any other rules you conveniently forgot to mention?"

"Nay, lass, I think that's the last of them." Valescar's face returned to normal, swiftly expelling the dark cloud that had briefly lingered. It was a strange thing. Despite treating her like family, the man refused to acknowledge such a simple, affectionate label. *Is it the difference in our stations? Is it because we aren't related by blood? Or is it because he doesn't want to get too close?*

If nothing else, it was a convenient way to push his buttons when she needed to. And perhaps that was all it amounted to—an annoying tick to distract the greatest military mind in the nation. But Sylette would contemplate that more later; of immediate import was the slow but steady failure of her strategy for victory.

Her greatest sin had been underestimating the size of the middle board and the tenacity of the neutral Terran army. While the side boards were of the usual eight by eight variety, the center field was twice as long at sixteen by eight. This left enough room for an entire extra force to further complicate an already difficult game.

Sylette's goal had been to play aggressively on the flanks to quickly grab pieces for a blitz down the center. After all, winning once was certainly easier than winning twice. However, since Valescar refused to engage the grey army from his side, she was bearing the full brunt of their fury. As piece after piece fell to her marching Eliade troopers, it was obvious that her attrition-style tactics would soon create a breakthrough.

But will I make it in time?

No, no she would not.

"Checkmate . . . and checkmate. I believe that makes this my win, right, Missy?"

The princess's jaw dropped in shock. Sylette had known she was in a tough position, that she was gradually losing the game, but to be defeated on *both* side boards in the same turn was beyond surprising. However, a quick glance confirmed that neither of her kings could escape. It was over.

"What? How? You haven't moved at all in the center, while my Eliade have defeated the grey army and are knocking on your door. How could I have lost the sides if I have more pieces in the middle?"

"Do ye have more? I wonder . . . " Valescar leaned back in his seat, exposing his more casual military fatigues. Absent was the full plate he normally wore, replaced by an off-center buttoned tunic with a high collar affixed with the diamond-shaped badges of his rank.

She set to counting immediately. Even knowing what the conclusion would be, her spirits sank when she finished, "You have ten more than I do."

"And how did I make ye think I had less?"

"You clustered them at the back of your side, barely moving them when your turn came to create the illusion that you had less control than you did." It was a simple trick, one Sylette would have noticed if she'd paid even slightly more attention to Valescar's moves. *I focused so much on my own strategy that I failed to consider his,* she realized.

"Exactly." Valescar beamed an approving smile at her correct deduction. Despite having lost the game, his praise made a joyful consolation prize. "Seven-sided chess ain't like ordinary chess, where there's one victory condition and multiple ways ta fulfill it. Instead, there's many ways ta win and tons of ways ta go about it. So, what's the simplest way ta play? Determine what your enemy is doin' and undermine them! Ye wanted the center board, so I gave it ta ye and focused on winnin' the side boards. And since I didn't make an enemy of the grey army, I didn't have ta move a muscle there ta stay in the game. Fight smart, Sylette, not hard, and remember—"

"The enemy always gets a say," she finished for him with a wink and a smirk.

"Just so, Missy, just so."

Despite losing, Sylette felt content. She had learned how to play the most advanced strategy game in the world, and her thrashing would make her not only a better chess practitioner, but a better leader as well. Valescar always framed his lessons as being related to contests they fought, books they read, or topics they studied. But the truth was that they were just as applicable to real life as the pastimes from which they originated.

The warm glow of new knowledge was shattered by a loud commotion in the hall outside. Valescar immediately turned toward the sound, rising from his chair, crimson cloak of office unfolding behind him as he reached for the sword on his left hip. It was the right response. The study in which they were playing was deep within the palace, accessible only by the royal family, their guests, and servants. No one without authorization should be able to reach this place, and there certainly shouldn't be people yelling, screaming, or rushing about, especially this late in the evening.

Something was wrong.

Quick as a mouse, Sylette jumped from her seat, raced around the table, and clutched the back of Valescar's cape. The top of her head barely reached his waist. At the tugging of her tiny hands, the rittermarschal glanced down with a comforting grin.

"Everything will be alright, little Missy. I'll protect ye."

Those words were almost enough to put her at ease before the double doors in front of them burst open, bouncing roughly off the ornate bookshelves to either side. Sylette's heart nearly beat out of her chest before she recognized the intruders.

"Instructor Boyle, Colonel Stetson, what brings ye and yer men here?" Valescar asked the men at the door, not yet deigning to remove his hand from the hilt of his blade. Sylette wondered why he might still be suspicious of them but didn't speak out herself. It wasn't a princess's role to intervene in matters like this.

The two men and the squad of rifle-armed soldiers with them were outlined as murky, dark shapes by the fading orange light from the courtyard windows at their backs. Then, as the electric lights in both the study and the hall came on together, their features resolved back to normal proportions. Even so, the expansive girth of Boyle, Sylette's overseer and tutor, and the cadaverous slimness of Stetson, the head of the royal guard, were anything but standard.

Not being a military man, the large teacher caught one glimpse of Valescar's tense stance and nearly fell over as he tried to hide behind the colonel. "Put that thing away, Valescar! It's an emergency!"

"Don't be a fool, Boyle. He hasn't even drawn his sword. And regardless of the circumstances, respectfully refer to him as rittermarschal." In the corridor beyond, another team of soldiers went rushing past, the mages in tow hoisting a medical gurney between them. Whatever was going on had the entire complex in a hubbub and seemed to involve someone, or someones, being injured.

Valescar appeared to reach the same conclusion that Sylette did, for he let go of his weapon and stalked toward Stetson and his guards. They immediately came to attention before being waved off by the rittermarschal. "Enough o' that. Ye said there was an emergency. What happened?"

Boyle opened his mouth to speak but was cut off by Stetson. Sylette stifled a giggle at her strict, stuffy tutor being put in his place. "His Majesty requires your presence, sir. Immediately. I'm not at liberty to say anything else at this time." He glanced quickly in Sylette's direction, but when he noticed the princess's return gaze, emitted a harsh cough. Stetson was known to be sickly, so she couldn't say whether the diversion was real or fake.

"Very well, lead on."

Saluting again, Stetson turned on his heel and led the squad of soldiers, dressed in light mail and royal colors, back through the door. Valescar followed closely, his large frame taking one step for every hurried two of theirs.

The door shut behind them, but not fast enough to block out the high-pitched shriek, litany of curses, and clank of chains that floated down the passageway from the left. Sylette couldn't make sense of the noises; they were simultaneously familiar and chilling.

She looked at Boyle, who was nervously biting his fingers at the sounds as he glanced back and forth between her and the door. "Instructor, just what is going on?" Her voice startled him, and he flinched backwards, his hands raised in a defensive posture. It took a full moment for him to regain his composure.

"Absolutely nothing, Princess Sylette. You needn't be so apprehensive."

"You're the one who looks scared, though."

"What have I told you about backtalk?" Her kindness erased Boyle's fear as his jowls flapped with indignation, and his usual, grating personality returned. "Do not presume to know what your elders are feeling. Remember that well, or next time, you'll be writing lines again!"

"Yes, Instructor." Though Sylette was confident she already knew as much, or more, than the rotund intellectual, Boyle had been installed in his position by her father. As a result, he was an immutable existence from which she could not escape. *But my father must have made him my teacher for a reason. I have to learn what I can from him, as he wants me to.*

Evidently reassured of his control of the situation, Boyle brushed aside the remaining chess pieces and pulled a large, leather-bound tome from inside the sizeable folds of his luxurious robe. "Then enough of these silly games. Tonight, you will be reading chapters one through twenty of wise Emperor Quintaris II's discourse on the anatomical differences between the aristocracy and laypeople of each race. Quite a refreshing read, one that might make you realize why you should act less like a rebel and more like a princess."

He set the book on the table and gestured expectantly at the seat in front of it. Without a word, Sylette climbed the cushions until she could open the book. As she surveyed her lengthy assignment, Boyle continued to disseminate at her back. "I swear, being around that commoner soldier has made you more and more . . . "

Sylette tuned him out, preferring to focus on the abysmally boring book before her than his ceaseless, self-important droning. The first page of useless information was quickly finished, and she turned to the second.

One page down, twenty chapters to go. Oh joy, oh joy, oh joy.

———◈———

"So, it looks like you're the one who got stuck with Ol' Fatty."

Sylette glanced up to see the grinning face of her eldest brother, Vasuron, staring back at her. He was completely inverted with his long legs hooked about one of the larger boughs of the oak the princess was leaning against. How he got there—as with most things the eccentric youth did—was a mystery.

"You mean Instructor Boyle? Why do you care?" The moniker was such a perfect fit that she didn't struggle in the slightest to make the connection. At the moment, the overseer in question was across the palace garden on the patio, attended by two maidservants and the princess's assigned guard. They were ostensibly here to watch Sylette during a short, *scheduled* break from her studies, but given their loud conversation and alcohol consumption—a near-empty pitcher of wine sat on a serving trolley nearby—they had all but forgotten their intended duty.

For her part, Sylette held little desire to engage with Vasuron. Of their siblings, the fifteen-year-old was by far the most immature and manipulative. It was a poor combination of traits in a brother. But even more than that, in her opinion, it was a *horrendous* combination of traits for a future leader. *And unless something untoward happens, he'll be the next emperor.*

Beyond that, though, she really just wanted to be left to spend her free time in peace. It wasn't like Sylette never got to be alone, but since the previous evening, the entire compound had been on edge. Security seemed to have doubled. Self-absorbed Boyle was watching her like a hawk—until he'd lost focus, at least. No one she talked to had heard anything from her father.

And strangest of all, her mother, Lanara, third consort to the emperor, was missing.

Or perhaps not missing. It was entirely possible that she had received a summons to spend the night with His Majesty. *Normally she would tell me where she was going, though.* Despite Sylette having maids and tutors to help raise and take care of her needs, Lanara tried her best to be there for her like any kind mother might. Instead of being tucked in by servants, the princess's mother would sit by her bed and recite stories, poems, or songs until she drifted off to sleep. Whenever Sylette hurt herself during martial arts or magic training, Lanara would come running, kneeling down to clean the wound and reciting a nonsensical spell of love to make everything better.

In their world, a realm of royal politics and familial intrigue, it was the closest thing to a normal mother-daughter relationship imaginable.

As Sylette pondered these troubling thoughts and clutched her pet crysahund, Tyxt, whose soft crystalline fur she'd been grooming, closer, Vasuron released his legs and backflipped down onto the manicured grass beside her. The execution of the technique was nigh perfect, and the first prince raised his arms in a victory pose. Sylette didn't deign to acknowledge the performance with so much as a clap.

"You could at least *pretend* to be impressed," Vasuron chided her with what was surely a faked air of dejection. "And, no, I couldn't care less, to tell the truth. But since I fired him as my teacher, it would appear that the refuse has run downhill . . . to you. My apologies, dearest sister."

"Do you ever get tired of lying?" Sensing Sylette's growing agitation, her crysahund, possessing the same protective instincts as its canine cousins, bared gleaming diamond fangs at Vasuron and snarled. "You aren't the least bit sorry."

"Fair point. But I figured someone should feign sympathy at the litany of misfortunes being heaped upon your head."

"What do you mean?" She massaged the animal's temples, calming Tyxt and prompting him to growl contentedly. Then Sylette released him so that one of them could enjoy the early afternoon tranquility while she dealt with Vasuron. His attention drawn by a family of geese parading toward a nearby pond, Tyxt dashed away at full speed.

"You mean you haven't heard?" Her brother's dark eyes widened in feigned surprise, and as if to add to the already extreme melodrama, the prince spun about the tree trunk. Sylette scooted in the opposite direction to maintain the distance between them.

"No, Vasu, I haven't." She purposely used the shortened nickname that he hated, and his brow twitched ever so slightly in response. *At least some small part of him is honest.* "Care to enlighten me?"

Vasuron ignored her for a moment, likely as some minor retribution for referring to him improperly. Instead, as a dark cloud materialized in the otherwise sunny sky above, he followed its shadow across the courtyard, dodging shrubs, flowerbeds, and statues as it weaved back and forth. Ultimately it came to the pond where Tyxt was stalking the geese, and Sylette thought for sure her brother would have to give up on it. But with the grace of a professional acrobat, Vasuron danced from exposed stone to stone until he reached the other side.

There he plucked a single fresh rose from a bush vibrantly bursting with scores of the pink blossoms. Sylette frequented this garden, hidden like a gem at the center of the palace, and of all the stunning vistas it offered, that stand of eglantines was her favorite. Set against the glistening waters of the lily-topped pool in the foreground, it was a scene unlike any other.

Dearer to her than transient beauty, however, were the memories of times spent here with her mother, year after year. *I wonder if she knows it's in bloom yet?* Spring was only just beginning, and soon the entire yard—not just the roses— would be flush with new life for them to marvel at.

As though aware of her thoughts, Vasuron returned the way he'd come, long-stemmed eglantine in hand, and presented it to the princess with a grand bow. "The first rose of spring for my lady."

The gesture was completely unlike the selfish youth. "Why? Are you trying to avoid my question?"

"The thought hadn't crossed my mind. In fact, I thought it appropriate that I present you with this, given that both you and the third consort cherish them." He used Lanara's official title, as if attempting to demean the woman in front of her own daughter. Sylette took the veiled insult in stride and reached for the flower. When her fingers touched the stem, Vasuron smirked—a wide, gleaming grin—and added, almost as an afterthought, "One should always bring a girl flowers when bearing bad news."

With a twist of her wrist, Sylette batted the rose away, knocking it to the ground where its petals came apart like shattering glass. A pinprick of blood welled on her skin from a thorn-inflicted scratch. That was secondary, though, compared to the clarity Vasuron's malicious comments gave her. "Where is my mother? What have they done to her?"

"The third consort is fine . . . for now. Though you might start thinking about looking for a new caregiver. I know! Maybe my mother could take you—"

Swift as a viper, her still-outstretched arm lashed at the prince's smug face.

His reflexes, however, were equally fast. Vasuron's fist caught Sylette's as it approached and clenched down tightly, causing the princess to cringe with pain as he bent it backwards. Red droplets from her open wound flew across the distance to dot his cheek, though the prince hardly seemed to notice. "Is that any way to repay my kindness? I'm being very generous, you know."

He pinched down harder, and Sylette's knees buckled as her body automatically tried to escape by flowing with the pressure. Concurrently, her mind reflected on his words. What he said *wasn't* wrong. In the Sarconian royal family, his offer, if genuine, was magnanimous.

To create generation after generation of strong leaders, the system had to be designed to produce the best genes possible. As a result, the emperor took as many mates as he desired and lay with them as many times as he wanted. If the offspring was adequate, the woman who bore it became the closest thing to his wife possible, a consort, and was kept close at hand for both whim and necessity. Love and feelings were not considered; ensuring the brightest future for the empire was paramount.

While they'd want for nothing if the union was successful, a consort could still be discarded at any time and for any reason. And if such a fall from grace occurred, their children would likely follow them, being the offshoot of a shamed parent. *And this is especially true of girls, who are not valuable successors like males.*

If Lanara had indeed incurred His Majesty's displeasure, Vasuron's own mother adopting her was no less than a rope of salvation dangling over a wide abyss.

Suddenly, as though on another of his impulses, the prince released her hand and stepped back, not a shred of anger or displeasure left on his countenance. His force removed, Sylette stumbled forward before catching her balance. She clutched her still-aching wrist while glaring daggers at her sadistic brother.

"You really don't have a gracious bone in your body, do you?" He clicked his tongue in disapproval. "Pity you weren't born a boy, with all that fire and venom. It would have been fun competing with you."

"I don't believe you."

"Come again?"

"I don't believe you. You always lie. You always play games. That's all this is." Sylette denied the situation with all her being. *It isn't true. Vasuron can't be trusted.* She needed to convince herself he was wrong. The alternative, even if the proof was eventually forced upon her, was . . .

"Hmm, I can't have my little sister think that . . . What should I do?" He paused for a moment before his eyes lit up with inspiration. "Why don't we go see for ourselves?"

"See what?"

"The trial, of course! They're making a big show of it and everything! Apparently she did something pretty terrible to warrant all the attention."

Her heart sank. Her fists clenched of their own accord, and the increased pressure caused a slim red trickle to continue flowing from the open cut on her knuckle. *It's a lie. A well-woven tale—perfectly logical but a lie nonetheless.* Even so, a voice behind all the others softly whispered, *What if it isn't? What will you do then?*

If against all odds it was true, then Sylette would have to do everything in her power to stop it, to free her mother. Unfortunately, her determination far eclipsed her capabilities. Thus, the rational thing to do was enlist assistance.

"Vasuron, please take me to the trial. And, if the worst should happen, please, I'm begging you, help me save Lanara. With the influence you have, you might be able to."

"That's an awful lot to ask. After all, it's likely that will entail going against father."

Sylette dropped to her tiny knees and bowed before him, hoping to appeal to her brother's ego. It was a pitiful sight, completely unbecoming of a royal, but it was the princess's only chance. "Please. I'll never poke fun at you again. I'll do whatever you ask of me. I'll treat you like the emperor himself. Just please, please protect my mother."

The prince sighed, looked up at the sky, then back at her. "Fine, fine. Now get up. The trial starts soon, so we haven't got all day. First, we have to get past your hanger-ons," Vasuron indicated Boyle and the guards, still caught up in merrymaking on the other side of the garden. "It may mean getting your dress dirty. Ready for a climb?"

Back on her feet, Sylette had already started wiping the grass and soil from her clothes when her brother finished speaking. "What do you mean?" she asked for the second time that day.

He grinned and pointed up, past the tree, to where a balcony could just be glimpsed astride its uppermost branches. "What comes down, without first going up, needs have come from somewhere. You first, dear sister."

⸺◈⸺

The Sarconian Senate chamber was filled to bursting. It went without saying that the senators were there, but in addition to them and the usual military elite, everyone who was anyone was packed together until hardly any standing room was left. Every minister, governor, officer, or well-connected noble in the capital seemed to have come to the trial of Lanara, third consort to the emperor.

"No one can look away from a burning wreck," Vasuron whispered in her ear as Sylette looked on in morbid horror. Through the small gap in the lavender curtains shielding their hiding place, she could see most of the expansive space, including the currently empty dais and throne. What disturbed her more than anything else she saw was how right her brother was. Almost all the people gathered were contentedly chatting to one another, using an event that might destroy her mother's life as another opportunity for making deals and connections.

She also marveled at how easy it had been to steal away here, behind the bulky drapes separating a side passageway from the head of the chamber. If she made the journey alone, Sylette would surely have been stopped and turned away. But with the first prince at her side, she'd received no more than a few curious glances. No matter who they were, all who came into contact with Vasuron knew who he was and assumed whatever he was doing was fine. *Or, more appropriately,* she thought, *that he can do no wrong.*

In their minds, if her brother was walking astride the daughter of a woman about to be condemned—for some offense or another—he obviously possessed a good reason for it.

However, once they reached the Senate building, he had wisely suggested that they remain out of sight. Since intruding upon a government session overseen by the emperor himself was something even Vasuron wouldn't come away unscathed from, it made sense to conceal their presence until absolutely necessary. And so they'd found a place as near to the seat of power as they possibly could without being detected.

Sylette was about to reply with a sarcastic remark about how unnecessary his comment was when an aged man in long, black robes walked up to the lectern situated left of the main dais. "Order! Order, I say!" His grating voice and simultaneous gavel banging quieted the legions of murmuring voices and brought all eyes to the fore. "This ninety-seventh emergency session of the Sarconian Senate for the purpose of trying Third Consort Lanara Martavis for high crimes against the state is now convened. May the accused and her accuser please step forward."

Everything Vasuron said was true. *High crimes against the state? What has my mother done?*

Barely had that thought crossed her mind than doors at opposite ends of the chamber opened in unison. From the nearer door behind the podium, dressed immaculately in a golden tunic and crimson robe, silver crown atop his head, emerged their father, Emperor Sychon Artorios. At first glance, he appeared normal, but on closer inspection, his skin was far too pale, and he moved with an uncharacteristic limp, even when supported by two attendants. As they gingerly helped His Majesty onto the throne, it became evident that an extra sash had been wrapped about his waist, perhaps to hide the cause of his obvious ailments.

And from the grand door at the front of the hall, bathed in the rays of late afternoon sun slanting through the lofty windows above, her mother was led forth. *Led* was indeed the correct term. Clad in naught but a simple, tan prison shift, her long, brown hair matted by both filth and blood, and with heavy manacles threatening to drag her to the ground below, Lanara was being pulled down the central aisle by a long, iron chain.

As if that wasn't enough to shatter Sylette's spirits, at the other end of the chain was none other than Rittermarschal Valescar. He acted like Lanara surely felt; his one good eye stared at the floor below, his steps were slow and leaden, and he jerked at the leash as if entirely unaware of what he was doing.

What's going on? Why is Valescar leading her? Why did they treat her so cruelly? Tears forced their way from Sylette's eyes, and against all good sense, she tried to break from their cover and rush out. She would figure out what was really happening, make the rittermarschal see sense, and snap her mother's hands free of their bonds. Somehow it would all work out.

Vasuron grabbed the princess's shoulder and roughly whipped her back. "Are you crazy? What will going out there now accomplish?" His insistent hissing, still quiet enough not to be heard beyond their alcove, snapped her back to reality.

"But—"

"No *buts*. Just watch and see what happens. Besides, the moment isn't right yet."

Sylette wondered just what he meant by that, but did her best to hold her passion in check—for now. *By Sarcon, they've been torturing her.* Her mouth went dry, and a sob caught in her throat. What act could possibly be deserving of such abuse?

When Lanara stumbled closer, the harsh treatment she'd suffered became increasingly apparent. Her left eye was blackened and crusted shut with dried ichor. Superheated brands had been applied to the skin of her face and neck. Gaping sores and gleaming whip marks stood out in contrast to the remnants of sackcloth on her shoulders and back. It was a miracle she could stand.

In that instant, Sylette understood the events of the day before. Valescar had been called away to take charge of Lanara's imprisonment. The clanking chains and screeching resulted from the guards dragging her away to the dungeons. And the medical gurney must have been for the emperor, who now bore a fresh injury.

The epiphany drove the princess to the stone floor, where she steadied herself with one hand as she leaned against the wall. Sylette's thoughts became a jumbled mess; logic warred with emotion as both struggled to make sense of the situation. Behind her, Vasuron said nothing nor made any move to help.

Then the jeering began.

"Foolish wench. How dare ye bite the hand that feeds ya!"

"The empire gives you everything, and this is how you act?"

"How could you? Do you want Rabban to win? Are you a spy?"

"Treason! Treason! Treason!"

They kept coming, voices rising, blending, seeking to overcome each other in an ever-rising cacophony of hatred. It was impossible to tell who was sincere and who wasn't. Every new insult seemed to egg the others on to greater heights of crass contempt.

"Death's too good for a whore like her!"

Sylette tried to tune the clamor out. She covered her ears, started humming to herself, even beat her head against the nearby bricks. None of it worked.

Only Vasuron's honeyed breath was louder. "Do you know why they do it? All of them are oh so glad it's her and not them. And the more insistent their cries, the more they dissociate from the thought that they could ever be in her shoes one day. Isn't our system lovely?"

It was the stinging, rhythmic whumping of the gavel that saved Sylette from contemplating her brother's statement. The banging continued until the masses quieted enough for the old speaker to be heard, at which point he continued to shout them down. "Order! We will have order in the court! Silence in the presence of His Majesty!"

Invoking the authority of the man behind him finally stilled the crowd. With the cessation of their vile calls, Sylette found the strength to stand back up, only to nearly crumple over once more at the sight.

There, at the foot of the dais, barely ten meters from the emperor, was her mother, on her knees and covered from head to foot in rotten filth and assorted detritus. Her detractors had not just cast barbed words at her but also the remnants of whatever food and garbage they carried with them. It was a pitiful sight—a thin, once beautiful woman of middle age, beaten, crushed, and ruined beyond all recognition, her neck pressed to the floor between the spearbutts of two soldiers she hadn't a hope in Oblivion of escaping from.

Why?

That was the single question Sylette's brain remained capable of processing, and it repeated over and over again in the depths of her sorrow-addled mind.

The response, as though taunting her, came immediately. "The third consort stands accused of treason, of conspiracy to overthrow the emperor, and, most heinously, of attempted regicide. Does her accuser agree with these charges?"

Gears turned; Sylette's thoughts started again, ever so slowly. *My mother tried to kill Father? Is that where his wound came from? Why?* She'd never shown any indication of being hostile toward the emperor. She'd never shared any cause for anger or resentment with her daughter. *Why?* The question refused to go away, despite having already been answered once.

Without looking up, Valescar intoned a simple, "Yes."

Why is Valescar the accuser? I thought he liked mother? I thought he cared for me? Why would he do this?

"Does His Majesty accept the charges as leveled?"

A weak nod—and what may have been a vengeful sneer—came from the man on the throne.

"Then this case of Emperor Sychon Artorios versus the third consort, Lanara Martavis, is hereby in session. Consort Martavis, do you have any words to offer in your defense?"

Sylette waited for an explanation, a reason, anything to help her understand how this impossible event occurred. There had to be an excuse, a misunderstanding, a mistake. *Please, Mother . . . please. I can't lose you . . .*

When a reply failed to come, she worried for Lanara's sanity, that she may have broken under the torture and torment. Then she saw the gag, the rage-filled eyes, and the tears streaming down her mother's face as she struggled almost imperceptibly within her bounds.

They had no intention of letting her speak. This was not a trial, but the start of an execution.

"It seems that Consort Martavis has correctly decided to accept her wicked crimes with silence. In which case do you, Rittermarschal Valescar, her accuser, have anything to add either for or against her?"

"No, Speaker."

"Then, having found Consort Martavis guilty on all counts, we ask that Emperor Artorios deliver fitting judgment upon her using the wisdom conferred to him by his forefathers and . . . "

This was wrong . . . entirely, completely wrong. Lanara was not being afforded an opportunity to object. There was no discussion of either motive or even the crime itself. And Valescar, supposedly Sylette's mentor and friend to both her and her mother, was the one leveling the charges.

She turned to Vasuron to ask him to step out and try to slow or halt the proceedings until a *proper* hearing could be held. In the middle of her maneuver, with Vasuron's jet black-hair and expanding smirk just coming into view, Sylette felt a sharp push against her side and midriff. As she stumbled backwards, confusion turned to understanding, granting the princess just enough time to express her disbelief aloud.

"Why?"

"Because *this* is the right moment, and *this* will be far, far more interesting than whatever *you* had planned."

The curtain parted behind her, then closed again across Vasuron's shadowed features and malicious, glinting eyes. Sylette rolled, once, twice, and then came to a stop face down on the white marble of the podium.

When she finally raised her head and stood, the chamber was hushed, with every eye staring at her in perplexed astonishment. Lanara and Valescar gazed at her with frozen terror. The speaker looked as though something unholy had stolen into his sacred assembly. Everyone else appeared simply bemused at her unexplained and sudden materialization.

Valescar broke the stillness with a cry like a wounded animal. "Why? Why are ye here, Princess Sylette? Yer not supposed ta be here!"

At that instant, on top of the pain she'd endured watching her mother's suffering, the realization that Valescar was truly a part of this debacle—to the point of trying to keep her in the dark about it—destroyed any sense of tact or reserve Sylette yet maintained.

"Why am I here? I'm here because you all tried to hide this from me! You attempted to convict and pass judgment on my mother without even letting her daughter know! And you did so without letting her talk, torturing her half to death beforehand—and with no presentation of evidence or testimony whatsoever! You call this a trial? This is a farce!"

The stunned silence continued for another minute, as no one quite knew how to respond to such an outburst from a ten-year-old girl who also happened to be their princess. Sylette, breath ragged from screaming at the top of her lungs, glanced over at her mother with a hopeful smile. But all she received in return were pleading eyes full of tears that kept darting between her, Valescar, and the emperor.

It was the latter who, despite his condition, clapped and laughed as he struggled to his feet. "Brave words, Sylette, brave words. You're certainly my child to be able to boldly condemn me and my court of our hypocrisy to our faces. So, I'll tell you what your mother did, and then we'll ask these gathered dignitaries what should be done about her crimes."

For the briefest of seconds, Sylette thought that she might succeed and that Lanara might actually get a fair inquiry from which she might be acquitted. Then the mighty voice of Sychon, her father, began extolling her sins with all the empathy of a headsman.

"The third consort, Lanara, your mother, attempted to kill me without warning by stabbing me in the stomach with a dagger. When the initial blow failed to finish me off, she drew a second blade and aimed for my heart to finish the job. Bleeding from my first wound, I managed to fend off the wench and call for my guards, who restrained her. This woman, regardless of her sanity or motivations, has clearly committed treason, for which the consequence is clear. So what say you, Senate? What should her punishment be?"

Their response was singular and overwhelming.

"Execute her! Execute her! Execute her!"

Sychon cut them off with a wave of one hand, then half grimaced, half grinned at Lanara and Valescar on the floor below. An unspoken exchange passed between them, after which his eyes locked with Sylette's. "And what of Princess Sylette, her daughter? She is the progeny of a traitor and has shown complete disrespect for decorum by interrupting a session of the Senate that she had no business being at. Furthermore, she has called into question both *my* authority and the power of this institution. Such acts border on treason themselves. What shall we do with her?"

Sylette finally understood her predicament, her mother's pitiable glances, and what game Vasuron had been playing from the beginning. Lanara had done the unthinkable but still tried to protect her child from the backlash. Meanwhile, her brother, desiring to get the utmost sick enjoyment out of the situation, had thrown the princess to the dragwyrms along with the consort.

"The glicka fruit doesn't fall far from the tree," a rotund man with admiral rank insignias called, slamming a meaty fist onto the desk in front of him. "They're both guilty!"

"Kill them! Purge the disease in our midst!" cried a short, bald minister across the center walkway.

Another, a token female senator in an elegantly flowing dress, bellowed from the eaves, "Neither has any value to the empire! Banishment is the least this calls for!"

How did such a body make the decisions that ran the nation? How did anything good come from the frenzied mob mentality by which they were so clearly driven? In Sylette's gut, disbelief turned to resentment, resentment became anger, and anger slowly morphed to hatred. *They're rotten, all of them:*

*this institution, the entire empire, my father, my brother, everything. It all . . . needs
. . . to burn.*

Silence descended with another gesture from the emperor. "Then their
punishment is decided. Execution for the third consort." He then paused, taking
a breath, drawing out the suspense with the same cruelty so evident in his eldest
son. "And banishment for the third princess. Both will be carried out tomorr—"

For her age, Sylette had an incredibly advanced grasp of the theory and
execution of the magical arts. However, the size of her men'ar network, determined
both by natural proficiency and the gradual development of the necessary blood
vessels to carry the energy, was below average. As a result, she currently couldn't
conjure more than two daggers at her best and most focused.

But right now, one was all she needed. *I'll figure out the rest afterwards.*

As the emperor spoke, staring past her at the masses on the marble rows to
either side, Sylette forced her spirit energy into the air and bid it form into as
many sharp, floating daggers as possible. The first manifested, then the second
took shape before fizzling back out of existence. *Good enough. Now to finish what
my mother started.*

She adjusted the trajectory slightly and sent it soaring at the emperor just as
shouts of surprise at its sudden appearance rippled through the crowd. *Too late,
you imbeciles.* Elation surged through the princess's mind, only to be replaced
with bitter disappointment as it was snatched from the air by a metal cable.

Sylette turned her rage-filled eyes on Valescar. "Why? Why defend him?"

While her heart was filled with fury and wrath, the rittermarschal's appeared
to hold nothing but sorrow and regret. Tears streamed openly from his eyes; his
cheeks were red from weeping. "For the good o' the empire."

Then Valescar's second cable, having snaked along the floor outside her
line of sight, gripped Sylette about her waist, raised her slight frame aloft, and
slammed it into unconsciousness against the hard floor.

<hr />

When the suffocating dark cowl was ripped from her head, Sylette was nearly
blinded by the intense, unfiltered sunlight coming from directly above. She tried
to avert her eyes, only to scuff the side of her face against the coarse wood of the

stocks about her neck. There was no give in the hand restraints either; moving any part of her body, even the feet, would only serve to further chaff her exposed skin.

Those attenuated movements were apparently all the excuse the vicious gaoler needed, for he swiftly rapped the shamed princess across her calves with a nail-studded pole. Sylette howled in pain and instinctively tried to arch away—to no avail in her solid binds. The biting metal ripped new sores on already brutalized flesh; the rivulets of blood dripping down her legs were evidence enough without being able to turn and see.

Black masked, with belt upon belt of torture implements strapped to his person, her keeper moved into Sylette's tear-lined vision. One stunted leg, defect or battle injury, dragged behind him. "There's no escape, girlie. You just stay put and wait for the main event."

She wanted to spit at him, to throw curse after curse at his disfigured wretchedness, but held the growing venom in check. A night in a dank cell with no food or water, after being beaten, stripped of all her possessions, and thrust into a threadbare tan smock, was enough to make even the most rebellious prisoner reflective. However, for one as intelligent as Sylette, her silence had another purpose.

Banishment. To most it was a death sentence—losing everything and being cast out into the world to perish, alone and unloved. In just a few short minutes, all this exile cherished would be gone. *Everything . . . except the hatred pulsing in my breast.*

Yes, Sylette now had a new purpose for living, and death could not claim her until she succeeded. With eyes now accustomed to the glare of the beautiful spring day—so laughably ironic given the execution about to take place—she gazed about her surroundings. The houses were mostly of old architecture, dilapidated here and there but still standing. Smoke rose from a thousand chimneys as one thick mass. Old cobble streets in every direction ran thick with traffic: animals, their handlers, and the refuse of both. The great technology of the empire's upper levels, so evident near the heart of the great city of Sarconia, was almost totally absent.

Perhaps I'll leave these people be when the time comes, thought Sylette, even as a grimy crowd gathered about the raised platform. These wretches, scorned by the rich and powerful above them, didn't share their crimes. Surely they would understand just how foolish the travesty taking place here was.

Then a boy in patchwork clothes, scarcely five or six years of age, chucked a rotten apfel at her using all the might contained in both his hands. It landed a meter short, breaking into rolling chunks that traveled a short ways before stopping. Sylette stared at the child in disbelief as the shabbily dressed woman next to him—likely his mother—handed him another piece of spoiled fruit. In her other hand rested a newborn wrapped in swaddling blankets.

The first shot fired, the massed peasants began slinging anything on hand toward the stage with reckless abandon. Vegetables, fruit, stones, parts of wagons and furniture, even feces came flying up at her. A piece of rock clipped Sylette's forehead, leaving a jagged slash. A potato with a bite missing hit her nose; blood began dripping from it almost instantly. Even the gaoler was not unaffected as several flung objects splattered against his outstretched arms and body.

"Stop, you idiots! We haven't even read the charges! And the woman to be executed hasn't been brought out yet!"

"Who cares?" shouted a fat woman with a stained baker's bonnet and apron on. "We know they're guilty as sin. Plus, the longer you drag this out the longer my storefront's blocked!"

A wrinkled old man, bent over a cane and with an outdated Sarconian army tricorn on his head, grumbled, "If yer executin' 'em down here, they're obviously spies and traitors. We know the drill; get on wit' it!"

"Get rid of the traitors!"

"For Sarconia!"

"My cart can't get through! Hurry the blasted thing along!"

"Glory to the empire!"

On and on the hail of diatribes and detritus came. A pile of ek droppings creamed Sylette's left ear, making her deaf on that side until it slipped off. Her face and body dripped with the pungent, burning juices of a dozen types of overripe produce. Every additional impact was further agony.

Naive. I'm so naive. As with her father, as with Vasuron, and even with Valescar, her trust had betrayed her. Regardless of how they looked, regardless of how those in power viewed them, these people were still Sarconian citizens. They were part of the system—*proud* of it, in fact. Theirs was the *greatest* nation in the world; so long as they got the merest scraps from the table above, they were content. Every passing moment was a new lesson for Sylette, and her tally of future targets only continued to expand.

"Back! Back, I say!" By the time the gaoler sent a squad of soldiers to drive back the throngs and establish a perimeter about the stand, the entire structure was slick with unidentifiable mush. Even this section of the outer Humbrad wall, against which the platform was constructed, was completely coated in goo. On top of that, when the guards took their sword-butts to a couple of unruly onlookers, a riot nearly broke out. Only the discharging of several rifles above the agitated crowd managed to diffuse the situation.

It would have been comical, if only the fervor of the masses hadn't brought the dreaded conclusion even faster than expected.

Sylette heard the soft, recognizable patter of her mother's feet before she saw her. Accompanied by the ghastly rattling of rusted chains, she was led behind the former princess and over to a scarlet-stained block directly in front of her. There the gaoler kicked Lanara's legs out from under her, causing her to crash to the wooden beams with a sickening crunch. The audience laughed with callous appreciation. Unable to bear the pain of watching, Sylette closed her eyes.

"This woman, of no name and no consequence, stands convicted of high treason and sedition against the Sarconian Empire. The punishment for such is death by beheading. Do you have any final words before the sentence is carried out?"

Evidently nothing about them was being revealed to the public, likely to prevent any unwanted questions about corruption—real or otherwise—within the imperial court and family. That mattered little to the two of them, though. Shortly, both would be beyond caring, one dead and the other bent on destroying this depraved establishment.

Lanara remained silent, and the ex-princess peeked once more. Despite it all, her mother was smiling brightly at Sylette, one good eye beaming and face full of concern. Her heart, deadened as the past day's events had made it, nearly revived and broke again. *Why? Why do you still look at me as though I'm the one in trouble? It's you they're going to kill, Mother . . .*

"Since the traitor has nothing to say, we shall begin the execution at once."

The gaoler struggled to bend down, but once on his knees, he strapped

Lanara's head and hands securely to the block. Her neck was aligned with a deep, worn line in the middle of the center groove. When he stood, his next words drove another stake through Sylette's heart. "Rittermarschal Valescar, you may carry out the punishment."

Slow, metal footfalls clanked past her, resolving into the back of a man she'd once loved. At the center of his large frame, on the cape he almost always wore, was the crest of the Sarconian Empire along with two crossed greatswords symbolic of the Ritter Order. It was an oddly appropriate image: two blades for Sylette and her mother, discarded by him for the sake of the empire, which reigned above all else.

He turned upon reaching Lanara, throwing back his cloak to reveal a large axe, which he hefted with both hands. Valescar hesitated for a moment, but since he was wearing a helmet, Sylette couldn't tell what he was thinking. Then he raised the weapon above his head.

Time slowed. The disgraced princess locked eyes with her mother: tarnished, tortured, yet still perfectly radiant. Lanara looked back with compassion and peace, emotions totally perplexing to Sylette given their state. Then tears burst forth from the older woman as she mouthed the words to her daughter's favorite song, one she'd sung a thousand times before:

> *My child, my child, how kindly thou must be,*
> *To grace the life of one undeserving such as me.*
> *I know not why my life has been so blessed,*
> *But know that, in my love, you always may find rest.*
> *My child, my child, your hands have healed my heart,*
> *And now we'll ever be together, even should we part.*
> *I know not why your smile heals my soul,*
> *But know that, because of you, I am now made who—*

The axe fell. The tune ceased. The crowd cheered.

Sylette screamed and raged against her shackles, mangling her wrists and ankles but not caring in the slightest.

After a few seconds, Lanara's head, freed from its body, fell into the bucket set before it. Her rich, brown hair, shorn by the fatal cut, was caught by a sudden gust and whisked away into the sky.

"Blast you, Valescar! I hope your fetid corpse rots in Oblivion! I'll put you there myself if I have to! You hear me you—"

As the unmoving metal effigy stared at her with what may have been pity, the gaoler's rod cracked the struggling Sylette brutally on the temple, causing her to descend into blissfully sweet darkness for the second time in twenty-four hours.

———⋖⋗⋄⋖⋗———

It would not require a significant exertion of force to throw a petite, ten-year-old girl through the air.

And yet it felt like the pair of guards put all the strength they could muster behind the toss. Sylette, her body worn, ragged, and emotionally drained, sailed several meters through the air before landing and rolling through the dust like a rag doll. She coughed blood, then wearily rose while clutching at a new scrape running the length of her left arm.

With these new injuries, on top of those she already possessed, it was a small miracle that Sylette could still move. Pain and hatred were the twin fuels keeping her going now. Agony indicated that she yet lived. And the second? Revenge was the only thing she had left to live for. The two were inextricably linked.

A pathetic haversack was cast at her feet by one of the guards. As it landed, something inside shattered, and the contents were quickly soaked. "Sorry about that. Looks like my hand slipped." One guard mocked an apology, after which both raucously chortled. To them, Sylette was just another peasant girl being cast out of the city for thievery.

She simply glowered in response, not even bothering to pick up the pathetic offering. Whatever was in there would barely sustain her for a day anyway. Despite being thoroughly robbed of everything but the tattered shift she wore, Sylette briefly considered using her remaining energy to summon daggers to kill the crude soldiers. However, such an act would see her dead in the ditch beside the road. *No, their time will come, along with the rest of this city.*

"What are you smilin' at? Go on. Get!" Apparently her pleasant thoughts had shown on her face, for the second man started waving his rifle at her threateningly. *Such brave souls, to feel threatened by a filthy little girl.*

Sylette took one last look around: at the tiny side gate they'd cast her from, at the towering inner wall—behind which rose majestic, opulent skyscrapers—and at the airships darting across the sky above. She saw in everything power, prestige, and grace. Then her mind set the mental image aflame. *Now it's perfect.*

An uncontrollable snigger escaped her lips at the thought, but before the guards could take further offense, she curtsied and turned away from the city. "I'm leaving," Sylette called jovially over her shoulder, "but I'll come back one day. I hope, when that time comes, you two will still be right here where I can find you."

When neither responded, the ex-princess looked at the dull horizon, breathed deeply, and took her first steps down the poorly kept highway. At that moment, she was struck by a sudden feeling of glee. It had nothing to do with leaving the city, setting out on an adventure, or just getting past the stench of the decrepit shantytown of war refugees outside its confines. Rather, Sylette's elation was born of something else entirely.

She was *free*.

Free of her father, free of her brother, free of responsibility, and free of all that tied her down, bad *or* good. Better still, those individuals expected her to perish. They figured casting a ten-year-old girl out into the world alone was a death sentence. How wrong they were! Sylette would take the escape they had given her and twist it into the noose from which to hang them.

With these thoughts in her head, she skipped down the path. Passersby shot her strange looks before continuing on their way. They had little time for what appeared to be a deranged child. Even those who would normally take advantage of a young girl paid her no heed—after all, she had nothing to steal.

It would be a hard journey. She'd have to start small, scavenging or stealing what she needed to live. But Sylette had her magic, a resource more important than any other. With that, her wits, and her training, she'd at least survive—perhaps thrive. Ultimately, when the time came to ignite the flames of her vengeance, the erstwhile princess even had her very name to sell.

Sylette would grow strong, obtain power, and then return to the place of her ignominy.

On that day, the empire will rue its greatest failure: letting me go free.

Chapter 19

Budding Hope

Hetrachia 11, 697 ABH
Etrus City, Sarconian Province of Darmatia

———◄═══◇═══►———

Midnight had come and gone. The fire in the hearth was long dead; only cinders remained. Martan, apparently tired of his work, listened with eyes closed to a small, illyrium-fed projectostand set on the corner of his desk.

But despite the late hour, none of those listening to Sylette's story felt tired. Well, except for Renar, who snored loudly while hunched over in his chair. Five immaculately cleaned dishes were scattered on the ground about his feet. At several points, Sylette had appeared ready to lay into him for his rude behavior, yet somehow maintained her temper. Perhaps it was the very nature of her tale that kept the former princess in check. No doubt such a small problem paled in comparison to the horrors she'd experienced.

When the conclusion came and passed, Matteo, just like everyone else, found himself stunned into silence. How trivial were his issues in comparison to hers? He glanced around the room at the comfortable trappings, seeing in the well-trimmed furniture, the fancy glassware, and the graceful chimney stonework the signs of a pleasant, if not extravagant, life. His hardworking, devoted father was dozing in the corner of the room, while his doting, tender mother slept upstairs.

Both his parents loved him dearly and were still alive, cleaning up his messes even now. Yet here was Sylette, this tormented soul who had been on her own since the age of ten, whose own father had tortured his mate and daughter to the edge of death before killing the former and exiling the latter. The difference in their fates couldn't be more ironic.

And I'm the one who wants to run away. The hypocritical statement kept replaying in Matteo's mind. Sylette lost *everything* but struggled on for the sake of avenging that loss. On the other hand, Matteo had all he could ask for. His heart, however, was weak. He was so frightened of what might happen that he was willing to abandon all of it and run away. *Can I ever be like her? Can I find the strength to protect the things I care about?*

Interrupting his thoughts, Velle set her hot compress, now dry and cold, aside as she stood. When she walked toward Sylette, arms out wide, the other woman took a slightly defensive stance, as though not sure how to react.

The hug caught her by surprise.

"Thank you for sharing your story with us, Sylette," Velle said. "What happened to you was very painful, and it's easy to see how you started down your current path. But are you sure you're doing it for the right reasons? Are you sure this is our fight?"

Her highness allowed the embrace to continue for all of two seconds before she broke Velle's grip and gently pushed her away. The cautious nudge suggested she cared just enough not to repeat Vallen's earlier mistake.

"I don't want your pity," Sylette said. "I want your understanding, for you to see that this isn't an enemy you can reason with or run away from. If the emperor would do that to his own family, what do you think he'll do with this country, or the rest of the world, for that matter, to get his way? That's right. There's nothing he'd hesitate to do if he thought it would benefit him.

"And don't think the rest of the empire, from Valescar to the lowest serf, isn't complicit in all of it. They've accepted, propagated, and even expanded upon his methods. It's corrupted all the way through. So if you want a future, yes, this is your fight too. Next to that *my* reasons are unimportant."

That rosy picture of events to come raced through Matteo's thoughts: trials and executions of innocent after innocent, croplands burning under fire launched from warships beyond count, cities in ruin with noncombatants crawling through the wreckage. He shuddered.

"See, at least the cowardly Professor seems to understand what's coming," Sylette remarked, correctly interpreting Matteo's shivering.

Velle appeared ready to come to his defense when Unter's deep voice interjected. "Set in stone, such outcome is not. Even were it, do what would you have us? But seven are we. If no plan, not only mountain fail to move shall we, but crushed by its weight will we be."

"Enough with the platitudes!" Sylette cried in exasperation. "If taking down the empire were easy, someone would have done it by now."

Disturbed from his slumber by the loud voices, Renar bolted awake while screaming incoherently at an imagined pursuer, "Gah! Don't chase me meat! I'm sorry for eating your family, but they were just so tasty!" He abruptly made to rise from his chair, but his left foot caught the leg of the seat. Both of them crashed back down in a tangled mess.

Velle giggled, but Sylette had only disdain for the uncouth display. "Glad you could join us, Renar."

He raised his head and smiled sheepishly. "Can we all agree to forget what just happened?"

"Oh no, we can't. You *are* trying to take the imbecile's title of most useless group member, right? This might be just what you need to put yourself over the top."

While Sylette's sarcasm was intended to be cutting, Velle and Lilith couldn't stop themselves from laughing uproariously. Even Matteo had a chuckle or two escape his lips. Unter seemed unaffected, but maybe Hues processed humor differently. After a moment, Sylette looked at each of them in bewilderment, unaware of what was so funny. Her reaction made the situation all the more humorous.

In the wake of the princess's tragic story and a night of riotous arguments, this brief moment of levity was *exactly* what they needed.

The Projectostand clicked over from the smooth sounds of a popular late-night jazz ensemble to a pre-recorded news segment. Following a short introduction reminding citizens of an ever-increasing list of Sarconian regulations, the familiar slick tones of Tannen Holler—the only anchor remaining at the only station sanctioned by the empire—came over the airwaves.

" . . . Tonight we'll be reading some mail from those tuning in. We've done this segment before, and I must admit we've been surprised by how much support our audience has for the new government. Rest assured that your thanks reach all the way to the top, as we have it on good authority that Emperor Artorios himself listens to this network. First up is one Armeen Maridaat, writing in from Weisvale in the cold northwest . . . "

"No reason to listen to this sell-out." Martan, also roused by their unruly discourse, leaned forward in his seat to turn off the jabbering device. Strangely,

Renar, face lit up by some unknown epiphany, jumped to his feet and rushed to stop him.

"Don't turn it off! He's about to read a secret message!"

Secret message? Matteo thought. *On a Sarconian-run broadcast?* It would be hard to believe coming from anyone, but the fact that those words left the mouth of Renar Iolus, whose grades had been lower than Vallen's, made it an even harder pill to swallow.

Matteo found himself expressing his incredulity before he could bite his tongue. "Are you sure you're not imagining things?"

"I'm not!" Renar shook his head animatedly, shaking loose a mat of black hair squished from being slept on. "That name, Armeen Maridaat, was a, you know, one of those mixed-up letter things . . . "

"Anagram," Unter supplied. Unlike the rest of them, he seemed to know where the former class bully was going with this.

"So what does this anagram do for us, if it means anything at all?" As she spoke, Sylette crossed her arms, a smirk of icy disapproval on her lips. The frigid chill emanating from the princess's body language was practically palpable.

Renar wilted slightly under her gaze before pressing on. "Remember our lesson on this year's military coding methods? Any message that comes through an unsecure channel will be headed by an . . . ana-anagram . . . of Nemare, Darmatia, the capital. Rearrange those words and you get Armeen Maridaat!" His look of unfiltered joy at that deduction was almost heartwarming.

Despite the evidence presented, Sylette was still ready to retort when Lilith cut her off. "Let's just listen to the rest of the message and then let Renar explain himself, okay?" The short brunette's amicable request was met with a huff and rolling of eyes, but the Sarconian exile relented by closing her mouth.

" . . . She's sent us a poem by Archelaus Heisden . . . "

"Is that an anagram too?" Matteo asked.

A swift glare from Renar was all it took to stymie any further questions from him. Though the commandant's son was out of the classroom now, his prowess as a former bully hadn't quite left him. *Of course, Sylette is scarier than both Renar and Vallen combined . . .*

" . . . He was a famous prose writer from over three hundred years ago. What a throwback! Armeen hopes that the beauty of this piece might warm your hearts and help us cooperate in preserving this wonderful land along with our Sarconian brothers. That's a great message, Armeen. Please send us more just like this in the future. Now, here's the poem:

> On distant shore, where mist abounds,
> The god of wind and sea is found.
> His jagged crest, worn and pocked,
> Is lined in shadow where none may dock.
> Beneath the yet eternal flame,
> The wooden trappings of mortals came,
> And only where his light did shine,
> Could they avoid the depth's confine.
> Stoic, stout, firm he stands,
> Protecting all beneath his hands.
> The serpents flee, their maws pull back,
> The sea hems and haws and must retract.
> Haze can but hide; the truth still remains.
> Both fear of man and hope to claim.
> If one can but survive the perilous quest,
> In the sea god's breast they may find rest.
> But tarry not too long inside,
> For presumptive guests he shan't abide.
> Hurry back to surface glare,
> Lest lack of air be thine final fare.
> Worse sleeps there are, than in the deep night,
> But for me, Darmatian sunlight shall be my last,
> most glorious sight.

"That was . . . a unique experience, Armeen! Very good poem, very inspirational. I'm sure all our listeners would agree that they, too, love the feel of the sun here in the province of Darmatia. On that note, let's segue to our next letter from a very excited Sarconian property developer. According to him, Darmatia hosts some of the best potential resort real estate on the continent, so I'm sure you'll be thrilled to hear some of his ideas . . . "

As Tannen Holler droned on, Martan shot Renar a plaintive look. Having heard enough, he nodded in the affirmative and Matteo's father shut the Projectostand off. With a wretched squeal, the turncoat celebrity caster died—well, his voice did at least.

"Did you get what you needed from that?" Sylette, still not convinced, leaned against the wall beside the fireplace. Its fading light cast large shadows of her against the curtained windows on the far side of the room.

Velle, the swelling on her cheek mostly gone, sat back down and twiddled her thumbs. "It was all gibberish to me."

Though almost all the remaining lamps or candles had gone out, there was still just enough illumination to see the smug look on Renar's face. "I know exactly what the poem was referring to."

Everyone looked at him expectantly, but he seemed content to hold them in suspense—probably because he'd never before known something his peers didn't. Matteo could relate. *I've always been at the other end of the spectrum, with my cowardice and poor athleticism.* However, motivation for Renar to speak came in the form of Sylette's threatening growl.

"Spit it out or I promise I'll use you for target practice the next time I'm itching to try out my daggers."

"Fine, fine." Renar raised his arms in a mock gesture of surrender. "Jeez, can't a guy enjoy his one and only moment of brilliance in peace anymore?" He nodded appreciatively at the looks of sympathy from Matteo and Velle before continuing.

"So that poem, considered by many to be the masterpiece of Archelaus Heisden, an author from the early fourth century, is titled 'The Sea God's Crest.' Despite how it sounds, it doesn't reference a person or an event, but a place. In his additional notes about the work, Heisden writes that he was enraptured by the "mundane elegance" of the site, a location simultaneously "sinister and alluring" in his—"

"Tell us where it is. We don't need a dissertation on your love of art and poetry. Besides, aren't you a guy?" If words were blades, Renar would've been pierced several times over. He did, in fact, stagger backwards as though wounded. Sylette was no doubt just being herself; even so, she was hitting too close to home by attacking the muscular youth, practically brimming with masculinity, for what appeared to be a gender-inappropriate hobby.

"Do you like things like poetry, codes, and puzzles, Renar?" came Velle's kind, soothing voice.

"Well, yes, I do, but my father, General Iolus, always told me to avoid such things, or at least keep them secret. That they . . . weren't going to help my image or career."

"He wasn't wrong," sighed the impatient Sylette, closing her eyes.

Lilith stood and moved to stand beside Renar, laying a small hand on his shoulder. They'd been squadmates for a long time, so it made sense that she would have a better handle on how to deal with him. "I, for one, don't think there's anything wrong with it." She glared pointedly at the princess, who didn't react, regardless of whether she saw the look or not. "Stereotypes are made to be broken. Besides, if you didn't know anything about that anagram or poem, we'd still be sitting here none the wiser."

"Undeniable fact, that is," Unter announced.

While Matteo couldn't quite bring himself to say something encouraging to the former bully, the pressure wielded by the rest of the group was enough to make Sylette fold. She pushed off the wall and turned her back to them. In the dim glow, he thought he could just make out a ragged series of scars on her exposed neck.

"Alright, I'm sorry." Her vexation, even in defeat, was obvious. "Now can you please tell us what the poem means?"

Renar recovered quickly, and, grinning broadly, picked up where he'd stopped. "Like I said, we're looking for a location. And the name of it is the same as the title: The Sea God's Crest. Filled with jagged reefs, high cliffs, and random, jutting islands, it's a treacherous stretch of coastline. That in and of itself isn't enough to go on, but there are a few more clues to help us."

A light bulb lit up in Matteo's mind. "Weisvale! It wasn't just a throwaway town for the fictitious Armeen to write from. There's only mountains north of it, so the shore we're seeking has to be south of it."

"Right," Renar said, acknowledging his correct answer, "but that only narrows it down to someplace on the Phar Coast between Etrus and there, which is a lot of ground to cover. However, there's one more hint in the poem itself."

"Eternal flame, light did shine, firm he stands . . . " Unter was bent over a piece of paper on the end table beside his seat. For a Terran, reading in the faint luminescence would be difficult, but for Hues, with their excellent night vision, it was an easy task.

From where Matteo sat, it looked like he had managed to transcribe the entire poem as it was read. Given his struggles with the Common Tongue, and the speed at which he would have had to write, his accomplishment was nothing short of amazing. "What did you find, Unter?"

"Looking for a house of light, we are."

"Bingo!" If Renar was disappointed that someone else figured out the missing piece of the puzzle before he told them, it didn't show on his face. "The place referred to in this poem is beside the sea, between Etrus and Weisvale, with a lighthouse built over top of it."

"And if this was submitted using a Darmatian military cipher . . . " Velle began, " . . . then that means whoever sent it wants other army survivors to go to this spot!" Lilith finished with an excited little dance of joy. Renar and the Sylph joined in her enthusiasm; how could they not be ecstatic that others had survived the battle at Aldona and still fought on?

Whereas Unter likely didn't celebrate because of the reserved nature of his kind, Matteo avoided partaking in their merriment for another reason entirely. *Do I want to go back? Do I want to keep fighting? Isn't there a safer, easier way out?* He'd been thinking the same thoughts for days, with no concrete conclusion. But now that there was a way for them to press forward without being alone, finding answers to those questions became all the more important.

"What proof do you have that this isn't a trap?" Sylette asked. "It could easily be bait by the empire to round up holdouts." She'd swung around to face them and moved her silver hair so that it covered the formerly exposed marks. Given her desire to battle the Sarconians—under any circumstances—her sudden opposition seemed counterproductive.

Renar shook his head. "No, that's not likely. It's a very old poem. Not many collectors still have a copy, let alone libraries. Only a well-read Darmatian scholar, or a fanatic like me, who also has knowledge of military protocol, could have sent the message. I think it's legit."

"Plus, Empire better telling us go someplace less remote. Easier on them. Have us go to Nemare, or big, other city."

Their two compelling arguments made a good case for the validity of the communication. As a result, for the first time since he'd met her, Matteo got to see Sylette smile genuinely. It was truly charming, enhancing the natural beauty of her pale skin and lustrous locks. Apparently nothing made her happier than moving a step closer to her vengeance.

"Well, what are we waiting for then? Let's go find them!" she said.

At that moment, the last of the candles blinked out, their final tendrils of smoke curling toward the ceiling. The fire was naught but ash; the only radiance left came from a pair of illyrium lamps, stalwartly struggling to push back the darkness. In their mute blaze it was impossible to see more than the outlines of both furniture and people.

"That decision will have to wait until tomorrow," Martan declared as he rose from his desk. He stretched gingerly before gesturing toward the hall. "It's already past two in the morning, and I don't have the candle reserves to bring out a second batch due to the new rationing rules. Let's pack it in and start again when it's light out."

A petite shape with shimmering tendrils, likely Sylette, started to object before being cut off by the rising blob of Unter. "Few things there are that till tomorrow cannot wait." His mass, along with the still enthusiastically talking others, shuffled from the room. Renar let out a few expletives as his foot encountered the leg of another chair.

Matteo was left alone with the silver-haired princess. As his eyes became more accustomed to the dark, he could almost swear she was crying. Sylette's voice, when it came, was naught but a whisper. "They don't understand, they just don't understand. Every minute wasted is a minute the empire is growing stronger. What if there isn't a tomorrow? What if . . . what if today is all we have? What then?"

Not seeming to notice him, she stalked from the room, off to sleep or, more likely, to prepare as best she could for the coming day.

However, sitting there in the shadows, surrounded by the comforts of his familiar life, Matteo was left with yet another question to ponder. It was a derivative of her own deepest musings, yet resonated with him all the same.

Is tomorrow worth fighting for, when it may mean giving up all I've ever known?

Chapter 20

Forced Hand

———◆———

Sylette usually loved to be proven right. However, in this specific instance, she would have preferred to forgo that pleasure. Saying "I told you so" wasn't much comfort when faced with an approaching platoon of Sarconian soldiers.

From her vantage point atop Matteo's house, the former princess could see rank upon rank of riflemen in red and gold livery marching up the main thoroughfare from the direction of the harbor. The rising sun at her back glinted off their chainmail, causing many to raise their arms or lower their helmets to block out the glare. At their fore drove a treaded, open-topped vehicle with several officers and one *very* familiar face: Grozza, the elderly Moravi to whom the cadets had "sold" their stolen ship.

Two for two. I figured he'd sell us out.

Whether due to the blinding light or the ivy-covered terrace behind which she hid, Sylette had not yet been spotted. As a result, instead of charging straight for their building, the convoy came to a halt a block away. There the man in charge, clad in a dress uniform instead of armor, stood at the rear of the car and began barking orders. Four different squads quickly formed before rushing to the doors of the nearest residences.

They immediately broke them down to force their way inside. A moment later they reemerged, dragging the occupants with them. Terran men, women, children, and even a token family of Sylphs, found themselves roughly hauled from their homes by their occupiers. Most were still in their nightclothes; others were naked, having not been given the chance to dress. *All* were frightened. One middle-aged man, in the garb of a dockworker, tried to break free and run to his daughter, only to be cracked across the head by a rifle butt. Once downed, the Sarconians continued beating him until he stopped trying to move.

When the structures were clear, their portals broken and front gardens devastated, the prisoners were lined up before the Sarconian commander. Evidently satisfied, he gestured to Grozza, who began assessing the stunned civilians. Some he eyed. Others he sniffed. A few he even tasted with his long, forked tongue. None were allowed to resist the Moravi's scrutiny; they were securely kept by soldiers who hefted their guns as if they had no qualms about using them. Reaching the end of the line, he shook his head—what they were looking for wasn't there.

I've seen enough; time to go. Sylette dropped from the raised bench where she'd been, wisely, it seemed, spending her nights and raced toward the stairs. Days prior, when she mentioned the need to set a watch to the others, they'd scoffed at her "paranoia." Now her caution would be their saving grace.

Silver hair flaring, Sylette nearly smacked into Unter on the second-floor landing. The blue giant was fully clothed, clad in the patchwork garb necessary to cover his unique frame. Despite her refusal to let him go outside—he stood out *far* more than the rest of them—the Hue always rose early in the morning.

"Is wrong, something is?"

"Wake the others. Grab the bags. There's a Sarconian patrol out front coming for us, and they'll be here soon." The ex-princess squeezed past his bulk and ran to the next stairwell, knocking violently on each door she passed. Time was of the essence; it would only take the soldiers five, ten minutes at most, to work their way here. Taking the stairs two at a time, Sylette dashed into the kitchen where she grabbed some of the gear they'd stored in the cabinets. *All-weather apparel . . . check . . . Batteries . . . check . . . Grenades . . . check . . . MREs . . . check . . . Vallen's metal rod . . . not that he'll be using it . . .*

She was nearly through the entire list—one she'd committed to memory—when the rest of the party, breathless and toting their equipment, burst into the room. Matteo's parents, also awakened by their frantic activity, were right behind them.

Sylette felt her blood boil almost instantly. "Why are you wasting time carrying that useless lump around?" The object in question was Vallen, clearly awake but lying limp in one of Unter's four arms all the same. Two others carried sacks of kit, leaving him with only one free limb.

"One of us he is. Couldn't just leave."

"Fine, whatever, not my problem. Matteo, is there another exit?"

The Professor, already shaking like a nervous wreck, pointed to the rear windows. "O-out the back. All of . . . the properties on the road . . . connect t-to an alley."

"Good. We'll take that way." It was almost certainly guarded as well, but facing a few enemies was a fair bit better than facing an entire mob of them. "Unter has point, I've got rear. Velle will be in the center as support. The rest of you fill the gaps. Do not, under any circumstance, break formation. Got it?"

A chorus of nods and affirmatives came in return, except from Vallen, who continued to stare straight ahead with blank eyes. *How pathetic can you get?* was the only thought Sylette would spare on him.

Martan, one arm protectively about his wife Anathea, halted them as they made for the rear door. "I realize you didn't have time to reach a proper decision before being forced to run away again. Even so, when you make it through, take some time to settle on something you're all at peace with. That's really all you can ask for in life."

"Anyway, take these, son." He passed Matteo a set of keys, one larger and blockier than the rest. One of its three sides was unevenly serrated, which would make it difficult to duplicate. "That's the activation pin to my private airship. It's in hangar three down at the docks. If you can make it there, I'm sure it'll help you escape. Now get going. We'll head out front and try to delay them a bit."

Tears pooled in their eyes as Martan talked, and when he finished Matteo wrapped them both in a passionate hug. Then, in a further waste of time, Velle, Lilith, Unter, and even Renar all took turns embracing their hosts. Sylette tapped her foot impatiently throughout the entire unnecessary display. When the waterworks were *finally* finished, she shoved the others outside. *How nice. How idyllic. How* sickening. *It's almost like they* want *to be captured.*

They crossed a modest patio, walked over a trim lawn, and arrived at the fence fronting the backstreet. On Sylette's signal, Unter threw the latch; they leapt through, weapons ready to face . . . nothing. There was naught but trash cans and mewling rodents in both directions.

Before she could breathe a sigh of relief, the plan came collapsing down about their heads. Rounding the corner from the direction of the approaching Sarconian detachment came two more Moravi followed by a small group of enemy troopers. Their eyes met then widened simultaneously as recognition dawned—they were the other lizards who'd been with Grozza the night they crashed.

"Grozza vaz rightz! Zer zneakin out ze back vay!"

"Quickly! Take them out before they alert the rest!"

The rose-colored one, Triz'ka, sucked in a deep breath and bent her back, preparing to let loose a warning undulation. Not hesitating in the slightest, Sylette took advantage of the confusion to send a swift wave of daggers cascading toward her. Most missed or clanked harmlessly off the armored soldiers to the rear, but one struck her unprotected abdomen point on. The reptile doubled over onto the ground with a watery gurgle.

Her comrade, well built with many varied bone protrusions that were desirable among their species, chose fight over flight. He rushed down the alley with razor-sharp teeth and claws bared. Unter, shields on three of his four arms, took the charge head on and easily knocked aside the smaller combatant.

Undeterred, the hissing lizard began shooting jagged bone segments from his wrists. At close range, it was nearly impossible to dodge, and several perforated the Hue's unprotected legs. Grunting with pain, the stalwart blue strongman managed to stay on his feet, and his teammates rushed to his aid.

"Don't use magic if you can avoid it!" Sylette shouted as the duo passed on either side of Unter. "We don't know how long we'll be fighting for!"

Heeding her warning, Lilith drew her rapier and harassed the larger foe with a swift series of jabs. High, low, high-high, low-high-low. None were intended to kill, but they drew tiny spurts of purple blood all the same. So focused was the Moravi on defending against the agile girl that he didn't notice Renar until it was too late. The mighty blow from the greatsword practically cleaved him in two.

"Shiel'retuv!"

A spinning white glyph spawned across the gap just in time to catch a barrage from the Sarconian infantry at the other end of the lane. Their guides down, they no longer had a reason to hold their fire. Only a timely barrier from Velle saved them from an evisceration.

On the verge of releasing a second salvo, the squad found themselves on the receiving end of their own bullets when the shield shot the absorbed lead right back at them. Not every shell hit, but two went down with cries of shock. The remainder quickly grabbed their fallen and retreated back around the walled corner.

The whole engagement had taken less than twenty seconds. On the surface, it could be considered a success—four enemies down in exchange for some minor wounds on their hardiest fighter. *However,* Sylette groaned internally, *it's actually the worst possible outcome.* With the loud retorts from the Sarconian firearms, the whole garrison now knew they were here.

"Woohoo! We showed them, didn't we!" True to form, Renar was holding his broadsword aloft and extolling their victory at the top of his lungs.

"Shut up, you idiot!" Sylette hissed at him. "We aren't even close to winning! For that matter, this isn't even a battle we can win. Now get moving!" When he started to walk toward where their opponents had fled, she jabbed a finger in his chest and pointed back up the hill.

"Where do you think you're going? That way!"

Matteo fidgeted anxiously, his mouth opening and closing. *Get on with it. We don't have time for your awkwardness.* Sylette pierced him with an icy glare and he rapidly spilled his guts. "But the docks are down below. Up is a dead end!"

"You're right, Matteo." She smiled at him before crushing his pitiful logic with the full weight of their reality. "That's also where all the enemy troops will be. And now they know where we are. So if you want to live, we're going to have to go up first. Got it?"

His meek "yes" was drowned out by the loud peals of a Projectomic system somewhere nearby. After a moment of painful static, a crisp, unaccented voice rang out across the neighborhood. "Darmatian rebels have been encountered in sector Charon-3. Additional forces arriving from the garrison are to take up posts along all routes below sector Bekur and work their way up through the city. Lethal force is authorized. Citizens, if you do not wish to become casualties, exit your homes and make for one of the newly erected checkpoints. Failure to cooperate with this directive will be seen as subversion of our mission, and you will be reclassified as a dissident. That is all."

Sylette didn't even bother to point out that, once again, she was right. Matteo was on the verge of tears—understandable, given the danger his parents were in and the fact that they were tearing up his hometown to search for them. Renar was also thoroughly cowed. He silently sheathed his blade and looked at her for further instructions. *If this is what it takes for them to listen to me, so be it, I guess.*

She gestured toward the end of the alley *not* clogged with bodies, and they took off at a brisk trot. Unter, his legs injured, stumbled every few steps but still kept up. Even though Sylette wanted to order the kind giant to abandon Vallen or some of their belongings, she knew he wouldn't do it. *I know which I'd ditch first. I just hope his compassion doesn't get us killed.*

As they traveled, the sounds of the Sarconian deployment faded into the distance, replaced instead by the growing panic of the populace itself. While the empire was content to slowly weave an unbreakable net in which to catch their prey, their recent announcement had thrown the people of Etrus into chaos. Even on the backstreets, individuals and families rushed past, clutching whatever precious things they could grab before escaping behind the supposed safety of their occupiers' cordon.

Some shot them weird glances as they passed, having noticed their openly displayed weapons or Unter's trail of blood. Many turned to glares of accusation as their minds reached the correct conclusion. Their eyes seemed to say, "You brought this on us." It wasn't true in the slightest; everything was the empire's fault for invading in the first place. However, that wasn't an argument Sylette cared to have, so she motioned their group to the side each time they ran into someone.

During one such encounter with a family of three, the father, upon seeing Unter's massive form in the front, lost his composure and roughly pulled his wife and daughter down a different path. The young girl, unprepared for the sudden jerk, lost her grip on a worn stuffed prickupine she was carrying. Her tiny hands instantly grabbed for it but couldn't reach. As she was dragged farther and farther from it, she bawled uncontrollably, her tears dripping to the cobblestones below. Even so, her fearful father showed no signs of turning back.

"Levi'tatum."

A shimmering platform the size of the toy materialized below it, raising the doll into the air and carrying the animal back into the grateful grasp of the little child. Her crying ceased, and she raised the hand grasping the dirt-covered prickupine to wave at them. Velle grinned warmly at her in return.

"I thought I said not to cast unnecessary spells?" Sylette chided the Sylph from the rear without slowing down.

"If we disturb their lives for our own benefit without helping them in return, are we any better than the Sarconians?"

Velle's response was the kind of naive nonsense the exile expected from someone unlearned in the cruelties of the world—as she indeed was—but before she could retort their column came to a screeching halt. Unable to stop her momentum, Sylette ran straight into Renar's unpleasantly firm shoulders.

Extricating herself from him, the ex-princess stepped to the side to see what had brought them to a standstill. There, in the middle of a filthy back alley filled with rancid garbage, surrounded by high fences and generous manses, stood a wrinkled old woman in a pure white habit. Her expression neutral, she did not seem put off in the slightest by their appearance, the ongoing manhunt, or anything else for that matter.

A slight smirk parted her withered gums. "Well said, young Velle. No matter what happens, you mustn't forget the people you're fighting for in the first place."

"Mother Junica! What are you doing here?"

Sylette hadn't met her before, though going off Matteo's outburst she was probably a nun in a local religious order. Her abrasive response, however, was anything but motherly. "What? You don't think an old hag can get around by herself? I'll have you know that I have every nook and cranny of this entire city committed to memory, and there isn't a single flea in five leagues that can sneeze without me—"

"He probably meant 'what are you doing here in this situation,'" Velle placated, nudging the flabbergasted Matteo out of the line of fire. "This would be a dangerous place to be for anyone, especially an elder like yourself, Mother."

For whatever reason, Junica didn't unload on the Sylph for attempting to calm her. Apparently just the Professor had earned her ire. *I can certainly sympathize*, Sylette thought. Instead the nun raised one gnarled hand and pointed at the closing sounds of the Sarconian advance.

"My advanced years are *exactly* why I'm here. None of them expect a shambling ancient like myself to be capable of anything, so I can come and go as I please. Now get along to the church at the summit. If you do, Abbott Kinloss will show you the way forward."

How will a church help us? How did this granny get here? Is she working with the empire? The questions kept mounting in Sylette's mind, and she would have answers. With a few swift steps she passed Velle and marched straight up to the venerable nun. At this short distance she stood a full head above the bent woman.

"Why are you helping us? I thought you ascetics believed in *peace* and *love* above all else." She put a sardonic emphasis on "peace" and "love." Those wishful ideals were a fantasy. "If you weren't aware, we're probably going to leave a trail of bodies behind us to escape. Are you alright with that?"

The wizened Junica didn't flinch or balk in the slightest. "I'm here for two reasons, missy. First, an old friend asked me for help, and I just couldn't say no. Second," she waved dismissively at the horizon, where a Sarconian cruiser could be seen ascending above the ruddy rooftops, likely to assist in the search, "those wahoos didn't make any friends among the faithful when they destroyed the Cathedral of Sariel in Nemare. And while we've taken an oath of non-violence, that doesn't mean we can't oppose the empire in . . . other capacities."

As she finished speaking, the Mother flashed Sylette a knowing wink and began shuffling past them back down the alleyway. *A spy. She's a spy. And a fearsome one at that.* A chill ran down the exile's spine. As Junica said, no Sarconian would suspect a frail religious sycophant—from their perspective—of sedition. It was the perfect cover.

"Best move along, young rebels. And if your travels happen to cross paths with Mother Superior Tabitha, tell her that her sister says hello."

Mother Superior was the title given to the woman at the top of a religious order of the faithful. *If that was the friend she mentioned,* Sylette contemplated with shock, *then the empire has made an enemy of the entire Way of the Will . . . of the entire Darmatian Church itself!*

It was a mind-blowing revelation, one that at once invigorated and frightened Sylette. Perhaps, if this was but the tip of the growing Darmatian resistance, there was hope for this country after all. Everyone but Matteo seemed thoughtful; it appeared they'd interpreted Junica's words as she had. However, while he might be book smart, common sense flew right over his head.

"Come with us, Mother," Matteo urged. "It's not safe to stay here."

Even though she didn't turn around, the nun's words carried in them the sound of her shrewd smirk. "Didn't I tell you I know everything about this city? Don't worry, I'll be seeing you again." And with that she was gone. Vanished into thin air. Matteo ran to the spot, trying to discern how she'd disappeared, to no avail. Whatever side passage, secret entrance, or trick had been employed, Mother Junica was simply gone.

At that moment, Sylette held but one regret.

I wish she could've worked that magic on us.

———⊰◈⊱———

The area about the church was a tactical nightmare.

Sure, the edifice itself was pleasant enough to look at, with a white facade contrasting against a black fence and a thick hedge in the foreground. However, past the twin marble effigies of Sariel, raised swords stretching toward the heavens, lay an empty dead zone. No matter which direction one approached the structure from, there was a space fifty meters wide of nothing but bare cobblestones. No buildings, no signposts, no people or vehicles. Completely empty.

They'd been in their current position for ten minutes. Hidden in the shadow of a modest government office building, Sylette had spent the intervening time trying to come up with a passable plan to get from here to there without being riddled with lead. So far she'd come up with no ideas that didn't end with casualties.

And while she pondered, the dragnet about them closed ever tighter. To their right, baking in the light of the midday sun, was the first imperial detachment to reach the center peak of the city. Granted the privilege of marching straight up the main road, the platoon had made it here before them, cutting off any possibility of them entering the chapel without being seen. Even though a fair number of them seemed to be slacking off—after all, their enemies were only a small group of provincial malcontents—there were more of them than they could hope to fend off once spotted.

Behind her, the others prepared as best they could. Velle had performed emergency first-aid on the perforations through Unter's legs, sealing up the skin and giving some moderate relief to the muscles and nerves inside. Several rough, pale splinters of Moravi bones came out in the process, but they didn't seem to have infected the wounds in any way. The others checked their weapons or kept to themselves; not many people knew just what to do in the calm before combat. Vallen and Matteo were the only exceptions, the former still dazed in his own little world, while the latter had no weapon.

Sylette finished thinking through the most recent simulation and shook her head in dejection. There was no way to do this with the resources on hand. She turned, thinking to ask one of the more reasonable party members like Unter or Lilith for advice, when she noticed a distortion in the darkness. Beneath the metal stairwell attached to the side of the building was a group of nearly imperceptible moving shapes. As she blinked, wondering whether her mind was playing tricks on her, an arm appeared from within one of the blobs. In its grasp flashed something metallic and silver. *Time's up, it seems.*

"Camouflage capes!" Sylette blurted, even as Lilith, having noticed the same thing, jumped into action. Her rapier took the first man in the throat; he collapsed soundlessly, his blood spraying across his companions.

Their cloaks rendered useless, the rest quickly threw them off, revealing another three assailants. The first pulled a short sword and swung at the fencer, only to have her duck the blow and impale his midsection. Instead of backing off, the burly soldier grinned, clamping down on her wrist with his free hand. Lilith tried to break his grip with little success. At the same time the darkly dressed attacker to her left pulled out a pistol and prepared to shoot her.

So focused was the gutted enemy on maintaining his grip that Sylette barely had to aim to send a gleaming blade slicing through his forehead. He went limp, allowing Lilith to jump back and retrieve her weapon.

"Thanks!" she yelled, before noticing the pistol aimed at her. The brunette flinched aside, but the shot never came as Renar charged in screaming to shoulder-slam its wielder against the far wall. Bones crunched. A scream tore from his lips. Then Sylette silenced him with a dagger to the head as well.

All eyes fell on their last foe, who, despite the loss of his comrades, was calmly raising a flare gun above his head. Sylette summoned and fired another dirk. Lilith and Renar ran toward him, weapons raised. Velle gestured, willing into existence a glyph to block the shot. Unter stumbled to his feet, far too slow, far too late to make a difference.

Even as all their techniques hit him, the flare whistled high into the air where it exploded in a roar of crimson shrapnel. A moment of silence followed. Then the collective noise of the hundreds of Sarconian soldiers within hearing reached their ears. They had been found; the enemy was coming.

"Move! Across the plaza, now!" Sylette charged out of the alleyway, hoping the others would be right behind her. They had the briefest window of opportunity before the entire garrison came crashing down upon them. Even if they took damage, now was the last chance they had.

"Who were they?" Matteo shouted above the rising din.

"RSF, Reconnaissance Special Forces, the eyes and ears of their army. Now shut up and run!"

From across the square came the staggered retort of several rifles. The rounds came nowhere close, either whizzing past them through the air or striking the stones at their feet. However, the Sarconian platoon was just coming alive. An officer with lieutenant's bars on his breastplate was running about behind them, whipping them into a firing line with the flat of a saber. In a few seconds their barrage would become a lot more effective.

So when they were but halfway to the church, Sylette brought them to a screeching halt.

"Velle, two barriers toward the enemy. Unter, drop Vallen and those bags and stand behind her spell to catch any stray bullets on your enhanced shields. Lilith, fire back some blasts in between volleys. Renar, grab one of the two rifles in that bag and shoot back."

Matteo glanced plaintively at her when his name wasn't called. "What about me?"

"Stay low and try not to get yourself killed."

Just as the first hail of bullets flew toward them, Velle's shimmering glyphs spawned into existence to halt their approach. The one or two that made it past glanced harmlessly from Unter's shields and magic-enhanced exterior. Then the Sylph dropped her incantation to allow their offensive duo to lash back.

"Exo'displova!"

Crack . . . crack . . . crack!

With a swing of Lilith's blade, two small orange projectiles whipped off toward the enemy lines. The first missed everything, striking a building to the left of the main road. Despite its small size, the ensuing explosion shattered both windows and walls, raining glass and masonry on the Sarconians below. The second fiery detonation, landing in the middle of their lines, sent bodies and weapons launching in all directions. Though most of them got back up again, the sheer volume and chaos of the blasts were enough to validate their effectiveness.

At the same time, Renar unloaded a clip through the growing smoke. The resultant cries, both as a result of his hits and Lilith's strike, showed that their efforts had made a mark.

"Woohoo!" he cheered as he swapped in a new magazine.

"Shields back up!" Sylette ordered.

"Shiel'baresh!"

Another ineffective volley bounced off Velle's defenses, and they retaliated in the same manner. Soldiers with melting chainmail rushed for the cover of nearby structures. The Lieutenant, his officer's cap gone and hair singed, was shouting for the troops to push the rubble they'd created into a makeshift barricade. Even their attackers' rifle retorts slowed to a trickle, so focused were they on protecting themselves.

Sylette's heart surged with elation. *Maybe, just maybe, we can do this.*

Then everything fell apart, as it was always going to.

"Panzcraft!" Unter bellowed, ducking behind his shields. A large shell whizzed past them, missing Velle's glyphs by centimeters. Sylette followed its path, watching it decapitate a Sariel statue before impacting one of the supports between the church's windows. The resulting blast was devastating. Stained glass in myriad colors shot forth on tendrils of flame, and huge stone chunks sailed impossibly high in the sky. Part of the roof caved in, cascading onto rent pews that now bore a closer resemblance to exposed ribs. When the carnage was finally over, a gaping maw one-fourth the size of the entire building laughed at them as though mocking their folly.

"Abbott Kinloss!" Matteo wailed, scrambling toward the wreckage. Sylette grabbed his collar and yanked him back, even as another storm of lead from the emboldened Sarconian infantry railed against Velle's shields.

"Do you want to die? Sit back down!" She refocused her attention back forward, looking through the swirling mists for the oncoming beast. And there it was, a metal monstrosity on tracks with two colossal cannons pointing directly at them. It lurched over the wreckage on the main road, crunching the flimsy concrete and stone beneath its armored mass, lumbering past its weaker kinsmen for a better shot. Lilith sent fire spell after fire spell at it, but they did nothing but scorch the grey paint or singe its rubber treads.

With a thunderous belch of smoke, the behemoth stopped and fired.

Both shells scored direct hits on Velle's shining barriers, and as they began to shatter, Unter thrust all four of his arms against them, feeding his men'ar directly into the failing shields to keep them going. Both of them heaved and grunted, throwing everything they had into maintaining their magic. It was almost enough . . . before the giant cartridges ran out of momentum—a condition that caused their explosive innards to engage.

Their techniques dissolved in a coursing inferno, the force of which tossed everyone backwards. Sylette flopped end over end, hitting her head and nearly blacking out. When she managed to stand, blood was dripping from a gash on her forehead, threatening to cloud her already distorted vision. The exile wiped it aside—a solution that barely stemmed the flow—and tried to take stock of their situation.

Everyone was breathing but hurt. Velle was pale, bruised, and drained, but that was understandable since she'd borne the greatest burden in their defense. Unter didn't seem much better off, his forearms coated with grisly burns, though the rest could probably go a few more rounds. Around them, obscuring their surroundings, was a slowly drifting wall of smog, a combination of residue from gunpowder, debris, and fire. From beyond it came the vague sounds of men and machinery being rushed into position.

Sounds that came from almost every direction.

A refreshing fall breeze swept through the square, taking hold of the smoke and blowing it off the summit. However, Sylette could not enjoy the crisp air's touch, for it was a capricious wind, one that had taken away the only protection standing between them and certain demise.

From behind the church had come an entirely new detachment of Sarconian soldiers. At least two platoons of riflemen situated behind hastily erected sandbags were now staring down iron sights at their party. Behind them idled not one but two newly arrived Panzcraft, steam rising from sloped rear decks as hot engines began to cool. Their four guns gazed dispassionately at what was no better than cornered prey. Officers, safe at the rear, shouted unnecessary orders to troops that already had the situation well in hand.

To make matters worse, their original foes had been reinforced. Two tarp-covered trucks at the top of the main street were emptying a stream of infantry to take up positions alongside those already there. One squad, likely led by an overeager sergeant, moved up alongside the first Panzcraft, which hadn't advanced since firing the shells that broke their resistance. Behind the bustling deployment, an armored car, all angles and topped by a commander's cupola, pulled to a stop with a screech.

All in all, over a hundred small-caliber guns, an indeterminate number of intermediary explosives and destructive implements, and six massive cannons stared at their small group of fugitives. They were outnumbered. They were outgunned. And they were surrounded on three sides with no hope of escape.

Is this . . . is this it? Is this the end?

A million possibilities, a thousand scenarios, and a hundred strategies rushed through Sylette's mind in an instant. None had a positive outcome. As that fact sank in, that there was truly no way out, fatigue and despair slammed down upon her like the weight of the sun. *Did I really come this far just for it to end this way? My efforts for revenge, my hatred, my yearnings . . . is this all they amounted to?*

Her knees buckled under the physical and mental strain; there was no point in resisting the inevitable any longer. However, her legs never touched the ground. On either side of Sylette, supporting her fragile frame, were red and blue arms. To the left, lithe, slender, was Velle. To the right, strong, steadfast, was Unter. They had borne the greatest injuries out of any of their group, yet here they were, holding her up when she thought all was lost. Despite the odds, these two were not ready to yield.

"So what's the plan this time, Sylette?"

"To the end, try will we. With breath, there is hope."

That's right. If I give up now, what was the point of everything that came before? As long as I draw breath, I will . . . fight . . . on. Sylette smiled, a broad, defiant grin, and stood back to her full height. Adrenaline surged through her, inducing a heady rush like no other. She was alive, there was still strength in her body, and she would fight on.

"Alright, here's what we'll do. One more defensive stand. We weather the storm, then in the split second when they pause to reload we make a break for the church. Crazy enough?"

"If it wasn't crazy, it wouldn't work," Lilith said without sarcasm, testing the heft of her now slightly bent rapier.

"I was hoping we'd leave the surrender option on the table," Renar said with a sigh, stuffing an illyrium grenade into his belt with one hand and hefting the rifle with the other. "But it doesn't seem like they'll be making any offers like that."

Matteo, last to speak, raised one hand as though asking a question. "Can I at least shoot this time?" He gestured at the other rifle on the ground nearby, its bag and the rest of its contents scattered about them.

Sylette shrugged. *What's the worst that could happen?* "Just make sure the barrel is pointed at *them*."

With a wave of her arms, Velle summoned six glyphs into being, two facing toward each group of enemies. A small grunt escaped the Sylph's lips at the strain of maintaining so many simultaneous barriers, but she held firm all the same. Unter brought his four shields together. As the metal touched, he used magic to expand and mold their shape until they became one massive, interlocked screen, which he braced against the ground in the direction of the double Panzcraft. Having done the best she could to fix her weapon, Lilith pointed it in the air to try to blast down incoming projectiles. Eyes to their sights, Matteo and Renar stood back to back, muzzles pointed through gaps in Velle's wall. Even Sylette, her daggers not well suited for defense, conjured all twelve and split them into spinning star-shaped groups of four to deflect bullets. The imbecile, still unmoving and nearly forgotten, lay at the middle of the formation.

Now we're as ready as we'll ever be.

Strangely, in spite of their obvious intent to keep fighting, the Sarconians seemed content to let them make all the preparations they desired—provided they didn't open fire. One minute passed, then two. Heavy breathing and coughing came from Velle and Unter as they struggled to maintain their incantations. To Sylette, it seemed more than a tactical decision by the enemy to let their men'ar reserves run dry. With an overwhelming numbers and firepower advantage, when they attacked hardly mattered. *No, they're definitely waiting on something else*, she reasoned.

Suddenly everything went dark. Not pitch-black, but shadowed, as though something were blocking the sun. Sylette glanced up. Sure enough, the imposing bulk of a Sarconian heavy cruiser had glided into position directly above them. Its T-shaped fuselage bristled with weaponry facing every direction, and no fewer than three belly turrets were trained on the square below—on them. As it took up a hovering stance, bow propulsion systems flared with the yellow glow of illyrium, halting its forward momentum.

Disbelief, rather than horror, was the first emotion Sylette felt at the vessel's appearance. *Do they seriously intend to fire on us? In the middle of the city? Have they gone mad?*

"Talk about overkill," Renar breathed. If that thing fired, they—and pretty much everything in the vicinity—would be obliterated.

However, its weapon systems remained dormant; there was no ruddy glow to indicate a transfer of energy to the underside guns. Instead, after a moment, a wheezy voice floated down from above, courtesy of projectostands somewhere aboard the airship, and suddenly everything made sense to Sylette. After all, that cautious man hated to stick his own scrawny neck out where it might be chopped off.

"This is Lt. Colonel Stetson, commander of the 232nd mechanized battalion attached to the Sarconian Fifth Fleet." Apparently he'd gotten demoted from his cushy palace post, but the cadaverous coward deserved far worse if he was party to the injustices heaped on Sylette and her mother. "You are surrounded with no hope of escape by either land or sky. If you turn over to us the silver-haired girl in your party, lay down your arms, and surrender peacefully, your lives will be spared. Furthermore, you will be granted a fair trial under Sarconian law. You have two minutes to decide."

With a staticky click, the broadcast stopped and a tense silence descended across the plaza. Fair trial? *Ha, if what my mother got was a "fair" trial, Sarconians don't know the meaning of the word,* Sylette scoffed inwardly. Or, more likely, they preferred to substitute their own definition: fair is whatever's best for us.

But Stetson had tipped the empire's hand. Whether or not he knew who "the silver-haired girl" actually was, they didn't care about the rest as long as they could get her. That knowledge also explained most of their actions to this point: trying to catch them sleeping, sending in RSF stealth squads, attempting to trap rather than kill their group, and so on. The Sarconians never spent that much effort dealing with ordinary rebels they could just burn out regardless of collateral damage.

Wait, Sylette thought, dread clasping her heart with icy fingers. *What if the others actually believe what he's saying?* She looked about, panic flowing into both her eyes and actions as she glared at each of her companions in turn. The sudden loss of focus caused her floating daggers to disintegrate back into the ether without ever being used.

Sylette's anxiety did not go unnoticed.

"Are you alright?" Velle, worn and pallid, placed one arm on her shoulder, the other still raised to maintain her glyphs. The former princess nearly jerked away from her touch before recognizing the legitimate concern resonating on her face.

"It's nothing, Velle. She's just worried we might still sell her out." Lilith, her tone bored and distant, didn't even turn around, which made her deduction all the more amazing. "Which is silly, considering we could've done it a dozen times already without going on an execution-worthy rampage first."

Her heart began to slow; Sylette's mind calmed along with it. *That's right, they stuck with me this far. If they wanted to betray me there were many better opportunities to do so.* It was just so hard to trust, especially after what she'd experienced in her past. *Maybe that's why I freaked out.* Gently, with a slight smile, she breathed a sigh of relief.

"You're right . . . I'm . . . sorry . . . about that." Sylette squeezed the words, strange and foreign, out of her mouth.

"Besides, even I'm not dumb enough to believe they'd actually let us live if we did what they ask. And if the second dumbest cadet in the group can see that, I'm sure all of us can." Renar flipped his thumb at Vallen as if to indicate that the immobile fool was, in fact, the least intelligent among them.

At that everyone except Unter and Matteo laughed. The former nodded in half-grinning agreement, while the latter stared mutely at the ground, his rifle in danger of falling from his trembling fingertips. He seemed to be wrestling with something or other, though exactly what was known to him and him alone.

Sylette's thoughts were cut short by the reengaging of the projectostands shouting down at them from the heavens. "Your two minutes are up. Since you have shown no indication of acquiescing to our demands, you will be taken into custody by force. Captain Graum, your troops may advance at will."

An officer, the one who had been with Grozza earlier, popped halfway out of the armored car's cupola and began belting orders. "Company, fix bayonets!" In unison, all the infantry soldiers around them pulled long metal blades from their belts, affixing them to a slot below their rifle muzzles. The simultaneous clinking was thunderous. "Take the silver-haired girl alive; kill the others if they resist. Company, advance!"

With a groan and a belch of white steam, the Panzcraft rolled forward once more. They came on with growing speed but didn't fire. As the Sarconian soldiers fell in behind them, careful to stay within their bulky silhouette, it became clear what their goal was. The impenetrable iron bunkers would lead the way; the lightly armored troopers would follow. And only when they were right in their foes' faces would they swarm out to overwhelm them.

Stetson had evidently received new orders from much higher up the chain. Based on the enemy's actions, Sylette now knew that for certain. Formerly they didn't care if their tactics caused some casualties in the process of bringing them down. Now the imperials were so apprehensive about firing a shot that they were willing to risk additional lives by engaging in hand-to-hand combat. For whatever reason, the emperor wanted his daughter back, and he wanted her in pristine condition.

Not waiting for a cue, Renar fired at their approaching adversaries in the lee of the original Panzcraft. *Crack . . . crack . . . crack!* The sharp banging of his discharges woke Matteo from his daze, and he began haphazardly sending his own lead downrange. *Crack . . . crack, crack!*

One unlucky Sarconian took a shot through his useless helmet. Dead on impact, he fell out of formation into an expanding pool of his own blood. The rest of their clips, including all of Matteo's poorly aimed barrage, pinged off the front and sides of the steadily closing monstrosity in the lead. Completely undeterred, the imperial column marched onward over the body.

No, no, NO! This isn't going to work! Sylette fumed with a grimace. Renar and Matteo popped in new clips, but their store was running dry. Each of them only had another reload or two at most. Lilith flung as many explosive spells as she could at the larger force on the other side, but the bend in her rapier was wreaking havoc on her accuracy. Some flared harmlessly in the sky, others blasted pitfalls in the pavement or scored microscopic channels in the Panzcrafts' armor. Only one, a truly lucky shot, went high into the air before rocketing down amid the exposed infantry. But before she could utter so much as a cheer, the smoke cleared to reveal merely a handful of burned soldiers being carried to the rear. The gap filled instantly; the highly trained imperial war machine came ever closer.

There were simply too many of them. Sylette knew that, in a few moments at most, they would reach Velle's barriers and grind them into ether. Then they would engage in close combat. Unter and Renar, with their size and strength, would get a few of them, maybe more. Even with her blade damaged, Lilith was skilled enough to down a half dozen alone. And at point-blank range, Sylette's own daggers would be able to target exposed flesh with vicious precision.

But none of it would be enough. No matter how many they killed, more would come to replace them. They'd get tired, sloppy, hemmed in to the point where they could barely move. When that happened . . . the others would die, pierced by countless bayonets from every angle, and Sylette . . . *I'll be captured and taken before my father, a reacquired pawn to serve my mother's killer for the rest of my life.*

That was an abhorrent, disgusting future. *I'd rather die than let that happen.* As that thought crossed Sylette's mind, in her weakness she briefly contemplated ending it then and there. A dagger to the back of her thin neck would be swift, painless, and prevent the familiar hardship to come.

The exile's fiery will crushed that pathetic notion. *I have not survived this long to quit here.* Besides, it would be a betrayal to those around her to take the easy way out. They were here, grimly fighting to the end because of her presence— because they had gotten caught up in her fight.

Next to their resolve, my pride is nothing.

The Sarconians were now but five meters away. Eagerness, adrenaline, and the desire to be unleashed after holding back for so long shone on the sweating faces of the closing soldiers. They gripped their weapons tightly, ready to charge, already imagining exacting vengeance after their earlier sufferings. Whether here for love of money or country, there was no hint of doubt in these troopers' minds at what they were about to do.

Their party would need a miracle to survive the coming assault. However, all the variables were accounted for; there was nothing on hand except the people and equipment they'd possessed all along. Renar, his ammo drained, threw the worthless instrument at the enemy with all his might. One dumbfounded private gasped in surprise as it smacked him in the face. A brief scuffle among his neighbors resulted as he was knocked backwards, but there was no other damage.

Then the barbarians were at the gates. With a loud cry they tore from cover, surrounding Velle's barriers on every side. Rifles rose and fell, bayonets stabbed, the battle was joined. Most rebounded harmlessly, but some found their way through the gaps, searching almost desperately for flesh to impale. Lilith took it upon herself to relieve those individuals of their weapons, pricking their overextended hands with her crooked rapier as best she could. Most yelped and let go immediately, leaving behind their gun, skin, and blood. As out of place as he was, Matteo came along behind the agile brunette, grabbing the discarded arms and placing them alongside Vallen in the center, well out of reach of their former owners.

Vallen . . . Vallen . . . VALLEN! There was still something—someone—that Sylette hadn't bothered to consider. But what use would that imbecile be at this point? If none of their efforts could turn the tide, how could the powers of one egotistical idiot? She pushed the thought away, preparing to summon her daggers and contribute as best she could to their last stand. Surely the erstwhile princess's best attempt would be better than whatever she could coax out of that self-pitying fool.

However, that mindset was as arrogant and prideful as one could be. *I will never see my vengeance realized if I'm unwilling to exhaust every last option available.* She soundlessly turned and rushed to Vallen's side. Only Matteo saw her go, but he didn't bother to say anything. The rest were too engaged to even notice.

To start, she tried slapping his cheeks until they were red, and while it was immensely pleasurable, the Triaron did not respond. So Sylette turned to what she was best at: verbal abuse.

"Wake up, you imbecile! Are you just going to lie there and die? Are you going to let the rest of your friends perish along with you? I thought you were angry at Leon's death? Are you willing to let that same thing happen another five times over?"

Vallen remained comatose. To the side, with a loud crash, one of the Panzcraft came charging through Sylette's wall. Upon impact, the rammed glyph shattered into thousands of glinting shards that quickly faded into nothingness. A cheer went up from the Sarconian infantry; they'd breached the barrier!

The grey steam-belching behemoth began withdrawing to make space for its comrades to rush in, but Unter quickly stepped into place. Before it could reverse, the Hue cast an incantation welding his four shields to the vehicle, digging his massive feet into the loose cobblestones and heaving with all his might. Red veins bulged beneath his pulsing muscles as he fought flesh versus metal with the Panzcraft. For now, the line held.

But it was not a permanent solution by any means. Already aggressive soldiers, the end in sight, were clambering atop the halted vehicle to drop into the cordon from above. Velle, half collapsed and bleeding from her nose, wearily raised one of her arms to seal off their egress. A brief flicker of light was the only evidence that the Sylph had even attempted a spell. Renar and Lilith rushed in, felling the first off-balance entrants. The bodies briefly made a new, slightly more morbid wall, until their compatriots dragged them back. Though no one else tried to get in that way, Unter, and Velle's remaining shields, could only last so long. Hundreds of cracks, growing ever larger, raced along the radiant screens.

"Come on, idiot! It's now or never! Do you think your death would make Leon happy? Do you think that would make the steward, your father, happy either? By the Void, I think I'd be the only one happy if you died, but unfortunately, I won't be around to celebrate it! Why, you ask? Because I'm going to get hauled off by my murdering father! I know you don't care, but do . . . something! Arrgghh!"

Sylette was at the end of her rope. She pounded her fists on his chest, hoping against all odds that he might wake up to stop her. But there was still no sign of awareness, despite his eyes being wide open. Vallen simply had no will to do anything.

In the background, Renar had a brilliant idea and slashed the rubber treads of the encroaching Panzcraft using his greatsword. Its wheels, attached to the treads by a series of gears, spun helplessly above the road with their traction removed. Unter was freed from his burden. However, as he stepped back, the commander popped out from the top of the vehicle, pistol in hand. Screaming, he discharged the entire magazine at the blue giant.

The first bullet went cleanly into his chest before the Hue could enhance his body to resist the remainder. As Unter fell, Lilith leapt up and dispatched the assailant, while Renar shoved the grenade he'd been carrying down the open hatch. Cries of panic echoed from inside, but the crew couldn't escape due to the dead weight of their superior blocking the way. Seconds later there was a muffled *whump* and the Panzcraft exploded from the inside out.

Though the detonation didn't extend far due to the thickness of the vehicle's armor, the shockwave was strong enough to damage Velle's neighboring barriers. A jagged seam appeared on both extending across their entire length, from which fault lines spread like the roots of a tree. It was clear they would fail in seconds.

Velle and Unter were both on their knees, unable to continue fighting. Matteo quivered nearby, either unsure how to contribute, afraid to struggle on, or both. Renar and Lilith were holding their own, but soon there'd be too many gaps for them to cover.

Everything came down to this. Sylette had one more card to play. Maybe, just maybe, it would work.

After all, it was the reason she'd kept fighting all these years.

"You're right, imbecile. All that isn't worth fighting for. Who cares what you have now. It isn't real. It isn't valuable. You know what really matters, though? Your past. The things that made you who you are. The things you loved and cherished. The things you had stolen from you, cruelly, ruthlessly, right out from under your nose. You fought to protect those things, those people, and what did it get you? A sharp dose of reality right through your heart. We aren't all powerful. We can't fight fate, we can't stop time, and we can't keep people from dying. But if all that's true, what can we do? We can destroy. We can hate. And we can take vengeance. We can stand back up and do to those who hurt us what they did to us. And we can make it painful, far more painful than it ever was when we felt the same way. Why? Because we're almost dead inside; we simply have nothing left to lose."

She continued. "It was the Sarconians who took Leon away from you. No amount of blaming yourself will change that fact, even if it's partially true. So take it out on them. If you project your anger, hate, and loathing onto someone—something—else, it will feel oh so much better. Burn it all. You tried fighting for others; now fight to avenge the hole in your chest. Besides, what else do you have to lose?"

While her time with the others had marginally softened her rough exterior, this was the mantra that Sylette believed in her heart of hearts. Throughout the long years since her mother's death, her banishment, and Valescar's betrayal, these thoughts were always with her. They were both her comfort and her guide.

At first, even that didn't seem to be enough. But as the barriers burst, the soldiers poured in, and Sylette began to give up hope that she'd get through to Vallen, a light began to resonate deep in his eyes. Suddenly he shot up, a grin on his face—the same cheeky, boyish, overconfident smirk he normally wore. Grabbing his metal rod from the remnants of the equipment bag beside him, he stood up amid the unfolding chaos as if he didn't have a care in the world.

"Thank you, your highness."

"For what?"

"For reminding me why I don't let anyone get close to me anymore."

With that Vallen winked roguishly, morphed his weapon into a massive warhammer, and set to his desired vengeance with relish.

Chapter 21

Upheaval

---

*T**huunnggg!*

Ah, what a glorious sound, Vallen exulted.

The note in question, caused by the crushing impact of metal on metal, reverberated melodically for but a second before being drowned out by the surrounding din of battle. As it faded, so too did the occupant of the now squashed helmet that had served as anvil to the initiating blow. Ironically, the Sarconian collapsed beside the same crouching Sylph he'd been about to impale, his rifle clattering away across the cobblestones.

Velle, barely cognizant, shot Vallen a weak smile of thanks, but he moved on without so much as registering her existence. He hadn't planted his warhammer in that soldier's skull to save a comrade. He had done it because he was the closest target—with his back foolishly turned to him on top of that.

More, I need more. That wasn't nearly satisfying enough. Velle's barriers were down. A flood of red and gold surged inwards from all directions. One charging trooper spotted him, coming to a halt and carefully aiming his rifle to eliminate any chance of missing; at five meters, it would be impossible for Vallen to dodge.

So he didn't even try. Shaking the stiffness out of his shoulders, particularly the still injured right, the Triaron merely activated his full-body electric field and strode straight at the man. Expecting his foe to react by doing anything *but* that, the private panicked, discharging his weapon immediately.

Crack! With shock-filled eyes, the soldier could do naught but gape as the bullet turned aside upon reaching his enemy's energy-coated chest, flying harmlessly off into the smoky air above the melee. Then Vallen reached him and put a permanent end to his confusion with the spiked reverse end of his weapon.

Too slow, much too slow. The adrenaline pumping through his veins, the elation of being in control, the simple feeling of the coarse alloy abrading his hands as he swung—all that sensory input made Vallen ecstatic beyond belief. But his hunger wasn't sated. The hole in his chest continued to demand more appeasement, *faster* satisfaction.

Out of the corner of his eye, a Sarconian officer wearing a black peaked cap gestured frantically at the Triaron with a saber. Four riflemen responded to his cries—completely unheard by Vallen, blood thundering in his ears—and fired on him together. *How foolish.* Pale blue light cascaded in bursts across his flesh, disintegrating or turning aside every shell. When their clips were empty, they drew back in terror, preparing to flee from a force they were incapable of dealing with.

However, a flight of daggers cut them and their leader down from behind. "Stop using your magic like it's bottomless. Do you want to run dry?" A brief glance to his right confirmed that Sylette had followed in his wake.

I don't need your help was Vallen's first thought, but instead he curtly replied, "As long as I take them down, how much men'ar I use doesn't matter." He began stalking toward the next group of enemies, who had encircled Unter and Renar in the lee of a burning Panzcraft. The two were holding their own, but only because none of their opponents were shooting for fear of hitting their comrades.

Sylette stayed on his tail. "You think you can beat them alone? Look around! This is an army! We need to get the others and go!"

Some tiny amount of her logic penetrated into the depths of Vallen's frenzied bloodlust. *If the rest survive, I'll be able to do more damage.* Besides, if he died here, that would be the end of his retribution, and there was *far* more enjoyment to be had. "Fine. If I can't erase them all, I'll break their resolve instead."

Vallen smiled eagerly. He hadn't tried what he was about to do in a long time. It was guaranteed to disrupt the enemy—temporarily, at least—if successful, but was a one-shot technique. A failure would see him use up most of his remaining energy, leaving him vulnerable to whatever foes were left.

Placated by the Triaron's seemingly controlled rage, Sylette left him to his devices, running back to grab Velle and drag her toward the relative safety of his shadow. Elsewhere, Lilith was standing guard over a cowering Matteo, somehow more useless in close combat than he was at range. She had eschewed her traditional rapier, damaged beyond repair, for a captured Sarconian saber and a detached bayonet. With one in each hand the petite girl waltzed about the small space, dealing injury or death to any that came too close. Blood flew, men cried out, yet the press drew ever closer. Soon she would have no room to move.

This information, along with everything else happening on the battlefield, was vital to Vallen's spell. Through the soles of his feet he felt the reverberations of stomping boots, clashing metal, and grinding treads. The breeze carried with it the rancid smell of sulfur, blowing south across the hilltop square. He noted the positions of as many things as he could: Sylette fending off soldiers behind him, his other trapped comrades, the two remaining Panzcraft blocking their escape to the rear.

Then the Triaron gathered his men'ar, forcing it from every part of his body down into the head of his warhammer. There he molded it, instilling it with his will and the sensory data he'd just obtained. Exhaustion threatened to overwhelm Vallen as he finished; however, he still needed to execute the incantation, one that their overconfident enemy would never see coming.

Let's see how they like this. With a groan inducing heave, the Triaron swung the weapon over his head before calling upon the power of the wind to bring it crashing back to earth. The cobbles shattered beneath the blow, burying the upper portion of the monstrous mallet entirely. At first nothing happened. But then, with a thunderous rending of stone and cement, the surface of the plaza erupted.

It was as though the ground had been released from a prison. Whole segments of manmade paving shot high into the sky before crashing down with impetuous force. Many unsuspecting Sarconians were tossed aloft by these unexpected updrafts, flying even higher because of their lighter mass. The soldiers' screams wailed across the melee until being silenced by the inevitable sickening impacts of their return to land. Even worse were the fates of those in the path of the dropping boulders; their comprehension of the situation would arrive but an instant prior to their squelching ends.

However, that wasn't enough to stop their enemy completely. While the infantry panicked and rushed to escape the area of the spell's effect, the heavily armored Panzcraft pushed forward unimpeded. A large chunk of rock fell directly on top of one's roof only to shatter into smaller bits with but a tiny indent left behind as evidence of its impact. Seeing this, most of the riflemen clustered around their frames so as to escape the worst of the remaining barrage.

In comparison, Vallen's comrades needed but move slightly one way or the other to avoid the tumultuous explosion of the square. He had purposely marked their locations to ensure that the terrain around them stayed firm. *But even I'm not* quite *perfect.* With his shields raised to the heavens, Unter was easily able to weather the storm of stones that couldn't be evaded by his large frame. Matteo, on the other hand, was compelled to scamper to the side to dodge a final cracking of the pavement that lifted past him and into the air.

As the last pieces of the surface layer crashed back down, it appeared as though the Sarconian detachment had weathered the worst Vallen could throw at them. Sylette, huddling near him while covering Velle as best she could, shot him a look of indignation that seemed to say, *For all your bragging, this is a pretty pathetic result.* In reply, the Triaron merely held a finger to his lips and pointed at the clustered groups of enemy soldiers. The majority of them were still gathered about their Panzcraft, while the rest were huddled in small bunches with rifles held at an angle above their heads to deflect falling debris. All eyes were on the skies—never suspecting that the next threat would once again come from below.

Suddenly the naked ground exposed by the displaced cobblestones shot upwards. Whole columns of earth, made of soil, clay, and packed minerals, blasted forth across the battlefield. None of these growths broke off to go flying into the air as before, but their very appearance proved disruptive. Terrified soldiers rose on pillars toward the heavens. Others were walled off from each other. The unluckiest found themselves nightmarishly ground between rising masses from which they couldn't escape, or slowly pierced by ancient stalagmites dredged up from beneath the town.

It was utter chaos. Officers shouted at their men to regroup, the few fortunate enough to be outside the spell limits alternately collapsed in shock or focused on naught but saving their own skin, and those trapped between or atop the new constructs cried for help as they struggled to wriggle free.

Even the Panzcraft were not unaffected. When Vallen spotted them in the confusion, one was already on its side, treads whirring uselessly, while the other was being overturned by a rapidly expanding cone of earth beneath it. Despite being near impervious to destruction, they faltered just as easily as anything else once robbed of their mobility.

When Vallen's incantation finally ran out of power, the sediment towers had reached a height of twenty meters. The church and town were only barely visible, glimpses of them glinting through small gaps in the seemingly random earthworks. His spell, the same one he'd used against Sylette in the graduation match a lifetime ago, had gone splendidly. Despite being on a completely different scale, its effects and sheer power were beyond expectations. *Pity it didn't go higher*, Vallen thought with a wide grin, looking up at the untouched cruiser still above.

Though the Triaron was content to leisurely observe his handiwork, others didn't share his enthusiasm. He felt a rough tug at his collar, at which he looked down to see Sylette doing her best to haul Velle in the direction of the chapel. "Are you planning to gape all day, or do you want to get a move on before they sort themselves out?" Apparently even doing exactly what he said he'd do wasn't enough to earn the slightest praise from this frigid woman.

Vallen opened his mouth to retort, only to find himself looking at the ground as he nearly fell flat on his face. A staggering step was all that saved him from a tumble. Darkness swirled at the edges of his vision, accompanied by a renewed throbbing in his right shoulder. After blinking away the clouds in his eyes—likely more imagined than real—he glanced at the wound to see that a red splotch had seeped through both hidden bandages and outer shirt. All these things, including Vallen's now racing heart, were symptoms of men'ar overuse.

The princess picked up on his weakness immediately. "Looks like it was too soon for you to push that hard. Well, at least it's stopped you from whatever *witty* reply you were about to make. Now get it together and drag yourself to the church if you have to." Without another glance, Sylette lurched past him, obviously struggling under the greater weight of the Sylph she carried.

Even the growing threat of slipping back into MIS wasn't enough for Vallen to take that one lying down. *Though technically I'm still standing, barely.* "Ha . . . if it weren't for . . . that *push* . . . as you put it . . . we'd be finished. I think . . . I deserve . . . at least a little . . . recognition for that." His exhausted rasp should've been loud enough to hear, even over the still shifting landscape about them, but Sylette was either too preoccupied with her task or simply ignoring him. *I'd bet on the latter every time.*

With the leaden pain of moving a body under the influence of the worst

413

hangover, Vallen turned and limped after her. There were plenty of Sarconian survivors around, and he certainly hadn't given up on avenging Leon, but as the silver-haired ice princess had correctly pointed out, there was a time and place for everything. If the Triaron didn't outright collapse in a few steps, he'd at least be useless for the rest of the day. Since most of the soldiers were focused on rescue efforts, for now—*for now*—it was best to simply survive while leaving them to their own devices.

From behind a nearby dirt bulwark came the sounds of intense exertion. Vallen briefly tensed up before the azure bulk of Unter was forced over the top of the barrier to collapse on the pavement beyond. Behind him came the mud-caked form of Renar, who groaned while flexing his muscles. The youth's greatsword, currently unneeded, had already been resheathed in the case on his back.

Unter was probably the worst for wear out of all of them. As he struggled to stand, Renar rushed to get under his left arms for support. The Hue's legs shook uncontrollably, still bleeding as a result of whatever chemical secretion coated the Moravi bones that had pierced them earlier. Add to that the chest wound, on top of taking the brunt of *multiple* Panzcraft rounds, and it was a miracle the giant was even breathing.

Since both of them made it through, that only leaves . . .

"Is there a reason you're still lugging that thing around?"

As was becoming common for her, Lilith materialized from nowhere at Vallen's side, pointing toward something at his feet. So fatigued was he that this time he didn't even react, neither to her sudden appearance, or the fact that the girl seemed to have no problem being coated with blood and grime from head to toe. Matteo, considerably cleaner, followed her with timid steps.

When he failed to respond—Vallen had missed what she'd said entirely—Lilith repeated the question, tapping her saber gently against the aforementioned object. "I said, why are you dragging that massive hammer? Wouldn't it be easier to carry in its normal form?"

At the pinging sound of metal hitting against metal, his gaze lowered to the ground where his chrome-tinted weapon, still in bulky warhammer mode, was scraping across the cobbles. *Oh*, Vallen thought. *That would explain why it's so difficult to move.* Since the strange device took on the properties of whatever Vallen was copying, a massive, crushing implement weighed significantly more than, say, a sword or dagger. Without a word he reverted the shape-shifting tool to its base, baton-like form.

Recognizing that the Triaron wasn't in the mood to chat further, Lilith made a playful face and rushed to catch up to the others. A single glare from Vallen sent Matteo scurrying after her. *If the Professor wasn't here, or could carry his own weight, we'd be so much better off.* However, just thinking about that inane fool made his head hurt, so he tried to focus on walking and nothing else. *Step left, step right, left, right. That's all I need to worry about.*

Vallen's faster gait saw him pass the awkward four-legged bundle of Unter and Renar as they reached the edge of the silt labyrinth. Though the duo was having a rough time of it, for obvious reasons, in his state the Triaron felt no compulsion to help them. After all, they were only making good on their escape thanks to him. *By the Veneer, I could've forgotten to leave an exit. I might've accidentally crushed someone too. I wonder if anybody realizes just how much they owe me?*

The sounds of their beleaguered foes faded behind the thick, meandering walls of earth they'd just left. Here, at the edge of his spell's area of effect, the dirt columns were only half formed. Some had collapsed entirely, spilling over into the church courtyard and burying most of the surrounding wrought-iron fence. The surviving Sariel statue stuck awkwardly from the sludge at a weird angle, while most of the garden was submerged beneath the mire. Only a solitary patch of stalwart neverfades, blooming astride the shadow of the now gaping wound in the chapel's side, remained untouched.

But none of them really cared about aesthetics right now. Their party stumbled across the rubble-strewn threshold, footing disturbed by both the debris and the jarring transition from foggy sunlight to murky darkness. As Vallen's eyes adjusted, he could see that the area around the breach was a mess inside too. The entire center segment of the modest temple was trashed: pews lay in myriad splinters, shredded holy books drifted across the ground and through the air, and shattered stained glass shone like muted stars amid the carnage.

While the windowpanes themselves were almost all broken, it was from their portals that the sanctuary's meager illumination came. But what they showed, beyond the destruction they'd already seen, wasn't hopeful. To their right was a pulpit and another, larger, bust of Sariel, his angelic wings spread to welcome the congregation, his long golden hair dropping down to arms held wide in benevolence. To their left were more, yet intact, pews, along with doors leading to what were likely offices or staff quarters.

Nothing visible looked worthy of the effort they'd spent getting here. In fact, they were just as trapped in here as out there.

Matteo's anxious shouting broke the dust-filled silence. "Abbot Kinloss! Are you here?"

A slight cough came from behind one of the rear pews, followed by the muffled whump of a large book being dropped on the ground. Sylette was immediately on guard, summoning a trio of daggers which hovered menacingly in the air between them and the noises. "Come out or get impaled!"

"No! Don't shoot! In the dark I thought you might be with the soldiers!" A frail, shadowed form stood up from behind the final row, wrinkled hands raised in surrender. The speaker quickly stepped into the center aisle, where the better lighting showed he was just an old Terran man in a brown habit. "See? I'm the one Mother Junica sent you to meet."

The princess wasn't quite convinced, but Matteo ran forward and hugged the clergyman despite the danger Sylette's blades still posed. "Abbot Kinloss! I'm so glad you're safe!"

"And I you," he managed to squeeze out through the embrace. "But we must hurry if we are to keep it that way. Oh my, you have a few injured." As the Abbot pried himself loose from the Professor, his gaze took in the state of Unter and Velle, temporarily resting on the benches nearby.

"Can you do something about that?" Lilith asked while cleaning her captured blade on a torn scrap of parchment she'd picked up.

"I'm afraid not. I have no magic training myself, and there's no one here but me so—"

"What do you mean there's no one here?" Sylette had dissolved her weapons, but her fiery temper seemed to be permanently engaged.

"Exactly that. I sent everyone away so they wouldn't be caught in the crossfire."

She stalked toward the monk until they were face to face. "Then what was the point of coming here? Where are the reinforcements? The weapons to help us fight back? A way to escape? This is nothing but a dead-end!"

Matteo, foolishly, tried to get between them. "Sylette, I think you might be overreacting a bit. There has to be a reason Mother Junica sent us—"

For his troubles he got an elbow to the chest, which left him staggering backwards until Renar steadied him. *Serves the coward right,* Vallen thought, not bothering to intervene as Sylette resumed her tirade.

"You stay out of this! So what's the *big plan* then, Abbot? Ask Sariel to negotiate on our behalf? Pray for the Sarconians to have a sudden change of heart?"

In spite of his age, the holy man seemed to possess some backbone. He turned and gestured for the group to follow him. "While we should always petition the Veneer and Creator for our foes to recognize their misdeeds, the current plan is indeed one of flight. If you will come with me, perhaps we can accomplish that before those outside recover their bearings."

Sylette rolled her eyes at the back of his head. However, even she wasn't going to balk at the only option left to them. She quickly bent down, hefting Velle onto her shoulder, this time with help from Lilith, before trailing after Kinloss. Renar and Matteo followed suit with Unter, leaving Vallen unburdened at the rear. Given his condition, though, it was only right that he not have to do any heavy lifting.

The Abbot led them through a set of wooden doors at the front of the hall and out into the adjoining foyer. Once the portals shut behind them, the sounds from outside grew even dimmer, softened by several solid layers of stone. Instead of going to the front entrance, perhaps to try to circumvent the Sarconian detachment by emerging past their lines, Kinloss headed to a single, unimpressive interior opening. He depressed the latch, pushed aside the sturdy oak door, and ushered them all into the chapel bathroom.

"You have got to be kidding me," Sylette breathed in exasperation. Normally Vallen would say something sarcastic right along with her, but since he was brutally weary, he settled for a heavy sigh. Even Matteo seemed confused by this strange turn of events.

"While I never pass up the chance to go, don't you think this is a bit much, Father?" Renar glanced at the stalls, underneath of which ran an empty— *thankfully*—waste trench that disappeared into the far wall. Lilith, nonplussed as always, walked over to the washbasin and began splashing water onto her blood-caked face and clothes.

"Relieve yourself if you need to, but our destination is over here." Kinloss strode through a thin curtain separating this room from the next. Vallen followed him and the others through the divide into, well, of course, the shower room. On this already weird adventure, it was the only destination that made sense. Fortunately, despite the opportunity presented by the four water spigots mounted in the walls around them, Lilith kept her clothes on. Her damp attire and body were still streaked with filth in hard to reach places, but apparently marginally clean was good enough for her.

Aside from the pipes and knobs necessary to operate the showers, the aqua-tiled chamber was almost completely bare. A towel rack adorned the far wall beneath a small, high-set window, and aside from that tiny aperture the only exit was the way they'd come in. Conclusion: it was the deadest part of an already very dead, dead-end.

And Sylette couldn't help but bite on that. "Look, I know you aren't used to this war and spy stuff, but hiding us here isn't going to help. They're going to search the entire church, and that flimsy little drape you've got across the entrance won't stop them. New plan, guys, we'll—"

"Do you ever pause to consider all the options, or is leaping before you look your go-to?" Not waiting for her response, Abbott Kinloss hitched up his habit and knelt in the center of the room. There, at the bottom of a slight incline, was a rusted metal drain cover, no bigger than Vallen's hand.

All of them, including Renar, seemed to catch onto the clergyman's scheme, and why it wouldn't work, at the same time. "No way we're fitting down that tiny hole."

"Of course not, but as you know, things aren't always what they seem." Kinloss impossibly thrust his hands through both the surrounding tiles and the metal hatch. At first Vallen thought the old man was just far more powerful than he appeared, but then his addled brain registered that the parts of his hands still exposed weren't bleeding from the impact. Furthermore, the image itself wasn't disturbed in the slightest. His hands had somehow pierced through the surface like it wasn't even there.

Like it wasn't even there.

"Morphic magic," Lilith whispered in muted awe. "Specifically, an illusion."

"Just so, my child. Now get me some younger, stronger arms down here to lift the real grate out."

"Who cast the spell?" Sylette asked as Matteo and Renar stooped to help Kinloss. The monk helped ease their disbelieving hands through the facade, guiding them to the truth behind the fiction.

"I'm not entirely sure. It was here when I took over this parish, and it will probably be here long after I'm gone. Could be the businessmen that founded Etrus, could be King Darmatus and his men from way, way back. All I know is that someone needed a way to escape unnoticed, and that the clergy here have kept it a secret for a long time."

With audible groaning, the two Terran youths heaved a slotted metal grate that was half a meter across out of the ground. As soon as the cover left its circular berth, the spell was disrupted and a dark hole wide enough for two men, or one Unter, was revealed. A series of rungs made a ladder on the near side that was visible for but a few meters before it was swallowed up by the gloom below.

"The incantation uses the connection between the grate and its slot as the trigger for activation, so when I push it back into place it'll look just like before. When the imperials search this place, even if they step on it, they shouldn't suspect a thing." The Abbot directed Matteo and Renar to set the cover at the edge of the hole, from whence he could more easily kick or push it back into place. Then he reached inside his voluminous sleeve and pulled out a yellowed scroll, which he handed to the Professor.

"This is a map of the Etrus waterways, the structure that this shaft leads to. This system was built to bring drinking water up from the valley to the top of this high hill, so while old, it should be reasonably clean and easy to navigate. Since Mother Junica made me aware that your goal is to escape by airship, I've already marked the quickest route to the harbor water processing plant, where you'll come up. Should be an easy dash to the hangars from there, since they are both in the same facility."

"What if they still manage to follow us?" Sylette would probably break down if she didn't ask *every* possible question about *every* little thing.

A knowing smile lit the monk's creased face. "In case that happens, I've already sent two of my brothers ahead. They've been instructed to head for the city's freshwater source near the Lyndwur Forest while making as easy a trail to follow as possible. Provided you stay in the water channel itself, which should only come to your waist at most, they should end up tracking the wrong group."

"Sounds good to me," Vallen said, finally speaking up. With the way forward clear, he had regained some of his earlier vigor. *Time to finally be free of this place.* He stepped toward the ladder, but Sylette stopped him with her outstretched arm.

"No, there'll be an order to this thing. Matteo has the map, so he goes first. After him will come Unter, followed by Renar. The two of them, on either side, will be responsible for making sure he doesn't fall. Then Lilith, Velle, and me, for the same reason. Since you're too tired to be useful, but not too worn to walk, you'll carry your own weight and come last. Got it?"

As with everything the exile said, her plan made a certain logical sense. *Plus I don't have to worry about anyone but myself.* Though it irked Vallen to acquiesce to Sylette about anything, he nodded in agreement.

"We still need light." Renar pointed at the pit, of which all but the top few meters were shrouded in shadows. Before losing most of their supplies in the recent battle—*Not my fault, of course,* Vallen determined—they'd had military-grade illyrium-powered glow rods. Now they didn't even have enough rations to last the rest of the day, let alone all their weapons.

"Maybe throw some candles down and hope they . . . don't . . . " Abbot Kinloss began but trailed off as Lilith purposefully walked over to the towel racks. With strength belying her small frame, she ripped both of them from the walls then took the discarded drying rags and wrapped them about one end of each. The remaining cloths she stuck onto the tip of her captured saber.

Next, to the amazement of all gathered, she recited a short chant and lit them ablaze. "These should do," Lilith stated matter-of-factly, returning to the shaft and dropping all three into the abyss below. They fell for just a few seconds—a good sign—before clattering to a halt against a solid surface. At this distance it was impossible to tell how many were still lit, but at least one continued to throw flickering light up the tunnel.

"We'll take the candles and a lighter too. Just in case," Sylette added, throwing Lilith one of her rare smiles.

After a short delay, during which Kinloss grabbed their additional supplies, they were ready to depart. Matteo, the first to descend, started onto the slippery top rungs before stopping to stare at the preacher aiding them. "What about you? Are you coming with us?"

"No. Someone has to stay behind and throw them off the scent. An empty church would be far too suspicious, and they would likely destroy the entire building in order to pick up your trail. No, I must remain here."

"They don't need an excuse to kill you, you know." Sylette's honesty was brutal, but from what Vallen knew of the Sarconians, absolutely correct. *It's what they did to Leon . . .*

"That may be, but regardless, I cannot leave my parish, my town, and my flock. Furthermore, I have to get the garden back to normal before you return. Maybe, at that time, everyone will come, not just Matteo and the Sylph girl."

"Don't do it, Abbot. Just leave! The flowers will be there when you get back," Matteo pleaded, clearly on the verge of tears. Before he could do something rash, Sylette guided the dazed Unter to the edge of the hole, forcing Matteo farther down the passage.

"There's no time!" Sylette insisted. "Leave him be. Renar, you're next."

When the entire party was in the hole, Kinloss bent over the gap to begin levering the cover back into place. Even at the top, as far away from Matteo as he could possibly be, Vallen could hear his pitiful cries echoing up from below. Since he had no way of silencing the idiot, his position in line was both a blessing and a curse.

When the grate was nearly closed, the clergyman leaned down, whispering through the gap. His face was so close to Vallen's that he could almost smell the man's breath. "Please take care of Matteo for me. He's a good lad, but his biggest flaw is that he cares too much. He can't decide what he cherishes the most and ends up frozen in fear, unable to prioritize anything. Teach him that there are things worth fighting for, and . . . that there are also some things that need to be let go of." *Yeah, sure thing,* Vallen thought, suppressing a snigger. *As if that coward will ever fight for anything. He'd sooner let everything slip through his fingers than stick his neck on the line.*

Vallen had no intention of responding, but even so Abbot Kinloss raised his voice loud enough to be heard by everyone in the shaft. "I will pray for your safety, my children, and may you do the same for me. Let the divine wisdom of Sariel guide all our steps, keep us safe, and, if the Creator wills it, allow us to meet again. Perhaps"—he smiled, a broad toothy grin visible to the Triaron and no one else—"next time it will be under circumstances far better than these . . . "

As his voice reverberated down the passage, a final shove resealed the entrance, dropping them into near total darkness and eliminating any chance of return. Vallen sighed and started descending carefully a rung at a time. Despite the Abbot's words, his only concern right now was not stepping on Sylette's fingers. The outburst that would ensue worried him far more than the prayers, petitions, and requests of any religious nutjob, helpful or otherwise.

Besides, faith in anyone but oneself is beyond worthless. Two people believed in me, and I in them. And what did that get them? What did that get me? Heh, nothing, that's what. But don't worry, I've got a new purpose now. I'll take it out on the ones responsible, exact vengeance for what they did, make them feel the same soul-crushing pain I've felt. And when I'm finished, neither of you will be lonely anymore . . . because they'll all have joined you in the place they truly belong . . .

Chapter 22

Purpose

The same thoughts replayed over and over in Matteo's head as they trudged through the waterways.

First was Leon's death. Then Unter and Velle got hurt when we were forced to run. Now my parents are almost certainly in danger, danger that I brought upon them. The same is true for Abbot Kinloss. Will they die for our—my—mistakes? Will all of us be killed?

Every waterlogged hallway looked the same, so much so that in his distracted state he'd already led them astray several times. First it was a dead-end overlooking a bottomless chasm. Then straying onto a series of passages that continuously looped back on themselves. When at last they hit the cavernous central drain, a massive chamber built as a reservoir for collecting unused runoff from the city above, Sylette snatched the map away from him. In retrospect, it was only fair— the room wasn't even remotely close to the thick red line denoting the path they were supposed to be following.

After an hour and several agonizing lectures later, they were almost to their destination. Despite several outbursts from Vallen, perhaps rightfully blaming him for their misfortune, the rest of the journey had passed in relative silence. Sylette, a stoic mountain of willpower and drive, led the way. At the princess's side was Lilith, the last of their makeshift torches flickering in her hand. Only her constant attention kept the flame from dying altogether. The rest of the party trailed behind them in partial darkness: Matteo carrying Velle on his back, Renar supporting the somehow unflagging Unter, and Vallen doing whatever he felt like.

Perhaps he was entitled to though, both to rag on him *and* act however he pleased. Without the Triaron's well-timed intervention everyone would surely be dead. Furthermore, Matteo himself had been worse than useless, getting in the way, forcing others to protect him, and simply being a burden no matter what he said or did. *A burden to my parents, to this town, to my friends, to—*

"You can't . . . no . . . shouldn't . . . become . . . like him."

A sudden listless whisper sounded directly into Matteo's right ear, startling him. His brief panic caused him to jump, and he nearly dumped Velle from his back. Realizing his mistake at the last second, he clamped down on her legs, which were twined about his waist, and lunged forward. That hasty movement did avert the Sylph's fall . . . but also pressed her body even tighter against his backside.

So soft . . . blast it, Matteo! What are you thinking about at a time like this? He shifted her weight, trying to ease her . . . ample . . . chest from its current location, but his attempts seemed to only make things worse. Matteo couldn't properly fix the situation without setting her down, which would take time, hold up the group . . . And it wasn't as though the feeling was entirely unpleasant.

The same voice spoke again, more insistent this time, snapping him out of his newest distraction. "It's me . . . Matteo, Velle. Stop freaking out . . . and just . . . keep walking."

"Velle, you're awake! That's, er, well, great!" He tried to keep his nervous embarrassment from his tone, but it slipped through just the same. Velle, in her weakened state, seemed to neither care nor notice. "H-how are you doing?"

"Fine, but . . . right now . . . I'm more worried . . . about you. You . . . seem to have this idea . . . that for your life to . . . have meaning . . . you have to be both brave . . . and powerful like Vallen."

Her words came in breathy bursts, as though it took considerable effort to think through and say each one. Obviously holding a conversation was something the debilitated Sylph shouldn't be doing. "Don't talk right now. You need to rest and save your energy—"

"If I . . . don't say anything . . . you're just going to keep . . . beating yourself up . . . which, in our . . . current circum—" Velle paused mid-word, coughing lightly until she could continue. Matteo felt each expulsion like small fists hitting between his shoulders and resisted the urge to stop her from speaking further. "—stances . . . hurts both of us."

When she finally got it out, her statement was baffling, so much so that Matteo simply puzzled over it for several moments without responding. *You're the one in real pain.* The group ahead turned down a side passageway, hopping back into the flow of water to do so. *Mine is just imagined; it's all in my head.* They had been out of the water on a raised side platform for a while now, so it would be annoying to hop back in with his nearly dry boots and socks, but Matteo followed just the same. Fortunately, though cold, this stream only came up to his knees, thus missing Velle entirely. *How does my self-doubt, my self-loathing, affect you?*

"What do you mean?" Matteo asked at length.

A short, hacking laugh followed. "I thought . . . knowing things . . . was *your* specialty."

The Sylph's comment was intended to be playful, but it just reminded Matteo of his inadequacies all over again. *Yeah, I'm just a brain. Not good for much else, and not even for that under pressure.* Matteo remained silent as he trudged, falling further behind the party both because of his burden and his divided focus. If they turned a corner now, he might even lose them.

"Come on . . . don't be like . . . that."

"Like what?"

"Mopey . . . depressed . . . this . . . "

One of Velle's hands, dangling limply around his neck, reached down and almost imperceptibly patted his chest for emphasis. *How am I acting different than normal?* Matteo's thoughts turned dark. *I've always thought Vallen was better, I've always wanted to be like him, I've—*

"And that's where you're wrong," Velle inserted forcefully, without rasping. "You used to think he was foolish, that he could improve, and that while there were things he was great at, there were things you could beat him at too."

"But what good are book smarts on a battlefield? What good is knowledge in a fight? What good . . . wait, did you just read my mind?" Matteo came to an abrupt halt in the middle of the gently running water. Part of his shock was regret—*I shouldn't be yelling at Velle*—but most of it was genuine awe . . . and fear at what she may have seen in his mind and heart.

"Not quite . . . and there's no need . . . to be afraid." The Sylph was back to split phrases. Talking normally was as much a burden on her right now as he'd thought it was. "Remember . . . I'm your friend . . . "

"So what are you doing then? How do you know what I'm thinking?" The light on the walls from ahead dimmed drastically, so Matteo rushed forward as he spoke, hoping that his sudden burst of movement wouldn't hurt his charge. In response, Velle wrapped her arms as securely about his chest as she could.

His choice to hurry proved fortunate, for they barely made it into view of the hobbling pair of Unter and Renar before they turned into another tunnel, this one sloping upwards toward the surface. If they lost the rest—on top of not having a map—it would be near impossible to escape this labyrinth of subterranean burrows.

With a large sigh, Matteo raced to the corner and clambered uphill after them. Apparently his efforts were comical, for Velle let out another giggle, this one less harsh than the last. "You know . . . I think I could . . . get used to being carried. It's nice . . . not having to walk . . . or climb up slopes. And then . . . you've always . . . got someone to talk to . . . which isn't bad either."

"It's not especially fun . . . for the one doing the carrying," Matteo gasped. He was bent nearly double going up the incline, to the point where anyone looking at them would almost think Velle was lying on a flat surface with legs. His only saving grace was that they were back on solid ground, and, even more of a boon, steps had been hewn into the stone to make the ascent easier. After suffering countless stair-running punishment drills at the academy, Matteo had never been more thankful to see a flight of them than at this moment. *Bless both the Veneer and the maintenance crews.*

In fact, for something akin to a sewer, the entire system was in magnificent shape. Since it was used for drinking, bathing, cooking, and other tasks, the water here was pure and nearly devoid of minerals. Drawn from an underground spring beneath the Lyndwur Forest, it was ferried against gravity by devices similar to the gravpads on airships, which used illyrium power to keep their charges afloat. Upon reaching the waterways, regular fluid mechanics took over, and a complex network of pipes and chutes carried the life-giving liquid to and from the surface.

Reaching the top of the incline, Matteo was forced into a squat to avoid banging Velle's head into one of those very same copper tubes. As thick as his head, it would've been a stinging blow, regardless of whether the water it carried was hot or cold. Rumor had it that one could tell how close ground level was by how thickly congregated the ducts were. With them practically strangling each other for space along the sides and ceiling of this passageway, it couldn't be that far off at all.

"That was a close call." Matteo felt his knees pop as he raised his body back up as high as he dared. Velle's sharp intake of breath indicated that her head was likely scraping the conduits above, so he set off after the others with a slight crook to his spine. With the excitement of catching up to the group past, Matteo decided to prod the Sylph once more about her earlier comment. "Velle, I don't mean to pry, but, well, just *how* did you know what I was thinking earlier?"

At that moment a fresh puff of wind, far different from the stale air they'd been forced to endure throughout the lower levels, blew at them from the front. Whether it came from a vent or an external opening, it was magnificently refreshing and smelled of the crispness of fall fading into winter. The cleaner draft also seemed to have a positive effect on Velle's condition. Her voice, though still faint, now spoke into his ear without wavering.

"That breeze is heavenly." The renewed expression in the girl's words, combined with the already close press of her body, served but to increase Matteo's discomfort. He shifted surreptitiously as he walked, hoping against hope that she wouldn't notice, but Velle's own slight movement in response made the friction between them all the more unbearable. "And there you go again. Please calm down, Matteo."

"I-I am calm!" he stuttered in response, once again bewildered by the Sylph's discovery of his inner agitation. *I barely moved. How does she keep figuring it out? And does she know why I'm excited, or merely* that *I'm excited? Has Velle always been able to see inside us like this?* The whirlwind of thoughts inside his head did serve to distract him from his rising yearnings, but also threatened to spiral out of control into incoherency if any more tangents piled upon those already spinning about. Mercifully, Velle's soothing voice cut through them all.

"Fine. This is partly my fault, and it's not that big of a secret anyway." She paused, as if waiting for his undivided attention before continuing. Only when Matteo's mind had quieted did she continue. "I, along with many of my kind, am an empath. In other words, we can see the emotions of others."

It would be a difficult concept to swallow if Matteo hadn't already felt the ability's effects. Even so, it came as a shock and forced him to reassess everything he knew about Velle: her actions, her words, and, more than anything else, her relationships. *Does Vallen know? Does she know his secrets—all our secrets?* "Is it always on? H-have you been able to see what we're thinking and feeling the entire time?"

"And this is why most Sylph don't tell anyone. Their first reaction is always panic." Velle shifted uneasily and dug her nails into the front of his shirt, almost as though his alarm were bleeding over into her. *Oh, right, it probably is.* Matteo refocused as much of his attention as he could on their surroundings. Watch that rubble pile, duck beneath the pressure valves there, make sure the party isn't getting too far ahead. The distraction seemed to work, for Velle gradually calmed. "I don't know how you put yourself under so much stress all the time. You are by far the most anxious person I've ever felt, but somehow it doesn't consume and destroy you. Matteo, you have a strength you don't realize."

He blushed, felt his cheeks reddening, and endeavored to still his mind even more. *Neutral thoughts. Neutral thoughts.* "Anyway," she continued. "I care about all of you, and my goal isn't to invade your privacy. That's why I tend to be wary of physical contact with others, unless I feel I can use my power to help them. You see, Sylph empath abilities stem from our capacity to control our blood. Since we can use that to read the flow of our own pulses, it stands to reason that we can interpret what those changing rhythms mean—what feelings they represent. Then it's a simple matter of connecting with another being and reading the cadence of their heart."

In spite of himself, Matteo began to feel more self-conscious about the sensuous weight on his back. "So you have to be touching a person for it to work?"

"Yes. A hug, an extended handshake . . . a several-hour paik-back ride," Velle said with a cute laugh, the irony of their situation clearly not lost on her. "The more direct skin contact, the better, and the same with the time of coupling."

Matteo nearly tripped at her choice of vocabulary, as it instantly sent his thoughts to all the wrong places. He gulped as he tried to regain his bearings. "So, uh, given how you specifically knew I was, er, thinking about Vallen before, d-does it just let you sense what emotion they're feeling, or, well, is it a little more exact?" He waited on bated breath for Velle's answer, since it would determine whether the beautiful woman he carried knew just how he felt about her.

The Sylph gently laid her bare cheek against his neck, her long, lustrous black hair falling across Matteo's aching shoulders. He knew it wasn't a romantic gesture, but just that minor contact sent lightning through his nerves to reinvigorate his tired body. "The best practitioners can see almost everything the target knows, both in their current thoughts and subconscious. It's one of the reasons you see the few Sylph outside of the Magerium in businesses revolving around trade and information.

"A nudge, a deal sealed with a clasp of hands, a warm caress or a night of passion, all of them yield the knowledge needed to succeed in the world outside our home. Furthermore, since we can manipulate the temperature of our bodies to some degree, it's also why many Sylph . . . prefer to wear as few garments as possible." She said the last part carefully, as though trying to bury the implications. For her part, Velle always dressed to fit the occasion, but that never stopped her allure from shining through.

"And how much can *you* see?" Matteo drove forward with a confidence that belied his usual trepidation. *Why is this so important to me? I could still drop it and let things return to normal.*

She sighed, and the breath passed across the flesh exposed beneath his collar, propelling a thrilling chill down his spine that took every ounce of Matteo's willpower to subdue. "A few words, a glimpse at the cause of the emotion, no more. And, of course, I feel, to some degree, the same things my partner does."

"So, umm, does that mean—"

"Yes, yes, it does." Velle's voice was compassionate, despite obviously knowing what he was referring to. "But it's a natural reaction to a situation like this, and you're sweet to be worried about how I'd take it. Besides, I know you don't mean any harm."

Another long slope, this one free of flowing water, stretched into the murk before them. From the flare of the torch some distance ahead, it was clear that a series of lights and electrical cables ran along the walls. Though they were off now, with no switch in sight, it was a promising clue that the group was near a maintenance access of some sort.

However, the added difficulty of the upwards traverse did little to stem Matteo's unique confusion. Equal parts relief, embarrassment, and dejection, his mind was in such turmoil that he could not find the words to respond. *She found out about my . . . weird thoughts but doesn't really care. Is that a good thing or a bad thing? Do I want her to care?*

A gentle touch at his chest broke his reverie once more. "Don't focus on that, Matteo. We can talk about it later. What can't wait is what started all this—our talk about Vallen."

The change of topic was a welcome one, though he tried his best to hide that sentiment. "Why does . . . Vallen matter?" He grunted as the path increased in angle by several degrees. Whoever designed this place had clearly not taken people carrying others into consideration.

"Because you've decided to use him as the illyriite standard for everything."

"That's not—"

"It is true and you know it. But he's not perfect. He's flawed just like the rest of us. Vallen has scars—deep, horrible scars—that hang him up and make him act irrationally and . . . " Velle's impassioned speech petered out, as though she were unsure how much she should be telling him. Matteo felt warm, wet drops on the nape of his neck. *She's crying?*

"It's alright, Velle, you can stop there. I—"

"No, you need to hear this." She slowly controlled her sobs, the movements of which he could feel through the connection between their bodies. Suddenly it occurred to Matteo that in spite of the perseverance and fortitude Velle had shown thus far, she might be just as overwhelmed as he was. For the first time he was able to see the girl beneath the woman—scared, unsure . . . and hurt.

"You see, it was his pain that first drew me to him. I . . . had my own issues that drove me away from home, and in Vallen I saw an opportunity, a chance to help someone in a way only one of my race can, and by doing so . . . also redeem myself. I tried to become what he needed, to change who I was to suit the moment. But in the end I failed. He chose escape over healing, and it's only gotten worse since Leon's death. You saw that last night when he broke down, and today when he fought like we didn't matter."

It was a lot to take in at once, especially in the middle of what was little better than a mountain climb in full kit. Yet Matteo did his best to internalize Velle's words—maybe helping her would save him, just as she had tried with Vallen. "You tried to salve his wounds with your presence, giving him the love and attention you thought he needed. But he rejected everything, and now you're left wondering if you should have tried in the first place."

The short snigger Velle gave was completely at odds with the tone of their discussion. "You know, you have a knack for this therapy thing. Maybe we can start a business. I'll be the secretary, and your patients can take turns riding around on your back through sewers, ruins, and such."

"You'd at least be full partner. You started this, remember?"

"True. But however will you carry both me and another person?"

"Just attach a wagon to my waist with a rope and we'll be set."

Imagining that sight set them both to laughing. So loud and boisterous were they that most of the group paused and glanced back at them. When they finally finished, the last of the echoing guffaws fading away, Matteo found himself wondering where his newfound self-assurance had come from. *Maybe that's the effect Velle has on me . . .*

Unable to wipe the tears of mirth from his eyes, he tried to blink them away while the Sylph returned to the previous topic. "But yes, you're right. I set out to try to bring Vallen up from his misery and at some point fell in love—not quite with him, but with the idea of saving him. And while it hurts, it seems either he doesn't want to be saved, or that I wasn't up to the task . . . "

Velle's voice cracked, and once again she seemed on the verge of tears. Before Matteo could attempt to comfort her, the Sylph continued, "And so my point is this: you're *you*, Matteo, as simple as that sounds. Don't try to be Vallen. You haven't lived his life, and he hasn't lived yours. Find your own path, your own goals, and your own reasons to accomplish them. With your kindness, strength, and will, I'm certain you can do it."

Sure, those were great motives to do something, but Matteo's problems were twofold. *Simply discovering what I want to do in the midst of this terrible situation won't be enough. I still lack the courage to see any of it through!* "Velle, that's perfectly good advice—"

"Nice of you two lovebirds to finally join us."

Matteo stumbled in surprise as he narrowly avoided walking straight into Sylette. Fortunately, Lilith was there to help, stepping forward to ease Velle from his back. However, she couldn't also save him from his own fate. First his left leg caught a loose floor slab, then the right banged a low pipe joint, and Matteo fell face first into the metal door ahead. The princess, who had sidestepped at the first sign of his graceful approach, clicked her tongue disapprovingly.

"If you had been paying attention, this wouldn't have happened. Do try to avoid adding yourself to the list of our injured." Sylette would likely have been more displeased with him if his collapse had made more noise, but the heavy old door barely registered the impact. With a groan, Matteo stood back up, one hand feeling at the sizeable welt already growing on his forehead. *As if I don't have enough to worry about.*

Since everybody else was standing around in varying degrees of exhaustion, this must be their destination. Besides, Sylette didn't seem like one to take a break mid-march. While Lilith sat Velle against a nearby wall, Renar applied the last of their bandages to Unter's wounds, all of which seemed to be getting worse, not better. Sickening yellow pus dripped from the chemically infected leg gashes, and since there wasn't an exit hole, a lead bullet was certainly lodged in the Hue's breast. Regardless of his race's hardiness, he would not last much longer without proper treatment.

Which, of course, Velle could give him if the Sylph wasn't on the edge herself. Despite being fully conscious now, using magic would simply fry her men'ar cells and leave her on death's door as well. That left Vallen, who, remarkably, was as useless as Matteo right now. Spent and lost in his own thoughts, he hadn't even bothered responding to Sylette's quip implying that he and Velle were more than friends. *It seems she was right—both about his priorities and his capabilities.*

Unbidden, Matteo's musing mind deposited an almost unthinkable idea on top of the previous one: *maybe, just maybe, this is my time to shine!*

"After a couple more minutes, we'll head through this door and out onto the tarmac. From there we'll locate the hangar our airship is in and fight our way to it. What's the number of the building we're looking for, Matteo?"

"H-hangar three," he stammered, caught off guard by Sylette addressing him directly. Glancing up at her, he noticed for the first time that there was a glass slit the size of a small board at the top of the door. From it filtered streams of elongated afternoon sunlight—a welcome sight given the hours they'd spent underground. More gratifying were the vents above the egress, which blasted refreshing air into the sealed room from outside.

Unfortunately, the ashen viewport also revealed disheartening news. They had come up at an access point near the water purification plant, but not in it. To their left were the grand silos, taking in the underground flows, processing them, then storing the clean fluid for use by the townsfolk. Beneath their long shadows were naught but a few maintenance trolleys, overflow barrels, and dilapidated forklift transports waiting to be disassembled for parts. In this age of magic automation, delivering water door to door was as archaic as drawing it from a well.

But while that side was clear and unguarded, the same could not be said of the hangars and army base on the other. Though Etrus didn't possess the most expansive harbor facilities, the Sarconians were certainly looking to change that. On top of the three existing, medium-sized hangars, a fourth and a fifth, both large enough to house heavy cruisers, were on their way up. In the week since the occupation began, the scaffolding had already risen twenty meters high, supporting solid metal frames that made the originals look flimsy by comparison.

Additionally, four anti air batteries were scattered about the warehouses, their cannons pointed to the sky as though begging the Darmatians to try and reclaim their abandoned facility. Sandbags surrounded those positions now, but concrete pillboxes were being constructed to replace them. More jarring still was the large pillar being constructed at the far end of the runway separating the plant and base. It rose above everything in the vicinity, thick at the bottom and topped by a small sphere at its thinner peak. The space between was filled with concentric rings that stood out from the core column, each about a meter distant from the last. Ironically, though it didn't appear to be much more than an oversized lightning rod, most of the base's ground defense—infantry units and several panzcraft—were clustered about it.

Figuring out exactly what the bronze pole was would have to wait. If only the perimeter forces were taken into account, Matteo knew they had next to zero chance of making it to his father's airship in their condition. It would be the summit battle all over again, this time without a convenient escape route to save them. However, the actual likelihood of success was worse than negative. Regardless of what Sylette believed, they simply weren't getting past the two cruisers resting on the tarmac, their thick armor and bristling armament glistening imposingly beneath the evening sun's rays.

So Matteo decided to do something unorthodox, something completely out of character for him. He decided to speak up. "Sylette, there has to be a better way."

He immediately regretted his choice, flinching back from the verbal—or physical—barrage that was sure to come. But the princess merely crossed her arms and gave a sardonic eye roll. "How else are we supposed to get there? We're out of equipment, half of us are injured, and this is the exit that monk marked on the map. We have to try. Or do you want to take the coward's way out and go back to the search party that's almost certainly found the entrance to the waterways we used?"

"I, for one, vote backtracking to the forest. It may be slow going, but we'll be alive," Renar interjected from his crouched position by Unter. He also raised his hand, as though starting a poll, before Lilith walked over and slapped it back down.

"We'd still have to cross the path we came on," she countered. "Either way we run into the Sarcs."

"Oh, right."

Matteo clenched down on the small fire of confidence simmering in his chest, using it to drive forward. "Say we reach the hangar. What if it's locked?" *Did you even consider whether or not our enemies would want to keep others from stealing their stuff?* He bit his tongue before saying the last sentence. Already walking an unfamiliar tightrope, he wasn't going to push harder than necessary, especially when dealing with Sylette's icy temper.

"Then we break in. The main door, the side door, the windows—whatever's necessary."

"The front entrance is fifty millimeters of Gestalt steel that takes two illyrium engines to slide apart. The side is only ten millimeters, but that's still pretty strong. All the windows are ten meters or higher from the ground." *Now tell me how you expect us to get in while under fire from a small army.*

To her credit, Matteo didn't need to add his silent conclusion for the princess to reach the same realization he had. In an unusual display of uncertainty, Sylette bit the left side of her lip then looked at him with a mix of frustration and expectation. "I take it you have a suggestion? We can't do nothing. Unter needs medical attention, Velle's not doing well either, and they'll find us eventually. We have to try something, sooner rather than later."

"Let me see the map of the waterways."

Without further complaint, Sylette drew the aged paper from a pouch on her belt. Matteo took it with a nod of thanks and scanned the area around their current location. Though it hadn't been his favorite thing to do, he had spent a lot of time at the harbor—and therefore in his father's hangar. *Carry these, Matteo. Tie those knots properly, Matteo. You're going to have to learn basic accounting to help me with the books, Matteo. Clean the place up, Matteo—we've got some important clients coming tomorrow.*

He remembered the interior layout perfectly. In fact, it had been ingrained into him, both because his father needed an extra, mostly unpaid, laborer, and because he had always hoped his son would take over the family business. *If I get out of this, perhaps I'll do just that.*

There! A small shaft leading directly below hangar three, right beneath the washroom used by Martan's employees. Matteo had known it needed a sizeable drain, just like the one in the church. After all, he spent his childhood scrubbing those showers until they gleamed. *Now we have to hope it's big enough to fit someone through.*

He reached down and dug some grime out of a gap between the floor slabs. *Can't blame the maintenance crews for skipping this.* It was mushy to the touch, being predominantly mud, and perfect for makeshift chalk. With a few quick swipes of a finger, the new route was marked.

"Lilith, can I ask you a favor?" Matteo held the map out in front of him until the brunette came and took it. "You're the smallest among us . . . o-of course, I don't mean that in a bad way . . . so I was hoping you could go and see whether we can make it down the path I've marked. It's not too far, down the hall and take the first turn."

The petite girl didn't seem to care whether he was implying something rude or not, for she simply nodded and dashed back down the passageway, failing torch in hand. Lilith returned a few minutes later, covered in grime, wet from head to toe, clothes torn. The torch was no longer with her.

"It's nothing like the hole beneath the chapel. I was barely able to fit through, and while I didn't go that far, it looks to be about the same size all the way through. There's no way everyone, especially Unter, is squeezing in there."

Despite Sylette shooting him the "what now?" glare, Matteo had been prepared for this to happen. There was still one way, dangerous and haphazard though it might be, for them to get into the hangar *and* distract an entire army.

However, it might mean destroying part of the company his father cherished.

Were his father here, he'd probably take that risk himself. *I can always rebuild Antares Shipping*, Martan would say. *What I can't replace are lives.* Imagining his broad grin and beaming face were all Matteo needed to make his decision. "Lilith, I want you to follow that path all the way to the end. If I'm reading this map correctly, at the end should be a vertical drain, much like the one built into the church. Hopefully shifting the grill isn't too difficult, but if you have to blast it out of the way, do so. Then find my father's store of synth-oil. Since it's a shipping company, there should be a decent amount. After that, you do what you do best—blow it up."

"You want to blow up the warehouse?" Sylette had remained calm through his explanation but now exploded just like the barrels of lubricant would in their incendiary solid form. "What will that accomplish?"

"It's the only way in. Either the blast knocks out a wall or the fire failsafes will kick off."

"What about your key?" The princess gestured at Matteo's pocket, where the airship activation pin, though small, weighed on him with the responsibility it entailed. "Why would your father give you the ship key but not the means to get to it?"

"Key . . . no open door. Code . . . for entrance . . . required . . . but changed it . . . has Empire. Martan told me such . . . thinking possible . . . for me to bypass . . . it was." Though Matteo hadn't considered hacking the security panel at the hangar's side access, it made sense that his father had told the magtech-savvy Unter about the workaround and not him. Anything beyond punching in the numbers on the pad would be out of his depth. However, the fading giant was in no condition to enact that plan either. Simply talking left him gasping for breath, a sign that one of his lungs had almost surely been perforated as a result of his chest wound.

"And what happens when the building comes crashing down? We could lose the airship!"

Despite the fact that her plan of inciting a base-wide firefight was *just* as likely to destroy their objective, Sylette continued to pick apart his plan. Though, considering that he was never the one who came up with ideas, Matteo could hardly blame her. "It's a possibility, but the transport should be on the opposite side of the warehouse from the synth-oil. Our goal in igniting a blast is to set off the fire system. Sprinklers will come on, alarms will sound, and all the doors will automatically open to let out the smoke. That's when we blend together with the rush of people going to fight the blaze and sneak in."

Lilith nodded her assent to the plan, and Sylette, though still skeptical, warmed to the idea. "That seems like a reasonable approach. But I can't quite fathom why such a simple plan would work. In the empire or Imperium, they'd never be foolish enough to allow something like a small fire to undo their security measures."

"Yes, well, as you've pointed out before, we aren't the best at war. Around here, everyone is in the business of making money, and protecting our stock comes first. Hence the automatic failsafe." *Let's just be happy something is working in our favor this time.*

As the lithe brunette ran off to resume her previous spelunking adventure, Matteo and Sylette set about getting the rest ready for a final dash, the signal for which was, of course, the giant detonation that would likely rock the entire complex. Checking the area outside one last time, he spotted several industrial hoses rolled up near the water towers, firefighting equipment probably left there by some lazy dockhand who was more worried about clocking out on time than following protocol. Several portable frames, along with canisters to place on them, were strewn about as well. Grabbing those items as they went would help solidify their cover.

While Renar helped Unter to his feet, Sylette was busy accosting Vallen into carrying Velle. It made sense to Matteo that he should have his hands free, given that this was his plan and he was the only one who could fly the ship, but some small part him felt annoyed that the Triaron should get to be close to the injured Sylph after everything he had done to hurt her. However, doing something about it would be impossible—both because he'd have to directly confront Vallen and because it would betray Velle's confidence in him. Which was worse, he couldn't say.

Strangely, Vallen, in his own way, seemed cowed by the silver-haired princess, for he quickly acceded to her demands and reluctantly hefted Velle onto his back. Matteo was also terrified of her impetuous fury and aggressive assertiveness, but their dynamic seemed somehow different. *If I didn't know better, I'd say they're so similar that neither can stand the other.*

Five minutes passed. Then ten. Matteo was beginning to think Lilith had run into trouble, either an impasse in the tunnel or an unexpected guard squad in the building. Simply imagining what such a failure would mean for them made him more and more nervous.

Almost instantly the ground began to shake, a tumultuous tremor even greater than the aftereffects of Vallen's earth spell. Dust shook loose from the ceiling, unsecure tiles vibrated free, and several pipes broke free of their moorings. One of Matteo's hands caught the door handle just in time to steady himself, while the others either fell or braced themselves against the wall. Barely had the rocking subsided than the shockwave hit, carrying with it a cracking snap that could be heard even within their cement bunker. To those outside it must have sounded like a blast from a dreadnought's main armament.

With his head still ringing, Matteo thrust down on the latch he had grabbed and threw open the metal hatch. "Go, go, go! Renar, grab a hose and toss it over Unter's shoulder! Sylette, get one of those backpack canisters!"

The light from above was momentarily blinding as his eyes adjusted from the murky darkness they'd been in for hours. Even so, he pointed as best he could in the direction of the nearby silos, hoping that his comrades would understand his intent.

Alarms blared across the complex, their shrill cries only adding to the throbbing in his skull. From here hangar three appeared normal, its walls still standing, but out of both the opening front entrance and rear poured thick, black smoke, evidence of a fierce fire brewing inside. *Opening front entrance . . .* Matteo thought. *By the Veneer, my plan worked!*

But there was no time for celebration. If they didn't capitalize on the confusion caused by the explosion, they'd be no better off than before. With the spry Sylette in the lead, they raced—as fast as possible given their injuries— to the water towers, grabbing whatever equipment they could. Renar took two thick loops of hose and draped them around the blue giant's lower arms. Unter, though weak, clutched them tightly to his waist. Vallen fidgeted in place. Even with Velle on his back, he seemed on the verge of breaking off to chase after the Sarconian soldiers rushing toward the burning warehouse.

For her part, Sylette seemed content to follow the plan to the letter. She bent down, grabbed a small twelve-liord barrel, and fastened it onto a wooden carrying frame set against one of the inoperable trolleys. Preparing to place it on her back, the princess swept her long locks out of the way, only to freeze with the majority still wrapped in her left hand.

"Renar, give me your shirt."

The bulky Terran, currently placing another roll of tubing about his free shoulder, shot her a look of utter disbelief. "What?"

"Your shirt. Now."

The princess's intent dawned on Velle first, who feebly raised her head to speak to the perplexed and reddening Renar. "Sylette's hair. It's her most defining feature, the one they're looking for. She needs to cover it up."

In retrospect, it made perfect sense, but the former bully remained self-conscious about it even so. "What about Vallen? Or Matteo?" While Matteo didn't like being brought into this, he was at least thankful that Renar hadn't suggested stripping the ailing Unter of his outerwear—which would be massively oversized besides. *And why she doesn't want Vallen's is as clear as day to everyone besides him, I think.*

"Stop complaining and give me the blasted shirt!"

Once the exchange had taken place, and Sylette had wrapped her unique silver strands beneath Renar's worn grey tunic, they were ready to tackle the next stage of Matteo's plan. A mass of soldiers was now gathered in front of the hangar, where beneath the fully open Gestalt doors a bucket chain to the next building over was forming. Though there was a perimeter guard in place, most of those attempting to fight the blaze, now visible through the high windows on the right side of the building, had abandoned their arms and armor on the ground.

"From here we head straight for the hangar doors. If anyone stops us, we say we're civilians who were helping build the new hangars and are trying to assist with the firefighting. Hopefully they buy it. Let's go."

Matteo, a decent sized pail in each hand, led the way across the tarmac. By this point, there was enough smoke in the air to partially block out the sun, bringing an early onset to the evening that was still several hours off. Velle and Unter shortly began coughing, the acrid vapors agitating their already impaired senses. Renar, without a shirt himself, tore strips from Unter's sleeves and pressed the light cloths to their mouths and noses. It wasn't a perfect solution, but it was better than nothing.

As they passed between the cruisers, one of them began lifting off. Matteo ducked halfway to the cement before realizing that there was absolutely no way it had anything to do with them. The vessel ascended into the smog, where its thrusters engaged, buffeting them with a warm backwash and temporarily clearing the area of gas. Then it glided out over the nearby harbor, descending to the surface with the armor plates about the lower decks retracted.

"They intend to flood the bottom levels and weapon emplacements, then dump the entirety onto the warehouse," Sylette announced by way of explanation. Matteo, glancing over at her, noted that even with her signature characteristic hidden she remained striking. If anything, the turban lent the exile an additional air of exotic glamour.

"It will take some time to restore those areas, especially since the water here has salt in it, but it seems they value this base enough to do so. You should be happy they care so much about your people, Matteo."

He caught the sarcasm in her voice, an indication that their goal was anything but the wellbeing of Etrus. *They care only about the strategic value of this installation. Nothing more.* Their actions this morning made it painfully clear that the empire didn't care who or what was in the way of their objectives.

At the edge of the unfolding chaos was a hastily erected checkpoint—really just a couple of soldiers fortunate enough to have been selected for security rather than manual labor. As their group approached, one guard stepped forward while removing a set of earplugs. Whether they had been issued to all the men, or he had simply chosen to ignore regulations and wear them, Matteo couldn't say.

"I don't recognize you lot. What group are you with, and what are you doin' here?"

On the scrawnier side, despite his cuirass and the chainmail beneath it, he seemed used to giving orders. The sneer he wore was probably a nigh permanent fixture, one far more easily read than the prominent rank insignia on his chest. In other words, he fell into yet another class of individuals Matteo struggled to deal with: superiors.

"Well, you see, we heard the explosion and, er, rushed over to, you know . . . help . . . out?"

The slight adjustment of the soldier's stance and narrowing of his eyes were obviously bad signs. "We've got enough people working already. Y'all just scamper back to town right quick before I book you for—"

"Sergeant, it seems there's been a misunderstanding," Sylette said, edging past Unter and Renar, whom she'd been hiding behind to avoid attention. While the princess was far better suited to dealing with military types than Matteo—ironic, given that he was a cadet himself—he could only pray she didn't blow their cover. "We're part of the crew working on the new hangars, assigned there on the orders of Lt. Colonel Stetson. If you want to validate our credentials with him, you're welcome to do so, but you know how much he *loathes* having his time wasted."

Invoking Stetson's name impacted the man like a bolt of lightning. His back straightened, his smirk disappeared, and he practically stumbled over himself making amends. "That won't be necessary, miss. I'm sure the commander needn't be bothered o'er something so trivial." Then his eyes focused on Velle and Unter, whereupon skepticism reentered his tone.

"But what about the Hue and Sylph you have with you? Orders from above are Terran work crews only, no exceptions."

"The blauer is one of the top architects in the city, while the feurgrer is a medic. They were brought in because of the limited personnel in those areas," Sylette smoothly lied, nonchalantly using the derogatory slang some Terrans used to reference the skin color of their races. While Matteo knew the words, Eliassi for "blue beast" and "crimson witch" respectively, he never expected to hear them from the lips of anyone he associated with. With his mouth hanging partially agape, the sergeant was clearly taken aback at her casual use of the terms.

"A-and their injuries?"

"Inflicted in a similar blast in the underground waterways where we were investigating the structural integrity of the base's foundation. It's probably how the terrorists got in and out."

Both the eyes of their questioner and his partner, who'd been listening silently, bulged out in surprise. "Terrorists! How do you know that?"

Playing the perfect haughty superior, Sylette rolled her eyes with disdain. "Who else do you think did this? Isn't it obvious? And shouldn't you be doing something about it? Send somebody into those tunnels. You could still catch the rebels who did this!" She emphasized her point by gesturing back toward the small stone building by the water purification plant they'd emerged from.

By the gleam in the sergeant's gaze, Matteo could easily discern the exact moment at which he fell for the princess's bait. Clearly writ there was *If I can catch those responsible, I'll be well rewarded.* "Corporal, gather up the squad and meet me o'er by the water plant. You lot get going—take care of the fire, get back to work, whatever. Just stay out of the way of the soldiers."

"Yes, sir." Sylette sketched a salute, which was completely ignored by the two men as they scrambled to assemble a task force to hunt down the very people they had just finished talking to. If the situation weren't so dire, Matteo would have laughed aloud at the sheer irony of it all.

The guard cordon broken, there was nothing of consequence left to overcome between them and the dark, smoking maw of the hangar. In that space flowed a teeming sea of red, gold, and beige, Sarconian soldiers stripped down to their tunics, or, in some cases, bare flesh. Those going into the building wore nothing but pants or undergarments, dousing themselves with buckets of water to stave off the heat for as long as possible. The root of that precaution, the fire they themselves had planned and set, was still deep within the warehouse, but crawling gleefully closer with every passing second.

"Anyone not on bucket duty should be grabbing anything you can out of the fire's path! We need to slow it down long enough for the *Impelus* to return!" An officer, his cap and saber eschewed for a hose and handheld projectomic, was shouting orders from the center of the chaos. Like his men, he was down to his skivvies and covered in dirt and soot, evidence that he had been working right alongside them.

At his orders, mattresses, shipping containers, cots, sacks, spare parts, and anything not bolted down were being removed from the hangar. Once out, the soldiers cast it anywhere they could before diving back into the smog. The ground was littered with the detritus of a lived-in barracks, a sign that the building had been converted to troop housing. Matteo's gut clenched out of worry for Lilith, both that she had survived her explosion and that she hadn't yet been discovered.

"You there! Stop gaping and get those buckets in there!"

A muscular, shirtless man with the face of a toad began filling Matteo's buckets from a small canister set atop a stand of crates. As soon as they were mostly full, he shoved the youth toward the entrance and motioned the next man forward. Unbeknownst to him, Matteo had stumbled into the pail line. But that was just as well; now he had an excuse to head inside.

Sylette, bending under the pantomimed weight of her carrying case and canister, was equally successful getting herself and the others through. Renar dumped the hoses with a group of grateful soldiers who began jury rigging them together to reach the next hangar over. Then, with their remaining equipment and injured comrades, they ducked through the smoke wall and into . . .

. . . a furnace. Matteo immediately dumped his buckets, bringing his hands up to protect his tearing eyes. *Clang!* The precious water within the overturned pails sloshed uselessly across the glossy floor. However, the loss of the precious liquid was secondary right now. Between the vapors and heat it felt like every orifice of his body was alternately melting or stinging—a spectrum of pain that left him briefly unable to think about anything else.

Then he felt something cold—well, cooler—thrust into his left hand. The voice of Sylette, dulled by the sound of the roaring flames, yelled at him from the same side. "Goggles! I got them from the soldiers! Put them on and let's go!"

With great difficulty, Matteo fumbled the pair of lenses onto his face, securing them with a strap that wrapped about his head. Then, only then, did he open his eyes, despite the residual aching he felt from the ashes already inside them. A maelstrom of flames cackled at the far side of the large main room; the hallway leading to the back rooms, offices, washroom, and stairs to the second level had already been consumed. All the places Matteo remembered, his father's office, the hidey hole beside the rear loading dock, everything, was gone. If he had time to, or if his tear ducts would've worked in this extreme heat, he might have cried.

No! That's not what I should be thinking about! Where's Lilith? The passageway at the center of the far wall was wreathed in fire. There was no way anyone was getting through that hell of whirling yellows and orange. If she wasn't already out of the fuel storage room, or the baths from which she emerged, the girl was probably . . .

"Snap out of it! There's the ship!"

Sylette began running toward the left side of the room. Vallen, following her, nearly bowled Matteo out of the way, and Renar and Unter weren't far behind. Ahead, under the eaves, was the transport they were looking for. Whether because they didn't have the key, or because they didn't have anywhere else to put it, the empire had kept it in its original docking berth.

The blaze, trapped at the rear of the warehouse for lack of anything combustible to consume—*at least the Sarconians did something right*—lapped at the neighboring stall and encroached upon it from the rafters. However, unable to cross the bare cement floor in between, or gain purchase upon the metal ceiling, it could not reach the craft. *Yet another small fortune in what has thus far been a calamitous journey.*

Matteo followed her, trying to ignore the oncoming dizziness and heat-induced fatigue that threatened to drop him to the scalding pavement. Every breath was agony, so he could only imagine how Velle and Unter felt right now. He drew on that thought, using their stalwart courage to boost his own as best he could.

When they not so much arrived but stumbled into the meager shadow of the ship, a figure detached itself from the darkness behind one of the four landing gear. "This is a pretty old ship. Are we sure it will fly?"

Before any of them could react, the shape resolved into a thoroughly dirtied, though now dry, Lilith. Matteo breathed a sigh of relief, and even Sylette seemed marginally pleased that the freckled brunette had survived her ordeal. Renar flashed her a big, warm smile, something Matteo would have thought him incapable of just a few weeks prior.

"I knew you'd be okay. Nobody on my team would let a little explosion do them in."

"Yeah, well, that's enough of the weepy reunion banter," Lilith replied with a grin. "Those guys over there are starting to get interested in what we're doing."

In the middle of a burning building it was easy to forget that not everyone fighting the flames might be your friends. With the inferno contained to the back third of the hangar, and much of what could be salvaged removed from its path, most of the Sarconians still inside were either tossing buckets of water at the undying conflagration or hauling in hoses that could do far more good. However, almost all the soldiers had goggles, and with nothing but a thin veil of reeking fumes between their group and the firefighters, they could see them almost as plain as day.

Several were already pointing in their direction and calling incoherent exclamations. Another couple were making for the gradually dissipating smog wall at the entrance. Regardless of which blew their cover, it was only a matter of time before their new pals became enemies once more.

"The key, Matteo. It's time to go!" Sylette gestured at the old ship, plainly expecting him to know how to get inside. His father had taken him flying on numerous occasions, but he'd never really paid attention to how the vessel worked. It was difficult to do so when you were afraid of both heights *and* crashing.

It was Lilith who once again saved the day. "Boarding ramp lock is right here." She stabbed a finger at a panel beside the nearest support strut. On it, visible even in the half-darkness caused by the circular brim of the transport, was a hole shaped to receive his activation pin.

As Matteo slid the key into the slot with an audible click, Sylette suddenly looked back at the wall of flames in horror. "What about fuel? What if the ship doesn't have any illyrium or synth-oil?"

"Way ahead of you." Lilith groaned as she pulled a couple of barrels from behind her earlier hiding spot. Both had caution signs on them and were color coded with yellow and black bands respectively. "I decided to save some before blowing the rest. Figured with our track record the ship would be running on empty."

With a twist of the pin, a pop sounded from the underbelly of the airship, and a hissing hydraulic system slowly lowered a thin ramp down to ground level. Sylette gestured Vallen and Renar aboard to secure their injured, then began helping Lilith with rolling the containers after them.

By now it had become apparent that their group was trying to steal a ship rather than help put out the fire. Two of the soldiers still inside, their bare chests slicked black with sweat and ash, sprinted toward them.

"What do you think you're doing!"

"Stop immediately! You know what happens to thieves!"

Since they hadn't been expecting intruders during an emergency, neither had weapons, but both appeared strong enough to permanently damage Matteo with their fists. Without a second thought he pulled out the key and raced up the ramp. Though he knew a fair bit of martial arts, he was far from confident in his skills—in fact, it had been his worst grade at the academy.

The hold, much smaller than the Sarconian transport they'd absconded with so recently, was barely large enough to hold Unter's massive frame. While Velle was strapped in near the cockpit door on the far end, the Hue was all but wedged between the two walls. As an extra measure, Renar was wrapping him in with straps from the floor, ones normally used to lash down cargo. A bob of brown hair jutted from a hole in the floor—Lilith either messing with the ship's innards or trying to connect up their fuel. Sylette was leaning over the hole, while Vallen paced aimlessly in the remaining square meter of space available to him.

"Two soldiers . . . no weapons . . . almost here!"

Vallen instantly stopped and thrust Matteo out of his way. He staggered into the bulkhead, nearly falling forward into the princess, but managed to regain his balance just short of that disaster. He watched the disappearing back of the Triaron as he walked down the gangway, followed by the brief sound of blows and screams once he left his field of view. A moment later, all he could hear was the sound of the raging, crackling blaze.

When Vallen returned, there was blood on his shirt and his knuckles were rent and oozing. Whether the soldiers were still alive or not wasn't even a question that needed to be asked. A chill went down Matteo's spine at the sight. *Is this really what I want to be like?* he thought, reflecting on his earlier conversation with Velle.

"Illyrium is connected to the power converter, and the synth-oil is in the sump pan. We're ready to fly." Lilith put her hands on either side of the access hatch and hauled herself up and out. In addition to her rent, soot-blackened clothes, her cute face was now speckled with grease, her arms coated with grimy tar. It would take an industrial shower to get her clean after the events she'd been through.

"It's your show, Matteo. Get us out of here." Sylette indicated the forward cockpit expectantly and followed him there once he started moving. *Well, at least she's a more competent co-pilot than Renar,* Matteo sighed inwardly.

Clambering around Unter was a chore, but in spite of his poor condition the giant did his best to squeeze tight against one of the walls as he passed. Then Matteo was on the threshold of the flight deck, preparing to once again take all their lives into his hands. It hadn't ended very well last time, but at least all of them had survived—excepting Leon, of course. *Am I ready? Can I do this?*

Before Sylette could threaten, accost, or physically force him into the pilot's chair, Matteo felt a delicate touch at his right hand. He looked down to see Velle's soft, crimson hand trying to clutch his. With a brief adjustment, Matteo instead grasped hers—even now, she was still trying to cheer him up.

"Don't worry, Matteo. You *are* ready. After all, this is something only you know how to do. Vallen can't save us, and neither can anyone else. Now, get up there and fly this ship."

Velle's gorgeous, benevolent smile was like the sun to Matteo, banishing the dark clouds of doubt to the far recesses of his mind. He grinned back at the Sylph, squeezed her hand, then strode through the portal to take his seat. Once there, he stuck the activation pin into the center of the dashboard, brought the power online, and started the engine.

Though the craft was several decades old and bore a strange half-moon design rarely seen anymore, she was still good enough to get them through. The vibrations from the engine quickly reached an optimal level, humming through the deck and providing enough background noise to drown out the fire beyond the viewport. Ash had begun falling onto the glass, but a quick flip of the wipers gave him enough room to see.

Then they were ready to go. And this time, Matteo wouldn't make the same mistakes he did before. Goggles off—check. Hover drives on—check. Landing gear and ramp retracted—check. Ground-level stabilizers—check. Puffs from jets on all sides of the vehicle kept him from ramming into the stall walls as he eased the stick forward. On the *Feywind* he had forgotten that handy tool, resulting in skidding across the ground and wall before reaching the open air. *Not this time.*

As he turned the vessel to face the hangar doors, an explosion from deep within the building buffeted their rear. Flames danced about the hull and around the cockpit window, but Matteo managed to steady the craft. At that moment, a number of dings, much like rain or hail, sounded from the front of the airship, and he looked down to see a squad of Sarconian riflemen peppering them with small-arms fire.

It was a useless gesture—even against a transport as outdated as this. However, Matteo didn't begrudge them it. Where Vallen or Sylette, who glared at them from the co-pilot's chair, might have attempted to *deal* with them, he knew they posed no threat. Besides, for better or worse, his father's ship didn't have any weapons.

With a nudge of the throttle, Matteo glided over them, their clanging blows shifting to the bottom, then the rear of the craft. One second . . . two seconds . . . and they were through the smoke wall, out of the hangar, and into the free sky.

Not so free! Not so free! Right in front of them was the second cruiser, lifting off the runway and moving to block their path. Even as he saw it Matteo was jamming the controls to the left, hoping to scrape past it and elevate before it could bring its weapons to bear.

"Evade! Evade!" Sylette shrieked, for once in her life slower than Matteo at reacting to something.

"I already am!"

"No! That one! Evade that one!"

Coming from the left, now on a collision course with them after his adjustment, was the returning *Impelus*. Its belly dripped fluid, liords jetting from countless seams, but its goal wasn't to shoot them down with waterlogged cannons—it was to ram them. As its T-shaped fuselage filled the viewport, individual windows, and the crewmen inside, visible at this range, Matteo jinked back right. There was a narrow channel, barely wide enough for a craft their size, between the two closing behemoths. The question was whether they'd make it through in time.

It was a risk Matteo would never normally take. But this time he threw full power to the engines and gunned for the fading blue sky beyond. To his right, Sylette looked more nervous than he'd ever seen her. Of course, she had every right to be nervous. Individual armor plates, bulkhead rivets, and even welds were now apparent on both ships. Worse, they were skimming above or below their broadside gun emplacements, so close that neither cruiser could fire for fear of blasting the other. Matteo swore he could see the equally frightened eyes of Sarconians watching them from their own posts. *Yes, everyone involved is scared out of their minds!*

Twenty meters to go. Ten meters. A sudden drag on the ship thrust their heads forward, and Renar's yelling wafted forward from the cargo compartment. Apparently he hadn't strapped in on this voyage either, but that was secondary to the sparks now flying from the transport's wings—a sign that he was scraping both sides of their contracting prison.

Matteo tilted the craft vertically. One wing went up, one went down, and suddenly they were looking at the world—the sky, actually—on its side. Renar screamed some more, Vallen cursed, and Lilith cried something about "crazy pilot, this or that." Whatever it was, Matteo didn't have time for it right now. The blood rushed into his left ear, he tried to twist his head as close to right side up as possible, and, above all else, he prayed fervently to the Veneer and the Creator that they would make it through.

And make it through they did.

With a whoop of joy unlike Matteo had ever unleashed before, they burst out the other side. He quickly returned the airship to its normal orientation, leveled out, and continued to elevate over the city while easing back on the throttle. The cruiser commanders behind them were sure to get an earful. A grinding of metal on metal, a shrieking cacophony of groaning plates that were never meant to be joined together, signaled that they had trapped not their intended target, but themselves.

Gods, was this a moment Matteo would never forget.

"Darmatian rebels, this . . . Lt. Colonel Stet . . . oadcasting over an . . . en channel. Ground your . . . and surrender immedia . . . Otherwise, be pre . . . uffer the consequ . . . "

The grating voice, garbled due to distance or faulty equipment, burst out of the comcrystal mounted near the middle of the dashboard. Matteo felt his euphoria drain away instantly, replaced by a creeping dread. *Do they have my family? Abbot Kinloss? Mother Junica? A-are they going to shoot us down?*

"He's bluffing. He can't do anything as long as I'm on this ship," Sylette huffed, her gaze, like his, on the third cruiser still orbiting the summit of Etrus. "Head out over the water. They won't be able to keep up with us in a footrace."

Stetson spoke again, this time far more clearly. Either he'd cleaned up the transmission or found the specific bandwidth their comcrystal was attuned to. "I have in my possession evidence linking one Abbot Kinloss and his priory to support of insurrectionist activities. Normally the empire would establish a court and let due process take its course, but given their overwhelming guilt I have decided to invoke my right as regional governor to adjudicate and pass judgment myself. As a result, if you rebels do not turn yourselves in, I will reduce the Abbot and his church to cinders, much as you have done to one of my precious hangars."

Matteo glanced in panic from the cruiser, to the barely visible chapel spire, to Sylette. "He-he's still blu . . . bluffing, right?"

"No." Her tone was deadpan, her silver eyes set like stone.

Without thinking, Matteo swung the ship toward the cruiser and jammed the engines back to full power. Sylette looked at him like he was crazy and began reaching for the controls. "What are you doing? We can't go back there!"

"I have to save him!"

"How? Shoot that warship down with no weapons? Ram it? Surrender?"

"Whatever gets the job done!"

He edged away from her grasping hands, trying to keep the stick and his arms out of her range. So Sylette unbuckled her harness, rose halfway to her feet . . . then slumped back into her chair.

"Look, Matteo. I'm going to try to reason with you. If you go back there, regardless of what option you choose, everyone dies. Everyone but me, in some of those outcomes. But not just everyone in our group. Once they have you, they have your parents, if they don't already know they're involved. Renar can be used to bring down his father, General Iolus, if he's still fighting. Vallen can be used to pressure Steward Metellus. And . . . and he's going to kill Kinloss no matter what. That . . . that's just the way Stetson is, trust me."

She continued, "Asking nicely isn't like me. To be perfectly honest, if someone else could fly this ship, I might just incapacitate or kill you to stop this foolish display. But there isn't, so I need you to make the right choice. Please let Kinloss go, Matteo. You know it's what he knew would happen all along."

Sylette, frigid ice princess of the Sarconian Empire, sat there gazing at him with the closest thing to compassion she was capable of. Her hands were clasped in her lap. Her back was straight. Her turban was removed and her smushed silver hair was plastered about an angular face that was trying to melt into the softest form it could. Then Sylette dropped her chin a degree and closed her eyes. It was as close to a formal bow as anyone living had probably seen her perform.

"Please, Matteo."

Sadly, she was right. Kinloss *had* known he would die from the second he got involved with a group of Darmatian cadets with nowhere else to turn. But that didn't erase Matteo's pain. The memories of a kind old man who was there for him when he needed him. A person to talk to when he was bullied at school, someone to comfort and advise him other than his parents, a caretaker who let him pass time in the church and garden he nursed so lovingly.

It was true these things weren't much—any teacher or holy man would be expected to do the same. However, there was no malice in his goodwill, no ulterior motive to malign his deeds. Matteo didn't know the Abbot's past, but to him he was a blessed individual—one of the few people in the world who lived up to the lofty virtues so many aspired to. His flowers—neverfades, rosarias, bloodlilies, aphroniles, blochesums, and so many others—were all but gone now. However, their beauty, *his* beauty, would live on in the hearts of all who had seen them.

And . . . in my heart especially.

Matteo swung the transport sixty degrees left, pointing its nose out to sea, the chapel and hovering cruiser still barely within view through the right side of the canopy. "We'll head over the water and up the coast. I only hope Renar remembers that poem so we can find the resistance base."

"Thank you, Matteo." Sylette wasn't one for gestures, but saying thank you was likely more than she had done for anyone in a long time. However, he didn't need gratitude. This was what Kinloss would have wanted.

In the fading evening light, glittering majestically across the incoming wave tops, a red glow from Stetson's cruiser could be seen. It pulsed from one end of the large warship to the other, then settled into a concentrated mass amidships as a massive barrel unfurled from its stomach. The cannon, nearly as large as those they'd seen on Sarconian dreadnoughts at Aldona, was pointed squarely at the summit of Etrus.

"I will take your sudden course change as a rejection of my magnanimous offer. Since you have chosen so poorly, please enjoy the fireworks."

The cannon bucked back in on itself as it spat a projectile too fast for the eye to see. Instantly a cloud of blinding orange flame burst from the top of Etrus, expanding outwards to incinerate everything in its path. It was impossible to see the full effects at this distance, but it was clear that the chapel—and Kinloss along with it—was no more. When the light faded, only smoke and distended buildings remained about the hilltop.

I have to remain strong. I have to fly the ship. I have to get everyone through this.

Despite those thoughts, Matteo found tears welling up in the corners of his eyes. He choked them back, cleared his nose, and did everything he could to hold back his emotions.

So focused was he on flying and *not* feeling that he didn't immediately notice the four hands placed against his back. When he finally registered their presence, he turned around to look . . . and at that instant burst into tears. How could he not when presented with the support of his friends?

They stayed like that for a minute: Velle being held up by Renar's free arm, Lilith leaning against the back of his chair, Sylette pressing a single finger to his right shoulder. Unter was too injured to move anymore, but Matteo knew he cared as well.

Even when the moment ended, and everyone went back to their own tasks, Matteo knew things were different. *They* were different. *He* was different. Each of them had come through a crucible—several crucibles, in fact—and been changed by them.

Now Matteo was ready to face the world. To choose his path.

He had, at long last, found something he was willing to risk his life to protect.

Epilogue

Creeping Rot

Hetrachia 12, 697 ABH
Nemare, Capital of the Sarconian Province of Darmatia

———◆———

Seb was drunk.

Not just tipsy. Hammered. The Sarconian guardsman could barely move, fell to the ground every time he tried, and even then couldn't crawl more than a meter in any direction without stopping to hurl. However, immobile, smashed Seb was somehow more loquacious than standing, sober Seb. From the wooden floorboards beside the bar he alternately wailed for more spirits, sang at the top of his lungs about his girlfriend Rose, or threw up on every space not already coated with his pungent expulsion.

It was therefore no surprise when the master of the establishment—ironically named the Desert Rose—threw them out. Tremon could have refused him, both because he dwarfed the tall man by a full head length, and because of Sarconian regulations prohibiting locals from denying service to imperial soldiers. But he didn't. His plastered partner was clearly in the wrong. As his mother hadn't raised a son who would cause needless trouble for honest folks, the burly Terran simply nodded to the proprietor, hefted Seb like a sack of potatoes, and ducked through the curtained doorway into the cool Darmatian night.

"Hic . . . we'll report dat . . . hic . . . bloke ta Lieu-lee-lieuteny Snyder firt thang . . . hic . . . tamarrow mornin," Seb stated matter-of-factly from his position on Tremon's wide shoulder. "He won't . . . hic . . . get away . . . hic . . . wid mistreatin us like dat! But fo' now . . . hic . . . onwards ta da next pub!"

Though his head never moved from the larger man's chest, one of Seb's arms lazily rose and waved in the general direction of the nearest tavern. It was

453

impressive, given his drunken state, that he got the correct line to the place despite the buildings and streets in between. Tremon sighed but grinned begrudgingly even so. "Yes, yes, brother. Off we go."

The two of them were not really siblings or blood related in any way. If they had been, perhaps they would not be as close as they were. Both had grown up in the same farming village, as far north of Sarconia as you could go—and then yet a little farther still. To proper city folk from the capital or farther south, they were the lowest of the low. Earth scratchers, country bumpkins, the bottom of the social totem pole. But separating the wheat from the chaff wasn't a condition exclusive to the upper stratums.

Yes, even wet, useful mud will try to distinguish itself from dry, cracked mud. So it was with Tremon. Born with an undiagnosed condition that caused him to quickly outstrip other Terrans his age in height and brawn, the youth had been ostracized by those around him. The village kids viewed him as some sort of monster and taunted him incessantly, both verbally and with sticks and stones hurled from a safe distance. Their parents sniggered under their breath about the blauer in Terran skin, the hulking brute that was dumb as rocks and only good for plowing fields, like an ek. His own mother and father didn't quite know what to do with him either. While his presence was a boon to farm labor, they steadily grew to fear his clumsiness, and that it might eventually turn to outright destructive impulses.

Of course, that was the fault of his constantly growing limbs. Since their size and strength were ever changing, Tremon would often have accidents, ranging from the very minor to the very dangerous. A dropped plate, a damaged door handle, bent silverware. A smashed stepstool, a broken window, a carelessly nudged gas lantern. The last had been the worst and final straw. While caring for the draft animals in the town stable, he had misjudged his reach and knocked over the lamp he'd been using as a light source. That year had been a dry one, and the dehydrated bales to be used as livestock feed went up like kindling. He tried to put it out, first with his hands and then with suffocating tarps and bags, but nothing worked.

When the entire barn lay in smoking ashes the following morning, the blame was leveled entirely against him—despite poor water supply and the dry season bearing some responsibility—and Tremon was exiled to a shack on the outskirts of town. He thought that would be the end of him, wasting away on the edge of civilization like some leper or Red Plague victim, but there was still one bright spot to his existence: Seb.

The boy, a couple years older than the towering giant, had the exact opposite problem—he was far shorter and more diminutive than those his age. As a result, he was practically useless for hard field work, couldn't perform the necessary cooking or cleaning duties of a woman, and, just like Tremon, had to have clothes specially tailored for his frame. However, while he was similarly picked on for his small stature, the danger he presented to the community was considerably less, and he could come and go as he pleased.

Where Tremon had become quiet and withdrawn because of his suffering, becoming the very vapid, mute titan people took him for, Seb had become charismatic to the point of obnoxiousness. He was a dreamer, filled with grand plans and goals that he never shut up about. Every time he brought food to Tremon's hut or went walking with him through the distant hills where they wouldn't be seen, he'd tell his huge friend of a dozen new schemes he'd come up with the past day.

Some were crazy: making an airship out of local bamboo and twine, stealing the mayor's prize sapphiritoise shell to see how much it would sell for, or traveling about the neighboring hamlets trying to sell their village well water as a cure-all. Others, though, were more reasonable, including the one they eventually agreed to pursue—leave everything behind on Seb's eighteenth birthday and join the Sarconian Army.

When the day came, neither was missed and nobody tried to stop them. The journey to the nearest recruiting station took several days, but the time passed quickly and joyously. Even an arduous trek was better than the life Tremon had been leading. On their arrival, the mustachioed major sitting behind the provincial headquarters desk had looked them up and down and smiled congenially. Though the massive youth was only sixteen, two years below the minimum enlistment age without academy training, the man never even asked for their ages. With a glimmer in his eyes, he stamped their enlistment papers without another thought. It was one of the first times someone had reacted positively to Tremon's size.

Now, two years later, they were part of the occupation force for the

Darmatian capital of Nemare. While Tremon didn't agree with all the decisions of his superiors and country, he had still done what he was told, fought where he was told to, shot his rifle at the people he was told to. To his knowledge he hadn't killed anyone yet, nor did he want to, at least deliberately. For that purpose, the gun line he often stood in was ideal, since the massed fire and smoke meant no one knew whose bullet had been the fatal shell. However, if it was necessary to protect Seb and his current existence, Tremon might. Though he was still subdued around everyone but his de facto brother, whether because of his size or his performance, they all treated him well. It was a good feeling, one he wasn't ready to relinquish just yet.

And for the person who set him on this path, Tremon was willing to be a bit indulgent and take him to one more watering hole. *What's the harm?* It was their first night off since they'd arrived over a week prior, and they also didn't have to report in for duty until early afternoon. Seb would probably still have an agonizing hangover then, but at least he'd be conscious enough to stand watch or patrol.

"Dat . . . hic . . . breeze sho do feel . . . hic . . . nize. I'm glad we . . . hic . . . gots a postin' down . . . hic . . . here." *And yet that desert chill is doing nothing to bring you back to your senses.* Though Tremon had only drunk two glasses of Ithran wine, his size and build meant that alcohol impacted him far less than, say, Seb, who was half as tall. Of course, the tiny soldier had also consumed twice as many beverages, which likely affected his current stupor as much as his short stature.

That aside, Tremon was also glad for their present assignment. Despite their low ranks, in this vibrant, wealthy city they were living like they never had before. Nobody shot at them, the lodgings were beyond anything he'd ever experienced, and the work was easy. Gone were the daily drills, the harsh metal airship bunks, the bug-infested hay and straw of both his original bed and army field cots. Similarly absent were the terrible military rations: hardened crackers and a gelatinous protein pack. Now they spent their days in ease, ensuring the locals didn't act up while enjoying real feather mattresses, exotic food, and drinks that didn't taste like raw sewage.

As for those Darmatians they watched, most seemed content with the new way of things. Crime was nonexistent. Former government officials were working amicably with the emperor and upper echelons to ensure a smooth transition of power. Even those on the street merely nodded their heads and moved out of the guardsmen's way. It seemed almost as though the brief war between the two nations had never been fought.

Tremon was so caught up in those thoughts that he nearly ran into the elderly man in front of him. At the last second, he saw the white turban atop the man's head and managed to check his momentum, tightening his grip on Seb to prevent him from tumbling forward. For his part, the drunk burped loudly but remained still and incoherent of his surroundings.

"Sorry, I didn't see you there."

The man, his face wrinkled and eyes sunken, slowly turned around, his gaze widening in surprise as he took in Tremon's size. Then his eyes narrowed, focusing on the crimson and gold Sarconian crest on the breast of the giant's tunic. Though the soldiers were in plainclothes, per regulations they were required to have some identification at all times, either a chest patch, an armband, or their military papers booklet.

The already bent man set to deeper bowing and scraping. "The fault is mine entirely, Your Grace. I apologize for blocking your path, but . . . " He turned and looked nervously over his shoulder where, in the middle of the narrow road, clogging the space between the flat-faced residences on either side, was a cart laden with goods. Wooden crates formed the bottom layer, while heavy-looking metal ringed barrels sat atop them. The entire structure was listing to the left, where two middle-aged men and a teenage girl were attempting to replace a broken wheel and strut. An untethered ek stood patiently nearby.

" . . . I'm afraid the street will be impassable for several more minutes. I do dearly hope that this incident causes no offense. We'll be gone short—"

Tremon held up his free hand to stop any further groveling by the aged man. The situation was an accident, plain as day. "You have done nothing wrong." He began to lower Seb, planning to set him on a nearby doorstep while he worked. "Here, let me help you so that you may be on your way."

"No, no, good sir! You mustn't do that!"

Instead of graciously accepting his aid, the white-robed man hopped forward, waving his arms frantically and stopping him from placing Seb down. "We're almost finished here. Better you wait and not dirty your hands. I wouldn't want you or any of your friends to think ill of us for forcing our labor upon you."

"I would never—"

"Nonetheless, I insist you lift not a finger, Your Grace. Please trouble yourself not over this simple task." His pleading was on a whole other level than Tremon had ever witnessed. Granted, he had never experienced ingratiation of any kind before, but surely this was unnecessary. *Is it because we're Sarconian soldiers? Is he worried we'll report the delay he created, the inconvenience they caused us?*

Since Tremon was out of his depth, he decided it was better to listen to the man. However, his presence was likely to be a nerve-wracking burden while they finished. Already the girl, perhaps the elder's granddaughter, was looking at them anxiously, fidgeting with her dress while biting her lip. He would quit the scene and find another route to their destination.

"Good evening then, sir. I wish you success with your repairs and travels."

Thankfully, there was an alleyway to the left of the blockage. Tremon bowed his head to the group, reaffixed Seb upon his shoulder, and squeezed his way through the deeper darkness. While Nemare's primary and secondary roads were well lit by illyrium-fed electric lamps, the backstreets and poorer sections were not as well maintained. Either they were illuminated by gas and torch or not at all. Tremon had heard rumors of a place called Sewertown that was purportedly even worse, though he had no desire to visit somewhere that might remind him of his youth.

The angled rays from the twin moons above proved enough to light his way. Occasionally little clouds would flow across them, reducing his visibility, but Tremon had come a long way from his clumsy childhood. Despite the trash, broken boxes, or fallen awnings that blocked the narrow route, he managed to step over or around each obstacle while keeping his shoulders half-turned.

Unfortunately, his focus on the ground meant that he lost track on what was both ahead and behind. Leaping over a final capsized drum that had spilled broken bottle glass across the ground, Tremon found himself in the middle of a small but bright courtyard. Well, perhaps less of a courtyard and more of an extra lot, the type of space that formed between blocks of buildings of different sizes. Flaming braziers had been set up in each of the four corners, casting flickering shadows on the sand-colored clay walls of the surrounding tenements. While the center was clear, the edges were cluttered with boards of varying length, discarded rusting pipes, and various other kinds of refuse and garbage.

But his surroundings were the least of his concern. Far more alarming were the beings filing in through the two additional passages, one to the front and one on Tremon's right. Of varying shapes and heights, they all wore full-body white robes crowned by a flattened hood similar to the headpiece of a nun he'd once seen. Unlike that nun, none of their faces could be seen, their races and skin colors hidden beneath dark veils and gloves that covered the flesh exposed by their garments.

After their somber entrance, they spread out in a half-moon formation to block Tremon's way forward. Though he had been unable to pinpoint their numbers as they exited the murky gloom, it was now clear that there were six of them. Suddenly the crackling of breaking glass came from behind him followed by whispered cursing. Tremon dashed into the space then spun so as to put as much distance between himself and all the mysterious men.

Hanging their heads apologetically, two more robed individuals entered from the alleyway he'd just exited and completed the encirclement. His heart beat faster and faster. His adrenaline pumped, and cold sweat beaded across his forearms. *If I hadn't moved, there's no telling what they would have done to me from behind.*

Almost as if ignoring his presence, they began to talk amongst themselves, their voices sounding strange and alien behind the thin veils they wore.

"He's a big one, isn't he?"

"But his companion is drunk. He can't do anything."

"Are we sure we want to do this?"

"Once we cross this line, we can't go back . . . "

"Losing your nerve already, Hendr—I mean brother?"

It was just as Tremon feared. By some twist of fate, these strange men—for they sounded like men—had come to kill them. And right now they were building up the courage to follow through on the deed. He glanced around, taking stock of the situation. *Three ways out, all guarded by at least two enemies. Pile drive past them? But they'd catch up when I have to slow down in the narrow corridor. The roofs are low enough for me to grab, but I'd need enough time to toss Seb over then haul myself up. Maybe I can talk my way—*

"Enough!"

One of them, not the tallest but bearing a gold-painted wooden staff, stepped forward while gesturing for silence. As he moved into the center, where the glow from all four fires framed his body, it became clear that a yellow seven-pointed star adorned the center of his otherwise immaculately pure habit. One of its tips, the top one directly below his hidden visage, was twice as large as the rest, perhaps denoting its greater position or importance.

Having calmed his subordinates, the man pointed the rod, likely a symbol of his authority, at Tremon. "You, Sarconian, do you know what crime you have committed?"

Tremon blinked twice with shock. *Crime?* "I have broken no laws."

"Perhaps that you know of. But what of your nation, your empire? What of the countless lives they've taken?"

Why was he on trial here? Could Tremon really manage to find a satisfactory explanation that would get them out of this? And where had he seen that symbol on their leader's chest before . . .

"I personally wish the loss of life could have been avoided, but that was war. A war without killing isn't possible!"

"If you don't agree with it, why do you wear that crest? Why do you march with their armies? Why do you not cherish all that the Creator and Veneer have given us?" When he said the word Creator, the whole lot of them bowed their heads and crossed themselves. The pattern they made traced the star on their master's chest, finishing with a line from their forehead to the top of the principal point.

That's when it clicked. *These are believers in the Church of Light, followers of the Creator and Veneer.* Though Tremon had never been religious—the Sarconian Empire actively attempted to stamp out faith in anything but the emperor and military—he had still heard enough about them to understand the basics. Since they sought a world of peace where all patiently awaited the return of the Creator without fostering violence, hardship, or strife, it was no wonder they disliked the imperial agenda. Not to mention that same empire had so recently destroyed the Cathedral of Sariel, one of their holy sites.

But at their core they were pacifists. What could compel them to corner soldiers like this? Tremon gulped, then played that card for all it was worth. "Do you think the Veneer would want you to do this? Won't killing us just perpetuate the cycle of violence?"

While Tremon didn't speak often or much—this was the most he'd said at once in weeks—no one who really knew the giant would accuse him of being dim. Despite his looks, he was probably the smartest man in his company. *Please let that logic work. Please!*

But the leader merely shook his head and laughed. "We, the Sect of Sariel, ascribe to a higher plane of thought than that. As Sariel's angelic golden hair turned midnight black to absorb the sins of mankind, so too will we absorb your malevolence into ourselves. The tranquil world the Creator, the Veneer, and Sariel desire has no room for scum like you that upset its balance. If we have to dirty our hands to achieve his righteous vision, so be it!"

Negotiations had broken down. Tremon backed further into his corner, then set Seb down gingerly. Even with everything going on around him, his soused brother was snoring lightly, his eyes closed shut. *Don't worry, I'll protect you.*

He reached for the sword at his belt . . . which was, of course, missing since they were off duty. *Looks like we're doing this the old-fashioned way.* Tremon flexed his considerable muscles, which rippled visibly even through his clothes. Several cultists fell back a step at the sight.

"I don't want to hurt any of you."

"Then we'll make this painless," the staff wielder intoned pitilessly, signaling his minions forward. "May you find redemption for the sins of your people in the Void."

The seven approaching men drew knives from inside their robes and advanced together. Tremon's first priority was to protect Seb. His second was to escape with him. On the left, one of the more eager participants drew inside the titan's considerable range. Without moving, his fist lashed out and buffeted the side of the faux monk's head. Bone crunched, teeth flew, and the man crumpled where he stood.

Six to go. From then on, they closed more warily, syncing up their movements so that he had to pay attention to them equally. Tremon went on the offensive. A low round-kick broke the knee of the rightmost assailant, who went down screaming. Two swift punches lifted his neighbor from the ground and sent him sailing across the lot to crash noisily amid the lumber and pipes. *Looks like my military martial training is serving me well,* Tremon thought, his spirits rising.

Yet even the army instructors couldn't give him eyes in the back of his head. Tremon felt several impossibly painful pricks at his back as blades rose and fell against his exposed flank. Each blow flared through his nerves like the worst bee sting he'd ever had—magnified by a hundred times.

But his blood was up now; he wouldn't be stopped. Pulsing red rimmed the massive Terran's vision, and he rounded on his attackers while roaring furiously. The first's neck he snapped with an elbow to the throat, the second he kicked with enough force to break the man's ribs. As Tremon killed his first men, he wondered if maybe, just maybe, his parents had been right all those long years prior about his savage predilections.

When those two dropped, he gazed about madly, trying to find the last of his foes. Their leader was still standing in the same place, somehow calm despite the terror Tremon was wreaking upon his men, while the remaining duo were making for the unconscious Seb.

"NO!" the wounded Terran roared. He abandoned all pretense at fighting form and rushed them, bowling the first into the nearby wall. His eyes went wide then filmed over as his spine snapped loudly and the brittle construct caved inwards under the blow.

Seeing the fate of his companion, the last cultist swiftly raised his dagger to strike a fatal blow. Unable to reach the man himself, Tremon took the stab through his meaty hand, grimacing as the thin cutting implement slashed skin, muscle, nerves, and bone before poking out the other side. Try as he might, the would-be murderer couldn't retract the weapon, and a few seconds later Tremon used his pierced hand to smash the assailant's face in with the blade's own handle.

That's it. They're all down. The large guardsman felt a moment of elation until another half-dozen sharp thrusts skewered his backside. Blood spurted unbidden from his lips, the result of considerable internal damage, and he turned to see that another dozen white-robed cultists had arrived, half of which had snuck up on him as he protected Seb.

There would be no escaping this. It was a miracle in and of itself that Tremon had downed six armed opponents with nothing but his bare hands. Nevertheless, this was where his luck ran out. With a mighty shout he bucked his current attackers off, grabbed Seb in one hand, and flung him atop the nearest roof. A grunt came from him as his body landed, then there was silence. Maybe he would wake up and escape. Maybe he would make it far enough to get aid. Maybe he would come rushing back here with their whole platoon in tow. *However, if he but lives, that will be enough.*

His enemies' shock wore off and they resumed their offensive, plunging their stinging blades into his flesh wherever they could find purchase. Tremon could no longer count the number of times he'd been impaled—truly, he could hardly feel them now. His ichor ran swift and thick to soak and pool on the sandy cobbles below. All his limbs had lost the will to move.

When he finally fell, he imagined it was like a great oak collapsing in the forest. Once, long ago, Tremon had cut one down, back when his father still taught him things and saw him as an asset rather than a burden. The axe blade chipped away at the trunk, bit by bit, piece by piece. At first the tree seemed to feel nothing. It took the blows and kept on stubbornly reaching for the heavens, stoically refusing to acknowledge the feeble efforts of the large Terran boy trying to bring it down. But after he was halfway through, the great forest giant began to tilt, and when he was three quarters done, it finally began to topple.

At first the motion was slow, gradual. Then it picked up speed, shattering the branches of its neighbors and threatening to drag them down as well. The impact was deafening—anyone in the forest that day would have been able to hear the crash and sense the shaking. Though once those faded, it was over. The magnificent oak was down, ready to be turned into lumber, then from lumber to fence posts, a plow, a house, or whatever else was needed. After all, the oak was dead. It no longer got a say.

So it was with Tremon. His legs failed before his consciousness, and he collapsed backward suddenly and without warning. When his body hit the ground, he had the faintest sensation that something was trapped beneath him, squirming and struggling to break free. Then it too, like him, went still.

Though he could no longer move his head, his unblinking eyes stared straight up at the night sky above. Light from the braziers tinted the edges of the scene with yellow and orange, but for the most part the visage was pure—a blue-black backdrop flecked with beaming stars and overshadowed by dull radiance from the overlapping, shimmering moons. It was as beautiful a view as Tremon had ever seen in his short, paradoxical life.

A white shift was thrown over his frame and a piece of paper placed atop it. Though his fading vision couldn't make out the reverse of the words written on the parchment, his final sight, since it was directly above his eyes, was of the symbol etched there: a seven-pointed star with its principal tip more prominent than the rest.

END OF REBIRTH

Glossary of the Unfamiliar and Arcane

ABH: Acronym for "After the Battle of Har'muth." Most Terran calendars use this event to delineate the start of the modern era.

League: A unit of length equivalent to the distance a Terran man could walk in about one hour.

Veneer: Seven immeasurably powerful deities formed from portions of the Creator's essence and fashioned after each of Lozaria's seven races. Their appearances, abilities, and personalities reflect the temperament and qualities of said race. They were originally Lozaria's stewards, its caretakers, but have long since vanished along with their maker.

Illyriite (Glows Green): Immensely potent spirit stone and an unlimited source of energy (men'ar) for performing magic. After the disappearance of the three Aurelian brothers (Sarcon, Darmatus, and Rabban), knowledge of existing shards was lost, and now Illyriite is considered little more than a fable.

Men'ar: Unconfirmed component dwelling within all forms of matter. In mortals, it has been theorized to be carried on blood vessels. It is by harnessing its latent connection to ambient men'ar in the environment that mages are capable of performing the miracles known as magic.

Illyrium (Glows Yellow): A weaker version of Illyriite that serves as the foundation of modern society. Everything from airships to catalysts to lamps use it as an energy source. Unlike Illyriite, this mineable yellow mineral breaks down over time, becoming dun and useless. Comprised of compressed men'ar somehow trapped within its crystalline structure.

Creator: Ultimate deity responsible for the creation of Lozaria and its people. His true name is unknown. Worshipped by the Church of Light, who depict him as a radiant pillar of light that burns away darkness. Church teaching cites that he and his Veneer are presently withdrawn from the world and its affairs.

Void or Oblivion: The twin names of the infinite nothingness from which life is said to have originated. Whether or not the Void is sentient is the subject of much debate, and there are religious sects that pay it homage instead of the Creator.

Sensor: Mage capable of sensing the flow of men'ar in living things. Sensor skills do not inhibit the development of any of the ten schools of magic.

Telepath: Mage who can project their essence into the minds of others, seeking to either directly communicate, persuade, or manipulate. Telepath skills do not inhibit the development of any of the ten schools of magic.

Red Plague (Glows Red): A vicious pestilence that swept across Lozaria during the second century EOA (Era of Abandonment). Infection first became apparent when the victim's veins changed from blue to red. Intense coughing fits and expulsion of blood from every orifice followed, along with the gradual, painful growth of crimson crystals within the bloodstream. Death occurred after the sprouting of these beautiful buds, which ejected a dense mist that was contagious for ten days after death. There are no records of recovery prior to its total eradication by the Aurelian brothers.

Dragwyrm: A rare interbreeding of the mighty land-bound wyrm and the graceful, semi-sentient dragons of the sky. While there is not a more powerful beast on the face of Lozaria, magic and magtech advancements have enabled mortals to hunt down or capture many of them. Most known dragwyrms are now bred in captivity, raised as servient haulers of artillery and other heavy cargo.

Empyrean Relics: Mythological weapons and mystical items rumored to have been wielded by the Veneer prior to their disappearance. References to them are confined to the realm of storybooks.

Firing-Arm: Prototype firearms engineered to fire piercing bolts using a series of springs and cables, much like a crossbow. Application of the user's men'ar increased their range, accuracy, and effectiveness.

Elysium (Glows Dark Purple): Seven obsidian shards of varying sizes and shapes said to have power over the very fabric of the universe. Legends tell of a ritual by which one may sacrifice a portion of one's soul—one's life force—to an Elysium fragment to have their deepest desires granted.

Scrying Orb: Illyrium infused hand-held recording device capable of capturing visual and audio data for later playback. Central crystal encodes information as men'ar waves—pure magical energy.

Lume: Luminescent barrier projected by a generator infused with men'ar, typically via direct transference from connected illyrium crystals. Capable of absorbing and dissipating an equivalent amount of physical or magical energy.

Esta and Exal: Lozaria's twin moons, considered female and male respectively. They are perpetually out of sync with each other, one waxing while the other wans and vice versa. The presence of these two bodies causes Lozaria's tidal patterns to be stronger than normal, and the effects of gravity have been lessened compared to a planet with fewer orbiting bodies. Their combined luminescence is enough to make nocturnal travel easy unless cloud cover is present.

Scrivening Magchine: An autonomous copying device powered by illyrium that can perform a range of scribing functions from copying to critique based on the enchantments applied to it.

Casting Catalyst: Weapon or accessory imprinted with illyrium dust in the form of runes and symbols. These etchings are tailored to the type of magic utilized by a mage, enabling them to bolster their internal men'ar with ambient energy absorbed from their surroundings. While the body's own men'ar reserves are more potent, since they are familiar to the user, casting spells with men'ar channeled through a catalyst will prevent destruction of the mage's physical vessel through MIS (Men'ar Imbalance Syndrome).

MIS (Men'ar Imbalance Syndrome): Degradation of the mind and flesh as a result of a body holding more or less men'ar than it is capable of. In other words, the size of the "soul" must match the sturdiness of its "container."

Projectomic: Input system that uses magic to convert auditory input into vibrations and waves that can be transmitted across varying distances. Handheld versions can modulate the speaker's volume, and brass knockers can be attached to send short-range, codified transmissions.

Projectostand: Output system that deciphers projectomic signals and converts them back to sound. Small, in-home units are becoming more popular for news and entertainment, but most still occupy stadiums and cities to quickly broadcast information to large crowds.

Telescriber: Screen based display system that projects visual data acquired by either scrying orb or recorb.

Recorbs: Short-range, direct transmission device consisting of a hovering sphere, a lens, and a low quality illyrium crystal that can only hold a few minutes of optical information at a time. Since they're cheaper than scrying orbs and can indirectly offload their data to nearby telescribers, they are often used to relay sporting events, speeches, or special events.

Flag-Brawl: A popular Lozarian sport played by two teams of four mages each. While the basic premise is the same as capture the flag, a children's game, its brutal execution involves far more rules and violence. Many professional players are former soldiers and mercenaries, a fact that is indicative of Lozaria's belligerent nature.

Eight Fleets: Nickname for the Sarconian navy—its world-renowned air fleet. Each fleet is commanded by a rittermarschal, one of the nation's preeminent mages and tacticians.

Great/Lost Magic: Capable of altering the landscape and leaving behind whole armies of mutilated corpses, these incredible spells were banned by a council of nations, never to again be used in war. Originally wielded by the Veneer before their disappearance, mortals were capable of duplicating them through the efforts of entire battalions of mages, most of whom perished or were deformed in the process.

Long Chants: Several dozen incantations translated from ancient Eliassi to Common over numerous generations. The difficulty of learning and casting them is made up for by their potency and effects—which often seem to possess minds of their own. Every boon they grant is balanced by a cost.

Afterplane: Grey, drab, endless space occupying the region between the physical realm—Lozaria—and Oblivion. The souls of the dead wait here, suspended in vacant emptiness, until they are claimed by either the Creator or the Void.

Seven Races of Lozaria

Terrans: A race of bipedal beings who, in comparison to their fellows, are average in almost every way. Lacking the brawn, longevity, or hardiness of other races, they have invested heavily in the development of magic and magtech. Though they lose out to the Sylph in the former and the Hues in the latter, their population far exceeds either, which has enabled them to expand all across Lozaria. Responsibility for many of the continent's conflicts can be laid at their feet, and the three principal Terran states—Darmatia, Sarconia, and Rabban— remain embroiled in what outsiders view as a "Terran Civil War."

Vladisvar: The most prepared warrior is the one whose arm *is* his sword.

The foremost of Lozaria's martial races, the Vladisvar possess an appropriately imposing physiology. Standing at almost three meters tall, they possess coarse, leathery grey skin, long claws, and horns growing from the sides of their temples. As tradition mandates, most Vladisvar, both male and female, are tattooed with a variety of permanent dyes as they age. These symbols, along with the armor plates their mercenaries graft to their flesh, tell the story of their life through recountings of important events. While their religion worships cosmic balance— equalizing good and evil in the world—most Vladisvar that stray from their nomadic origins take work as mercenaries. Though outsiders speculate on their apparent hypocrisy, no one can say for sure why they almost desperately seek battle.

Hue/Haead: Give a Hue—or Haead, as they call themselves—a new invention, and she'll return it to you a few days later with two improvements you'd thought of and three you hadn't.

471

This matriarchal society of four-armed, blue-skinned beings occupy half of the Etrus Peninsula, a territory they grudgingly share with the Sylph. The largest, tallest beings on Lozaria, they are quick-witted and deft with their many limbs, making them the continent's foremost authority on magtech. It is believed that their obsession with technology stemmed from a population with a low men'ar factor. While every living creature possesses men'ar, not all can wield it, and a Hue child capable of wielding magic is a rarity. Even should a Hue develop magic, sorceries are frowned upon in their society, perhaps because of their country's proximity to the men'ar adored Sylph. The practice of 'Alteration,' enhancing one's body with magtech implants and grafts, is a newly popular trend to overcome magical deficiencies, though there is considerable pushback against it by traditionalists.

In addition, it should be noted that Hue gender roles are flipped not just in government, but across the spectrum. Males are viewed as breeding stock first and individuals second, and their advancement in society is only at the whims of their female superiors or mates.

Sylph: Grace and elegance are paramount to a Sylph. If you are born with magic and beauty, you'll go far in life. If you must choose just one, pick magic, for with it you can grasp the other. But if you have neither . . . slavery or a swift death are the best you can hope for.

Like their neighbors, the Hues, the Sylph are particularly isolationist, believing themselves superior to the other races. Their base features are similar to Terrans, with the exception of their red pigmentation, the curvature of their ears, and their innate ability to manipulate their body structure using the men'ar in their blood. By doing so, they can sprout wings, expand their muscles, and even rearrange their organs to avoid or mitigate lethal wounds. This ability stems from their command of magic, which is—as a collective race—only second to the Eliade.

Since political power stems from magical aptitude, magtech is almost completely banned within their borders. Foreigners are confined to a special district in their cities. Visiting dignitaries are suffered rather than honored. Though a tenuous peace currently exists between them and the Hues, their disputed ownership of the Tesset Lode, a massive illyrium deposit sitting astride the border between them, means that a renewal of hostilities is all but guaranteed.

Eliade: What is the difference between Illyriite and Eliade? While a person is unlikely to encounter either in their lifetime, Eliade are *supposed* to still exist. However, none have been seen since the Illyriite War, so accounts of them are confined to myths and fables.

Their bodies are wispy, almost ethereal. Solid substance makes up their core, but everything beyond that—their roving sensory appendages, clothing, and skin—is hazy, like flowing mist. It is theorized that this nebulous state brings them closer to ambient men'ar than any other creature, thereby enabling them to wield incredibly potent magic.

When they did engage in mortal affairs, their immortal council, the Eliassa, governed over the other races like a stern parent. Their longevity, which brought them to the cusp of divinity, gave them the right to rule. Now, like the Veneer they worked alongside, they have all but vanished from Lozaria.

Moravi: There is no deal a Moravi won't make, nor cesspit to which he will not travel to make it.

An extremely prolific reptilian race hailing from the southern atoll that bears their name, the Moravi, once conquerors, are now proficient traders. They can walk on two or four legs, using their tail for balance in the former orientation. Similar to the Sylph, Moravi can rapidly produce bone marrow within their bodies, enabling them to modify or eject portions of their skeleton. This ability is handy during a variety of situations, including combat. The color, size, and positioning of their scales and spinal spikes is the primary distinguisher of sex. To outsiders, the slight bulge of a Moravi female's chest is practically imperceptible. In addition to being highly sensitive, their long, forked tongue plays a role in intraspecies communication.

Though they previously dominated much of present Rabban, Darmatia, and the Etrus Peninsula, the Moravi have since been driven back to their isles, where the aristocracy enjoy lives of indolence and the most ambitious travel far afield as merchants and crime bosses. Since each clan-pack numbers in the hundreds, and clan-packs often pursue the same interests, the organizations Moravi establish are incredibly powerful.

Trillith: The individual is nothing; the Hive is all.

Trillith culture is almost as mysterious as that of the Eliade. They certainly *do* exist; their silk products, spun from gossamer threads certain members of their species produce, can be found adorning manses and palaces all across Lozaria. Yet the expansive diffusion of these wondrous fabrics and tapestries is misleading. A foreign merchant wishing to establish a trade relationship with them will not succeed in his lifetime. In fact, it's possible that his grandchildren may still be struggling to earn the Trillith's trust generations later. The only outsiders the insectoid beings truly accept are those who are outsiders no longer. Even a Hue or Vladisvar who willingly relinquishes their sense of self and melds with the collective Hive may join them, at which point they are merely one more appendage of a million limbed whole.

There are as many kinds of Trillith as there are communal roles to be fulfilled. Some have six legs and walk low to the ground. Others are bipedal, and still others fly. The only commonality is that they all go through larva, pupa, and adult stages, with the latter possessing a chitin exoskeleton. Most communicate mind to mind telepathically, through the Hive, but some few possess . . . unsettling features similar to other races, such as vocal cords and distorted faces to go along with them. Scholars speculate that these evolutions were developed to interact with other races, but remain uncertain—or unwilling to guess—how the adaptations were acquired.

The principal Trillith nesting grounds are the Great Southern Forest and the Badlands. Other Hives have yet to be confirmed.

Principal Styles of Magic Use

Engravate (Tier 1 caster): A mage who uses a paired catalyst—on which is carved illyrium infused runes often laced with their own blood—to cast spells by drawing upon the ambient men'ar in their environment. They must establish a special bond with the catalyst in order for the transference of men'ar from surroundings, to device, to caster to function properly. Most still use a verbal incantation to direct their spells and reduce men'ar consumption.

Invoker (Tier 2 caster): A mage, typically an Engravate, who can cast spells without using a spoken incantation. Instead, they compute the directives of their magic (type, spread, range, potency, target, etc.) internally using a second "injection" of men'ar. This process is best examined using two analogies. While the men'ar for the incantation is molded separately from the men'ar for the physical formula, like two hearts beating in parallel, Invoking is akin to holding one's breath during the swiftest of sprints. Approximately twice the men'ar will be consumed for the spell—all directly from the user's bloodstream. The benefits from Invoking a spell (speed and secrecy) must always be weighed against its cost, as Invokers are far more likely to suffer MIS (Men'ar Imbalance Syndrome) than any other type of mage. It should be noted that an Invoker is *not* required to Invoke with every cast. Provided they recall the Eliassi diction, they can revert to utilizing verbal methods of invocation.

Armsmage (Tier 2 caster): Armsmages are the inverse of Invokers in that they can cast spells utilizing any tool or weapon—including their own body, in many cases. Though practitioners of some schools of magic are known for tattooing their bodies with runes after the style of Engraving, neither an Armsmage's flesh nor weapon needs be covered in arcane symbols. They can pick up a stick and wield it just as effectively as an enchanted blade. In fact, their magic is expelled from the "Arms" themselves, whether by swing or block, stab or shot. However, as with Invokers, this convenience comes with an increased drain on men'ar, one accomplished by crafting a men'ar link between their essence and the implement. The perception of both merges, and, for an instant, they become extensions of each other.

Triaron (Tier 3 caster): The Triaron is a classification of mage referring to an elementalist sorcerer who possesses the properties of both an Invoker and Armsmage. When all of these are used in conjunction, the Triaron can cast any elemental spell from any weapon without an Engraved or verbal catalyst. While this does make the wielder extremely versatile, capable of launching wave after wave of magic with no warning or delay between them, they are still bound by the laws of men'ar usage. Where an Invoker exhausts men'ar at twice the rate of an ordinary mage, the Triaron will expend it at three times that speed. There are rumors that Darmatus Aurelian, the first Triaron, found a way to circumvent this severe handicap, but contemporary magic scientists have yet to uncover the secrets of his power. Aside from Darmatus, only one other Triaron has ever been identified.

NOTE: Tier 0 casting requires a series of formulaic drawings and the chanting of a lengthy quotation. This archaic method of casting has been accelerated in the modern era, where magtech and a mage's individual skill combine to evolve their casting into a flowing, graceful art.

Gerjunia Halsruf's Classification of Magical Attributes
(Ten Schools of Magic)

———◆———

Elemental: The School of Physical Manifestation
Time and Space: The School of Axial Manipulation
Curative: The School of Rejuvenation
Blood: The School of Seals and Pacts
Enhancive: The School of Reinforcement
Morphic: The School of Alteration and Perception
Degenerative: The School of Separation
Necromantic: The School of Preservation
Dark: The School of Shadows and Eternity
Light: The School of Radiance and Infinity

The vast majority of mages fall into one of these categories. Those that don't, approximately a percent of known magic users or less, are grouped in an eleventh set called "Unique." Unlike the vast array of abilities comprising the ten main schools, there is no common ground among the powers of Unique mages. One may be able to control quantities of metal with magnetism, while another might use soothing song and dance to manipulate people's actions and feelings. Why or how these marked deviations manifest has yet to be determined.

Seven Blessings (Seven Holy Tenets)

———◆———

Order (Justice) — Trillith
Understanding (Charity) — Moravi
Strength (Honor) — Vladisvar
Curiosity (Knowledge) — Hue/Haead
Knowledge (Dedication) — Sylph
Wisdom (Unity) — Eliade
Will (Conviction) — Terran

Each Blessing, bestowed as a boon upon a specific race by the Creator, is paired with a related Tenet: an aspiration or ideal that they should strive to achieve. Part of a faithful believer's responsibility is to meditate on how to live a life that will connect the two. Any adherent to the Church of Light should endeavor to practice all seven Tenets, but, whether because of racial schisms or the difficulty of that task, most choose to focus on the one directly associated with their race and Veneer.

Knowledge is both a Blessing and a Tenet, a curious occurrence that many priests point to as a sign of its importance. Divisiveness between various races and factions of the Church has led to the marginalization of this teaching outside of Nemare and other prominent centers of learning.

Lozarian Calendar

Jenuvant

Illyssuil

Charkur

Ithnaris

Kusselaf

Venare

Fulminos

Orpexaz

Festivus

Hetrachia

Adamantele

Mesmeri

Order of Military Ranks
for Embattled Nations

Sarconian Empire

Gefreiter

Unteroffizer

Sergeant

Ritterbruder Second Class (Equivalent to regular army captain)

Ritterbruder First Class (Equivalent to regular army major)

Rittermark (Equivalent to regular army colonel)

Vice Admiral

General or Admiral

Rittermarschal

Grand Marschal

Kingdom of Darmatia

Private

Corporal

(Not active duty) Cadet

(Not active duty) Senior Cadet

Ensign

Lieutenant

Captain

Major

Lieutenant Colonel

Colonel

General or Admiral

Airship Classifications Ordered by Size and Crew Complement

Civilian

    Skimmer

    Yacht

    Freighter / Transport

Military

    Hoverskiff (fighter)

    Hoverjet (fighter)

    Transport / Lander

    Light Cruiser / Corvette

    Heavy Cruiser / Frigate

    Carrier

    Dreadnought (Capital Ship)

About the Author

Christopher Russell (native of Williamsburg, VA) is a 28-year-old mechanical and aerospace engineer (graduate of the University of Virginia) who has loved reading since the day he picked up a book and writing since he could scrawl his first letters. After voraciously consuming titles from every genre—ranging from *Star Wars* to *Lord of the Rings*—he decided to combine the expertise from his professional education, passions, and Christian faith into a fantasy epic bridging the gap between magic and science. He currently resides in Charlottesville, Virginia, with his loyal dog, Vallen, named after the protagonist of his first work. For behind-the-scenes information on all of Christopher Russell's works, visit christopherrussellauthor.com.

CPSIA information can be obtained
at www.ICGtesting.com
Printed in the USA
JSHW021058270820
7517JS00001BA/1

9 781642 798876